Praise for Nathan Hill's

WELLNESS

"A modern take on love, marriage, and society's obsession on improving almost every aspect of our lives—and the impact technology and social media have on our culture and in our lives. This brilliant novel will leave you thinking about the truth of your own life and the stories we tell ourselves and each other."
—Oprah Winfrey

"*Wellness* has an insistent pull. . . . The beauty of Hill's second novel is that every character is at least a little strange and no one is unworthy of sympathy."
—*The Washington Post*

"*Wellness* is a perfect novel for our age. . . . Hill is an immensely talented writer; he has a gift for prose that's elegant but unshowy, and his dialogue consistently rings true to life. . . . A stunning novel about the stories that we tell about our lives and our loves, and how we sustain relationships throughout time."
—NPR

"I read Hill's novel with excitement and close to a sense of disbelief that there is still a writer out there who is intrigued by amplitude and by what fiction can do if pushed far enough."
—Daphne Merkin, *The Atlantic*

"A hilarious and moving exploration of a modern marriage that astounds in its breadth and intimacy."
—Brit Bennett, author of *The Vanishing Half*

NATHAN HILL

WELLNESS

Nathan Hill's bestselling debut novel, *The Nix*, was named the number one book of 2016 by *Entertainment Weekly* and one of the year's best books by *The New York Times*, *The Washington Post*, NPR, *Slate*, and many others. It was the winner of the Art Seidenbaum Award for First Fiction from the *Los Angeles Times* and was published worldwide in more than two dozen languages. A native Iowan, Hill lives with his wife in Naples, Florida.

nathanhill.net

WELLNESS

WELLNESS

A NOVEL

NATHAN HILL

VINTAGE BOOKS
A Division of Penguin Random House LLC
New York

Image on p. 113 is adapted from *Natural Lipstick: Close Up of the Face
of Young Woman with New Shiny Lipstick on Her Lips* by
Yakobchuk Olena/stock.adobe.com.

Image on p. 181 is from *Three Essays: On Picturesque Beauty;
on Picturesque Travel; and on Sketching Landscape: To Which Is Added a Poem,
on Landscape Painting* by William Gilpin. London: R. Blamire, 1794.

The Library of Congress has cataloged the Knopf edition as follows:
Names: Hill, Nathan, [date] author.
Title: Wellness / Nathan Hill.
Description: First edition. | New York : Alfred A. Knopf, 2023.
Identifiers: LCCN 2022052632 (print) | LCCN 2022052633 (ebook)
Classification: LCC PS3608.I436 W45 2023 (print) | LCC PS3608.I436 (ebook) |
DDC 813/.6—dc23
LC record available at https://lccn.loc.gov/2022052632
LC ebook record available at https://lccn.loc.gov/2022052633

Vintage Books Trade Paperback ISBN: 978-0-593-46983-5
eBook ISBN: 978-0-593-53612-4

Book design by Maggie Hinders

vintagebooks.com

Printed in the United States of America
1st Printing

For my parents

COME WITH

HE LIVES ALONE on the fourth floor of an old brick building with no view of the sky. When he looks out his window, all he can see is her window—across the alley, an arm's length away, where she lives alone on the fourth floor of her own old building. They don't know each other's names. They have never spoken. It is winter in Chicago.

Barely any light enters the narrow alley between them, and barely any rain either, or snow or sleet or fog or that crackling wet January stuff the locals call "wintry mix." The alley is dark and still and without weather. It seems to have no atmosphere at all, a hollow stitched into the city for the singular purpose of separating things from things, like outer space.

She first appeared to him on Christmas Eve. He'd gone to bed early that night feeling horribly sorry for himself—the only soul in his whole raucous building with nowhere else to be—when a light snapped on across the alley, and a small warm glow replaced his window's usual yawning dark. He sat up, walked to the window, peeked out. There she was, a flurry of movement, arranging, unpacking, pulling small vibrant dresses from large matching suitcases. Her window was so close to him, and *she* was so close to him—their apartments separated by the distance of a single ambitious jump—that he scooted back a few feet to more fully submerge himself in his darkness. He sat there on his heels and stared for a short while, until the staring felt improper and indecent and he contritely returned to bed. But he has, in the weeks since, come back to the theater of this window, and more often than he'd like to admit. He sometimes sits here, hidden, and, for a few minutes at a time, he watches.

To say that he finds her beautiful is too simple. Of course he finds her beautiful—objectively, classically, *obviously* beautiful. Even just the way she walks—with a kind of buoyancy, a cheerful jaunty bounce—has him thoroughly charmed. She glides across the floor of her apartment in thick socks, occasionally doing an impromptu twirl, the skirt of her dress billowing briefly around her. In this drab and filthy place, she prefers dresses—bright flowered sundresses incongruous amid the grit of this neighborhood, the cold of this winter. She tucks her legs under them as she sits in her plush velvet armchair, a few candles glowing nearby, her face impassive and cool, holding a book in one hand, the other hand idly tracing the lip of a wineglass. He watches her touch that glass and wonders how a little fingertip can inspire such a large torment.

Her apartment is decorated with postcards from places he assumes she's been—Paris, Venice, Barcelona, Rome—and framed posters of art he assumes she's seen in person: the statue of David, the *Pietà*, *The Last Supper*, *Guernica*. Her tastes are manifold and intimidating; meanwhile, he's never even seen an ocean.

She reads inordinately, at all hours, flicking on her yellow bedside lamp at two o'clock in the morning to page through large and unwieldy textbooks—biology, neurology, psychology, microeconomics—or various stage plays, or collections of poetry, or thick histories of wars and empires, or scientific journals with inscrutable names and bland gray bindings. She listens to music he assumes is classical for the way her head sways to it. He strains to identify book jackets and album covers, then rushes to the public library the next day to read all the authors that rouse and unsleep her, and listen to all the symphonies she seems to have on repeat: the *Haffner*, the *Eroica*, the *New World*, the *Unfinished*, the *Fantastique*. He imagines that if they ever actually speak, he will drop some morsel of *Symphonie Fantastique* knowledge and she will be impressed with him and fall in love.

If they ever actually speak.

She's exactly the kind of person—cultured, worldly—that he came to this frighteningly big city to find. The obvious flaw in the plan, he realizes now, is that a woman so cultured and worldly would never be interested in a guy as uncultured, as provincial, as backward and coarse as him.

Only once has he seen her entertain a guest. A man. She spent an appalling amount of time in the bathroom before he arrived, and tried on six dresses, finally picking the tightest one—a purple one. She pulled her hair back. She put on makeup, washed it off, put it back on. She took two showers. She looked like a stranger. The man arrived with a six-pack of beer and they spent what seemed like an awkward and humorless two hours together. Then he left with a handshake. He never came back.

Afterward, she changed into a ratty old T-shirt and sat around all evening eating cold cereal in a fit of private sloth. She didn't cry. She just sat there.

He watched her, across their oxygenless alley, thinking that she was, in this moment, beautiful, though that word *beautiful* seemed suddenly too narrow to contain the situation. Beauty has both public and private faces, he thought, and it is difficult for one not to annul the other. He wrote her a note on the back of a Chicago postcard: *You would never have to pretend with me.* Then he threw it away and tried again: *You would never have to be someone trying to be someone else.* But he didn't send them. He never sends them.

Sometimes her apartment is dark, and he goes about his night— his ordinary, hermetic night—wondering where she might be.

That's when she's watching him.

She sits at her window, in the darkness, and he cannot see her.

She studies him, observes him, notes his stillness, his tranquility, the admirable way he sits cross-legged on his bed and, persistently, for hours, just reads. He is always alone in there. His apartment—a desolate little box of unadorned white walls and a cinder-block bookshelf and a futon condemned to the floor—is not a home that anticipates guests. Loneliness, it seems, holds him like a buttonhole.

To say that she finds him handsome is too simple. Rather, she finds him handsome insofar as he seems unaware that he could be handsome—a dark goatee obscuring a delicate baby face, big sweaters disguising a waifish body. His hair is a few years past clean-cut and now falls in oily ropes over his eyes and down to his chin. His fashions are fully apocalyptic: threadbare black shirts and black combat boots and dark jeans in urgent need of patching. She's seen no evidence that he owns a single necktie.

Sometimes he stands in front of the mirror shirtless, ashen, disapproving. He is *so small*—short and anemic and skinny as an addict. He survives on cigarettes and the occasional meal—boxed and plastic-wrapped and microwavable, usually, or sometimes powdered and rehydrated into borderline edible things. Witnessing this makes her feel as she does while watching reckless pigeons alight on the El's deadly electrified lines.

He needs vegetables in his life.

Potassium and iron. Fiber and fructose. Dense chewy grains and colorful juices. All the elements and elixirs of good health. She wants to wrap a pineapple in ribbon. She'd send it with a note. A new fruit every week. It would say: *Don't do this to yourself.*

For almost a month she's watched as tattoos spread ivy-like across his back, now connecting in a riot of pattern and color that's migrating down his slender arms, and she thinks: *I could live with that.* In fact, there's something reassuring about an assertive tattoo, especially a tattoo that's visible even while wearing a collared work shirt. It speaks to a confidence of personality, she thinks, a person with the strength of his convictions—a person *with* convictions—contrary to her own everyday inner crisis, and the question that's dogged her since moving to Chicago: *Who will I become?* Or maybe more accurately: *Which of my many selves is the true one?* The boy with the aggressive tattoo seems to provide a new way forward, an antidote to the anxiety of incoherence.

He's an artist—that much is clear, for he can most often be found mixing paints and solvents, inks and dyes, plucking photo papers out of chemical baths or leaning over a light box inspecting film negatives through a small round magnifier. She's amazed at how long he can look. He'll spend an hour comparing just two frames, staring at one, then the other, and then the first again, searching for the more perfect image. And when he's found it, he circles the frame with a red grease pencil, every other negative is x-ed out, and she applauds his decisiveness: when he chooses a picture, or a tattoo, or a certain bohemian lifestyle, he chooses devotedly. It is a quality that she—who cannot decide on even the simplest things: what to wear, what to study, where to live, whom to love, *what to do with her life*—both envies and covets. This boy has a mind calmed by high purpose; she feels like a bean jumping against its pod.

He's exactly the kind of person—defiant, passionate—that she came to this remote city to find. The obvious flaw in the plan, she realizes now, is that a man so defiant and passionate would never be interested in a girl as conventional, as conformist, as dull and bourgeois as her.

Thus, they do not speak, and the winter nights pass slowly, glacially, the ice coating tree branches like barnacles. All season it's the same: when his light is off, he is watching her; when her light is off, she is watching him. And on the nights she isn't home, he sits there feeling dejected, desperate, maybe even a little pathetic, and he gazes upon her window and feels like time is zipping away, opportunities gone, feels like he is losing a race with the life he wishes he could lead. And on the nights he isn't home, she sits there feeling forsaken, feeling once again so bluntly dented by the world, and she examines his window like it's an aquarium, hoping to see some wonderful thing erupt from the gloom.

And so here they are, lingering in the shadows. Outside, the snow falls plump and quiet. Inside, they are alone in their separate little studios, in their crumbling old buildings. Both their lights are off. They both watch for the other's return. They sit near their windows and wait. They stare across the alley, into dark apartments, and they don't know it, but they're staring at each other.

THEIR BUILDINGS were never meant to be habitable. His was, originally, a factory. Hers, a warehouse. Whoever built these structures did not predict people living here, and so did not give those people a view. Both buildings were constructed in the 1890s, profitable until the 1950s, abandoned in the 1960s, and dormant thereafter. That is, until now, January 1993, when suddenly they've been seized and resuscitated into new purpose—cheap apartments and studio space for the city's starving artists—and his job is to document it.

He is to be the building's memory, capturing the wretchedness before the rehabilitation. Very soon, crews of workers—*worker* here being a word used pretty laxly to describe the poets and painters and bass guitarists who do this labor in exchange for reduced rent—will begin the cleaning and sanding and painting and waste removal necessary to make the place generally livable. And so here he is, in the foulest, most unmended reaches of the former factory, wandering with a borrowed camera and documenting the ruins.

He's up on the fifth floor, walking the long hallways, each footfall stirring up a fog of powder and filth. He photographs the dirt, and the allover rubble of collapsed ceiling tiles and plaster and brick. He photographs the elaborate graffiti. He photographs the broken windows, the curtains decomposed to fibrous ribbons. He's worried about stumbling onto a sleeping squatter, and debating whether it's better in this situation to be quiet or loud. If he's quiet, maybe he can avoid a confrontation. But if he's loud, maybe the squatter will wake and scare off.

He stops when something catches his eye: sunlight on a wall, streaking across antique paint that's peeling, slowly, crinklingly, with a thousand tiny fissures and clefts. A hundred years after its application, this paint is now liberating itself, and the texture reminds him of the surface craquelure of old portraits by Dutch masters. It also reminds him, more prosaically, of that small pond on his father's land back home, the one that would go dry during drought summers to expose the wet mud underneath, the mud hardening in the sun and cracking into jumbled little fractals in the dirt. The paint up here looks like that, like the riven earth, and he shoots it in profile so as to channel a viewer's gaze along its deep, exfoliated edges—less a photograph *of* something than a photograph *about* something: age, change, transfiguration.

He moves on. He decides to be loud, not confident he can effectively sneak while wearing these boots—thick and steel-reinforced, purchased cheaply at the Army/Navy surplus, necessary given the nails sticking straight up from the floor, and the broken glass that is the evidence of some raucous night involving shattered beer bottles. He should also be wearing a mask, he thinks, because of the dust in the air, the dust and dirt and probably mold and mildew and toxic lead and unfriendly microbes, a still and hazy particulate cloud that turns the sunlight coming in via windows to glimmering streaks that in landscape photography would be called God beams but are much more blasphemous here. Gunk beams, maybe.

And then there are the needles. He finds a lot of these, clustered in small methodical piles in some dark back corner, tenaciously amassed and emptied but for a scrap of dark sludge at the tips, and he photographs them with the shallowest depth of field this lens is capable of, so that the picture is almost entirely blurry, which he thinks cleverly evokes what it might have felt like for whatever poor soul was here, craving the needle. Heroin inspires an odd love-hate relationship in the neighborhood—people mildly complain about the hypodermics they find in the park, and about the abandoned buildings down the street known widely as shooting galleries for how many junkies can be found there. And yet? Among the artists who live in his building and who occasionally complain about the heroin, most of them also sort of look like they do it. And often. They have that skinny, stringy-haired, sunken-eyed, colorless look of the frequently high. And in fact this was how he came to be living here; the landlord found him at his first gallery showing and asked: "Are you Jack Baker?"

"I am," he said.

"You're the photographer?"

"Yep."

It was an autumn show at the School of the Art Institute of Chicago. On display were pieces by the school's incoming studio art majors, and among the roughly two dozen freshmen, Jack was the only one who worked primarily in landscape photos. The other students were expressionist painters of exorbitant talent, or they assembled elaborate sculptures from mixed objects, or they worked in video art, their installations built of complexly interconnected televisions and VCRs.

Jack, meanwhile, took Polaroids.

Of trees.

Trees back home, out on the prairie, growing as they did when they were exposed to the weather: tilted, their trunks swept sideways by the unyielding wind.

Nine of these Polaroids were taped in a three-by-three grid on the gallery's white wall, Jack standing nearby waiting for anyone to engage with him on the matter of his art, which nobody did. Dozens of well-dressed collectors had passed him by when this pale man in a ragged white sweater and unlaced work boots introduced himself. His name was Benjamin Quince, and he was a graduate student, a master's candidate in new media studies, now in his seventh year in the program, working on a thesis, which, to a freshman like Jack, all sounded like an unfathomable level of academic achievement. Benjamin was literally the first person to ask Jack a question, the question being: "So. Trees?"

"The wind blows hard where I come from," Jack said. "It makes the trees grow up crooked."

"I see," Benjamin said, squinting behind big round eyeglasses, idly rubbing his chin of wiry patchwork scruff. His wool sweater was stretched and honeycombed and doilied in places. His wispy hair was unwashed and hay-bale brown and of a particular length that required diligent ear retucking. He said: "And where do you come from?"

"Kansas," Jack said.

"Ah," he said, nodding, as if this confirmed something important. "The heartland."

"Yes."

"America's breadbasket."

"That's right."

"Kansas. Is that corn or wheat? I'm struggling to picture it."

"You know the song 'Home on the Range'?"

"Sure."

"That's basically where I'm from."

"Good job getting out," Benjamin said, winking, then he studied the Polaroids for a moment. "I'll bet nobody's interested in these pictures."

"Thanks so much."

"I'm not making a value judgment. Just saying, these images are probably not popular with this particular crowd. Am I right?"

"Most people linger for between one and three seconds before smiling pleasantly and moving on."

"And do you understand why?"

"Not really."

"Because Polaroids are not appreciable assets."

"Sorry?"

"They don't sell. A Polaroid has never once been auctioned at Sotheby's. Polaroids are mass-produced, instant, cheap, impermanent. The chemicals will degrade, the image will dissolve. A Polaroid is not a durable good. These people here?" Benjamin motioned vaguely to everyone else in the room. "They describe themselves as collectors, but a better word would be *investors*. They're capitalist stooges. Materialistic tools. They're looking to buy low and sell high. Your problem is that a Polaroid will never sell high."

"Honestly I hadn't thought about that."

"Good for you."

"Mostly I just liked those trees."

"I have to say I admire your authenticity. You're not another of these pandering sluts. I dig that." Then Benjamin came closer, put a hand on Jack's shoulder, whisper-spoke: "Listen. I own a building in Wicker Park. An abandoned old ironworks. I bought it for a dollar. The bank just wanted to get it off the books. You know about Wicker Park?"

"Not really."

"North Side. About fifteen minutes on the train. Take the Blue Line six stops and it's a completely different world."

"Different how?"

"Primarily, it's real. It is a place of substance. That's where the real art is happening, unlike this donor-pleasing bullshit. And real music too, not the fake corporate crap on the radio. I'm renovating my building, a total gut job, turning it into a co-op for creatives. I'm calling it the Foundry. Very exclusive, invitation only, nothing mainstream, nothing conventional, nothing frat boy, no yuppies allowed."

"Sounds nice."

"Do you do heroin?"

"No."

"But it *looks* like you do heroin. Which is perfect. You want in?"

It was the first time in his life that being skinny and frail worked somewhat in Jack's favor—it got him this apartment in Wicker Park, where he's living rent-free in exchange for photographic services, living among musicians and artists and writers who mostly also look like they do heroin. It's a thrilling place to have landed, and Jack finds that despite the poor condition of his apartment building, despite the darkness and bleakness and shivering cold of a real Chicago winter, despite the neighborhood's frequent muggings, and the alleged dealers stalking the park, and the gangs with their complex rivalries and occasional disputes, he loves it. It is his first winter away from home and he cannot believe how alive he feels here, how utterly, truly, and unprecedentedly free. The city is noisy and dirty and dangerous and expensive and he loves it. He loves the noise in particular, the roar of the elevated trains, the honks of impatient cabbies, the shriek of police sirens, the moaning of lake ice grinding against concrete embankments. And he loves those nights when the noise stops, when the city is shut down and muffled by a storm dropping the fattest, slowest snow he has ever seen, and cars are buried on the curbs, and the sky is a scrim of reflected orange street-light, and each footfall is greeted with a satisfying eluvial crunch. He loves the city at night, especially when he exits the Art Institute and looks upon Michigan Avenue and the great skyline beyond, the buildings that touch the clouds on thickly overcast days, their colos-sal flat faces inscribed with hundreds of tiny yellow squares where the business of the city works overtime.

It is an odd feeling, to sense one's aliveness, for perhaps the very first time, to understand that life up until this point was not being lived, exactly; it was being endured.

In Chicago, he's seeing art in person (museums being unavail-able where he comes from); and he's watching theater (never having attended a school that even once put on a play); and he's eating foods he's never eaten before (foods he had not once encountered until now: pesto, pita, empanadas, pierogi, baba ghanoush); and he's lis-tening to classmates sincerely debate who's better: John Ashbery or Frank O'Hara? Arne Naess or Noam Chomsky? David Bowie or lit-erally anybody else? (Debates that would earn nothing from people back home but blank stares and possibly beatings.) For the rest of his life, the songs released this winter will always call him back to these feelings of expansiveness and freedom—Rage Against the Machine screaming "Fuck you, I won't do what you tell me!" being the verse that most accurately embodies his new uncaged ethos right now, but even the cheesy commercial radio hits feel special and meaningful, songs like "Life Is a Highway" and "Right Now" and "Finally" and that *Aladdin* tune that's getting interminable airplay and seems to Jack almost like his own Chicago anthem: it is, indeed, *a whole new world*.

(Not that he would admit to anyone—ever—that he secretly hums and sometimes actually sings a song from a Disney cartoon while he's in the shower and, further, that he finds great strength in it. No, he'll take that to the grave.)

He loves the noise of the city because there's something reassur-ing about it—the evidence of other people, neighbors, compatriots. And also there's something grand about becoming insusceptible to the noise, sleeping peacefully through the urban night without flinching at the beeps and voices and car alarms and police sirens outside—it's an important marker of transcendence. Back home, the only noise was the constant low breath of the wind, a prairie wind relentless and monotonous. But sometimes, under the wind, after sunset, one could hear the barking and howling of the coyotes that scavenged the countryside each night. And every once in a while, the howling of a pack would become suddenly and hauntingly reduced, only one voice, and the howling would become more urgent, more like yelping, and then more plaintive, more like whining, and Jack, still awake and hearing all of this despite the covers pulled up way over his head, knew exactly what was going on. A coyote was trapped on the fence.

What happens is this: when coyotes leap over a barbed-wire fence, sometimes they don't leap high enough, and they get caught on the top wire, right at the spot where their hind legs attach to their body, which on canines forms a kind of unfortunate hook. Their front paws will be reaching, swimming, not quite touching the ground, their back legs bucking, and they'll hang there despite fierce kicking because coyotes are not biologically equipped with the joints or flexibility that might enable other animals to free themselves from a wire fence. Coyotes cannot twist enough, cannot maneuver back legs that are really meant only for driving forward, and so they dangle there, all night. And because they're dangling on barbed wire, there's a very good chance they came down upon—and were impaled by—the fence's knifelike talons, which are now digging into their softest, most tender spot, and the more they thrash and kick and wriggle, the more the spikes stir up their insides, and this is, eventually, how they die: bleeding out from stabs to the belly, their screams carried for miles on the wind. Jack would see them in the morning, hanging like clothes from a line.

Compared to that, the sirens of Chicago are a blessing. Even the muggings are a reasonable toll for entry into this world.

Jack has not yet been mugged. He has, since moving to Wicker Park, perfected a look that he hopes is a mugger deterrent, a dangerous-seeming impression built from secondhand clothes purchased at the

Salvation Army and an armload of tattoos and unkempt hair and an urban sort of strut and a steely, determined stare over a cigarette that's very nearly always in his mouth—all of which communicates, he hopes, *Fuck off*. He does not want to be mugged, and yet he is also aware that the possibility of being mugged is, in a weird way, part of the draw, part of this neighborhood's particular attraction. The artists who come out here are not here despite the neighborhood's danger but because of it. They are here to embrace it. Wicker Park is, according to Benjamin Quince (who can really get going on this subject and talk just about all night long), Chicago's answer to Montmartre: cheap and dirty and run-down and, therefore, alive.

So the filthiness is roundly celebrated, hence Jack's photos, which try to capture exactly this quality: the grit, the gunk. He searches the hallways and former offices and storage rooms of the fifth floor looking for evidence of life on the edge. The cracked paint. The left-behind hypodermics. The broken windows. The browned curtains. The crumbling walls. The dust that's settled so thickly after so many years that it's now less like dust and more like sand.

"That is so raw," Benjamin says later, inspecting the photos.

The two of them are standing on the roof of the co-op on a deep-winter day. Jack is blowing warm air into his cold, cupped hands. He's wearing his usual thin black peacoat, under which is every sweater he owns. Benjamin wears a big parka so puffy it looks balloonish. His cheeks are watermelon pink, and his coat looks warm and soft and probably filled with down, a material Jack has heard of but could not define specifically.

Benjamin looks at the photos, and Jack looks at the gray neighborhood around them, the occasional pedestrian or car, the mounds of dirty snow, the streets and alleys running perfectly straight all the way to their vanishing points at the lake. They're on the east side of the building, the side that faces the girl in the window. The nameless her. Jack looks down into her apartment. She's not home right now, but this new view from above is strangely thrilling. He sees a rug she's placed on the floor near the window, not visible from his usual vantage on the fourth floor. And he imbues this new fact about her with great meaning: *She is a woman who buys rugs.*

He wants to know everything about her. But he has not asked anyone anything about the girl in the window because he can't figure out how to ask about her without also revealing that he occasionally spies on her, a practice he is ashamed of only insofar as he knows that others would shame him for it.

Benjamin, still admiring the photos, says: "We gotta put these on the internet."

"Okay," Jack says as, directly below them, a man walks into the alley. He's carrying a large black duffel bag, and judging by the way he's stumbling along, it seems that either the bag is so heavy it's impeding his balance or he is very drunk.

Jack says: "What's the internet?"

Benjamin looks up from the photos. "Seriously?"

"Yeah. What is that?"

"The internet. You know. The information superhighway. The digital hypertextual global cyberspace thing."

Jack nods, then says: "To be honest I'm not entirely clear on those terms either."

Benjamin laughs. "They don't have computers in Kansas yet?"

"My family never really saw the point."

"Okay, well, the internet. How to explain it?" He thinks for a moment, then says: "You know those flyers for bands that people staple to all the telephone poles?"

"Yeah."

"The internet is like those flyers, except imagine they're not on the telephone pole but in it."

"You lost me."

"Imagine they're inside the telephone *wires*, traveling at the speed of light, all of them connected, dynamic, communicating, accessible to anyone in the world."

"Anyone?"

"Anyone with a computer and a phone line. I've gotten visitors from England, Australia, Japan."

"Why do people in Japan care about your flyer?"

"There are outcasts everywhere, my friend. The misunderstood, the unpopular, the dissidents, malcontents, freaks. With the internet, we find each other. It's like this amazing alternative world. You don't have to prostrate yourself to the usual conformist rules. You're free to be your weird and wild self. So it's a more honest place, less fraudulent, more real."

"More real than what?"

"The world. The manufactured fishbowl construct we live in. The whole mind-control commercialized oppression apparatus."

"Wow. That must be one hell of a flyer you made."

"It's absolutely state-of-the-art."

"And it's a flyer about what? The Foundry?"

"Sort of, but it's also about the neighborhood, and the energy in the neighborhood, our antiestablishment vibe. You want to see it?"

"Sure."

"I'll tutor you. I'll be your internet sherpa. Pull you out of the eighties."

"Thanks."

"Hey, you should work for me. I need visuals. Photos of bars, bands, parties. Cool people being cool. That kind of thing. Could you do that?"

"I guess."

"Great!" Benjamin says, which is how Jack comes to be employed in the New Economy despite not understanding exactly what's new about it.

Beneath them, the man with the duffel bag stops at the bike rack behind the co-op. He stands there considering the many bicycles locked to the bar, wobbling a little on unsteady feet. Then he puts down his bag, unzips it, and pulls out a large bolt cutter, with which he quickly and cleanly snips the lock off one of the more expensive-looking ten-speeds.

"Hey!" Jack yells.

The man turns around, frightened, and looks down the alley. Then he searches the windows of the building, and then, his palm shielding his eyes from the light, he finally spots them, on the roof, six stories up, at which point the man smiles at them, and waves. A big friendly wave, like they're all old pals.

And what can they do? Jack and Benjamin wave back. And then

they watch the man stow his bolt cutter in the duffel bag, which he slings around his back before hopping on the freed bicycle and riding crookedly away.

Benjamin smiles and looks at Jack and says: "That was so fucking real."

S HE'S STANDING in the far-back corner of another loud bar, invited here by another guy of large opinions, here to see another band she's been told she must love. Tonight she's at the Empty Bottle, that bar on Western Avenue with the big sign out front for Old Style beer and an awning that says MUSIC / FRIENDLY / DANCING.

Right now, only one of those three things seems accurate.

There is indeed music, though it is not danceable, and it is certainly not friendly. She's listening to a band she doesn't know the name of because she could not hear it above the noise of the band. Her date yelled it at her, the band's name, inches from her ear, *twice*, but no luck. The band's drummer and lead guitarist both seem obsessed with preventing any behavior that isn't the strict paying of total attention to them. Even the song's lyrics—which feature something about the lead singer's world-sundering spiritual pain and disaffection—are mostly lost in a bellow of power chords, while the manic drummer seems capable of only one simple maneuver, and it involves a lot of cymbal. People stand around not so much dancing as flinching in rhythm. Drinks at the bar must be ordered via gesture.

Whenever the door opens, there's a burst of cold air, and so she's still wearing her scarf, her mittens, her woolen winter hat, which she pulls way down over her ears to muffle the onstage pandemonium by a few blessed decibels. Just outside are roughly half the bar's patrons, those who chose the cold over the noise. They stand stiffly, their arms and legs pulled tight to their torsos, mummies out in the snow. It's the kind of Chicago deep-winter evening that's so beyond frigid it causes despair, so bitter it triggers spontaneous sidewalk lamentation: "*Fuck,* it's cold!" the people out there say, stamping their feet. It's the kind of cold that gets into your boots and stays there all night.

The band she's listening to is not the band she came here for. The last act is, allegedly, tonight's big draw, though her date refuses to tell her anything about it. He doesn't want to spoil it for her. He wants her experience of listening to this music for the very first time to be, he says, pristine. He's managing her entire experience, and he probably thinks she appreciates it. She stands next to him, sips her beer, and, unable to converse due to the surrounding ruckus, she waits.

The walls of the Empty Bottle are brick and covered in most places by posters or flyers or stickers in such quantity and density that it causes a kind of cognitive overload looking at them too closely. The ceiling is tin-tiled except for the area above the stage, where sheets of foam sound-absorbers—those shaped like egg cartons—hang a few feet over the musicians' heads. The stage is painted matte black and flanked by stacks of enormous amplifiers. At the bar, there are a total of nine beers on tap, and they all cost a dollar fifty.

It's one of several local venues known for serious music that she's recently been persuaded to visit, invited by guys eager to impress her. Tonight's guy—serious; studied; somber; a particular gravitas that one might call *clenched*; an upperclassman whose blond hair is parted down his scalp's exact middle; John Lennon glasses; patterned sweater over differently patterned shirt; name of Bradley; *Call me Brad*—had sat down next to her in this morning's microeconomics lecture, the arms of their big winter coats pressing into each other the full fifty minutes, the dirty snowmelt puddles under their respective boots eventually joining as one. After the lecture—which was a deep dive into expected utility and risk aversion and how people make choices in conditions of uncertain information—she could feel him looking at her as they packed up, and when she glanced at him he gave her this big exasperated roll of the eyes and said "*Booooor-ring*," and she smiled at that even though she didn't find the class boring at all, and he followed her out of the lecture hall asking if she had plans tonight, because if she didn't, there was this brilliant new band playing at the Empty Bottle, where he happened to know the bartender—the implication being that she could drink despite being underage—and when she expressed a hint of interest, he got all elaborate, told her how she absolutely needed to hear this band, right now, tonight, when the band's music was still pure, before word got out about them, before the malevolent forces of popularity and money changed them and ruined them. So, okay, fine, she agreed to meet Brad here at nine, and when she arrived, he ordered beers and said: "So, you like music?" And she said: "Sure, I like music." And then he basically forced her to prove it. He began testing her: Do you know this band, do you know that band? Fugazi, Pavement, the Replacements, Big Star, Tortoise, Pixies, Hüsker Dü—pronouncing this last one so exactingly that she could actually hear the umlauts—and when she said she didn't know a single one of them, he shook his head pityingly and then offered, of course, to teach her. It turned out that Call-me-Brad had a large collection of rare vinyl that he really wanted to tell her about—and wanted even more to show her, in person, back at his place—a full wall of his apartment dedicated to only the most scarce, most genius, most iconoclastic records, sacred records that almost nobody else had heard of or properly appreciated—

Honestly she had stopped listening. Brad required no more encouragement to continue monologuing—the sexual anxiety was *radiating* off him, a throbbing low-grade panic—and so her attention just kind of detached until the band's expressive guitarist interrupted with a strenuous riff, whereupon Brad shut up and the howling set began.

What she hasn't told Brad is that the only reason the rumor of a brilliant new band piqued her interest was the high probability of seeing *him*, the boy in the window, the boy from across the alley, at the show. And indeed she walked in tonight and there he was, up in the front row, with his camera, and she felt a kind of heaving sensation in her gut that might be the experience people are describing when they say "My heart leapt," though that description sounds pleasant and enjoyable, certainly much more enjoyable than this current sensation, which is less like leaping and more like being liquefied.

Whenever she sees him out in the world, she tends to become shy, even though she does not consider herself a shy person. She'll spot him late at night at the Empty Bottle, or Rainbo Club, or Lounge Ax, or Phyllis' Musical Inn, with his camera, at work, and she'll watch him until her scrutiny and interest become unbearable: *Why don't you notice me?* It feels like there's a spotlight on her face that gets brighter the longer she stares at him, but he never sees it. He's always in the front row, engrossed with his camera, shooting from his knees up at lead singers and solo guitarists to make them look, in his photos, monumental.

She's seen his work on the internet, on one of those electronic bulletin boards, which is also how she finally figured out his name: *Photography by Jack Baker.* He's always up there by the stage—sometimes even onstage, shooting the crowd from the position of the drummer—whenever the best acts are playing, the locally famous bands that he usually leaves the bar with, which convinces her that he's firmly out of her league.

She is, here in Chicago, a nobody.

She does not get invited to the after-parties she knows are elsewhere happening. And she knows they're happening because she's seen them on that bulletin board, photos by Jack Baker capturing debaucheries occurring somewhere in the neighborhood, who knows where. Is there any worse anguish than this? To know that fun is being had but not being invited to also have it? Her name is Elizabeth Augustine—*of the Litchfield Augustines*—though her family's reputation holds cachet only in particular circles, and these circles do not extend way out here. She's merely an anonymous student now, a freshman at DePaul, a lowly outsider stuck in the farback corner, a woman not exactly plugged into the local music scene and so to know where she might find Jack Baker and the rest of the neighborhood's in-crowd she needs the help of aficionados, guys like Brad, who now leans into her during a subdued moment when the guitarist is tuning and explains certain things about tonight's brilliant band, how their sound is distinct from *rock* or *alternative* or *grunge* in ways she knows she can't identify. It all sounds like noise to her, but Brad insists that, no, in fact the Seattle sound now taking over the radio and Billboard charts is nothing like the Chicago sound, which is, he says, less commercial, more true to native jazz roots, less mainstream, more indie. It's a break from East Coast hardcore, which sold out long ago, and a break from West Coast grunge, which is right now in the process of selling out. It is its own thing, nurtured in forgotten flyover country, unmolested by the larger moneyed interests. She has never before thought about a rock song's *terroir*, but she has been giving a lot of thought lately to the crippling effects of money, and in fact escaping the greed and wealth of her family—and the associated inhuman behavior and endless striving and competitive immolation that such greed and wealth demands—had been one of the primary reasons she left everyone she ever knew and came to Chicago.

It would be, she vowed, her final move. She had promised herself, even before arriving in this city, that she would stay here for good, that she would at last build a permanent life—*her own life, a compassionate and decent life*—this after a childhood of ceaseless moving: she had spent her adolescence living in the wealthy outer suburbs of the big East Coast metros, attending innumerable private day schools, moving from place to place to place as her father marauded this company, then that company, auditing, acquiring, raiding, poaching, liquidating, cashing in, moving on, profiting wildly while leaving nothing behind but insolvency and angry litigants, which was something of a family tradition.

And so she was delighted to find this particular crowd in Chicago, who rejected such crass mercantilism; anyone who pursued wealth was shunned for "selling out," cast aside for being a "sheep."

She does not want to be a sellout.

She does not want to be a sheep.

And yet, she'd really like to be invited to those parties.

The band, meanwhile, kicks into its next noisy offering, and Jack photographs the lead singer, shooting him first from the side, in profile, then from behind, then from down in front, kneeling on the dance floor, shooting upward, at which point, as if choreographed, the singer leans way out over the stage, microphone pressed to his lips in a pose that she is sure will look, in the photo, fucking heroic, and the singer whispers something into the mic that's unintelligible now that the wanton guitarist comes in and overpowers the whole moment. She senses a kind of sibling rivalry between the singer and the guitarist. She decides there's no need to learn the name of this band, as it will almost definitely break up, and probably before spring. Jack, meanwhile, stands and sheds his sweater, the heavy black one that's about two sizes too large for him, the sweater that's essentially his everyday winter uniform, holes worn in the back from sitting on it. Beneath that sweater, he's wearing another, thinner black sweater.

What is it about this boy that's so compelling to her? It's surely not just that he happens to live across the alley. She can imagine that most guys would prompt her to do nothing more than close the curtains. But with this boy there's an unaccountable feeling of recognition, like he has some important quality that she's looking for but cannot quite name. Elizabeth had come to Chicago intending to melt, with full abandon, into its lively bohemia: to drink with poets and sleep with artists. (Or vice versa, whatever.) And not even good poets or good artists; the only criteria she really has for going home with a guy is that he is a good and interesting and selfless man who deserves it.

Which is a condition the guys of Chicago have thus far failed to meet.

But the boy in the window seems different: he exudes a kindness and gentleness and restraint that's a radical departure from the world-dominating ethos she moved to Chicago to escape. Jack Baker is considerate—or at least she believes him to be considerate, believes he would be a considerate person, a considerate lover. She believes this because of the many private scenes she's witnessed from her place at the window, his many small moments of careful attentiveness: the books of literature and poetry and philosophy he reads late into the night, the way he patiently looks at so many negatives until he's found the right one, the way he hides sheepishly behind his long bangs. Even his choice of career—photographer— strikes her as pleasingly self-effacing. He will always be on the outskirts, watching. By definition, the photographer will never be the center of attention. She's dated guys who were always the center of attention, guys like these guys up onstage, guys like Brad, and she's found that eventually their need becomes crushing.

The band finishes the set, finally, with a great detonative roar that's similar to its ongoing previous roar except for the strength and frequency of its cymbal-banging. It's impossible to "crescendo" when you've been at max volume the whole time, so the band just goes faster, their beat getting so compressed that everything coming out of those big amps turns to mush. And then with a final orgasmic bucking of the guitarist's hips, they come to their screeching end, at which point the lead singer—in what is his first intelligible speech of the night—says "Thank you, Chicago!" as if he's talking to a sold-out Soldier Field and not a dozen people in a dive bar hiding from the cold.

The musicians unplug and Brad turns to her, says, "So what did you think?" Then he crosses his arms and waits for her to answer, and Elizabeth understands that whatever her answer is, his opinion about it will be fierce.

"On a scale of one to ten," she says, "how much would you say your parents loved you?"

"What?"

"On a scale of one to ten."

"Wow!" he says, laughing uncomfortably. "Ha ha!"

"I'm serious."

"You," he says, pointing at her, shaking his head, grinning a wide stupid grin, "you are a spitfire! You know that? You are *sassy*."

After which he goes for more beer.

At the other end of the bar, Jack is mingling. He approaches various groups standing at the bar and says a few words and then takes their picture. She's seen these photos too, online, portraits of people out at bars. They remind her of that part of the society magazines back home where for upward of six glossy pages it's nothing more than snapshots of people who recently attended important local soirees and fundraisers. The difference between those photos and these being that the Chicago subjects tend to be more ironically detached. They don't smile, and mostly don't even look at the camera. They have a bearing that makes it seem like they're aware their photograph is being taken but don't care to participate. Jack thanks them and moves along.

He's walking her way now, toward the front of the bar, searching for a new subject, his gaze landing on this person, then that person, evaluating them, and Elizabeth wonders if this is the moment he'll finally notice her, the moment he'll finally want to take *her* picture. And she decides she does not care how obvious she is or how liquid it makes her insides feel, she's going to look at him, look directly at him, she's going to demand his attention. And this for some reason feels really risky and scary and threatening to her, and when his eyes sweep over her, she has this almost instinctive response to hide. It's the boldest she's ever stared at him, which is how she sees him quickly inspect her and then, just as quickly, dismiss her. He moves along, with no recognition, or interest, whatsoever.

She feels, in this moment, sort of like someone never invited to the prom.

She watches him go outside, and when he opens the door, there's that arctic surge that makes everyone around her curl up, which is when she realizes: her hat is pulled down to her eyes, her scarf is covering her mouth. She is practically *in disguise*.

So she takes off her scarf and hat, runs her fingers through her hair, and looks out the window behind her. She brings her face right up to it, close enough to feel the chill of the outside air. She sees Jack, his figure made wavy and rippled, distorted by the thick glass. He's standing at the curb—he shoots, then sidesteps, then shoots again from a new angle, sidesteps again, shoots again. People are pretending not to notice him and yet always angling their bodies contrapposto to the camera. He's pointing that camera right at Elizabeth, but between them is the huddled crowd, the blowing snow, this cloudy block of glass, and so he hasn't seen her—or maybe he's ignoring her; she can't be sure.

Just then there's a sound from the other end of the bar, a guitar playing a few simple chords, repeatedly, quietly. Elizabeth glances at the stage to see what band is next and is surprised to see it's only one woman. She's short—barely five feet tall—and blond, skinny, young, wearing jeans with a tank top tucked in and a cream-colored cardigan, her hair in a plain shoulder-length cut. She does not, in other words, look like a rock star. Her presentation is contrary to that of the band that was up there minutes ago, all those outlandish guys. She looks so unassuming that Elizabeth thinks it's possible she's a patron who's drunkenly taken the guitar and will soon be escorted offstage by the bartender. But no, the bartender does not move, and at her first sound, Jack Baker comes in from the cold and immediately begins photographing her, and it's clear that the girl isn't warming up but has actually already begun her set, that she has no band and no instrumentation other than the guitar she's holding, which is not plugged into the giant speaker apparatus but rather into one small amp at her feet, so it's hard to hear her over the small crowd that isn't shutting up. Elizabeth leans forward and listens to her, her strangely monotone voice, her song, which seems to describe a man with tastes so ravenous he can no longer really appreciate anything:

> *I bet you've long since passed understanding*
> *What it takes to be satisfied*

She's not exactly singing the lyrics but also not exactly talking—it's a peculiar timbre somewhere in between. And her pitch is not what you'd call in tune, but it's not flat either. And she strums her guitar so modestly, and she sings so matter-of-factly, without any of the ornamentation and melodrama and vocal scratch of your typical rock-and-roll singer dudes. When Brad returns, Elizabeth whispers: "Who is this?"

He looks at the stage, surprised, as if he had not yet noticed anyone up there. "Nobody," he says. "Filler."

"Filler?" she says.

"The headliners are running late. She's killing time."

And with a dismissive wave, Brad resumes his discourse, this time a litany of his top-five concert experiences ever. Around them, people chat loudly and rudely, Elizabeth straining to hear the music. Over at the bar, the four guys from the previous band are now laughing, almost advertising how much they're ignoring the singer's performance. And this is how the short song goes: the woman strumming her unadorned guitar, her humble sound competing with the ambient noise of an indifferent crowd.

"Number five? The Rolling Stones at the Silverdome," Brad is saying. "It would have been higher on the list but it was 1989 and the Stones were obviously no longer at their peak and anyway the Silverdome is as lifeless as a mental ward."

"Uh-huh."

"Number four was Soul Asylum at Metro in July, which could have easily been number three on the list or maybe even number two if the bar weren't filled with all these yuppies yelling *Runaway Train!* like it was the only song they knew."

And Brad continues his long countdown, Elizabeth thinking that for a guy who claims to love music, Brad sure seems to also hate a lot about it. And the singer continues her song about this insatiable man who's no longer capable of happiness, and Elizabeth listens to the lyrics and giggles, at which point Brad stops his ponderous clucking and looks at her a little defensively—he's not a man who likes being laughed at—and says: "What's so funny?"

"This song," Elizabeth says, "it's about you."

"Really?" he says, genuinely excited, listening finally as the woman sing-speaks in her dark monotone:

> *You're like a vine that keeps climbing higher*
> *But all the money in the world is not enough*

Brad is now thoroughly confused, but Elizabeth doesn't care. It's as if this song were written just for her, a song describing all the greed she has made it her life's mission to escape.

Then the door opens and there's that stab of cold air and in walk three guys who could only be the headline band, dressed as eccentrically as they are. She clocks the lead singer immediately, in thick plastic sunglasses and what looks to be a ruffled baby-blue tuxedo shirt from the seventies—conspicuously uncool, which of course makes it really cool—the top four buttons calculatedly undone. The guys enter the bar with a swagger that makes the crowd instinctively part.

"They're here!" Brad says. "That's them!"

Onstage, the singer wraps up her song, then shrugs as if to apologize and says, "I guess that's it," to dispersed polite clapping. And Elizabeth watches as the singer packs up her guitar and, together with Jack—who had been photographing her all this time—they walk toward the bar's exit. The singer, Jack, and the singer's small entourage, all of them off to whatever wondrous after-party awaits.

And she's following Jack with her eyes as Brad continues to explain why Elizabeth is so lucky to be here tonight, experiencing for the first time this new band, with him, and she's nodding but continuing to stare at the baby-faced photographer, and right at the moment that Jack crosses paths with the headliners, he looks up at the band, and then *past* the band, at this table of nobodies in the far-back corner, and his eyes lock onto Elizabeth's. She sees him seeing her, now that she's without scarf and hat, and there's this shiver of recognition between them as he smiles and waves, and she smiles and waves, and Brad looks at her, puzzled, and the relief she feels is just about knee-breaking.

And what does Jack do? He walks *right past* the band, he walks right up to Elizabeth, he ignores the brilliant musicians and ignores the now puckered Brad and he extends his hand and utters the first two words he'll ever say to her.

They are: "Come with."

C OME WITH.

What an odd and curious and delightful thing to say. *Come with.*

She'd never heard anyone ever say it like that before. None of Elizabeth's friends in those many private schools would ever say it like that, nor would her parents, nor any of the guests her parents often entertained. They'd never leave that word *with* hanging at the end of a sentence, unresolved. They'd say it correctly: *Do you want to come with us?*

It would be proper and complete: *Would you care to leave this place?*

A fully literate and well educated and finished phrase: *Please give us the pleasure of your company.*

But Jack had said, simply, *Come with,* which to her ears sounded refreshingly—and charmingly—imperfect. He held out a hand and looked at her with no guile whatsoever, with no knowledge that he'd said something either funny or strange, which filled her with tenderness.

Come with would turn into a mantra between them, a kind of abracadabra calling back the thrill and surprise and exuberance of this first night. "Come with," he will say a few days later, when he takes her to the Art Institute and they hold hands and stare at all his favorite modernists. "Come with," she'll say a week after that, when she gets student rush tickets and they watch *La Bohème* at Lyric Opera and he pretends not to be embarrassed by his cheap sweater amid all those suits and ties. "Come with," she'll say a few summers later, when they go to Italy and look at every painting and textile and statue that Venice has to offer. And years after that, on a certain significant night when he gets down on one knee and opens a black velvet box with a tasteful engagement ring inside, he will do everything exactly according to tradition except that when he proposes, he won't say, "Marry me," he'll say, "Come with."

It all starts on this night, with Jack holding out his hand at the Empty Bottle and saying, "Come with," this incomplete sentence that Elizabeth completes by taking his hand and nodding *yes*, and together they walk through the blowing snow and the freezing cold, and for the very first time that winter the subzero temperature seems not oppressive but rather *hilarious*, how they keep ducking into vestibules and alleys to escape the wind, rubbing their hands together, laughing, sprinting to the next hiding spot, traveling in this preposterous manner all the way to a bar on Division, where during a conversation about how much they both loved tonight's singer they actually lose track of the singer, and the singer's entourage, looking up for a moment and realizing they're alone, they've been abandoned, then laughing about this, not really caring, talking more, establishing the essential facts about each other: She's Elizabeth; she's from New England. He's Jack; he's from the Great Plains. He's studying photography at the Art Institute. She's at DePaul majoring in cognitive psychology, and also behavioral economics, and also evolutionary biology, and also neuroscience—

"Wait," he says. "You have four majors?"

"Five majors if you count theater, which I have no talent for but enjoy nonetheless."

"So you're a genius."

"Mostly I'm just tenacious," she says. "I have a good brain supplemented by a better work ethic."

"That's exactly what a genius would say."

"I'm also minoring in music theory, for fun. And I'll probably audit a few courses in ethnographic sociology. Basically, I'm studying the whole human condition. Coming at it from every possible angle."

And the blip of silence that follows makes her immediately regret saying it like that—*I'm studying the whole human condition*—how pompous! how pretentious! Jack eyes her for a terrifyingly long moment and she worries that either she has ruined the evening by being arrogant or he is about to ruin the evening by being one of those disappointing guys intimidated by her ambition. But then he says, "Are you hungry?" and the answer is "Yes!" because, first, she is actually sincerely hungry, but also, second, she knows that getting food with Jack elevates and advances the night—it means they're now *kind of on a date,* that they've moved beyond the category of *random bar encounter,* that she has not in fact ruined anything, that he is not in fact intimidated—and so they totter all the way to that bistro on Milwaukee she's never once entered because it's called Earwax, which, *gross,* but he convinces her to eat at this Earwax place and they share a black bean burger and a soy milkshake and he tells her that he's thinking about becoming a vegetarian, that he couldn't be a vegetarian in the backward beef-eating place he grew up in but is free to be a vegetarian here, in Chicago, whereupon she admits that in Chicago she is now free to indulge her deep and abiding cravings for very fatty and very sweet dessert-type foods, these things having been strongly discouraged back home due to parents who had a weird fixation on her diet, on eating only those foods whose fats had been complexly rearranged and chemically substituted—tasteless low-fat cheeses and diet yogurts and margarines and cereal bars—at which point Jack smiles the confident smile of a man with a very good idea and takes her to that hot-dog place next door called Swank Frank and orders the deep-fried Twinkie, which they also share, and which is goddamn heavenly, meanwhile talking about how life should always be full of exactly these kinds of simple yet profound pleasures (screw whatever her parents said about her waistline, her figure), which leads them—wildly gesticulating hands sticky with filling, laughing powdered-sugar lips—to a disquisition on all their favorite things, all of life's best and simplest pleasures—

"Back rubs," she says without even pausing to think about it. "Long and luxurious and totally aimless back rubs."

"Hot showers," he says. "Incredibly hot. Like, use-all-the-hot-water-in-the-whole-building hot."

"The first sip of water when you're really thirsty."

"The first sip of coffee in the morning."

"The smell of dryer exhaust."

"The smell of hot asphalt at an amusement park."

"Sprinting into the ocean."

"A hayride at sunset."

"Lobster rolls, warm, with melted butter."

"Cheese ravioli out of a can."

"Whoopie pies with marshmallow fluff."

"Tater Tots with mayonnaise."

"The moment everyone at a wedding stands up at the first few notes of the bridal march."

"When you stare at a Rothko so long it looks like it's vibrating."

"The statue of David."

"*American Gothic.*"

"The beginning of Mozart Forty."

"Rage Against the Machine."

"The violin solo from *Scheherazade.*"

"The idée fixe of *Symphonie Fantastique.*"

"Autumn leaf-peeping in the White Mountains."

"Watching a Polaroid develop."

"The purple shimmer on the inside of an oyster."

"The green sky before a tornado."

"Skinny-dipping in the morning."

"Skinny-dipping *anytime.*"

It's an altogether manic and ceaseless conversation, a conversation that feels sometimes like falling down stairs, barely keeping upright, taken by gravity, skipping, grasping, and then somehow landing, magically, on one's feet, intact and triumphant.

They walk the few blocks up North Avenue to Urbus Orbis, the coffee shop with the delightfully rude waitresses, the one place in the neighborhood where everyone gathers nightly, the place that is now, at two o'clock in the morning, teeming with the local after-bar crowd, and the two of them manage to find a table way in the back corner and they order their dollar coffees and smoke their cigarettes and they stare at each other for a long moment, and that's when Elizabeth asks: "On a scale of one to ten, how much did your parents love you?"

Jack laughs. "And thus concludes the small talk."

"I don't like to waste time. I want to know everything I need to know, right up front."

"Reasonable," Jack says, nodding, smiling, and then he seems to turn inward for a second, looking into his coffee, and the smile turns into a sad smile that makes Elizabeth feel a new warmth for him and he says: "That's a hard question to answer. I suppose, with my dad, it's sort of indeterminate."

"Indeterminate?"

"It's like dividing zero by zero. The answer isn't real. It's one of those paradoxes. It doesn't fall anywhere on your scale. What I mean is, it would not be accurate to say my dad doesn't love *me*, specifically, because he doesn't love *anything*. The man does not feel. Not anymore. He's numb. He's one of those guys who's like, *I'm fine, I don't want to talk about it, leave me alone.*"

"Oh, I see," she says, and she reaches across the table and touches him, lightly, on the arm, just a graze, just a small show of sympathy and care, though there is much meaning and purpose in that touch, and they both know it.

Jack smiles at her. "Yeah, my dad, he's this big rancher guy, this real silent type. Never showed any emotion at all. The only thing that ever got him going was talking about the land. He loved the prairie, and he knew everything about it. We'd go out walking and he'd teach me how to identify things, like, *That's bluestem grass, that's Indian grass, that's a baby elm tree*. It was nice."

"It sounds nice."

"But that was a long time ago. He doesn't do that anymore. He quit ranching about ten years ago and has spent roughly all his time since on the couch, watching sports, feeling nothing."

"And your mom?"

"My mom was less concerned with me than with my mortal soul, which, she said, was wicked. So her love was conditioned upon whether I was saved."

"And were you? Saved?"

"She said going to art school in Chicago was basically the equivalent of going to a whorehouse in Gomorrah, so I guess not." He rolls his eyes. "Her whole church is praying for me."

"What are they praying for?"

"I don't know. That I'm saved. That I don't fall into temptation."

"And how is that going?"

"I think I've resisted temptation pretty well," he says. "You know, so far." And this is when he touches her arm, ever so lightly, a reciprocal graze, slightly above the wrist, but the signal is powerfully sent, the interest is mutual, and they both blush hard and he quickly pivots: "How about you? Your parents? Scale of one to ten?"

"Well," she says, grinning, flushing, her face hot, "I'd say their love was in the middling range provided I kept quiet and followed them gamely around the country. We moved a lot—Boston, New York, D.C., back to Boston, then Westport, then Philly I think was next, a few weird months in the Hudson Valley, back again to Boston, another little stint in D.C. . . ."

"How many places have you lived?"

"I have never in my life had a friend for longer than eighteen months."

"Wow."

"We would always move sometime before eighteen months."

"Why? What did your parents do?"

"My mom studied history at Wellesley and then did nothing afterward except curate elaborate personal collections of antique jewelry and old furniture."

"Okay. And your dad?"

"Climbing the corporate ladder is, I believe, the relevant term."

"Gotcha."

"Advancing the family fortune. I come from a long line of criminally successful people."

"Successful doing what?"

"Whatever awful thing they wanted. Seriously, my family tree is a tangle of bad behavior. Swindlers. Sharks. Harvesters of quarterly profits. Financially clever but morally bleak. Their wealth was built a few generations ago via graft and fraud, and little has changed since. I wanted nothing to do with it."

"They must hate that you're here."

"They said if I moved away, they were cutting me off. Which was fine. I don't want that money anyway. The money was a kind of control. I don't want to be beholden to it, or to them."

"Some people," Jack says, nodding, "are just born into the wrong family."

"That's right."

"Some people have to create their own family."

"That's exactly right."

"My mom, my dad," Jack says, "they never really *got* me."

"Oh, same here."

"They were too busy feeding their misery. I don't think my parents enjoyed a single moment they spent together, ever."

"Mine are one hundred percent the same," Elizabeth says.

"I don't understand it. I mean, if your marriage doesn't fill you with joy, what's the point?"

"They say that marriage is hard, but it seems to me if it's that hard then you're probably doing it wrong."

"Yes, exactly!"

"If it's that hard, stop doing it."

"Yes! If every day isn't joyous, then leave. Get out."

"And that's what I did," she said. "I left. I had to escape."

"Me too. Never to return."

"Never to return."

And this, they realize as they stare at each other, amazed, this is why each of them feels so powerfully familiar to the other, why they recognized each other and understood each other so easily: they are both in Chicago to become orphans.

They smile at each other then, and refill their coffees, and light more cigarettes, and Elizabeth continues her interrogation, a thorough inventory of probing and alarmingly personal questions.

"Describe the first object you ever loved," she asks.

And then: "Tell me about a time when you were laughed at in public."

And: "When did you last cry in front of another person?"

And so on: "Describe the moment in your life when you were most afraid."

"Do you have a hunch about how you're going to die?"

"If you died tonight, what would be your biggest regret?"

"Describe exactly what you find most physically attractive about me."

They will eventually forget exactly how they answered all these questions, but they will never forget the much more important thing: that the questions were, indeed, answered. That they each had this impulse to talk and talk and talk that was categorically different from the guarded way they usually conducted themselves around new people. Which, in the moment, together, at the coffee shop, seems like a pretty important sign. *It's love,* they think. *This must be how it feels.*

By now they're shutting down the Orbis, and it's probably three thirty or four in the morning, and the two of them are exuberant, jittery, caffeinated, and Elizabeth asks her final question: "Do you believe in love at first sight?"

And with no hesitation whatsoever, Jack says, emphatically, "*Yes.*"

"You seem pretty confident about that."

"Sometimes you just know."

"But how?"

"You can feel it, here," he says, placing a palm over his chest. "It's obvious."

It's the kind of gesture—and the kind of sentiment—that might have sent her fleeing were it coming from someone else. Any other guy would have annoyed her for assuming she was the type of person who would fall for a line like that. But from Jack it doesn't sound like a line. His soft eyes stare earnestly out from under his long tousled bangs.

"How about you?" he says. "Love at first sight. What do you think?"

She smiles at him then, and, by way of an answer, she pulls him out of his chair, out of the Urbus Orbis, back into the cold, and pressing tightly together for warmth, they make their way home. They stop at the mouth of the alley that separates their apartments, these two ruined buildings now caught mid-rehab, and they look at each other, eye to eye, and he's nervous and quiet, doesn't know what to do next, and so she says, "Come with" and takes him up to her apartment, where he sleeps that night, entwined with her in her little bed, and the next night, and the next night too, and for countless nights thereafter, for the rest of the year, and the next many winters, and all the baffling time to come.

THE DUAL MASTERS

PERHAPS it was the frequent use of the word *forever* that made these meetings feel so fraught. As in, "This is your *forever home*," a phrase invoked by builders and designers and architects and real estate agents whenever some costly new extravagance was proposed. The implication was clear: If this is the home you'll die in, maybe go ahead and splurge. Maybe go ahead and buy the real marble tiles rather than the bargain porcelain knockoffs. Maybe buy the actual reclaimed barnwood instead of the replica laminate distressed at the factory. Maybe build those cabinet doors not from cheap MDF but from a premium exotic like, perhaps, *ipe*.

It goes without saying that all parties involved took commissions and kickbacks on these materials, and so there were certain strong incentives vis-à-vis the upselling.

Their *forever home* was a three-bedroom condo in the northern suburb of Park Shore, in a building that would be christened the Shipworks after renovations were complete, so named for its original owner, a long-defunct boatbuilding company. The Shipworks was currently undergoing a full gut and restoration—the last time Jack had dropped by, the place had been reduced to nothing but its original iron shell. Their future condo was, right now, literally just air—just a rectangle in the sky, six stories up—though that bit of sky was thoroughly defined and demarcated in the loan-approval paperwork it had taken many tedious hours to complete. Renters all their adult lives, Jack and Elizabeth were finally becoming homeowners, were finally "putting down roots," was how the mortgage broker described it, which Jack quietly resented; he and Elizabeth had met in 1993, and it was now 2014, and he personally thought more than two decades in the city meant they were already pretty well *rooted*, thank you very much.

They'd spent a whole afternoon reading and initialing and signing and notarizing loan-related affidavits, after which they were, at last, approved, and they'd celebrated by standing outside the construction fences and toasting what would eventually become the Shipworks. They were on the brink of homeownership, buyers of real estate that was not yet technically "real" but was circumscribed and plotted with NASA-like precision somewhere within the four hundred pages of loan-application documents Jack carried under his arm. Signing the papers had felt like an order of magnitude more important than any other single thing they'd ever done; even getting married, even having a child, required far less documentation, and far fewer approvals, than securing a mortgage for a condo that did not yet, per se, exist. They stared up at its general location. Jack thought that in previous generations his job here would have been to scoop up his wife and carry her across the threshold, but of course there was no threshold, and Elizabeth had no use for time-worn gestures, and anyway Jack had never been a big enough guy to carry anyone.

"We're going to be living *right there*," he said, pointing at the void their home would soon occupy and inflecting his voice reverently to give the moment its proper gravitas. "Toby will grow up right there."

Elizabeth squinted and frowned. "I thought the condo was *there*," she said, pointing to an entirely different spot in the sky.

"Really? I could've sworn it was *there*."

It was the first of many minor disagreements. It turned out that when designing a full home from scratch, there are innumerable unanticipated questions, and Jack surprised himself at how much he cared about all of them. Like, for example, Elizabeth wanted to forgo wall cabinets in the kitchen in favor of open shelves, an idea that struck Jack with the force of heresy, even though he had not once in his whole life given any thought to the subject of kitchen cabinetry.

"Open shelves?" Jack said, appalled.

"Yes!"

"You want all our stuff just"—he waved his hands vaguely in the air—"*out*?"

"It would be beautiful."

"It would be embarrassing!"

"No, look." She fetched her laptop and showed him a photo of such a kitchen. It was one of many hundreds of kitchen photos she'd collected and organized and tabulated, along with dozens of book-marked web pages and saved YouTube videos—she had, as usual, done her "Elizabeth thing," researching and attacking a subject from all possible angles. The photo Jack looked at now showed a kitchen with dark walnut shelves on which white plates and white bowls and white coffee mugs were tastefully stacked and nested among small pieces of whimsical art. It was a kitchen where most everything was either white or wood-toned, where all the dishes matched, where there were no greasy streaks on any surface, where the wide farm-house sink was clean and empty, and where all the typical kitchen implements—toaster, microwave, coffee maker—had been ban-ished. It was a kitchen that seemed designed more for reflection and meditation than actual food prep.

"See?" Elizabeth said. "Isn't that beautiful?"

Jack nodded. "Okay, yeah, very nice," he said, trying to be dip-lomatic. "But I suspect that has more to do with the million-dollar budget than the open shelves specifically."

They were sitting at the counter of their small, cluttered Wicker Park kitchen, its generic sink water-spot-stippled and full of the dirty dishes neither he nor Elizabeth ever had much enthusiasm for cleaning, the refrigerator dotted with fingerprints from an eight-year-old who routinely forgot to wash his hands after playing or eating, the toaster atop a rubble of what must have been at least a quarter cup of burnt breadcrumbs, the coffeepot with the more or less permanent bong water–esque haze on its once-clear glass, the microwave with its interior red crusty canopy, the result of a genera-tion of exploding tomato sauces: there was such a gap between their lives and the lives of people with open shelves.

"Let me offer a quick demonstration," Jack said, whereupon he stood and walked to the upper wall cabinet where they stored all the plastic plates and plastic cutlery and plastic sippy cups amassed during Toby's toddler years, along with the total madness of the Tupperware collection, an agglomeration of eclectically sized plastic containers and their (occasionally) respective lids, all jammed together so tightly that as soon as Jack opened the cabinet, one of the larger containers fell out and bounced hollowly on the counter, as he knew it would. This was followed by a kind of Tupperware cascade as the pile lost its structural integrity and slid out of the cabinet and all over the floor in what ended up being a way more effective demonstration than Jack could have ever hoped for.

He looked at Elizabeth. She stared back at him. She said: "I believe I understand what you're getting at."

"What makes you think we could have open shelves?"

"I said I understand."

"We need to be realistic," Jack said. "I mean, do you seriously want all this out? For everybody to see?"

"Okay, first? Who's *everybody*?"

"I don't know. Guests."

"When's the last time we had guests?"

"We sometimes have guests."

"And second? If we had open shelves, it wouldn't look like that," she said, gesturing at the mess on the floor. "It would look better. We would be better."

Which ended up being the basic philosophical divide between them: whether their new home should reflect their current reality or their future aspirations. Should it be designed based on how they actually lived or how they wanted to live? For Elizabeth, this new condo was a chance for all of them to *upgrade*, and not only their residence but their entire modus. She wanted their new home to have, for example, an "arts-and-crafts nook" even though nobody in the family had ever been particularly crafty; and she wanted a "rec room" for the playing of nostalgic, analog-type games like Parcheesi and Uno and Go Fish even though Toby seemed interested in games only when he was watching other people play them online; and she wanted the new condo to be "free of television" even though most nights she fell asleep in front of one. And it was hard for Jack to hear these things and not think that Elizabeth was externalizing all her irritations into the very architecture of their new home, baking her disapproval into the walls of the Shipworks.

"I want a fireplace," she said one night over dinner, as they silently ate salads and scrolled through their phones' profuse feeds.

"A fireplace?" he said, looking up at her.

She nodded. "Like this," showing him the photograph on her screen, a picture from an architecture magazine, a middle-aged couple curled up in bed, at night, reading books, a crackling fire at their feet. This couple might have been in a log cabin. They might have been in the woods. They had the contented, untroubled expressions of people with well-thought-out retirement plans.

"I'm not sure that's exactly our style," Jack said.

"I love it," she said. "I want that fireplace. And also? I want to read more."

"But you read all the time."

"For pleasure, I mean. Not for work. And both of us, you and me, together. I'd like us to read lots more."

"You think I don't read enough?"

"I'm just saying, doesn't this look nice? Wouldn't this be fun?"

He set down his phone and his fork, clasped his hands together, stared at her for a moment. "Is everything okay?" he said.

"Of course."

"You're not discontented?"

"I'm fine, Jack."

"Because it seems like you're discontented."

"I'm really perfectly fine."

"It's just, all the adjustments you want to make to the new place. The open shelves. The no TV. The game room. Your new minimalist aesthetic."

"What's wrong with my aesthetic?"

"It's not very recognizably *us*. It makes it seem like you're maybe unsatisfied, maybe a little unhappy."

"I am not unhappy," Elizabeth said, patting him on the arm. "Or, at least, I am not abnormally unhappy."

"Not abnormally. What does that mean?"

"It means I'm exactly as happy as I should expect myself to be, at this stage of life."

"And which stage is that?"

"At the bottom of the U-shaped curve."

Yes, of course, the U-shaped curve—she'd been mentioning that a lot lately, whenever Jack prodded her in this way. It was a phenomenon well known among certain economists and behavioral psychologists, that happiness, in general, over a lifetime, tended to follow a familiar pattern: people were most happy when they were young and when they were old, and least happy in the middle. It seemed that happiness spiked around age twenty, spiked again around age sixty, but bottomed out in between, which was where Jack and Elizabeth now found themselves, at the bottom of that curve, in midlife, a period that was notable not for its well-publicized "crisis" (actually a pretty rare phenomenon—only 10 percent of people reported having one) but for its slow ebb into a quiet and often befuddling restlessness and dissatisfaction. This was, Elizabeth insisted, a universal constant: the U-shaped curve pertained to both men and women, both the married and unmarried, the rich and poor, the employed and unemployed, the educated and uneducated, the parents and the child-free, in every country, every culture, every ethnicity, for all the decades that researchers had done this work—the science showed that people in midlife were carrying around with them, all the time, a feeling that was, statistically speaking, the equivalent of someone close to them having recently died. That's how it felt, she said, that's how far you were from your early-twenties peak, according to objective measures of well-being. Elizabeth suspected it had something to do with biology, natural selection, evolutionary pressures millions of years ago, as it had been recently shown by primatologists that great apes also experienced the exact same happiness curve, which suggested that this particular midlife sadness must have provided some kind of prehistoric advantage, must have helped our ancient primate ancestors survive. Perhaps, Elizabeth hypothesized, it was because the most vulnerable members of any troop were the young and the old, and so it was important for them to feel happy and content and satisfied—the more satisfied they felt, the fewer risks they would take, and thus more of them would survive. Whereas those in middle age needed to feel the opposite: a great inner unrest, a turmoil so unpleasant that it made going off into the dangerous world seem preferable in comparison. There needed to be someone, after all, who got shit done.

Elizabeth seemed to think this was comforting, that a midlife lull was more biological hardwiring than evidence of something specifically wrong with one's marriage or life. But for Jack, it was not comforting at all. It just confirmed his fears. All he heard was: his wife was sad.

"But I won't be sad forever," Elizabeth said. "Eventually, in our sixties, we'll both be exactly as happy as when we first met. That's what the science says, anyway. And isn't that exciting? Isn't that something to look forward to?"

"That's kind of a long time to wait, darling."

"In the meantime, it's important to do things to manage our emotional reality. Like, we should pursue new adventures, new experiences, and make little revisions here and there to our daily routines. To keep things fresh and interesting."

"Hence the fireplace?"

"I believe that we would be motivated to read more books together if we had a fireplace to read in front of. That's all."

"Well," Jack said, picking up his fork again, "I don't like fireplaces."

She stared at him for a moment. "Really?" she said.

"Really."

"You don't like fireplaces. How did I not know this?"

Jack shrugged. "Never came up."

"Who doesn't like fireplaces?"

"I don't."

"But why?"

"They're dirty," he said. "They're hazardous."

"Hazardous?"

"Because of the, you know, the smoke. It's bad for Toby. The particulates."

She squinted at him, confused. "You don't like fireplaces because of the *particulates*?"

There were ultimately so many such quibbles and dumb flare-ups that they settled on curating separate Pinterest pages and giving these pages to the Shipworks project manager, who would arbitrate.

They asked him to combine and synthesize these two collages, creating a home that would be, basically, an amalgamation of two other amalgamations. And now here they were in the manager's office, ready to tour their new home for the first time.

The manager—also the lead salesman and finance officer and real estate agent for all Shipworks properties—was Jack's old friend and landlord, Benjamin Quince, who had finally abandoned that master's thesis in new media when it became obvious he'd find much more success in an altogether different field: real estate. It turned out that putting those photos on the internet had served as an effective—if accidental—advertisement, drawing exactly the kind of mainstream interest Benjamin had moved to the neighborhood to resist. He'd loudly complained about the myriad waves of yuppie newcomers until he realized how much he could charge them in rent, after which he poured his new Foundry profits into more ventures—buying other old buildings to renovate and lease—then expanding into similarly transforming neighborhoods nearby, and eventually founding his own company, which specialized in the planning, financing, and building of Chicago-area condos, its headquarters downtown. It was Benjamin who'd alerted them to this opportunity at the Shipworks.

"Jack, Elizabeth, so good to see you," Benjamin said now in his big bright office that overlooked the river. "Can I get you something to drink? I have a case of raw hydrogen water back here. It's anti-inflammatory, antioxidant, absolutely gem-grade stuff. So much better for the body than the trash-garbage that comes out of the tap."

When Jack first met him, so long ago, Benjamin had the gaunt, pale, sunken look of devoted malnourishment and vitamin-indifference. Now he was rugged, ripped, a man who ran half-marathons and did Tough Mudders, who led meditation classes every morning out of this very office, who was fanatical about ingesting only organic and natural and authentic foods and supplements, refusing to put in his body anything that was in any way processed or manufactured or artificial or advertised or publicized. It was like his college-era anti-establishment stance had, over the years, radically narrowed, and now pertained strictly in the area of his diet. His skin had the enameled quality of inveterate moisturization. His beard was long but neat, square and rigorously barbered, fading into salt-and-pepper stubble on his cheeks and head. His muscular shoulders stretched his sport coat taut. When he hugged Jack, he squeezed so hard that Jack issued a little involuntary *oof*.

"Please," Benjamin said, smiling, motioning Jack and Elizabeth toward two black leather Eames chairs. His teeth were the high-wattage alabaster color of advanced dental work. The skin on his face was somehow more reflective and effulgent than the skin on the rest of his body. He said: "Sit. Get comfortable. It's the big day, yes? The big reveal? I am so excited."

The walls of Benjamin's office were decorated in large-scale renderings of what the Shipworks would look like once construction was complete, most of these pictures depicting a bustling sidewalk scene with dog-walkers and bike-riders out at twilight, the building glowing invitingly, orangely, behind them. It was a mixed-use building designed following certain New Urbanist principles, primarily that it was environmentally low-impact and contained a multiplicity of dwellings: there were live-work units on the ground floor, massive penthouses on the top floor, and between them a couple dozen units of varying size—two-bedrooms, three-bedrooms, some set aside for low-income housing, for which there was a federal grant. Buying in the Shipworks was the only way Jack and Elizabeth could ever afford to live in Park Shore, Illinois, a place where the housing stock was otherwise all big grassy estates, extravagant manors that had once been country enclaves for the Gilded Age rich, now routinely selling in the seven figures. It was a place well beyond their income's reach—Jack earned only a meager salary from part-time teaching gigs, while Elizabeth ran a small and decidedly humble nonprofit. Their budget had always been tight, their paychecks swallowed by rent and childcare. The only money they'd ever managed to save was from one incredible windfall, one epic freelance job awarded to Elizabeth a few years earlier, for which she was paid an enormous sum that had, ever since, sat idle in a savings account that Jack would occasionally stare at, on his computer, late at night, logging onto their bank's website and looking at this profound number: more money than he'd ever had in his life. It had functioned as a kind of symbolic bulkhead or retaining wall, this money, a large heavy thing that protected them from the pressures of the world. It let them breathe, let them relax, knowing it was there, this emergency nest egg.

And Elizabeth convinced Jack to liquidate the entire thing, to drop it all into their brand-new forever home at the Shipworks.

The Shipworks had gotten its name from the fact that it had once served as the showroom for the Chicago Shipworks, a boat company founded in the 1880s that operated a factory on the shores of Lake Michigan. The factory burned down under suspicious circumstances involving bankruptcy and insurance sometime in the 1950s, but this showroom was left untouched and abandoned. It had once been a beautiful brick building, with ceilings high enough to accommodate a sail's mast, and floors varnished and shellacked to the shine of a sailboat's hull, and a plaster facade sculpted to evoke the prow of a ship. After purchasing it, Benjamin had committed to returning the building to its turn-of-the-century glory. He had of course wanted to preserve the original wood floors, which were notable for being built from teak boat-decking rather than your usual maple or oak, but engineers had found that the decking had mostly rotted away in the last few decades and was now too brittle to salvage, and so the architects decided to build new floors from a synthetic composite called *Permateek* that looked pretty much exactly like the original boat-decking but was much longer-lasting. Then the original brick walls were found, after a city health department–mandated inspection, to contain toxic chemicals in the mortar that far exceeded modern legal levels, and so all the walls came down and plans were drawn up to replace them with modern walls stamped and painted to look like the original brick. And then it turned out that the beautiful plaster ship's-prow facade, after enduring the intense freeze-and-thaw cycles of many brutal Illinois winters, had begun crumbling and collapsing from the inside, and so the whole thing had to be demolished and engineers were right now 3D printing a new facade from complex polymers using photos of the old facade for guidance.

The point being, the Shipworks would look more or less exactly as it had in 1890, even though literally everything that actually *made* the Shipworks would be new. Thus its catchphrase, "Vintage Living, Modern Luxury," which was displayed on every poster in the room in a large blue nautical font.

"Not gonna lie," Benjamin said, smiling at them from behind his big desk, "I am exquisitely, extravagantly, almost arrogantly proud of this design. I've had my very best people working on it. Are you ready to be thrilled? Yes? Okay, then please put these on." And he handed them two big virtual reality headsets, which was when Jack understood how they would be taking a "tour" of a condo that had not yet been built.

"This is better technology than they use in Hollywood, by the way," Benjamin said as he helped them strap on their VR gear. "It's absolutely state-of-the-art."

After the masks were properly attached, and after Benjamin had asked "Okay, you ready?" and tapped something on his keyboard, the twin screens in front of Jack's eyes glowed to life and suddenly he was standing in what he had to admit was a pretty lifelike and three-dimensional and photorealistic depiction of a living room.

A coolly minimalist living room.

Everything in white and walnut.

Jack sighed and looked around. He found that as he moved his head, the view in his goggles changed accordingly. He saw a white leather couch that would probably be really beautiful for approximately eight minutes before it met with some heartbreaking accident involving Toby and grape juice. And white floor-to-ceiling bookcases decorated sparsely with color-coordinated books stacked horizontally next to vases and picture frames and assorted objets d'art. And exposed brick walls with no sign of a television anywhere. Instead, there were paintings adorning the walls, much bigger and more expensive-looking paintings than any he and Elizabeth actually owned. And a credenza behind the couch topped with fine and almost certainly fragile pottery. And, beyond all that, a big kitchen with vast open shelves.

"Welcome," Benjamin said, "to your *forever home*."

"It's so beautiful," he heard Elizabeth say from somewhere beyond the goggles. "The kitchen is perfect. And I adore that accent wall," she said, probably about a wall at the far end of the living room that was covered with planks of distressed and sun-bleached and weathered wood, wood of old age and high character.

"That is recycled barnwood," Benjamin said. "Actual wood from the genuine barns of America's heartland. I have a great supplier."

"It's gorgeous."

"Solid hardwood, of course, so no formaldehyde off-gassing. And the floor tiles are handmade encaustic with absolutely no artificial additives. And you notice how the walls seem to sparkle? That's because they're covered with a pro-energizing crystal paint blend that mimics the sun's specific wavelengths, for circadian rhythm reasons. And there's a water-filtration system optimized for Chicago's specific toxic soup of plastics and heavy metals. Pollution-free induction stove. UV sanitizing lights in all showers. Air purifiers that cleanse each room of industrial poisons. Do you have any idea how many chemicals there are on one speck of dust? It's in the five digits, not even kidding. Our corporate overlords don't want us to know how unhealthy it is to *breathe* these days, so most people have no idea. They just go merrily along. Cooking with gas. Sheep in an abattoir, am I right? But you won't have to worry about that. This will be a home that's aligned with your natural body. Think of it as a detox diet *for life*. I know that wasn't on your list, but I took the liberty. It is, after all, your forever home."

"It's wonderful," Elizabeth said. "I love it."

"And how about you, Jack?" Benjamin said. "You're being real quiet."

"I'm just looking," Jack said in a kind of singsong tone, trying to keep the edge out of his voice.

"He hates it," Elizabeth said.

"I don't hate it," he said. "It's just—this design doesn't seem to reflect any of my input."

"Oh, sure," Benjamin said. "That's because you haven't seen your master yet."

"My what?"

"Your master. C'mon."

And suddenly Jack was moving, from the living room through the kitchen and down a hallway, the view bobbing lightly as if to simulate his real gait, Jack feeling the tiniest bit dizzy and disoriented from the sensation of walking without really physically walking. He floated into a room that was notable for how dreary and bleak and off-putting it was: chunky furniture made from what looked like a dark oak, walls painted in a deep maroon, hunter-green sheets over what looked to be a waterbed, curtains that were perhaps actually black, a dartboard on the wall, a beer fridge. It was a room that was very masculine and very unfashionable, making Jack wonder if this was how he was perceived from the outside, as someone in need of a man cave.

"Welcome to your master," Benjamin said.

"I don't understand. I have my own room?"

"Yep, your very own suite."

"And Elizabeth sleeps where, exactly?"

"In her own suite. Waaay at the other end of the condo."

"Seriously?"

"That is also where I put the fireplace."

"Hold on." Jack ripped the Velcro straps apart and removed the goggles. "We have separate bedrooms?"

"Technically it's called 'dual masters,'" Benjamin said with finger quotes. "It was on your wife's Pinterest page."

"It's kind of a trend," said Elizabeth, now removing her own mask.

"A trend."

"Yeah. Separate master bedrooms. A lot of people are doing it."

"You want to sleep separately?" Jack said. "Like it's the fifties? Like we're Lucy and Ricky?"

"Note that we wouldn't *have* to sleep separately," Elizabeth said. "This merely gives us the *option* to sleep separately those nights when we want to."

"But what if we never want to?"

"Jack," she said gently, "we already do."

Which was, in his opinion, a little too much information to reveal in front of Benjamin, there, even if she was right, that the two of them had slowly, over the years, established a habit of sleeping apart most nights. It had begun when Toby was a toddler and going through a maddening picky-eating phase that caused Elizabeth a great amount of stress, so much stress that she was waking up in the middle of the night, every night, then lying there anguishing and worrying in that particular three a.m. way in which all anguishes and worries are hugely magnified, meanwhile Jack resting quite peacefully next to her and often crowding her and smothering her in his sleep. Elizabeth described a sort of slow-motion chase that was apparently happening every night in their queen-size bed whereby Jack would unconsciously roll toward Elizabeth and cover her with one or two or (sometimes, somehow) three limbs, surrounding her and encasing her and occasionally literally clasping and hanging on to her, and she would soon need to pull herself free and roll away from him because there was no chance of her falling asleep in that burdened position, and then eventually—and usually right at the moment she was finally drifting off—Jack would seek her out again, rolling toward her and draping himself heavily atop her, and she would once again need to extract herself and roll away, and this exhausting game would continue until Elizabeth was left with only the smallest sliver of bed, right there on the edge of the mattress, totally untenable, sleepwise, and so she'd finally get up and go sleep on the hide-a-bed in the room that functioned as their home office, Jack oblivious to all of this until he woke up, once again, alone. This had been happening now for almost seven years. Jack would wake up to find himself abandoned in the night. Or, on those evenings Elizabeth went to bed early because of pressing morning responsibilities, Jack would go ahead and sleep in the office himself, on the hide-a-bed, sparing Elizabeth the whole ordeal. And even though this practice had been ingrained and habitualized over the years, Jack realized right at this moment that he nevertheless still thought of it as a phase, one of those temporary relationship bumps to overcome so that he and Elizabeth could get back to the intimate, entangled way they used to sleep together, when they were young.

However, inscribing it into the layout of their *forever home* meant it was categorically not a phase. He imagined the rest of his life as a cold and lonely void where he shared his days not with a wife but with a glorified lodger. He thought about his own parents, who had slept in twin beds for as long as Jack could remember.

"I think on the matter of dual masters," he said, "I'm a hard no."

"You're not completely satisfied," Benjamin said. "I understand. I hear your gripe. But it could take months to revise the design, and there are a few things we really ought to consider before going back to the drawing board. A few, let's say, externalities."

"Okay."

"I'm thinking of two externalities in particular. First, there's the issue of risk."

"Risk?"

"As in, how to control it. How to spread it around and diffuse it. As you're aware, we've encountered a few construction snags, a few building snafus, sudden budget-ballooning costs, non-amortized, unfortunate, unforeseen. It's increased our risk. The investors are nervous. The project suddenly doesn't look like the safe hedging vehicle they need it to be. They could pull out."

"And torpedo the whole thing?"

"Perhaps, yes, but probably more likely it would delay construction for however long it takes to settle the inevitable lawsuits. Six months? Maybe a year, tops?"

"A *year*?"

"Actually maybe two years."

"But we've already paid for it!"

"And that was very shrewd of you. You helped control the project's risk, by taking on risk yourself. Good job."

"Ben, we drained our savings account."

"And I appreciate how that must feel upsetting. But I don't think you appreciate the significance of controlling risk. I mean it. No important thing has ever been done without controlling risk."

"It's our *entire savings*. All of it. We cannot afford to pay both mortgage and rent for a year."

"Jack, do you know what the oldest book in the world is?"

"No."

"It's a ledger, written in Mesopotamia, six thousand years ago. That's before the invention of literature, by the way, and before government, before religion. Do you know what it is? Do you know what we needed to invent before we could invent all those other things? *Insurance*, Jack. Indemnification. Project financing. Limits on liability. Do you understand what I'm saying?"

"Honestly not a clue."

"Building big things is *risky*, Jack, and humanity couldn't do it until we figured out how to spread that risk around. The Sumerians were the first to crack it, and thus became the world's first empire. They devised a way to insure all those expeditions into unmapped country, all those ships and caravans facing unknown peril. History remembers the travelers themselves, the Marco Polos and Magellans and such, but the real heroes of those stories are the underwriters."

"As in, people like you."

"I don't mean to brag, but yeah, this is where I really excel, alchemizing so many motley interests, the investors and sponsors and purchasers and suppliers and lenders and contractors and such. My projects are vast creatures of shocking complexity—intricate, unruly, asynchronous, a little baroque. It takes serious craftsmanship, project-financing on this scale. But that's always been my special talent, bringing people together. It turned out I was a mediocre artist, but great at logistics, and a fucking Mozart of risk management. So don't you worry. I'll figure this out."

"Okay. Fine. What do we do?"

"We finalize *now*. We approve plans for as many units as possible, as quickly as possible, to minimize the investors' exposure to risk. That's the first externality."

"And what's the second?"

"The second is divorce."

"Excuse me?"

"Not that I'm implying anything specifically about *you guys*," Benjamin said, smiling broadly. "It's just, you know, fifty percent of all marriages?"

"Uh-huh."

"And a lot of couples now choose to cohabit after a divorce. For the kids."

"They keep living together after they break up?"

"Oh sure. Many couples find it ideal. They have their own bedrooms, their own separate entrances. So in the event of divorce you can continue living in the same place with minimal traumatic disruption for Toby. And how nice would that be for him? No weekends away from home, no dispiriting sleepovers at Dad's depressing little empty apartment."

Jack looked at his wife. "Are you planning on getting a divorce?" he asked.

"Jack, it's our forever home," she said. "Shouldn't it accommodate all possibilities?"

"You didn't answer the question."

"It's not an indictment of our marriage. It's just about sleep health."

"If I may?" Benjamin said. "Try to think of it less like marriage criticism and more like marriage insurance. By that I mean, you don't purchase boat insurance because you *want* your ship to sink, right? Same principle."

"But," Jack said, "it seems so, I don't know, so unromantic. So pragmatic."

"Aren't you always saying we should be realistic?" Elizabeth said.

"Yes."

"Well, here I am, being realistic."

"And this is the *one thing* you choose to be realistic about? This?"

How had they so suddenly and so profoundly switched roles? Now Jack found himself the aspirational one, wanting their home to reflect not their real life but an idealized version of it, one in which he and Elizabeth fell asleep together and woke up together and agreed on all things. He longed to capture again the intensity and electricity and ease and unification of their first years together.

That winter they began dating, so long ago, Jack had spent every night in her small apartment, sleeping with her in her tiny twin bed. They'd wake in the morning sore from holding each other so tightly.

Jack thought about that winter, how for months they were separated by the distance of an alley. All they wanted back then was to eliminate the space between them. And now here they were, twenty years later, putting it back.

THE SONG that all the little children were right now exuberantly singing was a popular dance number about a woman getting really drunk at a nightclub and having haphazard sex with a stranger and then blacking out so she doesn't remember any of it the next day.

Except, no, that wasn't exactly right. The song the children were actually dancing to and performing in front of their parents was—you had to listen carefully—a remake of that other more debauched song, this new version having been superficially edited, the adult singer replaced with a dulcet preteen, the most raunchy lyrics replaced with family-friendly alternatives. It was now a song sung by children, for children, part of a series of child-appropriate pop covers that was the only music ever broadcast during these playdates at Brandie's big suburban Park Shore house. It murmured low in the background, usually, unless the kids decided, as they had today, that they wanted to put on a show. And so here they were, the kids, eight of them, ages six to eleven, all twirling, hopping, hands in the air, sometimes bobbing up and down in a kind of proto-twerk, staging in the living room their vague impression of how pop stars act in music videos. Meanwhile, the parents watched, clapped, hooted, and generally displayed maximal self-esteem-boosting support and encouragement.

Elizabeth studied them, the parents. She watched them watching the children. She was looking for any exterior sign of discomfort or unease that the kids were being exposed to—were, alas, *performing*—this particular song. The song was of that dance music subgenre that might as well be called "Look at Me I'm in a Club!" It was music that you heard in the club, about the club, on the subject of being seen in the club—basically up-tempo drunken solipsism, with sporadic sexual depravity.

"It's going down!" the kids sang. "I'm yelling timber!" Which in the original version of the song was a description of falling down drunk, and maybe also a reference to giving a blow job—the lyric was ambidextrous that way. But the parents didn't seem to notice anything untoward, and that's probably because many of the song's key phrases had been changed—a word here, a word there—so that the new lines often meant something exactly the opposite of the original, even if the original still existed in Elizabeth's ear as a kind of epistemic echo.

"Let's make a day you will remember," sang the children.

"Let's make a night you won't remember," sang the echo.

"One more dance, another town," sang the children.

"One more shot, another round," sang the echo.

The song had so many such redacted, edited, and ambiguous lyrics that it had little residual meaning left over from the original. It was a nonsense song now, fully censored and decontextualized. Elizabeth wondered how many such small changes could be made to a song before its story was obscured, how many altered words— ten? twenty?—before the song was a new song.

Elizabeth sat by herself, a short distance from the larger group. She watched as the children danced and sang, and she watched as the parents obligingly humored them, and she watched her own son, Toby, himself also sitting a short distance from everyone else, on the kitchen floor, his back to the wall, curled up so that his knees hid his face, staring at the screen of his little tablet computer, ignoring everything, playing Minecraft, alone, as usual. It was what he did during these playdates; Elizabeth longed for him to finally join the other kids, but Toby preferred withdrawal. She'd been bringing him to these gatherings for a month now, and still her son refused to integrate. Instead, he built elaborate structures—castles, cathedrals, cities—on his private little screen, in his fake digital world, far away from the other children.

She felt a familiar ache, seeing this. Toby was, at eight years old, the "new kid in school," and she remembered, vividly, what that felt like. Growing up, she had been the new kid in school so many times, and she could still feel it in her body, the anxiety and distress and foreboding of entering another unfamiliar place, midsemester, all social arrangements already settled, all cliques very well established, Elizabeth entering this milieu as an automatic outcast, pariah, curiosity, wandering hallways idiotically searching for a locker, walking into classrooms many minutes late, always the oppressive feeling of being ambiently watched, appraised, judged. The horror the outsider feels in a cafeteria with few available seats. The terrible choice between sitting leprously alone or asking to join a group—"Can I sit here?"—thereby risking public rejection and eternal humiliation. The feeling of this—it was so easy to summon it, in her body, it was still so close to the surface—the feeling was like that of her car hydroplaning on a wet road, that sensation when you first lose control and all your muscles tighten and harden and hunch up as you brace for disaster. That's what it felt like, all the time, when you were the new kid.

So she could sympathize. She understood why Toby might want to sit alone, far away. She had wanted that too, when she was his age. She could still recall a certain picture book she had read over and over when she was young, even younger than Toby was now: it was called *Sylvester and the Magic Pebble*, and it was about a boy—actually a donkey, but whatever—who finds a magic pebble that grants wishes. And one day while holding the pebble, he encounters a hungry lion and, terrified of being devoured, screams, "I wish I were a rock!" And he turns into a rock. A large pinkish-gray boulder. After which there comes much sadness because, even though he's safe from the lion, he can't ever again pick up the pebble and wish himself back to normal (due to: no arms) and so he stays like that, a rock. People look for him for many days, and he observes them, silently, as they walk right by. Eventually, of course, he transforms back into Sylvester and all ends well, but Elizabeth usually preferred to stop reading before that part; she preferred the part before the ending, when everyone is still looking for Sylvester but nobody can find him. This was honestly her favorite part of the story: being a rock, being unseen, ignored. The way the lion looked at the rock helplessly before leaving it be—this was basically what Elizabeth wanted most whenever she was the new kid. To be left alone. Or, if not left alone, to at least have that rock's same stoicism and indifference and emotionless flat facade during those moments she was being paid attention to disagreeably. To achieve such a surface hardness and gray blankness that she could not be perturbed.

And now, so many years later, here was Toby, hiding behind his computer, doing the same thing.

The children continued their dancing, their singing, and Elizabeth walked over to Toby and sat down next to him, looked over his shoulder at the screen, where his fingers moved with the speed and dexterity and complex intertwining of a pianist: he twirled the in-game camera with one hand while rummaging through his digital inventory with the other while somehow also manipulating Minecraft's digital building blocks with various available fingertips. It was all so fast and blurred that Elizabeth never had any strong idea what he was actually doing.

"Hey buddy," she said. "You want to maybe go play with the other kids?"

She waited for him to respond, but he kept at it, quietly running his fingers across the screen, moving these pixelated, many-colored boxes from one place to another place, ignoring her.

"The kids sure are having a lot of fun," she said.

Still nothing.

"What are you making there?" she asked.

"My secret hideout," he said. "It's underground."

"Underground?" she said, feigning enthusiasm. "*Wow.*"

"Yeah, look." He zoomed in to show her. "Here's the hidden entrance, under this tree. And then you go down these steps to the front door. It's made of pure netherite and it has a big lock on it and booby traps."

"Your front door is booby-trapped?"

"I put pressure plates on the ground, with dynamite underneath. See?"

And he lifted a square of what looked to be regular gray floor to reveal a hollow below, inside of which he had, sure enough, hidden a large stash—kind of uncomfortably large, kind of a psychotically large stash—of TNT. Bright red bundled sticks of TNT going down farther than she could even see.

"Honey," she said, "why would you do that?"

"Nobody knows it's there," he said. "So if anyone comes in, the whole place *blows up*."

"Right, but, honey? Why would you *do* that?"

He looked up at her. "So nobody can get in," he said. "So they leave me alone."

"But wouldn't your hideout be more fun if you invited friends?"

He stared at her for a moment, confused. Toby had inherited so much from her—her unruly blond hair, her slouchy posture, her penchant for solitude—but when he focused on her like this, it was undeniable that he had Jack's dark, searching eyes.

"What do you think is better," he finally said, "diamonds or netherite?"

"What's netherite?"

"A metal from a different dimension."

"What kind of dimension?"

"A dark place, with no daylight or weather."

"Okay, then I guess I'd say diamonds?"

"No," he said, shaking his head, turning back to his screen. "Netherite's better."

"Okay."

"It's stronger, and it doesn't burn."

Then he returned to his silent assembling, ignoring her once again.

It had seemed like such a good and judicious and even responsible parenting decision, letting Toby play Minecraft. The game was, after all, so innocent: you just built things. It was digital Legos, digital Lincoln Logs, digital blocks—how sweet, Elizabeth had thought, how very wholesome. Plus, she'd seen research showing that Minecraft could actually *help* kids who experienced attention- and anxiety-related behavioral problems, that it could coach them to focus on a single task, to break down problems into their step-by-step constituent parts, teach them the benefits of patience and delayed gratification. And while it was definitely true that, in Minecraft, Toby did indeed exhibit the patience and industry and creativity and focus that Elizabeth had always hoped for—he often built huge, cavernous worlds painstakingly over the course of weeks, whole cities filled with everything but people—it was also true that this patience and industry manifested strictly in the world of Minecraft, and nowhere else. In every other area of life, Toby was as impulsive and occasionally explosive as he'd always been. Only now there was this new thing that maximally triggered his tantrums: Minecraft, and when (or whether) he was allowed to play it.

The game seemed to overwhelm all of Toby's other concerns, seemed to drown out the real world entirely. It was his primary— and sometimes *only*—topic of conversation: describing his current Minecraft creation, or his next Minecraft creation, or what people were creating on the many Minecraft YouTube channels he followed. He had even started a channel himself, doing what he called "reaction videos." He would watch other people play Minecraft, and he would react to them, often dramatically. Elizabeth could not fundamentally understand this: Toby was not playing the game but instead reacting to other people playing the game, which apparently still other people found attention-worthy, which was ludicrous. When Elizabeth was growing up, the conventional wisdom was that playing video games was the height of laziness. Then a few years ago, it became popular to watch other people play video games online rather than play them yourself, which seemed even lazier. And now people were watching other people watching other people play video games. It was like a Darwin fish parade of sloth. But Elizabeth kept all this to herself. It gave Toby a great deal of pride that his channel, which he called "the Tobinator," had recently eclipsed a thousand followers, and he insisted that a little more growth would bring some ad revenue, which seemed to delight him, and so she resisted the occasionally strong urge to take his tablet computer and throw it in the lake.

"Ten more minutes," she told Toby as the children concluded their show and began taking deep bows, to the parents' generous applause. "Ten more minutes of screen time, okay? And then you're playing with the other kids," she said, to no visible reaction.

She'd been trying this last month to explain to her son how to make friends with new people. She had, at first, naïvely suggested that he just go up and start talking to them, but she was forced to retract and revise that particular direction after she watched Toby barge into a conversation, walking right up to this group of children and intruding on their chat with something irrelevant and off-topic and weird and Minecraft-related—"Do you want to watch me explode a cow?"—and all the kids stared at him confused for a moment before closing ranks and returning to their previous conversation. And so Elizabeth modified her earlier instruction to suggest that before he went up and started talking to people, Toby should first figure out what those people were talking about so that he could participate and add to the discussion rather than rudely derail it or cut it off. But this also required amendments when she saw Toby wander up to a group in mid-conversation and stand there, less than an arm's length away from them, watching them and staring at them creep- ily until, very quickly, the children noticed him and became visibly uncomfortable and all of them moved in a very obvious manner far away from the awkward new staring kid.

Which was when Elizabeth realized she needed to take the entire conversation-entering process that she had intuitively perfected all those times she was the new kid in school and break it down for Toby into manageable, followable micro-steps (honestly this was pretty fun for her; behavioral psychologists tend to love their flow- charts). The first step was *Observe, Watch, Study, and Eavesdrop*. She told Toby that before he approached any group, he should first make sure it was a group he indeed wanted to approach, should verify that the group was speaking in a nice way and generally being kind and not bullying or teasing anyone either inside or outside the group. (Toby was, she knew, a bit of a socially awkward boy, and therefore probably an easy target for bullying or teasing, and it broke her heart imagining him enduring exactly the kind of abuse she herself had occasionally endured as a child when she'd found herself trying to enter social circles in which she really did not belong.) So, yes, first observe the group and eavesdrop on the group to make sure the group was not cruel or vulgar or troublemaking—*but*, she quickly added, there was also Step 2, which basically occurred simultaneous to Step 1, which was: *Be Inconspicuous.* She told Toby that most people did not like to be stared at and found the experience of being stared at unsettling and sometimes even threatening. So Elizabeth suggested using a prop—Toby's tablet computer could function in this manner—some object that he could look at while eavesdropping in order to give the impression that his attention was otherwise occupied. After which Step 3, *Identify the Topic of Conversation*, followed as a matter of course. The point here, she said, was to suss out what the group was currently talking about and assess whether he had anything valuable to add; ergo, if the group happened to be talking about Minecraft, then by all means it would be perfectly appropriate for Toby to jump in and tell them about exploding a cow, but this was *literally the only circumstance* in which he should lead with Minecraft stuff and in every other circumstance he should enter the conversation by trying to bolster that conversation in an honestly helpful and supporting way.

But not before Step 4: *Locate the Leader.*

It had been Elizabeth's experience that all social groups—no matter how egalitarian they seemed on the surface—had one person who was, at any given moment, on some deep and perhaps even unconscious level, in charge. A kind of social conductor that the group tacitly elevated. Elizabeth began understanding this during all those mortifying lonely cafeteria lunches when she sat by herself, pretending not to care, pretending to be a flat gray rock. She'd look around with the objective, dispassionate eyes of the scientist she would one day become, and she began noticing this pattern: she'd watch a group of friends talking, and at some point one member of the group would excuse themselves to go to the bathroom or grab a dessert or something like that, and if the group continued their conversation effortlessly and without hiccup, Elizabeth knew that the person who'd departed was not the leader. But if the group seemed to struggle, if conversation suddenly seemed fragile, if people stared at each other silently for a moment, filling the space with empty transition words—"So, um, yeah, well, anyway . . ."—like a record skipping until it finds its groove, she could tell that the group had lost its captain and was now grasping for a new one.

This observation was, years later, borne out by research she did at Wellness, where she found that people expressed all sorts of tiny, subconscious behaviors when in the presence of a personality they perceived as larger or more important or more powerful than their own: they angled their shoulders differently, mimicked body language, raised the frequency of their voice by a few hertz, tilted their head down a couple of degrees—deferential gestures that were almost, but not quite, imperceptible.

There was so much you could decode about people if you watched them closely enough. This was what Elizabeth learned as she passed the time during so many lonely childhood lunches and recesses and study halls and solo homecoming dances: people revealed themselves constantly, but unconsciously, and in the very smallest of ways.

And she was explaining all of this to Toby, and she hadn't even yet gotten to Steps 5 and 6 and 7—which were, respectively: *Wait for a Pause in the Conversation; Say Something Helpful;* and, finally, *Lie If Necessary,* which was a step she'd reveal to Toby but perhaps not to Jack, who was so righteously sincere and genuine about all things and would not understand how the practice of strategic dishonesty had been usefully deployed in her own complicated adolescence—when Toby declared that this was all hopelessly difficult and well beyond his capacities and he henceforth sat far away from the group, playing Minecraft, not even attempting to socially engage, which was a pretty big backfire, Elizabeth had to admit. It seemed to happen like this so often, that her parenting of Toby ended up producing exactly the opposite behavior of the one she was working so hard to cultivate.

"Well, you watch me," she'd told him, because even if Toby wasn't going to follow her tried-and-true seven-step schema, Elizabeth certainly would. She was even doing it right now, as she walked back into the living room following the kids' brief performance:

Step 1: Observe, Watch, Study, and Eavesdrop

The parents who frequented these playdates all lived nearby, and thus tended to converse mostly about the things they naturally had in common: the kids, or the school, or issues of local civics. Elizabeth had gathered from previous conversations that there was an effort underway to expand the town's recycling program, and a campaign to get the city council to pass a symbolic resolution declaring its support for global refugees. Before this last month, Elizabeth had never once set foot in Park Shore, Illinois, and when she'd first asked Benjamin what the place was like, he'd described it as "the confluence of real estate's three magic *l*'s."

"And what are the three magic *l*'s?" she'd asked.

"Liberal, leafy, and loaded."

It was a place of grand old country homes, most of which now featured rainbow flag signs in their big picture windows declaring that all people were welcome here. It was a place of tanklike SUVs with "Coexist" bumper stickers. Lawns as soft and thick as carpets, landscaped exclusively with native and noninvasive plants, maintained without the use of any chemicals that might be harmful to bees or bee colonies. There was a quaint downtown with cute shops and restaurants, an active weekend farmers market, an express train into the city, a compost program whereby the town's collective yard clippings and leaf litter was dumped in the summer and autumn to become, in the spring, healthy nutritious loamy soil that could be used by local amateur gardeners, gratis. When Elizabeth heard about this, she thought that maybe, for the first time in her life, she might garden. Maybe she and Toby could build a little garden together, on the rooftop of the Shipworks. Maybe they could sprout seeds or something, grow tomatoes, pick herbs, all that, tend to real life—*real efflorescent life*—rather than the digital life that obsessed him on his screen, those pixelated plants and animals of Minecraft whose existence was purely instrumental ("Why would you explode a cow?" she had asked Toby. "To get meat and leather" was his simple answer).

What a surprise, after so much time in the city, to finally come out to the suburbs and find this: community, comfort, acceptance, ease, optimism.

She had begun to feel so crowded in Chicago, and not only physically crowded—bumped into on the sidewalk, jostled on the train—but also sort of mentally crowded. It had begun to feel like Jack and Toby's presence in their inescapably small apartment was overwhelming. If they were in the same room with her, even when they were being perfectly still and quiet, it was as if they were playing bongos for how much Elizabeth could focus on anything else. She felt under constant benevolent surveillance at home, felt like Jack noticed everything—she couldn't even bring home a new brand of pickles without undergoing a tedious cross-examination: Did she not enjoy the other brand of pickles? What specifically did she not like about those pickles? What was it about the new pickles that attracted her? Would she like to sample other kinds of pickles in order to figure out which pickles were in fact her favorite pickles? And on and on—it was all so incredibly, so excruciatingly boring.

Jack had been particularly, almost maniacally, ever-present as of late, following her around when she left the room, sitting at her hip when she was reading, asking her what she was looking at when she was looking at her phone, not proactively doing chores but swooping in to finish chores whenever he caught her doing them, telling her to go relax on the couch maybe, or in bed, or, perhaps, in a bubble bath that, of course, he would happily draw for her. Plus he'd been sending her these cheesy little love texts throughout the day, occasionally even hiding a real paper note in her purse that said "Just wanted to let you know how much I love you," then asking her about it, later, after work ("Did you get my note?"), his face full of expectation and need. Or sometimes they'd be reading together in the living room and she'd look up from her book to discover him staring right at her and she'd say "What?" and he'd smile like a doomed lamb and say "Love you!" and it drove her completely bonkers. She supposed that in another context, these things might have been cute—early in their relationship, certainly, Jack's big romantic gestures had struck her as spontaneous and grand—but now all his mighty efforts just smacked of desperation. *Chill out,* she wanted to tell him. *Back off.* But there was no way to say that without hurting her gentle husband's big feelings, so instead she smiled and said

"Thank you for the note," and then changed the subject, meanwhile longing for space, for larger and more private space—the roomy condo at the Shipworks and her own separate bedroom and the trees and grassy vast openness of suburban Park Shore.

The story they'd always told themselves in their twenties was that suburban life was stifling and oppressive, but that's not how it felt to her now. What it felt like now was liberation.

Elizabeth was walking back into the living room, eavesdropping on the other parents while also staring at her phone—per *Step 2: Be Inconspicuous*—idly skimming the headlines of the day, which were all variations on some kind of deep dread: There was an Ebola outbreak overseas . . . would it go global? There was civil war in the Middle East . . . would it spread? There was a dip in the stock market . . . would it lead to a recession? Elizabeth let her eyes go unfocused, stared past the headlines instead of at them, and she listened.

Step 3: Identify the Topic of Conversation

It was Brandie holding forth right now, effusively praising the kids' lip-synched performance and asking them if they might enjoy making vision boards about their interest in music, insisting that the best way their song-and-dance dreams might one day become reality was for them to visualize those dreams via aspirational collages, adding that she just so happened to have a large collection of pop culture magazines she kept stashed away for exactly this purpose, plus, of course, enough markers and stickers and scissors and paste sticks to go around.

Brandie did this kind of thing a lot: she took any interest the kids showed in any subject and supercharged it. She was the one who organized these playdates, and held them at her own big house, and usually thought up amusing and inventive things for the kids to do together, and Elizabeth didn't need to spend any time whatsoever on *Step 4: Locate the Leader*, for Brandie was undoubtedly it. Elizabeth had spotted it right away, how when the other parents spoke, even when they were all in a big group, they tended to speak to Brandie, at Brandie, for Brandie, glancing her way when they finished speaking, a little approval-seeking gesture that Elizabeth had long been trained to see. If Brandie happened to cross her arms, the others tended to cross their arms too, in unconscious mimicry. If Brandie smiled at something, the others smiled as well, and their smiles were those genuine smiles that recruited the muscles around the eyes, meaning that they weren't producing fake mouth-smiles for Brandie's benefit but actually sincerely taking on the same positive affect as their leader.

Brandie had been in corporate sales and marketing for many years but had given it up when her children were born so she could full-time parent. That's how she said it. Not "I am a full-time parent," but rather "I full-time parent." Now she sat on every available school committee, organized every school fundraiser, attended every field trip, was the parents' representative at every meeting of the board, and even led cleanup efforts at the local beaches. In the small world of suburban Park Shore, Brandie was like a compassionate and generous and bighearted Bond villain: her fingers were in *everything*.

She seemed religious but in an ill-defined and unassertive way, more like just in the way she was always talking about sending her good thoughts to people who needed them. Her house was early turn-of-the-century, designed by some historically important architect, the style an American take on a French château, large but not ostentatious, chic but not gaudy, elegant but also restrained, decorated in that particular neo-Nordic way that managed to be austere and cozy at the same time: lots of blond wood, muted neutral colors, fluffy hand-knitted blankets draped invitingly over the backs of couches and chairs. There was a wall devoted to the kids' many arts-and-crafts projects. There was a big kitchen with long open shelves.

Brandie always seemed to be dressed in a manner that was, above all, *appropriate*: season-appropriate, occasion-appropriate, age-appropriate. Today she wore a summery white cotton T-shirt tucked into slim white jeans—clothes so virginally white they seemed to have somehow never been touched by the messy, smudgy tasks of child-rearing—accessorized via a small gold wristwatch and a straw tote bag. She always seemed to have a designer straw tote bag with her, and always a new one; the woman must have had a lavish collection of expensive straw tote bags, from which she pulled, like magic, whatever mom-thing was needed: wet wipes, Band-Aids, a sewing kit, tweezers, a stain remover pen, gauze. Elizabeth was listening to Brandie and the other parents converse, and pursuant to *Step 5: Wait for a Pause in the Conversation*, Elizabeth was poised to speak whenever a good opportunity presented itself, when Brandie glanced over at her and suddenly made it unnecessary.

"Oh, Elizabeth!" she said. "I have something for you."

And then Brandie was striding her way and reaching into her tote and pulling out a small, carefully folded brown paper lunch bag with Toby's name written, in calligraphy, on the front.

"What's this?" Elizabeth said, taking the bag.

"Apple turnovers," Brandie said triumphantly.

"Really?" Elizabeth said, opening the bag and looking at the triangular pastries inside, golden brown, dotted lightly with sugar.

"They're for Toby," Brandie said. "Consider it a welcome gift. I'm so sorry it's taken us this long to get him one. It's been a whole month already—that's inexcusable!"

"You made apple turnovers?"

"*We* made apple turnovers," she said, "the kids and I."

"Wow. Thank you."

"You're very welcome! It was fun. And anyway we absolutely had to use the apples before they went bad. Our garden is *bursting*."

"That's very kind of you."

"We thought it would be a nice thing, since Toby likes them so much."

"He does?"

"Oh, sure! They're his favorite."

"They are?"

"His favorite dessert in the world!" Brandie said, directing this toward Toby in the kitchen. "Isn't that right, kiddo?"

And Elizabeth turned around and saw that Toby was no longer staring at his screen but in fact was staring at them, nodding and staring at Elizabeth, or perhaps staring at what Elizabeth held in her hand, this bag heavy with apple turnovers, a food she was surprised her son even knew existed, much less liked, much less favored above all others.

"Of course," Elizabeth said, nodding. "Turnovers, yeah."

"Just warm them up in the oven," Brandie said. "Five minutes at four hundred degrees ought to do it."

And then all the kids were running back into the living room, announcing that they had another show to perform, that all the adults should soon gather around for this exciting second act. Brandie gave a little clap and said, "Oh, yay!" and Elizabeth remembered *Step 6: Say Something Helpful,* and so she said to Brandie, "I think Toby should join them," and she walked toward her son, who, when he saw her coming, looked again at his computer and curled up a little tighter against the wall. She squatted down next to him and said, "Screen time is over now," to no reaction whatsoever, then, "Toby, it's time to play with the other kids," to, again, no reaction, and so she reached out to take his tablet away from him, and she had barely grasped it and begun to pull it gently toward her when Toby suddenly, and without any warning or ramp-up, screamed.

It was the kind of scream she hated most, that high-pitched, ear-shredding noise that was always the leading edge of a large, unstoppable meltdown, a shriek that triggered instant panic, Elizabeth already saying, "No, no, no, no" almost involuntarily as Toby's body went rigid and his face squished up and turned crimson and out came that other person Toby turned into during these episodes, that inconsolable not-Toby who disconnected from the world and lived entirely within his uproar. He'd been doing it since he was a toddler, and Elizabeth had long hoped that she might somehow find a way to parent him out of it, or, failing that, that he would simply grow out of it—but, so far, no luck. The tantrums persisted, and she understood by now that the best way to deal with such a meltdown was not to reward it or punish it but to simply show care and empathy and attend to him with loving patience, which Elizabeth could manage successfully in the privacy of their home, but when the tantrums happened in public, on trains or in grocery stores or, now, here, in front of other parents, Elizabeth felt all those eyes on her pressingly, staring at her with the kind of horror mixed with grim fascination that brought her right back to those lonely cafeterias of her youth, enduring the grotesque curiosity of a strange new student body, which, in its cruel gaze, was telling her: *You do not belong here*. She felt their stares as Toby's scream silenced the room, and Elizabeth felt the urgent need to *do something*, to make it stop, to perform some kind of magical feat of motherhood, but of course there was no way to make it stop, nothing to do but plead with Toby—"It's okay, it's okay"—and hope this meltdown wouldn't be a long one, hope it wouldn't be one of those where Toby struggled to breathe through overpowering sobs.

Who knows how bad it might have gotten had Brandie not swooped in right at the moment Toby's scream was about to crest, appearing suddenly at his side and saying with unexpected enthusiasm and gladness: "Who needs a brain break?"

Which somehow shut him right up.

"You need a little time to yourself there, kiddo?" Brandie asked him.

And Toby looked up at her, maybe startled at her quick appearance and unlikely cheer, and said, "Uh-huh," his big eyes already glistening.

"There are some weighted blankets in the quiet room," she said. "You go on in there and have yourself a brain break, okay?"

"Okay," Toby said, standing, sniffling.

"That's right," Brandie said. "You squish those bad thoughts all the way down to your shoes!"

Which made Toby, unbelievably, giggle.

And then the boy was walking away, and Brandie picked up his computer, which he had left behind, and handed it to Elizabeth.

"Thank you," Elizabeth said.

"What a sweetheart," Brandie said as the two of them watched him go.

"How did you do that?"

Brandie shrugged. "I sent him my peaceful thoughts."

"That's it? You sent your thoughts?"

"Yes, that's it. It's really very simple. I said to myself: *I am the peace amid the chaos.* I thought that, and believed it, and then the universe made it true. You should try it. Say it out loud, and when you do, try to really, honestly believe it."

And Elizabeth looked at her host like, *Seriously?* But then she saw Brandie's big open guileless grin, and she recalled *Step 7: Lie If Necessary*, and so Elizabeth nodded and smiled.

"I am the peace amid the chaos," she said, trying to smile genuinely, with both her mouth and her eyes.

NONE of the most authoritative-seeming sources on the World Wide Web could agree on something as simple as how to train a bicep. On the straightforward question of how to make one's biceps bigger, it was, online, chaos. When Jack first googled this subject and clicked on the top result, he foolishly thought he had it all under control. It sounded pretty simple: you made a bicep bigger by lifting moderate weights many, many times—four sets, twelve reps, weight at 45 percent the muscle's upper lifting limit, sixty seconds mindful resting between sets, done two to three times weekly—which was said to activate something called the sarcoplasmic fluid within the muscle, thereby making it bigger. And Jack tried this for about a month until he grew impatient with his lack of results and went back to the web to discover that, actually, he'd been doing everything *all wrong*. The secret to making a bicep bigger was not to lift moderate weights but rather enormous ones, and only a few times—just three sets, lift until you fail, a weight at 85 percent the muscle's max, a two-and-one-half-minute rest between the sets, exactly twice a week—which allegedly shocked the muscle's myofibril tissues into growing back larger. So Jack tried this for about a month, until he again grew impatient at his biceps' complete lack of change or growth and went back to the web and learned that, once more, he'd been doing everything *all wrong*. The key to real muscle building, he discovered, was progressive weighting—where you start with the weights that are lightest and ramp to the weights that are heaviest, lifting them seven to twenty times each—which was supposed to work both the slow-twitch endurance-type muscle fibers and the fast-twitch power-type muscle fibers that were present in some ratio in every muscle. So, okay, Jack spent a month progressively weighting all his workouts, then went back to the web when, once more, there was no change in the size or shape of his biceps, nor triceps, delts, quads, or any of the other major muscle groups he'd been, as advised, "targeting," and this was because, once again, he'd been doing everything *all wrong*, that according to a totally different website it didn't really matter how heavy or light or progressive your weights were if you weren't also supporting your weight lifting with the proper diet, that if you were restricting calories in an effort to shed pounds (which Jack was, naturally, doing), then you weren't providing your energy-hungry muscles enough sustenance to build themselves up with, and so weight lifting at a caloric deficit meant that, perversely, the body burned muscle fiber to make up for the deficit that working the muscle fiber created in the first place, a sort of biologic Penelope paradox whereby Jack's body would undo at night all the work he had done during the day. So Jack needed to follow a more weight-lifting-friendly diet, which required him first to establish the baseline metabolic rate for a person of his age and gender and height and weight and body fat percentage as determined by skinfold caliper measurements at his waist, neck, and back, but when he inputted all this data into four online "Basal Metabolic Rate Calculators" he was given four wildly divergent numbers, with a gap between the lowest and highest numbers being the caloric equivalent of a large daily pepperoni pizza, which seemed pretty odd, to get such inconsistent results from the same data, not to mention irritating, that the whole point of buying something like *skinfold calipers* in the first place was to make his weight-loss and muscle-building plan scientifically exact, which seemed necessary since too few calories would prevent muscle-building but too many calories would encourage gut-gaining, and so consuming the proper number of daily calories felt like threading an impossible needle, dietwise. He ultimately just took an average of the four separate numbers and used that result to extrapolate his daily macronutrient needs, the most important of which according to almost everyone was protein, which was necessary in monstrous quantities—when he calculated his alleged protein requirement he found that to satisfy it he'd basically have to eat three whole chickens a day, which seemed both unlikely and weird, which was why everyone online advocated for a daily protein powder smoothie or two, to supplement one's normal protein consumption, which led him down yet another dizzying online labyrinth where proponents of protein powders made from whey or bone or soy or hemp or peas or rice or something ambiguously called "superfoods" all argued that their protein powder was the correct protein powder and that if you were using any other protein powder you were doing it *all wrong*.

Jack was a man with an advanced degree from a good school, and yet the whole enterprise of working out and losing weight seemed hopelessly complicated and convoluted and beyond his capacities. It was like the more online research he did, the fewer objectively true things he knew. Which was why he finally purchased the System.

Ads for the System began appearing after Jack's first foray down the internet's weight-loss rabbit hole, after his very first Google search: *How to lose belly fat.* This search had coincided with the planning of the new condo at the Shipworks and Elizabeth's subsequent critique of their whole way of life. One of the changes she wanted—along with the arts-and-crafts nook and open shelving and such—was a "home gym," a little exercise alcove that would include a treadmill and a weight rack and one of those machines with complexly configured cables that allowed you to do like thirty different exercises, plus one of those giant rubber balls that people writhed around on in ways that supposedly worked their core. And, as usual, Jack didn't really understand why Elizabeth wanted to make this change, given that she did all her exercise at the gym.

"Why do you also need a gym at home?" he'd asked.

"I thought it could be for"—little pause to search for a delicate way to put it—"*both* of us."

Meaning, of course, that it was for him.

"You think I need to exercise?" he said, surprised.

"I know you've always loathed the gym."

"Yes."

"But, well, we're getting older," she said, and then she went through a short disquisition on the special needs of people of advancing age regarding, like, bone density, hip strength, that sort of thing, framing the home gym in terms of longevity, even though she and Jack were just now barely into their forties.

The next morning, though, in the shower—standing in that old gray claw-foot tub he hated, how the vinyl curtain would always draw itself in during a shower and cling to him like a cold jellyfish—Jack examined his belly. He pinched at and prodded his belly. He finished his shower and stood in front of the bathroom's long mirror and looked at himself—really *looked*—and what he saw could be called, maybe, uncharitably, a gut. There was a slight swell, he observed, a *pooch*. Strangely, it was the first time he could recall seeing it. He'd always had such a small and slight figure, and had always known himself as such a skinny guy, a frail guy, that he hadn't paid attention to this bulkier guy quietly creeping forth.

That very day, he searched the web for ways to tone one's belly, which was when ads for the System began their assault. He saw the first one on Facebook, between two posts from his father in which, as usual, the old man was ranting, angrily, in all capital letters. That month's worrying headlines had delivered so much grist for the elder Baker's mayhemed mind: there was rioting in Missouri (*TERRORISTS!*), and airstrikes in the Middle East (*DIVERSION!*), and migrants drowning in the Mediterranean (*CRISIS ACTORS!*), and Ebola surging in Africa (*CORPORATE PLOT!*).

Jack, as usual, debated and commented and fought with his father, but ignored the ad.

Then he saw it again, this cryptic ad for something called the System, it suddenly appeared outside of Facebook, on some random website, up there in the top banner, and then the ad began following Jack around the web, showing up all over the place, cycling through slogans until it found the one that called to him most:

DON'T WORK HARDER, WORK SMARTER
HUGE GAINS, NO NOISE
THE DATA-DRIVEN ROUTE TO RIPPED ABS

And so on.

The System's whole allure seemed built on the promise that it somehow peered into your body and extracted the most consequential data, data that would then be used to build a personalized, optimized workout program. Which had been persuasive enough to lead Jack here, to the gym, one of several people at the gym today who was #OnTheSystem. You could always tell which people were #OnTheSystem because, first, they all had the same wearable—a wristband that looked like a watch without a face, in the System's signature color, tiger orange—and, second, because they would all occasionally, suddenly, sit up very straight. It was because of the app's posture notification, which let you know when you were slouching, which Jack was doing all the time, apparently, because roughly every ten to twelve minutes the bracelet would buzz to let him know he was, again, drooping, and his phone would light up with another message about spinal health or neck stiffness or energy flow or something similarly posture-related. A gym full of people randomly doing this—popping up powerfully erect—had a whack-a-mole quality that reminded Jack of prairie dog towns back on the Kansas plains.

How the bracelet knew he was slouching was a mystery, as was how it knew his blood oxygenation level, sweat pH, skin plasticity, hydration, lactic acid levels, diabetes risk, UV exposure, even his current mood. The bracelet kept track of all these things, as well as more explicable data like heart rate and steps walked and sleep quality. He received a report each morning about the previous night's sleep, the bracelet having monitored his tossing and turning all night. It even had a microphone that would record him snoring, which the app would play back for him the following day, his occasional snores, which he always found surprising. He had not known he was a snorer.

The System quantified everything, and not only hard numbers like calories consumed and waist circumference and bicep size but also softer and more abstract measurements, like Jack's feelings of well-being, optimism, passion, whether he was, as the app put it, *flourishing*. The System asked him to describe his work life and his home life, and so he went ahead and typed up a comprehensive essay about his career, how it had looked so promising following his graduation with a master's degree, when he'd been hired at one of the local universities as an adjunct professor teaching undergraduate Intro to American Art and Intro to Photography classes, a part-time position he was, in his midtwenties, super grateful for, figuring he'd get a little teaching experience under his belt so he'd be ready to pounce on whatever area full-time academic jobs came open when the current professors moved or quit or retired. And indeed the local academic market had experienced its usual employment churn, but the problem for Jack was that the universities in and around Chicago had almost universally decided to fill those positions not with more full-time tenure-track professors but rather with part-time low-cost adjuncts, hired, as Jack was, on a semester-by-semester basis, paid roughly one-tenth of what the professors made to teach exactly the same classes, with no health insurance, no retirement plan, and no guarantee that they'd be hired again the next semester. Jack now cobbled together as many Art History and Intro to Photography classes as he could, doing essentially the same job he'd done when he was recently out of school, only now feeling far less grateful for it.

Jack keyed all this into his phone—slowly, as he had never mastered typing on his phone the way he saw Toby doing it, with two thumbs and at blazing speed—hoping that the app would have some kind of magic answer for him, some solution to the problem of his stagnant career.

It sent him a coupon for a seminar he could take to become a Realtor.

Which, okay, fair enough.

Regarding Elizabeth, Jack was far less specific, mentioning only that he felt a worrying distance from his wife, a strange small lurking antagonism, that she'd been expressing latent domestic frustrations since they'd purchased the new condo and that, more generally, he feared that the exigencies of parenthood had slowly transformed their marriage into one that was focused on family administration rather than romance, that there was, lately, a distressing lack of spark.

After which the app sent him a coupon for a vibrator.

The Madagascar, it was called, because of its shape: a thin tip giving way to a thick and bulbous middle, which allowed the thing to provide "fully enveloping stimulation," allegedly. It was part of a line of geography-inspired sex toys (there was a prostate massager called the Mexico that was downright intimidating). And Jack, feeling a little desperate, went ahead and bought the Madagascar and presented it to Elizabeth with the suggestion that maybe they use it, together, and she said they'd definitely have to do that someday, and she put it in the drawer of her bedside table, where it remained, still, untouched.

Jack had been surprised that the System was so interested in his marriage. It asked him to record his spouse's daily moods along with his own: whether she was happy or sad, distant or affectionate, sexually interested or sexually unavailable, and so on. The app was, after all, a health tracker, and, according to the data, there was no other variable that affected one's health more than a high-quality, high-satisfaction, long-term pair-bonded intimate sexual relationship. The System sent him loads of information on this subject, how a good marriage was the number one single predictor of good health—apparently, the difference between a bad marriage and a good one was, health outcomes–wise, the same as the difference between smoking and not smoking. People in happy marriages had higher life expectancies, fewer cases of depression, heart disease, Alzheimer's, arthritis, were generally less *inflamed*. And being lonely in one's marriage was the health equivalent—all else being equal—of having diabetes. It turned out that feeling isolated and alone and unsatisfied in one's marriage was not only emotionally damaging but also damaging for one's physical bodily health, and so the health tracker took the quality of Jack's relationship very seriously indeed.

The System collected all of Jack's subjective happiness data, plus all of the objective data the bracelet accumulated, and, using what it called a "deep learning AI," delivered not only the personalized workout routine Jack had been expecting but also a personalized *life* routine. The System recommended optimal daily meals, the times he should optimally eat them, how much water to optimally drink with them. The System recommended the optimal time to go to sleep, the optimal time to wake up. And it recommended ways to optimize his marriage. There was actually an elaborate subsystem dedicated to improving what the app called his Love Score, which involved "gamifying" the rituals common to high-satisfaction relationships. He received points and badges and other such rewards for completing specific tasks: *Acts of Service* were chore-type things—taking out the trash, doing dishes, cleaning the bathroom—basically the drudgery of domestic maintenance; *Romantic Gestures* were those stolen, thinking-of-you-type moments expressed over the course of an otherwise normal day—a sexy text message, a love note hidden in a purse or briefcase, a secretly mouthed *I love you* from across the room; and then there was *Special Memory-Making*, which involved planning elaborate date nights or travels abroad or hiking trips or weekends in isolated forest cabins, all of which Jack had recently recommended. In fact, according to the System's online leaderboard, Jack knew that he was personally in the ninety-ninth percentile in all of these "giving" metrics, and so it was really discouraging that his relationship's total cumulative score hovered in the midfifties, mostly dragged down by two things: first, his very low *Need Fulfillment* count, as he had not recorded meeting any of Elizabeth's specific needs for at least a month now—and not because he wasn't trying, but because she didn't seem to have them. Needs. She could go weeks without expressing a single desire, a single difficulty he could maybe help her with. Years ago, he had fallen in love with exactly this quality—her independence, her poise and self-sufficiency—but now, more often than not, it made him feel peripheral, like he was just sitting around wondering: *Do you need me yet? Do you need me ever?*

And then, second, there was the matter of their *Intimacy Quotient*, which was lower than average as calculated by the frequency of their sexual encounters, plus the wearable's measurements during their occasional couplings, as the bracelet's interior accelerometer could sense when sex happened, and the device tracked the duration of the sex, his heart rate during the sex, calories burned by having the sex, and the decibel level of bed squeaks and what it called *female copulatory vocalizations*, about which there were whole separate analytics. Jack felt a little queasy letting the System have access to their most private, most personal information and utterances, but as the app often reminded him: *You can't improve what you don't measure.* And so Jack went ahead and measured everything. (There was even an attachment one could purchase on the System's website, a "smartring" that fit around the base of one's penis that tracked the number of thrusts during sex and the g-force achieved by each thrust, but Jack had held off on buying that particular item, for probably obvious reasons.)

He was frustrated by the lack of progress on these fronts—neither his body nor his marriage had shown much improvement, despite the System's many rigors. Elizabeth still operated as if the point of each day was to all-out sprint toward evening's exhaustion. She was always busy, running from here to there, her schedule a mad gridlock of work and playdates and extracurriculars and chores. But Jack kept at it, hoping that, eventually, all the exercise and acts of service and romantic gestures would function as a kind of elaborate flypaper, holding Elizabeth still, and he would finally see the change he wanted to see, which was not exactly *change* but rather a kind of reversion—he wanted his joyful wife back; he wanted his skinny body back. And so he kept following the System's advice, which was why he was at the gym, right now, doing something called "burpees."

He would have felt foolish doing burpees were it not for the many people at the gym currently also doing them—at least a dozen others, all wearing the same orange bracelets, all doing this objectively absurd-looking exercise, a push-up fused with a jumping jack. He looked around at all the other people doing burpees. To Jack, it felt like they were all in this together, doing this silly thing. They were a club. The burpee club. And as he rested between burpee sets, he kept trying to catch someone's eye so he could shrug and smile and make a face like *I too think this is ridiculous*. But he couldn't catch anyone's eye because, he had noticed, when people were at the gym, they did not tarry. They were not sociable, nor approachable. The women especially, who, when they walked from station to station, stared so hard at the floor it was like they were trying to crack the concrete with their minds. When people at the gym exercised, they did so with expressions of deep inner focus and concentration. When they rested, they looked at their devices. And the entire time they were in the gym, they wore headphones, some of them DJ-huge.

This might not have seemed all that unusual except that the gym was housed in the same building where, many years ago, there had been a coffee shop, the Urbus Orbis, which was the beating heart of Wicker Park when Jack first moved here, a place where people would sit all night nursing an infinitely refillable dollar coffee and commune. It was where you went to *not* feel alone, which was maybe why Jack's failed attempts at connecting with the other burpee-doers felt weirdly important, because a place once known for fellowship was now serving the private, solitary, and narcissistic impulse to look hot.

It was where Jack and Elizabeth had their first date, this building. The memory of it was still so near, that night so momentous—he always thought they deserved their own plaque on the wall: *It all started here.* The place was, for Jack, just a bog of nostalgia. But few others still remembered it as the Orbis building. After the Orbis went bankrupt (which was blamed mostly on its refills policy, which encouraged customers to take up tables for several hours while spending only one dollar), the building was transformed into an elaborate condo and used as the main set during the eleventh season of MTV's *The Real World*, which drove everyone in the neighborhood batty. And not only because of the squadron of cameras following the seven roommates all over the place, but also because the locals knew their bohemian neighborhood was going to become way less bohemian once it was colonized by something as corporate as Viacom. They were incensed about it. They protested it. Jack remembered one night when a small crowd had gathered at the *Real World* condo's front door and everyone was chanting "We're real! You're not! We're real! You're not!" and one of the cast members (maybe it was Kyle?) came home trailing his big television-production posse, and he was unlocking the front door as the crowd hurled this abuse at him—"We're real! You're not! We're real! You're not!"—and he stopped fiddling with the lock and stood there for a moment, hanging his head, staring at his shoes, looking all sad and dejected and injured and victimized, and Jack suddenly felt a bolt of sympathy for this poor guy, who, after all, never asked to be dropped into such a conspicuous building, in such a surly place, but then the cast member (or maybe it was Chris?) suddenly popped his head up and asked one of the cameramen, "Did you get that? Please tell me you got that." And the cameraman gave him a big thumbs-up, and one of the producers stepped in and said to the crowd, "That was *so amazing*! Great job, everyone! Now we need to get that from a different angle, so please keep doing exactly what you're doing. It's *fantastic*!" And the producer clapped his hands and smiled a big smile and the cameramen darted to new positions and the crowd—sort of confused now, looking at each other like *Do we still do this?*—kept chanting with maybe one-third of their previous enthusiasm, and they all watched as the cast member once again bowed his head and looked for all the world to be really sad and anguished, and Jack listened to the crowd saying "We're real, you're not. We're real, you're not" and he thought that, in this moment, none of them were real.

Now, years later, just about every quaint storefront in the neighborhood had been replaced with some chain. Like that fantastic vegetarian café, Earwax, which had lasted a few years longer than Jack's own vegetarianism, that place was now a Doc Martens. And his favorite art gallery was now an Urban Outfitters. And the Swank Frank hot-dog stand where he and Elizabeth would get a fried Twinkie after all the bars had closed, that was now a Bank of America.

Their bohemian neighborhood had turned into a yuppie neighborhood with a bohemian theme.

His phone buzzed with a new alert, *Tasty Hack Saves Carbs*, about how substituting pureed cauliflower for mashed potatoes would be a carb-free way to save a few hundred calories, on average, it said. And then it offered him a coupon for cauliflower at the nearby Jewel-Osco. This was what the System's app did during his rests between exercises: sent him life hacks. The idea here was that if Jack had to rest for two minutes between burpee sets, then he might as well be productive with those two minutes. He might as well learn a thing or two while he waited, in order to reach what the System often called *Peak Efficiency* (thus, its tips for optimization were, themselves, optimized). The hacks he received were often listicles that gave him the plummeting sense that he was fucking up at literally everything in life, even the easiest things: "6 Mistakes You're Making in the Shower" and "9 Ways You're Sleeping Wrong" and "The 7 Hidden Dangers of Sitting." That was a System favorite: *Sitting Is the New Smoking*, it said several times weekly. The System was very strongly opposed to sitting at a desk all day, preferring instead that its users *stand* at a desk all day, or, even better, *walk* at a desk all day by installing a slow-moving treadmill beneath their desks so that during an eight-hour workday they could also complete what would end up being the equivalent of a 10K. The app would send a coupon for these desk/treadmill combo things, which cost, on average, almost exactly Jack's salary for an entire semester.

He did another burpee.

Push up, stand up, jump up, repeat.

Ahead of him were at least two more sets of burpees, followed by bicep curls, squats, and a series of demented twisty maneuvers involving foam rollers that would strengthen his *core*, an ill-defined, unseen, inner part of him that was, according to the System, in dire need of improvement. He'd been told this on his first day with the new wearable, when he'd completed the System's initial fitness evaluation. *Problem Area: Core*, it had said, which reminded him of something his mother used to tell him. "You're rotten to the core, Jack Baker." Apparently, the AI agreed.

Maybe, he thought, he'd go ahead and buy that cauliflower.

Maybe he'd come home tonight with cauliflower and a lean protein—almost certainly chicken breast—and he'd puree the cauliflower into a gooey paste, and when Elizabeth asked him what he was doing, he'd explain to her how cauliflower was a delicious and carb-free alternative to mashed potatoes, which he thought would be impressive, his dietary knowledge. And then if Toby liked the taste of it? If Toby ate his whole portion without complaining? Bonanza. A real husband-win. And then maybe there'd be a little bedroom action tonight. Maybe he'd suggest they give the Madagascar a whirl, and maybe she'd love it.

Except, come to think of it, Elizabeth most likely had tonight's meal already thoroughly organized. She was probably thawing some frozen thing right at this moment. If he came home with spontaneous food ideas, it would probably stress her out, because then she'd have to alter the plan, and she wouldn't have gone to all that trouble if she'd known he was cooking, or something like that. Jack's attempts to contribute domestically always seemed to fizzle somehow. Elizabeth consistently implied that she'd like him to do more of the meal prep, and yet she also kept a ten-day rolling menu in her head, deviations from which caused her great aggravation. It was like she wanted him to contribute, but only in the exact and precise and singular way she imagined but never once articulated.

Maybe he wouldn't bring home the cauliflower. Maybe instead he'd mention the thing about the cauliflower, to get it into her head, for the future. Maybe just sharing the cauliflower hack would be enough of a domestic contribution to allow for some Madagascar possibilities later in the evening.

He finished his final set of burpees while imagining that he looked as serious and professional as everyone else. Then the bicep curls, the squats, the copious horrible core-working drills. On his way out, he logged the circumference of his waist and his biceps using the tape measure the gym provided for everyone #OnTheSystem.

And, as usual, there had been no change.

THE IDEA came to her as she was preparing the turnovers.

Brandie's apple turnovers. They had just gone into the oven—five minutes, four hundred degrees—and Toby was sitting at their small cluttered kitchen table waiting for his snack, staring at the oven, when he looked up at Elizabeth and asked, "How many can I have?" Which was when she recalled that study she'd read, so long ago, the one at Stanford, the one about kids and marshmallows and patience.

"We're going to play a game," she said.

The kitchen air was already sweet with the scents of apple and cinnamon and caramelized sugar. Elizabeth removed the pastries from the oven, and she transferred the whole steaming batch to a glass container, all of them save one, which she placed poignantly on a large white plate. She placed the plate in front of Toby, at a small distance, reachable if he stood on his chair. Next to it, she set a glass of milk.

"I'm going to leave the kitchen," she said, "and then I'll come back in fifteen minutes. During that time, you are allowed to eat this snack."

She saw him look at the turnover, saw a seriousness overtake him.

"However," she said, and he looked back up at her, "if that snack is still here when I come back, then I'll let you eat *two* snacks. Do you understand?"

He nodded.

"So you can either have one turnover now or two turnovers in fifteen minutes."

"Okay," Toby said.

"I hope you take some time to really consider your decision."

After which she walked out of the kitchen, leaving Toby alone with his predicament. She went to her bedroom. Opened her laptop. She set the timer for fifteen minutes. And she waited.

Any first-year psych major would have known about this study. Elizabeth herself had first encountered it in her freshman-year social science seminar. It was an experiment about self-control and delayed gratification among small children, wherein researchers had presented their subjects with an excruciating dilemma: the kids could either eat one marshmallow now or two marshmallows in fifteen minutes. The researchers found that some kids could successfully wait the fifteen minutes, while others could not. Then they tracked these kids through adolescence, into adulthood, and what they discovered was that the kids who had resisted the marshmallow for fifteen minutes were the ones who did far better, later, in life. They did better in high school, scored better on the SATs, were admitted to better colleges, got higher-paying jobs, had fewer unwanted pregnancies, fewer encounters with the law, fewer heart attacks and strokes, were less depressed—it was amazing how their futures could be read, like tea leaves, in this one moment when they were children and they were presented with a marshmallow and a choice.

Toby's pediatrician had encouraged Jack and Elizabeth to try things that might help Toby practice his patience and restraint and frustration-tolerance. This was after a private meeting where Elizabeth had brought in her own copy of the *DSM-5* with several highlighted passages about oppositional defiant disorder and disruptive mood dysregulation disorder and intermittent explosive disorder and various sensory processing disorders and the doctor said: "I don't know, maybe?" The problem was that Toby never quite met the criteria for any one diagnosable thing. Like, for example, to be officially identified as having ADHD you had to show six or more specific symptoms of hyperactivity-impulsivity, of which Toby showed only four. And this type of thing happened with all of Toby's screenings and tests and evaluations: there was never a definite positive, and for every presenting symptom, there were also contraindications. Yes, he had trouble remaining in his seat, and yes, he often fidgeted and tapped his hands or feet, and he was sensitive to unexpected noises, and he seemed afraid of new people and new social situations, and he had unpredictable tantrums that would reduce him to painful, suffocating sobs; but then again he also seemed to feel sincerely ashamed and embarrassed and apologetic following his meltdowns, and he scored in the upper percentiles on tests of empathy and theory of mind, and he was often really observant and insightful even about total strangers, and he could sometimes sense from the next room when a bad mood settled over her and suddenly he'd be right there asking, "What's wrong, Mom?" So the doctors shrugged. Which was a relief for Elizabeth, sort of. She was glad that Toby did not seem to have a disorder, but then again, if he did have a disorder, she would at least know what to do. There would be a treatment, best practices, a script to follow. But with Toby, there were no such practices, no such script, no assurances whatsoever. They just had to figure it out.

Elizabeth sat on her bed, staring at her computer, waiting. She had fully intended to use this brief moment of solitude to get a little work done but instead found herself on Instagram, cruising through Brandie's feed. Elizabeth had searched for Brandie's Instagram almost immediately after they'd first met a month ago, and since then Elizabeth had been lightly, but consistently, watching, studying, lurking. There was already a photo posted of today's playdate performance. And next to that, a picture uploaded yesterday of Brandie's children in their big white sun-drenched kitchen cutting up apples and laying out puff pastry and smiling the big smiles of harmonious loving family togetherness. Below that, Brandie meditating in her garden, the words *Shift your focus, shift your life* written atop the image. Next to that, a selfie with Brandie and her husband, arms around each other, all dressed up, on a date. The husband was some kind of banker. His name was Mike. He wore polo shirts that fit snugly around his impressively buff chest and arms. *Love this man so much*, Brandie had written, and she'd followed that with three of those emojis with hearts for eyes.

The timer's sudden alarm surprised her—it made Elizabeth realize that she'd gone into one of those little internet reveries, that a more-than-expected amount of time had passed, and that she'd been staring at Brandie's husband (the man was seriously fit) for longer than was probably couth.

She returned to the kitchen, and she was not altogether surprised to find that both her son and the turnover were gone.

He was in his room, watching YouTube. She brought him back into the kitchen and told him they were going to try it again. This time she raised the stakes: if he waited the fifteen minutes, he could have *two more* turnovers, plus some extra screen time that night. But if he could not resist, if he broke down and ate the one extra snack she was now offering him, then he would have no screen time whatsoever, and he would be going to bed early.

"You understand the consequences of your actions?" she said. He nodded. "All you have to do is restrain yourself for fifteen minutes." He nodded again.

She went back to her bedroom, set a timer, waited.

The thing about those kids who could resist the marshmallow was that they had ways to distract themselves and disassociate themselves from their desires, to pretend like their desires were something separable from their selves, and to picture themselves in the future and empathize with the people they would be in fifteen minutes' time, which was a surprisingly tricky thing to do. Recent neuroimaging research showed that when people imagined their future selves, they used a different part of their brain than the part they used when imagining their present selves. When imagining their future selves, they used a part of the brain they also used when imagining, say, the inner life of a celebrity, or the thoughts of a character in a book. In other words, forgoing a marshmallow now to eat it in the future felt, in the moment, in a certain part of the brain, literally like just giving the marshmallow to someone else.

The trick, she knew, was being able to live more fully in your imagination. To reduce the mental gap between you and the person you would soon become. To tell a story about the future that was more compelling than the present, which was something Elizabeth seemed to have a special knack for. It was one of her superpowers. And not only lately—in the way she had been assembling their upcoming life at the Shipworks, engineering their condo to maximize future satisfaction—but it was also her basic disposition while growing up, moving from place to place, school to school, starting over constantly, friendless once again, lonely, it had become an essential skill just to get by, just to endure. Elizabeth needed to invent stories about herself and her future that were more bearable than her present, more hopeful than her past, and in the meantime simply wait and wait and wait.

So creating elaborate and optimistic forecasts for herself—that was basically where Elizabeth had lived all her life. In her imagination. In her head. It was her only permanent address.

Not so much for Toby. Toby tended to be passionately, recklessly in the moment. He was—she hated to admit it—an eat-the-marshmallow-right-now kind of boy. And these boys, the ones who were unable to contain their fleeting impulses, tended to be the guys who, later, you needed to avoid. And she did not want Toby becoming one of them.

The timer went off. She returned to the kitchen, where, once again, her son was gone. And, once again, so was the turnover.

"I'm going to teach you a little trick," she said after finding him at the computer and bringing him back to the kitchen. "Try to pretend it's not actually real food."

Toby was confused.

"Pretend it's a *picture* of food," she said, "on a piece of paper. You wouldn't want to eat a piece of paper, would you?"

Toby shook his head.

"That would be gross, wouldn't it?" She was trying to sound flippant, happy. "Eating a piece of paper with a snack drawn on it? Yuck!"

The boy laughed.

"Pretend it's a piece of paper, and if you don't eat it after fifteen minutes, then I'll let you have as many turnovers as you want!" She opened her mouth and goofily shook her head around in a kind of joyful *Isn't-that-amazing?!* expression.

"As many as I want?" Toby said, looking at her dubiously, with scrunched-up eyes. They both knew that sugary foods were, in this family, highly regulated, minimally apportioned.

"As many as you want," Elizabeth assured him. "And imagine what that would be like. Think about how happy you'll be in fifteen minutes, eating as many turnovers as you want. Are you imagining it?"

He closed his eyes and tipped his head up, as if in a pleasant daydream.

"Yes," he said.

"Are you happy, in your imagination?"

"Yes."

"Great. Now think *only* about how happy you'll be in the future. Keep that feeling in mind, and if you can wait fifteen minutes, you can feel that way in real life. Okay?"

"Okay!"

"Okay. Your time starts now."

And she left the kitchen, but this time she left the door open a crack, so she could watch him, and what she saw was that, as soon as he thought the door was closed, at the very first moment he was left alone, he reached across the table and grabbed the turnover and stuffed it, whole, into his mouth.

She burst back into the kitchen. "What the hell are you doing?"

Toby was cowed by her appearance, and her sudden anger. He stopped chewing mid-chew, crumbs falling from his lips.

"Why are you eating that?"

"You said I could!"

"You're supposed to wait!"

"You said I could eat it if I wanted to!"

"But you're not supposed to want to!"

And Elizabeth was about to open the garbage bin and dramatically dump the rest of the turnovers into the trash when she heard the front door open, heard Jack's happy voice—"I'm home!"—and then her husband was gliding into the kitchen, wearing his workout clothes, hopped up on post-exercise energy, saying "My *god*, it smells *great* in here!" and kissing Elizabeth on the cheek and sliding over to the counter and grabbing two turnovers and eating them immediately—one might even say *impulsively*—closing his eyes and going, "Mmmmm" while Elizabeth and Toby just stared at him, silent.

Sometimes, especially on the more frustrating days, Jack's ability to so easily sate and enjoy himself without complication or guilt seemed contrived solely to mock her.

"So," Jack said after finishing the turnovers, slapping the counter lightly with his palms for emphasis, "I heard the most interesting thing about *cauliflower*."

Later that night, after dinner, and after cleaning up the kitchen, and after preparing tomorrow's lunches, and after taking out the trash and recycling, and after helping Toby with his homework, they commenced the elaborate nightly bedtime ritual. Jack read to Toby for about half an hour—right now they were making their way through Narnia—and then Elizabeth took her turn, and her primary job was to soothe and comfort Toby, who, most nights, dreaded falling asleep.

If Toby was unable to wait fifteen minutes to eat a snack, it was not, she knew, because he was unable to imagine himself in the future, because on these nights, when she tucked him in, he described a future that was vivid with all the horrible things that might happen as he slept. He worried about burglars bursting into his room or bugs crawling across his face. He worried about having bad dreams, worried about not waking up in the morning. Going to sleep seemed, for Toby, like a difficult exercise in trust. Trust in the world not to be cruel while he was unaware. He was so vulnerable these nights, so stricken with doubt and fear, that however challenging and disagreeable he might have been during the day, however many tantrums he might have thrown, Elizabeth immediately forgave him—all that mattered was soothing the terror in his heart.

"Mom?" Toby said tonight. "How do I know that you and Dad will be here when I wake up?"

"Sweetie, we're always here when you wake up."

"But how do I know that tomorrow will be the same? Maybe tomorrow you'll be gone."

"Toby, I promise, we will be here when you wake up."

"Both of you?"

"Well, one of us might be at work or running errands or some-thing. But we'll be right back."

"No, not gone like that. Like *gone*. Like, really gone. Forever."

"Honey, that would never happen."

"But what if you can't help it? What if in your sleep you disappear?"

Elizabeth nodded. He'd probably seen something on TV, or on the internet, or in a comic book, or maybe there had been some-thing tonight in Narnia, something about people blinking out of existence. That was the paradox of Toby at this age—or, for that mat-ter, people at any age: they could be so rational and levelheaded in one area but so paranoid and delusional in another. And she knew from her own research at Wellness on this very subject that the most effective way to approach people with an irrational belief was to rebut that belief from both inside and outside its own frame.

First, outside the frame: "Honey, people in real life don't disap-pear. That's just made up. That's just a story. You don't have to worry about that."

And Toby nodded in a half-hearted and unconvinced way, which was when Elizabeth shifted to the second prong: inside the frame.

"But even if we did disappear," she said, "you know what would happen next?"

"What?" Toby said, his eyes lighting up, suddenly interested.

"We would come back."

"You would?"

"We would fight so hard to come back. And do you know why?"

"Why?"

"Because we would miss *you* so much," she said, touching a finger lightly to his chest.

"Really?"

"We would miss you so much that we would reappear. That's how much we love you. We love you so much that we would come right back. Okay?"

"Okay," he said, now satisfied. And Elizabeth took him in her arms and he put his head in the nook of her shoulder and she held him there until his breathing began to slow and she got up and pulled the covers over him and kissed him on the forehead and said her customary farewell, which was not "Good night" or "Sweet dreams" or anything like that. Those tended to agitate Toby, who generally considered nighttime to be scary and treacherous. No, the way she said goodbye to him each night was the way everyone signed off on all of the YouTube channels he followed, which Toby found weirdly comforting:

"Don't forget to subscribe," she whispered softly, near his ear.

"Don't forget to subscribe," he said, facedown, his words muffled by the pillow.

She closed his door and walked to her bedroom, where she found that Jack was undressed, and the lights were turned low. Mood lighting. Sexy lighting. Jack had bought these special light bulbs that he could control with his phone. They were all over the place, LED bulbs, Wi-Fi connected and multihued, so that he could change the apartment's color temperature throughout the day, to match the sun: the cool bluish-white light of high noon, the more buttery-white light of late afternoon, the warm amber-white light of early evening. There were so many kinds of white light. It had something to do with the Kelvin scale. It was all very important to Jack; his training in photography made him sensitive to color temperature, he said. But the way he had the lamps tuned in the bedroom right now, they were of no naturally occurring cosmic color. It looked more like a brothel. Like a red-light district. Like a strip club. Scarlets and maroons and purples.

He was sitting on the bed, waiting. He had taken off his shirt, his pants, shoes, socks, even that silly orange thing on his wrist he called a *wearable*, which was right now lying askew on the bedside table. Jack wore nothing but his boxer shorts, and when he turned to her, she saw what he held in his hand: the vibrator he'd bought for her. He wiggled the toy slightly, saying: "I thought we could maybe . . . ?"

Which made her feel this sharp, guilty tumble inside, the same guilt she always felt when he was in the mood and she just wasn't. She hated being that person: the dowdy, exhausted wife who says no. What a cliché.

"You wouldn't have to do anything," he said, sensing her hesitation. "You could just lie there and enjoy yourself. I'll do all the work."

"The *work*?" she said, teasing him.

"You know what I mean. I'll be the giver. Your only job is to lie there and receive. No other responsibilities."

He'd always been like this, even when they'd first met: so attentive, so willing to hear her and please her. Jack wasn't like the guys she'd encountered before, who mostly blundered blindly forward doing whatever strange things they thought she should like—things that usually involved the twisting of various parts, the thwapping of various parts, the fiddling, squeezing, rubbing, handling—and then blaming her when she didn't really enjoy any of it. No, Jack was utterly up-front that he needed her to teach him how to touch her in the particular way she wanted. She could guide him, she could correct him, she could give him direction, and he wasn't threatened by it, wouldn't get angry about it, which at the time felt like a goddamn miracle. But now she wondered why she'd been so impressed: a guy who did what you asked him to do—shouldn't that be just the basic standard? Shouldn't that be routine? Unremarkable? And how low were her expectations at age eighteen that Jack's simply asking "What do you like?" made him seem like a hero?

Not that any of it mattered now. It was merely another way that she looked back at the person she used to be and found that person to be distressingly alien.

Jack had remained an attentive and considerate lover, all through the years. And their sex life was consistent and enjoyable, perhaps not as robust as it used to be, but then again, who could expect that? They had more sex than some married couples, and less than others. She did not put a number on it, she was not quantitative, she didn't think of it in terms of *x number of times per week* or whatever, because that was both crude and inaccurate. They had sex when they wanted to and were able to, and this was sometimes frequently, sometimes infrequently, depending on a host of other variables, chief among them how taxing the day's parenting had been, and how distant her mom-brain felt from her sex-brain, and how many stressful items were on her mind's ongoing to-do list, and how depleted she felt her inner emotional reserves to be.

She sat down next to Jack, leaned into him. "Thank you," she said, "but I'm just, you know—"

"You're not in the headspace."

"Not even close to the headspace," she said. "Not in the same galaxy. I'm sorry."

"It's okay."

"It's just that the day has been long and trying."

"It's really okay."

"I would like to be sexually pleased," she said, "but maybe sometime later in the week."

Jack laughed. "I'll contact your secretary, get it on your calendar."

"Right," she said. "Sorry." She knew Jack preferred sex to be passionately spontaneous, but that had been difficult after Toby, when the exigencies of jobs and parenthood erased most spontaneity. It used to be that they *seduced* each other. Now it was more like they just *asked* each other. An element of planning had entered their sex life, and she understood that Jack probably grieved about this. It probably seemed, to a romantic like him, a little dull. Pragmatic. Dreary.

He stood up, grabbed his phone, tapped a few things, and the lights in the room changed, from the dark sultry red to a pale anemic halogen.

"Toby's having an existential crisis," Elizabeth said.

"A what?"

"He thinks one of us will stop existing."

"Like, as in, die?"

"No. Not die. Just suddenly not be. Disappear."

"Oh," Jack said. "Has that church lady in the suburbs been telling him things about the Rapture?"

"Brandie is not that kind of church lady. She's more New Agey, I think, more *woo*. And besides, she wouldn't do that. She's really nice. She made us the apple turnovers."

"That's always how they start, church people. With food. To gain your trust."

"Oh stop it."

"First they give you food. Then they come for your soul."

"It's not like that. Brandie seems into that positive-thinking stuff. That power-of-the-mind-type stuff. Which, you know, is not totally irrational."

"It's not?"

"If you're a positive person, it tends to make people react better to you, and it increases your confidence, decreases your stress. It's a kind of self-fulfilling prophecy."

"Yeah, well, as long as she's not giving Toby any strange pamphlets to read."

"She's harmless."

"Fine."

"Jack, I'm sorry I'm not in the mood tonight."

"It's really okay," he said. Then he put the vibrator back in the bedside table's drawer and put on sweatpants and a T-shirt and kissed Elizabeth and told her good night, and as he walked out the door, he glanced back at her and said, in a little singsong voice: "Love you."

She made a smile for him. "Love you too."

Then he closed the door, went to his office, off to do whatever he did on the computer after hours.

That night, Elizabeth fell asleep quickly, as usual, and then, also as usual, she woke up at some point thereafter, either late at night or early in the morning. It was still dark out. She was alone in the bed. Jack must have stayed in the office again, on the pull-out couch. It could have been one a.m., or three, or five—she didn't check her phone because she didn't want to know. It happened this way all the time now, that she was no longer able to sleep through the night. She consistently woke up at some awful hour, her mind spinning: about work, about Jack, about Toby, about Toby's new school and new friends, about the move to the suburbs, or sometimes just about the stupidest things—there was a package of chicken in the fridge that was nearing its expiration date, and so she'd have to remember to do something today with that chicken, and she wondered whether she should get up and make a note about the chicken or if she would remember it in the morning on her own, without the note, and then all the chicken-related recipes she had in her head suddenly sort of unspooled before her, and she thought about which chicken dishes they'd eaten recently, and which ones Toby refused to eat, and which ones were healthiest, and so on and so forth. This kind of thing, at three o'clock in the morning, could occupy her for an hour, this dumb thing about chicken.

But she had discovered a routine that allowed her to avoid all this worrying and aggravation. She had found that a combination of benzos and physical release would generally put her right back to sleep. So she drank a little water, took a Xanax, and then reached into the bedside table for the vibrator, the Madagascar, which, despite its ridiculous geographical conceit, was actually a pretty remarkable tool. She brought the thing under the covers and clicked on her favorite setting, something called Tectonic Shift, which was, as usual, enough to finish her within minutes.

THE SIX-HOUR SEMINAR that Jack was forced to attend at the beginning of each new semester had been called Orientation until a few years ago, when the university changed the seminar's name to Onboarding. The name change coincided with a revamp of the orientation curriculum, which had bloated into this all-day human resources horror during which members of the HR team attempted, at unmerciful length, to "socialize the mission statement's DNA," is how they put it. They were referring to the many-planked mission statement the university had spent two years and countless consultant dollars developing in a campus-wide effort to express everything the university did in just one sentence. This was the brainchild of the university's new CFO, who told the faculty in all seriousness that developing a mission statement that captured everything the university did in just one sentence was akin to their "moonshot," and he asked for their help in this endeavor "not because it is easy, but because it is hard." Why the university needed to corral its collective intelligence and creativity and energy for the task of expressing everything it did in just one sentence was a mystery to most faculty, but this did not stop their administrator bosses from enthusiastically assigning them to "mission statement working groups" so that they could have a voice (unpaid) in developing this one magical sentence, this one statement that would distill everything everyone did into a phrase ideally small enough for letterhead.

"This organization desperately needs to level-set," the CFO said at a meeting of the faculty body. "We can *hope* that we're all on the same page, but, to be frank, hope is not a strategy."

That the university even had a CFO rather than a more traditional dean was also a new development, but the faculty mostly let this pass because they could see the much more important writing on the wall: that if the university had a codified "mission statement," the university could also terminate those faculty who did not advance it. This was a pretty big threat to the more checked-out professors, who for years had enjoyed the leeway and soft responsibilities of tenure. And, indeed, Jack had never seen certain faculty so interested in their jobs as when they joined their mission statement working groups, where their singular, overriding goal was: *turf protection*. One guy from the geography department, for example, who'd been tenured since the seventies and whose sole contribution to the field in the last decade had been a one-man campaign to get the city of Chicago to switch to the metric system (his constant whining and complaining and letter writing on this subject was the reason his neighborhood was the only one in the city where the signs said SPEED LIMIT 48 KPH, that's how much of a pain in the ass he was to his alderman), this guy, who had not attended a single department meeting in four years, who had not volunteered for a single committee assignment since the beginning of the twenty-first century, now fought with choleric fury to get some mention of the metric system into the mission statement. He was literally the only person on campus who cared about this subject, but still he crusaded to make it one of everybody's guiding principles.

And the thing is? *He got it.* In one of the mission statement's several planks, he successfully lobbied to insert language about "conforming to global standards," language that he believed was specific enough to protect his particular interests, after which he vanished once again.

And this happened all over, in every working group, idiosyncratic professors from two dozen academic departments all fighting for explicit mission-statement representation. So, in the end, it was pretty easy to understand why the mission statement came out looking the way it did: a compound-complex, multi-semicoloned, many-branching grammatical nightmare that forced the English department to stage a collective symbolic walkout when the faculty senate approved it.

Since then, all new employees have had to endure this "onboarding" symposium at which HR painstakingly explained all of the mission statement's many phrases and planks and dependent clauses, which took about six hours, total. And the really criminal thing was that this was the ninth time Jack had done it, the ninth time he had been "onboarded." This was mostly due to a software glitch. As a part-time faculty member, Jack was, technically, according to the computer, "fired" at the end of each semester. Then, at the beginning of the next semester, he was "hired" once again. This was to circumvent the faculty's collective bargaining agreement, which mandated that anybody hired for more than a specified number of weeks per year had to be given health insurance and a pension. So all of the school's adjuncts were summarily fired two and sometimes three times a year so that the university could avoid the cost of giving them benefits. And the software glitch manifested when they were hired again the next term: when they resumed work, they showed up in the system as a "new employee." And all new employees had to be onboarded.

So here was Jack, sitting at a conference table in the richly appointed luxury ballroom that was usually the setting for university fundraising events, being onboarded for the ninth time. Around him were familiar faces, all the other adjuncts he recognized from years of onboarding, all of them right now looking about as bored and uninterested as the college students they sometimes complained about. There was only one person at Jack's big circular ten-seat table who was genuinely new, a man sitting next to Jack whose name tag said "Carl / Assistant Professor / Engineering," which Jack may have momentarily scowled at, that "Assistant Professor" bit, how it implied full-time employment, tenure, security, success, validation. The university rarely approved these full-time positions anymore, but when it did, the jobs were almost always in math or science or technology—basically the departments that dependably brought in research grant money and therefore, according to the CFO, "earned their keep." Carl was young, probably late twenties/early thirties, probably a recent PhD, with short ruffled hair and a barely-there mustache and a wrinkle-free shirt the color of a summer sky. He'd endearingly taken careful notes for the first hour of onboarding but had since stopped and now merely sat there like the rest of them, abiding. They had just finished covering the mission statement's third plank, clause four, subclause nine, the part about a "safe campus environment," which was where the HR team put the sexual harassment training. This consisted of a thorough explanation of the legal definition of sexual harassment, followed by an "opportunity to leverage your learnings," as the HR folks put it, where they would all watch a series of videos that showed two actors depicting behavior that may or may not have been sexual harassment. The idea was that each of the ballroom's many tablefuls of new employees needed to decide among themselves whether the behavior shown in the video cleared the legal bar to be considered sexual harassment. To which the answer was: yes. It did. Every time. Every video definitely depicted sexual harassment. But each time they went through this exercise in each successive onboarding seminar, this one dipshit from the philosophy department would inevitably try to split hairs about whether some behavior was technically, legally, actually sexual harassment, trying to justify and defend the most borderline cases, to really "tease out the gray areas," as he liked to say. This was a guy who regularly antagonized on Twitter, diving into trending fights regardless of the subject, the kind of guy who most often selected "Reply All" on his overbearing emails. And the HR people listened to him patiently with neutral facial expressions and then reminded him that, no, the videos were not really hair-splittable. The videos were a blunt instrument. And everyone sat back and rolled their eyes as fucking Jerry from Philosophy got all Socratic again, delaying lunch.

Lunch was submarine sandwiches that were roughly 95 percent white bread, with a gray layer of turkey or ham for the meat eaters, or American cheese for the vegetarians, or a single diaphanous leaf of wet lettuce for the vegans. The assigned activity during lunch was a getting-to-know-you game where each person had to describe their "life's work," and describe it in the way they would describe it to a normal, nonacademic "regular guy on the street," is how it was explained by the university's CFO, a man with a degree in, seriously, just "Business," who thought it was really important that academics step out of their ivory towers and connect with nonelite, normal, salt-of-the-earth-type folks.

"I'm a photographer" was all Jack said when his turn came, keeping it vague and simple.

And the rest of the table, having listened to Jack's strained explanations in previous seminars, asked no further questions—all of them except Carl from Engineering, who of course had not heard this before and was therefore genuinely curious: "What do you photograph?"

"Actually, nothing," Jack said. "I don't photograph *things*. I don't have subjects, not in the traditional sense."

Which produced the usual frown and forehead crinkle that Jack saw on anybody subjected to an explanation of his art. "I'm confused," Carl said.

"I'm a photographer, but I do not use a camera."

"Then . . . how?"

"What I do is pour chemicals onto light-sensitive photo paper to achieve interesting results."

"Okay."

"I use emulsions and developers and fixers and various reagents and sometimes also light the way a painter might use paint."

"Uh-huh."

"And instead of using a canvas, I work on reactive silver bromide paper."

"Uh-huh."

"So you could say my work is sort of at the intersection of photography and painting, and maybe alchemy, with a few printmaking techniques thrown in as well. I call it a *photochemigram*."

"I see," said Carl, who was staring at Jack and absently tapping his fingers on the table. "And what does it . . . mean?"

"I don't follow."

"What's your hidden meaning? What's your art *about*?"

"Oh, well, I guess if I had to define it, I'd say the subject of my photography is the photographic process itself. Like, its chemistry?"

"Uh-huh."

"But the images themselves don't *mean* anything. Not strictly speaking. The pictures aren't *of* anything. They're nonfigurative, nonrepresentational, nonobjective, totally abstract."

"I always thought art was supposed to have hidden meaning."

"My art is about form and balance and texture. It's pure image, I guess you could say. Decoupled from meaning."

"I see." There was a pause now as Carl the engineer processed this. "Quick question, though?"

"You want to know why."

"A little."

"Why the hell is this my life's work?"

"I might have said it nicer."

"Let's just leave it at: some of my pictures look really cool, okay?"

"What do they look like?"

"So there are these, like, big fields of shadow and color, this swath through the bottom, and also these dark, like, I suppose you could call them blobby drippy things in the middle, with all these evocative, like, little black streaky bits."

"Uh-huh."

"It's obviously hard to describe."

"Obviously."

"I guess you have to see it for yourself."

"I guess."

"Here, have a look."

And Jack pulled out his phone and retrieved the scan he'd made of his most recent work, a really successful example, Jack thought, with a central splotch that had achieved all these surprisingly interesting and cool swooping tendril things—and he was explaining how the central splotch was made, by placing unfixed reactive photo paper in a tray and filling the tray with water and then, using an eyedropper, releasing little dabs of chemical developer onto the surface of the water, which then diffused and diluted so that when it finally made contact with the paper at the bottom of the tray, it resulted in these cool forms that were all wispy and kinetic and cloudlike and ethereal—when Carl suddenly interrupted: "It looks like a bird," he said.

"Okay," Jack said. "Well, it's not a bird."

"But it really looks like a bird."

"It's not supposed to look like anything. It's abstract."

"I see a bird," Carl said. "Don't you see a bird?" And now he handed the phone to his neighbor, who nodded, and then the phone made its slow way around the table as everyone agreed that, yeah, it sort of looked like a bird.

"And what is your field?" Jack said, finally taking his phone back, desperate to change the subject.

"Engineering," Carl said.

"Right, I got that already," pointing at the name tag.

"Materials."

"Okay."

And Carl just sat there staring at him, as if this perfectly answered the question.

"Any particular one?" Jack said.

"Plastics," Carl said.

"Well," Jack said, nodding. "Thank you for your service."

They spent the rest of lunch chewing their dry sandwiches and looking at their phones.

Jack had an #OnTheSystem update about his snoring—apparently, he'd been doing it again, last night. And he listened to a brief recording the bracelet had taken of his snores, which sounded like he was rhythmically going *UH-uhhhhh-UH-uhhhhh* without even breathing, which was pretty weird.

There was also a new email from Benjamin—subject line: *We might have a problem*—with several attached photos of what appeared to be the construction barrier surrounding the Shipworks. This wall had been bare plywood a few days ago but was now covered, all the way around, with a single message, repeated many times, applied via spray paint and stencil:

SAVE HISTORIC PARK SHORE!
STOP THE SHIPWORKS!

But Jack didn't have time to give the email any further thought, as the CFO had now come back to the lectern and was announcing the inauguration of an exciting new policy regarding the evaluation of faculty. "This will let us make more informed choices about who to hire, who to fire, and who to promote."

Which certainly got everyone's full attention.

"Gone are the days when college professors could insulate themselves in the ivory tower," the CFO said, invoking one of his two favorite phrases—*ivory tower*—which he used pejoratively at least three times per speech. His other favorite phrase was *to be frank*, which he used prior to saying something rude, as he did right now: "To be frank, faculty are out of touch with what's important to real people in the real world."

Normally this would have brought much more mirth to the assembled part-timers, as there was a popular drinking game they'd developed that depended on the phrases *ivory tower* and *to be frank* being used in close proximity. But now they were far too worried about what the CFO was getting at here to engage in their usual sardonic side-eye.

"For too long, academics have published in obscure journals that are read by, to be frank, no one," the CFO continued. "For too long, universities have subsidized scholarship that's important to only a handful of elites. And, *to be perfectly frank,* that has to change."

The HR team began handing out sealed envelopes to each employee. Jack's had his name and rank written on the front and a red stamp over the seal that said "Confidential."

The CFO continued: "Modern marketing departments know how to spend their money wisely, how to achieve a return on their investment, how to leverage attention to maximize their impact. And, to be frank, it's time we bring that wisdom into the ivory tower."

He touched something at his lectern, and behind him a big television screen lit up with a stock photograph of a group of businesspeople in smart suits, laughing. The photo seemed to have very little to do with the big words that appeared above the photo—*The Impact Algorithm*—written in an ugly, chunky typeface that Jack recognized as Impact.

"The Impact algorithm is a tool that tells us the exact value of each employee's contribution to the world," the CFO said, then the

PowerPoint advanced to the next slide, a list of things people do on social media and what each of those things was worth:

Facebook Share: 4 dollars
Facebook Like: 19 cents
Instagram Follower: 2 cents
Twitter Mention: 30 cents
Common Retweet: 7 dollars
Celebrity Retweet (e.g., Kardashian): 4,650 dollars

"The Impact algorithm can quantify exactly how important your work is, based on how many times other people mention it," the CFO said. "For example, did you get a shout-out on *The Today Show*? High impact. Were you cited only by obscure academic journals? Low impact. The algorithm lets us be absolutely transparent in our hiring decisions. We simply compare your salary to your impact, which reveals whether we're getting a return on our investment. Easy. Now please open your envelopes."

Sudden aggressive tearing and ripping sounds—evoking perhaps impulsive children on Christmas morning—filled the ballroom.

"We've taken the liberty of computing everyone's Impact Score over the last year," the CFO said. "If it's higher than your current salary, good job and keep it up. If it's lower, well, to be frank, you have some work to do."

And looking at his own number confirmed all of Jack's fears: his photography had not been reviewed, nor cited, nor tweeted, nor liked, nor shared, anywhere. In fact, the algorithm could find only one mention of Jack Baker's art: on an obscure YouTube gaming channel called the Tobinator, where the child host occasionally acknowledged that the art existed. This was, according to the algorithm, worth thirteen dollars.

His full impact on the world: thirteen dollars.

Meanwhile, across the room, Jerry from Philosophy shouted, "Oh yeah!" and raised his arms in Rocky-like victory. Then he began showing everyone his own very high score.

Jack could feel himself slumping down in his chair, and he was waiting for the corresponding posture-alert buzz from the System's bracelet—which did not come. It did not come because, he realized now, looking down at his wrist, he wasn't wearing the bracelet.

Why wasn't he wearing the bracelet?

He thought back and remembered taking it off in the bedroom last night, before his spectacularly failed attempt at seducing Elizabeth. It must have been there still, on the bedside table. Which made him wonder further: How could the bracelet have recorded him snoring if it had been in the bedroom with Elizabeth and not in the office, where he'd slept again on the pull-out couch?

He opened the app and listened once more, and it did not take long for him to figure it out: that wasn't the sound of snoring. That was the sound of a vibrator.

NEW RELATIONSHIP ENERGY

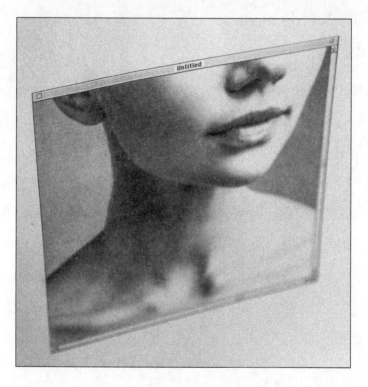

HERE THEY ARE, Jack and Elizabeth, entwined in her little bed, twisted up in the sheets. She's lying facedown, propped up on her elbows, chin resting on her hands, an enormous *Introduction to Psychology* textbook open on the mattress below her, and she's reading, occasionally taking a note, flipping a page, Jack's head resting on her lower back, his legs crossed, one foot hanging off the twin mattress, and he has a cigarette in one hand and a paperback in the other, a book of impenetrable philosophy he's reading for an art class, a beat-up copy he found used at Myopic, and the only sounds are pages turning, and the two of them breathing, and the occasional drag on a cigarette and the associated small crackle as it burns. It's late on a Sunday. They have homework to do for Monday. They've neglected it all weekend because it seems vulgar to give their attention to anything but each other.

By now they are long past their first date, and second date, and third date, and are well established in the we've-had-enough-dates-to-stop-counting-the-dates dates. They're doing that thing new couples do, attending to each other so devotedly and exclusively that they've dropped out of the wider world. They spend all their time together, and thus they've developed odd and novel habits, a shared language, a bizarre kingdom of two. One of their favorite new pastimes is to imagine that the inanimate objects of Elizabeth's small apartment are actually alive, that the clutter of their private world is full of names and eccentric personalities and elaborate backstories. The dinnerware, the couch, various socks and hats, various scarves and mittens, and coffee mugs, water pitchers, candleholders—all these things awaken, as in a Disney movie, when Jack and Elizabeth are home, together, in bed, pillow-talking, breathing magic into their tiny world. All the inside jokes, all the references that only the other person gets, the adorable private nicknames, the way their stubborn dedication to this immaculate new organism—*the couple*—can border on cultlike, this according to Elizabeth's psych professor and mentor, Dr. Otto Sanborne, whose current research specialization is, in fact, the complicated psychology of love at first sight. He says new couples employ basically the same tactics that cults do—they reinforce a collective identity via shared rituals, insider vocabulary, a sense of superiority over the whole outside world—but lack a true cult's impulse to recruit and brainwash followers.

"The only difference between a cult and a couple is ambition" is something he likes to say.

And, yeah, true—Jack and Elizabeth, these first few weeks, have been utterly exclusive and private, spending full weekends in bed together, unclothed, uncovered, hours that pass in beautifully long and unhurried drips, time that begins to feel to them as if it is, yes, holy, sacred. They lie together and read. They turn pages. Whenever one expresses the tiniest reaction—only a slight "Hm" or the hint of a laugh—the other will stop reading and look over and say, "What?" It seems disallowable that they are reading separate books and, therefore, having separate experiences. They long to be in each other's heads, to know each other totally and completely. How could homework ever compete? Eventually the attraction is too much to bear, and the books aren't picked back up. They forget about class tomorrow. They play this game where they hover over each other's bodies and study. They are explorers and cartographers, their bodies the frontier, and when they find something interesting, they touch it gently with a fingertip and say, "What's this?" The white flecks of skin on his left elbow, evidence of childhood chicken pox. The scars on the soles of his feet, from a Boy Scouts accident where he stupidly walked into a smoldering campfire. The constellation of cowlicks on his head that make his black hair swirl like a map of ocean currents. It turns out that she is double-jointed, and can make her fingers bend witchlike. She insists that one of her earlobes is slightly larger than the other, and he doesn't believe her at first, not until they get out the ruler and measure. Her body, he discovers, has three shades of blond hair: gold atop her head, straw on her arms, bronze down below. He can spell out words by drawing each letter onto the skin of her shoulder blades, and she is unusually good at deciphering them. She has a very slight divot on the bridge of her nose—imperceptible when one is looking at her head-on, visible only in profile—the result, she says, of a sports injury in high school.

"Which sport?" he asks.

"Tennis."

"Tennis, right, such a violent sport."

"I understand it's unlikely."

"How'd it happen?"

"It was at practice. I wasn't watching where I was going and, well—forehead, meet backswing."

"Ouch," he says, then he lightly kisses her divot, which is henceforth nicknamed the Wimbledon Trench.

She leans into the kiss and they make out—leisurely, then passionately, then tenderly, then back to passionately—just kissing for forty-five minutes straight, then big laughter when the heavy textbook falls from the bed with a startling thud, then another cigarette, the smoke glowing blue in the apartment's lamplight, lying on each other and talking until limbs grow numb, then a brief and unanticipated nap, then waking in the dark, famished, scrambling some eggs, eating them while still talking, always talking, late into the night, even till *dawn*—

"Is it morning?" she says when the alley outside her apartment's lone window begins to blush.

Yes, how holy this is. And how unholy it feels to finally separate. How profane it is when they have to leave that room, put on clothes, get on a bus, *with other people,* go to school. After two days of sex and touch and talk under warm woolen blankets, how blasphemous is the bus. She looks around and sees all these irritated people, all these people not aglow as she is aglow, and she thinks: *You are all doing it wrong.*

And then sitting in her psych class and realizing she hasn't heard a single thing the teacher has said for thirty minutes. She's been imagining Jack's hands on her waist, his mouth on her neck. She walks around campus in this state of light daydream—until she remembers, all at once, *shit,* she has a lunch date today. With a girl named Agatha, a drama major Elizabeth met at orientation. Agatha was studying to be an actor, and Elizabeth had vague notions of someday writing plays; it was a perfect match, is what Agatha had decided. "We're going to be best friends!" she'd declared. But now Elizabeth hasn't seen Agatha in a few weeks, and she's completely forgotten their lunch date, and so she races to the café where they'd planned to meet, arriving thirty minutes late and finding Agatha sitting alone, sandwich crumbs on the table in front of her, and she's crying.

"I'm so sorry!" Elizabeth says, hugging her, sitting down next to her. "I totally spaced out. Please forgive me."

Agatha looks at her with red, wet, puffy eyes and a balled-up chin. "*Noooooo,*" she says. "It's not *youuuuuu.*" Her words are coming out with a kind of musical fall to them, like bagpipes deflating.

"Uh-oh," Elizabeth says. Despite having known Agatha for only a few months now, she has come to understand that Agatha requires her friends to participate in, and get all entangled with, her dramas—theater folks are sometimes like that, each tragedy needing to be imparted upon an audience. Elizabeth finds it both endearing and utterly foreign; she's never been so messy with her emotions, and certainly never so overt.

Elizabeth studies Agatha's tortured, crying face and says: "Grandparent?"

Agatha shakes her head no.

"Boyfriend?"

Again, no.

"Oh," Elizabeth says. "Audition."

To which Agatha slumps down in the chair and says, "God, I am the *worst,*" then buries her head in her arms like people do when they fall asleep at the library.

"You are not the worst."

"I am," she says, her voice muffled. "I am literally the worst."

"You'll get the next part."

"That's what you said last time."

"Eventually I'll be right. You'll see."

"In high school, I was Emily in *Our Town*," she says. "I was Maria in *West Side Story*. I was Antigone in *Antigone*! What the fuck is wrong?"

Elizabeth smiles. She strokes her friend lightly on the arm. What she likes most about Agatha is that there is absolutely nothing guarded about her, nothing that feels hidden or mercenary. She comes from a small town in middle Illinois and wears plain T-shirts and big chunky Doc Martens and really sincerely considers plaid boxer shorts an acceptable outerwear choice. Instead of wearing skirts, she ties big sweaters or flannel shirts around her waist as a sort of skirt-suggestion. Her hairstyle is of the pulled-out-of-the-way genre. She wears bulky sweaters and old jeans that aren't even cutting-edge in her little hometown, a place that—not even kidding—is called Normal.

"Listen," Elizabeth says, "you are a beautiful and amazing person who will find happiness and success. I know it. For sure. It's all going to come together for you, and probably when you least expect it. You'll be minding your own business and *pow*, lightning bolt, suddenly out of nowhere someone will recognize how great you really are. They'll *see* you. You just have to be ready for it. You have to be open to it. You have to appreciate the moment you're in. Like, look at this day! Look at this sunlight! Isn't it grand?"

And Agatha lifts her head off her arms and stares at Elizabeth for a moment, perplexed.

"What is up with *you*?" she asks. Then she looks Elizabeth up and down and draws up straight and says: "Oh my god!"

"What?"

"There's something different about you!"

"There is?"

"You're, like, radiant."

"I am?"

"It's like your wall has come completely down."

"I have a wall?"

"Is this why I haven't seen you in so long? Is there someone new? There is, isn't there. Tell me. Confess."

After which Elizabeth spills the whole long tale, feeling charmed and giddy about her new boyfriend, sure, but also a little embarrassed that she's become this person: lovesick, love-drunk. She wonders if Jack is thinking about her this much, then feels actually wounded when she considers that he might not be. How this causes so much suffering. And that's when the worries begin, when Elizabeth's thoughts darken. In one moment, she's picturing her beautiful sensitive artist boyfriend and reliving their long delightful days together, and in the next, this poison question impolitely intrudes: *What if he goes away?*

What if it all goes away?

It seems impossible, unacceptable, terrifying even, that this love—which has become so important to her, which feels, at this point, sort of biologically essential, something that she would *literally die without*—is also so uncertain. It could go away. She has no control over that. He could just leave. And she begins replaying their time together over the past weekend and scouring it for mistakes: had she really scrambled eggs naked? *While he watched?* She imagines her body horribly jiggling, and she's mortified.

Then the dread on the bus ride home. Steeling herself for disappointment. Telling herself it'll be okay if he suddenly breaks up with her, no big deal if he disappears. They've been dating only a few weeks. She'd get over him. Feeling herself sort of detaching and withdrawing from her own body, as if she's merely watching herself as she walks to her building and climbs the four flights of stairs and enters her apartment and callously goes to the window, expecting the worst. But then she looks across the alley and there he is, waiting for her, Jack, standing there at his own window, and he's written something in paint right on the glass. It says, I CAN'T STOP THINKING ABOUT YOU, which makes her feel as if her spirit has suddenly returned, snapping her back into human place.

Across the dark alley, they wave at each other at exactly the same time. Laugh at exactly the same time. Put their hands over their mouths in exactly the same bashful way. She beckons him over with a small nod. He dashes out of his apartment, dashes into hers.

"It's like you're in my head," he says. "It's like I'm suddenly sharing my mind."

"That's exactly what I was going to say!"

"See what I mean?"

"I've been doing some research," she says.

"About what?"

"Love."

He laughs. "You've been researching it?" And she gives him a look like *Duh* and he shuts up, smiles. "Of course you've been researching it," he says. "Attacking it from all angles."

"It's part of my internship. We're studying it, love. I've been doing a lot of reading lately—cultural ethnography, psychological anthropology—"

"Doing your Elizabeth thing."

"Yes."

"And?"

"And what's interesting to me is that so many different cultures had such similar ideas about it. People all over the planet, completely independent of each other, separated by continents and oceans and time, having never spoken to each other even once, all decided basically the same thing about love. Which is kind of beautiful, I think."

"What did they decide?"

"That love is both part of the body and separate from the body. It's intrinsic to us but also divisible from us."

"I don't understand."

"They thought love was stored somewhere inside us," she says, "in some real place. Like a liquid in a bowl. Which, if you think about it, is a pretty brilliant metaphor. It's a way to explain why love feels almost physical, biological."

At this he squeezes her, as if to emphasize the point. She squeezes back and continues: "But it also explains why love sometimes feels fleeting, why it seems to occasionally go away. Because it's a *thing*. And things can run out."

"Where is it located? What's the bowl?"

"Most people thought the heart. Also the hair, or the kidneys, or the blood, or inside a tiny animal that lives within you."

And at this he sits up, stares at her searchingly, now very interested. "Tell me about that one."

"The animal?"

"Yeah. Tell me about that."

"Okay, well, before we knew anything about the brain or the nervous system, people believed that the reason they were alive was because there was something else alive within them. This was how they explained consciousness, that there was something inside them that moved them and controlled them. The animal within the animal."

"Like a soul?"

"There were different names for it, but yeah, basically. It was the essence or distillation of a person, the person's truest self, usually in the form of a bird or bat or snake or butterfly or some other important local creature."

And Jack nods and looks into his own lap and it seems, behind his long black bangs, that a sadness overtakes him, visible in the pale skin now furrowed around his dark eyes.

"What's wrong?" she says.

"Nothing," he says. "It's just, I heard this story once. When I was a kid. I thought it was made up."

"What is it?"

"That when you're asleep, your soul leaves your body and goes out and explores the world."

"Okay."

"So when you're dreaming, what you're actually seeing is your soul out wandering. Sometimes your soul is a bird, flying around, or sometimes it's a mouse. It takes the form of an animal and explores."

"Yeah, that's it exactly. That's what people believed."

"And the story I heard was that sometimes—rarely, but sometimes—your soul encounters other souls out on their own journeys. And so when you meet someone in real life who feels really familiar to you, who feels just, *bam*, instantly recognizable, it's because your souls have already met, at night."

"How wonderful."

"I thought so too."

"Did you believe it?"

"I didn't believe it . . . before," he says, letting the implication of that just sort of thrillingly hang there.

"Before what?" she says.

He smiles. "Before *you*."

And oh how she longs to love like that: grandly, instinctively, without self-consciousness or hesitation or that constant unwelcome burrowing doubt. It all seems so easy for him, loving without worry of repercussion. He simply speaks his heart authentically, unfiltered by fear, which seems to Elizabeth like a kind of impossible sorcery.

He does it again a few nights later, at his art opening. It's his first solo show, at a gallery on the ground floor of the Flat Iron Building, one of several new neighborhood spaces whose events are drawing more and more outsiders each passing month, strangers who emerge from expensive cars driven in from rich suburbs asking whether it's safe to park here. Nervous people who are transparently worried about the safety of their person and possessions but also drawn to Wicker Park's growing reputation, its undeniable scene. There's a rumor that a critic from the *Tribune* will be coming to Jack's opening—Benjamin Quince had written a press release about how "the young photographer capturing Wicker Park's cultural explosion" now had his first show—and the whole neighborhood is agog.

The show is called *Girl in Window: By Jack Baker*. What Jack has done is to photograph, tightly and diagonally and oddly askew, computer screens, on which there are open windows, all showing images of women in differing states of undress. The photographs were taken at such nearness, and at such angles, and with such a shallow depth of field, that the bodies look weirdly distended and fuzzy and textured and abstract. Jack then printed these images on large canvases, so that a face or a body that on a computer monitor might have been the size of a postage stamp is now titanic. It sometimes makes it difficult to understand what you're looking at, this transposition of scale. People stare at Jack's photos, confused, until, all at once, the image resolves, and they realize with some shock that they are looking at a nude in super-super-super close-up.

Everyone is there that night: all the eccentric painters and poets and actors and filmmakers and other sundry oddballs Elizabeth has seen in the halls of the co-op; and many of the musicians she's seen in bars, the rock bands that Jack so triumphantly photographed; and a larger-than-usual contingent of thirty- and fortysomethings venturing into Wicker Park from their large apartments on the lake, or down from big homes in Evanston, or into the city from suburban points west. It is this audience in particular that seems to delight Benjamin, who is downright giddy at having drawn suburbanites to his squalid neighborhood to look at smut. "We're shocking the squares," he whispers to any local who will listen.

Elizabeth stands next to Jack as he explains his philosophy to interested viewers. "The job of the artist now, in the nineties, at the end of history, is not to create but to *re-create*," Jack is saying to an older couple, collectors, maybe. "To remix, reconstruct, recontextualize. In a world where the subjects for art are all exhausted, where everything has been photographed to the point of cliché, the task of art is to make things strange"—the couple is nodding, smiling, absolutely eating this up—"thus my use of online nudes," Jack continues, encouraged. "It isn't the nude itself that interests me, but rather its ubiquity, that the new internet is filled with these bodies. And I wanted to perform a kind of transubstantiation upon them, turning the 2D surface of a computer screen into an object in 3D space, turning ephemeral digital code back into something palpably real."

"Can we buy one?" they ask, and Elizabeth smiles, kisses Jack on the cheek, and moves along. She walks among the crowd, eavesdrops, makes her way to the catering area, which is really just a keg with help-yourself plastic cups stacked upon it. She doesn't know anybody here, or at least doesn't know them well enough to walk up and mingle. So she is at the keg, alone, drawing an overly sudsy beer when Benjamin announces that tonight's artist wants to make a toast, and then there's Jack hopping onto a table and looking around the room and hollering, "Where's Elizabeth?" And then he spots her, and the crowd between them seems to part, and he smiles and raises his glass in her direction and says to everyone, "I'd like to dedicate this night to Elizabeth, the most brilliant person I've ever known, my inspiration, my muse, my Edie Sedgwick, my Juliet," which produces a collective *Awwwww* even among the otherwise pretty cynical members of this crowd.

After that, the feeling is like being scooped up and sanctified by the whole neighborhood.

It's the moment Jack and Elizabeth's relationship turns from private to public, after which everyone wants to talk to her, everyone wants to include her. They knock on her apartment door at all hours and beg her to join them in some new escapade, mostly involving some great band at one of the many neighborhood bars, some band whose musicians stand onstage in secondhand sweaters and stare straight down at the floor, their long hair obscuring every distinguishing feature—faceless, flaccid, blasé, bent over howling guitars—Elizabeth down below, listening, beer in one hand, cigarette in the other, nodding in time, just outside the edge of an incidental mosh pit.

These are the shows they'll speak of so reverently in the years to come, these nights they see some particular band while that band is still a neighborhood secret, playing in a dive bar for a crowd of ten, before all the record deals arrive, before the band migrates to MTV. They see Veruca Salt at the Double Door. The Jesus Lizard at Czar Bar. Urge Overkill at Lounge Ax. Wesley Willis just out on the sidewalk with his keyboard playing for anybody who will listen. Smashing Pumpkins at Metro. Liz Phair at the Empty Bottle. And all of them *before they were famous*. It will be a kind of glue between them, the fellowship of shared experience, the camaraderie of so many late nights, so many parties, after-parties, hanging with the band, crashing drunkenly at one another's apartments. Then hungover coffee and hash at Leo's Lunchroom, and long afternoons searching for vintage finds at Ragstock, the patchouli-scented clothing store with racks so stuffed it's often difficult to pry out even a single hanger. Or browsing the narrow crooked shelves at Myopic, the wood floors creaking with every footfall. Or hanging around Quimby's reading the local zines or the X-rated comics or the newest edition of *Adbusters* magazine. Or occasionally, when they need a change of neighborhood scenery, they all hop on the train—one of them distracts the attendant while the rest jump the turnstiles, just leap clear over the bars like elk ("We're like elk!" Elizabeth exclaims), a game that never seems to get old—and they basically colonize a full car on the El (usually the last one, the most empty one) and head out to innumerable cheap adventures about town: to the lake, or free concerts in Grant Park, or the jazz clubs in Uptown, or the gay bars in Boystown, or the dive bars in Logan Square (where those who are underage manage to procure alcohol in a nightly dare with bartenders and bouncers and local law enforcement), or they head to the tiny indie movie theaters that dot Chicago, little rooms with screens no bigger than a bedsheet where Elizabeth sees *A Clockwork Orange* and *The Cabinet of Dr. Caligari* and Fellini retrospectives and a midnight showing of *Beach Babes from Beyond* that they all absolutely howl through.

Sometimes they pile into one of their few working cars and venture out to one of the North Side malls to spend an afternoon among the yuppies. There is this game they play with employees of the Gap where the whole point is to walk through the store, touch the store's back wall, and then get out of the store without any of the store's employees asking, "Can I help you?" This is harder than it seems, because the Gap almost definitely has some corporate mandate instructing employees to promptly engage with every customer who walks in the door. The "Gapopticon," they call it: a brightly lit retail prison where you're constantly surveilled. Benjamin, in particular, can get all revved up about this subject: how the modern incarnation of the panoptic surveillance state is, in fact, a shopping mall, how a shopping mall's many employees and security guards and closed-circuit cameras teach you not only how to be watched but also how to watch yourself, how all those fitting-room mirrors are meant to make you think constantly about how you look to other people, to see yourself at a one-step remove, to submit to the tyranny of the gaze, and to understand that the gaze always finds you lacking.

"Being seen makes you less yourself," he often says, which makes the Gap challenge not only a fun game but also a kind of symbolic performance art, to enter and exit the Gap without being seen. To do it successfully, you have to innocently stand outside the store, waiting for the moment the employees are all looking elsewhere, then dart in and hide behind the racks of denim skirts until the coast is clear, then scoot on toward the halter tops and duck behind the flip-flops, then follow that lane all the way to the back wall, then leap out and touch the wall while the fitting-room attendant is otherwise occupied, then hurry out without running—because running always draws unwanted "Can I help you?" attention—while the rest of the group watches from just outside the Gap's doors and narrates the action like a bunch of ironic Bob Costases: "Oh, close one there, Bob." "Indeed, Bob, but a brilliant pivot near the rompers narrowly averted disaster!"

It is all *so funny*.

It becomes one of their favorite pastimes, pranking mass-market retail. They call it "culture jamming." It's sort of a thing. It's a way to resist the homogenizing, Earth-destroying corporate capitalist machine, but with a sense of humor. They do things like dare each other to spend two hours sincerely pretending to shop for a Dodge Caravan without the salesman realizing it's a gag, or, after that grows tiresome, they pose as employees of global retail chains and explicitly voice the crass consumer messages that are often implicit in the chain's popular advertising. Distinguished examples of this genre include the time one of them pretends to give out perfume samples at Saks, saying, "This scent will keep the darkness away." And the time in the Marshall Field's men's department when one of them stalks the Tommy Hilfiger sweater section saying, "It's one hundred percent wool, for one hundred percent sheep." And the time one of them pretends to sell push-up bras at Victoria's Secret and tells customers, "The higher your boobs, the greater your worth!" And the time they all go in full activewear to the Nike store and tell shoppers, "Don't worry about slave labor. Just do it!" They place stickers on mall cash registers and on ATMs and on fitting-room mirrors that espouse assorted anticorporate messaging:

Don't believe what they tell you
Shut the system down
Stick it to the man
Don't be a sheep
QUESTION EVERYTHING

Then they return to the Foundry at night and gather in its first-floor gallery and drink cheap beer and smoke clove cigarettes and give each other back rubs. All of them, in twos and threes and fours, working one another's deltoids to mush. They are all new here, all of them plunked down into this neighborhood from faraway places, and they band together like this, through communal touch. And yes, it's true, they do sort of resemble a troop of chimpanzees cleaning one another of ticks and fleas, and yes, several residents in fact make this precise joke and call them names that are Jane Goodall–related, but they don't care. They are intertwined; they eat together, drink together, sometimes sleep together. In a biology class, Elizabeth learned a new word: *inosculation*. It describes a phenomenon in which blood vessels from a transplanted organ or skin graft bind with and get entangled in a body's existing blood vessels, creating an entirely new vascular system. And this, she thinks, describes them perfectly, her inosculated friends, all intertwined, all binding together. When they go see the Breeders at Lollapalooza, they all look poignantly at one another during "Cannonball" and mouth that one perfect lyric—*I'll be your whatever you want*—like it was written for them, about them.

Why back rubs? *Why not?* They are all *in the arts*, for god's sake. They are making an insanely poor decision in this trickle-down economy. And what you do when you are making big mistakes is find other people to make them with you. If you are going to be destitute for the rest of your life, well, it might as well be pleasurable, you might as well have a good time along the way, you might as well say yes to what feels good. And back rubs feel good. And pot brownies, also, they feel good. And belting out Ani DiFranco and Tori Amos songs while standing and sometimes jumping or even dancing on the couch, that feels really good. And drinking absinthe and reading poetry aloud: feels good. And doing shots of pulverized hallucinogenic mushrooms mixed with lemon juice: tastes bad but feels good. And doing whippits: feels mostly good except for that moment right after you inhale when it feels like your head very quickly shrinks and then just as quickly explodes. There's a term used to describe the microsecond after the big bang when the known universe grew from a microscopically small speck to an infinitely large expanse—the term is *cosmic inflation*, and that's the expression they use to describe what their heads do on whippits, and what their hearts do when they're together.

Elizabeth is not accustomed to making such open and sincere declarations of friendship and intimacy. But she has come to realize that for the first time in her life, there will be nothing tearing her away from these people. There is no imperious father to one day announce that the family is again moving to a new city. And so she can discard her usual guarded and aloof manner, her usual disaster-preparedness. These people will not go away. She will not go away. She can, finally, allow herself to love.

And so it is that one Sunday a few weeks after Jack's show, they are all taking the outbound Red Line, colonizing the train's last car, a big group of about a dozen of them, on one of the first pleasant days of spring, and they are heading out for an afternoon scouring the thrift stores in Andersonville. Elizabeth sits leaning against Agatha, who is working out some tension in Elizabeth's neck with an iron grip that is, at the moment, positively Vulcan. The train has dipped into a tunnel at this point in the line, and so the bright sunlight has given way to a view of rushing gray walls. Then Benjamin stands up and clears his throat and they all look at him and he says: "Since none of you philistines read the newspaper, I guess I'll be the one to break it to you."

"Break what?" Elizabeth says.

And then Benjamin pulls out that day's *Tribune,* the Arts section, the cover of which features a big photograph of Jack and Elizabeth holding hands near one of the more PG-rated *Girl in Window* images. It had been taken the night of his show, and the attendant story—which Benjamin promptly reads aloud—is all about the trendy and exploding arts scene in Wicker Park. The reviewer names the Foundry in particular as a locus of this transformational energy, the center of life in this otherwise blighted neighborhood, and then toward the end of the story the writer describes Jack's show specifically and says the gallery has sold every single one of Jack's photographs, the reviewer declaring that "Jack Baker is the most exciting new artist in Chicago."

And as Benjamin finishes reading, they all look at one another, silent and amazed. And then the train squeals to a stop, the Grand Avenue stop, which couldn't be more perfect, because when the train stops and the doors slide open, the conductor announces over the speakers, "This is Grand," and Elizabeth hears the pun for the first time, never before having registered it until this very moment. And she looks around the car at her beautiful friends, all laughing (and Jack, in true sensitive-guy form, sitting there blushing), and she feels like they are all the candlewick of history, the bright, glowing, ember-hot beacons of change and progress, these few commuters, being spirited under the city on mass transit. She is more certain than ever that she's in love with Jack, and in love with these friends, and with this city, and with this bright Sunday in spring.

It is precisely as the train conductor said.

It is, indeed, grand.

AND THEN one day, they began losing friends. What had been, in their early twenties, a thrilling accumulation of new people and new experiences and more or less constant amusement became, in their late twenties, a contraction, as friends took jobs out of town or left the city to join significant others elsewhere. At first, these individual changes seemed discrete—just singular losses, not a pattern, not a trend—and so the basic contours of everyone's lives remained mostly the same. But then, seemingly all at once, the babies arrived. Jack and Elizabeth's friends began reproducing, and did so with such amazing synchrony it was as if they had all agreed, in secret, behind Elizabeth's back, to get pregnant during a small window between the ages of twenty-eight and thirty-two. It felt, to Elizabeth, like she'd been double-crossed. She was astonished that these co-op people, these artists and rebels who in the nineties raged hard against the mainstream, would, only ten years later, so obediently join it. Most of them left Wicker Park, decamping for cheaper rents elsewhere, for places where they could "spread out," was how they put it. The first time Elizabeth attended a Dora the Explorer–themed birthday party in a suburban backyard she felt utterly betrayed. Her closest friends—friends from college, friends she had lived with, partied with, gotten drunk with, traveled with, did recreational drugs with—were disappearing from her life, one by one. It was dismaying how swiftly this sometimes happened, how efficiently her friends could detach. Take Agatha, for example, probably Elizabeth's closest friend—Elizabeth and Jack regularly went to Agatha's place for dinners and movie nights, regularly took road trips with Agatha and her husband to Saugatuck or Door County. Then Agatha got pregnant and talk turned to how much the baby would adore Auntie Elizabeth, Agatha swearing that the child would not interfere with their friendship one bit, a promise that she could not keep for even thirty minutes after giving birth, Elizabeth getting a text late at night saying *It's a boy!* and Elizabeth writing *What???* and Agatha replying *Preemie! Surprise!!!* and Elizabeth writing *OMG, congrats! I'm on my way!!!* and Agatha saying *Actually, the baby's a little fragile right now and so to prevent infection we're only allowing family.*

And that's how quickly Elizabeth had become unnecessary. That's how quickly Agatha's new tribe—this *family*—had taken precedence. Elizabeth read this message and ached. *I thought we were family too* is what she wanted to say.

This happened each time another of their close friends had children: the prenatal promises all postpartumly broken, each set of new parents receding from view while Elizabeth struggled to hold on to fraying friendships. She would plan brunches with old friends only to have them say: *Sorry, that's during nap time.* She'd plan lunches and they'd say: *That's usually when the kids melt down.* She'd plan dinners and they'd say: *Right in the middle of bedtime.* She'd plan drinks after bedtime, even going so far as to offer to bring her own alcohol and her own cocktail shaker and her own coupe glasses to her friends' houses so they had literally no responsibilities whatsoever, could simply sit back and drink and visit, but they'd still decline: *Sorry, we're totally wiped out.*

And even those rare nights when she and Jack successfully weaseled their way into their friends' homes for a little face-to-face social interaction, these nights tended to end without any quality conversation whatsoever as the presence of new people in the house seemed to serve as a kind of trigger for children to get aggressively and sometimes violently attention-seeking, and the parents, perhaps on their best behavior and not wanting to discipline their children harshly in the presence of friends, would just let it all kind of happen, and the kids, testing their delicious newfound freedom, would start acting up and shouting and roughhousing, whereby the parents would become even more frustrated, and the whole spiraling thing made Elizabeth feel guilty for being there at all. It made her feel like a bother. It made her feel like her invitations and visits were *annoying* her friends. Eventually she stopped asking. Eventually it was just Elizabeth and Jack, looking at the expanse of the next several decades, together, the two of them, alone, connecting with friends only distractedly during occasional chaotic birthday parties.

And yet her friends did not seem exactly distressed about this new life. On the contrary, Elizabeth could not help but notice that her friends seemed to prefer it, seemed to really enjoy the larger houses and suburban backyards they'd upgraded to. They were altogether pretty satisfied with the situation. They had a child, and sometimes they had another. They were a unit, a fellowship, a family. They kept asking Elizabeth when she would have a family too. It made her feel like she was maybe missing out on something, that maybe the ideals of her early twenties were blinding her to this fundamentally important life experience. She thought about her behavior back when she was young, her occasionally dreadful behavior, how she and her friends would all go out to suburban malls and spend the whole day mocking. It felt so satisfying back then, so hilarious, even kind of important—"culture jamming" was their name for it, giving it the sparkle of high-minded virtuous resistance: the capitalist machine was plainly immoral, they thought, and therefore the people who were complicit within that machine were also plainly immoral, and therefore she did not have to feel bad for making fun of, or feeling superior to, these people. That is seductive logic when you're in your twenties, but now Elizabeth looked back on it and felt embarrassed. Their whole project seemed snotty to her. Arrogant. Sanctimonious. Even sort of grossly entitled: that was a pre-globalized world, a pre-9/11 world, a pre–housing bubble world, a world before the Great Recession, when they all sort of understood implicitly that however much they resented and resisted the mass economy, they would also have little trouble eventually finding a job and a livelihood within it. It made Elizabeth think that maybe those friends who'd migrated to the suburbs were in fact the most enlightened ones. They'd been the first to see through the delusion.

She and Jack had moved to Chicago to become orphans, to cut themselves loose from incompatible birth families and create a new family among the like-minded people of the co-op. And they had succeeded, for a time. But what they hadn't considered was that people don't stay like-minded forever. And when their minds changed, so did the family.

Elizabeth should have seen it coming. She understood how many people a single person could, over a lifetime, be. She'd been so many different Elizabeths in the many schools she'd attended growing up. In one place, she was a math geek. In another, she took up the cello and became a music nerd. In the next place, she joined the ecology club and committed to becoming a forest ranger. Then it was theater, and she began writing plays and monologues. At the next school, she joined the debate team and planned to be a lawyer. And the weird thing was: *All of these selves felt true at the time.* At each school, she took this test, this inventory of interests and passions that told you what career you might want to pursue, and every year, the test spit out a different answer. One year, it really said she should be a mathematician. The next, a music teacher. The next, a forest ranger, a playwright, a lawyer. Even her answer to the simplest question—"Where are you from?"—shifted from place to place, Elizabeth adopting whatever town she'd most recently come from as her new hometown. She was aware that one's self could change and evolve like that, and so it was not unimaginable that she was now evolving again, becoming someone new: a parent, maybe, a mother.

She started bringing it up with Jack, began wondering out loud whether they should consider having a child. And when he hesitated, she asked whether their reluctance to have a family was possibly a symptom of their own difficult childhoods, suggesting that maybe they were afraid of duplicating exactly the conditions that drove each of them away from their own families, that allowing these fears to prevail was sort of like letting their own awful families somehow win, and that being aware of these outcomes might in fact be an inoculation against them.

Eventually he agreed, and when Toby was born, Elizabeth came to finally understand exactly where all her friends had gone. She was astounded by how her priorities shifted, all at once, immediately, how any task other than keeping Toby safe, keeping Toby healthy, seemed like a diversion, or an interruption. She understood with some remorse that if one of her childless friends insisted on coming over during bedtime for martinis and conversation, it wouldn't feel exactly unwelcome, but it would feel a little irrelevant. Like Sisyphus pushing the boulder up the mountain but then stopping for tea. She realized that her old friends had not abandoned her, or at least had not done so in any volitional way; it was just that their attention had been seized, their love redirected, the purpose of each day reoriented, unavoidably and involuntarily. She finally comprehended parenthood's strange paradox: that it was deeply annihilating while at the same time also somehow deeply comforting. It was both soul-devouring and soul-filling.

She quietly forgave her old friends. And she quietly chastised herself for being impatient with them, and for being a person they could so promptly drop, a person who had probably made it irritatingly obvious at all those birthday parties that she was only partially there, with one foot out the door. She'd always lived like this: late for lunches, taking too long to write back, not calling for long spells, double-booking herself accidentally. It was like she was unconsciously advertising *I don't really need you that much.*

She made her peace with the losses as best she could, vowed to be a better person henceforth, and searched for new friends the way most parents do: among the mothers and fathers at her kid's school.

Which was why she was here, standing near the blacktop driveway of Park Shore Country Day with Brandie one late-summer morning, watching parents drop off kids, listening to Brandie describe, like a butler in a Jane Austen novel, each new arriving family.

"Mr. Keith Masterson and Mrs. Julie Masterson, of Forest Hills," Brandie said, nodding in the direction of a silver Toyota Sequoia now entering the circular drive. "They are both dentists. If you ever make a dessert for their son, Brax, be absolutely sure that it's sugar-free."

"Got it," Elizabeth said. "Thanks."

"Mr. Bryan Green and Mrs. Penelope Green, of Evanston," Brandie said, pointing at a new incoming car. "She is a lifelong vegan. Word of advice? Never ask how she gets enough iron in that diet. It seems to trigger her and she becomes unnecessarily intense and sort of activist."

"Okay, good to know."

Park Shore Country Day School was not actually located in the country. Nor was it, strictly speaking, a day school. It was a K–12 private school located in a converted former Carnegie library, right there in Park Shore's quaint downtown, a few blocks from where the Shipworks was currently under construction. Its guiding philosophy was that it took the old "country day school" model as an inspiration, a pedagogical starting point. What this meant in practice was that children of different ages all learned together in the same rooms and that teachers taught a multidisciplinary curriculum rather than specializing in any one field. The idea—as explained in the school's colorful marketing pamphlets—was that this format returned education to what it looked like before schools were taken over by the ethos of the assembly line, before education turned into a kind of Fordist factory that treated students as machines and teachers as assembly workers each overseeing a narrow component of that machine: science, math, reading, writing, etc. At Park Shore, everything was sort of smashed together, which better reflected how kids really learned, evolutionarily, naturally, allegedly.

Elizabeth and Jack had enrolled Toby at Park Shore Country Day because of its reputation as a place suited to Toby's particular challenging disposition: with its fluid approach to teaching, its lack of rigid rules, its focus on student movement and sensory activities, it was an environment in which Toby seemed able to relax, to remain steady and calm. He had fewer outbursts in this school, fewer tantrums, fewer violent episodes. Toby was not a boy who could sit at a desk all day and listen, and Park Shore seemed ideologically opposed to all-day sitting, or, for that matter, desks. So it was a good fit.

"Mr. Anthony Forrester and Mrs. Martha Forrester, of Northbrook," Brandie said. "She's in HR for United Airlines. He's been 'in between jobs' for like three years. We've mostly stopped asking him about it."

"Gotcha."

"Mr. Theodore Norman and Mrs. Carrie Norman-Ward, of Win-netka. Though she's soon to be just Carrie Ward again, without the hyphen. They're getting a divorce."

"Oh no."

"That's not gossip, by the way. They are very forthcoming about it. They even posted about it on Facebook, this really long essay they cowrote together explaining how they grew distant from each other and now they're separating with deep respect and thanks and friendliness."

"How evolved."

"They had been going to a couples counselor until they realized they couldn't save the marriage, at which point they switched to an uncoupling counselor, who, conveniently, worked in the same office. They're really trying to make the divorce as seamless and ethical as possible, for the kids."

Elizabeth nodded. "The part about them growing distant from each other—what happened?"

"What do you mean?"

"How did they get so distant? What was the cause?"

"Nothing really happened, or nothing in particular, as far as I know. They just stopped feeling as strongly as they once did. It's that thing, I suppose, that happens to so many couples. The passion faded, the spark died. There really ought to be a name for that."

"There is a name for that."

"There is?"

"Hypoactive marital attachment disorder."

"No kidding?"

"It's a condition," Elizabeth said. "I'm actually studying it at work. It's the fancy diagnostic term for the phenomenon you're describing: the cooling of romantic love over time."

"I had no idea."

"We're testing a cure."

"A cure? So you've invented, what, a love potion?"

"Technically it's a dopamine neurotransmitter targeting a very specific genetic polymorphism, but, yeah, around the office we call it Love Potion Number Nine."

"How interesting!"

"It's a cocktail of several important peptides that hopefully can help people connect with how they used to feel about their spouse."

"Love in a bottle. How about that," Brandie said, then quickly added: "Mike and I renew our vows at least once a year."

"Yeah, I've seen the pictures on Instagram. That's beautiful."

"It's our way of saying *I would marry you all over again*. It's how we keep the romance alive."

"Good for you."

Then Brandie spotted a new family, arriving in a bright red electric car that now crept past them making no sound whatsoever, and she leaned in toward Elizabeth and said: "Well, speak of the devil. Here come the lovebirds. I suppose you know about the lovebirds?"

She was talking about Kate and Kyle, recently transplanted to Illinois from Silicon Valley, a couple who'd become, in their short time here, a bit of a curiosity among the parents of Park Shore. Kyle was in his midforties, father to nine-year-old Camilla; Kate was in her midtwenties, the stepmom, everyone assumed. Whenever Kate and Kyle parted—like right now, as he dropped Kate and Camilla off at school—they would, in plain view of their daughter and her teachers and whatever other parents and pedestrians were around to see it, make out. They would full-on snog. Heavily, and with tongue, like teenagers on prom night.

"Wow," Brandie whispered, watching them going at it. Kate had her arms wrapped around Kyle, a stocky man with a body that looked perfectly engineered for rugby, and was kissing him longingly, deeply, and unselfconsciously. And when they were done kissing, Kyle gave Kate a spank, a quick flirty pat on the fanny, rather loud, right there in front of all the children.

"*Wow,*" Brandie said again.

Kate had been a surprising addition to the school's community, first because of her age. She was only twenty-five, which may have felt odd to the thirty- and fortysomethings, that someone so fresh-faced was also parenting, mothering, adulting. And Kate had probably intuited the group's disquiet, because she often made offhand comments meant to draw attention to this very divide, one of her favorite maneuvers being to begin a sentence with: "Well, for people of *my* generation . . ."

One time, Kate had actually told Elizabeth: "You're like the cool mom I never had," which caused Elizabeth a surprising amount of displeasure, privately, for several days.

Kate worked at the new Google hub that had recently opened in the West Loop, though it was unclear what she did there. "It involves a lot of math and a lot of programming," she had said. "I beg you not to ask me about it. It's so boring." She was friendly, and kind, and very outgoing, and seemed to have an excellent relationship with her stepdaughter, but some of the parents had come to find her a little strange, a little daunting, mostly because Kate and her husband had an open marriage, and Kate was perfectly open about this. Actually, openness was probably her defining quality: she was absolutely forthright and honest about subjects most of them would talk about only while in therapy or drunk. For example, they had all come to know that Kate hooked up with—and sometimes dated, and occasionally even went on out-of-town vacations with—men who were not her husband. She spoke of this regularly, and with no shame whatsoever, like it was the most normal thing in the world. And maybe it *was* normal—for a Californian, or a millennial. Honestly they didn't know. But it was a bit of a scandal among some of the older parents, most of whom were of Midwestern stock and so their comfort discussing matters private and sexual tended to fall somewhere between timidity and horror.

"Ladies," Kate said as she approached, "I apologize for looking so shook this morning, but I had a sleepover last night that went real late. You are *literally* witnessing my walk of shame."

It was true that Kate's long ashen hair—it looked like it was naturally brunette but she dyed it gray, for some reason—was still wet from the shower, but otherwise she looked as she always did, which was improbably stylish and cool and radiant and glowing and young. Kate had this ability to take certain scorned fashions and upcycle them into respectability. Like the gray hair, for example, which looked amazing and striking on her. And she wore these enormous glasses that should have been much too large for her face, square glasses with thick frames that would have been considered irredeemably nerdy when Elizabeth was a kid but nevertheless looked really hip on Kate. The glasses kept sliding down her nose, and so Kate's most frequent tic was pushing them back up every two to five seconds, and even this seemed endearing. She also wore pants that Elizabeth wouldn't have been caught dead in, these high-waisted things from the eighties that Elizabeth would have described as "mom jeans" and that looked absolutely terrible on everyone except, somehow, young women like Kate.

"You had a, sorry, a sleepover?" Brandie said.

Kate looked at them gravely over the rim of her big glasses. "And I am low-key *suffering*, seriously."

"What do you mean, 'sleepover'?"

"Oh, okay, well, most people my age use the term 'hookup,' but in the case of your generation, maybe 'one-night stand' would be the right nomenclature?"

"I see."

"Yeah, Kyle took one look at me this morning and literally loled."

"Your husband," Brandie said, "he doesn't mind that you have . . . sleepovers?"

"Oh, no, of course not. He has sleepovers too. And, you know, *thank god*. Because I don't know how I could possibly be a good parent without his girlfriends around to help out. Which is why I really respect moms like you two, doing it all on your own. That is amazing."

"I would not be okay with my husband having girlfriends," Brandie said.

"But they're wonderful!" Brandie said. "It's like we're all in this big extended family together. Plus I have about a dozen built-in babysitters."

"A *dozen*?"

Kate shrugged. "It takes a village! Anyway, I prefer the term 'sleepover' to 'hookup' because 'sleepover' makes it easier to explain to Camilla, why there's someone spending the night."

"Okay, but, is that ever confusing for her? Having a stranger in the house?"

"Oh, she loves it! It's like, in the morning she suddenly has a brand-new friend!"

"Uh-huh."

"Or, as in today, two friends!"

"Well," Brandie said, tightly gripping the handles of her straw tote bag, "it's like I always say: you need to give love to get love."

"Okay then!" Kate said, and then she bid them farewell and went off in search of coffee, Elizabeth and Brandie watching her go.

"Bless her heart," Brandie said. "I mean, I wouldn't let her anywhere near my family. But bless her heart."

And then the bell rang and the school day was starting and Brandie hugged Elizabeth goodbye and Elizabeth decided to stay a moment in Park Shore rather than fight traffic back into the city, and so she strolled the sidewalks of downtown, eventually passing the local coffee shop, and through the front window she saw Kate, sitting at a table, an immense latte in front of her, and after a moment's deliberation, Elizabeth went inside.

"Excuse me?"

Kate looked up. "Oh, hi!"

"Hi, yeah, so, we don't know each other very well, but can I ask you something?"

"Of course."

"It's personal. It's about you and your husband."

"Okay."

"It's about what you . . . do."

"Like, for a living?"

"No. I mean, what you do, romantically."

"Oh, you mean our sleeping around."

"Yes."

"Sure. Ask me anything."

"I guess what I want to know is, the way you described it, I mean, does it really feel like that?"

"Like what?"

"Like an extended family."

Kate grinned. "Actually, yeah. I mean, obviously there are powerful emotions that need to be clearly communicated and managed. But for the most part, yes, it's a big family."

Elizabeth nodded.

"Why do you ask?" Kate said.

"It sounds kind of nice."

"It *is* nice."

"I haven't felt like part of something like that in years. I really miss it."

"Well sit down!" Kate said. "I *love* converting people."

They spent the rest of the morning at that coffee shop, Elizabeth listening to Kate's fierce critique of modern marriage.

"It's stupid," Kate said. "Marriage is just stupid. Or at least the way we currently practice marriage, how we currently conceptualize it, in the West. It's so idiotic. We're stuck in this useless heuristic. I think it's time to sunset the whole idea."

"You want to get rid of marriage?"

"I want to update it. I want to beta test new models. I want to break it and start all over. The way I think of it is: marriage is just a technology that was never quite future-proof. Like, it may have been a good tool in Victorian England or whatever. But for us? Now? Not so much. We have these twenty-first-century relationships running eighteenth-century software. So it's glitchy and it crashes all the time. Typically with any technology we try to innovate and update and improve it, but with marriage we seem to refuse all progress. We've convinced ourselves that, actually, we *like* all those glitches. We *prefer* all the crashes. *If it weren't so hard to use, it wouldn't be worth it.* We've been persuaded that the bugs are features. It's so dumb."

"But what are the bugs? Specifically?"

"Well, the biggest one, obviously, is this thing about how there's this one superhuman person who, like, completes you. This one person who meets all your needs. Which, historically speaking, is an absurd notion. A total aberration. I mean, take the Greeks. Like, as in, the ancient Greeks, like Plato. In Plato's time, a husband's job was to provide financial security for his wife. That was his role. She, meanwhile, had lovers for her sexual needs, and the temple for her spiritual needs, and the in-laws for her child-rearing needs, and the village for her social needs. Then centuries later we decided that, actually, no, all those needs should be met by one person: this magical spouse, who is supposed to do what used to be the job of the whole big ménage, all alone. It's *literally* insane."

"But when I first met Jack, it really did feel like magic. I know it sounds cheesy, but that's how it felt at the time, like . . . soulmates."

"That's just NRE."

"What's NRE?"

"New relationship energy. It's when you're feeling those first fits of interest in another person. You know, that heightened, exuberant, all-encompassing, *my-god-I-want-to-merge-with-you-completely*—"

"I'm familiar with it," Elizabeth said.

"The NRE feeling generally lasts six months to a year. At most, in the very best of situations, it can last three years. How long have you and Jack been together?"

"Married for fifteen years, together for twenty."

"So you understand. I mean, when was the last time you felt that way about him? That kind of thrilling, bubbly, erotic—"

"Yeah, okay, you've made your point."

"Don't feel bad. It happens to everyone. It's not your fault. You're just operating a technology that is out of date and broken and maybe even sort of abusive in how it makes people feel like failures and frauds. I mean, there's a good reason why marriage had nothing to do with romance or sex or love for most of history. You ever wonder why arranged marriages were, like, *the norm* for centuries?"

"I'd say patriarchy."

"Okay, yeah, but also? It's because NRE feelings of romantic love are strong but *fleeting*. And a marriage needs to be dependable, long-lasting, resilient. So people all throughout history thought it was actually dangerous to have too much romance within marriage."

"Hence letting the parents decide."

"That's right. People do crazy shit because of NRE. They cannot be counted on to be rational. Do you know what a sea squirt is?"

"A sea squirt? No."

"It's a marine invertebrate that floats around the ocean looking for coral to attach itself to. Once it's found a good anchor, it settles down and eats its own brain."

"I assume there's a metaphor in there."

"For the sea squirt, finding security makes thinking unnecessary. People do this too, when they've found *the one*."

"Thanks."

"Hey, Plato said the same thing, that romantic love was irrational and fickle. Plato thought the most stable kind of love was more, like, friendship-type love, more, you know . . ."

"Platonic?"

"Exactly. So it's best not to mix something as temporary as romance with something as permanent as marriage. And I'd say, given our current divorce statistics, that Plato was onto something. Half of all marriages end badly, and another quarter persist only for the sake of the kids. Did you know that seventy percent of all married people have affairs?"

"I did not."

"It is a complete disaster. And the reason is that we all expect way too much from marriage. It's like, till death do us part? Forsaking all others? No, that's fucking impossible. And yet people think *I'm* the crazy one. And, you know, I understand. I've seen the looks. I know I don't get invited to the playdates. But the way I see it, what my husband and I do is actually quite conservative. We're trying to maintain stability, maintain a family, we're trying to *preserve marriage* by not asking it to bear quite so much."

"But why even get married in the first place? If you're so against it?"

"Because we have two competing impulses alive within us: the need for novelty and the need for stability. It's this constant push-pull. When I have too many hookups, I crave stability. When I have too many nights chilling on the couch, I crave novelty. The key is to celebrate the contradiction."

"Which you can't do in a normal marriage?"

"The, quote, unquote, 'normal' monogamous marriage was not invented for people like you and me. Monogamy was invented for another user altogether. Monogamy was a necessary invention to placate the saddest, most undesirable, most bottom-rung inept and pitiful dudes out there."

"Okay. Wow."

"Think about it. Patriarchy plus capitalism is an unstable system without monogamy. Capitalism ensures that wealth gets more and more concentrated, and patriarchy ensures that it's concentrated among men. It's a system that incentivizes women to marry older powerful guys, and if you don't have monogamy to level the playing field, you'll just have droves of pathetic young men unable to find wives. And as we all know, nothing is worse for the social fabric than a loser dude who can't get laid. So monogamy had to be introduced as a kind of elaborate software patch."

"I've never thought about it that way."

"Marriage is a technology. And some technologies amplify human abilities, while other technologies restrict them. A lever is a technology that amplifies, while a lock is one that restricts. And all I want to do is turn marriage from a lock into a lever. I want it to enable me to occasionally experience that romantic NRE rush without feeling like a failed spouse."

"But I've seen you with your husband. You do not lack for romance."

"Seriously, Elizabeth, go have an affair. Or better yet, tell Jack to have an affair. Afterward, he will be a thousand percent more attractive to you. It's like witchcraft."

"I'm not sure Jack would agree to that arrangement."

"Let's go out, the four of us! A double date! My husband is really good at talking about this stuff. It'll be fun!"

"I don't know."

"Text Jack right now. Tell him you have an idea for a new adventure. He'll be so happy."

"No, he really won't. Having separate lovers? This week I suggested we have separate master bedrooms and he freaked out."

"Separate bedrooms is a great idea, but I think *master* is a problematic word."

"Really? How?"

"C'mon, Elizabeth. *Master*. Doesn't it have connotations?"

"I hadn't thought of that."

"People of your generation often don't."

"My point is, Jack and I have been together for so long, I can't just introduce something like this, something this . . . radical. It would be really unfair."

"Do you know what I do for a living?"

"Some kind of math."

"It's called algebraic topology."

"Which is?"

"A branch of mathematics that mostly studies the intrinsic qualitative aspects of spatial objects undergoing homeomorphic transformations."

"Okay."

"Basically, it's the mathematics of deformation and change. Like, the way I explain it is: imagine a basketball. What's the shape of a basketball?"

"A circle."

"Not quite."

"I mean, a sphere."

"There you go. But what if I deflated the basketball?"

"It's no longer a sphere."

"Right. And according to geometry, it's now a new object. But we all know intuitively it's not a new object. It's still the same object. A basketball. You can deflate a basketball into the shape of a bowl and it's still fundamentally a basketball. You can fold it like a slice of pizza and it's still fundamentally a basketball. But what if you ripped the thing in two?"

"Then it's no longer a basketball?"

"And it's also not two basketballs. It has been transformed into genuinely different things, two new objects. And that's what my math does. At its most simplistic, it describes how much you can deform an object before it becomes a new object."

"Got it."

"This also has implications for big data, though I beg you not to ask about that."

"Your point is?"

"Things change. That is a given. The real question is how much change is bearable. What you have to ask yourself is how much can your marriage change before it's no longer fundamentally itself."

"Like, if I ask Jack to do this, will it rip the basketball?"

"Actually, what I was thinking was, are you sure it hasn't already been ripped?"

Elizabeth nodded. "Okay, maybe I'll talk to Jack," she said. "A new adventure—that sounds pretty good. I think we could use something like that."

"Yay!" Kate said, clapping.

"Thank you for this. It was all very enlightening."

"You're so welcome. Now can I ask you a question?"

"Sure."

"I was curious about something you said. About how you once believed you and Jack were soulmates."

"Yes."

"Do you still believe it?"

"Well, what you have to know is that Jack is wonderful. Thoughtful, smart, good with Toby, a deeply decent man."

"But do you believe he's your soulmate?"

"Actually, no, not anymore."

"When did you stop believing it?"

"Tuesday, November 4, 2008."

"That is remarkably specific."

"It was a memorable day."

"What happened?"

"It's a bit of a tale," Elizabeth said. "Let's just leave it at: that was the day I sort of unraveled."

THE UNRAVELING

I T BEGAN at noon on a Tuesday, in 2008, and it began with Toby refusing his food, again.

He had just gotten up from a nap—Toby was two years old at the time and no longer really in the habit of napping, but on this particular Tuesday, for whatever reason, he went down for ninety whole silent minutes, and Elizabeth spent the time cooking, and thinking. She was thinking about work. Specifically about a new client who had come to her with an odd request.

Elizabeth worked at a DePaul research lab that specialized in the placebo effect. The lab was technically called the Institute for Placebo Studies, but it was better known by its front organization: Wellness. What they did at Wellness was test claims made by specious health-related products to see if the products achieved results any better than placebo. Basically they were a watchdog group, a subcontractor for the FDA and FTC, sniffing out bullshit. In 2008, some of the more well-known products that had come through the lab included: the SlimSkirt, a miniskirt made of some tight, rubbery, tensile material that felt like a big rubber band around your legs, which claimed to give your glutes a significant, fat-burning work-out if you just walked around in it; Skechers Shape-ups, shoes that had these big half-moon bottoms and supposedly helped tone your butt if (again) you just walked around in them; the Smartshake, a low-fat, low-calorie meal-replacement weight-loss smoothie thing; and a detox diet called the Master Cleanse where you'd ingest nothing but tea, lemonade, maple syrup, and, for some reason, cayenne pepper, usually all at once, which claimed to flush all the toxins and cholesterol and fat right out of your body.

The reason Wellness was needed to test these particular products was that each of them had been shown to be, in one way or another, effective. Some of the people who used or consumed them reported, confidently, that the products did what they claimed to do, that they actually worked, that they were not bullshit—these people often said they felt 100 percent healthier and even thinner after using them. And sometimes their physical results did indeed match their enthusiasm: some of the women who walked around for a month in the SlimSkirt really did lose weight to a degree that was if not life-changing, at least statistically significant.

So the question the folks at Wellness needed to answer was: Were these benefits the result of the product, or the result of placebo?

Because it had been pretty well established by 2008 that the placebo effect was real, and that it was strangely, almost shockingly, powerful. The field of placebo studies had been jump-started by Elizabeth's own boss, Dr. Otto Sanborne, a psychology professor at DePaul who first demonstrated—repeatedly and conclusively—that when patients in hospitals believe a medicine will be more effective, it tends to become more effective, whereas if they believe it will fail, it's more likely to fail (Sanborne, 1975). Since then, he had shown in a series of pretty creative experiments how susceptible people were to suggestion and placebo. For example, take someone suffering from chronic back pain. If you gave this person a sugar pill but told them it was a painkiller, it tended to *work better* than giving them a painkiller but telling them it was a sugar pill (Sanborne, 1976). Or sometimes the subjects didn't even need the right story but merely the right ambiance, the right tableau, the correct set of unconscious psychosocial signifiers: like, a doctor wearing a clean white lab coat administering placebo pills was more effective at treating pain than the same doctor administering the same pills while wearing a dirty old T-shirt (Sanborne, 1977). In other words, the study of placebo was really the study of context and expectation and faith and symbol and metaphor and story, which could lead people to believe any number of delusions.

At least, that was Sanborne's original hypothesis, that these subjects were experiencing delusions, hallucinations. He assumed that the placebo effect was, as the saying goes, *all in your head*. But other researchers had taken up the work and muddied the model. They showed that placebos sometimes had actual physical manifestations. For example, people exposed to fake poison ivy developed real rashes (Barber, 1978). And people given fake caffeine experienced real heart-rate jolts (Flaten & Blumenthal, 1999). And if you told blue-collar workers that what they did at their jobs counted as "intensive exercise," the workers would begin to slim down and get stronger without actually changing one thing about their lifestyle (Crum & Langer, 2007). And while the neurobiological mechanism for all this was still a bit murky, everyone understood that the key to placebo's strange and remarkable effectiveness was *belief*. The subjects needed to believe the story they were being told. Which was why, incidentally, Elizabeth's lab was not ever explicitly called the Institute for Placebo Studies, for as soon as people saw that on the door and understood they were getting a placebo, they stopped believing in the placebo's story, and thus the placebo effect no longer applied. Hence the vague and intentionally generic name, *Wellness,* a word that had a certain semantic flexibility (it could mean really anything they wanted it to mean), convenient for a job where the primary duty was to invent alternate stories for people to believe in, and then test the efficacy of those stories.

For example: How do you test whether the SlimSkirt is a good product or merely a good story? You change the story. What if instead of telling people it's a leg-strengthening skirt, you told them it's a *movement-inhibiting* skirt? What if you told them—as Elizabeth did, in a particularly satisfying and elegant study—that the skirt was designed for people with leg injuries to prevent them from over-working their leg muscles? And then you had them walk around in what Elizabeth told them was the RestrictiSkirt for a month? What would happen?

What happened was that these people came back complaining that their leg muscles had atrophied, and that they felt tired, and lazy, and that they'd gained weight, which, by the way, they had.

So, bingo. The SlimSkirt was effective due not to the thing itself but to the story surrounding the thing.

Ditto the Smartshake, the one-hundred-and-fifty-calorie health smoothie, which, if you told people it was actually a six-hundred-calorie dessert called the Feast, tended to produce, rather than prevent, weight gain.

And this was honestly the most fun part of the job, coming up with these substitute truths. It made Elizabeth feel weirdly powerful, that a fiction she invented could be absorbed into someone's very flesh and made real.

And so on that particular Tuesday in 2008, she was giving careful and serious thought to her work. Specifically, to this strange new client: United Airlines, the Chicago-based air carrier, which had come to her with a problem. It turned out that United's customers were, in general, not very happy to be flying United. To be fair, there wasn't a single large airline that travelers weren't unhappy with at the time, as various economies of scale were at work that pretty much demanded the airlines undergo a series of cost-cutting efficiency measures that had resulted in, to use United's lingo, "disaffected and sometimes even hostile customer outcomes." These measures included adding more seats to already crowded planes, restricting legroom to cagelike minimums. Also laying off ground personnel at ticket counters and gates, which increased wait times. And a revamp of the in-flight meals and snacks that, compared to customers' memories of the previous meals and snacks, now felt downright miserly. And since United could not reverse any of these measures without facing serious blowback from shareholders, the company came to Elizabeth with a request: How could they get their customers to feel happy about the appalling things that were happening to them? United wasn't going to change the situation, so they wondered if Elizabeth could help them change how their customers *thought* about the situation.

In other words, Wellness was being asked, for the first time, not to identify bullshit but to create it.

Which Dr. Sanborne outright refused to do, citing professional ethics: the lab, he said, couldn't very well produce exactly the kinds of delusions that the lab was in most other respects trying to eliminate.

But the question had stuck with Elizabeth and she found herself, on this Tuesday, turning it around in her head, interested in it for two overriding reasons: first, because she was only recently back after a long maternity leave and frankly anything remotely brain-teasing was a welcome relief after the many months of emotionally gratifying but—let's be honest—intellectually dismal work of infant caregiving; and second, because of the fee.

The exorbitant fee that United Airlines was offering to pay for this work was several orders of magnitude greater than what the slashed budgets of the FDA or FTC could ever give to Wellness. This substantial sum did not mean much to Dr. Sanborne, who had been famous in his field for decades and who, at seventy-five years old, would be retiring very soon, and very comfortably. But for Jack and Elizabeth? For Toby? That money meant quite a lot indeed.

So it was on her mind that day: How could she make those unhappy customers happy without changing their material conditions at all? It was a question she pondered as she stirred the rice in the rice cooker, and steamed the broccoli over the water bath on the stove's back burner, and tasted the red-pepper relish now bubbling on the stove's front burner, and whirled the chickpeas to a paste in the blender, and microwaved the microwavable mac and cheese, which, despite being unnaturally orange and detestable, would be the only food item on this whole buffet that Toby would eat.

For Toby had become, all at once, at two years old, *picky*.

A picky, fussy, hypercritical eater, refusing every food except for mac and cheese and insisting he wanted nothing but mac and cheese for the rest of his life. In response, Elizabeth dove into the research. She read every relevant study, considered every relevant review. This was how she problem-solved, not only during Toby's new toddler phase but also throughout pregnancy: her approach to motherhood was scientifically rigorous and exact. Her parenting was informed by only the best, most respected, most thoroughly peer-reviewed research, and was therefore immune to personal bias or the whims of pop psychology or the passing fads on display in the bookstore's intimidatingly large Parenthood section. And so after reading many editions of the *Journal of the American Dietetic Association* and the *Journal of the Academy of Nutrition and Dietetics* and the *Journal of Eating Behaviors* and the *Journal of Clinical Nutrition* and *Appetite*, she discovered, among other things, that it was necessary to help Toby overcome his pickiness *right now*. Immediately. ASAP. Because it turned out that eating habits established at

Toby's age were, in the words of the researchers doing longitudinal work on this problem, "resistant to change," that the foods children refused to eat at age two would still be refused years later (Skinner et al., 2002), that children afraid of new foods were likely to grow into adults afraid of new situations and new places and even new people (Pliner & Hobden, 1992), that eating habits established right now were very likely to track all the way into adulthood (Kelder et al., 1994; Singer et al., 1995; Resnicow et al., 1998), which gave Elizabeth waking nightmares that Toby might be telling the truth about his mac-and-cheese plans, that he might really eat only mac and cheese forever, and Elizabeth imagined him after years of this diet, malnourished, obese, friendless, lonely, his brain fueled not by vitamins and minerals but by saturated fat, his skin and hair tinted a synthetic orange.

It was one of the more unfortunate compulsions of parenthood: to take any unwanted behavior and extrapolate how Toby's life would be ruined if the behavior persisted and enlarged and deformed into its worst incarnation. She did this all the time. Like, if Toby stared too long at her laptop screen, Elizabeth worried about his possible future internet addiction. If Toby pushed another child on the playground, she worried about violent masculinity and Toby's future juvenile delinquency. She evaluated any behavior based on what would happen if it were universalized. And she wished she could operate without such threatening categorical imperatives, but she found it impossible not to worry, especially when the research lined up with—and therefore validated—her fears. As was the case with the crisis of Toby's diet, and the crucial need to train him—*promptly*—to eat like a normally functioning omnivore.

The term in the scientific literature for picky eating was "neophobia"—the fear of something new. And according to the literature, the best way to overcome it was to prepare meals that included bites of new and novel foods along with servings of familiar foods, and to do this consistently with many diverse foods until your toddler eventually began eating everything on his plate willingly and happily (basically the advice of Carruth, Ziegler, Gordon & Barr, 2004; also Sullivan & Birch, 1994; also Birch & Marlin, 1982). The key was, simply, *exposure*. Like the treatment for many other phobias, the way to reduce one's fear of a food is to be exposed to that food in small quantities, in nonthreatening ways, repeatedly. According to the research, children Toby's age needed to taste a food between eight and twenty times before they grew to like and accept it (Wardle et al., 2003), and therefore it was important to continue feeding Toby new and novel foods even if he claimed not to like them, hence his lunch that day: sushi rice (which he had tasted and rejected five times previously; Elizabeth kept notes), hummus (eight rejections), red-pepper relish (four rejections), a sliced-up dill pickle (six rejections), steamed broccoli (eleven-going-on-twelve rejections), and the mac and cheese, a dietary staple for many months now.

All of this had taken a little more than an hour to prepare, and she proudly put all of it on two white plastic plates, and she set the plates on the table, and she put Toby—still warm from napping—into his high chair in front of one plate, and she took the seat across from him in front of her own identical plate, and she said, "Bon appétit," which was what she always said to officially commence family mealtime.

"No," said Toby, which was what he usually said in response.

It was noon on a Tuesday. Jack was at school, teaching. Elizabeth's job at Wellness was flexible enough to accommodate the duties of childcare, so mostly these afternoons with Toby fell to her. Their schedule today, as it appeared on her calendar, was:

10:30—Nap?
12:00—Lunch
12:30—Grocery store

She remembered a time in the years before Toby when things like eating lunch or shopping for groceries did not need to be elaborately planned, did not need the calendar's sanctification. These were the easy tasks that got taken care of naturally, inevitably: she'd grab lunch at some point, pop into the grocery store at some point. But now, with Toby, the day needed to be rigorously blueprinted—there was no *grabbing lunch* with a toddler, no *popping in* anywhere. She had looked at her calendar that morning and experienced—though she would never admit this—a feeling of lightness and happiness at the 10:30-to-noon block, when Toby would, hopefully, sleep, and she could be alone. Everything thereafter, she knew, would abrade with its usual friction.

Elizabeth calmly pointed at each food on Toby's plate and spoke its name aloud. "Hummus," she said, trying to imbue the word with excitement and temptation, trying to distract him from the disagreeable mood he seemed to have woken up in. "Pickle. Broccoli."

Toby stared at his plate for a moment, and, as if he were seeing it now for the first time, said: "Oh, pretty."

"Thank you," Elizabeth said. And he was right. It *was* pretty. She had read (in Sobal & Wansink, 2007, on what they called "tablescapes" and "platescapes" and other "microgeographies of built food environments") that the manner in which a meal is presented provides important cues about eating it. And so the six foods served in today's lunch were presented *beautifully,* in perfectly round portions—Elizabeth had used a small ring mold to keep everything nicely contained—which, with the backdrop of the spotless white plate, looked very pretty indeed. The red peppers were diced into a uniform brunoise. The hummus was sculpted into her best quenelle. The pickles were julienned. It looked like an interesting amuse-bouche at a Michelin-level restaurant. She didn't just serve lunch; she *plated* it.

"Remember," she said, "one bite of everything." Toby nodded. "Let's start with the hummus."

He watched as she dipped a spoon into the smooth beige dollop on her plate, then he looked up at her. Sometimes an expression would wash over his face that seemed far too adult for a toddler, an expression that seemed to be, like, layered. And the face he made right now, if she had to describe it, was, maybe, *anguished*.

Not sad, or enraged, or any other first-order emotion. But more like a complicated, layered, almost spiritual feeling of anguish.

He let his spoon fall to the floor. He began to weep. It was 12:02.

It helped in moments like this to think about insights from the field of evolutionary psychology regarding the sometimes baffling behavior of children. Specifically, Elizabeth appreciated the theory that food neophobia was an evolutionary adaptation, that toddlers afraid of new foods were merely behaving in a way mandated by a million years of natural selection. The argument (most clearly described in Cashdan, 1998) went like this: throughout our biologic history, human children around the age of two generally stopped breastfeeding and began eating the solid foods that would sustain them throughout adulthood. However, the food environment for our hominid ancestors was treacherous, full of poisonous plants and rotted meat. How could a young weaning omnivore survive? By becoming, suddenly, at age two, an excessively picky and fussy and choosy eater. Basically, natural selection transformed toddlers into these persnickety little snobs compelled to eat only those things they'd eaten many times before while barely nibbling at new foods until those foods showed themselves, over time, to be safe. In other words, being afraid of food helped kids survive.

And this whole evolutionary explanation allowed Elizabeth to mentally reframe Toby's pickiness and fussiness at mealtime and think of her son not as *difficult* or *intransigent* or *bad,* but rather as a boy fighting deep hardwired impulses that no longer made sense in this modern age of food abundance and safety.

Which made it easier to deal with, in a sort of cognitive behavioral therapy sort of way.

(Though honestly this reframing was occasionally hard to maintain during the more trying moments, such as just the other day, when she saw a mom on the playground ask her own toddler, "Do you like raisins?" and the boy took the raisins and chewed them happily and asked for more, which ignited a bolt of jealousy inside Elizabeth because Toby's consistent reaction to raisins was to scream at them and refuse to touch them and weep until she removed them from his sight.)

Elizabeth picked up Toby's spoon and washed it. She placed it next to his plate. She sat down and said, "Maybe let's have some mac and cheese?"

Toby looked at her. He stopped crying. Toddlers could stop crying *so quickly*. All at once, done.

"Macka cheese?" he said, suddenly happy again. And Elizabeth nodded and smiled as Toby took one successful bite of that orange, gooey, completely execrable processed microwavable macaroni-and-cheese product.

It felt like a kind of victory. Getting Toby soothed enough and acquiescent enough at the table to accept a bite of food—really any food at all—*was* a victory, though a complicated one, maybe even an embarrassing one. Convincing your picky toddler to eat food was not exactly the stuff of epics. Nobody ever wrote an opera about a mother heroically getting her baby to like hummus. It seemed beneath the threshold of caring, and, indeed, whenever she might bring it up with her younger colleagues at work, she saw within minutes how something in their eyes seemed to sort of gloss over, and she'd apologize—"Sorry, I'm sure this is so boring"—and her gracious coworkers would insist that it wasn't boring at all even though they almost always steered the conversation to any other subject.

Operas were written about great drama; what Elizabeth faced were a million dumb domestic dramas, every day. Even that word *domestic* was, she thought, a little sinister, how it literally meant "of the home" but also implied "boring." She remembered this one woman, a classmate in a screenwriting course Elizabeth had taken in college, a nontraditional student in her forties who was coming back to earn a degree—while the rest of the students were turning in scripts heavy on murder and apocalypse, this woman was writing about couples and breakups and children. "Little stories" was how the teacher described (and dismissed) them, "domestic dramas," comments that prompted the woman to turn in some kind of bad space thriller the next time around.

And the thing is? Elizabeth had been one of the people sneering at and privately making fun of this woman's work. Elizabeth might have even shown the script to her friends at the co-op, and they might have all acted it out one night in this terrible, arrogant way. It made Elizabeth so ashamed now, thinking about it. Also it made her feel even more resolved not to share her own little domestic stories, not to submit them to the criticism of others. These were victories she would keep to herself.

The problem, of course, was that victories you have to keep secret don't feel like true victories. When victories can't be shared with others, they begin to feel like a different kind of defeat.

Elizabeth dipped her spoon into the red-pepper relish, took a bite. Toby watched her, then looked at his own identical plate, stared for a moment, then dropped his spoon, letting it clatter onto the table.

"Can't?" he said.

"Do you want some help?"

She went to him and picked up his spoon, which prompted immediate fury: "No!" he screamed. "Is mine!"

"Okay," she said, and she handed him the spoon, which he grabbed tightly. She sat down again, took another bite, this time from the small pile of rice. "Now it's your turn."

He dropped the spoon on the table again, at roughly the same spot it had landed before. He looked at Elizabeth and shrugged. "Can't?" he said.

"I'll help you," she said, and as she dipped her own spoon into the red-pepper relish on Toby's plate, he screamed once more—"No! No! No!"—and with a great swipe of his arm, he knocked the whole plate, and all his food, to the floor.

Elizabeth took a deep breath. She sat down again, in front of her own plate. The reason she had fixed herself an identical plate was that, according to the relevant research, toddlers tended to take dietary cues from their parents (Carruth, Ziegler, Gordon & Hendricks, 2004), meaning they tended to watch and mimic what their parents did at the dinner table (see also Visalberghi & Addessi, 2000), which was why at this moment Elizabeth did not react to the plate's violent shove, nor the smear of hummus and mac and cheese on the kitchen's immaculate floor—immaculate because, according to the research, a toddler overcomes food fussiness when the kitchen is a clean, sanitary, inviting, social, and fun place (Horodynski & Stommel, 2005)—nor did she react to the spray of pickle and broccoli bits she'd have to later mop up. Instead, she calmly took another bite of her own sushi rice—the idea here was that toddlers tended to respond better to a parent modeling appropriate behavior versus getting scolded for inappropriate behavior (Solomon & Serres, 1999), which was why she would never say out loud to Toby that he was *being bad* or *being a little fucking shithead* even though she thought it, honestly, all the time.

But no, she would never label him out loud as a *fussy kid* or even a *picky eater* because once you label a child, the label tends to become self-reinforcing (Ambady et al., 2001), that the power of a label is that a child will internalize the label and make it true, will strive to become what you already believe he is (it's a phenomenon known as "stereotype susceptibility"), which was why if Elizabeth ever did verbally describe Toby to Toby, she would do it in a way designed to encourage better behavior, calling him a "good boy" or, maybe, "a good boy who loves his hummus."

Anyway, this parenting strategy was called "modeling" or "cuing" in the scientific literature.

And the emotional state she was trying really hard to model and cue right now was: *calm.* She was trying to evoke calmness in the face of Toby's regular outbursts, calmness while he was in the throes of this horrific neophobic phase, calmness at the fact that she spent hours each day preparing foods that had only one real point: to be rejected. It was especially, poignantly bad when Toby refused some food that last week he had loved—it felt like he was doing it on purpose, raising her hopes only so that he could smash them. It felt weirdly abusive, when he'd scatter previously accepted food on the floor, or when she'd lean in to hold him and he'd slap at her, or when she said "I love you" and he screamed "No!" It was hard not to feel like Toby was doing all this on purpose, that it was a sort of gaslighting tactic he wielded just to needle her and disrespect her. Though she tried really hard to resist this inner narrative because she knew that one of the things parents who were depressed had in common (according to Cornish et al., 2006) was that they attributed agency to their toddlers' misbehavior, that the misbehavior was filtered through a bleak and hopeless "depression distortion," and so merely thinking *He's doing this to me on purpose* was the first step down a dark, dark path.

So, above all, calm.

She calmly ate some rice. She calmly said: "You don't see Mommy throwing her food, do you?"

Toby looked at the floor. He seemed genuinely surprised to find such a big mess down there. He pointed and said: "Macka cheese?"

None of his sentences were any longer than three words. He also had a tendency to pronounce most sentences—even the declarative ones—like questions.

Elizabeth said: "Would you like some mac and cheese?"

"Where?" he said, shrugging, as if he had no idea why his food was no longer in front of him, as if he were not, at twenty-four months, old enough to understand not only simple cause-and-effect but also higher-order relational principles and inductive reasoning (which, according to Schulz et al., 2007, he totally was).

"I have mac and cheese on my plate," Elizabeth said. "Would you like to eat off my plate?"

"Okay," Toby said, nodding thoughtfully, as if this were an excellent compromise.

She set the plate in front of him. She told him to remember their one basic mealtime rule: that he could eat whatever he wanted, but he had to try at least one bite of everything. She knew he'd go straight for the mac and cheese, but she also knew it was important not to force him to eat the more nourishing, non-mac-and-cheese things, that the old "Eat your vegetables!" dictum tended (according to Dovey et al., 2008) to have the perverse effect of backfiring and making children hate their vegetables. Further, she knew she couldn't use the mac and cheese as a kind of reward for the eating of vegetables, because then Toby would begin interpreting his own behavior as "I must not like vegetables very much if I need a reward for eating them," according to just basic overjustification theory (see Lepper & Greene, 1978).

Toby looked at the food on the plate in front of him. Then he looked up at Elizabeth. He said: "Bubbles?"

Elizabeth sighed. "No," she said. He meant that he wanted to watch a screen saver on Elizabeth's laptop, this particular animation that appeared when the computer was idle: bubbles floating around the screen, colliding with each other and bouncing off the edges of the screen and also occasionally popping. It was so dumb and simple, and yet when Toby was an infant, those bubbles held him spellbound. And, back then, Elizabeth would go ahead and let him stare, after having read (in Chiang & Wynn, 2000) about how infants learn the concept of object permanence, how tracking visual objects across a visual field and watching those objects move and intersect could teach babies the essence of real-world "object-hood." But of course that was more than a year ago, and Toby continued to love this screen saver even now, long after he should have outgrown it.

"Bubbles?" he said again.

"Not right now," she said. "It's mealtime."

Which was an unbudgeable rule: no media during meals. No TV, no computers, no phones. Because when kids eat while watching a screen (according to Serra-Majem et al., 2002), they pay attention to the screen and not their bodies, ignoring crucial self-regulating signals and thus eating gluttonously, mindlessly. And Toby knew this rule—he had never watched Bubbles during mealtime, not even once—but still his face pinched in rage, and he shrieked and pounded his fists on the plate, splashing even more food onto the floor as he screamed the word *Bubbles*.

Was it reasonable to disrespect your own toddler's *tastes*? Like, Toby had so many other wonderful and enriching options to read and watch and play with, yet this was what he wanted most: to watch popping digital bubbles, on a screen saver. This dumb thing could absolutely bewitch him. Was it wrong that Elizabeth found this sort of . . . lame?

"You can watch Bubbles later," she said. "Right now it's time to eat."

She knew that Toby didn't really have the strongest grasp on the concept of "later," that toddlers tended to misunderstand the future tense (Harner, 1975, and 1980, and also 1982), experiencing the world in what she imagined as a kind of goldfishian everlasting present. Sometime in the next year or two he would really begin to understand the unfolding nature of time, but for now he was still all impulse, all immediate desire, had not yet learned how to displace that desire, how to map it onto the future. That would come later—for now, Elizabeth had to bear Toby's tantrums, and wait.

It was 12:15 p.m.

"Bubbles *now*," he growled at her with a strange kind of authority, like suddenly he was possessed by a drill sergeant. She wondered where he'd learned to do that, how he'd learned to produce such a dominant, almost despotic expression on his otherwise baby-soft face.

"Shouting won't help," she said. "Please eat your food."

"No!"

"Do you want different food?"

"No!"

"Are you hungry?"

"No!"

"Well, *I'm* hungry," Elizabeth said. "Can *I* eat your food?"

She was trying to be a little silly, to lighten the mood, to *model appropriate mealtime behavior*—she wanted Toby to see her happily eating this food, since watching other people consume food can provide neophobic eaters with a kind of "exposure-by-proxy" to that food, reducing their rejection of it (Hobden & Pliner, 1995). But as she reached for the plate, and as she said, "Mmmm, looks so good," suddenly the boy's face grew bewildered and terrified and he looked at her with these shocked, wide-open, dewy eyes and said, full of betrayal and hurt: "Is *mine!*"

And then all memory that he had thrown his own food onto the floor, and all memory that he had just seconds ago claimed to not want any food whatsoever, all that had been ejected. Now he was living inside the envelope of a brand-new moment, one in which his mother was trying to steal his precious lunch.

"Very . . . bad . . . mommy," he choked out through heartbreaking sobs. "Is *mine!*"

Elizabeth knew (primarily through a study on mother-toddler dyads by Laible & Thompson, 2002) that mothers experience conflict with their toddlers, on average, every three minutes. That's twenty conflicts per hour, every hour, all day long. On average. That same study found that certain dysfunctional dyads can experience upward of fifty conflicts per hour—one fight every seventy-two seconds—which felt, to Elizabeth, distressingly accurate. And, further, she knew that this was only the beginning, that mother-child conflicts reached a peak at exactly Toby's age and stayed right there, peaking, miserably, until age four (this from a Klimes-Dougan & Kopp, 1999 paper that made her heart sink when she found it in a developmental psych quarterly), which meant that Elizabeth was looking at two more years of this.

Two full years. That was how long it had taken her to get a master's degree. Two years at age twenty-three was an enormous, personality-shaping span. But now, as the mother of a toddler, it was just something to get through, to endure, to hopefully, mostly, forget.

Toby, meanwhile, had pitched himself forward and was now pitifully resting his head on the edge of his plate, his arms hiding his face, his back shaking with uncontrolled weeping, saying over and over: "Is mine. Is mine."

Eventually, between the melancholic swoons, Toby ate three bites of mac and cheese, one bite of hummus, and one bite of broccoli that he chewed for an optimistic ten seconds but ultimately spit out and put back on the plate in exactly the spot it had come from. Elizabeth noted the progress in her "New Foods Log." She pulled Toby out of his high chair and cleaned his face and hands and shirt. It was 12:21.

They had three more conflicts in the next few minutes: one when Toby started crying because he didn't want Elizabeth watching him while he played with a coloring book; another when he started crying when Elizabeth left him alone with said coloring book; and another when he remembered his wish to watch Bubbles at exactly the moment Elizabeth told him it was time to go to the grocery store.

Often on days like this she remembered advice she'd read from a therapist about helping people afraid of airplane turbulence: instead of dwelling on all the bumps yet to come, try to celebrate the bumps that have passed. So whenever you experience another midair bump, think of it like *Yay! That's one less bump!* Which was roughly what Elizabeth was saying to herself on the way to the grocery store, as Toby wailed the word *Bubbles* in the back seat, she thought: *Here is another fight I no longer need to have, another fight now overcome.*

She'd rarely taken Toby to the grocery store until recently, when the neophobia really seriously set in and she began researching strategies to subdue it and found (in Larson et al., 2006) that when children participate in the entire food-preparation process, they tend to eat the foods they help prepare, tend to be slightly more adventurous eaters, tend to feel a kind of "ownership" over the food—the food wasn't merely a thing that appeared on a plate but rather had a full and exciting context. According to one survey (Casey & Rozin, 1989), parents reported that the most effective way to help kids overcome food fussiness was to let the kids help buy and prepare the food—this was twice as effective as giving them a reward for eating new foods, and almost ten times more effective than telling them that all this food drama was making their mother depressed.

Elizabeth had fantasized about bringing Toby to the grocery store, where he would help her pick out handfuls of, say, edamame. Then he'd help her to shell the edamame back home, becoming really familiar with and charmed by the edamame, which would hopefully lead to a reduction in his fear of basically all green things. That was the idea, anyway, that the grocery store should be considered an extension of the kitchen, that all of it taken together—the whole food-procuring and -preparing and -consuming cycle and all its miscellaneous influences, the whole obesogenic ecology, the many overlapping and interactive and built and natural and sociocultural and political and economic and micro- and macro-level food-environment domains, as it was all described in the overwhelming literature on this subject (like fucking Rosenkranz & Dzewaltowski, 2008)—was a kind of single organism that, when unhealthy, manifested in sick kids.

And, as usual, Elizabeth's fantasy of quality parenting and charming edamame adventure was laughably far from reality. Like, for example, it took three more conflicts to get Toby out of the car and into the grocery store: first he didn't want her to unbuckle the straps on the car seat, crying when she even touched the buckles because she had once, while buckling him in, accidentally caught the skin between his thumb and index finger in the buckle and pinched it hard enough to leave a mark, and now he never let her fucking forget it; then he did that floppy-body thing that made it almost impossible to get him out of the car seat, going so limp and flaccid that pulling him out was like lifting a thirty-pound bag of water, Elizabeth all the while saying, "Help me, Toby. Please help me. Help me get you out," to no discernible effect; and finally, once out of the car, he didn't want to walk.

"Kangaroo?" he said, his arms aloft, by which he meant that he wanted to ride around in the wrap.

The wrap was just three meters of woven purple fabric that she twisted around her back and shoulders and torso in a complicated knot that ultimately created a marsupial pouch on her chest, hence the name for this technique in the child-rearing literature: Kangaroo Care. She had purchased the wrap when Toby was a baby, after reading about the soothing, quieting, trust-building benefits—for both infants and parents—of skin-to-skin contact (Feldman et al., 2003). To "kangaroo" meant to bundle Toby up in the wrap and carry him around with his face pressed closely to Elizabeth's chest. Which had been delightful until recently, when Toby had gotten way too big for the wrap, heavy enough that the load tended to leave her shoulders and back aching, tall enough that his forehead occasionally knocked into her chin, unwieldy enough that he strained the wrap's tolerances. But she had not yet retired the wrap from duty, and today, with Toby acting so belligerent and fussy, the idea of making him walk around when he did not want to was a fight she preferred to avoid. So into the wrap he went, and for a little while the kangarooing was pretty smooth. He calmly pointed at the apples and said, "Apples?" He pointed at the bananas and said, "'Nanas?" He pointed at the avocados and said, "Acados?" And Elizabeth praised him generously each time he identified a fruit or vegetable, happy that, at the very least, he knew the names of the things he refused to eat.

But she also, secretly, wished he'd stop talking like that, phrasing all his statements like they were questions. He did it all the time. He'd been doing it since he began forming words and sentences. It was like a tic of his, this tendency known colloquially as "upspeak" but described by linguists as the "high rising terminal." She disliked it strongly because, first, Toby seemed so young and pristine and new that his having already developed anything that could be called a "tic" seemed tragic. Second, because it made him sound like the toddler equivalent of a Valley girl and she worried that if he kept talking like that nobody would ever take him seriously. And finally, because this tic was, she knew, entirely her fault. She'd put it there. The pediatrician had more or less confirmed it after she'd asked: "Why does everything coming out of Toby's mouth sound like a question?"

"Well," the doctor said, trying to be diplomatic, "kids tend to mimic the speech of their parents."

"But I don't talk that way."

"You don't talk that way to adults," the doctor said. "But maybe you talk that way *to him*."

"I don't understand."

"Do you, for example, ask him a lot of questions?"

The answer to which was: *Oh my god yes*. She hadn't even realized—not until the next day when she was really mindful about it—that just about everything she said to Toby was a question: What sound does a duck make? Where's your belly button? What do we say to the nice lady? Do we throw things in the house? What color is the stop sign? Where does guacamole come from? What animal says moo? It was a kind of idle habit—at any given moment, there was always something she could teach him. She'd ask him to identify fruits and vegetables and colors and body parts. She'd take him to work and quiz him on her coworkers' names. Even the actual demands and instructions she gave him had turned into questions: Aren't you sleepy? Isn't it time to go night-night? She hadn't realized that her dominant mode had become interrogative. And so, yeah, of course Toby talked this way. He phrased everything as a question because *that's how he thought people talked*.

Elizabeth had wanted to teach him about the world, but instead she'd given him a tic.

As if she needed any more evidence that she could so easily fail at motherhood.

They were in the boxed food aisle when Toby, looking over her shoulder and pointing at something behind Elizabeth, said: "Some?" Which, translated, meant "I want to eat some of that," which was always a welcome and hopeful thing for Elizabeth to hear. So she turned around to see what Toby was pointing at and saw that it was the mac and cheese. And not even the organic, real-cheese, quasi-healthy version. No, Toby would eat only the most processed, most artificially orange kind possible. "Some?" he said again.

"Honey, you just ate."

"Some?"

"If you wanted mac and cheese, you shouldn't have thrown it on the floor."

"Macka cheese now?"

"No."

Toby looked at her with these big moist eyes and grabbed his belly in imitation of maybe a person starving and said: "I . . . so . . . *hungry.*"

And then he started crying.

It was sometimes hard to believe that Toby wasn't doing this kind of shit out of conscious cruelty. Because even though she knew it was unfair ascribing premeditation and real malice to the chaos of a toddler's wants, still it seemed a little fishy that Toby was able to so precisely, so consistently make her feel rage. And every time she felt the rage gathering—because Toby was once again doing exactly what was needed to deliver it—she'd have to remind herself that these were *bad thoughts,* these were the thoughts of a depressed parent, that all her work with the placebo effect had shown her that reality could be created by the stories you believed, and thus it was important to pick the right stories. No matter how incontrovertible the evidence was that Toby was punishing her—regularly, intentionally, calculatingly—she knew she *must not believe it.* Because if she believed it, then other terrifying behaviors would follow. And she'd read *all* the research here: she knew that depressed parents, when presented with a *conflict episode,* when presented with a child like Toby right now exhibiting *highly negative affect,* tended to respond, in the lingo of family science, *destructively.* These were the parents most likely to threaten and criticize and scold (Lovejoy et al., 2000), most likely to use physical coercion (Smith & Brooks-Gunn, 1997), least likely to use reason (Bluestone & Tamis-LeMonda, 1999), most likely to yell (Dumas & Wekerle, 1995), most likely to say things that were critical and guilt-inducing (Hamilton et al., 1993), most likely to feel strong hostility toward their children (Lyons-Ruth et al., 1986), most likely to perceive their children as more difficult or malicious or wicked than they objectively were (McGrath et al., 2007), all of which were behaviors that, if she gave in to them, would leave Toby seriously maladjusted and aggressive and noncompliant and antisocial and basically fucked up later in life (Ingoldsby et al., 2006; Scaramella & Leve, 2004; Dishion & Patterson, 1997; Herrenkohl et al., 1997; Strassberg et al., 1994; etc., etc., etc.).

And so when she felt the rage really coming on strong and she noticed that panicky sensation where it was like she was suddenly made claustrophobic by the pressure of her very own skin, she would stuff all of it way down, all the destructive impulses, she would bury them and focus on modeling external serenity and calm while mentally crossing out the bad story—

~~TOBY IS DOING THIS TO ME ON PURPOSE~~

—and replacing it with better stories:

TOBY NEEDS MY LOVE AND SUPPORT
I AM GOOD AT BEING HIS MOTHER
I CHOSE THIS

"I understand you're hungry, sweetie," she said, looking into his big eyes in an effort to really connect and relate and empathize with him. "We'll make a snack when we get home."

"Some now?" he said.

"No. When we get home."

"Now?"

"When we get home."

"Please now?"

"I said no."

And that was when he hit her.

As they were bundled so closely, the path to her face was, of course, unobstructed. And the strike came so suddenly and so surprisingly that it was, for Elizabeth, unavoidable and unblockable. The butt of Toby's palm connected with the point of Elizabeth's cheek, hard.

It was unclear whether this hit was malevolent and deliberate or whether it was the accidental side effect of Toby's tendency to, in heightened emotional states, get all twitchy. His arms flailed, his legs kicked, his head lurched—he had no bodily control during these tantrums. So it was possible that the hit was the result of one of these paroxysms, or possible that he did it on purpose. Either way, it hurt, and Elizabeth registered that hurt by saying "Ow!" and putting up her arms to prevent any further haymakers from landing. "No hitting!" she said angrily.

He began wailing and pushing away from her and kicking his legs trying to escape the wrap. Instead of hitting his mother, Toby was now sort of hitting himself, which, together with the loud lamentations, reminded Elizabeth of certain foreign funeral practices, those agonizing physical expressions of intolerable grief.

People, meanwhile, were staring.

And Elizabeth once again tried to model profound calmness while repeating one of her inner feel-good mantras—

TOBY NEEDS MY LOVE AND SUPPORT

—except that this mantra, while generally endorsed in the scientific literature, did not seem specifically endorsed in her particular case. That Toby needed any of her love or support was a supposition that lacked empirical evidence, in other words. For Elizabeth had poured as much love and as much support as she could possibly muster into this boy and yet here they were, Toby crying and flailing and drawing everyone's attention. It was hard to ignore that Elizabeth's love/support and Toby's crying/flailing seemed to be positively correlated, that they seemed to move in tandem, one driving the other: Toby would get upset and Elizabeth would express love and support and Toby would get much, much worse. It was like when a doctor induced high blood pressure in a patient by testing the patient for high blood pressure, a well-known medical paradox called the "measurement effect" (see Landray & Lip, 1999) where you create exactly what you're looking for, by looking for it, bringing into being something that would have never existed if you hadn't tried to find it. And maybe, among certain dysfunctional mother-toddler dyads, the relationship was similarly contrapositive—*If not x, then not y*—and maybe it would be best to *withdraw* her love and support, maybe her attempts to correct Toby's behavioral problems were actually causing those problems in the first place, and she recalled a flowchart she once saw (in Goodman & Gotlib, 1999) that had "Depressed Mother" on one side and "Disordered Child" on the other side and between them a chaos of psychological dysfunctions and maladaptive habits and situational stressors all connected via bidirectional arrows going back and forth between all of it—meaning, basically, that the whole thing was a single, dynamic, mutually reinforcing cause-effect system where the inordinate stress a mother felt about interacting with her misbehaving child made that mother feel depressed, and that depression made the child more anxious and thus more badly behaved, and that misbehavior further fueled the mother's stress, which made her feel even more deeply depressed, which caused yet more misbehavior, and so on and so forth in a *continuous, spiraling cycle* (as it was horrifically described in Cummings & Davies, 1994), which made her feel that maybe if she called it quits on motherhood and totally disengaged and ceased all love and all support, then Toby could be a normally functioning kid without his mother's clumsy interference (which, you know, citation needed), leading her to mantra number two—

I AM GOOD AT BEING HIS MOTHER

—which was *definitely* empirically false and had been false since literally her first minute of motherhood, right there in the birthing suite at the hospital, where she'd intended to have a natural and intervention-free birth with no unnecessary, over-prescribed medications or surgeries, but then, several hours into a difficult and stubborn labor, she experienced a sudden spike in blood pressure, and the baby's heartbeat crashed, and the doctor insisted on an emergency C-section to help the now "in distress" infant, and so they pumped her full of analgesics and performed the necessary surgery, after which she was so cold and nauseous and exhausted that she promptly passed out for one full hour, during which time Toby lay in an incubator, alone. And the thing about Kangaroo Care? The really awful thing about newborn skin-to-skin contact? It's that, according to the science, the benefits manifested only if the infant received the essential physical contact within sixty minutes of being born. It was right there in the research. They called it the "Sacred Hour," a crucial developmental moment that was *literally once-in-a-lifetime*. And Elizabeth had slept right through it.

She imagined Toby in that incubator—scared, abandoned, traumatized, making those horrible noises that researchers really actually characterized as "mammalian protest despair," borrowing a term used to describe the sounds that chimps made while trapped in small cages (Bergman et al., 2004). No wonder infants who missed out on the Sacred Hour were more violent later in life, more depressed, more anxious, more suicidal (Phillips, 2013)—in their first terrifying experience of the world, they had been taught a brutal, unforgettable lesson: *You are alone.*

Worse still was the fact that the Sacred Hour was also essential *for mothers* (De Chateau & Wiberg, way back in 19-fucking-77), that mothers who missed this profound bonding moment also missed the associated release of key maternal hormones that would have made them feel more comfortable and confident caring for their babies, would have made them kiss their babies more, spend more time staring into their infant's eyes—even a year after birth, mothers who had enjoyed the Sacred Hour held their babies more often, had more positive speaking behaviors with them, kept more doctor's appointments, breastfed longer. In one chilling study from Russia (Bystrova, 2008), skipping immediate postpartum skin-to-skin contact "decreased the *mother's* ability for positive affective involvement"—or, in other words, doing exactly what Elizabeth had done made her less capable of *love*.

"That's bullshit," Jack had said when Elizabeth told him about it.

"How would you know?" she said. Because, honestly, there was no way to be aware if her capacity for love was lacking. Love being such a subjective experience, there was no way to be sure that other mothers didn't feel more of it. It was like wondering if the red that other people saw was *more red*. She could never know. All she could do was look at the hard evidence, the way her particular love rooted in Toby and bloomed as a multiplex of maladaptive behaviors. He had never really mastered suckling, for example, and Elizabeth's body never ultimately produced much milk anyway, and so breast-feeding turned out to be a spectacular failure, which, incidentally, was a pretty well-known consequence of skipping the Sacred Hour (Widström et al., 1990). So Toby went on formula pretty early, and at the time Elizabeth was disappointed about that, but she became downright despondent when she discovered (in Galloway et al., 2003) that when children weren't breastfed, one of the common side effects was: *food neophobia*.

And so maybe, yeah, she could admit it was possible that she had taken such a deep dive into the neophobia research, and treated Toby's neophobia problem with such urgency, because the neophobia was, ultimately, her fault. And that it was probably pretty likely that every bad thing in Toby—the low impulse control, the generalized anxiety, the extreme pickiness, the verbal tic—every broken thing had been put there by her.

This, it turned out, was the most savage, most hurtful thing about being a parent: it wasn't just coming face-to-face with all your own shortcomings and inadequacies, but it was also seeing those shortcomings embodied in your child. It was knowing that any random moment when she wasn't vigilant and attentive and cautious was a moment that could deform Toby forever.

Which was why, as he melted down right there in the boxed food aisle, as he strained against the fabric of the wrap and tried to pull himself out of it, Elizabeth was mindful of containing and burying her most destructive impulses—primarily the one to hurt him. To emotionally hurt him. Exactly as he had hurt her. To say something devastating—this was a pretty strong impulse right now. To mock him and sneer at his pain. To roll her eyes at his stupid weeping. *You think you have a bad parent? You have no fucking idea. Try growing up with mine* is what she wanted to say, which struck Elizabeth immediately as something her own father would have said to her, and maybe actually did say to her, sometime when Elizabeth was Toby's age, which was maybe how Elizabeth learned to so effectively hide all her suffering. Because it was clear growing up in that house that any display of attention-getting emotion turned into a competition her father would always win. So eventually Elizabeth, as a child, stopped trying to compete and became, above all, nice.

Steady.

Placid.

Calm.

Industrious.

All through adolescence, she modeled the same external calmness and serenity that she modeled for Toby right now: "It's okay, sweetie. There, there. Everything is fine," she said, even though she did not feel this way on the inside, that everything was fine. What she felt on the inside was definitely *not fine*. It was more of an all-encompassing full-body dread that cascaded through her as she remembered again that she had *two more years of this*: fifty conflicts per hour, six hundred conflicts per day, two hundred thousand conflicts per year.

This was her immediate future: half a million fights.

Half a million opportunities to respond destructively.

It was unrelenting. It was unthinkable.

Toby screamed at her and she thought: *I am never going to make it.*

"Excuse me?" came a voice from behind her, and Elizabeth turned to find an old woman smiling gently. She had frizzy white hair and shoulders curled into a permanent shrug and a small fabric grocery bag that she held, meekly, in both hands, in front of her.

"Yes?" Elizabeth said.

"Do you need help?"

"No. Why?"

"Because," the woman said, all full of sympathy and compassion, "it looks like you're unraveling."

Which—fuck it—that was *enough*.

"*HOW DID YOU KNOW?*" Elizabeth cried, her voice breaking. This was all she could take on this day, in this hour. She had reached her capacity, could endure no more abuse. Here she thought she'd been projecting perfect maternal calmness and serenity and it turned out that this woman, this *stranger*, could see right through her, could see how Elizabeth was, indeed, coming completely apart.

"What?" said the woman, flinching and sort of jumping backward. "No, I mean"—she pointed at the floor—"your wrap, it's unraveling."

And Elizabeth looked at where she was pointing and saw about four feet of purple fabric bunched around her shoes.

"Oh," Elizabeth said, quietly. But it was too late. The tears were already coming.

They sat together in the grocery store's bakery section for a good twenty minutes, the woman buying a cupcake for Toby and playing with him and otherwise occupying him while Elizabeth sat there having a nice long cry that the lady pretended to ignore. And while she cried, she thought about her final feel-good mantra:

I CHOSE THIS

She had chosen, willingly, freely, to have a child, and therefore, by implication, she had also chosen to give up countless luxuries and comforts: entire nights of restful sleep, a clean and spotless house, disposable income, relaxed and languid days without any conflict or rage. All of these pleasures she had sacrificed. And not only had she sacrificed them but, because she had chosen to do this, because she had done this to herself, she now pretended to be happy and contented at their absence.

And this tickled something in her brain, and she felt a sudden epiphanic flash, that way the mind sometimes reveals it's been working on a problem beneath the surface and you realize it only when the answer pushes its way into consciousness: the perfect placebo, she suddenly understood, was *choice*.

If you chose to do something, you would endure all manner of mistreatment and still tell yourself: *This was the right choice*.

Here, Elizabeth thought, was an answer for her strange new client. How could United Airlines make its customers happy with a below-average experience? By making the experience much, much worse, and making people voluntarily choose to endure it.

This was the solution! Make the seats even narrower, the lines even longer, the competition for overhead space even more cutthroat—make it all famously bad and then tell people that they could avoid all of it and have a more or less normally below-average experience *for a modest fee*. Thus, if they knew beforehand that the experience would be dreadful but they didn't pay the fee to avoid it, they would be less unhappy about the dreadful experience because, ultimately, they chose to have it. They did it to themselves.

It was her eureka moment, the moment that changed everything, the moment that led to her pitching the idea to United Airlines and collecting their fee, a fee so substantial that she and Jack could finally afford to make a down payment on a home—their forever home, out in the suburbs.

It had all started here, at one p.m. on a Tuesday in 2008.

A WEEK LATER, right around the time that Elizabeth was beginning to find some humor in the whole grocery store episode, right around the time that she'd given the anecdote its own name—"the Unraveling"—in advance of soon entertaining her friends with the story, she was back in the kitchen, at noon, feeding Toby. It was his usual plate—five novel foods, plus mac and cheese—and Toby was refusing it in his usual stubborn way.

Jack was still home, rushing around, late for work. He kissed Elizabeth goodbye, kissed Toby goodbye, then noticed the plate of untouched food.

"Hey, check it out," he said. He removed his phone from his pocket, held it above Toby's lunch, and took a picture. He showed the photograph to Toby, who nodded at it and said: "Ooh, pretty."

Then, unbelievably, the boy began to eat.

He ate the rice, the pickle, the red-pepper relish, the hummus. He ate it all—quickly and happily. Elizabeth looked at Jack, astonished. "How did you . . . ?" she said, unable in this moment to form a complete sentence.

"Turns out," Jack said, "he thinks the food is pretty."

"Pretty?"

"Yeah. He doesn't want to ruin such a pretty thing by eating it."

Elizabeth watched Toby chewing his broccoli and swallowing it and reaching for more. He was now eating everything on his plate *except* the mac and cheese.

"If you take a picture," Jack said, "then the pretty food is captured forever, and therefore he can eat it without ruining it. He really has a keen sense of aesthetics. Maybe he gets it from me?"

"Why isn't he eating the macaroni?"

"Oh, he doesn't really like it," Jack said. "He only eats it because he thinks it's an ugly mess. Thus, there's nothing to ruin."

"How long have you known this?"

"A couple weeks. Sorry, forgot to tell you!"

And then he was out the door, and Elizabeth was left with Toby, watching him eat with exactly the appetite she had been wishing for him to one day achieve. It was everything she'd been working toward, everything she'd been hoping for, delivered in a single instant—and yet she did not feel happy about it. Not one bit.

Every couple has a story they tell themselves about themselves, a story that hums beneath them as a kind of engine, motoring them through trouble and into the future. For Jack and Elizabeth, that story was about falling in love at first sight, about two dreamers discovering their other half, two orphans finding a home, two people who understood each other—who just *got* each other—easily and immediately.

But stories have power only insofar as they're believed, and suddenly, sitting there, watching Toby happily eat, Elizabeth wondered if her and Jack's story wasn't in fact just another highly embellished placebo, just a fiction they both believed because of how good and special it made them feel. And maybe all love was like that, a placebo, and maybe every marriage ceremony was part of that placebo's elaborate ornamentation, its therapeutic context. And as soon as she considered this, it was as if the curtain came down, and just like her clients at Wellness upon being told the truth about their fake therapies, the story no longer compelled.

It was the day she lost belief. It was the day the fantasy she'd known as "Jack and Elizabeth, Soulmates" had—in the lingo of the relevant research on this subject—lost its efficacy.

FAILURE TO THRIVE

A DISTRESSING FACT that Jack Baker's mother never hesitated to bring up throughout his childhood was that, for all intents and purposes, he should not have been born.

He should not have even been *conceived,* she would tell him. Partly because of her age: she was thirty-seven at the time, and while women now routinely have children at thirty-seven, this was Kansas in 1974. And women in Kansas in 1974 did not have children at thirty-seven. In rural Flint Hills especially. Thus the doctor's horrible term for it: a *geriatric pregnancy.* And the doctor warned her about all the ways her geriatric pregnancy could go wrong— stillbirth, deformities, defects—warned her in a way that sounded, to her, at that moment, like an accusation, like she had waited all this time to get pregnant only to make this doctor's life difficult. She felt shamed for being pregnant so geriatrically. She told the doctor that she'd never intended to get pregnant again, never wanted to get pregnant again. She and Lawrence weren't even *intimate* anymore, and had not been intimate for a very long time. "I know that being together just once is all it takes to get pregnant," she told the doctor, "but, c'mon, what are the damn odds of getting pregnant after being together *just once*?"

"Especially at your age," the doctor added, unhelpfully.

But that's exactly what had happened: Ruth and Lawrence Baker had not spent any time in each other's beds in years, save on one evening that spring when a rare coupling had resulted, incredibly, unluckily, in Jack.

Unluckily because the Bakers did not need any more kids, did not want any more kids. Money was tight, the house was small, and anyway, as Ruth would tell Jack many times when he was growing up, they already had Evelyn, the implication being that one would never need another child when one already had a child as incredible as Evelyn.

Evelyn had been conceived when Ruth was in her twenties, in perfect maternal health, her body in its biologic prime. And, in Evelyn, it showed. Jack's earliest memories of his big sister were of watching her standing high above him on a float in the homecoming parade, in her dress and sash and tiara, smiling, waving. Actually, the word *float* is a little grand for what was in fact a flatbed trailer with paper streamers taped to its sides. The trailer was pulled slowly by a tractor driven by Jack's father, a quiet and impassive man whose pride in Evelyn was the only thing that regularly broke his otherwise deadpan veneer—he sat up there on his tractor with an uncharacteristically satisfied grin. Just about everyone in the county would come out to watch, carrying their own lawn chairs, occupying two blocks of Main Street, watching a parade that consisted of tractors pulling flatbeds, plus one fire engine, one sheriff's car, two clowns throwing candy, and the VFW guys on their body-rumbling motorcycles. And up above them all, Jack's big sister, homecoming queen three years running, valedictorian of her admittedly modest ten-person class, and star of the high school girls basketball team. Theirs was a school so small it could compete only in basketball, as there were literally not enough students to fill out a team in any other sport. Thus, basketball was a pretty big deal, and some of Jack's earliest memories were of watching his sister in that small, hot gymnasium, listening to the local ranchers who filled the bleachers cheering hard for Evelyn. Seeing her on the basketball court, you would almost think that she was aloof for how casual she often looked, like she was jogging. That is, until you saw her side by side with the other girls—their heads down, sprinting, spitting air—and you realized that Evelyn was just racing by them, easily, calmly, fluidly. The other girls were all flailing limbs pumping to keep up, like old jalopy engines shaking in their mounts. Evelyn was a comet. She took two steps and all of a sudden there she was, under the basket, laying it in for another easy goal.

But as much as she captivated on the basketball court, it was her art that everyone talked about. Evelyn was a phenomenally gifted painter, one of those painters able to evoke a landscape or a building or a person with only a few brushstrokes, the barest dabs of color.

Classmates and neighbors would sit for a portrait and after only a dozen flicks of her paintbrush they'd exclaim: "My word, that's me!" She had this ability to take the world and reduce it to its elemental shapes. Her favorite subject was the land itself, the prairie surrounding their ranch. Jack remembers Evelyn sitting in those fields every night at sunset, painting the same scene again and again in the varying, diminishing light: the summer land all rich and abundant; the winter land all browned and bony; the springtime land all scorched after the season's prescribed burns.

Evelyn was a talent. Everyone knew it. The way their mother described it to Jack, it was like Ruth's womb had only a finite number of resources, and Evelyn had nabbed them all. Which was why Ruth was not altogether surprised to hear the doctor's dire warnings, and why she was also not surprised when the symptoms started. Her sudden raging headaches, her general allover fatigue, an ache in her lower back that seemed kidney-related. She was not gaining weight, and, crucially, neither was this baby inside her. At each doctor's visit, she discovered that Jack had again missed all his developmental milestones. When he was supposed to be the size of a walnut, he was the size of a pea. When he was supposed to be the size of a grapefruit, he was the size of a plum. He was always disappointing. And the doctor would ask Ruth questions that once again sounded like accusations: Are you eating? Are you taking your vitamins? Are you exposing yourself to toxins or poisons? Yes, yes, and no, of course not—she was doing everything correctly, had been doing everything correctly, except, obviously for getting pregnant in the first place, as the doctor always reminded her.

Then test results came back with unsettling news. There was some key marker, some trace protein, present in the amniotic fluid, which suggested—the odds were roughly fifty-fifty—that the baby might be *abnormal*. He might have problems. He might be slow. He might be challenged by the basic functioning of life. Ruth didn't know precisely what medical condition the doctor was implying here, only that it was serious enough that he slipped her a piece of paper with the names and phone numbers of four Wichita family planning centers that she knew to be abortion clinics.

As Ruth would later tell Jack many times, this was, in Kansas in 1974, not as controversial as you might think. It was, in fact, not really controversial at all. Abortion in Kansas in 1974 was, actually, pretty well accepted, pretty unexceptional. Kansas had legalized the procedure statewide well before the Supreme Court legalized it for the rest of the country. Women who found it difficult to obtain an abortion in neighboring Oklahoma or Missouri or Nebraska would routinely come to Kansas instead. Kansas even elected to Congress a doctor who had himself performed abortions—the only state to do that, before or since. His name was Bill Roy, he was from Topeka, and in late 1974, in an election Ruth would sit out due to pregnancy-related complications, this congressman would come within a few thousand votes of ending the political career of a first-term senator named Bob Dole.

This is all just to say that your typical Kansas woman in 1974 experiencing a complicated geriatric pregnancy and given a list of abortion providers by her doctor would not have found that odd. She would not have spoken of it to anyone, of course, but not because she thought it was wrong. She would not have spoken of it because it was private, and Midwesterners respect one another's privacy.

So this is another reason Jack Baker should not have been born, as Ruth would later never hesitate to tell him: if he'd been conceived by your typical Kansas woman in 1974, he would have been silently, unproblematically, terminated. But Ruth Baker was not a typical Kansas woman, because she attended the Flint Hills Calvary Church, a small nondenominational ministry that met in a former feed store not far from the Baker ranch. And the Calvary pastor's Sunday sermons were limited to three basic subjects: avoiding impure thoughts, preparing for the end times, and abortion. Specifically that abortion was murder, and having an abortion was a "grade A violation of God's will."

He said that kind of thing a lot, how some bit of scripture was "grade A" or "prime" or "choice"; his flock was made up mostly of cattle ranchers and the families of cattle ranchers, so the pastor often spoke in their vernacular. And Jack would sit with his mother in church on Sunday mornings listening to these sermons, and whenever the pastor started going on about abortion—which became more and more frequent during Jack's adolescence, the sermons becoming more angry, the parishioners more aggressive and activist—Ruth would look at her son with this expression like *Aren't you lucky?* She seemed to imply that if it weren't for the accidental fact of her attendance at these very Calvary Church services and the idiosyncrasies of this pastor's faith, she would have aborted Jack for sure. It was her weird way of getting him devoted to the church. It had literally saved his life.

So Jack was born—as implausible as that was—six weeks early, in mid-November, tiny and jaundiced. The hospital kept him under ultraviolet lights for a week—it was supposed to help with the jaundice—during which time his mother and father watched him, this tiny unlikely creature, this quiet mouselike child, their urine-yellow baby.

The jaundice, it turned out, was only the beginning of Jack's problems. The four years following his birth felt to Ruth and Lawrence like an endless cycle of illness and fever and disease and infirmity—four years where they felt submerged in milk vomit and stomach acid and camphor oil and Vaseline and chalky barium shakes and calamine lotion and infectious-pink-eye goo and ice-water baths and hydrogen peroxide for earaches that ultimately required tubes—during which time their state of mind could probably have been best described as *prepared for loss.* Jack's parents were, this whole time, preemptively bracing themselves for the real possibility of this baby's passing—trying not to get too emotionally attached to him, always studying his behavior for symptoms of some new disaster, some harbinger of death. He was a sickly, skinny boy, could barely keep food down, would vomit in long eruptive jets that seemed unlikely for something so small. He screamed more or less all the time. He never seemed to grow.

The doctors had a brand-new horrible term for all of this: *failure to thrive.* This child was failing to thrive, and they didn't know why. So they asked Ruth more accusatory questions, questions whose central premise seemed to be that since they could not figure out what was going on with her baby, it was, again, most likely her fault.

"Are you feeding him?" asked many, many nurses and pediatricians and even a few nosy parents.

"Of course I'm feeding him."

"Are you sure you're doing it right?"

"Of course I'm doing it right."

"Show me. I want to see how you do it."

Ruth Baker began dreading Jack's visits to the specialists he required. And not only because these visits were frequent, and not only because they were expensive, but also because each new specialist required her to endure the exhausting failure-to-thrive interrogation once again: the judgmental questions, the dubious frowns, the raised eyebrows. What she wanted more than anything was to skip all of these appointments forever, but of course she couldn't do that because that would confirm to the doctors that she was exactly the kind of mother they already suspected her to be. So she kept going, kept answering the doctors' rude inquiries, kept imploring Jack to just, please, *grow*. Just be healthy. Because when he was not healthy, the blame seemed to fall squarely on her.

And so by the time Jack was roughly three years old, he could sense from his parents—though he would never be able to articulate it, either out loud or to himself—a palpable low hum of resentment. It was just there in the background, so constant that one stopped consciously acknowledging it. All Jack understood was that when he felt sick, his parents would get upset. When he couldn't stomach his food, his parents would get upset. When the doctor checked his height and found that it had not changed, his parents would get upset. And when they got upset, they would sort of detach from him—it was their old guardedness coming back, their old mental strategy, preparing for loss. But what this felt like to Jack—not that he was wise enough to reflect on it, just that he knew it felt fundamentally true to him, as true as the floor feeling solid and the summer feeling hot, so true it wasn't even remarkable—what it felt like was *loneliness*.

He felt truly and profoundly alone, which, for a three-year-old, is terrifying. It causes actual terror. It was simply not bearable for Jack to feel so discarded and estranged from his parents, his only source of care in the world. But of course he didn't have the power to change his parents, which was also unbearable. And so his psyche, in search of any explanation that would make the world seem more bearable, willing to believe any illusion that provided comfort and security, did its little dance. If Jack could not change his parents, he began believing that they did not need to be changed. That they were correct to feel what they felt, to do what they did. And that if anyone needed changing, it was him. Jack himself was the only variable he could control, and thus changing himself was the only way he could change the situation, the only way he could exert a little agency: to accept wholeheartedly the blame for his parents' misery. Because then he could end that misery by being better, by being good, was the story he began telling himself, quite unintentionally. Jack began to believe that if he could just be the best little boy he could be, then his parents would not be upset, would not detach from him, and therefore he would not be alone. And so a simple sort of algorithm started running in Jack's head, way below the level of conscious thought, one of those automatic processes that's working in the background, all the time, filtering everything, a simple script that took all of this anxiety and reflexively distilled it into two words: *My fault.*

If his mother was upset, he thought: *My fault.* If his father disappeared for weeks at a time, he thought: *My fault.* If his parents were fighting again, he thought: *My fault.*

It was not comfortable, this feeling, but it was more comfortable than being alone. His psyche eagerly deformed reality to avoid that which it found intolerable.

So Jack, without ever really knowing it, began automatically accepting all the fault and blame for any drama or pain in that house. It was like an instinct, to be exactly who they wanted him to be, to never make anyone the least bit upset. This reached a kind of masochistic peak around his fourth birthday, when, once again, he got sick.

It started as a slight twinge in his throat. An ongoing low-grade ache paired with only minor anguish when swallowing. It was, for the most part, ignorable. But then a few days later it transformed itself into exquisite little spikes of pain whenever he ate or spoke, this coupled with a slight shift in his senses that made even water taste odd, and made voices sound generally echoey and underwater. It was worrying, this progression, but still manageable—and definitely not rising to the level of telling Mom about. But another few days later he awoke with the sensation that the pain had somehow bloomed, that this thing in his throat was now on the move: he felt a constant throbbing misery creeping into his jaw and neck and shoulders. He eventually had to stop turning his head because it activated this pain that groaned through him and felt like the teeth of a small, persistent animal gnawing at the meat of his upper back.

Still, he did not say anything. Still, he hoped it would all pass on its own and he wouldn't have to upset his mother yet again. But it did not pass, and days later he found it difficult to move his head at all, found it difficult even to stay awake—his vision was cloudy and swimming, his forehead hot, the rest of him shivering, and even the thought of food made him involuntarily gag.

This was how his mother found him one morning, sweating and shaking, and just touching him made him weep, and she took his temperature and found it to be a hundred and three, and she scooped him up out of bed and he promptly vomited bile over both of them, and she rushed him to the local doctor, all the while thinking: *This is it.* The moment she'd been waiting for and preparing for all this time: little Jack was not going to make it.

The doctor took one look at Jack's symptoms—the nausea and vomiting, the fever, the confusion, the headaches and muscle pain and stiff neck—and diagnosed him with spinal meningitis. It was the stiff neck, he told Ruth, a dead giveaway. He sent them to Wichita that very day for tests and treatment, Jack falling into and out of consciousness the entire ride there. He opened his eyes and saw the soft rolling hills and swaying brown grass of the prairie in November, his parents in the front seat, glancing back at him with tight faces. Then he blinked and they were passing by the lake in El Dorado, trees poking out of the water where the Army Corps of Engineers had flooded the land, thick black trunks now drowned and dead and dissolving. Then he blinked again and they were in

Wichita, he was in the hospital, people were asking him to stand up, he was dizzy and cold, he looked down to find he was in a wheelchair, he was wearing one of those hospital gowns, wrinkled, papery, he was in a room with white walls and a bed at its center, and the people around him were asking him to stand and lean over this bed. Two nurses helped him, their touches like fire on his arms, and then he was standing and feeling the room begin to tumble end over end, colder now as he looked down once more to find that the hospital gown was open in the back, shivering as he leaned over the bed and rested his cheek on the bed's scratchy blanket and saw, through a window that looked into some secondary room, his parents, standing there with a few more doctors, arms crossed, watching, and the doctor was telling him to be calm, that it would be over very quickly, that what they were about to do was called a *spinal tap* and it was very important that during this procedure he be very still, that he not move at all, not one muscle, and that he definitely should not jerk or flail around, and the doctor said this in the really soothing voice that Jack had learned from countless other doctor visits to immediately distrust: "Can you do that for me, champ? Can you stay absolutely still?" And Jack, still staring at his parents, nodded, and then he felt hands on the small of his back, probing at the soft tender spot between two vertebrae, down where his spine was most curled and thus this spot maximally exposed, and he watched as his mother put a hand over her mouth as if to stop from screaming as he felt, in his back, on the spot the doctor had been prodding, a sudden strange pop, followed by a new and large and terrible presence. He would remember it as the most painful thing he'd ever endured, though it was not in fact painful. *Pain* was merely the easiest way to describe the feeling, which was not pain but had many of the same qualities of pain, primarily that he wanted more than anything for it to end. He began crying. The doctor told him to stay calm, that he was doing a great job, that it was almost over. The intrusion in his back then seemed to burst, fingers of ice shooting up his spine, pins and needles in his legs, numbness in his feet, he felt wobbly, tipsy, he was going to fall over, collapse with a needle in his spine, and he was trying to warn the doctor and implore him to remove the needle before he fell when the doctor clapped his hands together and said, "All done!" And then they were helping Jack into the bed, telling him to keep the same position, curled, fetal, Jack lying there confused because even though the needle was no longer in him, still he felt it, that puncture, that cold ache, which he would have asked the nurses about if he hadn't promptly passed out.

The tests of his cerebrospinal fluid came back negative for meningitis, which stumped the doctors. It was a minor medical mystery until one of them had the idea of looking down Jack's throat, and what he found there shocked him: tonsils so infected and inflamed that they were about three times bigger than even the most unhealthy tonsils the doctor had ever seen. Nobody had thought to look at Jack's tonsils because tonsillitis usually presented as a sore throat. Kids usually complained about it when it was at the sore throat stage. None of the doctors had ever heard of a child waiting so long that the symptoms grew to meningitis proportions. Why would he do that?

"They told me he'd be slow," said Ruth, feeling unfairly accused once again, feeling like maybe this kid had hidden his sickness just to torment her.

Jack woke up as he was being wheeled into surgery. A tonsillectomy was a simple matter, but he didn't know that. All he knew was that he had gotten sick, again, and his parents were with him, again, in the hospital, again, and they were upset, again, and that old familiar feeling—*My fault*—came back to him now, and even though his whole body hurt and his back still ached from where it had been punctured and his throat screamed in pain when he spoke, still he looked at parents with his big, liquid eyes and said: "I'm sorry."

WHEN A BIRD that had been swooping and soaring out over the Chicago River suddenly veered into one of the city's many large glass buildings, the twenty men on the other side of the glass mostly ignored it. All but one of them kept their eyes closed, despite the loud thud. They kept sitting there on yoga mats, on the floor, lightly stretching their necks, working their shoulders, twisting their torsos, lengthening their spines. They were dressed in full business attire—button-down shirts in white or blue, sport coats, dress slacks, a few neckties—though each man had slipped off his shoes upon entering the room, and set them down along the back wall, where there was now an agglomeration of shiny loafers and oxfords and brogues.

It was a room on the tenth floor of an office building on Upper Wacker Drive, a high-rise built on the spot where the river split into its north and south branches. The front of the building had been designed in the traditional rectilinear manner—straight lines and right angles where it fit into the downtown grid—but the back of the building was not rectilinear at all. It was, instead, one long and graceful curve that exactly mimicked the curve of the river below it. And the building's blue-green mirrored glass had been selected to exactly mimic the color of the water. It was a building created to perfectly fit into and reflect its particular surroundings, and most everyone agreed that it was one of Chicago's most beautiful and clever buildings, but it was a disaster for the local birds, who literally could not tell the difference between sky and water and glass, and so office life in this building was characterized by the violent frequent whumping sound when a window halted the flight of some unfortunate sparrow or warbler or duck.

There was only one man in the room not participating in today's breath practice, and that was Jack, who stood in the back, among the shoes, checking Facebook on his phone and trying to ignore the vague scent of moist leather and collective feet. Before him sat all these men on their yoga mats, beyond them the front windows, the view of the river, the Merchandise Mart across the river, the morning's frenzied rush-hour sidewalk bustle. Jack had been surprised by the bird's sudden impact and glanced up at the noise—he was the only one in the room who did—just in time to see a small dark creature hang still in the air for a split second before beginning its flaccid fall.

At the front of the room, facing everyone, was Benjamin Quince, sitting in full lotus pose, currently doing some side stretches, eyes closed, shirtless. His pecs were bulbous and his biceps were round and he had, all over, the rigid-but-also-swollen look of buff older men. After a moment, he opened his eyes and said: "Let's begin."

Then Benjamin inhaled—a deep and deliberate and even sort of gymnastic breath—getting his entire body involved, rearing way back, as far back as he could while still remaining balanced and upright, and then he threw himself forward and expelled his air in a great large gust, opening his mouth wide and sticking his tongue way out and making this sound like he was saying the word *ha* but never actually ending the word, staying inside the word's long open vowel until his lungs seemed fully spent, and right at the moment when it seemed like he might start gagging from the effort, he drew himself back and began breathing in these intense staccato little bursts, breathing furiously and in triple time, doing this for so long that Jack began feeling dizzy just watching it. Then all the men on their yoga mats followed suit: the long emphatic exhale, the many zealous inhales, after which everyone got real quiet and the room swayed drunkenly.

"Oh yeah," said Benjamin. "You feel that? That is *nice*."

It was a workshop on psychedelic self-microdosing that Benjamin led each weekday morning. The whole idea was that people would do this strange breathing thing right before work, activating some kind of chemical in the brain—not exactly LSD but LSD-adjacent, some kind of all-natural LSD cousin. This breathing practice would apparently release this hallucinogenic molecule in small, sub-hallucinatory amounts, a tiny dose that apparently had all sorts of workplace benefits involving enhanced creativity and improved focus and boosted mood and so on. People were supposed to do this whenever they were brainstorming on a new work project, or giving an important presentation, or asking for a raise, or doing basically anything on the job that was in any way difficult.

"Remember to stay in your body," Benjamin said, his head lightly rocking, bobbing, his long neat beard all aquiver.

He ran these classes before each workday, along with lunchtime sessions on advanced biohacking and occasional happy-hour lectures on how Buddhism can help you "crush work." His clients were mostly businessmen from the nearby buildings, employed in tech or advertising or law firms or brokerages, though Benjamin was currently trying to leverage his local popularity into something more viral: he was starting a channel, seeking a TED Talk, developing a method.

"Be gentle with yourself," said Benjamin, his left hand now doing a kind of weird groping thing on his own bare chest. "I have, you should know, fainted during this practice, once or twice."

Then everyone in the room did the whole thing one more time.

While Jack waited, he again checked the Facebook app on his phone. He was expecting, any moment now, an angry and likely unhinged response from his father. The previous evening, Elizabeth had gone to bed early and Jack had done what he usually did on the computer at night: write exasperated posts on Facebook rebutting whatever new nutty conspiracy theory his father currently believed in. Right now it was the Ebola virus that had, for some reason, snagged the old man's paranoid imagination. His father had a tendency to share—reflexively, thoughtlessly, without much examination or due diligence—any story or meme that immediately triggered his outrage. His feed was one of terrible first impressions, often accompanied by horrible videos in which Lawrence would rant into the camera, his body gaunt after years of couch-sitting, his bony face in close-up, the frame filled by two agape and terrified eyeballs. Today the stories were all about Ebola: that a town in Texas was currently under illegal CDC lockdown after just one family tested positive; that the government was secretly anticipating high U.S. Ebola casualties, the proof for which was the "fact" that it had purchased a billion dollars' worth of plastic coffins, all of them now stacked on a highway outside Atlanta; that the CDC had a patent on the Ebola virus and planned to unleash its sickness upon America in order to profit from the vaccine; and finally that Ebola could be cured by high doses of vitamin C.

Regarding the Texas town, Jack clicked on the link and discovered that the story had originated on an ambiguously named website called the National Report, which, upon close inspection, seemed to be a satire site intended to fool people who weren't paying attention, which Jack gleefully shared with his father, urging him to, as he told his students, "check your sources." As for the coffins, Jack informed his father that the exact same photo of stacked plastic coffins had been used a few years earlier in a completely separate online conspiracy theory, one alleging that the government was planning a martial-law massacre of millions of Americans, and Jack's father *had believed that one too*, had even posted about it, and Jack searched the archive until he found that post, and then he helpfully provided his father with the link. Regarding those last two items, Jack merely pointed out that it was impossible both were true—that is, if the CDC would make billions on a cure, then the cure couldn't also be vitamin C, and vice versa, adding that it was "interesting" that his father found both things simultaneously plausible, inviting him to "maybe think a little more critically" about his "logical reasoning."

After which it was well past midnight, and Elizabeth was almost certainly asleep, and so Jack did the other thing he did most nights on the computer: he looked at porn.

Now it was morning, and he felt a little bleary, not to mention ashamed that he'd stayed up so late on the computer. He had to teach a class soon, an art history class a few blocks away, but first he wanted to see Benjamin, here at his office, to get an update on the Shipworks.

"Feel your body," Benjamin said from the front of the room. "Feel where it connects to the floor, feel grounded on the spot where you sit atop the earth, feel the chi passing into you and reducing your inflammation. Remember that our ancestors walked on the grass and felt the stones with their bare skin. They earthed themselves daily. Follow their example."

He was touching himself again, running his fingers across his abs.

"Feel the grass, nestle in the dirt, carry a rock in your pocket and collect its ions. Remember that we are one with the earth," he said, and just at that moment, right behind him, a common pigeon suddenly swerved into the glass, clunked against the window, and fluttered there furiously, surprised, before flying awkwardly away.

Benjamin opened his eyes, smiled, clapped his hands. "Dominate your day, gentlemen."

And then everyone was standing—some very slowly, groggily— and Benjamin was striding over to Jack. He gave him a fist bump and a slap on the back and said: "Jack, buddy, could you do me a favor?"

"Okay."

"Smell my breath."

"What?"

"Does it smell like fruit to you?"

"I don't understand."

"Does it smell, specifically, like a stone fruit that's slightly past its prime? I think I've achieved ketosis. That's how you can tell, the odor."

"I don't know," Jack said, leaning toward him and taking a small, exploratory sniff. "Maybe?"

"Excellent! C'mon, walk with me."

And he led Jack into the adjoining room, Benjamin's office, the one with the posters everywhere of what the Shipworks would one day become, and they took their seats and Benjamin glanced at Jack's wrist, at the spot where the tiger-orange wearable used to be, and said: "Are you no longer on the System?"

Jack had in fact boxed up that wearable and put it in the back of his closet soon after listening to its recording of Elizabeth and her evening with the Madagascar. He had not mentioned this recording to her—nor would he—but he had casually left the wearable sitting on that bedside table the next night, and it had recorded Elizabeth using the vibrator again, and again the next night, and again the next. She had never once used this thing with Jack, but she was using it by herself, apparently every single night. After which, Jack had no interest in hearing anything like that ever again.

"I don't know how accurate that thing is," Jack said. "I mean, according to its metrics, I am depressed, quite depressed, even though I don't personally believe that I am. Or if I am depressed, it's probably more like a normal kind of depressed, like a midlife thing, bottom of the U-shaped curve, you know?"

Benjamin squinted at him. "That's probably the bacteria talking."

"The what?"

"You have a billion bacteria in your body right now. Did you know that? And they are constantly urinating and defecating all over your insides."

"That's really gross."

"Which is why you have to purify, Jack. Every day. Get rid of those toxins. Depression is the body's way of telling you it's drowning in poison. Are you getting enough sleep?"

"Not really."

"Well, there you go. You need at least nine hours to reliably flush out the bad."

"Ben, could you maybe put on a shirt?"

Benjamin leaned forward in his chair and flexed his chest muscles real tight. "Look at me, man. Best shape of my life." He stood up and fetched a dress shirt from a nearby hat rack, put it on, was buttoning it up, saying: "People at the gym ask me what kind of steroids I'm on. And I tell them I'm on farm-raised chicken breast and organic broccoli. I'm on two hundred daily ounces of raw water and several good reasons to live. That's all the drugs I need."

He sat back behind his desk, popped his feet up, crossed his arms. "Now, I assume you're here to talk about the Shipworks?"

"Yes."

"And all the new turmoil and agitation and bellyaching and such?"

"Yes, please. What is going on with that?"

"That is a story that begins in 1956."

"Okay, unexpected."

"In 1956, the federal government passed a highway bill to expand the nation's interstate system. And local governments, who at the time were almost entirely white, decided to put those highways right through neighborhoods that were, at the time, almost entirely Black, which meant, you know, bye-bye neighborhood."

"I understand."

"Then about a decade later, states passed civil rights legislation that allowed local people to sue developers to preserve neighborhood integrity. These were well-intentioned laws, I should say, but it turns out that actually using them requires a lot of time and coordination and effort and money, and so the only citizens who ever actually take advantage of these statutes are, perversely, wealthy white people protecting their property values. Which is what's happening right now in Park Shore. Lawsuits have been filed, injunctions are being ordered."

"So all this stuff about preserving Park Shore's history?"

"That is a smoke screen. That is pure PR. The folks organizing against us just don't want to admit what they're really afraid of."

"And what are they really afraid of?"

"Renters."

"That's it?"

"That's a lot. Think about it. Lower-income people living in a place like Park Shore? It might damage real estate prices. It might change the town's, quote, unquote, 'complexion.' Listen, we're trying to stick a high-density mixed-use building into a low-density affluent suburb. There was bound to be some pushback."

"Fine. So what now?"

"Fortunately, I specialize in this kind of thing. Risk management. It's kind of what I do."

"Meaning?"

"Well, I won't burden you with the specifics—it's phenomenally complicated work—but maybe just think about it this way. Think of risk as a kind of toxin, okay? Risk is like the gluten of project financing. It's poison. And it's everywhere, man, it's all around us. It's like gluten, plus all the added sugars, plus the soy filler, the *excipients*, and also the genetically modified seeds, the aluminum deodorant, the antibioticed cow, the 5G. I mean, do you know how much garbage there is in our food supply? In our drinking water? In the air? You avoid these toxins as best you can, but you can't avoid them all, so you have to dilute and expel and eliminate them."

"Yeah, but how?"

"Oh, have you not seen my stash?"

And Benjamin popped out of his chair and opened a cabinet on the wall behind him. Inside, in a mirror-backed cubby where previous generations of businessmen might have kept a decanter of whiskey, were dozens of small glass tincture bottles, dropper bottles, pill bottles, plastic packets with labels that were all glossy white and green.

"These are my superfoods," Benjamin said. "Natural, organic, and—this is essential—one hundred percent *bioavailable*."

He picked up one of the bottles and unscrewed its dropper cap—"This is concentrated red algae"—then he squirted the maroon liquid into his mouth—"It's for oxidative stress"—then another bottle—"These are citrus bioflavonoids"—and another squirt into his mouth, then more bottles, more squirts—"This is pure camu camu"—"These are adaptogenic herbs"—"This is for drippy gut"—"This awakens the lymph"—"This is something I got from this Serbian guy and I don't even know what it is"—"This is turpentine, which is a great antiparasitic"—Benjamin gulped down all these shots, his cheeks meanwhile flushing first to a light rose pink, then to a glowing ruby. "That is, *wow*," he said, eyes wide, shaking his head. "That really opens you up."

"How much of that stuff are you supposed to take?"

"Supposed to? I don't know. I do all this intuitively. I just dose until it feels right. The body knows, man. Trust it."

Then he grabbed what looked like a test tube of something dark green. "This is liquid chlorophyll. It soaks up all the heavy metals in your body." He unstoppered the vial, made a motion to Jack like *Cheers!* and tipped it back, swallowed. "Plus it also—oh, man, that is, whoa, *strong*—it also improves focus."

"Ben, are we still talking about the Shipworks here?"

"Oh, right. Anyway, my point is that project financing works on roughly the same principles. Wherever there's risk, you find ways to soak it up. This little hiccup in Park Shore simply means I need to disperse the risk via new investors and/or find different investors whose risk tolerance is more, let's say, robust. But nothing to worry about, okay? It's under control."

"Okay, great, good to know."

"You leave it all to me. And Jack?"

"Yeah?"

"Seriously, practice some self-care. You look like shit."

On his way out of the building, Jack had to step around several songbirds, all lying terribly still on the sidewalk of Upper Wacker Drive.

It was a twenty-minute walk to his classroom on Michigan Avenue. He was teaching an Intro to American Art class that met at nine a.m. in a basement room that was often too dark and too warm, thus the biggest challenge was to keep everyone engaged enough that they wouldn't fall asleep. They were currently studying the epic landscapes of the Hudson River School, and the students' assignment for the day had been to go look at a particular Thomas Cole painting, *New England Scenery*, which was on display at the Art Institute. Jack was mentally reviewing his lecture notes—he was planning a talk today on the Hudson River School's dictum that all landscapes must be *beautiful*, *sublime*, and *picturesque*, explicating what each of those terms meant in context—when he reached the door of his classroom and found, waiting for him there, in a navy suit, carrying a briefcase, the university's CFO.

"Can I help you?" Jack said.

"I'm waiting for the teacher."

"That's me."

"Oh!" The CFO took a quick skeptical glance at Jack's tattoos. Then he smiled. "Great! Well, I assume you know who I am."

"Yes."

"I'm going around putting in a little face time, just getting some one-on-ones with our school's very valuable adjuncts."

"Okay."

"Specifically, I wanted to meet with those adjuncts who have the lowest scores, according to the Impact algorithm. The lowest impact scores in the whole school, to be frank. Out of everybody. And I wanted you to know: *I am on your side.*"

"Thanks."

"So I wanted to touch base regarding that score, and see how you plan to, you know, kick it on up there, at least into the range of acceptability."

"I'm working on it."

"Because those pictures of yours? As much as we might personally like them, they aren't making an impact in the wider world. To be perfectly frank."

"I'm aware."

"Have you thought about maybe switching mediums?"

"What?"

"Everyone's pivoting to video these days. It has much higher engagement."

"No, I haven't really thought about that."

"Well, I don't claim to understand art. But I do understand CRM."

"What's CRM?"

"Customer relationship management. We have CRM software packages that let us track our customers as they journey through our website. And you know what we've found?"

"By customers, do you mean students?"

"Plus their parents. And what we've found is that when they reach your faculty page, well, let's just say it has a higher-than-usual bounce rate."

"And this is something I need to correct?"

"Yes, and I have a thought, a suggestion. Call it a growth hack.

What I strongly recommend is for you to try a bunch of new things, like a big bunch of very different new things, artistically. Like really flood the zone."

"Do what?"

"Basically a shotgun strategy. You start posting like crazy. Any little thought that flits through your mind, any possible new artistic direction, you get it all online and then watch your analytics. Whatever people are clicking on, that's your path."

"So my art should be about what exactly?"

"Doesn't matter! The basic idea is that it's very hard to predict what people will engage with, but with the Impact algorithm it's easy to *reveal* it."

"Flood the zone."

"It's a technique invented by the Russians. They are so exquisitely, almost admirably, good at this kind of thing. Just a thought!"

"Thanks, I'll work on that."

"Anyway, I wanted to let you know that we're rooting for you, partner. Wouldn't want to have to let you go!"

And with a firm handshake and a slap on the shoulder, the CFO took his leave.

Jack entered the classroom, turned down the lights, flipped on the overhead projector. On the wall behind him there appeared the large image of today's lecture subject, *New England Scenery,* a pleasant and pastoral view of the White Mountains at sunset, a big leafy tree in the foreground, a church in the middle distance, little dots of life all over: a hunter in the woods, a horse-drawn carriage, dogs at play, a child staring at a tree. Jack looked at the painting and then out at his twenty-five students. He took a deep breath. He said: "If you think that artists are free to make whatever they want, you're wrong. Artists have to do what they're told."

A couple of curious looks from students, heads cocked, a few people glancing up from their phones.

"Take this picture here," Jack said, pointing to the landscape behind him. "This thing is such bullshit."

Which got everyone's attention. He continued: "Landscape artists were not free to simply find a thing they liked and paint it. They were not free to depict whatever they wanted. They had to construct a *view*. And who was the view for? The collectors. The benefactors. It was for the people with money."

Jack was aware that a note of bitterness had entered his voice, but he kept going. He explained to his students how the landscape artists they were studying did not paint what the world really looked like, but instead were told by the wealthy what the world *ought* to look like and then went searching for examples. Landscape artists, he said, were not painting the world as it was, because between the painter and the landscape was a school of thought about what a landscape should be. They saw the land through a lens of doctrine and dogma. Which required them to travel enormous distances to find appropriate subjects, vistas that overlooked a scene close to the ideal: something that evoked the beauty of God's creation but not the actual tangled mess of real unruly nature; something that triggered feelings of awe but not in a way that would make a rich art collector feel small or ignoble. Often, of course, the world did not cooperate, and so the painters would invent their own scenes, taking elements from a real landscape to establish a kind of local "truth" and then surrounding them with fabrications.

"Like, for example, you'll often see paintings of Kansas with big herds of bison and Native Americans on horseback. But the thing is? Those were mostly painted *after* the bison and the Native Americans were wiped out. It's just that, by then, the collectors back East had a thing for buffalo and Indians, a kind of fetish, and so the artists obliged."

He called up another slide, of two drawings, the lower one showing plain grasslands and hills and sky, the upper one showing those same hills but adorned with bushes and birds and roads and people, an image ornamented with palpable life.

"These were drawn in 1792 by a British priest who was trying to establish basic rules for landscape art," Jack said. "This priest declared that the landscape on the bottom was not picturesque and should not be depicted, while the landscape on the top was picturesque and should be emulated. And do you know why? Because the one on top looked like where he lived, and the one on the bottom didn't. That's it. It was simply more familiar to this one guy. But then this standard became universal, and pretty soon everyone's land-scapes had to look like that."

The students in this class were mostly freshmen and sophomores taking the course out of a desire to satisfy a humanities credit rather than any abiding interest in American art per se. They were all star-ing at him very quietly. Little bits of dust floated in front of the pro-jector and glittered.

Jack crossed his arms, shook his head. "First it was the church telling artists what to do, then it was the wealthy. And these days, apparently, that job is being taken up by algorithms."

The students were now totally confused, exchanging concerned glances with one another. Jack decided to end the lecture early. The students filed quickly out and soon Jack was alone in that dark room, staring at those two images: the landscape with adornment, and the landscape without. He studied the image on the bottom—the grassland with no details, no features, no ornamentation, no stuff—and he thought what he usually thought each time he saw it, which was that the picture looked exactly like home. The wide-open prairie where he grew up, it looked just like that drawing, like bare space, like emptiness.

Some things, he thought, were not worthy of depiction.

Just then, as if Kansas could sense that he was right now thinking about it, there came an update from the plains. His phone's buzz alerted him to it: Jack's father had posted, once again, something tediously long and furious. Jack sighed. He imagined the old man, leaning over an out-of-date PC in that lonely house, the windswept grass outside growing wildly untended, the angriest of all possible television news playing eighteen hours a day in the background, Jack's father digesting the worst garbage on the internet and typ-ing away whole afternoons in spasms of reflexive rage. Now it was a post about how illegal immigrants were bringing the Ebola virus into America, and, reading the diatribe, seeing immediately its many logical gaps and falsehoods and offensive misinformation, Jack now understood how he would be spending roughly the next hour: hunched over his own aging computer—the one the university bestowed upon its adjuncts—researching and googling, constructing an impenetrable and overwhelming rebuttal, bringing all his vast academic training to bear against his father, refuting point by idiotic point his father's most deficient thinking, hoping that this time, maybe, the man would finally really listen.

THE THING about a prairie is that it's easily mistaken for nothingness.

That's what travelers often say, at any rate—"There's nothing here!"—driving through the Flint Hills of east-central Kansas and seeing no towns, no trees, no houses, nothing at all to interrupt the horizon, just grass everywhere in every direction for what looks like a million miles. People see this landscape and what it looks like to them is *nothing*. It looks empty. It looks like what land looks like before something else is done to it.

A prairie does not have the grandeur of a mountain range, nor the austerity of a desert, nor the gothic mystery of a forest, nor the romance of the sea. A prairie is a *lawn*, and it's hard to have extravagant feelings about a lawn.

Jack has a theory about this, about why the prairie is a disrespected landscape, why when we see it, we don't really *see* it: it's because you can't capture a prairie in a picture. It is notoriously difficult to depict a prairie two-dimensionally. Even to the naked eye, it already looks flat—this despite the fact that walking the Flint Hills can be exhausting, that a landscape that seems level at a distance can take your breath away when you're actually trudging up it. It's a great foreshortening that fools the eye, an illusion you keep on seeing even after you know it's an illusion. And then if you try to paint it or photograph it, this already flat land is even further flattened. With nothing to provide perspective, a prairie, transposed onto a 2D plane, becomes almost abstract, a Rothko-like field of tan and green. Just pure color, disconnected from the physical world. Unlike the forests of the east or the mountains of the west, a prairie has no dimension, nothing in relief, very little visual drama, no contours for the light to sculpt, none of the things that create what we might traditionally call a *view*.

As an object of beauty to hang on your wall, in other words, a prairie is a tough sell.

Of the many landscape paintings at the Art Institute, only one depicts the prairie. (And this in Chicago, which used to *be* prairie.) The museum's collection is instead dominated by dazzling autumnal East Coast forests, most of them in New England except for a few at Niagara Falls, all courtesy of the Hudson River School. There's Winslow Homer's rocky Maine coastline, and the dunes of Long Island from William Merritt Chase, and George Inness's Catskills, and the sandy beaches of Nahant and Nantasket via Thomas Doughty and Emil Carlsen, and then the museum's enthusiasm seems to fly right over flyover country and land at Georgia O'Keeffe, her mesas and bright flowers and white skulls. There is but one Great Plains landscape on offer in the whole place; it's by Alvan Fisher, and it's called, appropriately, *The Prairie on Fire*.

Appropriate because we only really see the prairie when we're doing something to obliterate it.

It's a lecture Jack gives to his Intro to Art class, during the chapter on American landscapes, how painters educated in the European tradition saw the endless tallgrass prairie of the Midwest and literally did not know what to do with it. They had no training that might have prepared them to depict something so monolithic. They were accustomed to scenes with easy scope and dimension: trees in the middle distance for perspective, rivers and valleys that made for convenient vanishing points, mountains on the horizon as an anchoring weight, all of it evocatively defined in light and shadow. But what do you do with a tallgrass prairie, where the middle distance and the far distance and the near distance are all flat and featureless and identical?

What these artists did, mostly, was ignore it. They kept traveling west until they reached the Rockies and were rewarded with landscapes that matched their schooling, which is why, in the canon of American landscape art, the prairie is so underrepresented. It's not because the prairie wasn't beautiful—most of the painters acknowledged, in letters and diaries, that it was very pretty indeed—but rather that the prairie did not accord with the traditional standards of what was specifically beautiful in landscape art. These painters came looking for the things they knew how to depict—forests and mountains and beaches—and when they found none of these, they declared the landscape "empty."

They did not see what was there. Instead, they saw what wasn't.

Jack means it to be a lesson on the difference between reality and the representation of reality. Beauty, he tells his students, is a constructed, not intrinsic, condition. The things we think are beautiful are only the things that have been depicted beautifully. And if it's not depicted, it's not seen. It never enters the imagination. It becomes a *nothing*.

Which is why the west got Yellowstone, and the prairie got destroyed.

His students nod and take notes during this lecture. He hopes to sincerely blow their minds with it, but he knows they're mostly wondering if this material will be on the test.

Sometimes, after this lecture, Jack will seek out that painting, *The Prairie on Fire*, and he'll stand there for a while and study it once again. It's situated on the ground floor, in one of the museum's quieter galleries. Upstairs is the daily ruckus surrounding *American Gothic*, the loud laughing parade of museumgoers grabbing selfies with Grant Wood's famous farm duo. Jack finds that he does not have the patience required in that room, not anymore. It tends to annoy him, the photo-hungry crowd, probably because he remembers a time when taking photographs was prohibited, when the museum was church-quiet and populated mostly by people who wanted to linger in front of art and lengthily consider it. Jack was one of these people, and he remembers looking on *American Gothic* for the first time, uninterrupted, for like half an hour, so long that his back and legs grew weary. *Art fatigue*, he calls it now, that particular spinal ache that happens after one stands for long hours in a museum holding stiff poses of observation and scrutiny.

That first time he saw *American Gothic* in real life, he was surprised at how small it was—only about two feet wide, less than three feet tall. It seemed impossible that such great fame came from such a little thing. Looking at it up close, he found that it was both more complicated and more crude than he'd previously believed. The farmer's round eyeglasses, for example, were a little squished on one side, a little asymmetrical, neither of the circular lenses an actual perfect circle. And the prongs of his metal pitchfork weren't straight, the points unaligned. And what at a distance appeared to be texture in the farmer's overcoat turned out to be, upon close inspection, clumsy-looking scratches. But then other flourishes impressed: how the pattern in the woman's dress was doubled in miniature in the curtains of the house, how the brushstrokes used on the farmer's forehead were angled in such a way as to evoke the wrinkles of someone who often raised his eyebrows dubiously—a lifetime of rural skepticism rutted into his skin, conjured here by an expert fold of paint.

This kind of long and measured study is, today, impossible. Jack's concentration keeps getting interrupted by people taking photographs. The museum tried to discourage this practice at first, but by the time everyone had a camera on their cell phone and a personal gallery online, asking them not to take pictures was like raking back the ocean. There was just no way.

Jack remembered his studio art classes in college, his professors insisting that all photographable subjects had been photographed, that the genre was now exhausted, that there was nothing new under the sun to take a picture of. These teachers had not anticipated smartphones. They had not anticipated selfies. Turns out, the way to make a photo new is just to put your own face in it.

Now the museum encourages photos, and asks its patrons to promote the institution when they post their pictures online by using the relevant hashtags. And so *American Gothic* is now mobbed all day by selfie sticks and tour groups and parents asking their children to pose in front of the painting and mimic it. The last time Jack spent any time with *American Gothic*, six different couples asked him to take their photograph in the span of ten minutes. Eventually, he had to abandon the whole thing.

The Prairie on Fire is, mercifully, not a famous painting. It's on a quiet wall of a quiet room where the most famous residents are minor works by John Singer Sargent. It's not the kind of room that inspires selfies, and so Jack prefers this room to the crowds upstairs, even if this makes him feel like a curmudgeonly old man not so dissimilar to the farmer in *American Gothic*—an antique character that people tend to prefer in a picture than in real life.

In *The Prairie on Fire,* the artist has solved the problem of portraying the prairie by, once again, avoiding it. It's a nighttime scene, so the otherwise tricky landscape is blackened and blotted out, save for the immediate foreground, where a group of travelers is being led through the tallgrass. In the distance, on the horizon, colossal fires burn. The smoke ascends into the air in great glowing swells of red and orange. The travelers look terrified. Even their horses look terrified. The fires are coming for them. They are in peril.

The painting is based on a scene from a James Fenimore Cooper novel that Jack has not read. There's something about a New York writer and a Boston painter attempting to depict the Midwest that seriously grates. It's a scene from the Kansas prairie painted by someone who had never been to Kansas, based on a novel by a writer who had also never been to Kansas, and Jack finds he resents it. It's similar to the resentment he felt years ago when city hipsters began ironically wearing the same John Deere hat that his own father actually, sincerely, wore: Jack was like, *Fuck you.* He's weirdly protective of the rural Midwest, even though, as a young man, he tried very hard to escape it.

"There's nothing dangerous about a prairie fire," Jack's father would say those years he was still setting them. "Not if you're careful."

Lawrence Baker was always careful. The burns he led each spring were famous among the local ranchers for their precision and control; he could set fire to a thousand acres of rangeland and not ignite a single unintended blade of grass. His burns were elegant, orchestrated things, and he was in demand all over the Flint Hills, contracted by ranchers as far south as Osage County and as far north as Pottawatomie. He visited their land each spring and set their hills ablaze.

"Fire in a prairie is like rain in a rainforest," he would tell Jack each April before leaving to go work the monthlong prescribed burn season. And Jack would know his father had begun his task when he smelled the cinders on the air, when he could see, at night, in the far distance, a faint orange glow.

In the years that the weather was cooperative, the burn season unfolded in an orderly, leisurely way. But other years were more challenging: if a prairie burn was to be reliably controlled, the grass had to be of a particular moisture, the wind below a threshold velocity, and those years when the Kansas springtime was dry and the air churned violent and swift, there might be only one day in twenty that was ideal, when conditions weren't hazardous, when it was finally safe for burning. And on those days, the Flint Hills felt like Pompeii. Every local rancher burned on the same day, and Jack would watch from his upstairs bedroom through glass that would slowly occlude with ash as the world was set on fire: the sky was a thick particulate fog, the ground was slowly blanketed as if by a blizzard, there was a charred smell in the house even though all windows were closed, and Jack would sit looking out at the gray plumes that rose across the horizon like the fingers of skyscrapers in a great American city.

It confused him, as a child, that before all the cattle came for their summer grazing, the grass would be burned away. It worried him, these scorched fields now devoid of the only cash crop this land had to offer: grass. Most of the ranchers in the Flint Hills did not themselves own cattle. Rather, they owned the calories the cattle feasted upon—the bluestem grass and Indian grass and switchgrass of the prairie, stuff so nutritious and dense that a yearling could gain four pounds a day eating it. And so the cattle came from all over, a million head every summer, shipped in eighteen-wheelers from Tennessee and Oklahoma and Texas and Mexico, to gorge on the tallgrass prairie of the Flint Hills for around ninety days before being shipped to the feedlots in late summer, and to the slaughterhouses sometime thereafter.

For the ranchers of the Flint Hills, cattle were machines that turned grass into money. And since these ranchers' livelihoods were based on how much weight the cattle gained over their summer grazing season, it was pretty important that their food source be as healthy and rich as possible. And it turned out that prairie grass was at its most deliciously healthful immediately following a fire.

And so it was that each spring, the old grass and thatch and thicket were burned away, and, like clockwork, exactly two weeks after a fire, the new shoots appeared, and the grass grew like crazy. In the span of just a few days, a blackened, sooty hillside became an efflorescence of vibrant, vivid green.

This happens at scale only in the Flint Hills, the last large tract of tallgrass prairie in America. At one point, this prairie covered the nation—north to Canada and south to Texas, west to the Rockies and east to Chicago. But the soil that proved so nourishing for grass and cattle also made it perfect for corn and wheat, and so the tallgrass prairie was slowly plowed over and replaced by crops—all of it, the entire continental expanse, everywhere, except for here, the Flint Hills of Kansas, the only large prairie in the country not converted to farmland because the plow could not penetrate this dense ground. The problem was the rock, the chert that gave this place its name. Stick a shovel in the ground anywhere in the Flint Hills uplands and you'll find, basically, gravel.

Jack tries to imagine what America's prairie looked like before the farms came: swells of grass rising above his head, swaying and rocking in the unstoppable summer wind, the same view in every direction, a perfectly straight and uninterrupted horizon. All of it, now gone. He wonders if this is also why travelers through the Flint Hills look around and see nothing, if maybe we call something "nothing" to avoid the knowledge that it's been lost.

But the prairie is not nothing. It is not empty. It is full. It is teeming. "There's more life in one cubic meter of Kansas tallgrass prairie than there is in the same amount of Brazilian rain forest," Lawrence would say. And he could see all of it, the land's covert citizens, the lichen and shrubs and grouse and wildflowers and hawks and sparrows and sandpipers and snakes and mice all thriving atop the ashes. He'd take Jack on long hikes that were like biology classes and history classes and chemistry classes all at once. He'd run his hand over the tassels of bluestem grass and then explain how the species was able to grow so tall here—because its fine roots could slip through tiny cracks in the rock layer and grow twenty feet down, all the way to the water table. He'd take a fingernail to the rocks sitting out, all over, on the sides of hills, ridges flecked with these white-blond boulders—"Nature's dandruff," he called them—rock that would scratch away at his touch. "It's limestone," he'd say, and he'd talk about how the Flint Hills used to be an inland sea, how they were right now standing on an ancient seafloor, where sometimes one could even find the imprint of a shell right there in the rock. That's why the hills here were so gentle: they had once been squashed by the weight of an ocean. He'd break off a chip of limestone and put it into a cup of vinegar back at home and together they'd watch it bubble.

He knew the names of everything, even the things that had more than one name. "That there is redroot," he said, pointing at a small shrub, three feet tall, one that dotted the hills and bloomed one year after a burn. It had white flowers that grew in tight, round bunches— "Your sister calls it wild snowball," his father said, and Jack smiled. Evelyn always had a way of making things a little more enchanting. "And during the Revolutionary War," Lawrence said, "when tea was hard to come by, the colonists steeped it in water. You can boil the flowers and the roots. That's why some folks call it New Jersey tea."

He was something of an amateur historian, naturalist, ecologist. He walked Jack to the edge of a little stream bordering their property, where elms and cottonwoods grew on the banks near the water, and he crouched down in front of what looked to Jack like a small brown branchless stick jammed vertically into the ground.

"That's a baby elm," his father said. "It's in the ecotone."

"In the what?"

"Ecotone. It means an in-between spot. Eco, like ecosystem. And tone, from *tonos*. That's Greek. It means 'tension.' So it's like the tension between ecosystems, you understand? The overlap between two worlds. Two worlds in conflict with each other. You see all that land behind us?" He pointed a thumb back at the soft rolling grassy hills. "That land wants to be prairie. But this here land in front of us, it wants to be forest. And this spot, this is where the prairie and the forest are fighting. And this little guy"—he brushed the baby elm gently with a finger—"he's the advance guard. There's a slow-motion war happening right here, Jack, beneath our feet, on a scale we can't even imagine."

Sometimes one of those expeditionary trees would take root far away from its cousins, way out among the grasses, unprotected by the windbreak made by the other trees, exposed to the near-constant southerly wind that blew vigorously across Kansas for much of the year. And if this tree were allowed to grow, it would grow up crooked, pushed so intently by the air that it eventually bent, and it would stay like that, even on the calmest days.

But these were rare, these windswept trees of the prairie. They were usually consumed by the annual burns long before they could grow too tall. It was fire that, over the many eons, had always kept the forests at bay.

"There's nothing unnatural about a prairie fire," Lawrence Baker used to say, "nothing unusual at all." And that was true until, one year, it wasn't. A spring burn in 1984, when Jack was nine years old, during a dry and cloudless April when the hot southern winds would not relent, the year Lawrence lit his last fire.

This is what Jack thinks about these afternoons he spends in that quiet corner at the museum, looking at this painting, *The Prairie on Fire,* studying the expressions of those travelers as they eye the approaching flames, their terrified faces full of panic and doom.

Paintings of the prairie aren't often accurate. But this one, Jack thinks, this one, unfortunately, is true.

THE HOUSE OF AT LEAST FOURTEEN GABLES

It is a fact that, in his later years, Alvin Augustine would boast to anyone willing to listen that the great Augustine fortune had come not from luck or providence but rather from his own toil and perseverance and personal ingenuity and inner vision and talent and pluck. However, most of his contemporaries—even those who happily joined him at the Gables for weekend galas or fox hunts—would have agreed that the Augustine fortune owed its existence in large part to the accidental and random convergence of three seemingly unrelated things: the church, the Civil War, and sweetened condensed milk.

As for the church: there are very few extant records referring to Alvin Augustine before 1858. In fact, there is but one, a single line in a church ledger written by a Greenwich Presbyterian minister indicating the transfer of land to one A. Augustine. The land in question was a narrow, one-hundred-acre tract south of Litchfield in the Shepaug River valley that was so densely wooded and rocky and mountainous and generally unnavigable that the land was literally useless: too forested for farming, too landlocked for a sawmill, too hilly for roads. It was given to Alvin (or perhaps sold at a remarkable discount; the records are unclear) during a time when the church was encouraging its parishioners to go forth into the still-wild portions of New England and tame them, a philosophical holdover from Puritan days when the woods were considered dark and uncivilized and godless, and so the cutting down of trees to make way for towns—with churches at their centers, naturally—served as a sort of proxy war against Satan himself.

Alvin's enthusiasm for engaging in this spiritual battle seemed only strong enough for him to remove the trees strictly necessary to erect a cabin, and no more. He built himself a one-room house deep in the woods south of Litchfield, after which he ceased all forestry operations and basically disappeared. This must have come as a bit of a shock to the townspeople, as Alvin's father was a respected writer, a well-known teacher, a staunch Calvinist; everyone had expected great things from the son. Alvin's father was Connecticut's leading scholar on the subject of Nathaniel Hawthorne—he had gone to Bowdoin with Hawthorne, become friends with Hawthorne, was still in contact with Hawthorne, and traveled regularly to New Haven to give lectures on Hawthorne. Alvin, meanwhile, had never really taken to fiction, nor reading, nor, for that matter, school, often claiming he was smart in ways you couldn't learn from books, which never failed to trigger a skeptical snort from Dad.

Alone in the woods in his little cabin, Alvin apparently commenced a slow decline into drink, which either had been his plan all along—to find a nice, quiet, out-of-the-way place where he would be free to do as he pleased without the sobriety-inducing stares of neighbors or the gossip endemic to the temperance hothouse that was rural western Connecticut—or was proof that the church's position regarding the forest's relationship with Satan and vice was, essentially, correct. And it might have been that Alvin was headed to an early and wet grave, because the first time he reappears in any records is at a bar: the Hem & Haw Tavern in Litchfield, where Alvin—by virtue of being at the right place at the right time—apparently found his way into a demonstration by one Gail Borden, a Texan who had recently invented a process by which he could condense milk and put it in a can, where it would never go bad. Borden had moved from Texas to the comparatively dairy-rich state of Connecticut to produce this new milk, which, he claimed, would change the world.

Keep in mind that these were the days before refrigeration, and so milk would routinely go bad in only a day or two. Sending it over long distances was impossible; steamships would have to bring their own cows to supply milk to passengers, but of course the cows, having no real evolutionary equipment with which to deal with the bobbing of water, would typically get outstandingly seasick, whereby their milk production would wane and then abruptly stop. So unspoilable milk in a can was, indeed, a million-dollar idea.

The problem was that nobody trusted poor Gail Borden, who'd spent nearly all his money on another food-preservation venture, the dubious Borden's Meat Biscuit, a sort of portable desiccated gluey beef loaf. Allegedly the only thing worse than how a Borden's Meat Biscuit looked was how it tasted, and so nobody had any interest whatsoever in trying out Borden's newest concoction, this thick and sort of ejaculate-yellow milk-syrup sludge. And even those present that night at the Hem & Haw Tavern who could be persuaded to taste it—who had to admit that yeah, okay, not bad—could not be convinced to invest in Borden's idea because why would they buy condensed milk when the taste of actual milk was so thoroughly superior? Who would willingly drink this when they could just as easily drink milk?

Alvin Augustine would later say that all these people lacked imagination, that they possessed only the very limited vision to understand what condensed milk tasted like to other people like them: other rich New England gentlemen. But Alvin, perhaps owing to his more hardscrabble life in the woods, could imagine what this milk would taste like to people who were not among the investor class, people who could not routinely afford fresh milk, people who had no easy access to the modern conveniences of the nation. Did America have many of these poor, deprived, out-of-the-way people? It was about to. For a war was afoot, *the* war, the great Civil War, and soon whole armies would be traveling south, and these armies would need to be supplied.

They would need, among other things, milk.

Milk that could survive a weeklong journey through the scorching hot South.

Alvin imagined what this condensed milk would taste like to a poor infantryman in godforsaken buggy and humid South Carolina. It would taste, Alvin decided, like deliverance.

None of the other men in the tavern that night thought this way, which was why, despite the great idea, Borden had managed to attract only a few investors, and had recently set up a factory in the only place he could afford to: middle-of-nowhere western Connecticut. And it turned out that Alvin Augustine owned the dense, rocky, useless forest immediately south of this new factory.

He did not have any money to invest in Borden's Condensed Milk, but he did have this sorry piece of land in the Shepaug River valley, and maybe lesser men—men without Alvin's creativity and vision, he would later say—would have simply sold the land for a modest sum and moved along. But Alvin Augustine did not do that. Instead, he offered Borden a deal: Borden could use Alvin's land for a rail line, and he could use it for free, in perpetuity, never paying any rent or fees, could rip up the land to construct a new railroad corridor that would connect his factory to the big Housatonic line in Hawleyville, which would then take his condensed-milk product, with speed, to all points south. Alvin's only stipulation, the only thing he required in exchange for letting construction crews do pretty much whatever they wanted to his land, was that the railroad that eventually ran on this line purchase the fuel for its steam engines—which, at that time, was lumber, in vast quantities—exclusively from the newly incorporated Augustine Railroad Supply Corp, whose only employee was Alvin, and whose only material asset was an axe.

And since Borden was in desperate need of shipping options, and since accepting Alvin's offer was substantially cheaper than buying the land outright, and since the railway would have to purchase its fuel from someone anyway, this all seemed like your classic winwin. A deal was made, and construction of the new Shepaug Rail Line began posthaste.

The prospect of wealth turned out to be a far better motivation for Alvin than the prospect of everlasting Christian salvation had ever been, and he went to work with great vigor, chopping down his trees and splitting them into logs small enough to fit into a locomotive's firebox. But this was slow and painful work, and as construction continued on the new rail line, it became clear that he would have only a few cords of firewood ready by the time the railroad was operational. So, blister-handed and aching, he traveled to Hartford and met with various banks' loan officers, who, being bankers, liked nothing more than a risk-free investment and so just loved Alvin's letter of guarantee from the railroad. They promptly agreed to accept Alvin's land as collateral in exchange for the cash he needed to hire a big expert crew of log cutters, who brought down the forest so fast it made the local clergy pretty proud.

Alvin's prediction was, of course, correct: the Civil War began in 1861, and soldiers in the field adored Borden's invention so much that Washington soon made sweetened condensed milk a required ration for every soldier in the Union army. Further, rumor had it that Confederate troops were stopping supply trains and robbing them of their condensed milk, meaning that this one small factory in Litchfield was supplying milk for two full armies, not to mention the fashionable restaurants of New York and DC, who were experimenting with Borden's concoction in cocktails and baked goods. In other words, demand for sweetened condensed milk was outrageous, and the only way to get it to the people who wanted it was via the brand-new Shepaug Rail Line, and each run of the Shepaug Line was fueled by timber provided by Alvin Augustine. And since Alvin knew that governments tended to have pretty deep pockets in times of war, and because Alvin's agreement with the railroad required it to purchase firewood from him *but did not explicitly set a price for that firewood,* Alvin charged an exorbitant and literally laugh-inducing sum for the wood, roughly twenty times fair market value. The accountant for the new Shepaug Line reported having a nice chuckle when he received his first bill from the Augustine Railroad Supply Corp, figuring that the ridiculous number at the bottom of the bill was an addition error and that the yokel who sent it must have been a little, let's say, math-challenged.

But it was not an error, Alvin insisted, and he invited the accountant to inspect their contract and pay up, which the railroad eventually did after much grumbling about a "gentleman's agreement" and "fair market prices" and "war profiteering" and so on. But there was nothing the railroad could do but hold its nose and pay Alvin what he billed because it was cheaper than moving the factory, and anyway they knew they wouldn't have to put up with Alvin for very long: there was only so much lumber a hundred acres could produce.

Alvin knew this as well. He was not, in fact, math-challenged. He was quite aware that your typical eight-wheel steam locomotive running at ten miles an hour—which was as fast as the tortuous Shepaug Line allowed—burned roughly twelve pounds of wood per mile, needing around four hundred pounds of wood to make the trip from Litchfield to Hawleyville, which was only about seventeen miles as the crow flies but needed about thirty-four miles of track to wind its way around the cliffs and buttes and valleys and other topographical challenges that made the trip a little nausea-inducing for the train's more delicate passengers.

And since it was necessary to make two round-trip runs per day, the line thus had a fuel requirement of right around sixteen hundred daily pounds of wood, which, given that your typical cord of dried red maple will weigh somewhere between thirty-five hundred and thirty-eight hundred pounds, meant that the Shepaug Line needed about half a cord every day. And since it was conventional wisdom that one acre of forest produced roughly one cord of firewood, it was pretty easy to calculate that Alvin's entire personal forest would be depleted in roughly two hundred days. A little more than six months. That's all the time he had to implement part two of what was increasingly looking like a kind of master plan, which involved finding all the other nearby owners of equally dense and rocky and wooded and worthless land and offering them the same deal that the banks in Hartford had given Alvin: namely, that Alvin would provide the landowners everything necessary to clear their land of its timber, holding their land in the meantime as collateral and allowing them to buy it back from him using their portion of the timber profits, which would be split fifty-fifty. And sure, the deal smelled a little odd to some of the landowners—why the need for collateral? why not simply come in and cut?—but Alvin insisted that this was just how it had to happen, paperworkwise, in order for his railroad supply company to technically, quote, unquote, "own" the wood and therefore mandate the Shepaug Line's buying of it. And he'd shake his head and frown at all the stupid unnecessary bureaucracy in Hartford in a way that made these guys—who were all, of course, isolated loners with a sort of libertarian suspicion of government—immediately trust him.

And indeed it seemed like a pretty good deal, that with minimal labor on their part, their property would be quickly transformed from worthless woods into valuable farmland. So they signed on varying dotted lines and more log-cutting crews were hired to clear out land as far west as the state line and as far north as Norfolk.

In the end, Alvin Augustine was responsible for the deforestation of pretty much all of western Connecticut, and at the same time he became the state's biggest land magnate, because after each parcel of woods had been fully cleared and the respective landowners came for their payment, Alvin paid them what had been specifically, clearly spelled out in the contract, which was 50 percent of the timber's "fair market value"—he had not told the landowners about the extraordinary markup he was levying on the Shepaug Line, an obligation that was exactly high enough to keep the railroad just barely solvent—and when the landowners then offered that cash to Alvin to purchase their property back from him, they were informed that they would need way, way more money than that, since the land was now being appraised at ten times what it was previously worth, owing to all the improvements that he, Alvin, had made to it. And so he gave them each ninety days to come up with the balance—which these people universally could not do—before serving eviction notices to all of them. Several of the landowners—or, rather, the shockingly now *former* landowners—took Alvin to court over this, and while the contracts stood up to legal scrutiny each time, more than one judge used the same word to describe Alvin Augustine: he was, they said, a *swindler*.

Eventually Gail Borden, who hated Alvin with an abiding and consuming passion, opened new factories closer to major shipping routes. And eventually steam locomotives stopped using wood for fuel and turned instead to bituminous coal. And eventually word got out about the swindle Alvin had pulled on the collective landowners and forests of New England, and so nobody trusted him enough to do a dime of business with the Augustine Railroad Supply

Corp ever again. But it was no matter: Alvin Augustine became one of the wealthiest men in western Connecticut, making millions in the rail and real estate and food industries even though he had basically no expertise in any of them. In his memoir, Gail Borden called the Shepaug Line the "crookedest rail line in New England, and not just because of the curves."

Alvin retired to that original tract of land he'd received from the church, south of Litchfield, where he built an outrageous house that would be both a monument to himself and a stick in the eye of his disapproving father, who could never hope to achieve such extravagant wealth in the field of Hawthorne studies. Alvin knew that his father's favorite novel was *The House of Seven Gables*, and even though Alvin had not read this novel, and even though he did not know exactly what a gable was, he knew for sure that he wanted to upstage and demoralize his father, and he would do so with a house that was at least twice as good as the house in that stupid book. So when the architect asked him his requirements for this grand new home, Alvin had but one: "I want at least fourteen gables."

EVERETT AUGUSTINE, 1870–1950

The eldest child of Alvin Augustine, Everett was, by all accounts, an anxious and lonely and fatalistic man. His weak constitution could perhaps be explained by the combination of his father's high expectations of him and the impossibility of meeting those expectations, due mostly to his father's own reputation. By the time Everett came of age and began searching in earnest for a career, he found that his father's swindles meant that most career paths were unavailable to him, or to anyone whose last name was Augustine: he could not go into the railroad industry, nor the food industry, nor real estate, banking, law, politics, even shipping. This of course did not stop the elder Augustine from complaining about his son's "indolence" and "poverty of vision" and "lack of mercantile instinct," which criticism perhaps caused Everett to foolhardily rush into a series of what turned out to be horribly misguided business ventures in what were maybe desperate attempts to earn his father's approval.

The first of these failures involved a substantial investment in cotton in early 1893, when Everett was in his early twenties and the recent recipient of a large sum of what his father called "seed money" that Everett was meant to substantially grow. Cotton prices had, at that time, been unstable and wildly fluctuating when Everett came across an offer to buy a warehouse full of what was advertised as *Luxurious Cotton Fabric Woven by Hand*, many hundreds of bolts of the softest white cotton muslin, many thousands of yards that Everett could imagine being used for couture gowns or wedding dresses, all of it now available in Atlanta at a deep discount—roughly 30 percent off recent highs. And based solely on one piece of advice he had received from a school pal who'd gone to work on Wall Street—that the secret to success in investing is to "buy the dips"—Everett decided to purchase the lot. Of course, he could have just as easily purchased cotton stocks or cotton futures if he'd really wanted to get into the cotton game, but instead he bought actual real physical cotton, because his father had always said that the wealth of the world was in material things: wood, land, real stuff you could put your hands on rather than abstract, fictional, made-up constructs like stocks and futures and even money. (Alvin had gotten a little paranoid in his later years about the legitimacy of paper money—this even before the country abandoned the gold standard—and believed that the banks and the government were together out to swindle him, and he believed this with a passion and a rage that seemed all out of proportion to the actual, on-the-ground facts.)

If Everett had done just a little research, he might have known that cotton prices were fluctuating due to a few unrelated but disastrous systemic developments—agricultural crop yield advances that had increased cotton production in the nation's south and heartland by an order of magnitude, plus the opening of trade barriers that brought in high-quality cotton from Egypt and India—both of which saturated the market and eventually cratered the value of cotton products. Further, the wild market fluctuations of early 1893 reached their conclusion later that year in a full-blown depression that was called the Panic, an almost decade-long period of stagnation and hardship that further served to weaken the prices of many retail staples, including, yes, cotton.

Plus it turned out, thanks to the tireless and noble efforts of the women in the ambiguously named League for the Protection of the Family, who at that time were advocating for the end of child labor in textile factories and mines, that the particular bolts of cotton muslin that Everett had purchased at what turned out to be a not-all-that-great discount had in fact been made by a whole sweatshop of impoverished, criminally underpaid, and prepubescent children, which meant that his warehouse of *Luxurious Cotton Fabric Woven by* (tiny) *Hand* would never be off-loadable to the fashion houses or theaters or even the burgeoning Hollywood costume designer scene, since none of them wanted anything to do with fabric tainted by the toxic whiff of forced Southern child labor.

So the warehouse and the cotton sat there on the books, losing money, Everett paying the rent each month while suffering his father's scorn and searching for other possible avenues to wealth. He thought he'd found one a few years later in the form of a brand-new health-sustaining miracle powder called Plasmon, made from the ground-up bits of dried milk albumen, one teaspoon of which was, allegedly, sixteen times more nutritious than a whole beefsteak while costing only pennies per serving. It was an invention that could solve world hunger, or so claimed the company's acting president and biggest investor, one Mark Twain, who'd written, with his usual wit, a glowing testimonial for Plasmon in which he said that when one ingests Plasmon, "the stomach will praise God and do the rest." The milk powder excited Everett, perhaps due to his father's milk-related success—it represented a kind of generational symmetry that likely pleased the younger Augustine, who worried constantly about measuring up. He was also likely seduced by celebrity, and entertained daydreams of bringing America's greatest writer to the Connecticut estate for a weekend of frivolity and pond-swimming, which would have done much to impress his father, who kept very careful records of each of the house's esteemed guests. And so Everett took his father's second round of seed money and invested it in this Mark Twain–approved milk powder, which was meant to be stirred into soup or oatmeal or cocoa as a kind of medicine: all the benefits of milk but without the fat. Plasmon had the consistency of something like talc and really needed to be stirred into other foods because on its own it was bitter and chalky and just completely unpalatable, which was probably why the company shortly thereafter went bankrupt and insolvent, and Everett Augustine lost his entire investment.

When he was given his third round of seed money, Everett was told by his father in no uncertain terms that this would be the very last, the very final bit of assistance and patronage Everett would ever receive for what Alvin called a doomed enterprise: the making of something that was at all financially viable, which was, Alvin saucily added, something perhaps better carried out by any of Everett's cousins, or even the kitchen staff.

And so Everett—who was by now feeling pretty thoroughly risk-averse—was on the lookout for an investment that was more of a sure thing, which he thought he'd found in the form of a Brooklyn financial services firm called the Franklin Syndicate, whose president claimed to have inside information about certain Wall Street stocks that enabled him to manipulate the market at will. This man was so confident in his moneymaking ability that not only did he guarantee an amazing 10 percent return *per week*, but he also guaranteed against the loss of the initial investment. In other words, it would be literally impossible for Everett to squander this final round of Augustine funding, which was music to his gun-shy ears.

Still, he started small: he made a one-hundred-dollar deposit, and when he returned to the Syndicate's Brooklyn offices a week later, sure enough, there were his earnings in the form of a crisp new ten-dollar note, waiting for him. And now he had a choice: he could either pocket the ten bucks or reinvest them with the fund. If he did the latter, then the return the following week would be slightly larger. Which indeed it was: eleven dollars, which he reinvested. The following week, he duly swept the resulting twelve dollars back into the account and collected, like clockwork, his thirteen dollars the next week. And so on. Some quick back-of-the-napkin math showed that any investment in the Syndicate would have a 520-percent return in only one year, which was why each time Everett visited the Syndicate's Brooklyn office, the lines at both the "deposits" and the "returns" windows were longer and longer: the word was out. And so, satisfied with the operation, Everett went ahead and invested the rest of his father's seed money, whereby the Syndicate offered him a 5 percent commission on any new investments he could send their way, and so he became a sort of full-time mouthpiece for the Syndicate, convincing friends and relations to buy into the outfit, collecting his commissions, and sweeping them into his portfolio, which, according to his receipts, was steadily growing so large that Everett realized he would outearn his own father in just a few years, a fact he delighted in telling the old man—who had bullheadedly refused to invest with the Syndicate—at family dinners.

Later, at the trial, it would come out that the Syndicate had never actually made a single penny from any of its customers' investments, and that when Everett collected that first ten-dollar return, it wasn't ten *new* dollars that the Syndicate had made but rather ten dollars from his original hundred. Same thing the next week, and the next. His investment's bottom line never actually changed, despite the Syndicate's wild claims about its growth. This is the kind of swindle that works really well provided nobody ever wants to withdraw their entire investment, which some people had begun to do, triggering the Syndicate's collapse. It was a con known as a pyramid scheme for a few years, until an Italian immigrant, who had an interest in international reply coupons and whose name was Charles Ponzi, sort of perfected it.

The president of the Syndicate went to prison, though none of his investors ever got their money back. And thus began what was, by all accounts, for Everett, a dark and lingering depression. He holed himself up on the fourth floor of the house, taking his meals alone and spending his days listening to vaudeville on the phonograph and, later, watching motion pictures. It was his interest in the movies that eventually inspired him to finally leave the house again, when a film director named David Griffith came to visit at Alvin's request. The invitation was sent not because Everett was a burgeoning film buff—Alvin had long since stopped caring about his failure of a son and his copious unprofitable hobbies—but because this particular moviemaker had recently become both rich and famous for a film that was currently sweeping the nation, a film that was the first-ever motion picture to be shown at the White House (apparently to a great review from the president himself), and Alvin tended to enjoy collecting people like that and adding their names to his home's walls. The film in question was called *The Birth of a Nation,* and showed a genteel post–Civil War South overrun with dangerous and crazy freed slaves, and in the climactic scene where one of these former slaves is just about to have his brutal way with the film's beautiful white heroine, in rushes, like the cavalry, a team of horsebacked Klansmen, all dressed in bright white robes and white pointy hats, to heroically save the day.

After the film, Alvin, who by this time was quite elderly and infirm, managed to stand all the way up and clapped and yelled, "Wonderful! Wonderful!" And the film's director told them that his movie had inspired a real resurrection of the Ku Klux Klan, which, the director was sure to add, was a softer and gentler version of the KKK than the one that had appeared in the Reconstruction South, more like a fraternal club, he said, like the Masons but with a slightly more focused mandate, which was the protection of real Americans and the American way of life from those outsiders who threatened it, namely Jews, Catholics, recent immigrants, ungrateful Blacks, and urban cosmopolitans. There were, the director said, already hundreds of local KKK chapters popping up all over the country, and they were mostly, and surprisingly, outside the South, concentrated in places like the upper Midwest and upstate New York and rural Pennsylvania, where the Klan's new motto, "100% American!" found a surprisingly receptive audience. The whole thing was becoming a real professional organization with real political power and a real official headquarters in Georgia, at which point Everett, usually pretty shy and ashamed in any gathering of successful men, suddenly spoke up, and asked what must have seemed to those in the room like a real non sequitur: "What's with the robes?"

And the director admitted that, yes, the original 1860s Klan wore no such getup, and that the whole white-robes-with-a-pointy-hat thing had been invented by the film's art and costume teams because, first, they needed some visual clue to let the audience know the Klansmen were heroes, and second, those particular costumes just looked really awesome on his grainy black-and-white film stock.

Everett then shocked the family by leaving the very next day for Georgia, where he met with the president—or, as he called himself, the Grand Wizard—of this new KKK and got a look at its Atlanta headquarters and organizational structure, which basically involved commission-based salesmen (called Kleagles) signing up new members (called Ghouls) who paid initiation fees that were then split by regional managers (called King Kleagles) and state-level managers (called Grand Dragons) and national operations managers (called Great Goblins), all of whom had further financial incentives to sign up still more members, and all of this was sounding—despite the dumb titles—pretty familiar to poor Everett, who had an intimate knowledge of pyramid schemes and was eager to finally be on the other side of the action. So he told this Grand Wizard, "I can help you," and when asked to explain, said: "You're gonna need robes."

The white robes and pointy hats from the film. Everett predicted that all of the Klan's new members would demand to dress up like the heroes from the blockbuster movie that had inspired their movement. And it just so happened that he, Everett, had, right here in Atlanta, a whole warehouse full of the highest-quality white cotton muslin.

And so Everett founded the Kavalry Klothing Korp and became the official clothier of the KKK, which, during its heyday between 1920 and 1928, was pretty lucrative indeed.

CORNELIUS AUGUSTINE, 1926–1980

There was really no way for Cornelius to win. The eldest son of Everett Augustine understood before he'd even reached the age of eighteen that he couldn't rely on his family's good name to survive in the world. Not when his grandfather's swindles still lingered in living memory, and definitely not when his own father had mass-produced the KKK's terrifying costumes. Which was why even after the Klan's membership collapsed around 1928 and Everett rebranded the Kavalry Klothing Korp (a rather unimaginative rebrand, in Cornelius's opinion, where his father simply turned all the Ks into Cs), he could find no willing customers. But it was no matter. Everett had made so much money during his Klan-affiliated years—and, conveniently, had kept it all as cash rather than investing it in the market, owing probably to his past investing-related traumas, and so had no money to lose when the market crashed in 1929—that he took an early retirement and waited out the Depression at the Gables, watching movies.

When Cornelius turned eighteen in 1944, in an effort to either improve the family name or join the one organization that didn't much care about the Augustines' tainted legacy, he enlisted in the military. The Marines. He saw some action the following year in Guam and Guadalcanal before he and the rest of the Second Division were loaded up and sent to Saipan, where they were given a few immunizations and a short course on the Japanese language. This clued them in about where they were likely headed next, sending a collective shiver down the spine of the Second Division because it was a well-known statistic that any direct frontal attack on the Japanese mainland would suffer an approximately 92 percent casualty rate, making the previous year's assault on Omaha Beach look, in comparison, like a day at the actual beach. And so it was with a complicated and yet profound sense of gratitude that they landed in Japan to discover that the United States had, days earlier, deployed atom bombs to annihilate two Japanese cities, and that the Japanese Empire had quickly surrendered, and that they would not be assaulting Japan but rather peacefully occupying it—it was as if the Marines of the Second Division had been simultaneously given the greatest full-body massage of all time, for how much their tension and stress and anxiety just all at once melted away. Cornelius's company landed near Nagasaki, one of the two cities to have been bombed, though from his vantage it was hard to tell anything was amiss other than a harrowing, eerie silence that hung in the air. Nagasaki is a city of valleys, and the bomb had been dropped on—and the damage mostly contained to—one of the inner valleys. Some of the guys on reconnaissance duty reported total and mind-fucking devastation—wastelands of debris and ash, skeletons lying in open fields—but for Cornelius, stationed back at the harbor, the deployment was a relatively easy and boring one. His job was to patrol the docks, which he did, quietly and lonesomely. For the first few days of this, he didn't see a soul. None of the locals had any interest in having any interaction whatsoever with the occupiers, owing of course to pretty reasonable bomb-related resentment, and also to the government's yearslong propaganda campaign that promised that any Americans who came ashore would immediately and viciously rape and kill them.

Cornelius didn't even see an actual Japanese person for a full week, not before an old gray-haired man, dressed in what looked to be very nice and very fancy clothes and not at all what Cornelius expected from, like, a war refugee, slowly and carefully approached Cornelius and said what sounded like either "Me Zoo" or "Me Shoe." Then the man pointed at his own chest, at a necklace he wore, a leather strap on which hung what looked to be a thick gold coin stamped with something foreign and incomprehensible—Cornelius figured it was some kind of family crest or seal or something, because the man pointed at it again and again said what Cornelius decided was "Me Shoe."

And so Cornelius pointed at his own chest and said, "Me Cornelius," and he felt kind of proud to be doing this, peacemaking, establishing friendly relations with recently bitter enemies.

The next day there was another man, a different man but dressed equally well with a similar gold coin around his neck, who pointed at it and said, "Me Shoe."

"Me Cornelius."

The next day there were three: two men in the morning, another in the afternoon, and instead of wearing the coins around their necks they carried them in small locked boxes, which they unlocked to show the coins to Cornelius, saying, "Me Shoe." By this time Cornelius thought he was making friends with one of the city's prominent families, the Shoe family, though they probably didn't spell it like that, Cornelius figured, and he took one of the coins and felt it denseness, its heaviness—it was almost assuredly real gold—and gave the men big nods of approval before handing them back the coins.

"Me Cornelius."

And that night in the temporary barracks the Second Division had constructed in the harbor, he mentioned that he'd gotten yet another visit from the Shoe family, whereupon a Marine asked him what the fuck he was talking about, and so Cornelius explained the whole thing and the Marine just about doubled over because, as he explained after a burst of uncontrollable laughter that Cornelius not-so-patiently suffered through, the locals weren't saying "Me Shoe," they were saying "mizu," which, as Cornelius would have known if he'd been paying any attention to the language lessons they got in Saipan, meant "water."

And suddenly Cornelius's old Augustine antennae went way up because he realized what was happening here: word had gotten out that the city's drinking water was probably radioactive and deadly, and so people were in desperate need of clean, potable, unpoisoned water, and they were willing to trade pure gold to get it.

When Cornelius returned home from the war, he did so with several footlockers full of coins, bars, cups, rings, necklaces, cutlery, sword scabbards, and even what may have been—though he had no interest in finding out for sure—tooth fillings. All of them gold or silver. All exchanged for the water Cornelius had procured for free. He established the Shoe Precious Metals Corp and worked diligently in the field of gold and silver and platinum and jewels for many years, never once admitting to his company's provenance, slowly building up the Augustines' good name, carefully patching his family's public persona and history, so that by the time his granddaughter Elizabeth was born, the only things people thought about the Augustines were, first, that the gold that passed through Cornelius's firm usually made its way to the necks of Hollywood's most popular starlets, and second, that the family was old money, having made all its wealth, somehow, in the previous century, from the railroads.

WELLNESS

ELIZABETH AUGUSTINE'S MARRIAGE to Jack Baker did not really begin on their wedding day, nor even on the day they met. It began the day that Elizabeth discovered the purpose that marriage served—what marriage was for, what love was for—which happened during her first month in Chicago, September 1992. It began when she spotted a flyer posted on the corkboard in the drama department. Amid all the other bulletins announcing auditions for local plays and student films and television commercials, there was this one strange ad:

ACTORS NEEDED FOR PSYCHOLOGY STUDY, it said at the top. Then, below: *What are the keys to unlocking the human heart? What are the conditions that create love at first sight? Can we persuade people to fall in love with complete strangers? We need actors to help us find out: college age, socially intuitive, with flexible personalities.*

At the bottom of the ad, the paper had been cut into strips that one could tear away, each containing relevant contact information. Elizabeth took one of these strips. She was the only one who had.

The next day, she prepared a résumé and walked to the address given on that paper, which was a small conference room in the psychology department with a placard that read:

DR. OTTO SANBORNE
PLACEBO STUDIES

The door was ajar, and through the gap Elizabeth saw him at his desk, reading. He was an older man with a very pink face and bright white hair, thin and wispy on his head, where he let it grow wildly away, but fuller and more well manicured on his chin, where he had trimmed it into a thick goatee. He wore round frameless eyeglasses, a long-sleeved, many-pocketed outdoorsy shirt with ventilation flaps in back, and old gray hiking pants with the zippers halfway up the thigh that could transform the hiking pants into hiking shorts. The way he was dressed, it was as if Sanborne believed that at any minute, right here in the middle of Chicago, he might be tempted by a nature walk.

There was a bicycle propped against the wall, near a haphazard stack of opened cardboard boxes. She tapped on the door. The professor glanced up from his book, eyebrows raised pleasantly, the look of a man accustomed to interruptions.

"I'm here about the study?" Elizabeth said, holding up the slip of paper. "Are you still looking for someone?"

"I am, I am," he said. "Come, please, sit."

Elizabeth sat across from him and produced her résumé, which he took. "I'm Elizabeth Augustine—"

"My dear, I'm sorry, just one moment," he said. "Forgive me, I'll be right back. Please, make yourself comfortable. Have a cookie," he added, picking up a bowl full of cookies and bringing it to her. "Please, I insist. They're my favorite."

And so she accepted the cookie—a pecan sandie—and Sanborne disappeared while she ate it, biting into the cookie and finding it sort of dry and stale, crumbling immediately. She wiped away the cookie's crumbs from the desk when she heard footsteps in the hallway, then Sanborne was back, sitting, nodding at her, picking up her résumé, saying, "Elizabeth Augustine, okay, hello."

"Hello, Dr. Sanborne."

"Please let me express how genuinely happy I am that you are here. Thrilled," he said, looking over her résumé now.

"Thank you, Dr. Sanborne."

"A very impressive academic record. Near-perfect SAT scores. Full scholarship. Yes, thrilling, indeed."

Elizabeth smiled. She was sitting up, her back very straight, hands clasped in front of her, elbows off the desk. It was the posture of the women she'd observed back home. All those elegant mothers sat exactly like this—still, erect, expressing mirth or curiosity or basically any emotion only from the neck up: tilting their heads to the right to indicate interest or to the left to signal sympathy, craning their long necks forward to say something in confidence, throwing their heads back to laugh. They were marionettes with one articulable joint, and Elizabeth recognized herself doing exactly this, whenever she met people of authority.

"May I ask you a question?" Sanborne said.

"Of course."

"It's rather a personal question."

"Okay."

"Why did you clean up your crumbs?"

She frowned. "My crumbs?"

"Yes, just now. All the little bits of cookie, you see? All the debris on the desk. You cleaned it all up."

"I suppose I did."

"Why?"

"I don't know."

"The desk is now spotless. You were really quite thorough. You don't know why?"

"Not really."

"Does that mean you cleaned it accidentally?"

"No."

"Automatically?"

"No."

"So there must have been some reason, some motivation."

She smiled at him. "Are you teasing me?"

"No, I'm very serious indeed. Describe your thought process. Please. You saw there were crumbs and you cleaned them up . . . why?"

"I guess it's polite?"

"Polite, yes, go on."

"Well, I think it's important to be a polite and considerate guest, to be thoughtful about how I conduct myself in public."

"And why is that?"

"Why be thoughtful?"

"Yes, exactly. Why?"

"To make a good impression, I guess. To make sure people think good things about me."

"And this is important to you, yes? The impression you leave on people?"

She leveled her eyes at him. "I suppose I was thinking that if you came back in here and saw the desk covered in crumbs, you'd think I was a slob."

"And you wouldn't want me thinking that."

"No, of course not."

"I'm honored that you hold my opinion in such high esteem," he said. "But I would not have thought you were a slob."

"It's something that's been drilled into me, I guess. Something my father always said."

"And what did your father say?"

"That small external blunders imply large internal defects."

"But, dear, don't we all sometimes blunder? Aren't we all, somewhere deep down, defective?"

"It was very important to him that I make a good impression. I come from a long line of shamefully successful people, and he wanted me to measure up."

She remembered the tours her father used to give his guests, the stories he used to tell about the family's grand house, how he'd stop in the Portrait Room long enough to tick through quick biographies of previous Augustine moguls—this guy made his money in the railroads, that one in textiles, this one in precious metals—never once mentioning all the exploitation and plundering that was the family's real bedrock specialty.

"My dad basically advocated a kind of personal broken windows theory," she said. "It's like, you can't overlook small failures, because small failures pave the way for large ones."

"And so you must police even the smallest failures."

"Right."

"That sounds very hard, my dear, very hard."

"Sometimes, yes," she said, but then—because it sounded like she was fishing for pity, and fishing for pity was exactly one of those small failures that needed policing—she changed the subject: "Why are you so interested in my crumbs?"

Sanborne smiled and leaned toward her, palms on the desktop, suddenly a little giddy. "What if I told you there was another reason you cleaned up this desk? What if I told you that the real reason you cleaned up those crumbs was something you are right now unaware of?"

And before she could even answer, he slapped the desktop excitedly with his palms and pushed himself up off his chair and walked over to the cardboard boxes along the wall, opened one, and said: "My dear, I present to you the real culprit!" And then he removed from the box a large bottle of bleach.

Clorox bleach. The bottle was uncapped, and she could hear the liquid sloshing around as Sanborne lifted it up and placed it on the desk.

"I don't understand," she said.

"Well, certainly not!" he said. "That's why it worked!"

Elizabeth stared at the bottle. "I cleaned up my crumbs because of a bottle of bleach?"

"Yes indeed! You felt the impulse to clean because of the associations you have with bleach."

"But I didn't even know it was there."

"Ah, but you *smelled* it."

And he was right—there it was now, that familiar sharp chlorine tang, appearing suddenly in her consciousness though she had not been aware of it before.

"In psychology, we call it 'priming,' " Sanborne said, sitting again. "It occurs when we are nudged by a subconscious stimulus, which prompts us to act when we otherwise might not. In this particular case, my dear, the nudge came from the associations you have with the smell of bleach."

"It smells like a bathroom after a very thorough cleaning."

"Exactly right. It is fresh, antiseptic, sterile, disinfected. And increasing the salience of these concepts motivated you to keep the desk spotless."

"Do you do this with all your students?"

"Ha!" he said, smiling broadly. "Yes! And for many years! I've found that students are roughly ten times more likely to clean up their crumbs when the smell of bleach is present."

"Wow."

"But that's not what really interests me."

"What really interests you?"

"I'm interested in the stories they make up about *why* they cleaned up the crumbs."

"The stories."

"Yes, when asked to explain themselves, people tend to invent exactly the same kinds of stories that you did. They talk about how they were raised, they describe lessons from their parents, they worry what I might think of them. Default explanations. Not a single person has ever talked about bleach, not even once."

"Nobody understood their real motivations."

"And isn't that the truth! Over the years, I've found that people tend to act automatically and think automatically, but when they're pressed to explain why they act or think a certain way, they rush into the void and invent a story. And then, incredibly, they *believe* that story."

"Even if the story isn't true."

"It doesn't need to be true. It merely needs to be satisfying. We all do it, to some extent. Between ourselves and the world is a story. Often it's a good story, a satisfying story, a personally appealing story. Take your father, for example."

"What about my father?"

"It's simply not accurate that small blunders equate with defect and failure. What is more likely is that it's satisfying for him to think of others as defective, and to think of *you*, in particular, as defective."

"Why would he want to think that?"

"Who knows what evil lurks in the hearts of men, my dear. All I understand for sure is that people have a very strong need to explain the world in ways that make them feel better, or safer, or more powerful, or more well liked, or more in control, but not necessarily in ways that are true. Alas, the truth is of very low importance, psychologically speaking. We're really very silly creatures."

Sanborne seemed greatly entertained by this, even sort of jolly. It was a quality Elizabeth would grow familiar with as she began working for him and, later, was mentored by him, interned for him, coauthored papers with him: whenever he uncovered new evidence of the human mind's ability to con and deceive itself, he turned into something like a benevolent, bighearted grandmother watching children play.

Most of their discussions centered on how people were generally, universally crazy. Or a whole lot crazier than her classes in economics had led Elizabeth to believe. In the world of economics, humans were rational agents, doggedly and intelligently pursuing their own self-interest. In Sanborne's world, humans were insane, suffering all sorts of delusions, prey to the smallest stimuli, easily tricked, contradictory, self-sabotaging, untrustworthy, malleable, impulsive, acting according to motivations unknown even to themselves, making everyone miserable. The world described in a microeconomics textbook was a rational and organized pursuit of maximized happiness. What Sanborne offered was a world in which happiness was a satisfying fiction set atop the mind's darker motivations, which accorded pretty well with Elizabeth's own observations, her bafflement at people's messy, careless, inconsistent affections.

"Take love, for example," Sanborne said on that day, the day of their first meeting. "Do you know, my dear, what's really happening to people in the midst of love?"

"Well, in my experience, they get nervous, giddy, they sweat a lot."

"Those are, yes, of course, true things that happen. But the nerves? The sweating? Those are exterior manifestations of an interior phenomenon. Do you know what that phenomenon is?"

"I guess I don't."

"Beyond all the poetry, beyond all the songs, love is this, my dear: it's an expansion of the self. It's when the boundaries of the self spread out to include someone else, and what used to be *them* now becomes *you*."

"That sounds kind of nice."

"It certainly feels nice! It feels quite wonderful, to identify some quality within another person—their charisma, their charm, their temperament, their point of view, their knowledge, their resources, their looks—you see this thing that they have and you want to have it too. And so the boundaries of the self ooze toward them, like an amoeba, like that blob from the movie about the blob. You glom on to them and surround them and subsume them, until you fully incorporate and digest this other person slowly over the course of many months."

"You've suddenly made it sound not so nice."

"You identify a thing you like in someone else, and you pull it within the conceptual borders of your own self. And the subjective experience of this process, the delusion the mind serves up to explain it, this is what we've given the name 'love.'"

"So," Elizabeth said, "I take it you're not one of those hopeless romantics."

"Ha! No! What other people call romance, I call annexation."

"So love is just selfish, is what you're saying? Marriage is just selfish?"

"Marriage, my dear, is a condition whereby you find so many qualities within another person that you want to have within you that you're willing to take on their flaws, which will, by extension, also be within you, for life."

"Have you ever been married, Dr. Sanborne?"

"Never."

"Have you ever been in love?"

"Too many times to count! Which brings me to the present study. Love, especially its beginning stages, that first lightning bolt, that Romeo-and-Juliet moment, is notoriously difficult to study in a controlled laboratory setting."

"Well, it's not like you can put two strangers in a room and tell them to fall in love."

"Precisely! But the question this study asks is: What if we can? If love springs forth from a feeling of interconnectedness between the self and an other, what if we can simulate that feeling?"

"How?"

"Through sustained, escalating, intensely intimate self-disclosure."

"And what does that mean, exactly?"

"I will give you a list of penetrating and inappropriately personal questions, which you will answer with a stranger."

"Questions such as what?"

"I'm still working that out, but the first question will most likely be: On a scale of one to ten, how much did your parents love you?"

"Wow, you really dive right in."

"It gets even more probing after that. The idea is that profoundly intimate revelations between two people in a very short amount of time can simulate the experience of love to a degree that's robust enough that we can study it. I will of course be working with you on the questions and the answers, to test the efficacy of both."

"I see."

"And that is, in a nutshell, the job, my dear. In short, you will be sharing intensely personal secrets with randomly selected men, and then we'll see if those men fall in love with you. Do you accept?"

Elizabeth started work the very next day.

THE WELLNESS STOREFRONT was located near DePaul's Lincoln Park campus, on a calm, tree-lined street very near the Health Sciences building, set within a row of outpatient clinics—there was a dentist, a physical therapist, a dermatologist, a med spa—on a block that had been zoned for commercial/medical. Wellness had moved to this location a few years ago after research had shown that the presence of these neighboring clinics seemed to prime clients in statistically significant ways—the vector being the increased salience of assorted signals involving health and medicine and professional expertise, probably—that improved the efficacy of most Wellness therapies by an average of 9 percent over results at its previous location, which was on busy Fullerton Avenue between a Firestone and an Arby's. The glass exterior of this new Wellness location was entirely frosted and opaque, with a sign hanging above the door that the staff changed daily depending on the clientele and the therapies under review. If a patient, for example, strongly believed in non-Western and alternative and what might be called indigenous forms of healing, and Wellness was testing some kind of Ayurvedic massage that balanced one's "primary life forces," then the clinic might put up the sign with the tribal typeface:

WELLNESS

Whereas if a client responded more to innovative bodily reprogramming and alchemical hacks—the keto folks were currently excellent examples of this, as the Bulletproof fans had been a few years earlier—the staff would put up the sign evoking something more sleek and futuristic:

WELLNESS

Or if the client was into things more quirky and artisanal and hip, as when Wellness was testing an oolong energy drink on a particular young tranche of urban professionals, then they might display the sign that looked like a silkscreened, handmade one-off:

Wellness

Some of their signs evoked class and heritage and old-money luxury, which was useful for certain essential oils involving pine or cedar or sandalwood, essentially the omnibus scent of expensive handmade carpentry:

Wellness

Other signs evoked a strict, ascetic minimalism, which of course was the underlying metaphor for any kind of cleanse—juice, celery, cabbage—the idea being that you were absolving yourself of every unwanted cell and molecule in your body, leaving behind only the cleanest, skinniest, most minimalist you, hence the sign:

Wellness

They had many such signs in their back storage room, each of which had been tested for its salience and efficacy.

This week, Wellness was working on a new diet supplement called Peat Bog Belly. The story behind this supplement was that archaeologists had recently uncovered the remains of a Paleolithic man in a peat bog somewhere in the northern UK, the man being so incredibly well preserved in the cold mire that forensic anthropologists were able to not only identify the specific bacteria present in his lower digestive tract but also clone and reproduce these bacteria. This was significant because such bacteria were the helpful critters that existed before the industrial wave of unnaturally processed food came along and genocided them out of our own modern guts.

And so what this supplement claimed to do was restore one's microbiome to the state nature and evolution had originally calibrated it, which was helpful in all sorts of ways involving digestion and immune system health and mental acuity and weight loss.

It was one of several new products to recently roll through Wellness related to microbiome and gut health, which was turning out to be *the* health trend of the year.

The supplement came in both pill and powder form—the latter meant for consumption via smoothie—and the job of Wellness was to evaluate which of many variables—color, smell, texture, taste, packaging, dosage, and what was called *therapeutic context*—made it most effective.

The sign out front was one of the many dimensions making up this last category—context—and after lengthy debates about the psychology related to the term *peat bog*, they had decided on the sign with the most old-timey British flavor:

Wellness

The thinking here was that the strongest association clients had with the word *peat* involved Scotch whisky, and so the most appropriate sign would be one that emphasized antique UK tradition, smartly leaning into the conceptual cluster surrounding *peat* rather than the one surrounding *bog*.

Elizabeth was sitting in the small conference room where new clients were evaluated. She had been interviewing patients all afternoon, people who had been referred to Wellness by a few select doctors around town, suffering from dyspeptic ailments that were relatively minor and non-life-threatening but also chronic and annoying—persistent indigestion, abdominal bloat, irritable bowels, unrestrained belching, mid-meal fatigue. Elizabeth was reading the intake form for her final patient of the day, someone named Gretchen who apparently had not been referred by anyone but had instead reached out independently and made her own appointment, which was rare. Wellness tended to keep an intentionally low profile, and Elizabeth was wondering how she might tactfully ask this Gretchen person what exactly she'd heard about Wellness when Gretchen walked in and Elizabeth realized it wouldn't be necessary.

"Brandie?" Elizabeth said upon seeing her Park Shore friend. "Hi there. Welcome. What a surprise."

Brandie was wearing big sunglasses, a silk scarf around her head, a flowy gray wrap—likely cashmere—around her shoulders. "Elizabeth, hello," she said, and they hugged and sat down, Brandie placing her big straw tote bag in her lap, as if she were hiding behind it. She took off the scarf, the sunglasses. "I'm sorry for all the cloak-and-dagger," she said. "I just didn't want anyone to know I was coming here. It's so embarrassing."

"It's fine," Elizabeth said. "Are you having some kind of problem? Some digestion thing?" Like most medical professionals, Elizabeth had been working in the field for so long that basically nothing regarding the body's biologic functioning (or malfunctioning) embarrassed her any longer. "It's okay, you can tell me."

"Oh, actually, no," Brandie said. "I mean, the peat bog thing? It sounds very interesting, but I'm not here for that."

"Okay. Then why are you here?"

Brandie took a big, deep breath. "I had an epiphany last night."

"An epiphany?"

"I was in my quiet room—have you seen my quiet room? It's this special room in my house, just off the living room, at the end of the hall. It's my oasis. I go there when I need to get away, to be alone with my thoughts."

"Sounds nice," Elizabeth said.

"It *is* nice. I find that I need a place to recalibrate, you know? A place to eliminate all the noise and get aligned with my next-level self. Mike built it for me, my quiet room. It's where I do my affirmations, listen to my subliminals, light my intention-setting candles, visualize. Do you have your own private place? A room just for you?"

"Our apartment is pretty cramped."

"But have you ever had a room like that? Your own special retreat?"

Elizabeth thought about it for a moment. "There was a room in my grandfather's house, in Connecticut. Every summer, no matter where we were living at the time, my family spent a month at that house. It's this huge estate in the woods, with a pond, and a tennis court."

"I'll bet it's beautiful."

"There was a room on the third floor that nobody ever used. And I would sometimes hide there, to be alone."

"Yes, that's exactly what I'm talking about. That kind of place. And here's what I recommend: close your eyes and picture yourself in that room. Really try to firmly believe you're in that space, okay?"

Elizabeth nodded. The last she'd heard, that room at the Gables had been demolished, along with the rest of the third and fourth floors. In the years since Elizabeth had left, the Augustine family estate had been systematically guillotined—but of course Brandie didn't need to know that.

"Okay," Elizabeth said, "I'm picturing it."

"Make this a regular practice of yours. Feel yourself in that room and spend some time mentally reflecting."

"Reflecting on what?"

"Things you want. Things you need. Things that would solve your troubles. You can call it prayer, or you can call it meditation. Whatever. Just picture what you want your life to be, in the future. I've been doing it a lot lately, and yesterday I was there in my quiet room and I had an epiphany. It was like this big intuition-bomb, you know? Like a sudden download from the universe."

"What was it?"

"You remember that drug you were testing? That love potion?"

"Yes."

"Well," Brandie said, and she took a deep breath. "I need it."

"You do?"

"Elizabeth, I need that love potion."

"But why?"

"My marriage—it's in trouble."

"It is?"

"Really big trouble."

"I don't understand. You and your husband, you two are *perfect*."

"I know it seems that way."

"Renewing your vows every year. Going on romantic dates. I've seen the photos on Instagram."

"Yeah, well, don't believe everything you see on Instagram," Brandie said, rolling her eyes. "The truth is, we haven't been good in a long time."

"How long?"

"*Long*."

"I had no idea."

"Can I tell you a secret?"

"Of course."

"Last year we had a . . . well, let's call it a little spot of infidelity."

"Oh."

"A little smidge of cheating, yeah. See, Mike was out of town, on a business trip, and he met someone, and, well, he insists that it happened only once and that it'll never happen again, but I still cannot get it out of my head."

"I'm so sorry."

"I know it's unproductive to think about it this much. I know it absolutely sends the wrong vibrations, to focus so powerfully on a negative thing. But I can't help it. Elizabeth, it got so bad that I actually installed this app on his phone, to track where he is."

"No kidding?"

"I'm not proud of it. I'm just terrified he's having another affair. Whenever he's gone, I check up on him, like"—and now she pulled her phone from her tote bag, swiped a few times—"here we go, it looks like he was at the office for about ninety minutes, then he drove home at an average speed of thirty-two miles per hour, and now he's downstairs taking no steps whatsoever, which probably means he's playing Call of Duty."

"Wow."

"The app was designed for parents to keep track of teenagers, but it works well for this purpose too."

"Okay."

Brandie tossed the phone back into her bag, hung her head. "It's pathetic, I know. And creepy. I really want to stop having these thoughts, but I feel so *angry* at him. Just *furious*. Like, every time we go on one of those dates, we barely talk, and we smile exactly once, to take a selfie that I can put on Instagram so I don't disappoint my followers, who would be *dev-as-tat-ed* if they found out that I have this shit marriage, that I am completely unable to 'practice loving-kindness' and forgive my own husband—they'd lose all faith in the universe, you know? And I have a responsibility to them, and to my kids, of course, and so I go ahead and smile real big and take the selfie and meanwhile my brain is *screaming*. Elizabeth, you have to help me."

Elizabeth took Brandie's hands in hers. "I'm really sorry. That sounds hard. Have you tried going to a therapist?"

"We have, sure, but it's the same problem. We talk and talk and talk about the affair. We focus on it *so much*. And I really believe that if you focus your attention on something terrible, you'll attract more of it. And we are already surrounded by so many terrible things, so much negativity, so much menace in the world, so much bleakness creeping in everywhere, and if you let even the tiniest bit of it into your life—"

Brandie, suddenly on the verge of tears, stopped for a moment, took a deep breath, composed herself, then continued: "Focusing on a problem preserves the problem, in your mind. I prefer to talk about solutions. Whenever I'm faced with a dilemma in my life, I ask myself a simple question: What would my next-level self do? I mean, would the version of myself who's conquered this problem still be sitting around moping and obsessing about it? No, of course not. That version of myself is out living her fabulous next-level life, because she *took action*. And that's why I thought of you."

"I wish I could help, I really do," Elizabeth said, "but the drug is simply not something we give out like that. There's a process involved, interviews, it's all quite rigorous. And the treatment is not officially approved by any regulatory body, it's still in the very earliest phases of research, and there's no guarantee—"

"Listen," Brandie said, "I will owe you, *so much*. I will be in your debt forever. Please?"

Elizabeth considered it for a moment, what it would mean for

Brandie to owe her a favor. Elizabeth's latent worry since moving Toby to Park Shore Country Day was that he might start having his meltdowns and tantrums in school, and while public schools had resources and professionals devoted to addressing behavioral problems, private schools tended to have a little less tolerance. They could simply insist that problematic students not return next term, no questions asked. And this fact troubled Elizabeth, that Toby might be summarily expelled and then forced to endure the new-kid-in-school ordeal all over again, somewhere else. But if Brandie were in her corner? The leader of the Park Shore PTA? The school's biggest fundraiser? The administration might be a little more accommodating, if Brandie asked them to be.

"I'll be right back," Elizabeth said, and she left the room, headed to the office storage closet, plucked a pill bottle from the small refrigerator there, and returned. She sat down across from Brandie and placed the bottle on the table between them. On its label, it said only this, in friendly Helvetica:

Dopamine Receptor D4/7R+ Polymorphism Neurotransmitter #9

"Here's how it works," Elizabeth said. "You believe you're angry at Mike because of the affair. Obviously. But it's also possible that the affair was a trigger for a larger, underlying, subconscious condition. And maybe it's this root condition that we need to treat."

And then she gave Brandie the long and involved explanation that she gave all her clients who were undergoing this very treatment: that their feelings of restlessness and tedium and loneliness and general marital blah, those urges toward anything at all different and exotic, that impatience and resentment they felt toward stasis and wedded monotony, might not reflect any real objective problem in their marriage. In fact, it was possible that all of these feelings could be explained by a biochemical feedback loop created eons ago within the most nomadic pockets of hunter-gatherer humans, those ancestors who migrated the farthest, or whose lives were most precarious, evolution had, over the ages, imprinted their very genetic code with exactly this compulsion: a suspicion of sameness. Those

Stone Age humans who, sixty thousand years ago, wandered away from the African breadbasket, walked through the Fertile Crescent, traversed the Indian subcontinent, traveled the distance of Asia on foot, crossed the land bridge to Alaska, who kept walking south, tracking game, avoiding the ice, following the seasons, scrounging, starving, moving on, always moving on—for these tribes, staying in one place for too long was literally a death sentence, and so nature selected for people apt to be *on the move,* people unafraid of new situations, people who in fact craved and needed new situations, and the evidence was right there in our DNA, in the eleventh chromosome, in the DRD4 gene, a dopamine receptor whose genetic sequence in most humans repeated either two or four or seven times, this last mutation, what was known as the 7R polymorphism, being strongly associated with novelty-seeking, risk-taking, openness to new experiences, stimulation-craving, even impatience, infidelity, promiscuity, impulsiveness, a strong desire to *leave*—all things under the umbrella of what might be called "exploratory behavior." And the 7R variant was seen most often in people whose ancestors were the most nomadic, who walked the greatest distances, who traveled the farthest away from home, who then bequeathed this genetic legacy to those who came later, creating people whose very biology pushed them toward something, anything, *new.*

In other words, as Elizabeth told her patients, it was possible that hypoactive marital attachment disorder did not reflect an actual problem within their marriage. It might just be that they were experiencing the cognitive dissonance of living a settled life with a migratory brain.

"Take one pill an hour before you spend time with Mike," Elizabeth said. "It's possible that you may, eventually, start to feel a change."

"Thank you!" said Brandie, all smiles. She stashed the bottle in her tote bag and hugged Elizabeth tightly. "I've been worried about this for so long, and I had no idea what to do, and then you showed up out of nowhere with this answer. And, well, it's a pretty unconventional answer, sure, not really what I was expecting, but, you know . . . When the universe sends you a rowboat!"

"That's right."

"Hey, you should come to my house this weekend! I'm having a gathering. There are people you need to meet."

"Great. Who?"

"It's a neighborhood group. We call ourselves the Community Corps. I organized it shortly after Mike's . . . unfaithfulness. I was going crazy at the time and felt like I had to do something, take action, inspired action. So it's a group of people who live in town, and we all work to make our town better, to up-level our little place in the world. If you're moving to Park Shore, you should definitely know them. Tell me you'll come. Please?"

"Yeah, okay, sure."

"Perfect! And Elizabeth?" she said as she patted the tote bag where her new pills resided, "*Thank you.*"

"You're welcome."

"You are such a good friend. I am so pleased you're in my life now. You and I, it's like we're vibrating at exactly the same frequency."

A kiss on the cheek, and Brandie was off.

What Elizabeth did not tell her—and what she had not told any of her other subjects, nor would she tell them until this research was complete—was that those pills contained nothing. Or nothing special. They were biologically inert. Just sugar pills. And that medical-sounding condition—hypoactive marital attachment disorder—was also a fiction. And even that story about nomadic wanderers and their genetic legacy was just a tapestry of miscellaneous facts and theories stitched together into a persuasive but scientifically unsupported narrative. The whole thing was nothing more than an elaborate placebo.

And yet, according to the data Wellness had so far collected, the charade often worked. It was effective for approximately 40 percent of patients. Roughly 40 percent reported a brightening of their mood, a weight lifted, a new feeling of marital openness and optimism and relief. And these reports were backed up by blood work, whereby these same patients showed altered levels of oxytocin and cortisol and other important neurological markers associated with mood, love, anxiety, and stress. In other words, the patients' subjective self-evaluations matched up with their objective brain chemistry. Something had biologically changed.

Elizabeth was always mindful of the specific words she used during these exchanges. She told her clients to take a pill, and then she told them they might start feeling better, but she never actually said it was the pill itself that would make them feel better. Her clients, of course, inferred exactly that, but Elizabeth was careful never to literally say it. Because she knew the pill could not make them feel better. The pill couldn't do anything. It had no active ingredients.

So she wasn't lying, per se. She was being honest when she said she believed they could be cured. It just wasn't the pill that cured them. What cured them, in the end, was belief. Belief in the full context of the encounter: the pills they assumed would make them feel better, this partly due to a lifetime's experience of taking pills that made them feel better; pills of a certain weight (five hundred milligrams) that felt appropriately substantial; pills of a certain color (bright red) that looked therapeutic; pills that were in capsule form (which people believed were more powerful than tablets); pills that were stored in a refrigerator (which people believed were more powerful than room-temperature pills on a shelf); pills prescribed by a medical (seeming) professional, in an office with an exterior sign and interior layout designed to be maximally reassuring—all of these factors meeting the patient's own strong desire to heal, which produced, finally, a confidence that they would be healed, a kind of confirmation bias that was the true and only source of this medicine. It was its single active ingredient: belief. Her patients were cured because, simply, they believed in the cure.

THE AUGUSTINE FAMILY'S large historic Connecticut home is named the Gables because, famously, it has a lot of them. Gables. At least fourteen, big and small, jutting out chaotically on each of the structure's four floors, some of these gables parallel to one another, others at sharp angles, making the house appear, from a distance, like a scramble of triangles and pyramids, like it's some difficult and abstract math object, a wood-and-stone dodecahedron right there in the Connecticut hills.

The Gables was built in 1865 by Elizabeth's great-great-grandfather, a man with particular and idiosyncratic architectural ideas. It's the kind of old New England mansion where every room has a story, and most of the rooms have names. On the first floor alone there's the Morgan Room (named after J. P. Morgan, who had, during a vacation in the summer of 1902, carved his initials into the underside of the enormous fireplace's enormous mantel), and the Vanderbilt Room (which features a framed, handwritten letter from Alice and Cornelius Vanderbilt inviting the Augustines to join them for summer at the Breakers), and the Cleveland Room (where hangs a photo of Grover Cleveland taken in that very room, when presumably it was named something else).

And then there's the Portrait Room, home to the slightly-larger-than-life-size paintings of the patriarchs of her family tree:

Alvin Augustine, her great-great-grandfather, who rose from total poverty to become a railroad industry tycoon.

Everett Augustine, her great-grandfather, a textiles tycoon.

Cornelius Augustine, her grandfather, a precious metals tycoon.

It is an important family fact that each generation of Augustinian tycoon did not, as her father often tells her, "rest on his family's laurels" but rather bravely made his own way in the world. Each entered some brand-new industry and—with the family's typical creativity and pluck—conquered it. It's a story about hard work and determination and success, a grand story for this equally grand house. Elizabeth's father loves giving guests the tour, explaining the significance of each room and telling the same tales every time to the various CEOs, various bureaucrats of significant government departments, chairmen of various boards who often descend on the Gables for summer visits. He'll guide them through each important room on the first floor, then up to the second, where all the rooms are bedrooms named for guests who have allegedly slept in them—the Walt Whitman, the Robert Frost, the Andrew Carnegie, the Meyer Guggenheim, the John Singer Sargent, the Henry Frick. Long before Elizabeth learned any of these names from either books or museums, she knew them here, as plaques on the walls of the Gables, the Augustine version of trophy heads from wild game hunts. She has always recognized the importance of those names, the function of those names, how they tell a story about her family beyond its obvious accomplishments: that her family is not only successful but also significant, inseparable from the progress of the nation, in fact part of the reason for the progress of the nation, a family that motors the nation forward—inextricable, powerful, prominent, American. Guests always have a fun time choosing which bedroom to stay in.

But there are certain rooms—and certain gables—that Elizabeth prefers. These are the servants' quarters, up on the third floor: three little bedrooms, only one with a window; a small bathroom; and an abandoned kitchenette. These rooms are walled off from the rest of the house—the only way into or out of the servants' quarters is a spiral staircase two stories tall that leads down to the pantry off the kitchen on the first floor. It is a design that makes clear how the home's architect thought the home should function: the servants would enter and exit through the side door, stay unseen in the kitchen, then retire to their separate and sovereign little bedrooms so that their employers could be, always, oblivious to their presence. Elizabeth imagines that they didn't live in the house so much as haunt its outskirts.

The family no longer retains live-in servants, and so this room is always empty, which is ideal for Elizabeth, who prefers to be alone.

This is where she goes to read, to daydream. It's a late-July morning, and Elizabeth is at the Gables for her family's traditional one-month summer stay, and she's hiding up here in the servants' quarters because she awoke with that unnamed melancholy that always accompanies and complicates this particular day. For today is her birthday. Today she is fourteen years old, and she is spending her birthday as she always does, at the Gables, with her parents—such is the tragedy of a summer birthday, that it's celebrated in isolation from friends. How she longs to spend one birthday with friends. How she longs, for that matter, to have friends. She has changed schools so frequently that, her whole life, she's never had a chance to know people for however long it takes for them to care about your birthday. She imagines herself as a small, forgettable blip in other people's more stable existence—at least, that's the pitiful way she tends to feel on the morning of her birthday, hence the hiding.

She's sitting under the window, on the floor, her back against the wall, reading. Next to her is a stack of books borrowed from the library at school. She had checked them out before the summer—partly to pass the time on these long days, partly to get a head start on next semester, when she'll be taking certain advanced upper-classmen courses in economics and philosophy and political science, for which she needed special permission to enroll, being a mere incoming freshman. The econ teacher was a special stickler on this front, requiring her to write a paper this summer on "The Invisible Hand." And she understands that all she really needs to do is regurgitate a little Adam Smith, just write a slavish thesis in praise of self-interest in laissez-faire free markets, but she's decided to widen the scope of her inquiry, to attack it from many new and different angles, and so this paper has expanded into a large dis-quisition on the grand subject of rational choice and human desire. And so this summer she's reading some Adam Smith, yes, but also some Jeremy Bentham, some Thomas Hobbes, some Descartes, some Plato, some John Stuart Mill, some William F. Buckley (this last one recommended to her by the poli-sci teacher, who has little framed pictures of Ronald Reagan on his desk where other teach-ers have pictures of their own children). And in a meaningful bit of happenstance, she's right now reading a passage on the question of desire—what do people want? What makes people happy?—and the answer seems to be, simply, *more*. More things. More stuff. "The natural desire of the individual for *more goods*" is how Buckley puts it, and this feels meaningful because today is Elizabeth's birthday, and this is what she knows to expect: more goods. Her father, every year, on this day, overwhelms her with goods, an annual spending spree she is not exactly looking forward to, despite what William F. Buckley says about people's *natural desire*.

Last year it was that big haul of expensive outdoorsy gear, this after Elizabeth had fallen in with an amateur ecology club at her previous junior high school in the Hudson Valley, and she'd spent her Saturday mornings volunteering in the Catskills, repairing trails, taking water samples from streams, examining animal tracks or birds' nests, sketching the colorful mushrooms she discovered upon the rotting trunks of fallen trees. Then her father found out about this new wilderness hobby, and that summer his birthday present to her was an ultralight backpack and ultralight hiking shoes and stretchy waterproof leggings and a rain jacket and wind pants and collapsible water bottles and dehydrated trail meals and a headlamp and a compass and carbon-fiber trekking poles and wool socks and sun-protective hats and a scale to weigh all of it—her father explaining that real hikers kept their packs at ten pounds or less, always, for speed and endurance reasons. Further, her father had purchased matching equipment for himself and announced that their goal for the upcoming year was to bag at least a dozen of the Adirondack High Peaks, a quest that lasted exactly one mountain when somewhere halfway up the Algonquin Elizabeth completely lost sight of him—he was walking that fast—and because he was carrying the map she didn't know which way to go when the trail split and thus had to sit down and wait, and he was annoyed that he'd needed to double back for her, and they'd lost all that time, and there was no way they were getting to the peak now, so they turned around and began their descent, her father making occasional comments all the way to the parking lot about who between them was the real hiker, and who was not.

After which she stopped all forest activities completely.

This year, at her new school, she had joined the tennis team, and apparently her father had found out about this new interest too, because sometime in the last year he'd had an actual full-sized tennis court installed in the backyard of the Gables. When she saw it for the first time, at the beginning of her stay here this summer, he said, "Surprise!" and she smiled at him and thanked him even as she felt her tennis-enthusiasm suddenly, wildly plummet.

It always happens this way: whenever she takes an interest in something, her father showers gifts upon that interest, which makes her lose the interest completely.

So, no, she is not exactly interested in *more goods*.

What she's most interested in right now is a note she's been reading and rereading all summer, a note from her new friend Maggie Percy—they'd worked on the school play together, got to know each other while building sets for *Pygmalion*. On the last day of school, Maggie had slipped her this note inviting Elizabeth to come with her family to New Hampshire on their leaf-peeping trip in the fall, exuberantly explaining how wonderful this trip was and how Elizabeth absolutely had to give them the pleasure of her company. Maggie had also given her one of those origami paper fortune tellers that the two of them liked to make—they did this all the time at school, folding flat sheets of paper into these diamond-shaped gadgets that supposedly predicted what career you would one day take up, or which boy you would marry, or how many children you would have. And this particular fortune teller asks whether Elizabeth will agree to go to New Hampshire this autumn, and the hilarious thing about it is that no matter which paper quadrant Elizabeth unfolds, the answer underneath is always the same: *Yes*.

She smiles now at the thought of it: a friend close enough to warrant an invitation like that. She returns William F. Buckley to his place on the pile. She leans out the window and lets the cool morning breeze brush across her face. She wishes she could be up here the whole day through, alone, undisturbed. She would read her books and write letters to Maggie and make her own funny fortune tellers all the way till twilight, when she'd lie on the floor and stare at the ceiling and listen for the nightly riot that comes from above, the scratching and clawing and fluttering of wings from the fourth floor.

For a few years now, nobody has been allowed on the fourth floor because of the infestation up there: a colony of bats that migrated down from the attic and overran the home's upper level. It happened sometime after the fourth floor had fallen out of use, after Elizabeth's grandfather passed away and the house stood empty for much of the year, used only sporadically by assorted members of the family coming here for summers or holidays. Elizabeth's father had put tarps over everything on the fourth floor and locked it all up and didn't think much of it until the following summer, when they first began hearing a disconcerting squeaking and scratching noise at dusk and dawn and realized that, at some point, while they weren't paying attention, the fourth floor had been seized. It's a nest that has so far resisted the family's many attempts at removal—every year, at the end of summer, the exterminators come and wipe out the horde, bombing the fourth floor and attic with poison, blocking every way in or out, every tiny entrance, with screens and insulation and plaster and caulk. And yet every year the bats return, sometimes a hundred of them, sometimes a thousand. One exterminator sent up there came back reporting huge stalactites of toxic, poisonous bat shit shimmering under his headlamp's light. Why did it shimmer? Because it was filled with fine and iridescent insect wings.

That's an image that has always stuck with Elizabeth. She imagines, just above her head, a million bats hanging upside down, asleep, while below them sit great mounds of guano exquisitely glittering in the morning's dappled light. She likes the ambivalence of that, a scene both beautiful and profane.

But now she hears her parents calling her name and the daydream is broken. She goes running down the spiral staircase, down through the pantry and into the kitchen, where she finds her mother, all dressed up: black slacks, a sharp gray blouse, pearl earrings. And it's exactly this kind of little thing that, on this day, brings out Elizabeth's strange melancholy—that even on her birthday, her mom has other things to do, other places to be.

She's off to an art auction in New York City. "I wish I didn't have to go, sweetie, but I'm expected." Then leaning in toward Elizabeth and whispering, "There's a chance the mayor's going to be there."

Her father, meanwhile, wants to know what Elizabeth would like to eat for her special birthday breakfast, and Elizabeth blurts out her favorite thing, "Banana pancakes," before she notices that a bowl is already out, batter already mixed, a waffle iron warming up on the counter.

"Oh," her father says. "I was making blueberry waffles. I thought you'd like that."

"No, *you'd* like that," her mother says to him. "That's *your* favorite, not *her* favorite."

"Well how was I supposed to know?" her father says.

"Maybe if you asked her first," her mother says. "Maybe if you paid attention to your own daughter."

"Hey, at least I'm sticking around for her birthday," her father says. "At least I'm not *abandoning her.*"

"Oh, do you want me to stay, sweetie?" her mother says, turning to her. "I can stay, if that's what you want."

"And do you really want banana pancakes?" her father says. "I can go to the store, pick up some bananas, throw out that batter, start all over. If that's what you want."

She looks at them both, one and then the other. They always seem to do this to her, make her feel as if just telling the truth, just saying what she honestly wants, is selfish and horrible.

"It's okay," she says. "Waffles are great, Dad. And Mom, you should go to New York. It's fine. We have all month to hang out."

And they smile the broad smiles of parents let off the hook, and her mother goes to catch a train, and her father finishes the waffles and leaves Elizabeth to eat them alone, returning with many birthday presents wrapped up in silver paper: tennis skirts and tennis blouses and tennis shoes, all of them bright white, and tennis hats and tennis balls and a tennis bag, within which is a new tennis racket, a Dunlop, black, with green triangles pointing up its neck.

"It's made of graphite," he says. "That's the same stick that Steffi Graf uses."

"Wow," Elizabeth says. "Thanks."

"C'mon," he says, "let's see how it works."

So they change into their tennis whites and take to the court in the backyard. He's bouncing on his toes, from foot to foot, and whipping his own new graphite racket over his head, loosening his shoulder. He's been taking lessons, he tells her. The guys at the club call him "the wall," he tells her, for how often he gets their shots back, which is *always*. Elizabeth nods and plays against him wordlessly, not talking even during the changeovers, speaking only when she calls out the score before each point. Otherwise, she stays silent and listens, for her father finds it necessary to point out—with the authority that comes from shallow knowledge—every mistake she makes.

And she makes a lot of them. The way her father plays, it's like winning the match is only a secondary concern, far less important than making every point as miserable as possible. He's a "junk-baller," as her tennis friends would say, his shots coming at her with so much spin that they hit the court's dusty surface and take off in strange directions, sometimes away from her, sometimes into her. He slices the ball with such force and at such extreme angles that, watching it float back slowly through the air, it looks more like an oval than a sphere, the round ball battered into donut shapes via outrageous RPMs. He does not attempt winners, does not even make her run, just hits these exasperating slow balls right at her feet, over and over, the balls whirling with backspin or sidespin, and she lines up to strike them back, intent on blowing at least one good forehand right by him, but the balls grab the court and bounce away and she lunges for them and she knows she looks like the most ridiculous person in the world. He doesn't simply want to win; he wants to win while also making her look foolish. And she does look foolish: she mishits balls, frames them, launches them into the trees or buries them in the net, and even if she does by some miracle return a ball into his court, it is never with any real pace or intention, and so her father easily hits her another twirling, gyrating shot, grunting as he takes his swing, carving the ball in some new way such that it bounces in yet another exasperating direction, and their match continues in this fashion for roughly the next hour and a half.

By the end of it, she feels as if she's boiling, and she's fighting back tears, and she can't even look at him as they approach each other at the net for their wordless mandatory sportsmanlike handshake. Then he tells her to get cleaned up because they're going to the mall, and so an hour later Elizabeth is in the passenger seat of her father's BMW, her new tennis racket in the seat behind her.

He asks her about school, about the classes she's enrolled in for the upcoming year. And she ticks them off one by one: AP economics, AP philosophy, AP political science, AP physics—

"What's AP?" he says.

"Advanced placement. It's an honors course. Like a college-prep course."

He nods, grips the steering wheel a little more tightly, silent. It's a well-known family fact—well known because Elizabeth's grandfather never let anyone forget it, talking about it whenever there was an opportunity—that Elizabeth's father was not cut out for the classroom. He barely graduated from high school, and never went to college. So AP classes would have been out of the question.

"I'm finding it really hard," Elizabeth says. "Maybe it's a little over my head. I don't know. I'm having to do a lot of reading this summer, to catch up."

Her father remains silent.

"I'm also taking theater," Elizabeth says. "Not AP. Just plain theater."

"Theater?" he says. "Why?"

"I don't know. I like the people, I guess. Plus I took this personality test last year, and it showed that maybe I'd be good at it."

"Oh, so it's theater now," he says. "That's your new thing?"

She's aware that she and her father had a similar conversation last summer, when she was at that school in the Hudson Valley and had other interests. Last year it was ecology; she was going to be a forest ranger.

"Your problem," he says, "is that you haven't found your calling. By the time I was your age, I knew *exactly* what I was going to do."

It's a story he loves to tell, how he barely skated by at one of those fancy boarding schools, with all those nerds and eggheads, none of whom had a clue about how the real world operates, all of their noses stuck in books, and while they studied their theories and abstractions, he was already out starting actual businesses, making real money, and thus had no time for the tests and quizzes and other bullshit of school—which is how he explained being so bad at it. School. He eventually started a company called, simply, Acquisitions, and as far as Elizabeth could tell, all it did was buy certain businesses, scramble them up in significant ways, and, at a later date, sell them. He said it was like playing with blocks, but on a global scale, that every company in the world was simply a structure made of many discrete units—like toy houses built of blocks—and so when he audited a company, he didn't care about the company so much as he cared about its blocks. And his great ability was to see how one particular block among all the other blocks would be more valuable in a different house. And so he'd acquire a company, liquidate all but one small unit of that company, add that unit to another company, and sell this new structure, at an unconscionable markup. This of course triggered outrage and lawsuits from all those abandoned and liquidated parts, but he generally ignored that and left it to the attorneys to clean up.

Anyway, this was his calling: to identify the stupidities and blunders and inefficiencies of the world, and exploit them.

"What's *your* calling?" he asks her now.

She shrugs.

"Not theater," he says. "The problem with doing theater is that it's a career with no guarantees. You could study your whole life to be a playwright and still never make it as a playwright. But if you study banking, *presto,* you're a banker. If you study the law, you're a lawyer. Leave the art-doing to the geniuses and prodigies. You need to study something practical."

"But I *like* it," she says.

"Well, if you really want to go into the industry, then don't be the playwright, be the producer. Don't own the play, own the theater. When everyone's digging for gold, it's best to be in the shovel business, understand?"

"Unless you don't like shovels."

"Irrelevant. The shovels are a means to an end, Elizabeth. Take your great-great-grandfather. Do you really think that Alvin Augustine cared one bit about condensed milk? Or railroads? No. He cared about *getting rich.*"

"But I don't care about getting rich."

"Spoken like someone who's already rich," he says. "And anyway it's not the money itself that's important, it's what the money gets you."

"What does it get you?"

"Status. Ease. Comfort. But most of all, it gets you freedom."

"Freedom?"

"The freedom to live your life as you see fit, to depend on no one, to live without constraint. *To walk free and own no superior,*" he says, now quoting Walt Whitman. She knows he's quoting Walt Whitman because this very quote is etched onto a plaque at the Gables, the one hanging outside the Walt Whitman bedroom. "Most people," he continues, "live small lives inside small boxes. But that's not us. *Walk free and own no superior.* Remember that, Elizabeth. Words to goddamn live by."

She nods and they fall silent until they reach their destination, whereupon he encounters the backed-up traffic and creeping chaos of a mall parking lot on a Saturday and a dark mood seems to overtake him. Frustration and anger and animosity blaze out of him. He is seized by two mutually exclusive imperatives. The first is to quickly finish the ordeal, to be out of the car as quickly as possible so he no longer has to abide all these other people, the slower drivers who can't seem to make up their fucking minds about where they're going, the shoppers with their big bags walking four abreast right down the middle of the goddamn road—"Fuck you!" he keeps screaming at them. "Fuck you!" And then he grows angry at the roads themselves, angry at the mall's very *engineering,* how a mall parking lot isn't designed as an easy-to-understand grid but rather as a kind of incomprehensible interlocking of complexly shaped mini-lots at unusual angles that funnel cars to crowded nodes where bumper-to-bumper traffic is more or less inevitable; yes, all this seems to agitate her father a great deal, and Elizabeth wants to tell him that he could avoid all this agitation so easily by pulling into the first open parking space he sees, but he does not do this because his second imperative seems to be to nab a spot *up front,* close to the mall's entrance, a sort of VIP spot that he keeps circling and circling the parking lot for, each time growing more impatient and more disbelieving that a space has not yet opened for him, like he's cursed, like this is the particular way the universe has chosen to punish him, and Elizabeth is in the passenger seat thinking about that word *freedom,* thinking that this right here, this cycle of circling and complaining in the parking lot, this is exactly what her father wants freedom from. He wants to be free of other people, free of their interference, free to do as he pleases without any obligations to anyone.

It strikes her that what he calls *freedom* could just as easily be called *domination.*

"Fucking *finally,*" he says when a space opens up, a real close one right next to the handicapped spaces. He shoves the gearshift into Park in a way that seems intended to teach it a lesson. He grabs her tennis racket and says, "Let's go."

Once inside the mall, he walks quickly, uninterested in spending any more time here than is absolutely, strictly necessary. They go into a sporting goods store and her father hands the tennis racket to the salesman and says: "This doesn't work."

The salesman frowns. "Doesn't work?"

"She can't use it. She keeps making errors. You said it would work."

"Maybe it's too heavy?"

"You think?"

After which they go into the bookstore, her father asking the clerk: "Do you have any AP study guides? They're for my daughter here. She needs a bit of a head start."

And then they go into a clothing boutique, her father saying: "My daughter here needs some new dresses. I'm having business associates over to the house. Formal but not too formal."

Elizabeth hasn't said anything this entire time, has merely allowed herself to be led from place to place to place, and her father seems to finally notice her silence and he looks at her and says: "Why are you so sour?"

And when she shrugs and remains quiet, he turns to the saleswoman, who's currently picking out dresses, and opens his arms wide in a *Why me?* gesture and says: "I buy her all these presents and this is how she treats me. Teenagers, eh?"

And then they're finally leaving, Elizabeth carrying two bags of clothes and two bags of books, her father carrying another new tennis racket, spinning it in his hands. She follows behind him as he walks onto the access road outside the mall, not even stopping for the slow-moving traffic, becoming exactly one of those pedestrians he had been cursing only an hour before. When he gets to the car, he stops and stares at it, his head cocked, and when she catches up to him she sees what's happened: the driver's-side door of his bright white car has a small dent in it, and within the dent, a smear of blue paint. He stares at his dinged door for what feels to Elizabeth like a very long time, then stares at the blue van parked in the neighboring handicapped space, a big blue van filled with complicated machinery that is probably some kind of wheelchair ramp or lift.

"Perfect," he says. "Just perfect."

Elizabeth doesn't dare say anything. Very quickly, and without making any eye contact, she rushes over to the passenger side of her father's car, dumps the bags on the floor, gets in, closes the door, and buckles herself in, as if everything is totally normal here, and she stares straight ahead so that she does not have to watch what she knows will happen next. She hears her father's footsteps outside the car as he paces around the van, then she hears his sudden grunt, the same sound he makes every time he swings a tennis racket, and then a loud and violent crack as her new racket, and the van's windshield, both shatter.

He opens the door of his BMW, tosses the crumpled racket into the back seat, sits behind the wheel, and, still not looking at her, says: "I have a job for you."

"Okay."

"I usually pay interns to do this kind of job, but if you don't appreciate free things anymore, maybe it's time you work for them."

"Doing what?"

"Discovery," he says.

He takes out his wallet and removes a ten-dollar bill. He gives it to her and explains that she is to go into Sears, buy a tape measure, and come back out and measure every disabled parking space in the mall's lot. All of them. In the whole lot. She will measure the widths of every handicapped space and she is instructed to note in particular those spaces narrower than ninety-six inches, which is the ADA-required width for handicapped parking spaces. Even if the spaces are only a half inch shy of the mandated ninety-six inches, her father wants to know about it.

"I'll be back in two hours," he says, and he leaves her there, alone.

And so she buys the tape measure and goes to work measuring parking spaces and finds that of the mall's twenty-three disabled spaces, two are not quite wide enough—one is ninety-five inches, another ninety-four—a fact that delights her father when he returns and pays her minimum wage for two hours' effort.

The following Monday, his lawyers issue a class action lawsuit against the mall on behalf of every disabled driver in the county, and he emerges a few weeks later with a quick settlement large enough to buy, among other things, a brand-new BMW.

THE FIRST THING that really should have put Elizabeth on notice, the first clue that something a little odd was happening on this night, was a certain strange declaration early in the evening, during the hors d'oeuvres hour, regarding the Ebola virus, and how it spreads.

Elizabeth had come up to Park Shore tonight to attend a meeting of what Brandie had called her Community Corps. Jack was home watching Toby while Elizabeth was here, in Brandie's large house, visiting with these people from Brandie's group, all of them right now standing around the dining room table watching CNN on a nearby television while also idly eating from a big spread of health-conscious snacks—a veggie tray with hummus, marinated tofu, several varieties of potato chip things made from ingredients that were not in fact potatoes: beet chips, kelp chips, chips of ancient grains.

The news that day was all about the Ebola outbreak now cascading through the small towns and villages of West Africa. The really big story was that an American doctor who had been on some kind of aid mission treating Ebola patients in Liberia had, himself, caught Ebola, and he had been promptly evacuated from Africa and flown back into the country—becoming, in the process, the very first Ebola patient within the United States—and he was now traveling, in an ambulance, at high speed, to a specialized medical facility in Atlanta. CNN was showing live footage, taken via helicopter, of this very ambulance, in a motorcade of other emergency vehicles, their lights flashing, racing down some interstate, passing everyone, and the people around the hors d'oeuvres table were riveted, silent, watching this scene unfold.

"What if it crashes?" someone finally said, and everyone nodded.

"This just doesn't seem safe."

"Couldn't he have been treated where he was? Did he really have to, you know, come back?"

"I hope they have him in a bubble."

"I hope they melt down that ambulance."

"I feel for the guy, I really do, but didn't he sort of bring this on himself?"

"Well, he spent all his time thinking about the virus, and then he got the virus. It shouldn't be a surprise. The universe gives you whatever you put out there. Equal and opposite reactions. It's simple physics."

Which made Elizabeth—who had once taken AP physics at a very good school—stop chewing on the carrot she was currently eating and cock her head, like *Huh?*

But the moment passed quickly—Brandie was soon turning off the television and herding everyone into the living room, where they all took their places on couches and love seats, Brandie saying, "Thanks for coming, everyone. Let's get started now." And then she walked over to Elizabeth and stood right next to her and put a hand lovingly on Elizabeth's back and said: "You know how sometimes you meet exactly the right person at exactly the right time in your life? Well, that's what happened with me and Elizabeth. She showed up at the very moment I needed her. It was just like, *wow,* pure synchronicity."

And then everyone in the room was smiling at Elizabeth and waving at her. There were ten of them at tonight's meeting: six women, four men, midthirties to midfifties, all of them with these open expressions of trust and reassurance and happy aplomb. Elizabeth smiled and waved back.

Brandie explained that this particular group had started as just a bunch of like-minded people who did their best to do good things around town.

"We love Park Shore so much, and we want to keep it beautiful, keep it exactly the way it is, for our kids," Brandie said. "So we're really active in the community, and whenever something comes along that might jeopardize what we've built here, we try to meet it with our positive vision."

"Jeopardize?" Elizabeth said. "What do you mean?"

"Oh, there was that store that tried to open downtown. The vape store. Can you imagine? A vape store right where our kids would see it? We got that squashed right away. And that restaurant—what was it called? The one where the waitresses dress like schoolgirls."

"Twisted Knickers," said someone in the group.

"That's the one. They tried to open a branch and we were like, *No way.*"

"I see," Elizabeth said.

"But I hope this doesn't make us sound like a bunch of scolds," Brandie said. "We're really a positive group, I promise. We try not to focus on negatives. The more you think negatively, the more negativity you attract. I mean, look at the internet. People on the internet are always howling about things they hate, and all it does is create more of those very same things. No, we consider ourselves more aligned with Mother Teresa."

"Mother Teresa?"

"That's right. Mother Teresa once said she would not go to an anti-war rally but she would go to a pro-peace rally. She understood that you have to focus on the thing you *want,* not the thing you're *against.* So we're not anti-vaping, we're pro-health. We're not anti-knickers, we're pro-decency. We're not anti–Styrofoam cup, we're pro-environment. We're not anti–leaf blower, we're pro–peace and quiet."

"I understand."

"You have to take a problem and turn it into an opportunity to express your positive values. And if you do that consistently, you can really up-level your town, *and* yourself. So that's what we try to do here. We all help each other be the most outstanding next-level versions of ourselves. And in this room, I gotta tell you, there are some pretty amazing success stories."

"Oh yeah? Like what?"

"Well, for example?" said a man to her right, a late-forties guy with a former football player's physique sitting in an armchair but bent way forward, elbows on his knees, like he was in a huddle. "I found this group when I was going through a really painful divorce.

And everything was looking horrible and bleak for me back then, but these folks helped me live life more positively and gracefully. And now? My ex-wife is coming back!"

Light applause followed for the divorced guy, who acknowledged it with a little salute.

"Wow," Elizabeth said. "That's great."

"And I'm getting my diabetes under control," said a woman across the room. "I joined this group and learned how to be at peace with my body and really sincerely love my body. And now my diabetes is going away!"

More light applause. "No kidding?" Elizabeth said.

After that, everyone in the living room shared their own personal story of growth and success: one woman had found this group after getting laid off from work, and, with the group's help, she was now in the process of landing her dream job, for which she was already buying a new wardrobe and a new car; and one man had a strained relationship with his adult daughter, but now the daughter was soon coming to visit, for the first time in years; and one woman came to the group worrying about her delinquent son, and now, with the group's help, that very same son would soon be going to Stanford. It seemed like everyone's tale followed this similar arc: they'd found the group at a moment of distress or desolation, and now, with the group's help, everything in their life was turning around, turning a corner, everything was at this moment soon becoming *great*.

"Pretty amazing, eh?" Brandie said.

And, yeah, Elizabeth had to agree. She was thinking that she hadn't experienced this particular kind of group dynamic—this vat of intense goodwill—since those days at the Foundry, her friends all sitting together in the ground-floor gallery, talking, laughing, giving each other back rubs. "Pretty amazing," she said.

Then Brandie clasped her hands together and said: "Now it's time to practice some gratitude!"

And she sat down right next to Elizabeth and leaned toward her in a posture of intense focused listening and said: "Okay. Go for it."

"What, me?" Elizabeth said.

"Yes, you! It's time to practice your gratitude. Go."

And Elizabeth looked around the room, at the group who was smiling at her, waiting for her. "I'm not sure exactly how to do that," she said, and everyone in the room gave a knowing little laugh.

"We've all been there," Brandie said, nodding sympathetically. "We have all been exactly where you are right now."

"Boy oh boy, is *that* ever true," said the divorced guy, which made everyone, for some reason, laugh real hard.

"Let's start simple," Brandie said. "Repeat after me. *I'm grateful for blank,* and fill in the blank."

"Okay," Elizabeth said. "I'm grateful for . . . my health."

"Okay, sure, but maybe that's a bit too easy?" Brandie said. "Maybe a bit obvious? It's pretty simple to feel gratitude for the pleasant stuff, but it's way more powerful to feel gratitude for the difficult stuff, the hard stuff. Here, observe."

And then she closed her eyes and took a deep, measured breath— long inhale, equally long exhale—and seemed to gather herself for a moment, then she said, quietly: "I'm grateful for all the challenges that have made me the person I am today. I'm grateful for all the pain that made me stronger. I'm grateful to Chester Fullerton, who broke my heart at the spring formal junior year. I'm grateful to Miss Godwyn, my camp counselor in eighth grade, who said I'd never amount to anything. I'm grateful to my dad, for being so bad with money, for all his failed schemes, his gambling. I'm grateful for those times we had to hide in our own home when the debt collectors came knocking. It made me envision a life of abundance, a life of peace and freedom, which is exactly the life I have now. I'm grateful to everyone who revealed my path, even if they did it by accident, or with malice. To them I want to say: *thank you.*"

The room was quiet. Brandie took another large breath, and then she smiled, and when she opened her eyes and looked at Elizabeth, it was with an expression of deep calm and serenity and Zen-like openness and ease.

"That was really beautiful," Elizabeth said.

"Now it's your turn. Try to find gratitude for something that's hard. What is hard in your life right now?"

"Well," Elizabeth said, "I suppose I'm worried about my son. He's starting at a new school."

"And what are you worried about?"

"That he'll fit in and be happy and, you know, adjust."

"And what would that look like?" Brandie said. "Close your eyes and describe it. Visualize it. Think about it as if it's already happened. What does it mean, that he fits in?"

Elizabeth closed her eyes. "I guess it means that he has lots of friends, and he looks forward to going to school every day, and he's no longer having so many episodes."

"Episodes?"

"He has tantrums, meltdowns, outbursts, that kind of thing."

"And these outbursts, they worry you?"

"Of course."

"Why?"

"Well, for one, I don't like to see him so upset. I feel bad for him."

"Obviously, sure. What else?"

"And I guess I worry that the outbursts will make it harder for him to learn in school, or make friends."

"Those are legitimate worries," Brandie said, "but those are reasons you're worried for *him*, worried on his behalf. Why are you worried for *you*?"

"What do you mean?"

"What worries do you have that are yours alone? Separate from him?"

Elizabeth sat there, eyes still closed. Her fists were clenched, she realized now, her fingers digging hard into the skin of her palms. She thought about Brandie's question and the image that called itself forth in her mind was of herself as a teenager, sitting quietly in her father's BMW, sitting there staring straight ahead as he smashed the window of a van next to her, smashed it using her brand-new tennis racket while Elizabeth was pressed into her seat doing that thing she did during any of his unpredictable eruptions—*going gray rock*, is what she called it—sitting there as if nothing mattered and nothing could disturb her.

"My dad had outbursts too," she said softly.

"Okay," said Brandie. Her voice was low and tender. "Now we're getting somewhere. Go on."

It was not something Elizabeth would normally have admitted, but Brandie's unexpected confession had her feeling more open, more forthcoming. "My dad had a temper," she said. "Anger issues. Impulse-control problems. That sort of thing. Random fury. It was kind of terrorizing."

"That must have been very challenging," said Brandie.

"He wasn't violent toward *people*. But walls got punched, things got smashed, objects got thrown. It wasn't violence directed at me— more like violence directed *around* me."

"That's terrible."

"Sometimes I see it in Toby, and it freaks me out."

"Of course."

Brandie's voice was so tender, so sympathetic, so full of care that Elizabeth found herself spilling more details. "I think he was always competitive with me," she said. "My dad. Anytime I beat him at anything, or outsmarted him, or just if I knew something that he didn't know, he'd get upset, and then sometimes things would get broken. He was the kind of guy who needed me to fail to feel good about himself, you know? And so I had to live by this unspoken rule: be perfect, but never too perfect. Be successful, but never threatening. Achieve, but never more than him."

She could still remember sitting in a classroom junior year, silently filling in bubbles on the SAT with her #2 pencil, and she'd been at it for almost three hours when she came to the exam's last question, another of those dumb word analogies: *replete* is to *fossilized* as *blank* is to *blank*. All morning she'd been solving these riddles, plus the reading questions before them, plus the assorted problems of algebra and geometry and trigonometry, and so far there hadn't been any problem that was remotely troubling. And she'd come to this final question with a full twelve minutes of time remaining, and as she stared at it the feeling she had was suddenly one of detaching. It wasn't that she didn't know the answer; it was more like she didn't care enough to think about it. It was roughly the same feeling she'd had when she'd decided not to write the easy four-page essay she was required to write in her music appreciation class. She had completed so many hundreds of school assignments by then, all of them perfectly, and then she was assigned this one lousy paper about the idée fixe in the *Symphonie Fantastique* and she just abandoned it. She ignored it. She simply did not do it. She took a zero, and thus her grade dropped from an A to an A-minus, and thus her GPA fell from 4.0 to 3.99, and that was the difference between valedictorian and not. And Elizabeth didn't care. Just as she didn't care as she sat in that classroom and her mind went blank for twelve minutes—it was the feeling of withdrawing, detaching, turning into a rock—and time was called and she turned in the SAT with this one question, the final question, unanswered.

Elizabeth continued: "I always had to sabotage myself to keep my father happy."

"But does it help you to dwell on it now?" Brandie said. "Does it really help you, staying way up there on your pain pedestal?"

"My what?"

"Is there a way you can feel gratitude, now, for your father? Can you be grateful for him and absolve him? Can you say thank you and I forgive you and I set you free? Because you have to declutter your heart, Elizabeth, just as much as you declutter your house. Take whatever is unnecessary and thank it for its service and let it go. Can you do that?"

"Well," Elizabeth said, her eyes still closed, "my father moved us around a lot, when I was a kid. I was always starting over at a new place. I suppose it made me unafraid of new situations. I suppose it made me brave."

"There you go," Brandie said. "That's how you practice real gratitude. You say to your father: Thank you for making me the brave person I am. And you say to your son: Thank you for teaching me about myself. And then I guarantee you, Toby's outbursts will stop. *I guarantee it.* Your son is cured."

"How is he cured?"

"By saying it. By saying it over and over. He is cured. You speak your truth into the universe and you will manifest it in your life, just like I manifested *you*."

"Wait," Elizabeth said, opening her eyes. "What?"

Brandie smiled at her. "If you want your life to change, you have to *believe* it will change, you have to envision the change, and then it will change. Speak of things as if they're true, and they will become true. That's exactly how I brought you into my life."

"You brought me?"

"Yes, with my thoughts."

"Okay," Elizabeth said, considering the group much more warily now. "But . . . how?"

"I asked the universe to solve my marriage problem, and I strongly believed that the universe would solve my marriage problem, and look what happened. You showed up."

"Ask, believe, receive," said the woman with the cured diabetes.

"That's how it all works!" said the divorced guy. "It's about getting aligned with the right vibrations. If your mind is vibrating right, the right things will be attracted to it. Like a magnet! It's a fundamental law of the universe. Einstein actually discovered it."

"But, did he though?"

"The key is to keep persisting inside your fantasy until the fantasy becomes a fact."

After which there came, from all quarters, a strained explanation of the mechanism for all of this, which, as far as Elizabeth could discern, had to do with quantum physics and thoughts transforming into energy and energy existing in positive and negative states and how one's energy sent vibrations out into space-time that produced either positive or negative changes in one's own reality, or something like that. Honestly, by the time the divorced guy was explaining how the universe was really one big hologram, Elizabeth found her spirits plummeting. She was feeling the way she sometimes felt at work when one of her clients was successfully duped by another of her sham Wellness treatments: disappointed, and even disdainful. That people were so easily persuaded and deluded made her occasionally feel sorry for these people, and also a little contemptuous of them, that they'd sacrifice truth for a story only because the story made them feel good. Elizabeth regarded herself as more disciplined than that, more dispassionate, objective, trained in a scientific world of confidence intervals and standard deviations and sigma values and the unbiased pursuit of fact. She would never believe a story like the one the divorced guy was right now telling, a story so devoid of hard evidence, a story that would never stand up to rigorous scrutiny. This was what she was thinking as she listened to him explain that what people experienced as "the real world" was actually a 3D hologram emanating from a 2D plane of energy and that our thoughts created mini-holograms within this more macro-hologram and altered the hologram to reproduce our thoughts in the perceivable world, and right at that moment Elizabeth interrupted him and said: "So, to be clear, your ex-wife. Is she actually coming back? Like, for real?"

"Yes, of course."

"Okay. Where is she right now?"

"Well," he said, a little defensively, "I mean, technically, officially, she's still, you know"—and here he raised his hands in finger quotes—"*living with Chad*."

"Right."

"But I know if I believe it hard enough, she'll be coming home very soon. It is all up to me. It is entirely within my control."

"That's exactly correct," Brandie said.

"What about you?" Elizabeth said, addressing the woman who had purchased the clothes and the car. "Your dream job? Is that a real thing?"

"What you have to understand," the woman said, "is that the universe responds to symbolic action. And what better way to signal to the universe that I am ready to accept its abundance than to buy things I totally cannot afford?"

"Oh my god," Elizabeth said. Then she looked at the woman with the cured diabetes. "And you? How's your health?"

"Well, my doctors keep telling me I have diabetes," she said, "and I keep insisting to them that I definitely do not."

"You are perfectly healthy," Brandie said, with sudden intensity. "Every cell and nerve and tissue of your pancreas is now being made whole and pure and perfect. Your entire body is being restored to health and harmony because you hold within yourself the power of total healing."

"Thank you," the woman said. "Thank you."

Elizabeth stood up and smoothed her shirt and said: "Can I use your bathroom?"

"It's just down the hall," Brandie said.

Elizabeth was worried that she might say something—something impulsive, something regrettable—worried that her disappointment might be made too plain to these people who would soon be, after all, friends, neighbors, colleagues. So she excused herself to go gather her thoughts, but then, at the end of the hall, she spotted a closed door with a sign upon it, a piece of what looked to be driftwood, lathed and sanded down, the words QUIET ROOM chiseled into it, hanging there on the door by a knotted piece of twine. Elizabeth considered this sign for a moment, glanced behind her to make sure no one was coming, then quickly opened the door.

Inside, the room had been decorated in a kind of serene beach vibe: there were shells and smooth river stones set sparsely on small tables of weathered wood. There were candles on the floor, in meticulous clusters near a large square pillow, cream-colored, big enough for meditating or napping upon. There was a rattan chair by the window, a few heavy blankets slung over its back. There were jagged bricks of pink salt glowing by some inner light, diffusing into the air.

But the room's dominant feature was the board. An immense corkboard that spanned three of the room's four walls, the whole thing a collage of drawings and photographs and pictures cut out of magazines and pages ripped from books with sentences highlighted or underlined. Elizabeth got up close to the board, near a spot where the name MIKE had been stenciled, where Brandie had tacked up, all over and even atop each other in sedimentary layers, pictures of couples, happy, together, embracing, holding hands. There were stills from Disney movies, princes and princesses, and photographs from magazines, advertisements, couples walking on beaches, or eating beautiful meals together, or lying in bed, one splayed over the other. And, distressingly, Elizabeth now saw that the faces of the people in some of these photos had been replaced, that Brandie's face or her husband's face had been taped or pasted over the original image.

A vision board, Elizabeth understood, was supposed to be an aspirational thing, but this one seemed more like a monument to suffering. She imagined all the hours Brandie must have spent here, fantasizing about a marriage more pleasing and secure than the one she actually had. It was like a road map of Brandie's injured psyche: how shattered she must have been by her husband's affair, how she probably went searching, desperate, for answers, discovered some pseudoscientific wisdom online, some philosophy that claimed she could control her life by controlling her thoughts, which must have appealed to her immensely, that she could personally dictate whether anything bad ever happened to her again.

Elizabeth moved along, to another wall, where a large white posterboard was hung, and at its center was a picture of Brandie's own house, her beautiful Park Shore château, and all around the house, extending in a big halo, she had written dozens—maybe even a hundred—short affirmations:

I will be HAPPY in this house.
This is my DREAM HOME.
I will ENJOY MY LIFE.
I WILL LOVE BEING HERE.
I WILL BE VERY, VERY HAPPY!!

And so on, Elizabeth reading all this and feeling bad—devious, even—like how it feels to stumble onto a friend's diary, like a violation and a betrayal. She left the quiet room, closed the door softly behind her.

Back out among the guests, Elizabeth invented some emergency at home—Jack had food poisoning, she said—and they all wished her well and invited her to come back anytime and assured her that her husband would be feeling better very soon, insisting that he'd probably be back to 100 percent even before she got home, because of course they were all now thinking about him, helping him, being positive for him, sending him their very best and most healthy vibrations.

ORIGIN STORIES

J ACK ALWAYS KNEW that burn season was close when he felt the wind turn. In December, January, February, the wind came mostly from the north, bringing to Kansas in weakened form whatever cold misery blew upon the Dakotas. But at some point in mid-March, the wind shifted southerly, and then it felt different, smelled different, and swept over the hills all at once. It was a wind that, in drought years, came gusting up so hard it felt like the whole Dust Bowl was coming with it, a dry and hot wind that bloomed forth from Texas and Oklahoma and tinted the sky the faint reddish hue of southern clay. The spring of 1984 was like that, a parched spring of daily wind advisories, when eighteen-wheelers actually tipped over on the Kansas Turnpike, the broad sides of their trailers catching the air like sails in a storm.

Jack loved it, the wind, loved watching how it interacted with the world, how the wind's shape was defined in the swirling grasses, in eddies that twirled twigs and spun up dust, tiny twisters that disappeared in seconds. Or how, in the sky, a line of starlings suddenly changed course midflight, their tight formation pummeled by a squall. Or how a hawk angled itself into the wind and hovered in place, unmoving, like a tethered kite, and then with a slight roll of its wing achieved a kind of blastoff in the exact opposite direction. Jack watched all these things, leaning out his upstairs bedroom window and looking upon a world that to the naked eye seemed empty and peaceful but he knew to be profuse and convulsing and agitated.

His father Lawrence was more hands-on. What Lawrence liked to do on the windiest days—those years he was still working, still communicative, still going outside—was play home run derby. He'd go to the north pasture, where the distance from the near fence to the far fence was about the distance between home plate and the center field wall at Royals Stadium, and he'd spend an hour pretending to be George Brett, launching fly balls into the jet stream and watching them carry illegitimately far.

Jack's job was to fetch the balls. He'd stand at the far fence wearing a tattered baseball glove that was laughably useless because even if he managed to maneuver himself beneath a fly ball, he would always, at the last minute, bail. He'd run away, screaming, arms protecting his skull like they did in school tornado drills. Watching that dense, unforgiving baseball hurtling right at him at what seemed like a thousand miles per hour was too much to bear. He could not place his body willingly in front of it. He didn't want to chicken out with his father watching, but some acts are not volitional, not when there's that much fear involved.

Lawrence was so far away that Jack would see the baseball shoot into the air well before he heard the crack of the bat (though it wasn't a crack, exactly; the sound of an aluminum bat striking a baseball is less a crack and more of a plink). The baseball would already be a hundred feet off the ground and soaring toward him with deadly intent when the plink finally arrived. And when the balls landed, they seemed to detonate in the grass—in all the many times they did this together, Jack never managed to make a catch, not even once—and the balls would bury themselves in the thatch, a layer several inches deep of basically hay: dead grass, dry and scratchy, a lair of spiders and mice and snakes. Jack would have to root around in it, terrified of attacks by biting things, and then he'd hear the plink of another projectile and feel a secondary terror that while he was looking for this buried baseball he'd get conked in the head by the next one. Then he'd collect all the baseballs in a bucket and drag the bucket over the uneven ground all the way back to his father. The north pasture was the larger of the two pastures—their house was built between these fields: a smaller one to the south, this large one to the north, separated by barbed-wire fence and gravel driveways and wide cattle trails that served as firebreaks. The north pasture was as big as a baseball stadium, and it took Jack several long minutes to drag that heavy bucket all the way back to his father, who ribbed him along the way—"C'mon, buddy, pick up the pace, let's go, let's go!"

But Lawrence was away on this particular windy spring after-noon, visiting ranches down south in preparation for the annual burns. Jack's mother was, as usual, holed up in her bedroom, watch-ing the full daytime lineup from the Wichita CBS affiliate, the only channel the television's bunny ears picked up. She'd been in bed since $25,000 Pyramid, was currently on Press Your Luck, and would likely be there through The Price Is Right, The Young and the Restless, As the World Turns, and all the way to Dan Rather at 5:30, when she would put some fish sticks in the oven and then return to the bed-room for prime time: Magnum P.I., Simon & Simon, Knots Landing.

Jack was upstairs, avoiding her, playing Dungeons & Dragons in his room, alone.

Theirs was a small house, a one-and-a-half-story frame house, the half story being an attic that had been turned into a bedroom. The main floor held his parents' room, and a den, and the small kitchen. And then there was the basement, which terrified him, a dirt floor and cold concrete walls, rickety and rotten plywood stairs, a dark place full of cobwebs, millipedes.

It was the first day of his school's spring vacation, and a week of nothingness unfolded before him. His mother rarely allowed him to leave the house, owing to his general sickliness, which also prompted her to keep him home from school at the merest cough, the slightest change of appetite. And so he had a lot of time to kill and generally nobody to kill it with—his mother watched televi-sion, his father worked, and even when his sister, Evelyn, had still been living at home, she was far too old to be a playmate. Then at a garage sale one weekend he'd spotted a Dungeons & Dragons guide with associated dice and figurines, and he found the book's cover completely beguiling: a knight with a glinting silver sword, a wizard summoning fire with his bare hands. And since he knew his mother would never buy it for him—she had been attending Calvary Church and had internalized its overwrought warnings that such high-fantasy role-play was obliquely sinister devilry—he stole it. When no one was looking, he pocketed the dice, and slid the book down the back of his trousers.

It did not even make him feel guilty, not anymore. He had no friends to play with, and so, in D&D, he could create them. He sat cross-legged on the floor of his bedroom surrounded by dice—the traditional six-sided dice plus the more complex many-faceted things—as well as many sheets of paper on which he'd written the names and vast histories and skill inventories of these made-up friends. There was a warrior, a wizard, a warlock, a cleric, a rogue. He played all these characters at once, plus the Dungeon Master. He was currently working through a campaign he'd created himself involving a large treasure guarded by mutant grassland creatures. He read from his Dungeon Master script: "There's a rabid coyote blocking your way to the treasure. Do you want to attack?" And then in a new voice—the deep Dirty Harry growl he reserved for the barbarian in the party—he said: "Waste him."

"Now, now," he said in the nasally voice of the thief, whom Jack suspected of secretly being a coward, "must we always resort to violence?"

"Perhaps we could reason with the beast," he said in the bored, aristocratic, slightly British voice of the wizard.

Then the warlock, a good-old-boy type who liked to get under people's skin, jumped in to accuse the wizard of being too cautious and cerebral, and the two of them spent a bunch of time arguing about the best course of action while the barbarian rolled his eyes in a kind of here-we-go-again manner because he'd heard this argument before and had learned to stay out of the way until it concluded as it always did, with a dice roll that pitted the warlock's persuasion skill against the sorcerer's willpower, with the warlock, this time, coming out on top.

"Yeehaw!" he exclaimed in the warlock's (for some reason) deep Southern accent.

Then came a shout—"Jack!"—from below, from his mother's room. He quickly hid all his D&D contraband in its spot behind the dresser, tiptoed down the stairs, tapped lightly on her door, and pushed it slowly open. Inside, the television howled, someone on-screen yelling "No whammy! No whammy!" to enthusiastic audience applause. His mother, in her twin bed, in a pink robe, sitting against the headboard, knees up, stared at the TV. The only evidence that she acknowledged his presence was that her head tilted a few degrees in his direction.

"I'm sorry," he said.

"What is all that commotion?"

"Nothing."

"I've been calling you for ten minutes!"

"I didn't hear."

"Of course not," she said. "Nobody ever pays attention to anything I say. Might as well not even be here."

"I was just playing a game," Jack said.

The air was quarantine-stale and smelled lightly of sweaty blanket and potpourri and that particular, unmistakable biologic scent of a parent's bedroom. His father's twin bed sat next to his mother's, and it was made—as it always was—tightly. The contestant on the TV yelled, "Stop!" and then everyone cheered. No whammy.

"What game were you playing?" his mother said.

"Nothing. Just pretending."

She took a deep, annoyed breath. "Always off in make-believe land."

"I'm sorry."

"Maybe if your head wasn't in the clouds, you'd be doing better in school."

His mother was idly twirling her hair around a finger, her long straight hair that used to be hazelnut brown but was now fully gray and in some places even white. She'd told Jack many times that he was basically responsible for this, that her first gray streaks appeared during his illness-addled infancy, such was the stress he put her under. On TV, the contestant continued imploring for "Big bucks!" and "No whammies!"

Jack said: "Can I go outside?"

"Why?" she said, still staring at the television, which sat heavily upon the storage bench at the foot of her twin bed.

Jack had seen this program, *Press Your Luck*, once or twice before. It was a game show where people took spins on what was essentially a highly embellished slot machine, which awarded them money and vacations and jewelry and cars and boats and state-of-the-art kitchen appliances. But the greedier they were, and the more spins they took, the greater the chance they'd lose everything and get bankrupted by the detestable "whammy," an animated bright red ambiguously humanoid creature that waltzed across the screen stealing all their money and prizes while cackling sinisterly. It was one of those game shows that required no skill or talent except for the ability to leverage one's low impulse control to occasionally, entertainingly, do stupid or embarrassing things, a TV trope (Jack would think, roughly a decade later) that was eventually adopted and perfected by *The Real World*.

He said: "I'm tired of being inside."

Just then, a gust of wind screamed along the edges of the house. The front screen door popped open and banged against its hinges.

"So now you're leaving me too?" she said.

Jack looked at the floor. One of the reasons he rarely spoke to his mother was that most anything he said seemed to accidentally hurt her. "Just for a minute," he said. "I'll be right back."

"Everyone's leaving me."

"No one is leaving you."

"Evelyn left me, a long time ago," she said. "And today your father's off god knows where."

"He's doing the burns."

"He *says* he's doing the burns."

She got this way each spring, right about the time that Lawrence began taking overnight trips to faraway ranches and preparing his fire plans for that year's prescribed burn. All of a sudden, Ruth Baker would become bleak and cynical and fatalistic.

The contestant on the television finally hit a whammy and the crowd groaned at his misfortune. His mother grinned.

"I'm only going outside," Jack said. "I'm not *leaving*."

"It's windy."

"I won't be out long."

"You have chores."

"What chores?"

"You have to get your room ready."

"For what?"

"Your sister's coming tonight."

"*Really?*" Jack said, smiling, unable in the moment to hide his excitement, which of course his mother took rueful note of.

"Wish you were ever that happy to see me," she said.

He looked at the floor again. "I am."

"Guess I'm not good enough for you, is that it?"

Jack shook his head and said nothing.

"We can't all be like Evelyn, you know."

"I know."

"Some of us have responsibilities," she said, turning back now to the television and resuming her long stare.

It was always this way with his mother: any fun he had seemed to come at her expense; any happiness he felt seemed to imply unhappiness with her. He could never admit to pleasure or cheer. If he enjoyed himself at a friend's birthday party, his mother took it as a criticism of her. If he enjoyed a meal at a restaurant, she took it as a rebuff of the meals she served at home. If he was proud of a decent test score, she accused him of implying she was stupid.

It required a careful emotional calibration. He could never appear too explicitly joyous about anything that did not directly involve her, otherwise she might take his joy as proof that he did not love her and say something awful: "If you're so happy without me, maybe I should just kill myself" being a favorite phrase.

And yet he could not advertise explicit unhappiness either, or else she might take that unhappiness also as proof that he did not love her: "If I make you so miserable, maybe I should just kill myself" being, again, a favorite phrase.

It was an ordeal, in other words. Never be too happy or too sad. He was right in the middle. He was fine. Everything was always fine.

"Go on now," his mother said, still staring at the television even though *Press Your Luck* had gone to commercial. "Get to work."

And so he left her bedroom and walked upstairs—not too quickly, nor in a manner that could be interpreted as "eager" or "hopeful" or "enthusiastic"—and he went about preparing his room for their special guest.

His big sister, Evelyn, was coming to visit.

Evelyn was already in her early teens when Jack was born, had moved out of the house before he'd even started elementary school, and so mostly what he knew of her came from these irregular visits, plus of course his mother's descriptions: charitably, his mother called Evelyn "a free spirit"; less charitably, she was "flighty" or "frivolous" or, simply, "different." She'd left Kansas immediately upon graduating high school, coming back only occasionally and unpredictably. Where she went the rest of the year, and what she did there, was something of a mystery. Every time she visited, it seemed like she had just come from some new and strange place. One year it was an island in Lake Superior, off the Upper Peninsula of Michigan, where she'd wintered at an artist colony, in a small cabin, the only heat coming from a woodstove that she regularly fed. Another year she'd just finished a stay on Cape Cod—all the way at the end of it, she said, at the iconoclastic tip—doing whatever one does at a *residency*. The year before, she'd been in the West Texas desert, at another artist colony, more stories of inspiring nights with writers and actors and painters and musicians. She'd come to the Baker ranch each year with tales of adventure in far-flung places: New York, San Francisco, the Florida Keys. Evelyn had never married, never had a family, never kept a job for more than a year, was always on the move.

"My daughter, the *artist*," Ruth would say, pronouncing the word with a great sarcastic French inflection: *ar-TEEST*.

They had a cold but accommodating relationship. During Evelyn's stays, they mostly let each other be. Ruth still spent most afternoons with her game shows and soaps, but when she emerged from her bedroom she found that Evelyn had added her own touches to the house: wildflowers began appearing in vases in every room, and windows that had been occluded by winter's grime were suddenly clean, the sunlight now surging in with renewed exuberance. While Ruth watched television, Evelyn went outside with her acrylics and painted landscapes. Or she spent days hiking the fields and collecting odd treasures, explaining her amazing discoveries over dinner: a shard of glass that was probably Depression era, a chip of bone that might have been bison, a piece of flint that was once almost certainly a Pawnee arrowhead. Ruth rolled her eyes.

"That's just a rock," she said.

"It's a rock with significance," Evelyn said, twirling the maybe-arrowhead in her fingers, her eyes aglow. "It's a rock with history."

"You always have to make things more than they are," Ruth said. "That's a rock. Plain and simple."

"The only thing at this table that's plain and simple," Evelyn said, smiling teasingly, "is you."

Indeed, *plainness* was the condition that Ruth seemed to strive for most. She still had the same haircut, at age forty-six, that she'd had in her high school pictures—which is to say long and straight and utterly neglected—whereas Evelyn came home each year with her bright blond hair done in a new style, and sometimes a new color. Ruth had no use for fashionable clothes, and had been wearing the same things—the same pink robe, the same few T-shirts—for several years, this despite the dresses that Evelyn brought each year as gifts, brightly colored dresses beautifully unsuited to life on a Kansas ranch. The two of them were the same height, though Ruth was a sloucher, her posture a kind of permanently weary quarter-bow, whereas Evelyn held a dancer's erect verticality, making her seem a good three or four inches taller than her mom. And where Ruth's general demeanor toward the rest of the world was basically *exasperation,* Evelyn seemed to be enchanted by everything.

Jack loved her visits. He loved the new vitality and life she brought to the house. It was odd how the addition of Evelyn did not make the small house feel more crowded but actually made it feel bigger, as if, during her stay, the house stretched and grew a few more rooms.

That night, after his chores were complete, Jack was eating fish sticks in the kitchen when he heard a car coming. The Baker ranch was located off a gravel road that had no name—it was designated Rural Route 13 by the post office, but that was mere paperwork, nothing real. Nobody came down this road unless they were coming to the ranch. The nearest house was ten miles away.

"She's here!" Jack yelled, and he went to the window to watch. His mother emerged from her bedroom, where the TV still blared, and stood next to him. They could see the car as a kind of aurora on the horizon, its headlights being the only light for miles save for the light of the house itself. They heard the crunch of tires interacting with the road, and the secondary pings and pops of stones driven upward and bouncing off an undercarriage and bumper.

"I wonder what crazy thing your sister did this year," his mother said. "That girl, she can never be still."

The headlights came into focus now, and Jack could tell right away that they were not the headlights of the economy car that Evelyn usually rented at the Wichita airport. They were instead the headlights of a truck—and a very distinctive truck, Lawrence Baker's 1973 F100, that boxy green Ford he'd driven as long as Jack could remember.

"What in the world?" said Ruth, who was now noticing the same thing. "Is that . . . ?"

Indeed it was. The truck pulled into the long dirt driveway and motored up to the house and there they were, Lawrence and Evelyn, getting out of the truck, talking, laughing at some private joke, Lawrence taking Evelyn's two big suitcases from the truck's bed and carrying them up to the porch. Evelyn looked as radiant as ever, her hair pulled back into a ponytail that bounced as she bounced, walking happily to the house wearing a red polka-dot dress. Lawrence was cleaned-up and sharp-looking—hair combed back rather than covered by his typical John Deere cap, a shirt with buttons, jeans unstained by ash or dirt, new-looking sneakers rather than his usual work boots. For a man usually so taciturn and neutral, it was refreshing to witness his smile.

Ruth met them at the front door, furious.

"Well *hello*," she said in a way that was unmistakably *not* a greeting. She did not like surprises.

Lawrence and Evelyn stopped just outside the door and they all three considered one another for an awkward moment before Evelyn, ignoring her mother's tone, opened the screen door and leaned in for a big hug. "It's been so long!"

Ruth directed an annoyed gaze at Lawrence. "What are *you* doing here?"

"Fetching Evelyn."

"I thought you were down south."

"Too windy," Lawrence said. "Can't do any burns in this damn wind."

"And you didn't think to tell *me*?" Ruth said.

"It's good to see you too, Mom," Evelyn said.

Ruth breathed in deeply and seemed to relent. "I'm always the last to know *everything*," she said, exasperated once more, then walked toward the kitchen. "Come in. I'll put on coffee."

"Oh my goodness!" Evelyn said when she spotted Jack, then rushed over to him and leaned way down low, hands on her knees, to speak with him face-to-face. "You've gotten *sooooooooo* much bigger!"

Jack knew this wasn't strictly true. His general inability to grow or put on weight was a topic of open discussion. Recently his mother had asked the doctor about maybe injecting him with growth hormone, something she understood was done to cattle and thought might also work with her son, her *little Jack Sprat,* which was her new and embarrassing nickname for him.

"Thanks," he said now, looking at the floor.

"You know what, big guy?" Evelyn said. "I have a *present* for *you!*"

She was talking in that measured, deliberate, singsong, condescending way you talk to people you believe are—and this would be his mom's word for it—*slow*. It was speech intended to be so sluggish that even the dimmest child could keep up.

"Thank you," Jack said.

"Give it to him later," Ruth said. Then, to Jack: "Go on. The adults are gonna talk."

Jack went upstairs and listened through the floor, but could hear only a vague murmur of voices. And so, satisfied that they'd be at coffee and conversation for a good long while, he did what he'd been doing lately anytime he was assured of lengthy isolation. He extracted that single Dungeons & Dragons game book from its hiding spot behind his dresser, removed all the loose notebook pages on which he'd drawn maps and quests and characters and creatures and notes for elaborate campaigns, and he played.

He picked up the game where he'd left it, with the barbarian facing down a monstrous rabid coyote, and Jack growled in the barbarian's delicious tenor: "Let's waste him."

Then he rolled six dice (agility test) and counted the result and recorded it in his notebook and then rolled five more dice (perception test) and counted that result and then rolled five dice again (skill test) and then four (defense test) and then two (strength test) and each time carefully recorded the results (all the while making the associated grunting and steel-shattering sound effects of battle), until finally he announced—again, in the warrior's deep voice—that the monster was, indeed, "Wasted."

"You got him!" he said in the frightened voice of the thief. "Impaled! Bleeding! Stuck him right through the solar plexus!"

"He's down but not out!" he said in a kind of radio-ad-guy voice that he used for the slightly annoying, socially awkward cleric of the bunch.

"Boy, is that dog ever mad," he said in the warlock's Southern twang. "Madder than a puffed toad!"

"Shall we please just finish him off," he said in the jaded voice of the wizard.

"Spittin' mad!" said the warlock. "Madder than a wet hen!"

"Okay, we get it," said the wizard. "He's mad."

"Madder than a mule chewin' on bumblebees!"

And it was at that moment that Jack heard a slight squeak in the floorboards and turned around to see Evelyn halfway in his room— she'd been there, watching him, for who knows how long.

Jack's face flushed, and he began collecting all the papers and dice in a sudden panic. "Sorry!" he said, though he didn't know exactly what he was sorry for. It was a reflex; if his mother caught him having this much fun, she'd be scandalized.

But Evelyn merely smiled at him and sat on the bed.

"What are you doing?" she said.

Jack shrugged and stared at the floor. "Nothing. Just playing."

"You do this a lot?" Her eyes were blue and alert and looked right at you, as opposed to Ruth, who typically seemed to stare about five degrees to either side of your head.

"I guess," he said. "Kind of a lot."

"What campaign?"

Jack looked at her then, surprised she knew that word *campaign*, lingo that implied familiarity.

"I don't know," he said. "I made it up."

"Show me," she said.

And so he showed her the maps he'd drawn, the monsters he'd created, the quests he'd invented. The problem with owning only one D&D book was that he ran out of material pretty quickly, and because he didn't dare ask his mother for more adventure guides, he had to invent the adventures himself.

"You did all this?" Evelyn asked, looking at the papers spread over the bedroom floor: blueprints of castles modeled on actual castles he'd seen in his geography textbook, illustrations of baroque evil creatures based on actual creatures he observed on the prairie: a red-tailed hawk, a copperhead snake, a pack of coyotes, all of them here fantastically enlarged and monstrous.

Jack looked over his creations, said: "Uh-huh."

"This is beautiful," she said, picking up the picture of the hawk and studying it. "So much detail."

"There's a hawk that lives in a tree outside my bedroom window. I watch him."

"You have a good eye."

"I'm at my bedroom window a lot," Jack said.

She nodded and returned the picture to its place on the floor, surveyed the mess of papers and dice. "Isn't this a difficult game to play by yourself?"

"Sort of," Jack said. "The biggest problem is playing both the Dungeon Master and the players at the same time."

"What do you mean?"

"Like, when I'm the Dungeon Master, I know all the surprises and secrets. Where the traps are, where the monsters hide, where the treasure is buried. But when I'm the players, I have to act like I don't know any of that."

"I can see how that would be confusing."

Jack gave a no-big-deal kind of shrug. "It's just one more level of pretend," he said. "Instead of being the Dungeon Master, it's more like I'm the Dungeon Master Master."

She smiled and studied him for a long moment, then stood up, said, "I'll leave you to it then." She was no longer talking in that ponderous way she'd talked to him downstairs. Now she spoke normally, as if to a normal person. She walked toward the door, but before leaving, she turned around and gave him one last long penetrating stare.

"Mom tells everyone that you're slow," she said.

"I know."

"But you're not slow at all, are you."

Jack shrugged again.

"I think you're going to surprise her," she said. "I think you're going to surprise everyone. I think you're going to knock their socks off."

Jack grinned. He could feel the heat gathering in his face, and a kind of lightness in his chest that he found almost unbearable in the way it made him want to both laugh and cry at the same time.

"Did you have a present for me?"

"Yes!" she said, her face brightening. "One second!"

She returned with a long brown cardboard tube.

"I thought you could use some more art in here," she said. "This room? It's a little drab."

It was true—the walls of Jack's bedroom were empty save for the old wallpaper that was the creamy aged color of something that was once white. When Evelyn was the occupant of this room, she filled it with all she found beautiful: pressed flowers and watercolor landscapes, scraps of wood threaded with rope and turned into mobiles, fossilized trilobites she'd discovered in the local chert—all of which Ruth removed as soon as Evelyn left home. Since then, Jack had never asked for anything to put on his walls, because anything he loved enough to put on a wall was also something he loved enough to keep private, far away from his mother's scrutiny or moods.

Evelyn opened the cardboard tube. Inside, rolled up, were several large glossy posters that Evelyn carefully removed and unspooled.

They were reproductions of paintings, some of which Jack even recognized. There was that picture of a man sitting by himself in a diner on an empty city street—"It's called *Nighthawks*," Evelyn said—and one of Monet's water lilies, this one all purple and green squiggles, and two more that were incomprehensible—one a chaos of crosshatches, the other a splattering of color—a de Kooning and a Rothko, Evelyn said, adding: "They're abstract. Someday I'll explain that to you."

Then she pulled out the last one. "My favorite," she said as she unrolled it, and right away Jack knew what it was. He could not say where specifically he'd seen it before, but he was already well acquainted with it: the farmer with his pitchfork, the stoic woman to his right, the white farmhouse behind them.

"*American Gothic*," Evelyn said. "The artist who painted this came from a very small town, way out in the country. Just like us."

Jack nodded. He was touching the poster with a fingertip, admiring its thickness, its smoothness—material that felt expensive.

"But he left his small town and moved to the city," Evelyn continued. "He went to school in Chicago, at an art school that's in a museum. Can you imagine? Going to school *in* a museum! Anyway, he became one of the most celebrated painters in the world."

"I've seen this picture before."

"Oh, sure, it's very famous. But look at it closely and tell me—who does the farmer remind you of?"

Jack studied him, and suddenly it was clear: the thin face, the close-cropped gray hair, the absolutely neutral and humorless affect—

"Dad," Jack said.

"Yes!" Evelyn said. "I thought so too! Look at him there, so quiet, so serious."

At the bottom of each poster, in gold-embossed type, it said: *The Art Institute of Chicago*. Jack ran his fingers across the lettering.

"That's where I've been this year," Evelyn said. "Chicago, mostly."

"You go everywhere," Jack said.

"Not quite *everywhere*, not yet, but I'm working on it."

"I only go to my window."

She smiled. "There's a big world out beyond these hills," she said. "Someday you'll see it. Someday you'll find where you belong."

Then she bounded to her feet. "Tomorrow, if you want, we can put these up."

Jack nodded. "Okay."

"Okay!" she said, and with a wave she bounded out the door and rejoined their parents downstairs.

He sat alone, staring at the blankness of his room. The posters were not yet up, but he could imagine them up, lit beautifully, framed elegantly against the vanilla walls—and suddenly, in his mind, he was strolling through the galleries of the Art Institute of Chicago, commenting smartly on each painting, walking with his band of best friends.

"An excellent example of an *abstract*," he said in the regal voice of the wizard.

"But it's just splotches of paint!" he complained in the low roar of the barbarian.

"I think it's real *purdy*," he said in the deep twang of the lovestruck warlock.

I T WAS because of Evelyn that Jack moved to Chicago. It was because of her that he applied to that school in the museum. It was her advice that led him to try to close that gap between feeling at home and feeling like he belonged.

And yet, in Chicago, he did not feel like he belonged. This was clear to him his very first week in the city, during the school's orientation, when he was introduced to the bewildering bureaucratic architecture of college, the many offices with names that meant nothing to him—words like *registrar* and *provost*—the dozen buildings of the spread-out Art Institute campus. Among the many things he would never admit to his new classmates was that up until that very moment, he had assumed college happened in one building. Because high school happened in one building. So did junior high, and grade school. He didn't even know he'd believed this until he was given a campus map with a confusing array of buildings and he turned to his neighbor and said, "Which one of these buildings is for school?"

To which the neighbor gave a sort of approving chuff of laughter and said, "I know, right?"

Why hadn't he been told that college happened in more than one building? Also, how did everyone already have their textbooks? In high school, the textbooks were waiting for you, on your desk, their corners curling from generational use. Also, how had everyone known to pack extravagantly for their dorm rooms? Jack had gotten off the bus from Emporia with nothing but a garbage bag full of clothes and his mother's steel typewriter, which came in a beat-up black plastic box with a handle like a briefcase. Everyone else had brought personal computers and cartons of ramen noodles, boxes of canned sodas, microwaves and tiny refrigerators, stereos with complexly arranged speakers, shelves specially designed to house giant collections of compact discs, posters for the walls. They seemed to have read some college life manual he had never been given. They seemed to have *money*, though this fact was not advertised explicitly. They all shopped at secondhand stores, just as Jack did, and they all complained about their low checking account balances, just as Jack did, and yet none of them needed a job. Jack was working part-time cleaning the art department three nights a week, a work-study job that had been advertised as "facilities management technician" but was more easily understood by its less euphemistic name: janitor. Jack was a janitor. He needed the money. Meanwhile he heard his classmates casually mention childhood trips to the fucking *Sorbonne,* and summers spent on European trains, and how their parents insisted on flying them to Christmas gatherings in Western ski towns, and Jack understood that despite surface appearances, these people were *different.* It almost felt like a betrayal, whenever he discovered some new evidence that they had not struggled as he struggled. He would hear them arguing about which of various foreign capitals were "overrated" and he wanted to say, *None of you ever went to bed in mittens because your family couldn't afford heat. None of you were ever dunked in a bathtub of ice when you had a fever because the hospital was too far away. None of you know what it's like to sincerely stop wanting things because wanting things makes your parents sad.*

But Jack didn't say any of this, of course. Mostly he sat back, quiet, ashamed, envious that these people had had such a massive head start in life regarding matters of culture and taste. They had interesting opinions about music he had never heard, books he had never read, art he had never seen, philosophies he had never known existed, cities he had never visited. This embarrassing fact—this obvious gigantic gap between their knowledge and his—was made most plain in Jack's studio photography class his first semester, a workshop in which the students were required to bring one of their own images each week to submit for "group critique," which turned out to be this insufferable process where the teacher—one Dr. Henry Laird, a middle-aged associate professor of art—would strongly imply that he had important connections with gallerists and tastemakers and collectors and critics who could launch a young artist's career, and so the students fell all over themselves trying to please him and agree with him. On the first day of these workshops, the first person to volunteer for critique showed a photograph he'd taken of Wrigley Field that included his own outstretched arm in the frame, his hand holding a postcard of that very view of Wrigley Field. It was a photograph that contained its own photograph. And even though this student had immediately volunteered to go first, still he acted like he wasn't all that satisfied with or impressed by his own work, shrugging and rolling his eyes and saying, "I don't know about this one. I think it might be too much of a cliché pomo gesture." And Laird nodded thoughtfully and the rest of the discussion about this photograph was about whether it was, indeed, a cliché pomo gesture, Jack all the while silent and thinking: *What the fuck is pomo?*

It sent him to the library after class, where he looked up *pomo* in the dictionary, and then in the encyclopedia, and in both sources found nothing, which deepened his conviction that his classmates were literally speaking a foreign language.

It took him three weeks to discover that *pomo* was short for *postmodern,* a word used most often by the students and professors who seemed really tired of, and exasperated by, art that Jack was only now seeing for the first time. Jack's inaugural stroll through the Art Institute felt wondrous: seeing his first Picasso ever, his first in-person water lily, his first Pollock drip painting, his first Rothko, his first Rembrandt, seeing van Gogh's self-portrait, seeing Grant Wood's *American Gothic.* All of these same paintings that seemed so exhilarating and soul-filling to Jack were, in his studio class, treated as camp, as tourist bait for the rubes coming in from the suburbs. It made Jack henceforth hesitate to ever admit he liked anything.

It felt mildly victorious to understand, finally, that *pomo* and *postmodern* were the same thing, but Jack's triumph was quickly diminished as soon as he tried to comprehend the meaning of *postmodern.* He would return again and again to the library—no class sent him to the library more than studio photography—to check out books written by the thinkers brought up in casual classroom conversation, and Jack discovered that getting through just one paragraph by fucking Jacques Derrida was an exercise in futility and masochism. Ditto Baudrillard, Lyotard, all of those occluded, incomprehensible, anxiety-producing books he brought home to read. Or, rather, to try to read, "reading" here being used only literally, only to describe the physical action of his eyes moving across lines of text, but without the understanding the word *reading* usually implied. Somewhere between the words and his mind was a blockage. The whole reader-writer mechanism felt like a plugged-up toilet, and Jack could not decide who, between thick reader and dense writer, was in this case the larger obstruction.

Eventually it became clear that a pomo photograph was usually less interested in its subject and more interested in itself as a photographic object. These photographs engaged in what Laird called a "contrapuntal unresolved Bakhtinian oscillation of cultural signifiers," which Jack dutifully wrote down in his notebook, word for word, next to which he spent the rest of class drawing a picture of his own severed head impaled on a pike. Photographs that were judged successful in group critiques were often photographs that "interrogated" some important intellectual and/or cultural idea: the artifice of photography, or the material conditions of art-viewing, or the simulacra of modern life. Professor Laird taught them that it was impossible to "take" photos in a world already overflowing with photos, that no image could be seen authentically because all images were at this point appropriating other images, that what a photographer did now was create pictures of pictures—that is, in a world where the subjects for art were exhausted, where there was nothing new under the sun to take a picture of, photographers no longer photographed, they *re-photographed*. In practice, this meant lots of ironic pictures of billboards, especially billboards hanging over the gridlocked Kennedy Expressway that promised some kind of spiritual escape through consumerism. Also photographs taken inside the Art Institute of people looking at art, particularly the crowd that gathered every day around *American Gothic*, a painting that, according to Professor Laird, was no longer a painting but rather a simulation of experience and a marker of shallow bourgeois taste.

"People no longer see *American Gothic*," he said. "Instead, what they see is"—and here his voice became deep and grand and bombastic, like a TV announcer introducing professional wrestlers—"*AMERICAN GOTHIC!*"

The students all nodded and smiled knowingly. Laird continued: "They cannot see *American Gothic* anymore because they cannot see it without also seeing its fame. They look at the painting and what they see is the *American Gothic* calendar in the gift shop, and the *American Gothic* coffee mug, and the *American Gothic* collectible framed poster with the Art Institute's name embossed in gold. The painting is no longer an authentic work of art. It is now a celebrity."

Introducing his own photography into this tableau felt, to Jack, almost dangerous. That first day of group critique, he had brought in his Polaroids, the ones showing trees out on the prairie, growing up crooked. In Kansas, one of the great forces of nature is the wind, the more or less constant wind that even on clear days, with no thunderstorms or wall clouds in sight, will still nudge you and press on you like a father's hand on your back. But of course there's no way to photograph the wind. The best you can do is photograph the evidence of the wind. These trees, for example, pushed so inexorably by the wind that they eventually relent and grow sideways.

The professor studied them. The class studied them. Many hands held chins, contemplatively. Finally, Laird said: "What exactly were you trying to say here?"

And Jack just voiced exactly what the pictures were already transparently saying: "That the wind is so strong the trees grow crooked."

Which Laird must have seen as a weak and wretched explanation, as he ignored it and quickly pivoted to questions about whether aestheticism in photography was inherently *naïve,* and about whether the heroic landscape photography of the early twentieth century was not in fact part of the rah-rah nationalism that abetted the Cold War, and wasn't it true that the iconic Ansel Adams portraits of the grand U.S. West in fact depoliticized and therefore colluded with Cold War–era American expansionism and patriarchy and violence?

(Judging by the way he posed these questions, it was clear the only answer Laird had in mind was: Yes.)

This is what it felt like to *not belong*: the anxiety, the constant low-level wariness, trying to avoid that shame Jack felt when it was revealed to him that he'd been doing something horribly crude, or thinking something horribly shallow. Like this photograph, which was apparently perpetuating violent American dominance, and here he'd thought it was a simple picture of a tree. His face burned.

It was with him all the time, this feeling that at any moment, in any encounter, he might accidentally do something or say something that proved to everyone here that he was not really one of them, that he was alien, idiotic, vulgar, fraudulent. It was the panic of being accountable to two competing masters: the person he wanted to be, and the person he really was. The attractive version of himself in the future, and the blundering version of himself from the past.

It's almost intolerably frightening, being stuck between those two selves.

Someday, he thought, he'll have digested enough Derrida, and he'll have read all the right books, and heard all the right music, and watched all the right films, and seen all the right art, and through a kind of inner alchemy he'll find himself being exactly who he right now hoped to become: publicly recognized, shown in galleries, reviewed ecstatically in the newspaper, talked about favorably among his peers—one day, he would be, like his sister, a real artist.

And that day, it turned out, came much sooner than he expected.

It began one morning in the co-op's ground-floor art gallery, a space that Benjamin Quince had created in what used to be a factory floor, which gave rise to the gallery's name: the Foundry. Jack and Benjamin were sitting at the gallery's only desk, on which were scattered dozens of slides from local artists hoping for a show, plus Jack's stack of rock-band photos taken recently at bars, and a big beige desktop computer.

This would be the first time Jack explored the World Wide Web—or maybe the first time he explored the *internet,* a word that seemed to be used interchangeably with *World Wide Web* but was distinct from it in mysterious ways. Jack had dropped off his photos and Benjamin suggested he stay a moment so they could get on the computer and Benjamin could show him "something cool." And so Jack waited as the computer's modem started its weird cadenza, beginning with the familiar sound of a dial tone and the beeps of a telephone number being dialed, followed by a garble of synthetic bleats and pings and whistles, then a low chirring, a buzz like static from a radio that's out of range, then cryptic blaps and blops that seemed more like cheesy audio effects from arcade games than the futuristic on-ramp to the information superhighway.

"Sounds like it's broken," Jack said, to which Benjamin laughed and said, "I know, right?"

Jack imagined that a hundred years ago this room would have been loud with the roar of industry. Today, the only sound was the cry of this little dial-up modem.

What Benjamin ended up showing him, finally, was something called a *hypertext*.

"It's a new way to read," Benjamin said as he stared at the screen, waiting for something to load. "It's a new way to experience stories, and probably even a new way to think: interactive, nonsequential, ergodic, polyvocal—"

"Stop using grad-school words."

"With hypertext, we're finally freed from the hegemony of the book."

"*Hegemony*? Ben, please, I'm begging you."

"Consider the book—and I mean the technology of the book, the actual physical form of the traditional printed codex book. You really have no choice but to read it in the way that's been prescribed to you, front to back, linearly, in order. You have no agency in that process. To access a book, you must submit to the tyranny of the author. Thus, readers of traditional books participate in their own oppression and subjugation."

"I had a high school English teacher who would probably agree with that last part."

"Why is this taking so long?" Benjamin said as he frowned at the screen and idly moved the mouse in quick short circles. "Anyway . . . what was I saying?"

"Books are oppressive."

"Yes, but in a hypertext you get to *follow links*, whatever links interest you. There's no gatekeeper. No overlord telling you what to do. You pick your own way through the story, navigating a sea of information, constructing personal meaning out of a big constellation of meanings—oh, hey, it's done loading. Here, sit."

Jack took his spot in front of the clicking, whirring computer. On its small screen, there was a crude map of the neighborhood.

"What exactly am I looking at?"

"It's my master's thesis," Benjamin said.

"Okay. And what's it about?"

"Ostensibly it's about Wicker Park. But really? It's about life."

"Life?"

"Totally."

"Whose life?"

"All our lives. Everybody's."

"Okay."

"The themes here are universal. Go ahead. Interact."

"I don't understand."

"Select a node."

"I'm not sure I know what that means."

"Use the mouse to click on the map. Try it."

"Why don't you just take me to the beginning."

"See, that's the beauty of hypertext. *There is no beginning.* You enter the network where you choose to enter it, and your path through the network is yours to make. The story isn't created by me, the story is created by *you.* You are its coauthor. Cool, right?"

"Cool," Jack said as he clicked on the map, on the shape representing the very building they were standing in right now—the former ironworks, Jack's current dilapidated home.

Up popped a new window containing a short paragraph, certain words underlined in bright blue:

The Foundry. It used to make **widgets.** Now it makes **art.**
Widgets are worth more. I bought the place for a **dollar.**

"Okay," Jack said. "Is there something I need to do now?"

"Yeah. Select one of the links."

"The what?"

"Those underlined words. They're hyperlinks. They take you between lexia."

"You say this like it means something to me."

"My god. You really are like decades behind."

"Fine. Whatever. I'm clicking," Jack said as he selected the word *dollar,* which took him to a new window, a new paragraph, more blue underlined words:

Dad always said a **penny** saved is a penny **earned.** He worked his whole life for not enough pennies. When he retired, they gave him an **ashtray.**

"The hyperlink, or '*link*,'" Benjamin said with condescending finger quotes, "takes you to other parts of the network. It's what makes all of this possible—hypertext, the web. I'm telling you, the hyperlink is the greatest invention since the printing press."

"Right," Jack said. He clicked on *ashtray*, revealing a new window, more text, more links:

The urn where my father's **ashes** are kept was the **second-cheapest** in the urn **catalog.**

"Whenever I see an ashtray," Benjamin said, softly, wistfully, "it reminds me of my father's urn."

"That's heavy."

"I'll be at the Orbis and I'll look down and see the ashtray on the table and I'll snap right back to my father's funeral. It's like I'm experiencing the two things at once, simultaneously."

"That's really heavy."

"Our lives are bound by time, but our memories are not. In the place where we actually experience our life, up here"—pointing to his forehead—"time does not exist. Something that happens right now could take you back to something that happened twenty years ago. And for a moment, in your mind, the distance between them vanishes. It's like there is no time."

"Gotcha."

"Did you know the Greeks had two words for time?"

"No."

"The first was *chronos*. It's where we get the word *chronology*. Chronos is countable forward time. Minutes, seconds, days, years."

"I understand."

"Like, the punch-clock. Henry Ford. Nine-to-five jobs. Quarterly reports. All very chronos."

"And the second word?"

"*Kairos,* which is the subjective felt experience of time. Like, a turning point in your life, a moment of truth, an important change, an opportunity, the feeling of the past bursting through to the present. When history slams into the now, that's a moment of kairos. It's a communion between the present and the past. My father's urn from ten years ago and the ashtray right in front of me—the two are, shall we say, *linked*. Hypertext embodies that sensation. The hyperlink literalizes it."

"Okay," Jack said, staring at the screen, "what now? Do I just keep clicking?"

"Yep."

"How do I know when I'm done?"

"You're never really, quote, unquote, 'done.' The story has no ending, no dramatic arc, no rising action, none of those manipulative book shenanigans. No edges, no boundaries, just branches, totally unconstrained, a map of meanings that you put together yourself. In that way, a hypertext operates in the same organic way the mind operates. So it's more real than a traditional book."

"Books seem pretty real."

"A book is a real object, sure, but the form of the book is artifice, a product of industrial mercantile nations nurturing good little middle-class consumers, sheep who learned to do what they were told: turn the page, turn the page, turn the page. Hypertext, on the other hand, presents an antiauthoritarian alternative. Readers of hypertext aren't passive consumers. They're creators."

"And what do they create?"

"Meaning. People can do what they want in a hypertext. There isn't an overbearing author telling them what to think. They have the freedom to think what they will. What you have to understand is that information technologies are really just vessels for ideology. Print books are authoritarian and fascist. Hypertexts are liberating and empowering. I'm telling you, dude, traditional storytelling is dying. In the future, all the important literature will be hypertext."

"And this is what the World Wide Web is for?" Jack said. "Hypertext?"

"The web seems good for two primary things, and the second is hypertext."

"What's the first?"

"Pornography."

"There's pornography on the web?"

"Oh my god," Benjamin said, shaking his head pityingly. "You really are truly backward."

He called up a new window and typed *BIG DICKS* into the search bar, but then looked at Jack curiously: "It is dicks, yeah? That is what you're into, right?"

"Uh, no."

"For real?"

"More into girls, actually."

"No shit? Wow. Unexpected."

Then Benjamin replaced *DICKS* with *TITS*, clicked something, and walked away, leaving Jack alone to peruse the literally thousands of Usenet groups that now appeared, each with a remarkably specific subject: porn-star tits and celebrity tits, Playboy tits and amateur tits, tits of certain sizes (big, bigger, *pendulous*), tits of certain shapes (teardrop, perky, pillowy), tits captured secretly through windows by voyeuristic neighbors, tits revealed accidentally by people out in public. And this was just on the first few pages. The results kept going for hundreds more, meaning there were literally thousands of groups that, as Jack read through them, became ever more particular and esoteric, like a pornographic Dewey decimal system. For Jack, who had survived an adolescence of oppressive Christian piety and denial, this abundance proved difficult to cope with. It was the equivalent of dropping one of our hunter-gatherer hominid ancestors into the middle of a modern American super-market: faced with such bounty—and after a lifetime spent nearly starving—he could maybe be forgiven for going a little crazy, for acting a little gluttonous, a little gauche.

Late that night, alone, in the art department, having finished his janitorial duties—emptying the trash bins in all the classrooms and offices, and sweeping up the plaster and Styrofoam and wax used that day in the sculpture workshop, and making sure all the chemicals in the photography darkroom were capped and properly stored—he retreated to the computer lab and sat in the dark and looked at porn until roughly dawn.

It became a kind of hobby of his: three nights a week, after completing his work-study tasks, he spent the rest of the night in front of a computer, indulging, for many, many hours. What took so long was a basic infrastructure problem, a basic impairment between supply and demand: the supply of porn seemed endless; his demand for porn felt endless; but the chokehold on the operation was the modem, clanking and buzzing along at 28.8 kilobytes per second, a number meaningless to Jack except in the way that it frustrated his attempts to look at all the porn he wanted to look at on any given night. His desire, it turned out, was several orders of magnitude larger than the modem's capacity. Most nights it went the same way: he clicked on a thumbnail image, and while that image loaded, he caught sight of another thumbnail he wanted to enlarge, and while that was loading, he saw another, and then another, until his computer screen was a mess of windows and half-downloaded pictures unscrambling themselves at a vexingly slow pace. The computer became really unresponsive then, taking full minutes to register a single mouse-click, or sometimes the machine seemed to abandon the effort, leaving the images all grainy and boxy and incomplete. One time Jack found a big file of images all involving a particular young woman whose body was at that moment strongly persuasive to him (something about how she didn't look like a porn star but rather like a regular girl talked into doing porn-star things for free, a quality he tried not to spend too much effort explaining but instead just sort of surfed its pleasant exterior veneer), and so he clicked on the compressed file, which promised to "uncompress" when it finished downloading, then he paced the room for a while, then checked the download bar, then emptied all of the building's pencil sharpeners, then checked the download bar, then washed all the chalkboards, then checked the download bar, then organized all the canvases and paintbrushes in the stockroom, then checked the download bar, then just sat there watching the download bar, unsure of whether it was actually moving, much like how he used to stare at stars wondering whether they were really crossing the sky, watching the bar's interminable creep to 100 percent, whereby the file uncompressed and promptly froze the computer, just locked it up completely, the only solution being to unplug the whole mechanism, which caused Jack so much rage he literally smacked the keyboard with his fist.

Professor Laird was stumped about how the keyboard had been cracked, but he never suspected Jack, whom everyone assumed was an industrious and hardworking and responsible guy; the art department hadn't been this clean in years.

It didn't take Jack very long to realize that the solution to his infrastructure problem was to get more computers involved. It was a light-bulb-over-his-head, bop-himself-on-the-skull kind of obvious moment, when he realized that instead of asking one computer to download fifteen images, he could recruit the lab's fifteen computers to download one image each. Then none of them would slow down or crash and he could achieve peak porn efficiency. And the first time he did this, he felt like a turn-of-the-century industrialist pacing his factory floor, going from station to station inspecting everyone's progress, listening to the music of fifteen modems crackling busily. He knew, of course, that it was risky. If anyone walked in while he was using only one computer—unlikely, this late at night, but still—it would be a simple matter to quickly close his window and pretend he was innocently checking email. But if anyone walked in while he was downloading porn on *literally every computer in the lab*, well, he tried not to think about it too much, and placed blocks of wood on the handles of the building's exterior doors, so if any-one entered he'd maybe hear the blocks fall and have a few minutes' warning to get the computers in order.

He sometimes wondered, after these nights, why he needed such extravagant variety, pornwise. In his youth he could be satisfied and sustained for a month by a single glimpse of cleavage, a half second of skin, the merest suggestion of a nipple under a thin or diaphanous shirt. But now, here, on the internet, he faced an odd paradox: the more images he found, the less any one of them was satisfying. It was more like they were satisfying only en masse, as an aggregate. He spent several hours downloading and looking at porn on the lab's fifteen computers and then trudged home slightly before dawn feeling drained and spent and sort of loopy, his brain buzzing with images of skin, his body leaping at the littlest pressure. And he got home and rolled into bed and started jerking away, just *jerk-jerk-jerking* faster and harder, in the dark, eyes closed, trying to queue up his favorite images of the night's expeditions, the perfect images with which to finish himself off—but weirdly all he could recall was a kind of abstract craving, as if on his walk home all the pictures he'd seen had melted themselves down into a shapeless, formless mass. An ingot of desire with no hard edges to grasp onto. He jerked at himself uselessly, wretchedly, well into morning.

Obviously he needed to get the images home with him.

The question, of course, was how? How would he get the pictures home? He couldn't save them onto the floppy disks he'd seen among students who actually owned computers. Jack stared forlornly at his mother's typewriter, its lack of electronics, its lack of a screen. No, he could not transport the images digitally. His solution, he decided, would have to be analog. He would have to take photographs of the photographs.

He'd been loaned a 35mm for his photography practicum. He'd been given a small supply of film and access to a darkroom in which to process it. He'd been taught how to properly develop film by Dr. Laird, who often spent the first several minutes of every class decrying the new digital cameras recently on the market for their lack of clarity or color or warmth or life, and admonishing computer screens for their lack of depth or sharpness or definition or humanity. Jack listened to these tirades and smiled pleasantly while imagining all the bodies he had access to online and thinking: *Disagree.*

So the next time Jack was on duty at the art department, he loaded up the fifteen computers with as much porn as they could each accommodate, then set up his tripod and camera in front of the best images, loaded film of a proper speed and grain, took a quick light reading, and shot about four rolls. Then he took the film into the darkroom for the long development process—the chemical solutions and fixing agents and stop baths, the washing of the negatives—then hanging them to dry overnight in the farthest back corner of the room. And he was feeling really good about this until the next day, when Professor Laird asked to meet with him after practicum.

"We need to talk," the professor said once they were in his office and the door was closed. "I want to give you a chance to explain something."

"Okay," Jack said, swallowing hard.

"One of our students noticed that there were some, let's say, *odd images* in the cache of one of the computers in the lab."

Jack didn't know what a *cache* was, but he could piece it together from context. He felt himself sinking into the chair.

"Yes, very odd images indeed," Laird said. "Very, let's say, *unsavory.*" He stared into his own lap, poignantly not making any kind of eye contact. "And then we found the same sort of . . . material, let's say, on *all* of the computers in the lab."

And here the professor gathered himself up and tried to act the part of a stern administrator.

"Do you know the material to which I'm referring?"

Jack nodded. "I think so."

"It's important to realize that I'm not *accusing* you of anything, Jack. I just wanted to give you an opportunity to explain."

And all the dread that Jack had been batting away these nights—all the guilt and horror about what would happen if somebody found out what he'd been doing—was flashing before his eyes as he stood up and decided to do the only thing he could think of to avoid getting publicly shamed forever.

"Come with me," he said to his professor. "I have something to show you."

Jack took him to the darkroom, to the far corner, where he had hidden his photos. They were still there, hanging upside down like meat on a hook. He removed them from their clips. Laird watched dispassionately under the room's single red bulb. Jack led him out of the darkroom, into the light, gave the professor a loupe with which to inspect the photos and said, "Look."

Laird did so, looking at one frame, then looking curiously at Jack, then inspecting another frame, and so on.

"I'm doing a reinterpretation of the nude," Jack said.

The professor kept looking, lingering a little longer on each frame.

"It's a project about the digital human form," Jack said, "about the immateriality of computer representation."

Desperate, Jack began regurgitating key words he heard often in class, words he was not entirely sure he was even using correctly: "I'm *recontextualizing* the images," he said, "in order to *interrogate* the *nonbeing* of the *mediated body*."

The professor kept looking.

"It's really about the *cultural production* of reality," Jack said. "Though I'm worried it might be a *cliché pomo gesture*."

Finally, his teacher reached the last image. He pulled away from the photos and turned to Jack and smiled.

"This," Laird said, tapping on the filmstrip, "Jack, this is brilliant."

ELIZABETH had planned it: a Friday-night double date with a new couple, Park Shore parents, who were coming into Wicker Park tonight and the four of them would be meeting at a craft cocktail bar nearby, one of those places that imitated a speakeasy from the 1930s, with a menu of Prohibition-era spirits, and a secret entrance, and no signage anywhere. This detail in particular seemed important, that there was no sign. You just had to *know*.

Jack was sitting on the bed looking at his phone. He had finished getting dressed well before Elizabeth (jeans, black T-shirt, sneakers—not a wardrobe requiring any time or thought), and had finished checking the news (an American doctor infected with Ebola was being successfully treated at a hospital in Atlanta), and had finished checking Facebook (Jack's father was insisting—furiously, passionately, and without any evidence—that this doctor was actually working for a pharmaceutical giant as part of an evil plan to spread the disease), and had finished checking his email (a new message from Benjamin saying that neighborhood resistance to the Shipworks had surprisingly vanished, that construction was full speed ahead), and now he was plotting their route to this cocktail bar via the map app: a ten-minute walk, the phone predicted, which Jack thought he could shave down to eight by cutting through certain alleys, and seven if their crosswalk-timing was fortuitous.

Elizabeth was in her closet, getting ready. "You're going to love Kate and Kyle," she called out to him. "They're great."

Jack nodded. He was now reading the reviews of tonight's bar. According to the app, the average rating was 3.9 stars, but that appeared to be artificially low, dragged down by people giving it one star when they couldn't find the entrance. He said: "Kate and Kyle. How do we know them?"

A pause as Elizabeth considered this. Then: "*We* don't know them. *I* know them."

It was one of her pet peeves, that thing that happens to couples when they stop saying "I" in favor of "We," as if they'd developed a shared couple-brain. Their togetherself. Jack would sometimes say "What do we want for dinner tonight?" and she'd stare at him and say "I know what *I* want for dinner. What do *you* want for dinner?" Or those moments when they'd spontaneously say exactly the same thing at exactly the same time, Elizabeth would frown and say "Stop it." She was a person who longed, at all times, for individuation.

Jack shoved his phone into his pocket and walked toward Elizabeth's closet. "What I meant was—" he said, but then he couldn't finish the sentence when he saw her, when he saw what she was wearing: a black bra, strapless, lacy, and matching underwear, a set he recognized as Elizabeth's last true attempt at purchasing anything resembling "lingerie." It had been a long time since he'd seen it, and Elizabeth turned around now, looked at him, looked at him looking at her, and he could almost hear her as she willed a silent message across the space between them: *Do not make a big deal out of this.*

"Remind me," he said. "Kate and Kyle. Who are they?"

"Parents at Toby's school. I've been talking with her lately. They're *very* interesting."

Her hand was touching a black dress that hung from one of those hangers that looked like a hanger and a pillow had merged: one of the *special* hangers. For a *special* dress. She looked at his T-shirt, his sneakers. "Are you going to wear that?" she said.

"Nope!" he said, and he retreated to his own closet to change.

When they arrived at the bar, he was in his coolest button-down shirt, wearing his coolest jeans, his coolest boots. The walk had taken them fifteen minutes (he hadn't accounted for Elizabeth walking in *heels*). And as promised, there was nothing on the street signaling the presence of a cocktail bar behind an anonymous wall of wooden planking, an elaborate street-art mural painted onto it, and a door that would have been obscured by the mural had they not been looking for it.

They passed into an entryway that was dark but for a small sign illuminated by a single light bulb: HOUSE RULES, it said, stamped onto parchment paper in a typeface that Jack associated with antique bookishness (almost definitely Garamond). The rules were very clear about the kind of clientele the bar favored: no baseball hats were allowed, no Jägerbombs would be served, and no Budweiser was on tap. Jack thought of his father, who wore a baseball hat every day and drank nothing but Budweiser. What would he make of this place? In the past, Lawrence might have shaken his head and smiled and made a light joke about "city folk," but now, given the websites he'd been reading lately, Jack was reasonably sure this bar would inspire another online rant about "class warfare." His father's Facebook feed was getting more and more difficult to read, his videos getting more unbearable as the old man talked himself into lengthy coughing fits, Jack watching and wondering when it would be appropriate to finally unfriend him.

Elizabeth brushed aside a big velvet curtain and Jack followed her into the bar's interior, an ornately Victorian-style room with lots of plush drapery and a crystal chandelier. People sat sipping drinks in high-backed chairs while the waitstaff hurried between them refilling water and clearing empty coupe glasses.

"There they are," Elizabeth said, pointing to the back corner where a woman and a man were standing and waving at them. The woman was surprisingly young, with dyed-silver hair and large thick-framed glasses and big friendly eyes that lit up when she saw them. She rushed over to hug Elizabeth ferociously and then said, "You must be Jack!" before leaning into him and kissing him right on the lips.

It happened before he even realized it was happening. It wasn't a long kiss, and she didn't linger—it was a playful kiss, but it was *on the mouth*. It was the first kiss Jack had shared with anyone who wasn't Elizabeth since the nineties.

"Oh, wow, cool tattoos," Kate said, lightly running her fingertips over his arms, tracing the designs in his skin.

Jack just nodded and smiled. He pulled his arms away, put his hands in his pockets. He was unaccustomed to being so forthrightly flirted with. He wasn't sure what to do, how to respond.

Kate, however, clearly thought nothing of it. She was already sitting, smiling, saying how good it was that they could all get together like this, one hand gesticulating wildly in the air, the other hand solidly clasping her husband's knee. This guy was her opposite in both physique and personality: quiet, stoic, bald, pasty, thickly muscled, a kind of no-nonsense psychopathic blankness that Jack for some reason associated with, like, the KGB. He had a round torso and stout legs and a pudgy neck and arms so big they looked like snakes digesting whole jugs of protein powder. Kyle sat there so silent, so unresponsive, so distant, that Jack thought it was a serious possibility that the man spoke no English.

They were the parents of a girl at Toby's school, apparently. "Toby is the most *delightful* young man," Kate said. "You must be so proud!"

"Of course, yes, definitely," Jack said.

"Such a handsome boy," Kate said, then she leaned toward him, put a hand on his knee. "Obviously he gets it from his dad."

"Gee," Jack said, "thanks."

And suddenly the evening felt terribly heightened. Kate's kiss, her flirtatiousness, Elizabeth's suggestive lingerie, they turned everything profoundly *meaningful*: every uttered sentence, every nod of Jack's head, even the way he was sitting—crossing this leg over that? arm around Elizabeth or in his lap?—all of it had become self-conscious and weird. It was as if he were suddenly watching himself playing a game with high stakes but unclear rules.

So naturally the drink order was an ordeal, one big test he could fail. When the server arrived—a freckled twentysomething with a thin red curly mustache and jeans tight as sausage casings—Jack was still studying the menu, which listed drinks with inventive names and ingredients he had never heard of and for sure didn't want to have to pronounce out loud: Eau-de-vie. Becherovka. Fernet. Cynar.

"Just give me something that's not too sweet," he told the server after a few hopeless moments skimming the menu looking for anything familiar. "Whatever you recommend."

"Actually?" the server said. "All the drinks here are *perfectly* balanced."

"Okay."

"There's nothing on the menu that's too sweet, or not too sweet.

Each drink is crafted to harmonize the sweet and sour, not to mention the bitter, spicy, salty, savory, and viscous sensations in your mouth."

"Viscous sensations?" Jack said, to which Kate added, in her suggestive, provocative way: "In your *mouth*."

"So you asking for something that's *not too sweet*?" the server continued. "That doesn't really make sense. Not in this context."

"I see."

"Perhaps you'd like more time with the menu?"

They were all looking at Jack now—Kate, Elizabeth, the server, quiet Kyle. They were looking at him and they were waiting. That is, until Kate said "Bring him what I'm having!" and then leaned into him and whispered, hand on his knee, "It's *delicious*." Wicked smile, little squeeze. Her dress drooped away from her body as she leaned in, but Jack's gaze remained fixed on her eyes, which were coffee-colored, her dark eyeliner applied in an exacting and sort of Cleopatran way.

They talked about school until the drinks came (Kate's selection was indeed delightful), and they clinked their glasses ("To new friends!"), and the waiter refilled Kyle's water (for Kyle had not asked for a drink, wordlessly shaking his head *no* when it was his turn to order), and there occurred a blip of silence—a pivot in the conversation, an awkward moment when some new subject needed to be introduced—and Kate clapped her hands and said: "Okay, lovebirds, tell us your origin story."

"Our what?" Elizabeth said.

"Your origin story! Your relationship genesis. How did you meet, start dating, fall in love, that stuff. You can tell a lot about a couple by their origin story."

This was easy and comfortable conversational territory. Like most couples, Jack and Elizabeth had told the story of themselves so many times that by now it was well-rehearsed shtick; Jack knew exactly when Elizabeth would interrupt to add a funny or poignant detail from her point of view, and vice versa, each detail landing at the correct moment for maximum impact. It began with Elizabeth:

"We met in college," she said. "We'd both moved to Chicago from far away. Jack was studying art, and I was studying everything."

"Everything?" Kate said.

"Psychology, economics, biology, neuroscience, theater, you name it," Elizabeth said. "Basically I had no idea what I wanted to do in life. Anyway, I was at this dive bar one night, on a really bad date, and Jack was there, taking pictures of the band. And I desperately wanted him to talk to me. He didn't know it, but I already had the biggest crush on him."

"Really?" Kate said. "How?"

"I'd been spying on him for months."

"What?" Kate said, which was the usual response to this little factoid.

"Yeah, we were neighbors," Elizabeth said. "My window looked onto his window. So I'd been watching him all winter."

It used to be, when they told this story, that Jack would begin. He'd be the first to describe watching Elizabeth through her apartment window. But somewhere along the way, sometime in the last few years, their audiences began to get uncomfortable with the details of that story: He'd been spying on her? Without her permission? For months? It began to sound a little invasive, a little predatory, a little stalkerish. What had not seemed so creepy in the nineties seemed, today, *very* creepy, and so they'd switched the order. Elizabeth was now the first to admit the peeping, which nobody seemed to have any problem with and which made the whole voyeurism dynamic feel more consensual and reciprocal and safe and therefore acceptable.

Which was why Jack waited until now to jump in: "I saw her in that bar that night, and she didn't know it, but I also had the biggest crush on *her*."

"What?!" Kate said. She was a good audience—enthusiastic, reactive—as opposed to her husband, who had no response at all, who seemed to be barely tolerating both the story and life. Jack was already imagining the joke he'd tell Elizabeth later: *It was like Kyle began existence as pure bicep tissue that eventually grew a head and achieved consciousness, only to be confused and confounded by our crazy world.* Yes, he thought, she'd like that one.

He continued: "I'd been watching her too, in her window, and I was hopelessly smitten."

"And I'd seen his photography," Elizabeth said. "He photographed all the cool bands, and hung out with rock stars. That was right here, in Wicker Park, early nineties."

"No fancy cocktail bars back then," Jack said.

"What was it like?" Kate asked.

"Very different," Jack said, leaning to see her now that the waiter had stepped between them to refill Kyle's water glass. "The neighborhood was abandoned. Nobody here but junkies and prostitutes and us, a bunch of artists and musicians."

"It was such a scene," Elizabeth said. "I was so intimidated to talk to him."

"And I was so intimidated to talk to her."

"So we didn't even speak for like a whole winter."

"Eventually," Jack said, "that night at the dive bar, I made a move."

"Thank god for that."

"And then we talked all night, till almost dawn. I'd never felt so excited to just talk to someone. I never thought a simple conversation could be such a rush."

"And we were inseparable after that."

"Everyone called us Romeo and Juliet."

"We were *that* couple."

"And the rest is history."

"Hooray!" Kate said, applauding the story. "That's so romantic!"

And indeed it was, Jack thought. It *was* romantic. He smiled at Elizabeth, who smiled back at him, and he felt relieved, happy to fall back into the safety of the past.

"And how about you guys?" Jack said. "How did you meet?"

"Oh," Kate said, looking at Kyle. "We met at an orgy."

Kyle gave her a knowing little smile and Jack realized that they too had a routine, a shtick.

"I'm sorry?" Jack said. "A what?"

"Well, not technically an 'orgy,'" Kate said. "More like a party that could accommodate an orgy, should one develop. I was there as a unicorn. Kyle was part of a polyamorous dating quad."

"I don't know any of those terms," Jack said.

"Oh, a unicorn is a single woman open to casual sex with committed couples. They're called unicorns because they're so difficult to find they might as well be mythical."

"Gotcha."

"And a quad is usually just two couples who are dating each other. It's important to note that not all quads are into group play, but this one was."

Jack looked at Elizabeth, expecting to see one expression—a *Can-you-believe-these-people?* smirk—but instead seeing another expression: a calm *I-told-you-so* smile. Elizabeth, he gathered, already knew. This was old information.

Kate continued: "Kyle and I had never met before, but we saw each other at the buffet table at this party. You remember?" she said, poking Kyle in the arm. "We started talking over the deviled eggs and never stopped. We talked all night long, until dawn. Everyone else was sleeping or going home, but we were still talking."

Jack wasn't sure what was more unbelievable: the part about the orgy, or the part where Kyle talked.

"We had so much in common," Kate said. "We were uninterested in traditional relationships. My mother is very Catholic, very sex negative. That just didn't work for me. I've never been able to stay faithful. I've never *wanted* to stay faithful. And Kyle felt the same way."

To which Kyle, in his first verbal contribution of the evening, added: "That's why the penis is shaped the way it is, you know?"

And Jack and Elizabeth stared at him for a moment, leaning in for an explanation, and Kyle stared back at them, blinking, silent.

"No!" Jack finally said. "We don't know!"

"Oh, okay, well, it's shaped like a plunger," Kyle said. "The penis. That's what it does. The human penis has evolved its particular odd shape to suction other men's sperm *out*. Which in a Darwinian sense implies that women have been, for all of human prehistory, basically cheating sluts—a term I use only in the most positive and affirming way. Because if monogamy were at all *natural,* then the penis wouldn't have to be shaped like that. But it is, which means that women were polyamorous for a million years, probably until the advent of agriculture, when we invented property. Then the rich needed to be able to hand down their land and titles from generation to generation, and so we created marriage and monogamy and chastity and started owning women's sex lives, to support the aristocracy and patriarchy, after which we exported that model via European colonization and wiped out all the world's other mating practices because they were, quote, unquote, 'wicked and uncivilized,' which means that not only is monogamy unnatural and toxic, but it's also a teensy white supremacist. And the kicker is that it doesn't even work. And we know this not only because of divorce statistics but also because of the contradiction that evolution has hardwired into our brains, which is that as soon as we get the thing we desire, we stop desiring it and start desiring something else, which probably served us well as hunter-gatherers but is a disaster for traditional marriage. Our desire for novelty is literally inexhaustible, which is why capitalism is a huge success and monogamy is not."

Then Kyle sat back and took a big dramatic breath, as if spent by this discursive spasm. He picked up his water and sucked the glass dry through a straw, the straw making a loud squelching sound as he removed the water in its totality.

"You know," Kate said once she was sure her husband had nothing more to add, "the math on this subject is fascinating. Like, given what we understand about life spans in the Pleistocene—about mortality rates and deaths due to starvation or lion or whatever—we've computed that the average length of any relationship for our human ancestors was eight years. For all of our evolutionary history, men and women only had eight years to meet, mate, and raise offspring before one of them died. Thus, evolution has wired us to feel very attached for eight years, but not so much after."

"What happens after?" Jack said.

"We tend to get antsy. We need something new. Do you know how long the average American marriage lasts?"

"No, but I'm gonna guess eight years."

"Bingo! We evolved to accommodate marriage for roughly eight years. After that, our brains wonder: Why am I still with *this* person? We long for a big change."

"But Elizabeth and I have been married for longer than eight years."

"Okay. What happened around the eight-year mark?"

"That's when we had Toby," Elizabeth said.

"Uh-huh. And eight years after that?"

Jack and Elizabeth looked at each other, Elizabeth offering him a sad smile. "That's right about now," she said.

Kate gave a sympathetic shrug, a gesture communicating *Obviously, I am correct*. "Kyle and I realized that we can't change human nature to accommodate our culture's idea of marriage, so we decided to change marriage to accommodate human nature. We sleep with other people, and we are honest and transparent about this."

Jack had of course heard of such arrangements before, but it was still pretty unsettling coming from a couple that Elizabeth had planned a double date with.

"Well," Jack said, "I'm not accustomed to our origin story being so quickly upstaged."

Kate laughed. "It all sounds really exciting, I know," she said, "but our life is actually just very normal. Like, everyone assumes we have orgies every night, but in reality, the orgies are only on Saturdays."

"Such admirable restraint," Jack said.

"Oh! You should come!"

"To an orgy?"

"Yes!" Kate grabbed Jack's knee again and leaned in very close. "Actually *orgy* is a pretty antique name for it. It's more like just a party that lacks certain important boundaries. You'll love it! It's so fun, and the people are *amazing*. It's at a private club, very classy, very low-pressure. You don't have to do anything you don't want to do. Just come and check out the scene. Tell me you will. *Please*?"

To be honest, Jack found himself feeling very attracted to Kate in this moment: the way she seemed to have this big inner supply of energy that animated her, as opposed to the way he and Elizabeth felt most days, which was *tired*. Worn-out. Run-down. Constantly in need of a chemical jolt. Kate seemed *alive*—she had big gestures, big opinions, she had big glasses and big hoop earrings. She said what she pleased, had sex with whom she pleased, was committed to being entirely, truthfully, unapologetically herself. Which was refreshing. Jack didn't think that he and Elizabeth lied to each other, exactly, but more like there was a kind of gulf between them full of diplomatically unspoken things. Their conversations dwelled instead on the banal details of planning, the errands that needed to be run, the groceries that needed to be purchased, the work and school schedules that needed to be coordinated, and questions—so many questions—about the facts of the day: What did she have for lunch? Did she like it? What was she reading? Did she like it? They didn't ignore each other, but he felt like the total bedrock honesty that Kate displayed had been replaced or subsumed by this other kind of sharing—not intimacy but rather a kind of comprehensive friendly wiretap. They were always aware of what the other was doing and saying. Less so what the other was *thinking*.

Example: Why had Elizabeth arranged this date? How many details of Kate and Kyle's adventurous sex life did she already know? Was this some kind of signal to him? Was she trying to tell him something? Did she now want to sleep with other people? And if so, did she already have someone in mind? And if so, was it Quiet-fucking-Kyle?

Jack smiled at Kate. "I don't think so," he said, then he took his wife's hand in his. "Elizabeth and I, we don't need anybody but each other."

Kate leaned back and seemed to exchange a poignant look with Elizabeth, then grinned broadly and said: "That is of course completely valid. What's most important is that you do what's right for *you*."

"And what's right for you," said, surprisingly, Kyle, "might be pretty vanilla."

"Vanilla?" Jack said.

"And that's *totally okay*, man."

"I don't know if I'd call it vanilla."

"If you change your mind," Kate said, "you're welcome to join us anytime."

After two more drinks, they called it a night. Kate kissed Jack goodbye—on the lips, again—and they were all heading toward the door when Jack felt someone grab him at the elbow. He turned to see their waiter.

"Hey," the guy said to Jack. "I heard you talking."

And Jack flushed red. He hadn't thought there'd been an audience for their conversation about orgies and male anatomy.

"And I think you should know," the waiter continued, "that what you were saying was really problematic."

"Listen, I think it's the other couple you really want to talk to—"

"No, it was you," he said. "I heard what you said about the neighborhood. And someone needs to call you out."

"What do you mean?"

"You said the neighborhood was *abandoned*."

"Okay. And?"

"I'm pretty sure it wasn't abandoned," the waiter said. "I'm pretty sure it was Puerto Rican."

Then he smiled at Jack in that self-satisfied way, that combination of *You're an asshole* and *You're welcome!*

"Whatever," Jack said to Elizabeth as they walked home, after he'd told her the story. "None of these shops were here, all of these buildings were empty. I don't know what else I'd call that but *abandoned*."

Elizabeth was walking out in front of him, walking much more quickly than she had on the way to the bar, and much less cautiously than she usually did in heels.

"I mean, I wasn't making a value judgment about it," Jack said. "I was only stating a neutral objective fact: the neighborhood was abandoned."

Elizabeth jumped into the street and jaywalked to avoid waiting at an intersection. Jack followed.

"I mean, it's not even *accurate* to say it was a Puerto Rican neighborhood, not in a historical sense, anyway."

Elizabeth dodged people on the sidewalk the way she did in airports when she had a tight connection: with speed and purpose and conviction.

"It was a Polish neighborhood before it was Puerto Rican," Jack said, juking around the other pedestrians as he tried to keep up. "And it was German before that."

He was waiting for her to defend him, expecting her to defend him and reassure him—*No, honey, you weren't being racially insensitive*—and the fact that she wasn't yet defending him and instead was walking way out ahead of him made him feel like maybe he had in fact been racially insensitive, which of course was his primary worry, that the waiter was correct. It made him feel pressingly, uncomfortably white, that perhaps this neighborhood circa 1992 was not in fact abandoned—maybe it was fully settled, fully occupied, but just in ways that Jack did not, or could not, see. He had come to Chicago during an era when the downtowns emptied and the suburbs swelled, and so he'd been able to think of himself, back then, as a progressive person, a good person, as opposed to those narrow-minded white-flight people escaping into the outer rings, cutting themselves off from the full range of humanity. But of course decades of gentrification followed, and now the thinking had changed: maybe what actually happened was that Jack and Benjamin and everyone else at the Foundry had barged into a party without an invitation, planted themselves at the center of the party, and then said, *You're so lucky to have us!*

What had not seemed questionable in the nineties seemed, again, questionable now. He felt exactly as he did when he first came to college: that, for reasons he was not aware of, he did not belong here.

"I don't know what I did wrong," Jack said. "I was broke, and someone offered me free rent and I said yes. Was that wrong? Does that make me a monster?"

Elizabeth didn't answer. If she had been going any faster, it would have been accurate to say she was *jogging*.

"Would you slow down?" Jack said, grabbing her hand. "What is going on with you?"

She stopped then and looked at him and seemed to take a moment to consider what to say. Her impatient expression was like the one she'd had when Toby was little and in that phase when he wouldn't stop asking *Why?*

"You know in the bar," she said, finally, "when you were ordering your drink?"

"Yes."

"And you couldn't decide?"

"Yes."

"And you got all embarrassed because you didn't know what to order?"

"Uh-huh."

"Nobody cared," she said. "Nobody gave a shit what you drank."

"Okay."

"You think everyone is watching you and judging you, but they're not."

Then she spun around and kept walking. Jack followed her in silence the rest of the way, and at home she disappeared into her closet and emerged in sweatpants and a T-shirt, told him she had some work to get done and not to wait up for her, and Jack understood that somewhere along the way he had screwed up. The evening had begun with lingerie, but it was ending like this, the two of them separated, Elizabeth in the office, in sweatpants.

Jack lay in bed wondering what he'd done wrong. Was it the "abandoned" comment? Was it the way he so aggressively defended himself after making the "abandoned" comment? Maybe it had nothing to do with the comment at all. Maybe he'd been too flirty with Kate, or too rude to Kyle. He played back the evening in his mind, reviewed everything he had said, searched for something to apologize for. He must have been in bed a full hour thinking about this before deciding that in the morning he would offer a sort of broad-based unspecific catchall apology and then use Elizabeth's reaction to deduce what she was upset about in particular.

He picked up his phone and opened the map app. He found tonight's cocktail bar and left a review. *Two stars*, he wrote. *Good drinks, but the waiters are pricks.*

HE'S SITTING in that airless classroom, in the back row, in the seat closest to the big hot window, sitting in the oppressive sunlight, not really listening to what's happening in class, focused instead on the back of his own hand. He's a small boy who looks too frail, too short, to be here, in the big building, among all these bigger boys, these sons of ranchers—broad-shouldered, big-biceped, hairy-lipped—boys with bodies swelled by puberty and work.

He doesn't fit in here, in this classroom, in this school, in the Flint Hills of Kansas, where boys grow up fast, and large.

And yet? Here he is, little Jack Baker, shorter even than all the girls in the room, sitting at a desk whose top bears the imprint of other boys' favorite things: *Lynyrd Skynyrd* carved into the wood with all the *y*'s shaped like lightning bolts, and *AC/DC* with the slash shaped like a lightning bolt, and lightning bolts, and pairs of big pendulous tits and a few Confederate flags and several oversized cocks with balls that are supposed to be hairy but look instead like they're covered in thorns; you can get only so much detail when your instrument is a hunting knife.

There's also this gross sheen on the wood, right at the two spots where most students' elbows would rest, two slight depressions made by decades of boredom as kids sat here, elbows on wood, chin in hand, smoothing out these divots with their friction and sweat and teenage sebum. It makes Jack gag a little, the thought of it. His elbows don't quite reach as far as the others, and so he's left to stare at these two notches, fossilized into his desk.

He is in "reading" class. All the students have their books open, and many are currently being used as fans. The room's large windows make the temperature in here greenhouse-like, and this has never been a school that could afford something as fancy as air-conditioning. So the students just sit and fan themselves and sweat.

Meanwhile, Daphne Carter is reading aloud, leaning way over and getting real close to the book, a small worn paperback, the same book they've been reading in class all week, a novelization of the movie *RoboCop*.

"Off . . . iss . . . ser Stark . . . weather . . . backed his . . . uh . . . Turbo . . . Cruiser? out of the alley," Daphne reads. "He wasn't . . . sssss . . . sure . . . he liked the . . . I . . . idea . . . of a robot . . . on the fork . . . er . . . force. . . . 'He's no more a cop than my . . . uh . . . blender.'"

Jack's left hand rests on the desk, next to one of the more amusing carvings, a dick with a hugely inflated cartoonish mushroom-head that someone else has drawn a happy face onto. He's holding a pencil. He's using the pencil's eraser to rub an inch-long gash into the back of his left hand, between the second and third knuckles. He's been doing this all morning, slowly abrading the skin, wearing it away, and now he's almost broken through. The skin under the eraser is, by now, as pink as the eraser itself.

He is a senior in high school, taking classes in the big building, which is where everyone goes from grades seven through twelve. The small building is for the younger kids, grades one through six. It's across the gravel parking lot from the big building. They call the small building a "building," but it is, in fact, just a house that's been shoddily converted—it's less of a school than a day care with a mild sense of purpose. Sitting here next to the window, Jack sometimes watches the kids at recess, screaming, running, throwing rocks, getting yelled at. But they're not at recess today because it's too hot, and so the only movement out that window is that of the oil pumps, six of them in the grassy field next to the parking lot, giving rise to the school's official mascot: they are the *Oilers*. Each pump bobs up and down to its own particular rhythm, and sometimes Jack will watch for hours to see the rare—but, he figures, mathematically inevitable—moment when all six pumps dive down and pop up again in perfect unison. Synchronized, like the Rockettes, he thinks, remembering those Thanksgivings he successfully maneuvered the television antenna to pick up the Macy's parade and his mother watched through the static and each passing float was some great new bewilderment.

"Oh, look," she'd say, "Snoopy."

"Oh, look," she'd say, minutes later, "the Rockettes."

It was a moment of pure pleasure for her, and, like most such moments, needed to be balanced out immediately thereafter by bitterness and recrimination: "I'll probably never see that again, since your father won't fix the damn antenna." Jack's mother had the ability to sour any happy moment by predicting it would never happen again, or complaining that it didn't happen enough. It was as if being momentarily happy threw off her equilibrium, and so her mood darkened as a kind of stabilizing ballast. As a result, the family had long ago given up trying to please her, all of them except Jack, who inherited the responsibility for his mother's moods through a kind of domestic fiat: no one else cared.

A single dot of blood appears under Jack's eraser. He pauses for a moment to examine it, the color of blood always a little surprising in its brilliance. He resumes rubbing, and the bright scarlet red smears and merges with the eraser shavings and turns a dirty maroon.

Daphne Carter, meanwhile, is still reading: "Robo saw . . . the time . . . for talk . . . was over. He . . . suhhh . . . switched . . . from his pub . . . lic . . . address mode . . . to his . . . uh . . . tar . . . get . . . ting . . . uh . . . second?"

"Sequence," Mrs. Brannon says. "Targeting sequence."

What they do in "reading" class is take turns reciting pages from whatever book Mrs. Brannon puts in front of them. The class is officially listed on the report card as American Literature, but Mrs. Brannon realized long ago that she couldn't teach literature to students who could barely read. Which puts her in a tough spot—she can't ask students to read real literature because the students cannot, and will inevitably flunk. And yet she can't flunk students in a school this small, not when most students don't make it to graduation anyway. There are, right now, only two seniors left in the whole school—Jack and Daphne—the remainder of their cohort, the roughly dozen others, lost along the way to various labor-intensive jobs or pregnancies or expulsion. Daphne Carter has been in Mrs. Brannon's class for four years, and even still she is hesitant as she reads, choppy, unsure, often wrong.

"Robo . . . uh . . . staaaarrrr, no, *stared* . . . at the do . . . nut shop. He had . . . never en . . . tered . . . the shop, and yet he . . . specially . . . remembered it."

"Not *specially*," says Mrs. Brannon. "Try again. Sound it out."

Daphne is a big, strong girl who carries all her schoolbooks in one prodigious purse that she hoists onto her left shoulder when she walks, swinging her right arm violently out to the side, as if she needs it for counterbalance, which is how she earned her nickname: the Thresher, or, sometimes, the Reaper. Daphne is presently trying to pronounce the word *specifically,* but it's coming out like the word *specially*. Daphne's readings all go this way—she sees a few letters within a word and her mind leaps to the nearest familiar word. It's not "reading" but instead a kind of impressionism and free association.

Jack assumes there's no real pedagogical purpose behind the reading-our-books-out-loud thing—it's simply that Mrs. Brannon wants to get through the day with slightly more dignity than the big building's other teachers, who mostly just show movies. Mrs. Brannon doesn't even bother to look at them while they read, and so she doesn't notice that Jack is erasing the skin of the back of his hand so hard that he's now full-on bleeding, that the raw skin has now broken open and whenever Jack stops erasing for a moment, the blood issues forth in little beads like those bubbles that appear on the surface of the ponds at the sulfur springs south of the school. He stares at it while Daphne slowly sounds out each syllable of the word *specifically*.

Mrs. Brannon has now gone quiet, leaving poor Daphne to get through this ordeal alone. Their teacher stares at the pages of *Robo-Cop* with her usual faraway expression, occasionally wiping her moist forehead with her arm. She hasn't noticed what she might call Jack's "misuse" of his eraser. Nor has she noticed that Rodney Snell is also using his eraser in this manner: to tear a hole in the skin of his hand. And so is Hunter Pierce. And Carl Kirkland. And both Aiden

Pryor and his younger brother Cole. Mrs. Brannon has not noticed that actually *every* boy in her class is now currently occupied by this one activity: erasing his own flesh. And it's probably best that she doesn't know this, because if she did know that her students found self-mutilation preferable to listening and paying attention in her class, it could be a pretty tremendous blow to an already wounded ego, Jack figures.

The eraser thing began that morning in the way most of these things begin: with one boy calling another boy a pussy, which is always followed by some test of manhood, usually something brutal and painful and stupid, sure, but also, Jack has to admit, occasionally really creative and interesting. Such as today's challenge: to rub away the skin on your hand until you've opened up a big wound, and then, at lunch, pour a whole packet of salt into your own open wound. The test, of course, is: Can you take it?

Except that Jack knows the real test has nothing to do with pain. The real test has to do with the courage necessary to face pain. Or maybe more accurately your *lack* of courage if you're afraid of pain, the cowardice of anyone who declines this test. The pain will be fleeting and forgettable, but that cowardice sticks to you forever.

Plus there's the fact that a boy refusing this test can expect to get beaten up, probably within a week. And this is Jack's real concern, his real everyday obsession: how to not get beaten up at school. He probably spends more brainpower on this than he does on actual school.

Because it's *so easy* to get beaten up. Fights happen, in this place, just about weekly. For any perceived misstep, any minor offense. Last week it was Hunter showing up to school wearing those new Reeboks with the air pump in the tongue. And, okay, maybe he should have known that coming to school in bright white clean flashy things like that would draw unwanted attention. And, indeed, Hunter didn't even make it to lunch—Rodney came up to him between first and second periods and said, "Nice shoes," which really should've tipped off Hunter right away. You could hear the menace in Rodney's voice, the threat just below the surface, and Jack spun around and quickly walked to his next class so that when the fight began—and he was sure a fight was coming—he'd be far away and not somehow get pulled into its orbit, as he'd seen happen before, boys standing on the periphery of a fight getting entangled in the fight when struck by some stray right hook or something. So the rest of this story Jack heard from other students, eyewitnesses, gawkers, who said Hunter smiled pleasantly at Rodney and looked down at his new sneakers and then back at Rodney and said, "Thanks?" And then Rodney asked: "They fit good?" And Hunter, still a little dense about what was happening here, said, "Sure." And Rodney said, "We'll see," then hip-checked him so hard it knocked Hunter right on his ass, legs up in the air, and Rodney grabbed one of those Reeboks and started tugging. And Jack can verify the next part of the story, because he was sitting in his second-period classroom, alone, when suddenly he saw Rodney pulling a screaming Hunter past the door, pulling him by the shoe all the way to the end of the hall, whereupon Hunter finally kicked himself free of Rodney's grip and popped to his feet and the two went at it, fistfighting to a draw before a teacher intervened.

The fight was such a usual thing that the subject everyone wanted to talk about afterward was the shoe. How it *never came off*. Despite Rodney's fierce yanking. That air-pump thing was the real deal, everyone agreed. Bravo, Reebok.

But Hunter hasn't worn those shoes to school since, which is smart—both for self-preservation and to prevent their inevitable vandalism. It's a universally held rule among the Oiler students that you never talk about money or act flashy about money, because nobody here has it. And showing up in fancy hundred-dollar shoes is, in its own way, talking about money, a way to advertise a little bit of wealth, to elevate oneself a little higher than the rest, and this kind of gesture will not go unpunished. It's like the school is a little communist enclave in otherwise patriotic Kansas, a place where manifest class divisions between people are vigorously—sometimes violently—erased. One kid came to school wearing nice mirrored Ray-Bans and was promptly punched in the nose, shattering the glasses. Last year, a senior put a high-dollar stereo in his car only to find his tires slashed by the end of the day. And when one girl returned from a trip to the shopping malls of Dallas wearing brand-new bright white Z. Cavariccis, she was immediately the victim of a lunchtime "accident" involving cranberry juice.

So no, you cannot stand out in certain important ways. Anyone who is flagrantly rich, or anyone who is too good at school, anyone conspicuously brainy or annoyingly gifted, is targeted and taught to comply, a socialization process that begins, usually, with those little rabbit punches right on that spot on the shoulder that makes it ache all day, then graduating to taunting and teasing and then raw violence if the kid can't take a hint. There was this one new boy, a city kid, who in his first week was extravagantly praised by the math teacher for his advanced algebra skills, and this kid was quickly shown on the bus what happens to teachers' pets, a lesson so effective that the kid's parents transferred him out of the school the next day.

It is an unspoken fact—and sometimes a weird source of pride—that the students of this school have, in general, very little money and very prescribed futures. They are not kids who are told to "dream big." And so they tend to treat anyone with either wealth or potential as an outsider. And it is this latter quality that makes Jack so nervous: his potential. Because he is leaving this place. Because he has recently been admitted to *college*—in the city of Chicago, for art—and word of this coup has surely reached his classmates' ears by now, and they are surely planning their thuggish response, and so Jack is going along with any dumb taunt just to stay off the collective's radar. His perpetual, unyielding mission each school day is to go unnoticed, to fit in, because as soon as one of the sadistic bigger boys—and they're all bigger than Jack, even the ninth graders—takes any interest in him, Jack knows there's nothing he can do to prevent his life from becoming a living hell. And so he goes along with all the dumb shit the other boys do, this eraser thing being the latest salvo in a long battle that pits wisdom against masculinity, a battle that, as far as Jack can tell, these boys will continue fighting the rest of their lives.

Surely the wound on his hand is big enough by now. Surely he can stop rubbing at it. Jack looks up to find that Daphne is no longer reading—the class has moved on to the next student, and Jack feels sort of disappointed that he missed how the whole "specifically" drama played out. He looks around and sees only a few of the other boys still grinding away—the rest are sitting there holding their own hands, their sweaty faces twisted and wincing.

They're in pain, Jack thinks, and he's a little worried about this because he knows that nothing makes a guy attack another guy's weakness more than feeling weak himself. Lunch will be difficult to navigate.

"Jack?" says Mrs. Brannon.

And Jack looks up and realizes it must be his turn to read. "Sorry," he says, flipping pages. "Where are we?"

Light snickering from the class. Jack has a reputation for being lost in thought. His own mother will tell anyone who listens how Jack has always been rather slow, and the kids in school love nothing more than confirmation of this defect.

"No, it's not your turn, Jack," Mrs. Brannon says. "I was just asking you to open the window."

"The window?"

"Yes, it's sweltering in here."

Jack looks at the window, an old wooden-framed, leaded-glass thing that's been painted so many times it barely has any clearance left to move, the frame surely swollen even more by today's heat and humidity, a window that must be eight feet tall and might as well weigh nine thousand pounds for all the likelihood that Jack will be able to lift it. He looks again at Mrs. Brannon.

"Me?" he says.

"Let's get some air in here," she says, then turns to whoever was reading. "Please continue."

And so Jack stands up while Layla Harris dutifully recites her page from *RoboCop,* a section where Robo is blowing away assorted bad guys, and Jack hopes the class is really into this scene and really transfixed by the sort of disturbingly specific descriptions of where each of Robo's bullets enters each of the bad guys' skulls, so mesmerized by the violence on the page that they won't watch Jack. He approaches the big window and takes it by what used to be two handholds but what generations of paint have made slippery round knobs, and he tries to angle his body and approximate what he thinks it means when he hears his father tell one of the ranch hands "Put your back into it," and he pushes. He pushes as hard as he can. And just as he predicted, the window doesn't budge. There's not even a *tock* of frame-on-case slippage.

He turns around. The whole class—excluding Layla, who's reading—is looking at him. The boys stare with hyena-like grins.

"It's stuck," Jack says.

To which Daphne responds by standing up with a big dramatic sigh, saying, "I'll get it." She strides over to Jack with a kind of pioneer woman's air of grit and strength and purpose, clutches the window by its curved grips, and, with a great pull of her big arms, pops it out of its frame and flings it fully open.

The class roars.

Mrs. Brannon tries to calm them down, but Jack knows they will not soon forget this. The boys in particular will *never* let it go, how he could not lift something that could be lifted by a girl. There is no greater embarrassment, and right at this moment Jack knows: he's going to get beaten up for sure.

DAD, I'M RECORDING," said Toby, annoyed, as Jack entered his son's bedroom early that Saturday morning. The boy was on his computer, wearing his bulbous headphones, watching the manic YouTube channel of a prominent Minecraft player and vigorously reacting to it.

Jack stood next to him, off camera, and studied the screen: the YouTuber—wearing his own large headphones, sitting in his own small bedroom—was in one of the computer's windows, this window inscribed within a larger window of the game the guy was presumably playing, this window inscribed within a still-larger window showing Toby's face as he looked into his computer's camera, this window being one of dozens currently open on Toby's desktop. Jack shook his head and smiled: windows within windows within windows, he thought, simulations inside of simulations—how perfectly, exquisitely pomo.

The YouTuber was one Jack recognized, one of Toby's favorite celebrities, a guy who couldn't have been more than eighteen years old and whose full-time job seemed to be playing Minecraft all day and streaming it to an enormous audience of mostly children. It was a job that must have paid pretty well, given the expensive tech and large gaming tchotchkes visible in the room behind him, not to mention all the logos. The guy's jacket was covered in logos—like a race car driver's—patches for his many sponsors, mostly computer-related, plus a few of those carbonated energy-type beverage things.

"You know, when I was young," Jack said, "none of my friends wanted corporate sponsorship."

"Why?"

"They called it *selling out*. It meant you were fake."

Toby snorted. "That's dumb."

"You think so?"

"It doesn't mean you're fake. It means you're good."

Jack studied the YouTuber's Minecraft creation, a dark and narrow stone room, low-ceilinged, with a tessellated floor covered in what looked like snakes.

"What's he making?" Jack said.

"An oubliette."

"A what?"

"It's the new viral challenge. Craft the worst room to die in."

"That's a little morbid."

"What do you think would be worse? Dying from snakes or dying from lava?"

"I'd definitely say snakes."

"Yeah," Toby said, nodding thoughtfully, "it'd be slower." Then he leaned in toward the camera and made his eyes go all big and googly as he scrunched up his face and raised his arms in fright and screamed with what sounded like real authentic terror: "*Snakes!*"

"Toby, your mom's still sleeping."

He looked at Jack, smiled bashfully. "But wasn't that a good reaction?"

Jack nodded. "That was a really good reaction."

"Yeah, that's a keeper."

"Now c'mon, put your shoes on. We're going to the farmers market."

It was their Saturday tradition, to let Elizabeth sleep in while they walked to the park and picked up their weekly allotment of vegetables and fruits and meats and whatever other surprises the good people of their farm share decided to put in the tote. It was a humid and overcast morning, sunlight streaking across the underbellies of clouds, the dark windows of shops sweating with dew, the air thick and mucky. They walked down Milwaukee until its meeting with Damen and North, one of Chicago's several confusing intersections where a normal ninety-degree grid was cleaved by a diagonal street. A driver arriving at this intersection had like five routes to choose from, making it, at rush hour, a squalling, omnidirectional horror. But Toby was used to it, having grown up with it. He pressed the Walk button on the appropriate stoplight and waited.

"What's today's mission?" Toby said. "Please make it a good one."

It was a game they played every Saturday morning, Jack giving Toby some cash and an ambiguous scavenger-hunt directive. Last week, he'd told Toby to "buy the rainbow," and the boy had come back with a bag of red and blue berries, orange and yellow citrus, one green cucumber, and one indigo eggplant. The week before, it was "things in shells," and Toby had returned with sugar snap peas and oysters. The rule was that they would have to incorporate all of his ingredients into a single dish later that day—often an adventurous meal, as Toby typically tried to sabotage it with at least one off-kilter item, which he found hilarious.

"Today's mission is," Jack said, doing a little mock drumroll, "*Mom's favorite breakfast.*"

Toby nodded and gave a thumbs-up. "Good one."

They waited for the walk signal. To their left was the gym where Jack's favorite coffee shop used to be.

"That's where I met your mom," he said.

"I know," Toby said.

"Right there. That's where we had our first date."

"Dad, you tell me that *all the time.*"

"I do?"

"How you and Mom met right here, a million years ago."

"Not quite a million," Jack said. "Do you know when it was?"

Toby looked up at him. "The late nineteen-hundreds?"

Jack laughed. "Yes, I met your mother in the late nineteen-hundreds."

Across the intersection was the Flatiron Building, previously home to Swank Frank, the hot-dog place; and Filter, the café whose windows were a jumble of many-colored flyers for bands and shows; and the art gallery where Jack had his first solo show—all of these now consumed by a single branch of Bank of America, where the only evidence of its former life as a gallery was the local art the manager consistently hung in the back, behind the waist-high table with the pens and deposit slips. Jack's show there had been the crowning achievement of his nascent career. *Girl in Window*, it was called—kudos to Professor Laird for coming up with that name, and for setting up the show with the gallery's owners, and for basically supplying Jack with the intellectual framework to explain why photographing internet pornography was innovative and important. The show had been an unexpected hit, covered even in the *Tribune,* where the reviewer declared that Jack Baker was "the most exciting new artist in Chicago," which of course Jack knew to be bullshit. So it was a strange and complicated feeling when people began treating him as if it *weren't* bullshit. People began, suddenly, for the first time, taking him seriously, asking his opinion, noticing when he entered a room. Even his photography workshop, which had been so intimidating to him, was, overnight, not so intimidating, as he noticed a swift change in the kinds of responses his art now inspired: high praise instead of the usual indifference. Further, he noticed an elevation of his own judgments, as the other students were, abruptly, amazingly, waiting to hear Jack's thoughts, and when they heard Jack's thoughts, they nodded, as if his thoughts were not crude or wrong or embarrassing.

Turns out, if all your companionship and social capital derives from being an important artist, it is frightfully easy to decide that you are one.

And so the fact that *Girl in Window* was born out of some pretty troubling porn-related obsessive-compulsive behaviors, that was discarded, mentally. History was rewritten. Jack began saying smug things in class that began with "When I came up with *Girl in Window . . .*" and actually *meaning* them.

They called him an important artist, and he made the mistake of believing them.

"Dad, let's go," Toby said, tugging at Jack's hand. The signal had finally changed.

They walked south on Damen, underneath the tracks of the Blue Line, past a wall of graffiti, right past the hidden entrance to last night's fancy cocktail bar. Seeing it, Jack felt momentarily ashamed—of his panicked behavior with Kate, the growing dread he'd felt about Kyle, the petulant review he'd left online. He resolved to delete that review later today.

"Hey, Toby?" he said. "Has Mom made any new friends up at the school?"

"I don't know."

"Has she been talking to a guy named Kyle?"

"I don't know."

"He's a big guy, like a thick muscly guy, with a shaved head. Have you seen him around?"

Toby shrugged and said, again: "I don't know."

"Okay. Forget it."

They crossed over into the park, where the many stalls of the farmers market were arranged to funnel people through a large central thoroughfare, in the middle of which Jack now saw Benjamin Quince, standing in front of a booth called Restorative Acres, sampling the greens. Ben had been a farmers market fixture for many years now and could often be heard lecturing the farmers themselves on clean eating and all-natural supplements and biodynamic food systems. Today he was wearing a muscle-fit tank top that said *Kale* across the chest in exactly the same font as those shirts that said *Yale*.

"Jack! Buddy!" Benjamin said, coming in for a hug, one of those guy-hugs that began as a handshake and transitioned.

Then he crouched down to Toby's level: "High five, little man! Hey, listen, you want to eat something weird?"

Toby's face lit up. "Okay!"

"Here," Benjamin said, handing Toby a small leaf about the size and shape of basil. "Try it."

And Toby popped it into his mouth and chewed for a moment before his face screwed up crossly and he said: "Ewwwww!"

"Another excellent reaction," Jack said.

"Thanks."

"That," Benjamin said, "is field pennycress."

"It tastes like rotten mustard!"

"Farmers call it stinkweed. It's actually in the cabbage family. Totally edible and good for you. Unlike those Monsanto horrors over there," Benjamin nodding contemptuously at another booth, one selling more traditional produce.

This seemed to be Benjamin's particular passion: strange plants with surprisingly dense nutritional qualities and complexly bitter flavors that were indigenous to the Midwest but had fallen out of favor with the big agro-industrial monopoly. He claimed that the only way to reliably eat real, untampered-with, genetically natural food was to choose those foods that had long ago been abandoned by capitalism, thus his preference for the Restorative Acres booth, filled with interesting and edible and esoteric weeds and shrubs—pennycress, purslane, clover, redroot, motherwort—its signs and brochures heavy on the use of the word *pure*. It was this obsession with *purity*—and, of course, its opposite: *pollution, contamination*—that occasionally reminded Jack of the sermons he'd heard at his mother's church back home, the pastor's exhortations against wicked thoughts and evil deeds. There was, Jack sometimes mused, a kind of church-like quality to the farmers market: a bunch of similarly minded people waking up a little earlier than they'd probably prefer to wake up on a weekend, coming to a place that offered salvation from an abstract bad guy—either Satan or late capitalism, depending. The stories were different, but the dominant aesthetic seemed about the same: both the church and the farmers market longed for a more pristine Earth, one as either God or nature originally intended, before humanity came along and fouled it all up.

"Dad?" said Toby, tugging on Jack's shirt. "Money, please?"

"Right." He gave Toby some cash and the usual instructions about not going anywhere Jack couldn't see him, and the boy hustled off with due urgency.

"So, real good news in Park Shore," Benjamin said. "The lawsuits have been dropped, the injunctions withdrawn, and construction continues apace. The Shipworks is back, and roughly on schedule."

"That's great. What changed?"

"Honestly? I have no idea. I'd love to take some credit here, but the truth is that sometimes the world's entropy works out in your favor. Best not to question it too much. Best to say thank you and march onward."

Jack watched Toby, who was right now at the booth that sold local rooftop honey. And there was something in the boy's gestures—his dramatic shrugs and big frowns—that gave Jack the strong sense that Toby was *haggling,* and he wondered where his son learned to do that.

"Let me ask you something, Ben. And please be honest."

"Okay."

"Would you describe me as . . . vanilla?"

"By 'vanilla' you mean what, exactly?"

"I don't know. *Normal.*"

"Oh, I see. Like, plain. Conventional."

"Yes."

"Boring. Humdrum. Not in any way kinky. Uninteresting. Mainstream. Basic."

"Yeah. Do you think that accurately describes me?"

"What you have to understand, Jack, is that there's nothing wrong with being vanilla."

"So you do. You think I'm vanilla."

"You should remember that vanilla is an excellent flavor. The most common flavor."

"This hurts, Ben."

"Actually that's probably another good synonym: *common.*"

"This cuts at my whole persona."

In college, Jack had gotten an extravagant tattoo, all up his arms and around his torso. He thought at the time that it was a bold statement, that it made him unique. And yet one look around the farmers market right now revealed how many people were equally bold and unique. The young man standing near Jack, for example, had red and orange dragons curling up his biceps, and was currently palpating an avocado.

Benjamin said: "Why do you ask?"

"I'm worried that somewhere along the way I turned into this person I never intended to be, this person that Elizabeth never expected to be married to, this, like, boring vanilla toxic untalented gentrifier."

"Jack, you are not a gentrifier."

"Thanks."

"You bet."

"And how about those other things?"

"I can't speak to those, but you are definitely not a gentrifier."

"Well I met a guy last night who really seemed to think that I was."

"That's cute, asking you to take responsibility for that. But no, you were just another cog, just the smallest possible pinion in the engine of global progress, one of mass culture's million tiny underwriters, dispersing risk."

"And how was I doing that, exactly?"

"It was your whole starving artist ethos, that whole rebel-without-a-cause motif. Back then, we really believed that the worst person in the entire soulless corporate machine was the man in the gray flannel suit, you know? The man in the small beige cubicle. But we were wrong about that. The truth is that tattooed hipsters are way, way worse."

"How do you figure?"

"Because they're capitalism's prospectors, mining the earth for the next trendy thing. Have you noticed how the corporations that profit most from art never create their own art? I'm talking about entertainment companies here, the cultural capital–type stuff—music, publishing, film and TV—the people who own those companies don't create a thing. And that's because creation is unpredictable. Only a few artists ever truly catch on. Trendiness is a bad investment. Too risky for companies that have to answer to shareholders and boards. And so they transfer that risk to us. They ask us to be starving artists, living in a garret, doing the work for free on the off chance of making it big. We thought we were so anti-corporate back then, in the nineties, at the Foundry, but actually we were each taking on our own little share of corporate risk. We were helping to outsource risk and diffuse it across the labor force. Then one artist out of a hundred becomes legitimately trendy, the corporations suck them up and make their standard profits, and the rest of us become, I don't know, adjuncts."

"Thanks, Ben."

"We were not the gentrifiers, Jack. And blaming you for what happened is like blaming a boat for causing the tide. No, the Foundry was a sweatshop, and we were its toiling, exploited workers. People think I've changed so much since college, but the way I see it, I'm now just doing deliberately what I was doing accidentally back then: managing and dispersing risk. And I feel no guilt about that whatsoever. Nor should you, though I expect you'll continue feeling guilty nonetheless, because you always do. Which is probably why you sent Toby to buy bananas, right?"

"What?"

"I expect you're bringing home bananas? And honey? For pancakes?"

"Actually yeah." It had been Jack's plan to get back to the apartment early enough that when Elizabeth stumbled out of the bedroom, she would find that they'd made her a huge stack of banana pancakes, which was Elizabeth's all-time favorite breakfast. He wanted to provide her with this, a big morning *gesture,* something thoughtful and affectionate and considerate and heartfelt and, okay, yeah, maybe a little desperate, maybe transparently sending a kind of *please like me* energy, but it was the only thing he could think to do after the troubles of the previous night: to overwhelm Elizabeth with tenderness and special breakfast treats.

"You do understand the irony?" Benjamin said. "Buying bananas at a farmers market, *in Illinois*? The only way those bananas are local is that somebody bought them at Jewel and took off the stickers and doubled the price."

"How did you know I was buying bananas?"

Benjamin smiled. "People have their patterns," he said.

When Jack and Toby returned home, they found that the apartment, in their absence, had come to life. Lights were on, coffee was brewing. They walked into the kitchen to find Elizabeth standing there, hip resting against the counter, having her usual breakfast: Greek yogurt, chia seeds, a tall glass of water.

"Mom, stop eating!" Toby yelled.

"What? Why?"

"'Cause we're making you pancakes!"

And so Elizabeth gamely observed them preparing this new breakfast: banana pancakes with honey and cinnamon and, also, for some reason, cantaloupe, which was Toby's subversive little recipe surprise. And then they all ate together while Elizabeth elaborately praised Toby's cooking skills, and she thanked them both for the delightful morning, after which she rewarded Toby with some bonus screen time, which was her signal—though the boy did not know it—that she wanted to talk to Jack, in private. So Toby scurried to his bedroom, and Elizabeth checked to make sure he was indeed wearing his big sound-muffling headphones, and she returned to the kitchen and looked at Jack and said: "So, banana pancakes?"

"Yes."

She laughed and shook her head. "That is so perfectly you, Jack. Like clockwork."

"Ben implied something similar. I don't get it."

"I was a jerk to you last night. I'm sorry about that."

"Okay, thanks."

"But it's noteworthy that when I'm a jerk to you, your response is to make me breakfast."

"Well, yeah, I guess."

"Why do you always do that?"

"I wouldn't say *always*."

"Okay, but do you remember the last time you made me banana pancakes?"

"No."

"Book club."

"Oh," he said, "okay." It was the last time he'd come to her reading group, the last time the women of her reading group had pleaded with their husbands and boyfriends to attend the group in a misguided effort to equalize the group's gender ratio. They were reading a novel about baseball—the guys really should have seen this as transparent pandering but, for some reason, didn't—and one of the husbands made a really nice point comparing the main character's quest to make the big leagues with Ahab's quest to kill his great white whale, and the women nodded encouragingly at this, and for some reason it all felt very challenging to Jack, like he was in danger of not being appreciated when other guys were being appreciated. And so even though he really had no opinion one way or the other, he suddenly spoke up and insisted that no, the author probably did *not* intend the *Moby-Dick* comparison, as Ahab is much less self-critical and much more self-delusional than this book's protagonist, and what you've got to know about Melville is—

A glance at Elizabeth, at the big frown on her face, shut him right up.

"What are you talking about?" she asked him in a way that made the group go quiet. And Jack sat there and stewed the rest of the night, and didn't speak to Elizabeth at home, and then woke up the next morning and, okay, sure, he made her banana pancakes.

"I remember," he said now.

"And do you remember the time before that?" she said.

"What are you getting at?"

"It was the night you found me in here vacuuming."

He definitely remembered that. It had been an attempt at debauchery, a few months ago, on an evening when Toby was at a friend's house and Jack and Elizabeth were home together, alone, and it seemed like everything was going well and really clicking: the candles were lit, a bottle of wine had been emptied, and they were in bed about to get everything started when she put her hand on his chest and said, "I'll be right back," and so he waited, and he waited, and finally he stopped waiting when he heard a small whir elsewhere in the apartment and left the bedroom to find Elizabeth in the kitchen, cleaning the floor with her little handheld vacuum.

She looked at him and turned off the machine. "There were crumbs," she said.

"We had plans."

"Yes, but I saw the crumbs and knew it would only take a second and then I could check it off the list."

He frowned. "If someone were to ask you to choose between vacuuming the kitchen floor and having sex with your husband, which would you choose?"

"I wouldn't exactly put it like that."

And the next morning he woke up early and felt worried about the whole thing and made, again, banana pancakes.

"Oh, okay," he said now, "so I'm a boring predictable guy because I wanted to make you pancakes?"

"It's just a quirk I've noticed."

"What a boring, conventional, *vanilla* guy I am, making you your favorite breakfast."

"Never mind. Forget it."

Jack stared at her for a moment, quiet. He hated making her feel bad—he always immediately regretted it.

"I'm sorry," he said. "That was mean."

"And I'm sorry I sprung Kate and Kyle on you," Elizabeth said. "I should have given you some warning."

"You're not sleeping with Kyle, are you?"

"Seriously? *No.* Of course not."

"Do you want to sleep with Kyle?"

"Is that what you're so worried about?"

"I don't know what to be worried about, Elizabeth. Sometimes I just have no idea what you're thinking. After all this time together, still, you can be a complete mystery to me."

She nodded and flicked her eyes to the floor, smiled in her private, fleeting way. "Agatha used to say that I put up a wall, and I suppose that's true. Forgive me. It's sort of my default mode."

"Yeah, so, explain something. Why were you angry last night, on the walk home? That's still a puzzle."

She sat down at their small kitchen table, looked at its old and faded surface, the blond wood scratched and gouged in places, stained in others. They'd discovered the table in an alley fifteen years ago and had sanded and oiled it back into respectability. Elizabeth had recently wanted to replace the table, but Jack couldn't part with it. He imagined that the table had, over its long service, absorbed the collective aroma of their kitchen, the omnibus background scent of a million loving meals.

Elizabeth looked at him and said: "I've been thinking a lot about our situation."

"What situation?"

"Our life situation, at the bottom of the U-shaped curve."

"Oh. That."

"And I've been doing some research—"

"Of course you have, doing your Elizabeth thing."

"And most of the studies show that the secret to happiness at this particular moment in life is to simply try new things. To have new adventures. To change the routine. And I feel like I'm trying to do that, here and there, but that you keep, well, resisting it, at every turn."

"How so?"

"In little ways. I suggest open shelves in the kitchen, and you're like, *No*. A fireplace? *No*. Separate sleeping areas? *No*. Even at your job—your boss is asking you to try something new, artistically, and you're like, *No*. You're not even exercising anymore, or wearing that orange wristband thing."

"Which you thought was ridiculous."

"And last night, at the mere suggestion of going to a party that you'd have to agree would at least be interesting, you were immediately like, *No*."

"I don't think *interesting* is the word I'd use to describe it."

"My point, Jack, is that you seem to want everything to stay exactly the way it is, with no changes whatsoever. And I guess that's why I got mad."

"Because you want things to change. You want *our marriage* to change."

"Jack, listen to me." She stood up and walked toward him, took his hands in hers. "I've found everything I ever wanted with you. I mean that. When I left home and came to Chicago, I had no idea what would happen. I just wanted to make a decent life, and I wanted to find a good guy, and maybe have a beautiful family together, and live in a nice home, and look what happened—I got all of that."

"And yet now you're bored."

"No, not bored. Just no longer seduced by the mystery of it all. Life's big hard questions—*What will happen? Who will I become?*— have largely been answered. And now I feel like there's this huge absence where the mystery used to be. And I guess that's really what I'm after."

"The mystery."

"The adventure of it. I don't know if Kate and Kyle are right. I don't know if marriage is a broken institution. But I do know that if we went to that party, I have no idea what would happen there. And that mystery feels kind of delicious."

Just then, their phones chimed—simultaneously—a message for both of them from, it turned out, Kate, who had written: *Such a pleasure meeting up with you lovebirds! Looking forward to our next encounter!*

Kate had punctuated her message with an emoji that Jack didn't know the meaning of, though Toby had tried once to teach him the intricate symbology of each weird glyph. This one was a yellow face with raised eyebrows looking slyly to the right and smiling. This could mean, if Jack's memory served, that Kate was maybe hungover, or sarcastic, or smug, or keeping a secret, or feeling attractive, or saying *Hey there* in a seductive or vulgar way.

Jack and Elizabeth rested their phones on the countertop and looked at each other.

"Do you really think," he said, "that attending some depraved party is going to fill your life with happiness?"

"Of course not," she said. "But I also know that life will not feel satisfying without some mystery, some adventure, some thrill. That's what the science says, anyway."

"And this is the particular thrill you want?"

"This is just the closest one at hand."

"I see."

"Let's go do a crazy thing. Okay? That's all this is. For the first time in a long time, let's not act like parents. Let's be like we used to be. Let's be unconventional. Let's not be so plain."

There was that word: *plain*. It brought him back to those evenings around the kitchen table with his mother and his sister, those times his sister was visiting and she would go off hiking in the Flint Hills all day and return with arrowheads or bits of quartz or shells fossilized to calcite or gray stones that she insisted were hardened chunks of magma pushed up from the center of the earth—miracles, she said, all of them. Evelyn was a person enchanted by everything. But

Ruth, enchanted by nothing, would snort: "Those are just *rocks*, plain and simple."

Jack had come to Chicago to be like Evelyn, but in parenthood, maybe, he thought now, he'd turned out more like Ruth. He had, unbeknownst even to himself, become plain. He had become simple. He had become vanilla.

"Fine," he said to Elizabeth now, "you're right. Let's do it. Okay? I'm in."

"Really?"

"Fuck it. Sure. Let's go have an adventure."

But even as Elizabeth hugged him, and even as she excitedly said she was calling Kate right now, Jack wondered if maybe it was another impulse he was honoring: not the impulse to be different, but the impulse to be the same. To go along with things. To be part of a herd. Maybe it was that old childish impulse to fit in, to hide, to appease. He remembered the lengths he used to go to as a boy, the horrible things he would do to be agreeable, to avoid fights. He never said no back then, never stood up for himself. He once rubbed the skin of his hand clear away—with a *pencil eraser*—so other boys would not notice him, so he could fit in.

He looked down at his hand, tilted it under the light. He found that if he made a fist and held it just so, he could still see the scar.

THE MEANING EFFECT

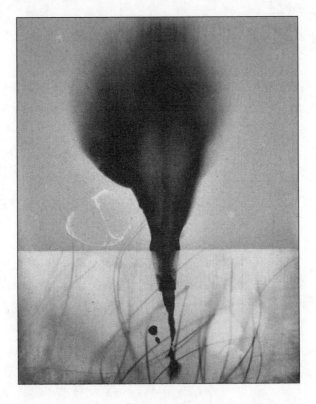

Two PATIENTS suffering from lower back pain visit an acupuncturist. The acupuncturist performs a long consultation with each patient that involves examining their tongue's color and shape and general tumescence for telltale signs of ill health, then measuring the rate and depth and force of their heartbeat in both the left and right wrists simultaneously, then pressing fingers into important pressure points searching for signals of bodily disturbance or bio-imbalance. And during this authoritative-seeming examination, it is explained to the patients that the specialized and tiny stainless steel acupuncture needles inserted precisely into the relevant nodes and meridians along their spine will unblock essential life forces, stimulating the body to release its effervescent healing energy, which will ultimately cure their back pain. Both patients agree to undergo treatment, but only one of them actually receives acupuncture. The other patient is secretly given a placebo treatment, the acupuncturist only pressing the skin of the back with a toothpick, which mimics the sensation of the needles' light prick but without their customary puncture. Thus, both patients believe they received real acupuncture. And it turns out that over time, both of them have *exactly* the same chance of being cured of their back pain. It turns out that it doesn't really matter whether they received real acupuncture or sham acupuncture—the outcome is the same.

Which, according to Dr. Otto Sanborne, proved that acupuncture—or at least the version of acupuncture practiced in the capitalist West—was fake. "Merely a placebo" was how Sanborne described it in his final report to the FDA, after the Wellness team had completed its study of a statistically significant number of lower-back-pain sufferers and found that the success rate of real acupuncture and fake acupuncture was basically identical: around 44 percent. Sanborne dispatched this report with great relish and then treated the office to celebratory drinks at a nearby bar after work; whenever he discovered some new phony treatment or nonsense medicine, he tended to be jolly for weeks, and when he spoke about this—especially after a few whiskeys—his eyes got wide and his face grew crayon pink, such was his exhilaration at exposing the mind's follies.

But that day, at the bar, Elizabeth found herself turning over the results in her head and thinking that the most interesting thing about the acupuncture finding was not necessarily that acupuncture had failed to perform any better than placebo. No, for Elizabeth, the most interesting thing was that placebo had actually performed quite well.

This was not long after Elizabeth's "unraveling" at the grocery store, and her subsequent triumph with the United Airlines gig, and so she'd already been thinking about the utility—not to mention profitability—of using placebo rather than eliminating it. For here was a back-pain treatment that required no surgery, no addictive drugs, nothing more expensive than a toothpick, had no side effects, and was successful almost *half the time*. It was the very definition of a quality medical intervention. And if a treatment was this effective, should we really worry about whether it was, technically, real? It made her wonder if instead of eliminating lies, maybe she could, somehow, harness them. Perhaps people weren't suckers for falling for a placebo. Perhaps falling for a placebo could be, in certain cases, helpful, useful, even ideal.

Example: oysters are not, in any real scientifically reproducible way, aphrodisiacs. If you give someone a dozen oysters and then measure their brain chemistry, you will find none of the specific hormones or neurotransmitters of sexual arousal. However, if you take a couple who believes that oysters are, in fact, aphrodisiacs, and you have them get all dressed up for a date night where they will be eating oysters together, and they go to a nice romantic restaurant that is famous for its oysters, and they pay a good amount of money for those oysters, and then you do a brain scan, you will find that their relevant glands have become hormonal geysers. In other words, by believing a story that was technically untrue, they created an elaborate ritual around that story, which had the effect of making the story true.

Or here's another one: chicken soup does not have any intrinsic properties that can cure the common cold. But when chicken soup is administered to a sick child by a caring mother who serves it with deep parental authority, the duration and severity of the child's cold will, generally, lessen.

Or the fact that absinthe never actually contained any hallucinogens. This even though all those great writers and artists of Paris—Baudelaire, Rimbaud, van Gogh, Manet, Toulouse-Lautrec—swore that it did. They all made poems and paintings about hallucinatory visits from "the green fairy" despite the fact that, scientifically speaking, absinthe had no special mind-altering qualities beyond that it was alcoholic. So how to explain these sincere collective accounts of hallucination? Elizabeth's theory: if you make absinthe a marker of insider status among an intellectual bohemian set that's rebelling against a repressive culture—in particular a culture that considers the drinking of absinthe decadent and degenerate—and if you then build an elaborate ceremony around reveling in the degeneracy of drinking absinthe that involves a special absinthe glass and a slotted absinthe spoon with cubed sugar set atop the spoon that is dissolved slowly drop by drop using exactly the correct ratio of absinthe and ice water in order to allegedly release the absinthe's hallucinatory essential oils, and if, further, you then *expect* and *believe* that this whole long ritual results in a concoction that will give you strange visions upon drinking enough of it, then, indeed, it probably will.

It was the *ritual* that was important—the acupuncturist's thorough examination, the couple's elaborate date, the mother's comforting home remedy, the ceremonial mixing of the absinthe. It was in these observances that the placebo effect activated and materialized: the transubstantiation of belief into reality, of story into truth, a metaphor made flesh.

Elizabeth called this phenomenon the "meaning effect," a term she much preferred to "placebo effect." Because to say that these effects arose from placebo implied that they arose from nothing—for that's what placebo traditionally was, an inert substance, literally and intentionally useless—when in fact the placebo effect was elicited by the strong sense of significance and substance surrounding the placebo itself: the context, story, ritual, metaphor, and beliefs associated with the placebo. The placebo effect was, in fact, the brain's response to finding meaning.

"Why not use it?" Elizabeth asked Sanborne that day at the bar. "Why not use placebos to help people?"

He frowned at her from behind his whiskey tumbler. Elizabeth continued: "If a placebo provides real relief, what's the big deal? Shouldn't people use whatever works for them?"

"But how do you know it was the placebo that caused the relief?"

"What else could it be?"

"Regression to the mean. The body's search for homeostasis. Feeling pain in your back is just a normal part of life, and it tends to come and go, naturally, sometimes waning immediately after it feels most severe. Therefore, if someone seeks out acupuncture at the moment the pain is worst—"

"Then they'll believe it was the acupuncture that cured them."

"When in fact they were going to get better anyway, on their own."

"I don't buy it. I interviewed these patients. Some of them had been suffering for *months*. They'd taken painkillers and muscle relaxants, they'd done physical therapy, they'd tried exercising differently, sleeping differently, and nothing worked. Then they tried acupuncture, and *presto*. Something about that worked."

"It worked because of a lie."

"So?"

"So when people are making decisions about their health, they should be able to trust that they're not being lied to."

"What if I told you: 'There is a good chance acupuncture will cure your back pain.' That is not a lie."

"But it's not the acupuncture doing the curing."

"Note that I'm not telling you *how* it will help, simply that it *will* help."

"That's lying by omission, my dear."

"What's worse: lying to the patient, or letting the patient suffer?"

He swirled the whiskey in his glass, thinking about this. "Even if it is ethical to help this one individual patient," he said, "the lie is unethical in a larger sense. If all doctors began to prescribe placebos, then all patients would naturally suspect they were getting one, and then patients would doubt all treatments. Which would undermine not only placebos but also real medicine. It can't work. It's not scalable."

"We're not talking about *all* doctors here, we're talking about you and me. Just us. And we've discovered that the brain is basically a medicine cabinet. We know this. It has incredible abilities to cure illness and relieve suffering, if only we can unlock it. And look what we have: a key. Wouldn't it be unethical *not* to use it?"

"But perhaps, my dear, that cabinet ought to remain locked."

"What do you mean?"

"Let's say you're right, that it wasn't regression to the mean, that our acupuncture patients somehow healed themselves. We provided the prompt, of course, but the healing was, strictly speaking, endogenous. The cure was inside them all along."

"Yes."

"So if they were capable of healing themselves, why didn't they do it sooner? Why did they need us at all?"

"I don't know."

"I don't either. But doesn't it imply that the pain was, in some way, useful? If the brain can cure the body but chooses not to, then maybe there's a good reason for the pain. Maybe the pain is necessary. Maybe the brain is saving its resources for something even more important, in the future."

"Like what?"

Sanborne smiled, swirled his whiskey, downed the rest of it. "That's for you to discover, my dear. Me? I'm much too old. Retirement beckons, but the work must go on!"

A few weeks later, Elizabeth was conducting an exit interview with a woman who'd participated in a Wellness study on juice cleanses. She was in her late twenties, from the suburbs, had moved to Chicago after college to work in the environmental advocacy sector, to "do some good" is how she put it, but was now deeply anxious that she hadn't really progressed up the nonprofit ladder much past intern, and hadn't yet found anybody to fall in love with despite literally hundreds of dates set up through literally every respectable dating website. Anyway, this woman had been told an elaborate story about the toxin-removing qualities of a particular line of cold-pressed juice blends that contained the most pure concentrates of the world's most nutritious whole foods—carrots, ginger, kale, beets, things like that—which Wellness provided her, in a five-day supply, in bottles with pure-white labels that said *Just Juice* and, crucially, had a price tag right there on the bottle: eighteen bucks *per serving.* The woman was instructed to consume only this juice in very particular and specific increments throughout the following five days, after which she returned to Wellness saying that this was the best she'd felt in *years,* that she had begun her cleanse as an unhealthy and perhaps even polluted person but had emerged bright and pure and new, that she was mentally focused at work and had all this available energy left over for her dating life, and she'd even taken up a new hobby and finished a few lingering tasks around her apartment, and her joints felt really fluid and lubricated, and even her ulcer pain had gone away, and she'd felt so great about the cleanse that she'd promptly gone online and joined several juicing communities and posted updates about her *juice journey,* and so on and so forth, Elizabeth's heart sinking because she knew she would have to tell this poor woman that she had not, in fact, been drinking juice at all, but rather she'd been drinking a placebo substance made of water and food coloring and some basic supplements that could be found in most any multivitamin, plus artificial flavors and sweeteners and thickening agents that mimicked the taste and mouthfeel of real juice. Elizabeth had to reveal this to her because it was the law: in order to receive any government or university funding, Wellness had to abide by professional ethics standards, one of which was that any study that deceived its subjects had to reveal the truth to those subjects upon the end of the study. Usually Wellness sent a letter, which informed its placebo patients that they'd received placebo. But now Elizabeth wanted to do this in person, to find out, up close, how the subjects responded.

How this particular subject responded was: not well.

"I don't believe you!" she said. "That's not possible!"

"I'm sorry," Elizabeth said, "but it's true."

"No, there's been some mistake. Check your paperwork. There is *no way*."

"I'm really sorry, but you were given a placebo."

"No I wasn't! I was given juice. Real juice. I can feel it. I'm a thousand percent confident about this."

"Confidence is rarely associated with accuracy, psychologically speaking."

"Check again. You've made a mistake."

Elizabeth recognized that the woman was in the first stage of grief—*denial*—and so figured *anger* would be coming along pretty soon, which it did immediately after Elizabeth made a big show of checking and rechecking the subject data and assuring the woman that, yes, she had indeed received a placebo.

"This is bullshit!"

"I apologize."

"Why did you do this to *me*? Why did you pick *me*? Were you trying to make me feel stupid?"

"No, of course not. It was a randomized, double-blind study. Nobody knew who was receiving what until it was all over."

"I bought a new juicer! It cost five hundred dollars! I put it on a credit card!"

"I'm sorry."

"And what am I going to tell people online?" she said. "My new juicing communities who were so supportive and wonderful. How am I going to face them now?"

Elizabeth nodded sympathetically and thought: *Bargaining*.

"I mean, I followed all the top juicers on Instagram! I posted about my cleanse! They followed me back! What am I supposed to say now? Like, sorry, it was all a big lie?"

"I don't know anything about that."

"Just yesterday some toxic jerk popped into our juicing subreddit and claimed juicing was a hoax and we fucking *annihilated him*! What am I going to tell these people?"

Elizabeth knew from the ethnographic research she'd read on the subject of cults that the thing that most effectively strengthened and deepened delusions was being surrounded by people who shared the same delusions. In these situations, alliances formed, enemies were identified, an us-versus-them dynamic was both encouraged and rigorously sustained. People were so much more apt to believe in something when they were immersed in a community of other believers, when they were surrounded by people speaking the same language, people with the same common referents. In this way, certain ideas—even bad ones, even false ones—had a kind of immune system: the more people they gathered into an ever tighter alliance, the more protected the ideas would be. You could think of an idea as a body, and the people who believed the idea as its white blood cells, attacking foreign invaders. When people expressed rage online, Elizabeth thought of it sometimes as the immune response of a threatened idea. But of course she chose to say none of this to the young woman, who was fully into the *depression* stage now, lightly crying, sniffling, forehead on the table.

"I just wanted to have *one good thing*," she said. "Like, just one thing in *life* that was good."

"I'm really so sorry."

"It's like I try and I try and I try, but nothing goes quite right. I mean, my job is shit, and my rent is so high, and I have tons of friends with benefits but no actual real friends, and everyone online is rude and angry to me, and no matter how much I advocate against coal plants the carbon in the atmosphere still goes up, and the seas are rising, and the droughts are coming, and the ice shelves are collapsing, and I thought, like, okay, no matter what happens, at least (*sniffle*) I'll have (*sniffle*) my juice."

And then the woman excused herself, complaining that her ulcer pain had, promptly, returned.

Perhaps it was cruel giving this woman a placebo, but it seemed in that moment more cruel to tell her the truth about it. What did it really matter if juice cleanses never achieved results better than placebo? *They still achieved results.*

Elizabeth began inserting new questions into the interviews she conducted with test subjects, questions that had nothing to do with the ostensible purpose of the study. The mandate at Wellness had been, for many years, to determine whether various health interventions could achieve results better than placebo. They'd been debunking junk wellness fads for so long, and yet it was hard not to notice that those fads kept coming, faster and faster, getting ever more popular and orthodox. Wellness had been fighting against this tide for years, and nothing had happened. It felt so futile. And so Elizabeth changed directions: instead of debunking junk treatments, she began investigating why they achieved good results at all. Among the people on whom placebos successfully operated, were there any common traits or conditions or contexts that explained the success?

And indeed there were. What she discovered, after she began asking questions about her subjects' home lives and careers and worldviews, was that people were, in general, totally confused and overwhelmed and tired and worn-out. They lived in a landscape full of despair and distrust, a world with toxic sludge seeping into the groundwater, particulates hanging in the air, oceans full of microplastics, a sky swamped with carbon and radiation, a food supply awash with pesticides and filler and garbage, doctors who had no time for them, politicians lying to them, PR flaks lying to them, TV journalists lying to them, unsatisfactorily employed, hopelessly in debt, one medical bill from bankruptcy, and nobody protecting them from any of it, government regulators in bed with the corporations they regulated, the powerful protecting the powerful while all the little guys suffered. And listening to these stories, Elizabeth decided that believing in fad diets or mystical chakras or energy crystals was actually a pretty rational and sane response to systemic collapse: If nobody else was going to protect you, you had to do the job yourself. You had to believe in something. You had to find, somewhere, hope.

When Dr. Sanborne finally did retire and Elizabeth took charge of Wellness, she began changing its direction and mission: fewer government contracts, less academic research, more focus on using all that they'd learned about placebo in order to actually help people. She gathered her small staff together and told them that the organization would be pivoting. She said to her colleagues' surprised faces that medical science, in its obsession with hard data and replicable results, had too long ignored the softer utility of placebo. When a treatment worked only because it told a compelling story, the medical establishment typically dismissed it in favor of more drugs, procedures, molecules, things they could repeat and explain. But a story could act on you just as strongly as a drug could. When you went to the theater, for example, and watched a play so good it made you weep, that was a sort of placebo: it was a story that changed your brain chemistry, and only the most blockheaded person would say, *Why are you crying? It's not even real.* What Wellness would be doing was not so different: creating fictive experiences that produced real physical and psychological responses. It would be biologic theater.

Elizabeth met with area doctors and asked for referrals, for patients who were lightly suffering—nothing life-threatening, nothing too serious—people with everyday pain: headaches, fatigue, insomnia, mental fuzziness, chills, hot flashes, stress, those symptoms that are modulated by the brain's perception engines rather than those created by foreign physical bodies like viruses or tumors or embolisms, against which placebos are almost never effective. Her team would then conduct telephone interviews with patients and arrange the office to create the context and aura that would most appeal to each patient's particular personality. She prescribed negative ion bracelets and probiotic chewing gums and lavender smelling salts and coconut-water baths and extra-strength turmeric pills and collagen supplements and weighted wrist bangles and superfood lattes and crystal-infused water bottles and pink-salt diffusers and bone-broth elixirs and paleo pomades and activated-charcoal toothpastes and CBD beard oils and pro-mitochondrial broccoli-extract patches and energizing alkaline smoothies and milk-thistle detoxifying powders and kombucha body washes and she didn't feel one bit guilty for deceiving her patients in this way. She figured you could give someone a synthetic opioid, or you could give them a placebo so compelling that it prompted the brain to release its own natural opioids—and wasn't that better for everyone? It was effective, it was cheap, nobody got addicted, nobody OD'd. And Wellness had a success rate at treating chronic pain that rivaled that of real medicine. Ditto fatigue, insomnia, anxiety, depression. After a few years of this, her results were incredible, and she would have written them up in an academic paper, but all these treatments violated just about every ethical protocol regarding medical placebo—specifically, the requirement to tell people they'd received a placebo, which of course would have ruined the treatment—and so Elizabeth's success remained a secret between her and the doctors who warily sent patients her way.

Then one day, a woman called the office with a request Elizabeth had not yet encountered: this woman asked Wellness to help her love her husband again.

The patient—thirty-eight years old, professional, mother of two, children nine and five, married eleven years—said that she was still deeply attached to her husband, who was a good person and a good friend about whom she cared very much. It was just that she didn't feel that particular *spark* anymore, didn't feel that thing that made her come alive inside like she had in their early days, before the kids. Divorce was out of the question—she wouldn't put her children through that trauma, and anyway there was nothing really *wrong*. She and her husband never fought; they instead just sort of existed, side by side, neutrally. She was in love with him, but that love no longer inspired passion. Could Wellness possibly help?

Which was when Elizabeth got into the love potion business.

She did not tell the staff she was interested in this woman's problem because of its regrettable similarity to her own personal home life—rather, she said it was an interesting new psychological challenge, plus a possibly lucrative profit vector given the well-known and common marital phenomenon of romantic love's cooling over time.

Elizabeth knew from the intake evaluation that the patient was a neat and ordered and rational person, very logical, very methodical, your classic ISTJ personality type, an IT manager at a local bank who, in other words, would not respond to anything very froufrou. No crystals, no ancient herbal remedies, for sure nothing exotically tantric. This woman saw herself as serious and dependable, practical, no-nonsense, she valued predictability and usefulness, and so before her visit to Wellness, Elizabeth arranged the office to look as generically corporate as possible: beige filing cabinets, gray chairs that were not entirely comfortable, those off-white adjustable-height desks with the rubber bumper running all the way around. The place looked basically like a copy shop, and Elizabeth's hope was to make the space feel as, quote, unquote, "normal" as possible, to make the patient feel normal, to make her think this treatment was just as normal and utilitarian and familiar as any other and not in fact a love potion that didn't really exist.

For the potion itself, there was some debate among the staff regarding its presentation and administration. A liquid infusion seemed obvious, some kind of thick elixir taken like a cough syrup, but that was ultimately dismissed because, often, when a problem felt intractable, the most effective solution was one that also felt difficult, and taking a shot of love juice was far too easy. An injection also didn't seem quite right. Injection placebos worked best when the problem was localized: knee pain, for example, or muscle spasms, both of which responded well to shot-based approaches. But a love drug injected anywhere on the body one could reasonably poke a needle would seem like a non sequitur. There was discussion of an IV drip that the patient would come in for every few weeks, in which case Wellness would nudge salient comparisons with dialysis, the subconscious messaging being that the IV slowly replaced the bad emotions with the good ones. And they were leaning in that direction when Elizabeth noticed in one of the interview transcripts that the woman said she often fell asleep with one of her husband's work shirts near her face, such was the comfort she still associated with his smell, and that's when Elizabeth realized that the solution would have to be: intranasal.

They prescribed the woman a no-nonsense medical-looking nasal spray, which they told her was filled with a cocktail of brain chemicals and hormones, explaining to her that what she experienced as *spark* in a relationship was simply the manifestation of ancient neuropeptides that governed our brain's *lust* and *attraction* systems, most notably dopamine and norepinephrine, and so what she needed to do was reassociate these brain systems with her husband. They compared it (in a nifty reframing of the patient's own IT background) to a computer that can't locate its printer—it does not mean that either the computer or the printer is broken, but simply that the driver needs to be updated. And this infusion of neurochemicals right up the nasal cavity and directly into the brain would function, they said, as that brand-new driver, allowing her to "connect" with her husband once again. Her instructions were to administer the intranasal dopamine spray (in reality it was, of course, just saline) whenever she would be, in the next hour, within sniffing distance of her husband. The effect of this, they said, would be to realign his scent and presence with her lust and attraction zones rather than the low-level-attachment and friend zones he currently occupied.

The reasons for these specific instructions were, first, to create a ritual—à la acupuncture and oysters—that felt to the patient authoritative and persuasive; and, second, to get the patient intimately contacting her husband at moments she *expected* to feel amorously toward him, figuring that in such contexts the lust stuff would probably take care of itself.

And indeed it did. In follow-up interviews, the woman reported a flourishing of her sex life and general all-around good feelings about her relationship, and she thanked Elizabeth profusely, requested regular refills, and sent Wellness an appreciative fruit basket every year at Christmas.

The staff celebrated the possibility of a new passive income stream while also feeling a little leery about their success. Around the office, people asked each other: Is this ethical? Lying to patients this way? Making them feel love under false pretenses? It was one thing to cure a headache, but tricking them into love? Didn't it sort of call into question the sincerity of that love?

Elizabeth's argument was that their treatments were akin, philosophically, to the treatments one might get at couples counseling, where a therapist would try to create new contexts to rekindle love. The difference here was only in the specific methodology, not in the underlying ethics. She compared it to teaching Toby to ride a bicycle: Elizabeth had run along behind him, assuring him that she was holding the bike upright, that she was preventing him from tipping over, when in fact she was doing no such thing. She wasn't touching the bike at all. He was actually riding it, really successfully balancing upon it, a feat he could not have accomplished without the confidence inspired by her lie. This was what they were doing at Wellness: they weren't creating love, but rather creating the conditions that allowed its expression.

Word got out among the city's therapists that Wellness had developed some kind of strange new love potion, and soon the office was fielding calls from husbands and wives all reporting basically the same symptoms: not exactly unhappy, but suffering nonetheless. They were friendly with their partners but not exactly passionate, loving but not romantic, faithful but also bored, thinking of their spouses as very devoted roommates, parents who acted toward each other less like lovers and more like cofounders of an at-home business whose products were children, not altogether miserable but strongly dissatisfied, not knowing quite what to do, disappointed, staying together for the kids.

For these patients, the Wellness team prescribed intranasal dopamine sprays or oxytocin patches or testosterone gels or cleansing estrogen scrubs or pheromone nebulizers or microdosed MDMA tinctures or DRD4 gene therapy pills—all of them placebo, of course—and in every follow-up interview with a thankful patient now really enjoying marriage again, Elizabeth would feel bolts of envy that the things she did to help other people would not help her. For it was a truism of placebo studies that the placebo effect obtained only if the patient was unaware of it, and so by definition Elizabeth could not partake of the treatments she herself invented. The stories that worked for others would never work on her.

But she tried. She tried doing things that were supposed to create the conditions for romance and intimacy. She and Jack had once booked a weekend getaway at a private cabin in the woods of Door County that had a deck out back where two claw-foot bathtubs sat next to each other overlooking a lake, and when they arrived at the cabin they found that the bathtubs had been recently filled with hot water and the water's surface covered elegantly with rose petals, and so, okay, they stripped off their clothes and got into the tubs and watched the sun set over the water while holding hands and occasionally glancing over and meeting the other's eye seductively in anticipation of romantic and spontaneous and vigorous lovemaking, Elizabeth meanwhile full of anxiety because she knew they were supposed to have really good sex that night and she was worried suddenly that the sex wouldn't be good enough to meet their big hopes for the moment, and then she was stressed out that the really good sex hadn't actually started yet, and then feeling awkward about how to actually initiate the really good sex while Jack just sat there, skin pruning, looking at her, waiting for her to, like, begin, and suddenly she didn't feel romantic and spontaneous at all.

It was always the same problem: she could no longer figure out how to be close to Jack without also feeling overwhelmed and suffocated by his expectations.

Not until, that is, she met Kate, who told a new story. According to Kate, the answer wasn't closeness but rather separateness. Separate bedrooms. Separate lovers. More separated lives. Elizabeth listened to Kate talk about how the problem with modern marriage was actually all that togetherness, all that intimacy, that stupid drive to merge completely with the other person, and that the only way a marriage could survive the decades was to inject some mystery and distance and emancipation, and as soon as Elizabeth heard this and imagined a life of total autonomy spiced up with the occasional fun and ethical fling with a handsome new stranger on a night free of the responsibilities of marriage or parenthood, she knew right away: here, finally, was a story she could believe in.

THERE WERE a few things they needed to know before attending an orgy.

The first was: don't call it an orgy.

"There's actually a pretty fierce debate about that online," Kate told Elizabeth during a phone call on the day of the party. "There's a very vocal faction on certain web forums arguing that *orgy* is in fact a misogynist term, that it's so, like, Playboy Mansion 1972. The word *orgy* sort of implies that everyone involved has a kind of blanket permission to touch whomever they want in any way they want, like at any moment you might be groped by *anyone,* which dudes seem to have no problem with, but it's a somewhat rare female request."

"So if not orgy," Elizabeth said, "what's the preferred term?"

"Oh, you can just be specific. Threesome, foursome, fivesome, sixsome. It's frankly pretty uncommon to go beyond six."

Elizabeth was sitting on the floor of her bedroom closet, the door closed, the phone's speaker muffled by her hand, Jack in the other room having promised to keep Toby fully occupied on a computer with the volume ideally turned way up—this was how much she did not want her son eavesdropping on this conversation.

"You should also think about how you want to identify," Kate said. "Like what kind of specific nonmonogamy do you want to practice?"

"I have no idea."

"Well, there's the classic don't-ask-don't-tell arrangement, and then there's the monogamish option, or the more transparent open marriage, also soft swapping, full swapping, hierarchical poly, nonhierarchical poly, polyfidelity, relationship anarchy, unicorn hunting—"

"I think we're just there to observe."

"Toe-dippers. Of course. You should know that tonight's party will be much more swinger than poly, which are two subcultures that don't always mix well."

"I would think they're both basically on the same team."

"Nope. Poly people tend to think that swingers make nonmonogamy look crude and unserious, whereas swingers think poly people make it look tedious and bureaucratic. The fights on Twitter about this subject are, let me tell you, vicious."

"This is beginning to seem a little overwhelming."

"Another thing you absolutely must do," Kate said, "is agree on an escape word."

"A what?"

"An escape word."

"What is that?"

"Well, you know how people in BDSM have a safe word?"

"I'm aware of the concept."

"An escape word is kind of like that. It's a signal to your partner that you want to stop doing whatever you're currently doing, *right now*. But whereas a safe word should be something you would never expect to hear during a sexual encounter—you know, so it stands out, so it's immediately recognizable in an otherwise heated moment—an escape word needs to be much more subtle. It should be something you can say in front of another couple without their noticing that you've said it."

"My god, how often do you have to do that?"

"Not often, actually, and almost never in the playroom."

"It's called a playroom?"

"Yeah. That's where the sex happens. The orgy, as it were."

"I don't think I can call it a playroom. That's way too childish. I can't handle the associations."

"I'm pretty sure it's supposed to imply that it's fun? Our language doesn't really have a word for this kind of activity, so we do the best we can. Like, you wouldn't call it the *love room*, right?"

"No, that's somehow even worse."

"As I was saying, once I'm in the playroom I almost never need to use the escape word. Consent is a big deal in this community, so everybody thoroughly discusses, *pre-consummation,* their boundaries and rules and preferences regarding touching and kissing and oral and swapping and kink and bisexual play and so on and so forth."

"This sounds phenomenally complicated."

"The only time I ever invoke the escape word is, actually, *before* the playroom, when I'm talking with a couple and realize I need to leave."

"Why would you need to leave?"

"Because drama. Some couples are oozing drama. Those are folks you really ought to avoid."

"Anything in particular I should be looking for, any warning signs?"

"Well, you'll find that most couples are there just having a sexy adventure, after which they'll go home and pay the babysitter and giggle privately about this crazy thing they did. But other couples are there because of some desperate need, some fracture in their relationship. And they think they can fix their marriage by doing this, which inevitably backfires. Things always explode, and, trust me, you do not want to be caught in the middle of *that.*"

"Good advice. Great. Thanks."

"As for attire, wear whatever you feel sexy in, and understand that no matter how outrageous you dress, someone else will be way more outrageous, and it will probably be Donna."

"Who's Donna?"

"You'll find out. Also the cover charge will be eighty dollars cash, plus one bottle of a top-shelf spirit. You'll understand when you get there."

"Fine."

"And the last thing you need to know," Kate said, "is ignore the protesters."

"There are *protesters*?"

"Sort of. Sometimes. Occasionally, when the weather is nice, there's a handful of people who will stand out front with judgmental signs. They're annoying but harmless. I guess they don't like that the club is located next to a day care. Anyway, we valet our car in back, via the alley, and we never even see them."

Which was exactly what Jack and Elizabeth did, driving in total nervous silence to this address in the suburbs, uncomfortably close to the borders of Park Shore, right there on the main thoroughfare connecting Park Shore to the expressways of the city, turning into an alley and driving until they saw a sign that said, simply, VALET, and veering into a large parking lot surrounded by a ten-foot privacy fence, pulling into a spot near the back of a three-story building with no exterior signage, a building whose windows were so darkly tinted that one could see only the faintest glimmers of what seemed to be the moving pinpricks of light scattering off a disco ball. Elizabeth had driven past this building so many times, on every trip to and from Park Shore, but had never, until this moment, seen it or noticed it.

"Welcome to the club," the valet said, and then they were escorted through the back entrance of a nightclub that seemed to have no name—unless the club's name was actually just the Club—into a kind of waiting room, a small holding area lit softly by a crystal chandelier with all these flickering LED candle things that mimicked real lit candles, which, together with the room's red walls and red velvet drapery and red satin curtains and what looked to be an actual antique art nouveau writing desk, gave the place a sort of Moulin Rouge quality. Behind the desk—which really was an outstanding piece of furniture art, Jack was thinking, with ornate inlaid carvings of flower stems and blossoms and such—sat a woman whose name tag said "Donna," who looked to be in her late sixties/early seventies, whose long gray hair was done up in a kind of volumized perm, whose low-cut black dress wasn't nearly as outrageous as Elizabeth had been told to expect, and who was right now looking for their names on a list. Jack and Elizabeth listened to the low throb of dance music playing on the other side of the door, and waited.

"Oh here you are," Donna said with a smoker's rasp. "Newbies, eh?"

Jack and Elizabeth nodded.

"Okay, there's some paperwork."

And Donna took them through all the administrative formalities necessary to gain entrance to this place, the name of which turned out to be, indeed, according to the documents, The Club: A Private Club. The paperwork was written in the dense, all-caps manner of software terms-of-use agreements, and the top page noted in bold and underlined ways that the eighty dollars they were paying tonight was not a "cover charge" but rather a one-night "membership fee" to The Club: A Private Club, Donna explaining that requiring a cover charge to a place where sexual activity occurred could run afoul of brothel-related statutes but that private social clubs had a different licensing structure that exempted them from all but the most aggressive prosecution. This brand-new membership to The Club: A Private Club would last, she said, exactly twelve hours, unless they wished to purchase quarterly or yearly memberships, the prices of which were absurd. Then another document informing them that if they entered the playroom tonight intending to engage in sexual activity, they were technically entering a space that they, themselves, Jack and Elizabeth, were *renting,* similar to how hotels rented out ballrooms for conferences without being held responsible for anything anyone at that conference said or did—"Legally, we're not offering a 'sex room' but rather renting you a space that you may or may not choose to have sex in," Donna said, "which, obviously, limits our liability"—so, okay, they signed and initialed the paperwork acknowledging that a portion of their membership money was actually the "rental fee" for said playroom, which fee was, of course, in the event that they did not partake in tonight's debauchery, nonrefundable. Then finally the alcohol waiver, Donna explaining that in the state of Illinois you cannot sell alcohol at an establishment where one might also encounter full-frontal nudity, which was why club members were required to bring their own alcohol, which meant that, technically, under a strict reading of state law, The Club: A Private Club was not illegally selling alcohol without a license but rather merely giving the alcohol you brought with you back to you, Donna meanwhile taking their bottle of Hendrick's and saying, "I'll send this to the bar," which was the last they saw of their gin.

"So I'm guessing Illinois has some pretty strict vice laws still?" Jack said, to which Donna blew out her cheeks and buzzed her lips and rolled her eyes like *Don't get me started*.

"Have a nice night!" she said, and she opened the interior door.

Inside, the club had a sort of eclectic and quirky Mad Hatter tea-time theme, with mismatched, whimsically painted furniture everywhere, and zany floral wallpaper on which hung antique mirrors and tilted antique picture frames and antique clocks all set to different times, also an effusion of flowers—almost certainly artificial—in pastel pinks and purples and yellows in vases at every table and strewn all over the shelves of the well-stocked bar. Along the outer walls were dark, private booths with high-backed couches of tufted velvet, all surrounding a black-and-white checkered dance floor lit from above by the soft, diffuse glow of string lights dangling around the disco ball. The music was notched perfectly to encourage dancing but also allow private conversation, and Jack leaned into Elizabeth and said: "What do we do now?"

She led him to one of the booths opposite the bar, and they sat on the plush sofa and, hidden back there, they watched.

The party hadn't started yet, as there were only a few dozen people here, and only four people on the dance floor—all women, all four of them taking turns twirling around the stripper pole in the dance floor's middle, spinning in ways that suggested much previous experience and possibly even classes and advanced training. They were in their forties or fifties, it looked like, and they were all wearing strapless dresses in loud neon colors that were so short that when they climbed the pole you could easily see who chose to wear underwear, and who didn't. When Jack noticed this, he immediately, out of respect, turned away.

Elizabeth, meanwhile, was feeling overdressed. She had chosen for tonight a little black number with spaghetti straps that was maybe two to three inches shorter than what she'd feel comfortable going to work in, but now she understood that in this particular environment such a dress was downright prudish. In this club, the flesh was aggressively, exultantly, unconcealed: skirts were minusculely mini; necklines dropped indecently to belly buttons; dresses were more suggestions of clothes rather than clothes per se; pasties seemed to be an acceptable "top"—and this not only on the fashion model bodies, of which there were a few, but on just about all the women here, the young and old and middle-aged, the large and small, youthful bodies and bodies touched by time or the swell of childbearing or the sagging of age; all was, here, unhidden. The woman presently spinning on the stripper pole, for example, her dress had, while sliding down the pole, rolled up to her rib cage, and so now everyone in the club could see exactly the way her belly drooped over her C-section scar, and she was laughing and twirling and just not giving a shit. Elizabeth found it surprisingly charming.

The men, on the other hand, almost exclusively wore the same outfit, the same combo of tight dark jeans and a tight black button-down, their body types almost exclusively what you might call "beefy," their heads almost exclusively shaved or bald. The sameness of it made Elizabeth laugh.

"If these wives are looking for variety," she said, "they won't find it here."

"Right?" Jack said. "I mean, do these guys all go to the same barber?"

"I wonder if they get a group discount on European clubwear."

"I'll bet their family portraits are all gym selfies."

"Research is definitely needed on whether the baldness gene also predicts wife swapping."

They smiled at each other then. It felt nice to be back here in this booth, privately riffing. It was like those college trips to the Gap; they were a team again. Elizabeth reached across the table and took Jack's hand.

Which was when Kate and Kyle found them.

"There you are!" said Kate, who wore a black leather miniskirt and large jewel-bedazzled eyeglasses and a top that was like a bikini crossed with a spiderweb, all strappy and netlike. She was also much, much taller than usual, owing to the eight-inch platform heels she was wearing, so that when she greeted them both (with quick kisses on the mouth, of course), she had to bend so far over that she nearly lost her balance and tumbled into their laps, which was probably the idea all along.

"Come with me, Romeo!" she said to Jack. "Let's get us some drinks."

Jack shot a glance at Elizabeth; *Romeo* was, in fact, their escape word. The agreement they'd come to was that if Elizabeth called him Romeo, or if he called her Juliet, that was the signal: drop everything, stop doing whatever they were currently doing, and escape.

Later, looking back on the evening, Jack would come to think that Kate's invoking their escape word in the first ten seconds was an important sign that they failed to acknowledge in the moment. Looking back on it, they would realize that their friends separating them like this—Kate taking Jack to the bar, Kyle sliding into the booth with Elizabeth—was actually some kind of advanced premeditated strategy, whereby Kate and Kyle could more easily evaluate each of them for playtime potential or, as it were, drama. But Jack and Elizabeth did not, of course, recognize this maneuver at the time. They just went with it. Sometimes, in the midst of information overload, it's hard to act like your normal wise, discerning self.

Jack, for example, could not possibly unpack the social dynamics at play in the moment, as all he was doing was basically repeating to himself: *Don't be creepy. Don't be creepy.* This one dictum pretty much occupied the whole of his working memory because, as he followed Kate to the bar and past the many women in their many flamboyant states of undress, he understood that each woman, each bit of exposed flesh, each breast emerging from a tank top, each nipple visible under a diaphanous or fishnet top, threatened to expose his deep, abiding, total creepiness. He longed to stare at the entire decadent scene, and it was the overwhelming power of this desire itself that made him feel like such a creep.

This was doubly so here with Kate, as Jack stood with her at the bar and got a good close-up view of just how much her strappy bra thing *did not entirely cover her* and he felt like there was not one single vector his eyes could travel without landing somewhere that would be interpreted as: creepy.

"Isn't this place beautiful?" Kate said.

"It sure is!" Jack said, staring hard at the drinks menu.

"I love how everyone here is so free."

"They sure are!" He was pretending to read the menu very, very carefully.

Definitely part of the issue here had to do with all of Jack's academic training vis-à-vis the male gaze, the problematic masculine impulse to objectify and dehumanize. He understood that there was something unbudgeably wrong with the way men often *perceived,* the manner in which they looked and saw and apprehended, which had to do with their tendency to deconstruct and reduce women to only their sexually relevant body parts, which, looking around the Club tonight, he thought: *Yeah, I'm totally doing that.* He knew that if he stared at the women here in the way he really sincerely wanted to, he would be looking in a selfish, lewd, purely objectifying manner, focused only on a woman's body versus her full human fullness, which made him gross. This was a familiar conflict for him, the same internal friction provoked by any voyeuristic opportunity that Jack would willfully, righteously, attempt to ignore. (Bike rides on the lakefront trail on those first summer days when it seemed like all the women of Chicago rushed to the beach in tiny bikinis were, my god, a nightmare of temptation and discipline.) His acute awareness of the toxic male gaze had the effect usually of making Jack deny exactly the things he wanted most, mentally resisting the very things he was most attracted to, though he honestly couldn't very well blame the academic scholarship for this, as when he first encountered this literature in college he already had the conviction—almost certainly owing to the miserable gender dynamics he grew up with—that one of the fundamental ways men injured women was by just *being themselves*. Just existing. Just inflicting their crude male agendas. And so when he encountered the critiques of the male gaze in college and read about how there was possibly something unchangeably wrong with him, he didn't really need all that much convincing. The readings tended to immediately confirm something he'd already suspected and known. For as long as he could remember, he had experienced this guilt-filled internal melodrama, this feeling that being attracted to a girl and paying attention to that girl was the emotional equivalent of coughing and sneezing all over her when he was sick. When he was attracted to a girl, he suddenly felt like that squid at the end of *Twenty Thousand Leagues Under the Sea*, all selfish grabby obnoxious need.

The women here in the Club, he understood, were dressed in explicitly revealing outfits not for the benefit of him and his gaze but rather for their own benefit, to embrace in a body-positive way their sexuality and femininity, and if he barged in with his creepy stare he'd disrupt this otherwise safe and empowering space, was the story going through his head right now.

"Are you okay?" Kate said.

"Yeah, sure, fine," Jack said. "Why?"

"Because you're staring at the menu like a crazy person."

Elizabeth, meanwhile, was tense.

"You seem tense," Kyle said.

"I'm not tense," she said, smiling a big tight cadaverous smile and shaking her head like *nah* in what was definitely a quick and manic and tense way. "Not tense at all!"

She was so tense.

Kyle had slid in next to her, had sidled right up on her, breaking all the usual norms of personal space, close enough that she could presently smell what was either cologne or aftershave or body lotion or all three, a compendium of musk. Like all the other guys in here, Kyle was beefy, and bald, and wearing a black button-down that had three fewer buttons buttoned than what would otherwise be considered normal, and so his collar flared open to reveal his keg-like chest and the blond chest hair that, judging by its absolutely uniform approximately two-millimeter length, Kyle must have shaved off completely three to five days ago. It was a strangely intimate fact to now know, that Kyle thought his own chest looked best when the hair was *exactly* this height.

"Tell me about Jack," he said.

"What do you want to know?"

"Tell me what made you fall in love with him."

Elizabeth smiled. It was not the conversational route she'd expected. She'd been tense because after Jack went off with Kate, and after Kyle slid all up in here, she'd assumed that Kyle would now expect her to be flirty and sexy and sexually available and so forth. She felt like the environment and the situation and the fact that coming to the Club had been her idea in the first place, it all sort of obliged her to be, in this moment, hot. Sensual. Seductive. And the problem was that nothing made her feel less like doing something seductive than when she was obliged to do it, when someone expected her to do it. And so all the charm and humor she'd felt while she and Jack were watching people from their dark booth, it all drained away when Kyle slid in here and looked at her with an expression she interpreted as: expectant.

But then here he was asking about Jack, which was a much safer subject, an assertion of fidelity to someone else, and so the question had the effect of slightly easing her tension.

(She did not know that Kate and Kyle often asked this question of new people, that they'd found it was easier to get vanillas to fucking relax when you got them talking about their commitment to each other. It was a strategy they had; it lubricated the foreplay, was their experience. Kate had, thus, at this exact same moment, also asked Jack the same question, about Elizabeth.)

"Well, when we first met," Elizabeth said, "we were in college, living in Wicker Park, surrounded by all these artists and musicians, all these people cultivating their self-conscious eccentricities. The place had a kind of *look-at-me!* vibe. But Jack wasn't like that. He didn't need the spotlight or attention. He was quiet, super romantic, even sort of chivalrous. Plus he was this tattooed artist guy with long tousled bangs, which obviously ignited the attraction."

"Why?" Kyle said.

"Why was the tattooed artist thing attractive?"

"Yeah, why did that detail in particular attract you?"

"I don't know. I just found it attractive."

"Yeah, but why?"

"I suppose, maybe, if I had to guess, I'd say it's because he was so different from everyone I knew, from all the people I grew up with. It was refreshing."

"How so?"

"I grew up in a very strict environment. Everyone was perfect."

"Oh, I see."

"Like, in my family you weren't allowed to fuck up. Ever."

"Okay."

"Any fuckup at all and it was like the world came down on your head. It was very high stakes."

Kyle nodded. "That sounds hard."

"It *was* hard," Elizabeth said, "but then here was Jack, with his tattoos and messy hair and exactly one outfit. He didn't care if he fucked up. His whole image was fucked up. He reveled in it."

"I understand now how that would be attractive," Kyle said.

"Yeah."

"How it could take the pressure off you, let you be yourself for once."

"Exactly."

Now that Elizabeth's tension was relenting, she could see that Kyle's expression was actually not *expectant* at all—it was more like *interested*. He was attending to her in a focused and interested but not necessarily expectant way, which was, frankly, unusual for a guy. Especially in a setting that could possibly involve sex or sexual conquest, it was pretty uncommon for a guy to separate his attention from what he hoped that attention would purchase, Elizabeth had found. To pay attention *for its own sake,* in other words, without asking for or expecting something in return, was, for guys, pretty rare. Kyle seemed to have a quality, Elizabeth was now coming to understand, whereby he did not care one way or the other if she became any more or less attracted to him during this interaction. The impression he was putting out was something like: *I already get so much female action via my adventures with (and without) my wife that my self-esteem does not depend in some fragile way on your reaction to me,* which therefore meant he could be calm and real and relaxed in his interactions with Elizabeth, so therefore those interactions were not infused with a kind of between-the-lines desperation and need, which Elizabeth would have inevitably picked up on and internally experienced as pressure or expectation, the lack of which was, she realized, also something that had attracted her to Jack all those years ago, which she now tried to explain to Kyle: "Jack wouldn't talk to me," she said, "which was, oddly, now that I think about it, also a draw."

Kyle arched a single blond eyebrow. "Go on."

"We kept seeing each other in the neighborhood, at bars and nightclubs, for months. And he always, like, ignored me."

"And this was attractive to you?"

"Isn't that strange? But yes, it was. It was like, the more he didn't need me, the more attractive he was."

"Because he seemed independent, strong, self-reliant, not one bit needy or clingy."

"Exactly."

"His lack of neediness was attractive because it was the opposite of your childhood experience, where you were subjected to other people's attention constantly."

"I suppose so."

"And other people's attention feels exhausting because their expectations come across as an impossible obligation."

"Right."

"You feel beholden to meet those expectations because you don't want to disappoint them. But their standards are so high that you end up disappointing them nonetheless. So you're screwed either way."

"Wow, yeah, exactly."

"In the end, you avoid the problem by being generally allergic to neediness."

"I had a psychology professor tell me once that the real definition of love is when we expand our sense of self outward to encompass a love object. Then some of their traits become our traits. And I guess I liked Jack's rebelliousness, his defiance of convention, his indifference to what people thought of him, and, yes, his independence, his lack of neediness. They were all traits I thought I lacked. He made me feel complete, I guess. We completed each other."

"Which I'm sure presents challenges now."

"What do you mean?"

"Just that Jack clearly needs you. Obviously he needs you very much." And Kyle tipped his head in the direction of the bar, where Jack was right now staring back at her, and catching him staring prompted him to give her a nervous little wave.

"Yes, he does," she said, waving back. Jack looked shorter than ever, standing there next to Kate, who seemed to tower over him in her platform shoes.

She turned back to Kyle. "Are you a therapist or something?"

"I'm in crypto."

"Okay."

Meanwhile, across the dance floor, Jack was at that moment telling Kate: "What first drew me to Elizabeth was her energy, I suppose."

"Her energy?"

"Her whole deal, her spirit. You know what I mean? Like, she was this smart, interesting, happy-go-lucky, go-with-the-flow type of person, down for anything, looking for an adventure."

Kate nodded. "Kyle is not so adventurous."

"Really?"

"I mean, we do *this* together," she said, motioning vaguely toward the mostly naked women around the stripper pole, "but I go elsewhere to meet other needs."

"What other needs?"

"Well, Kyle isn't really into power play, so when I want to sub, I have Larry, and when I want to dom, I have Marcus. I'm a switch, you see."

"I see."

"For serious impact play I have Bill, who's experienced and careful. And there's Paulie for pegging and rimming, which I *only* do with him. Malcolm is an amazing cuddler. Movie nights are with Kristian the Canadian cinephile. I go to restaurants with John the culinary hedonist. I'm less bisexual and more what you might call bicomfortable, but sometimes I just really need Brittney. And then there's Jason—I'm not exactly into crush fetishes myself, but I dig how much Jason is."

"What even is that?"

"Oh, it varies, but in Jason's case he likes it when I take any kind of fruit or vegetable that has a thick outer rind and, with my foot, *crush it.*"

"Wow. You have a whole, like, harem."

"I prefer to think of it as a portfolio that is properly diversified. What you and Elizabeth do—putting literally every emotional egg in one basket—it's so risky. People change, they flake out, they move on, they get bored, they die. I'm aware that at any moment anyone can up and leave. Nothing is permanent. Not even Kyle. Which is why I don't believe in *the one.* I don't want just one. I want a team of extraordinary people all doing their little part to support the gig economy of my heart."

"But isn't there something to be said for, I don't know, stability?"

"Stability is a midcentury fantasy. Stability came from a time when everyone had one job and one sexual partner their whole life. But now? Getting randomly fired after another merger, that's basically how business is done. And forget one sexual partner—now we sleep with dozens of people before marriage, plus we get married several times. No, stability only works when everyone agrees to take good care of each other for the long haul. The current epoch is much more like move-fast-and-break-things. It's a swipe-left era, you know? Stability just has a bad ROI these days. So the most essential value now is not stability, it's *flexibility,* plus a certain individualistic pluck."

"The ethos you're describing is basically the same one my boss has."

"Mine too! I work in tech, which is maybe why this lifestyle appeals. Open marriages are disruptive. Actually a lot of people in tech do the nonmonogamy thing. Like, those four women at the stripper pole right now? All coders."

"Really?"

"Really."

"I would have never guessed."

"People in tech tend to be data-driven, solutions-oriented. When they look at conventional marriage, what they see is a product that fails for seventy-five percent of its users. So they iterate and problem-solve."

"By sleeping around?"

"I prefer to think of it less like 'sleeping around' and more like 'maximizing value-added synergies.'"

"I see."

"So what are you into?"

"What do you mean?"

"What are your kinks?"

"Oh, I don't have any kinks."

"C'mon. Everyone has *something*."

The Club was getting a little more crowded, most of the booths now filled with foursomes talking and drinking and laughing and, in at least one case, making out. A few more people were braving the dance floor, and a line was forming near the bar, where, at a table along the wall, food was set out in a kind of low-key buffet: home-made sandwiches, salad stuff, something in a Crock-Pot.

Over in their booth, Elizabeth was showing Kyle photos on her phone: "This is Toby," she said, flipping through the folder in which she saved all his cutest pictures.

"Aw," Kyle said. "He's adorable."

"My little man," Elizabeth said, beaming.

Kyle, it turned out, was an incredible listener. What she'd initially thought of as personal-space-invading closeness was actually just an expression of his desire to listen to her better. He sat very close to her and looked her directly in the eyes with an intensity and an expression that was like *I am HERE for you*. And he wasn't merely looking *at* her eyes but actually more like *into* her eyes or *within* her eyes, like he was appreciating both the surface of the ocean and the ocean's floor, simultaneously, such was the quality of his attention. He'd asked her about herself, starting with her job, and so she'd told him all about Wellness, about her placebo research, her clients coming in with problems curable through phantom medicine. Then he'd asked about Toby, and so she was now telling him about Toby's gaming channel, which, like every other thing she'd told him, Kyle seemed to find entirely absorbing.

"Sometimes," she said, "I catch Toby making these funny faces in the mirror and I ask him what in the world he's doing, and he says—get this—'I'm practicing my reactions.'"

"That's amazing."

"Right?"

"And probably healthy."

"You think?"

"Sure. He's training himself to let his emotions out sincerely. It's a form of honesty most of us will probably never achieve."

"Huh. I never thought of it that way."

"Do you have pictures of your husband's art? I'd like to see it."

And so Elizabeth showed him Jack's work, the photochemigrams, the abstract images Jack created using the solvents and fixers involved in photographic processing. She flipped from photo to photo—all of them looking basically the same: a big central blob amid wild black streaks—and Kyle nodded and rubbed his chin and eventually said: "They're all so similar."

And she explained that actually there were interesting differences among them, places where the chemicals dripped differently, set differently, mixed in slightly different ways. But, yes, Kyle had a point. They all sort of looked the same, had the same essential motif: a big central blob amid wild black streaks.

"He's been doing this for how long?" Kyle asked.

"Since before we got married," Elizabeth said. "Like fifteen years."

"The same basic image for fifteen years?"

"Yep."

"I wonder what it means."

"That's the thing. It doesn't *mean* anything. It's not supposed to. There's no subject, it's not a picture of anything. It's a picture of nothing. It's pure abstraction, pure form, separate from meaning."

"I find it deeply meaningful."

"You do?"

"Yeah. The symmetry of it."

"What symmetry?"

"Think about it. Your husband photographs nothing, and you prescribe nothing. He captures nothing on film, and you capture nothing in pills. He practices the art of nothingness, while you practice the science of nothingness. You're both obsessed with it: nothingness, emptiness, blankness, absence. Don't you find that really meaningful?"

Elizabeth didn't know. She had never before considered it in just this way, but the sudden obviousness of Kyle's insight made her feel strangely nervous. She looked over toward the bar. She said: "Where are our drinks?"

Their drinks had been sitting on the bar for quite some time, slowly diluting as the ice melted, but Kate refused to bring them back to the table until Jack could admit to one weird kink he was personally into.

"Seriously, there's nothing!" he pleaded. "I like to have sex with my wife. That's my kink."

"I don't believe you."

"It's true!"

"You're not turned on by anything else? Literally nothing but having missionary sex with your lawful wife turns you on?"

"Well, I mean, *sure,* some things do."

"Like what? C'mon, you've gotta give me something here. Role-play? Spanking? Domination? Submission? Blindfolds? Gang bangs? Cuckolding? Cosplay? Pissing? Feet?"

"Why does it have to be exotic? Can't I just like the usual things?"

At that moment, a cheer came from the dance floor as Donna from the front desk appeared, having changed out of her black dress and into what appeared to be a see-through romper made entirely of . . . well, it wasn't altogether clear what it was made of.

"What is that made of?" Jack said.

"Condoms," Kate said. Then, louder, "You go, Donna!"

And, yeah, Kate was right. It appeared that Donna had taken hundreds of condoms—still rolled up in circles—and connected them all with twist ties into a shape she could wear.

"She says it's an evolution of the macramé she did in her youth," Kate said.

And now Donna was at the stripper pole, dancing like the elderly dance, not so much dancing as stiffly, carefully, bobbing. The crowd surrounded her and cheered.

Kate turned back to Jack. "When you say you are only turned on by the one thing our repressive culture permits us to be turned on by, it makes me think you're either not being honest with me or not being honest with yourself."

"I guess you could say I'm an omnivore."

"An omnivore?"

"Meaning, all those things you mentioned? All those kinks? I'd be into them if my partner were into them. I'd go with it."

"That's an evasion."

"No it isn't."

"I think you're just afraid of what you want. I think there's something you really like, something you don't want to admit to, and I'll bet it's filthy."

In fact there was something like this, something that absorbed and thrilled him on the porn sites he visited. These were websites that allowed users to post comments on—and apply search-term labels to—any image or video on the site, and there was one such hashtag that consistently captured Jack's attention, one he found himself searching for those times he was alone, on his computer, late in the night: it was called #WishMyWifeDidThis. Pictures in the #WishMyWifeDidThis genre could hold Jack's interest all evening, and not because of the particular acts that were portrayed—acts that ran the gamut from basic missionary to the most extreme debauchery. No, the only thing all the photos and videos in the great wide #WishMyWifeDidThis universe had in common was that the woman featured in each of these scenes was, always, happy. Ecstatic, even. These were scenes that depicted a man (or, often, men, several) who wanted to do certain things to a woman, and the woman feeling just super happy to oblige. And it did not even matter what the things were, what she actually physically did—only that she did it enthusiastically. This is what, apparently, the men of the English-speaking world secretly wanted from their wives: acceptance, accommodation, joy.

Elizabeth had said, during the few times they'd watched a little porn together, early in their relationship, that it was such a gross male fantasy: women so grateful to be servile and submissive and weak. And of course he had agreed with her—for he sincerely believed, intellectually, that women should not have to be servile or submissive or weak, even though his body, sexually, reacted very positively to exactly these servile women, a fact that brought him much guilt and torment and confusion for many years and made him believe that deep down he was a maybe broken and awful guy, that there were deformed and unjust things that seeped into your lizard-like brain stem if you were male growing up in a patriarchy, and his job would be to resist and tamp down these ugly masculine imperatives forever.

Except now he wasn't so sure. Because when he really thought about it and examined it, he decided it couldn't be the weakness or servility that turned him on. After all, it had never been his experience that people who feel themselves to be actually servile or weak ever act very happy about it. He remembered the way his put-upon mother treated his father: all bitterness and resentment and daily gloom. No, what interested Jack was this happiness, this enthusiasm, not because it implied weakness but because it implied the opposite: strength. What he imagined when he saw the women of #WishMyWifeDidThis were people so secure and so healthy and so confident that they could bear being servile *in this moment,* could bear to have a little fun being objectified for a few minutes, without feeling shattered. In other words, Jack saw women so strong he could not hurt them by being freely himself, and thus he did not have to feel guilty inflicting his problematic needs upon them.

But he could not convince Elizabeth, who, when he tried to explain it to her, gave him this look like she thought it was a line, like it was some bullshit rationalization. He could not persuade her that she had it wrong, that she was looking only at porn's surface details—its young and obedient bodies, its cliché acrobatic sex— and not seeing its real latent meaning.

"Well, whatever you're into," Kate continued, "whatever unspeakable thing it is, I hope Elizabeth does it for you."

Which produced a little involuntary "Ha!" from Jack.

"No," he said, shaking his head, "that will not be happening."

"Why not?"

"That is just not on the table."

"You should ask her! Didn't you say yourself that she's so adventurous? So happy-go-lucky? Up for anything?"

"Yeah, turns out? Not really."

And looking around now at Donna bouncing in her prophylactic dress, and the grinding and twerking happening on the dance floor, and the foursomes casually kissing in booths and corners, and just the free and easy and uncomplicated lust of the place—this in contrast to Jack's many nights sleeping alone on the couch, or nervously approaching Elizabeth with his seductive-but-also-cautious overtures—it all made him suddenly feel like a fool. The bitterness flooded his mouth.

"Elizabeth's sense of adventure," he said, "comes with prerequisites. Like, for example, that her workday was not overly tedious or stressful, that she does not have outstanding duties involving email or childcare, that ideally the dishes are all clean and put away, the clothes laundered, the sheets on the bed recently washed, the bathroom sink and toilet spotless and disinfected, the crumbs in the kitchen vacuumed up, plus she needs twenty-four and sometimes up to forty-eight hours' notice that maybe it's time to have sex so that she can, as she puts it, get in the right 'headspace' for sex, and frankly it's kind of difficult keeping my libido chugging along for two full days while I tidy and clean and wait and hope, so it's usually easier not to mention any of this, to keep everything to myself until I can find twenty minutes of private time with my computer to, as it were, take care of it."

"Oh," Kate said, softly. "I understand."

"Understand what?"

"Your dynamic. How your marriage works."

"Okay."

"Like, every marriage is governed at its deepest level by a fundamental OS, a very simple and usually unspoken command that keeps the machine running. A kind of cosmic if-then statement."

"And ours is what, exactly?"

"Easy. If a boy is afraid of what he wants, then he will be most comfortable with a girl who's afraid to be wanted. It's actually pretty seamless, what you two have done."

Which was roughly the same conclusion that Kyle was coming to over in the booth.

"People usually look for new relationships that are antidotes to whatever problems they had in previous relationships," Kyle said, "but in so doing we often end up, paradoxically, in relationships that have exactly those same problems."

Elizabeth nodded at him, riveted, staring sort of dumbstruck and spellbound by this beefy guy who seemed to have an eerie, uncanny understanding of her and her marriage.

"Like, for example, you wanted a romantic partner who wasn't all needy and clingy," he said. "But as soon as you found that guy who was not needy and not clingy, he slowly began to need you and cling to you. That's just the nature of intimacy. And so you began registering his need and slightly pulling back from it, which was probably confusing for him and so he reached out more, which felt to you even more like need, so you pulled back more, so he reached out more, and so on and so forth in a kind of perpetual motion machine of neediness and avoidance until eventually it seemed like you were partnered with exactly the kind of needy, clingy person you tried so hard to escape in the first place."

"I now kind of doubt there was ever a time he was not needy," Elizabeth said. "Not for real, anyway." She was thinking about the banana pancakes, Jack's reward for her when she was cruel. She knew, objectively, that it was a really sweet gesture, one she should appreciate, but honestly it made her furious every time.

"Oh, yeah, that happens a lot," Kyle said. "When people fear or despise something about themselves, they usually put up this front that is the opposite of the thing they fear and despise. They do this especially with romantic interests. So a person who despises his own neediness will present himself as independent. A person who fears his own perversion will present himself as chivalrous. A person who worries he's conventional and ordinary will adopt a kind of simulation of rebellion."

"Oh my god."

"And the problem, of course, and the great irony of the whole thing, is that then someone like you comes along sincerely looking for independence and chivalry and nonconformity, and so you're attracted to this guy's surface features because those are the ones that are most important to you. But as you slowly get to know him over time, bit by bit it's revealed that he's exactly the one-hundred-percent opposite of the person you were really looking for."

"Oh my *god*."

"It's a dynamic that is, unfortunately, really common."

"And you picked up on it in fifteen minutes?"

"You said earlier that you and Jack 'complete' each other. But by definition that means that each of you is, by yourself, incomplete. And maybe that's why you're both so obsessed with nothingness, because you both have this gigantic sense of *absence*. You long for whatever it is that, if you had it, would make you feel less lacking and fragmentary. And maybe you and Jack glommed on to something in each other that you hoped would fill that absence in yourselves, but that didn't ultimately work out and so here you are looking for new people to glom on to, new people to recruit into your conspiracy."

"Conspiracy seems a bit harsh."

"Can I tell you a joke?"

"Fine."

"A cop finds this guy crawling around a lamppost one night. The cop says, 'What are you doing?' and the guy says, 'Looking for my keys.' The cop says, 'You lost them under the lamppost?' and the guy says, 'No, but this is where the light is.'"

"I think I would find that more funny if I wasn't pretty sure the guy is supposed to be me."

"You're crawling around looking in only the obvious places. You're thinking, *Maybe a new condo will fix things! Maybe an affair! Maybe an orgy!* And sure, those things might make you feel good for a while, but the way-deep-down truth is that the absence you feel in your marriage, whatever it is, will still be there, and as long as you don't acknowledge it, it will always be there, a hollow at its center, and maybe you don't even know exactly what it is, this absence, but you know it is big, and it is deep, and it is raw, and, I promise you, it is festering."

He glanced over at the dance floor then—the first time he'd broken his intense eye contact all night—and he saw dancing Donna and smiled at her costume. "That's my theory, anyway," he said. "I could be wrong."

Elizabeth looked beyond the dance floor at Jack, who was still standing at the bar with Kate, though now he was bending slightly forward, his head in his hands, Kate's hand on his back, her expression one of deep care and concern.

"I thought Elizabeth was this relaxed, happy-go-lucky woman," Jack was saying, "but she's actually this total dictatorial perfectionist."

"It's okay," Kate said, "let it out."

"I thought she was this buoyant, cheerful person, but really she's stressed out *all the time.*"

He glanced up at the booth then and saw Elizabeth staring right back at him, and they locked eyes—between them was the mania of the dance floor, the dozens of bouncing, liberated bodies, the music's bass thumping, laughter from all quarters—and they stared at each other for a moment, across that busy space, and they didn't know it, but they were right now thinking exactly the same thing, which was: *You are so wrong for me.*

"C'mon," Kate said, and then she and Jack were walking back to the booth, placing the sweaty cocktails on the table, and Kate and Kyle clinked glasses and said—at exactly the same time and with exactly the same kind of weird tonal urgency—"Hungry?"

And they giggled and nodded and then Kate was telling Jack and Elizabeth: "You two have loads of fun tonight, okay?" And she and Kyle wandered in the direction of the buffet, and Elizabeth understood immediately, just by the weird way they'd said it and the way they'd reacted to each other after they said it, that *hungry* was, for sure, their escape word.

The word they used to escape toxic, dramatic couples.

Kate and Kyle had just used it on *them*.

Jack sat down across the table, and he and Elizabeth couldn't even really look at each other, instead staring vaguely at the blank surface between them, seeming to anybody paying attention like two punch-drunk boxers. Finally Elizabeth said, "I need to get some air," and Jack nodded, and she made her way through the now dense crowd, toward the front door, exiting onto the sidewalk and closing the door behind her, muffling the music, breathing in the warm night, then looking up the street and suddenly finding herself facing—she had forgotten all about them until just this moment—the protesters.

There were only a few of them, maybe ten, dressed in suits and ties and long, tasteful dresses. They carried large white signs with handwritten messages. CHEATING WON'T MAKE YOU HAPPY, said one. YOU DESERVE REAL LOVE, said another. GO HOME AND UP-LEVEL YOUR FAMILY. And so on. The protesters were quietly looking at her, probably a little stunned to be encountering an actual person from inside the sex club. She avoided all eye contact with them and quickly turned to go back inside when suddenly she heard it:

"Elizabeth?"

And then, like a bad dream, she appeared, emerging from the small sidewalk crowd, the queen of the Park Shore PTA: Brandie, looking horrified, standing there with what Elizabeth now understood was her Community Corps, holding a sign that said THINK OF THE CHILDREN.

THE PLACEBO MARRIAGE

WHEN JACK BAKER was a young man, he thought of himself as very different.

But different from what?

He knew he was different from other people. From everybody else. From that great mass of normal American people out there. Honestly he wasn't entirely sure. It was just this large disconnected feeling, a bewilderment that the things most other people seemed to love and enjoy were things he tended to despise. He felt so detached, trying to watch the television shows that everyone else was watching, the sitcoms, police procedurals, talk shows, game shows, soaps, all of which he abhorred. He strongly disliked playing sports or watching sports. He understood there were many people who rooted hard for NASCAR or WWF or the athletic teams of their proximate geographic region, and he knew he was not like these people. He seemed to dislike all the popular pleasures, and one might have thought him an elitist, except that he hated elite things too—he had no use for haute couture, haute cuisine. In the glossy culture magazines he occasionally skimmed, he was happy to note that none of the ads were directed at him, nor were the articles about dressing nice for work or managing your 401(k). He delighted in not knowing what a 401(k) even was. He delighted in knowing there were millions of people out there who had 401(k)'s and he was, he knew, different from them.

He did not have much of a philosophy other than this, being different. In fact, what drew him to certain philosophies was how they made him feel different from those people he yearned to be different from. In high school, he went through a phase where he wore only black and listened to bands that were, allegedly, satanic—Black Sabbath and Iron Maiden and AC/DC and Mötley Crüe and even INXS was acceptable with that one song "Devil Inside"—this even though he was, himself, personally, uninterested in satanism. Mostly he listened to these bands not because he liked them but because so many normal people didn't. Then in college he encountered subversive professors who used words like *dialectical* and *ontological* and *hegemony* and *panopticon*, who encouraged their students to use art as a means to "dismantle" and "destabilize" and "interrogate" and "critique," to lay bare the world's diabolical secret truth: that there was, in fact, no truth, that everything real was artificially constructed, that all solid ground was nothing but thin air. And Jack thought that the very language used to describe this process—multisyllabic words he had never heard uttered by anyone back home—was infuriating, and yet also satisfyingly exclusive. He spent his first college semesters learning this new language—that is, until he found another philosophy that seemed even more radical than the philosophy of his radical professors: the hypertext, the vehicle of new media, nonlinear, aleatory, ergodic, polyvocal (so many excellent words). It was the newest new thing, and he began writing papers that were digital compilations of disassembled thought, collages of image and text, ephemeral bits all linked together via hypertext markup language in a vast map of meanings that, conveniently, the professors did not quite know how to read or evaluate or grade. He argued that the professors' traditional mode of thinking—and he relished the ability to call his avant-garde professors "traditional," which is the special privilege of youth—that their favored style of making arguments in linear, chronological, hierarchical ways, was itself a social construct, probably authoritarian, maybe fascist, whereas hypertexts located their truth in diffusion and dispersal: the emergent democratic revelations of the network.

His professors could only helplessly nod and give him an A, so cowed were they in the face of the new fetish. It was, after all, an era of deconstruction, where student philosophers were trained to reveal the world's building blocks—and shred them. What happens to a text when you eliminate logical order? What happens to stories when you eliminate causality and linear time? What happens to art when you eliminate the subject? What happens to photography when you eliminate the camera? What happens to the world when you eliminate objective truth? This is what he did. This is who he was.

To really advertise the point, to show how independent he sincerely felt himself to be, to enact his guiding philosophy upon his body as something materially and physically real, the young Jack Baker resolved to get a tattoo. A big, outrageous tattoo. His friends told him he'd regret it. They said he should not get a tattoo so big and outrageous. He told his friends he would never become the kind of person who would regret this tattoo. "If I ever do regret it," he told his friends, "it means I'm no longer myself." He decided that only someone young and bold and peculiar would find pleasure in such a tattoo. If he ever stopped enjoying his tattoo, it meant he was no longer young and bold and peculiar and, therefore, no longer essentially himself. It meant he had turned into someone that he, the young Jack, hated. Thus the tattoo was a calculated insult thrown into the future. He was picking a fight with that other person: the awful older Jack the younger Jack could someday become.

The tattoo was enormous. It was a bright and shocking tattoo, an aggressively inappropriate tattoo: a curling, sinuous, many-colored maze of concentric overlapping organic forms, as if some alien planet's invasive shrub had taken root on his spine and rampaged across his back and down his arms, wrapping him in its neon growth. Jack loved it. People asked him about it all the time. They wondered: What does it mean? It doesn't mean anything, he would tell them. At least, it doesn't mean anything *in the traditional way*. The only meaning of this very odd tattoo was to show that Jack was the kind of guy who would get it.

Then many years went by.

Jack progressed academically. He met a woman, and it seemed the two of them were different in many similar ways. He fell in love with her. He was awarded advanced degrees in his field. He took a job that failed to pay him what he thought he was worth, though he could find no better job. He gained a little weight. Then a little more. He cut his hair short when it began turning gray at the temples. He had a son, and he delighted in watching him, first as a baby, trying to roll over, then later, as he began spitting out words, then taking tumbling classes, gymnastics classes, even ballet classes. Jack would have never believed he could enjoy ballet classes, but if the kid thought he wanted to be a dancer, who was Jack to argue? He couldn't believe how many other cornball things suddenly seemed perfectly charming. Like pushing the stroller around the mall race-car style, making engine noises, his son giggling. Or the two of them practicing pirouettes ridiculously in the living room. Or staying home Saturday nights to watch the popular sitcoms.

And so it was that one morning, Jack Baker—now not so young anymore—stepped out of the shower and looked in the mirror and saw the tattoo and felt, for the first time, regret.

He was running late that morning, and he needed to get his son to school on time, needed to make sure the boy was showered, fed, had his backpack, and why would he think of the tattoo now? He rarely thought about it at all anymore. He was used to it. It had become part of him, part of his body, something so usual that he rarely noted its existence. The tattoo was no longer very bright, and it was distorted in places where his flesh had swelled or slightly sagged. He remembered a time in his youth when getting the tattoo was the most important thing in the world. He was another person back then. He was, he knew now, a fool. He hadn't yet seen the world, lived life, fallen in love. His desire to be different was a pose, an elaborate emotional defense mechanism, a way to seem unique and special to other people when he himself, emotionally, in his heart, did not feel all that unique or special. He had realized sometime in his early thirties that maybe he'd been acting out against his distant parents, rejecting all the symbols he associated with them. He'd hated, so much, how he was made to attend to his mother as she wasted her days in front of the television, and so he'd relocated that hatred and placed it on the television itself. And he'd hated, so much, how his father had disconnected from life, how all the interest his father used to show in the outside world, walking with Jack across the prairie and illuminating it for him, was now directed exclusively at sports—Chiefs football, Royals baseball, Jayhawks basketball, the seasons of the Flint Hills now tied to which particular games were on TV—and thus Jack began to hate sports.

He'd merely been rejecting the things he secretly desired but could not have. He would have loved to be a big guy who was good at sports, but he was small and sickly instead. He would have loved to have enough money to afford haute couture, haute cuisine, a 401(k), but he was penniless instead.

It was sour grapes, recast as a philosophy of life.

His wife and son helped him appreciate the popular pleasures. They watched TV, went to the park, the mall—and he liked it. He realized that popular pleasures are such not because they are cliché but because they are often sincerely pleasurable.

So yes, when he was a young man, he was naïve and arrogant. So it goes. Most people, in their youth, are naïve and arrogant.

But most people don't have tattoos like this. And just then, as he thought that, staring in the mirror, wearing nothing but a soggy towel, a wave of hatred came over him.

But hatred of what?

Did he hate the young man he once was? That selfish and cocky brat? Or did he hate the older man he had become? In a way, he hated both. He saw his older self through the eyes of his younger self, and he felt betrayed. He had a mortgage now, and a 401(k), a job that he dressed nicely for, a marriage, a child. His older self had abandoned all his younger self's principles. He cut coupons. He woke up early. He wore slacks. He owned a watch. And he regretted this tattoo.

How could two such dissimilar people ever inhabit the same body?

The tattoo had not fundamentally changed, but he had fundamentally changed around it. It had happened bit by bit. Little compromises here and there, little concessions to the needs of the larger world. He had never, for example, thought of himself as the marrying type, but then eventually he realized that all his friends were married, and that he'd been living for years as if he were married, and anyway he really needed the health insurance, so, okay, he put that piece of him—the not-marrying piece—he put that away. Then another piece was removed when his son was born and he understood the necessity of the 401(k). Then another, when he decided he wanted to advance at work and began dressing as a respectable teacher—he put the piece of him that would never bow to fashion in that drawer with his old baggy black sweaters and combat boots.

And in this manner, a whole person can be transformed.

He realized that people, and marriages, and neighborhoods, were all modular things, with pieces that could be swapped out at any moment. Out on the street, a mom-and-pop store shutters, is replaced by a global retail chain, and if this happens a few times every year, eventually the block becomes unrecognizable. People were like that too, with all sorts of contradictions inside them waiting to get out. He realized that his current self—which seemed to him pretty stable and suitable and more or less true—was no more true than his younger self. Someday another person would emerge, a total stranger, and around him new friends would emerge and a new city would emerge and a new wife and a new son would emerge and they'd be an entirely new family. The people he loved, he thought, were visitors, and waiting inside them was the possibility of someone better or someone worse, someone good or someone wretched, someone intimate or someone strange. His wife, son, friends, coworkers—he could not count on any of them to be consistently themselves.

And this saddened him.

He got dressed. He covered the tattoo as best he could, though its tendrils were still visible above his shirt collar and down his wrists. He walked into the kitchen, where he found his wife and son. They were both eating cereal, both still wearing pajamas—the green pajamas with Minecraft glyphs on Toby, Elizabeth wearing brown shorts and a baggy blue sweater that clashed. He remembered a time, long ago, when she would have been mortified to wear an outfit like that around him. He remembered how she once wanted to spend every free minute with him. Now she wanted her own bedroom, her own space, her own lovers, her own life.

And Toby no longer attended ballet classes, no longer wanted to be seen with his dad at the mall, racing around in a shopping cart. Now all that seemed to hold the boy's attention was on a computer screen, videos and memes that were, to Jack, bewildering and inaccessible.

His wife and son were becoming other people, new people, people who found Jack more and more unnecessary.

He did not like this new family they were becoming; he wanted that other family back; he wanted to return to their better previous version.

"You're not dressed," Jack said, the words coming out a bit more sharp and angry than he'd meant them.

"Guilty!" Toby said, putting his hands above his head in the *don't shoot* pose he'd seen countless times on TV.

"Not funny."

"Okay," Elizabeth said. "You're right." He watched his wife rise to her feet with the grunt she made when her back was stiff. "I'll change," she said.

"I'll change too," said the boy.

Jack watched them walk away. He said "Hurry," but what he really wanted to say was: *Don't.*

E LIZABETH was driving Toby to Park Shore when she noticed that autumn had, at some point, happened.

"When did it get so colorful out?" she said, looking at a crisp blue sky set against the orange-yellow riot in the trees.

"Pretty," said Toby, who was in the back seat playing Minecraft, blinking from the game to the trees and back to the game.

"All at once," Elizabeth said. "All of a sudden, *boom*, autumn."

She knew that wasn't really true, of course, but that was how it *felt*. It was like she'd missed the season's slow ebb entirely. Why? Well, she'd been a little preoccupied.

Elizabeth was not surprised to find, in the days following their encounter at the Club, that Brandie had stopped inviting her to playdates. It happened very quietly, with no contact or explanation from Brandie, just the passive implication that Elizabeth was no longer welcome. It had made her, these past few weeks, lean hard into parenthood. She'd never been such a committed tutor for Toby as she'd recently been, making sure he did his homework and sitting there patiently every night helping him with it.

And any free moment she wasn't tutoring, she was cleaning. She was cleaning the whole apartment. By herself. In what was a pretty transparent guilt-related purifying ritual, she spent full days dusting and mopping and sweeping away all the dirt and grime deposited by the animals who lived in this apartment—three shedding and sweaty and careless human animals, two of them boys, the most careless of all. She began with the bathroom's tiled floor, which was, she noticed, harboring wayward clusters of hair in the grout lines and wall corners. A medley of thin and light and airy female hairs, along with the thick stubby male hairs that escaped Jack's electric razor, plus the curly dark pubic hairs of ambiguous gender—how had she not noticed all this *hair*? How had it been collecting here underfoot, all this time? She pumped some cleaning liquid onto paper towels, which lifted most of the hair but left some of it wet and clinging to the floor. She tried to pick up these hairs first with a sponge, then with a vacuum, then with her fingers, which mostly moved the hairs around but did not release them from the moist tile. She would wait until they dried and go at them again, she decided as she moved on to the toilet, a new horror: the pink streak deposited at the waterline, the light-yellow pee-related staining of the nearby grout and caulking. She sacrificed three toothbrushes and untold amounts of disinfectant to return the bathroom to its original unsullied state, the water in her cleaning bucket, meanwhile, slowly becoming a thin dark gravy.

She vacuumed the rugs (covered with little leaf fragments blown in from outside) and cleaned the microwave (the inside coated with what seemed like tree rings of grease and pasta sauces) and rubbed the char from the stove's metal grate and gathered an unlikely quantity of breadcrumbs from beneath, around, and inside the toaster. There were gross water spots on all the bathroom's chrome fixtures, and some kind of black growth in the drains, and mineralized deposits on the showerhead nozzles that required dunking the nozzles in a pail of vinegar. She rued all the little things she and Jack had meant to do in this bathroom, things they'd sworn to do when they moved in; the windowsills were thick with the many layers and little stalactites of paint that they'd promised to remove, exposing the old wood, which they planned to sand and oil and polish to restore its original beauty. She stared at the windows, still fat with the paint they never removed. She dug at the paint with her fingernails and found other colors underneath, colors popular in previous eras— there was turquoise, there was pink.

She hated these windows.

She hated that they'd done nothing to these windows. She hated that they'd had plans they could not live up to. She hated that soon they'd be abandoning these plans, moving to their new unblemished Park Shore home and therefore leaving all this imperfection unattended to. A claw-foot bathtub they'd slowly worn down, the white turning a cloudy gray under their feet—they had planned to reglaze it but never did. It became a sort of metaphor for everything she and

Jack had done wrong in their long relationship. They did not solve their problems; they merely became accustomed to them.

This was how she missed autumn.

She'd been cleaning again earlier today, scrubbing at the back-splash behind the kitchen sink, feeling miserable and ashamed about the mold that had been growing there, all this time, right under her nose. And she was scrubbing with such ardor that she did not notice the passing of the hours, not until Toby padded into the kitchen and said, quietly, "Mom?"

"Yes?" she said, digging with a scouring pad at the last stubborn remaining blackened spots.

"I was just wondering, are we going to leave soon?"

"Leave for where?"

"It's Saturday."

Of course. She had forgotten. Saturday afternoons were now reserved for board games at the Park Shore bookstore. Toby had begun getting together with four or five new school friends and playing this game that, to Elizabeth, was incomprehensible, involving hundreds of tiny plastic playing pieces and several decks of cards and interchangeable sections of maps and many-sided dice of exotic geometries. The point of the game seemed to be to colonize an alien planet and strip it of its natural resources, which required a lot of war and diplomacy and backstabbing and treaties as the kids wrestled for control of various points of late-game strategic interest. The whole thing was a kind of six-dimensional Monopoly on an interstellar scale, and Elizabeth wanted no part of it.

But all the kids' parents agreed that they preferred board games to video games, and they preferred the kids being in a bookstore to sitting alone staring at phones or televisions, so they each took turns managing the weird excursion.

And today was Elizabeth's turn. And she had forgotten.

"Yes," Elizabeth said, pulling off her yellow plastic gloves with a wet pop. "Let's go."

Her fingers were still pruned when they reached the bookstore, her hair tied back, her face un-made-up, her clothes of the just-thrown-on variety, and she apologized to the other parents for her tardiness and appearance, and the other parents gave sympathetic variations on "We've all been there" and then promptly escaped to enjoy their child-free day.

The store was one of those places where a bookstore and a toy store and an accessories boutique and a coffee shop had all sort of conglomerated. It was less a bookstore than a lifestyle emporium with a literary theme. Her only duties here were: first, feed the children; second, serve as impartial moderator for any rule-related board game squabbles; and third, make sure the children were not kidnapped or propositioned by perverts. The most difficult of these duties, by far, was the food. They all stood in line—Elizabeth and Toby and Toby's five friends—and just getting six boys to focus and make lunch-related decisions when all they really wanted to do was roughhouse—hitting each other on the arms or thwacking each other's earlobes seemed to be a weirdly popular and perhaps even instinctive thing for small males to do—that was tricky enough, not to mention the matter of remembering each kid's food restrictions and allergies and whether their parents were pro- or anti-potato chip, which was important because each sandwich came with two side dishes that the kids chose from a menu of a dozen possible side dishes—half of which nodded in the direction of what parents wanted their kids to eat (fruits and low-sugar yogurts), the other half being what kids actually wanted to eat, the menu's willpower-free id region, as it were, potato chips and cookies and such—which ignited a new debate when the kids whose parents were okay with potato chips had the bright idea to use the potato chips as leverage in the board game they were about to begin playing, as in "I'll give you my chips if you give me your first uranium mine," and Elizabeth had not yet decided whether to correct this behavior or applaud its ingenuity before the kids realized that their board game had now begun and that *all* their foodstuffs were on the table, negotiations-wise, and so they started asking the cashier for sandwiches that were half this, half that in order to boost their meals' temptation quotient, which sent the café's poor cashier into a sort of tailspin as he hunted around for the buttons and tried to key in what was suddenly six very specialized and demanding off-the-menu orders, which required further negotiations with Elizabeth about whether the cafe's "two-for-one" deal applied to half sandwiches or only whole sandwiches, which required the cashier to go fetch a manager to do something he called an "override," meanwhile the kids' drink orders had not even been taken yet, and so while the manager was being fetched Elizabeth tried to corral the group and make a list of what everyone wanted to drink, and that's when the guy standing next to her in line, whom she had not even noticed until right now, said in a voice loud enough for every single person standing in line behind them to hear: "Jesus, lady, it's not the invasion of Normandy."

He was a middle-aged man, balding, jeans and brightly colored cross-trainers, a barrel-chested guy who looked like a former jock who'd let his muscles go all saggy.

"Excuse me?" she said.

"Just order," he said. "It's not that hard."

All she could do was give a little chuff of disbelief before the manager arrived and their order was completed and the kids went to play their game and Elizabeth sat down to enjoy a little quality time with a book she'd been wanting to read but found that she could not focus on the book because the only thing she could think about was that fucking guy, that fucking asshole, who was not wearing a wedding ring and probably did not have kids and so had no idea what the fuck he was talking about.

How dare he? she kept thinking. How dare he criticize her like that, in public, in front of her child? She congratulated herself for not making a scene in front of Toby, but she wanted to make a pretty big scene right now. It was like the generalized frustration of the last few weeks had suddenly found a convenient target. She wanted to find the man with the tacky shoes and make him feel real bad about himself. She practiced a little speech in her head: *Keep your uninformed opinions to yourself.* She imagined other people in the bookstore's café nodding at her in grave agreement. She realized she had been imagining the bookstore's other customers as a kind of impromptu jury that she was performing for. She criticized herself for caring so much about what other people thought, then criticized herself again for always criticizing herself. She knew the man was at this moment not going through these mental spirals, was not deconstructing the interaction and litigating it before a fake jury. That's the thing about assholes—they are assholes unreflectively. No asshole thinks to himself: *Yeah, that was a quality asshole move.* No, they just *are.* They go around just *being,* in perfect clueless bliss.

She went to go find him. She returned to the café, but he was no longer there. She searched for him in the magazine stacks, with no luck. She decided to go up and down the bookstore's individual rows—she wasn't entirely sure what she was going to say to him, but she could see the general shape of it and she trusted herself to fill in the specifics in the moment—and she turned a corner into the "Current Events" row and that's when she saw not the man, but Brandie.

She was dressed in a fashion that Elizabeth would describe as "autumn chic"—knee-high boots over black tights, slim skirt, caramel-colored sweater, pumpkin spice latte as both beverage *and* accessory—and she looked now at Elizabeth and seemed entirely unsurprised to be seeing her.

"We just keep bumping into each other," Brandie said, smiling broadly.

"Hi, Brandie."

"Aren't you supposed to be watching the children?"

"Yes. I was headed there right now."

"Well, I was just dropping off the boys," she said, and then gave Elizabeth a kind of head-to-toe sweep with her eyes. "You want me to stay with the kids today?"

The implication being that she, Elizabeth, looked like shit and could probably use a day off, is how she, Brandie, probably meant it.

"Thanks, no, I've got it."

"You sure?"

"It's not a problem."

"Suit yourself," Brandie said, standing there with her hands clasped around her coffee, smiling her pleasant smile, rocking slightly back and forth, not leaving.

"Really," Elizabeth said, "I've got it."

"Great!"

Brandie continued her long stare, her stiff smile.

"It's okay, you can leave."

"I think it might be best if I stayed," Brandie said. "I think I'll be staying."

Which was when Elizabeth finally understood: Brandie did not trust her around the children. In Brandie's mind, Elizabeth was, herself, now the pervert the kids needed protection from.

"Brandie, listen—"

"I just wanted to thank you, Elizabeth. Really, sincerely, from the bottom of my heart. Thank you so much."

"Okay. For what?"

"Those pills you gave me. They're *amazing*. I've been taking them every day. And you know what happened? Mike came up to me yesterday and he wrapped his arms around me and he said *I love you* and for the first time since I can't even remember, I wasn't angry at him. His touch didn't make my skin crawl. It felt, actually, nice. I hugged him back. And we stayed that way, for a long time."

"That's great."

"I feel like maybe our marriage is back on track now. I feel like maybe I can finally forgive him. And I have *you* to thank for that."

"I'm so happy to hear it."

"Which is why it makes me sad to say that you and I can never speak to each other ever again." Brandie cocked her head and frowned. "So sad. Really. I'm so sad about this."

"Brandie, if this is about that night outside the club, what you need to know is—"

"I am not judging you, Elizabeth. I'm really not. You are free to do whatever deviant thing you please. If you and your husband want to stray on each other, that is entirely your business. It's just that Mike and I are on the right path again, and we're at this really fragile moment, and I can't have that kind of thinking invading my vortex."

"Your vortex?"

"It sends the wrong vibrations. I hope you understand. But I want you to know that I forgive you."

"You *forgive* me?"

"Yes, I do. Because forgiveness sends a very powerful signal. Forgiveness clears out the negative energy. So, Elizabeth, I'm going to say a little prayer for you. I'm going to say thank you, and I forgive you, and now I set you free."

And she reached out with one hand and squeezed Elizabeth lightly on the shoulder, smiled, patted her twice, then walked in the direction of the kids at the back of the store.

"Brandie, listen. I know things have been hard for you. I know you're not very happy."

Brandie swiveled around. "I am *so* happy."

"Yeah, you say that, but I don't think it's true. I saw your quiet room. I saw the vision board. I know you're suffering. Would you like to talk about it? Like, *really* talk about it?"

Brandie stood up a little straighter. "Elizabeth, I manifested you into my life to serve a specific purpose, and now you've served that purpose. Thank you."

"You didn't manifest me. I just showed up. It was a coincidence."

"There are no coincidences. There are only resonances, attracting and repelling each other. Which is why it's so important for me to be surrounded exclusively by people who support my future vision of myself. And you don't, Elizabeth, not anymore. But that's okay. The time we spent together was so precious. And you did your little part to help me become the next-level version of myself. So thank you, truly. But now our time has come to an end."

"The purpose of my life isn't to serve yours," Elizabeth said. "People aren't widgets for you to discard like that."

"I'd recommend you worry less about me and more about your own vortex. I mean, if Jack wants to cheat on you, and Toby is always angry with you, then maybe ask yourself what you're doing wrong."

"Excuse me?"

"You create your own reality, Elizabeth. And so every negative thing that's ever happened to you, you probably, in some way, asked for it."

"No. Sometimes bad things happen, and it's random."

"There's no such thing as random."

"Okay, fine," Elizabeth said, now hearing a note of exasperation creep into her own voice. "Let's say you're right, that bad things happen because our thoughts make them happen. If that's true, then how do you explain your husband's affair? Why would you manifest *that*?"

Elizabeth was using the same maneuver she often used on Toby at bedtime, when the boy was frightened by some imaginary thing: to persuade someone out of a delusion, try critiquing the delusion from inside its own frame. "If you never imagined Mike cheating," Elizabeth said, "then why did it still happen?"

Brandie nodded thoughtfully. "I've wondered about that too," she said. "I've done some real soul-searching on that very question, and what I realized was, it's not my fault. The unfortunate energy that created temptation in Mike, that was not coming from me."

"Then where was it coming from?"

"The world. All the negativity we're exposed to every day, out there," she said, jutting her chin in the direction of the bookstore's large front windows.

"Out where? What are you talking about?"

"You'll see it once you really tune in, Elizabeth, all the pressures that can lead us down the wrong path. They might seem small at first, like just tiny suggestions in, say, the music we listen to, or the TV shows we watch, or in the car while going into the city where for example my husband drives right by your perverse club every day on his way to work."

Brandie crossed her arms, tightened her jaw, as if the mere mention of the Club were a personal affront. "They may seem small," she continued, "but they add up. It's like, even a little water can crumble the strongest foundation, if you let it keep dripping, if you're not paying attention. I wasn't paying attention back then. I was on autopilot. But I'm damn sure paying attention now."

"But do you really think that if you simply block the things you don't approve of, if you censor the music in your house and protest the businesses you don't like, then nothing bad will ever happen again?"

"I just want to be certain that the only energy reaching my family is positive energy. I want to be certain that the only thoughts we have are positive thoughts. A year ago we almost fell apart, but since then we've been focused *only* on our future happiness, and look where it's gotten us. We're better than ever."

And Elizabeth was about to protest this—on the grounds that there's a big difference between sincere happiness and just bluntly ignoring unhappy thoughts—when she recalled something she had said to Toby not long ago, the afternoon she was giving him those apple turnovers: *Think only about how happy you'll be in the future.* She had tried, that day, to teach Toby how to displace his moment-to-moment desire, to untether his desire from the present and stow it somewhere downstream. For wasn't that precisely what Elizabeth had always done? Hadn't that always worked for her—looking to the future, envisioning a future better than her present? She remembered all that time she spent upstairs at the Gables imagining her future life, pretending she was somewhere else, someone else. She was enamored, then, with those little origami fortune tellers she made with her friends—it was such a thrill, every time, opening a flap of paper to reveal her future: where she would live, whom she would marry, what she would do, who she would eventually be. Looking back on it now, it suddenly seemed to Elizabeth that she'd been taking a kind of cosmic marshmallow test her entire life, always delaying and delaying, always waiting for a future better than the present, whatever that present happened to be. Growing up, she thought: *If only I could get away from my parents, then I'd be happy.* Then she got away from her parents, came to Chicago, and thought: *If only I could find the right friends, the right neighborhood, the right career, the right guy, then I'd be happy.* And then she found all of those things and she thought: *If only I got married, then I'd be happy.* And then, once married, she thought: *If only we had a family, then I'd be happy.* And finally: *If only we were living in a better home, the perfect home, a forever home, then I'd be happy.* She thought about all her elaborate schemes of late—the Shipworks, the Club—and wondered how different they were, really, from Brandie's excessive vision-boarding. Here Elizabeth was thinking herself so much more grounded than Brandie, so much less deluded, but maybe, in one crucial way, they were exactly the same. They both dealt with the pain of today by investing everything in a fantasy of tomorrow.

"Brandie," Elizabeth said, "there's something you should know."

"Okay."

"Those pills I gave you?"

"Yes?"

"They're not real."

Brandie narrowed her eyes and frowned. "What?"

"They're placebo," Elizabeth said. "They're just sugar pills. They don't actually do anything."

"*What?*" Brandie said, louder now.

"I'm sorry. I shouldn't have lied to you."

"No, that can't be right. Those pills work. I can *feel* it."

"That's in your head. Trust me, the pills, and the whole story about the pills—it's all fiction."

"I don't understand. Why would you do that?"

"I used to think I was helping people, but now . . . I don't know."

Elizabeth thought about Kyle's words at the Club that night, his strange diagnosis, that she was obsessed with a powerful absence, a hollow, a *nothingness,* festering and unacknowledged. Maybe, she thought now, it was time to stop ignoring it, whatever *it* was.

She looked at Brandie. "I think if you want to be angry at your husband, then be angry at your husband."

"What?"

"Be furious at your husband. He deserves it. *You* deserve it. A shitty thing happened, and you deserve to feel shitty about it. There's nothing wrong with that. And all this nonsense about vibrations and negative energy is just, I'm sorry, I think it's just avoidance and escapism."

Brandie gave a little chuff of disbelief and stared contemptuously at Elizabeth for a moment, but then she seemed to compose herself, took a deep breath, clasped her hands in front of her, smiled a strained but diplomatic smile.

"I knew that building of yours was going to be trouble," Brandie said.

"What building?"

"The Shipworks. We should have never ended our campaign."

"What campaign?"

"My group, my Community Corps, we were protesting the construction."

"That was *you*?"

"We stopped after we met you. I thought, okay, she's nice, maybe this won't be so bad. I can see now I was quite mistaken."

"But why were you against it?"

"Elizabeth, I try so hard to make sure my kids are surrounded by goodness and abundance. Do you seriously think I want them walking by that building every day on their way to school? A building full of—and let's be honest here—deficiency and lack? I mean, how does having a bunch of low-vibration people all over town help me become the next-level version of myself? How does it help my kids? No, I don't want that anywhere near them."

"That's a really awful thing to say about people who just aren't as wealthy as you."

"Wealth is the physical embodiment of one's mental state," Brandie said. "Money is the way the universe rewards you for being a positive and deserving person."

"Right," Elizabeth said. And suddenly, as she stared into Brandie's serene and unblinking eyes, it was like she was looking upon all those generations of Augustine patriarchs up there in their ostentatious portraits, people who would do the most vile things to get rich and then congratulate themselves for being clever enough to do them.

But before Elizabeth could say anything else, there came a call from the back of the store, Toby's loud cry: "Mom!" The way he'd turned it into a two-syllable word with a kind of minor musical fall between the notes—*MAH-umm*!—told her that something was wrong. She rushed to investigate. Turned out, one of the kids had used his nuclear arsenal to threaten and intimidate another kid into giving up his potato chips—a maneuver that was neither specifically forbidden nor specifically allowed according to the game's rules—and she was being called on to intercede. And so she sat down with the kids and the game's vast rule book, flipping pages and occasionally glancing across the bookstore at Brandie, who glowered back at her, and kept a vigilant watch going all day long.

SHORTLY THEREAFTER, construction on the Shipworks abruptly stops.

Notices appear taped to the barriers surrounding the building, immediately prohibiting—in dense and frightening legal language—all Shipworks operations, pursuant to several newly filed lawsuits and injunctions. The many contractors and subcontractors hired to tile and roof and floor the building sit around all day, doing nothing. Stacks of drywall melt whitely in the rain.

Jack and Elizabeth are on one of the middle floors, summoned here by Benjamin, walking through the unfinished space of a condo that, until now, they'd known only in digital or blueprint form. Toby is running down its long hallways, shoes off, sliding in his socks on the new and satisfyingly slippery Permateek floors. Major construction is by now largely complete—the plumbing is done, as is the wiring, and even the Wi-Fi—though the building is far from finished. The exterior is still surrounded by scaffolding, the elevator is not yet operational, mounds of tile and brick and stone sit atop splintered pallets, and dust is everywhere—drywall dust, concrete dust—a chalky white film on all surfaces, a fine airborne haze outlined in every shaft of light.

In their unit, doors are in place but lack hardware, base cabinets in the kitchen are without faces, capped-off electrical wires dangle where major appliances will one day go, walls have been erected but not yet painted, with large gaps showing at the floor, soon to be hidden by trim. In the dining room, bundles of salvaged barnwood—aged, weathered, marvelously distressed—are stacked, awaiting installation.

"We were making excellent progress," Benjamin says, stepping over the boards, his leather loafers protected from the dust by disposable blue cotton booties. "Ahead of schedule, even. And then, well, things got rather snarled."

They'd spoken to Benjamin soon after their visit to the Club, approving his design for the condo and its plan for dual master bedrooms, plus adding separate entrances for the two of them, in case their marriage came disastrously apart in the coming years, or months, or days—one could no longer be sure—so that in the event of irreconcilable separation, the condo could function as a kind of duplex, where Jack and Elizabeth lived their parallel lives without needing to interact at all, except of course in the kitchen, which would serve as a kind of neutral zone between the two sundered wings. Jack had quietly agreed to this plan, putting up no resistance at all. Since that night at the Club, it was like he needed to amputate all conflict from his life: he agreed with whatever Elizabeth wanted for their new condo; and he let his students get away with just about anything, no matter how lame their excuses; and he'd even cut off his dad on Facebook, unfriending him after the man's latest conspiracy nonsense appeared and Jack realized he no longer had the emotional reserves to continue their fierce, unproductive arguing.

"Turns out," Benjamin says, "there is a substantial community resistance that I greatly underestimated. I actually thought they'd disappeared months ago, but now they're back, and in a big way, and wow are they ever creative."

"Creative how?" Jack says.

"Those lawsuits about preserving neighborhood integrity, those are all back, plus new ones regarding historical significance. Apparently this group—the Community Corps is their quaint name for themselves—they're maneuvering to get the Shipworks listed on the state register of historic places, which would require that any little change we make to the building be approved by a fifteen-member commission in Springfield."

Benjamin leads them into the living room just as Toby zooms by, still in his socks, skating along the floor like it's an ice rink, screaming "This is so awesome!" as he disappears around a corner.

"And then there are the environmental impact statements," Benjamin says. "The city of Park Shore has now declared that the entire town—literally everything within its city limits—is a protected sanctuary for the endangered gray timber wolf, a species that hasn't actually been spotted in Illinois since the 1800s, which is something we'll definitely argue in court, someday, but until then it makes any new construction within city limits conveniently illegal. Plus there's an injunction alleging that the Shipworks is an essential nesting site for some threatened migratory bird, a bird that, again, *very conveniently* only passes through Illinois in early summer, and so now we have to sit around and do nothing and wait for almost a year to see if this bird, indeed, nests. It's all quite maddening, but I also sort of respect it, the gumption."

"Is there anything we can do?"

"It's all playing out in the courts now, and online, naturally. A Facebook group has been created. Preserve Park Shore, it's called. It's where they're organizing. It's also where, by the way, we've been doxed. Like, all of us. Our names are out there, on the internet, in public. Me, you, even some of the investors and financiers. Have you been contacted yet?"

"No."

"Because every day for the last week I have been getting a small piece of the Shipworks mailed to me at my personal house."

"Seriously?"

"One day it's a brick, the next a toilet handle, then a snip of copper wiring, a light bulb, a knob. I'm like, *Oh, swell. I wonder where this came from!* It's really gonna eat into our discretionary budget, if this practice persists."

They follow him down a hallway into Elizabeth's wing, into the room that would be, someday, her very own individual bedroom.

"The investors are worried," Benjamin says. "They would like to remain silent partners. They prefer to stay in the shadows, these particular stakeholders."

"And why is that?"

"Mostly because they're shell companies."

"They're what?"

"Oh, you know, offshore accounts, anonymous beneficiaries, that type of thing. More real estate money comes from abroad than you might think, which always requires a little legal finagling, a few creative lines on the deed."

"How creative, Ben?"

"Hey, I told you that project financing was a baroque business, all about finding exactly the right alchemy, and sometimes that perfect mix comes from strange places. Though I have recently come to wonder why in America they're called *tycoons* but in Russia they're called *oligarchs*. Isn't that strange?"

"Our home is financed by Russians?"

"Oh, ha ha, gosh, I've signed intimidating nondisclosure agreements on that subject, so I'm gonna go ahead and neither confirm nor deny, okay?"

"But it's all legal, right?"

"Sure, sure. It's just that our investors maintain a tax status that may or may not hold up to the intense scrutiny of an IRS audit. Thus they try to avoid calling any attention to themselves. Which is why these particular lawsuits are something of a big hiccup."

Toby appears again, sliding up to the bedroom door, exhilarated. "Dad, you know what we should do?" he says, cheeks flushed. "We should camp here! Overnight!"

"Sure, buddy, sounds like fun."

"No, no!" Benjamin says. "No, no, no! Under no circumstances should you be here without my knowledge, okay? The property is off-limits."

"Right," Jack says. "You don't want us tripping over something, getting injured. It's a liability problem, right?"

"Actually, we have very good insurance. Very, very good."

"Okay."

"Like *really* good."

"Gotcha."

"It's just that this remains a live construction zone, and, well, you just never know what might happen."

Benjamin looks gravely at Jack, tilts his head down and repeats, slowly, "*You just never know*."

"Okay, sure," Jack says. "You never know."

And then Benjamin's phone chimes and, upon looking at it, he says: "Well, speak of the devil! Our friends are at it once again. Some new action online. Would you excuse me for a moment?"

Whereupon Elizabeth removes from her bag the small tablet computer she always keeps there for those moments Toby is getting riled up and impatient and needs immediate digital distraction.

"Hey, Toby?" she says. "Would you check the Wi-Fi?"

"Cool!" he says, always happy for extra screen time.

"Check every room, okay? In fact, check the whole floor."

The boy dashes off, and Jack looks at Elizabeth. "What's up?" he says.

She takes a long, heavy breath. "It's Brandie," she says.

"Brandie. The church lady?"

"Yeah."

"What about her?"

"I'm pretty sure this is all her doing. The injunctions, the lawsuits."

"Seriously?" Jack says. "Brandie?"

"Uh-huh."

"Why?"

"She and I . . . we may have had a falling-out."

"You may have?"

"We did. We had a falling-out. She's angry at me. And this is her special way of showing it."

"What did you do to her?"

"We had a disagreement, okay? Let's not dwell."

"Okay, but this thing you did to her, can you undo it? Can you apologize?"

"Why do you assume I'm the one who should apologize? Maybe she needs to apologize to me. Why do you immediately think I'm the one to blame?"

"I'm only wondering if there's a way to fix this."

"It would just be nice if you were a little more on my side."

"Honey, whatever happened between you two, I'm sure it's going to blow over."

"It's not going to blow over."

"Okay."

"We're going to lose our home, and lose our nest egg, and Toby will get kicked out of school."

"We're not going to lose our home," Jack says, smiling, trying to be optimistic in the face of Elizabeth's sudden angst. "And even if we do lose the home, we can always find another one. Benjamin will get us our money back, you'll see. And then we'll put Toby into a new school. No big deal."

"No big deal? We'll make him start again? Be the new kid, one more time!"

"Relax. It'll be fine. Toby will be fine."

"That's it? That's your answer? He'll be fine?"

"Yes, he'll be fine, and it'll all work out. Let's take a step back and consider where we are, okay? It's you and me, in our forever home. This should be a happy moment. We should be, like, dancing."

"Dancing," she says, shaking her head. "Oh my god, that is just a perfectly Jack thing to say. That is textbook you."

"What is that supposed to mean?"

They stare at each other for a moment. It's quiet and they're alone and it's dusty and there might as well be little clumps of tumbleweed bouncing between them for how much this suddenly resembles the marital equivalent of a duel: two sharpshooters sizing each other up. Like most married couples, they have a mostly unspoken set of ground rules about how to fight—specifically, what it means to fight fair or fight dirty, to fight productively or fight unproductively. And one of the dirtiest and most unproductive ways to fight is, they know, to fight in generalities, in global abstractions, to take something done or said in a discrete moment and insist that it's "always" that way, to use a small misdemeanor as cause to shoot large holes in the other's personality or character. Elizabeth's assertion here— *That is just a perfectly Jack thing to say*—approaches this more dirty style of fighting; it's a violation of marital etiquette. Thus, Jack's question—*What is that supposed to mean?*—can be read primarily as an acknowledgment of this fact (he's noticed it too) and an invitation to either take it back or proceed. To walk away or draw, as it were.

She opts for the latter. "Do you know how hard this transition has been for Toby? Do you know how awful it's been to watch? And here you are . . . I mean, dancing? Are you serious? Maybe if you were a little more concerned with your son's well-being, maybe if you were a little more involved in his life, then I wouldn't have to do all this alone. Maybe I could have had some help with Brandie, if you weren't so absent. And then maybe none of this would have happened." (As an opening volley, it's a pretty deadly one, aiming immediately at Jack's biggest vulnerability, the fact that he himself grew up with a father who was largely emotionally absent, Elizabeth now implying that Jack is repeating that painful pattern and, by extension, injuring their son in exactly the way Jack was injured; she is not fucking around.)

"So it's my fault now?" Jack says. "Just like that? Wow, Elizabeth, that's creative."

"You leave everything to me. It's always my responsibility. I have to do everything alone, by myself." (Like most fights, the subtext here, from both participants, is, roughly: *You are inconsiderate and selfish, whereas I am generous and kind.* It's the basic ground from which they both start.)

Jack says: "Name one thing you have to do by yourself."

"I'm the one spending my mornings at that school."

"Which you do voluntarily."

"And I'm the one putting in face time with the other parents."

"Which, again, you do by choice. Honestly, Elizabeth, I don't understand how you can be angry at me for stuff nobody is making you do but yourself." (Totally calm and neutral and steady-voiced here. It's a classic husband maneuver, meeting his wife's rising emotion with the appearance of cold rationality and logic, the underlying implication being that all of her hysterical female agitation is preventing her from thinking straight; the fight is on, attacks and reprisals, strikes and counterstrikes.)

"All of the homework," she says (ignoring it), "the chores, the playdates—they all fall on me, all the time."

"Hold on. Just because I don't obsess over every little detail of Toby's life doesn't mean I'm not involved. I don't have to constantly freak out to feel like I'm a good parent." (Upping the ante, twisting the knife.)

"Don't tell me I freak out, don't minimize it like that." (No longer ignoring it.)

"But you do! You freak out, Elizabeth, you've been freaking out ever since he was little. I swear to god, as soon as he was born, you turned into this weird other person, this overbearing tyrannical perfectionist." (Pivoting to his advantage. Now he's targeting her biggest vulnerability, accusing an overachiever of failing, accusing a mother of being a bad mother; he can fight fire with lots more fire.)

"And you never changed at all!" (Sensing her edge slipping, moving to higher ground.) "You never grew up one bit! The same job for fifteen years. The same lectures for fifteen years. The same meaningless art for fifteen years."

"Meaningless?"

"You keep complaining about how nobody appreciates your work, but then you keep doing the same thing over and over and over. Maybe it's time for a change."

"Or maybe I'm not as comfortable with hypocrisy as you are." (His defensiveness suddenly morphs into piety, a flaw turned into a virtue, saintliness weaponized.)

"What does *that* mean?"

"At least I have some principles. Tell me, Elizabeth, what's *your* big accomplishment, eh? What's your claim to fame? It's that you made airplanes more crowded. Bravo. You made flying shittier. You got paid for making people miserable. Congratulations! You're a real Augustine after all."

(It's like their two decades of intimacy have equipped them perfectly for this moment, furnishing them with exactly the advanced weaponry needed to inflict maximum devastation; it's become less of a shoot-out now, more like a regional civil war.)

She says: "One of us had to make some money." (Passive-aggressive emasculation.)

He says: "If you wanted money, you should have stayed in New England, married some boring banker." (Retaliatory victimization.)

She says: "Oh, I wish I could go back and make some different choices. I really do. Sometimes I fantasize about a cosmic do-over." (Staunch fortification.)

He says: "No you don't. You don't mean that. You're just in fight-

or-flight mode. This is your amygdala talking." (Infantilizing her, treating her like a medical patient rather than a spouse.)

She says: "Oh, okay, honey, whatever you say." (Actually patting him on the top of the head, like a mother might a little child, the message being *I can infantilize you even more.*)

He swats her hand away, goes over to the window, crosses his arms, stares out at the rainy day (as if he's so disgusted he can't even bear to look at her). Their phones have each begun to chirp and buzz during their quarrel, messages arriving first in a trickle that is now becoming a wave, but they ignore it. Jack says: "Even if you got that do-over and you married that banker, you know what would happen? You'd end up in exactly the same place. You'd be frustrated and angry and stressed out and alone, no matter what, no matter who you were with. And do you know why?"

"I can't wait to hear this."

"It's because you have no idea how to love, Elizabeth. You're simply incapable of it."

She's silent for a moment (a silence without agenda or ulterior motive; she's finally genuinely hurt). Rain taps against the window. Eventually she says, softly, "What?"

"I try and I try and I try with you, but it's hopeless. Twenty years we've been together and I still feel like you've got one foot out the door. And I have no idea why. Whenever I try to figure it out, you just deactivate. You're a vault, Elizabeth. Sometimes I think I never even had a chance with you. Sometimes I think you'd genuinely prefer to be alone—just you, and maybe your vibrator, forever. That little piece of plastic—the one you're using every night?—that's your perfect companion. Uncomplicated and undemanding. It's all your tiny heart has room for."

For a moment there is no sound except the rain and the chiming of their phones, coming on even stronger now, which they both continue to ignore. He looks at her again, and feels, as he always does whenever he hurts her, immediately penitent.

"I'm sorry," he says, stepping toward her. "I didn't mean that."

She knows what will happen now. He'll come in for a cautious and careful embrace, and if she agrees to it, he'll eventually draw his lips to hers for a light kiss, and if she agrees to it, the kissing will get stronger, deeper, more insistent, and if she agrees to it, he'll be angling for make-up sex tonight after Toby goes to bed, and if she agrees to it, he'll be planning special date nights by tomorrow, and he'll try to engage her in flirty text messaging all throughout the day, and he'll stop her whenever they cross paths in the apartment for lengthy, tender cuddling even though she has work to do, and it will all be so exhausting, so draining. It's like this with Jack: whenever she rises to meet one of his requests, it only creates more requests. The way she experiences it, inside, is that she's already doing the very best she can attending to everyone's needs while also feeling herself at the extreme outer limits of her own energy and capability, and still it is never enough. *She* is never enough. He is never satisfied. He always demands more. Every intimacy she gives comes back greatly magnified, and so she finds herself sort of parceling out the intimacies, meanwhile strategically withdrawing from him in a way that won't trigger his disappointment or panic, and, right now, in this moment, in this dusty room, it no longer seems worth it, the emotional gymnastics required to be married to this man.

"My *god*," she says in a tone that stops his advance cold. "You're like an emotional hydra, Jack. You really are this sucking pit of need."

"Elizabeth, honey."

"You put on this big romantic show, but really, at the center of it all, you're just a terrified child who wants attention. You're a little frightened boy clinging to the first person who ever showed any interest—me."

"That's not fair."

"You thought if you married a rich girl, it meant you weren't the country bumpkin you're so afraid you really are."

"Okay, and you thought if you married an artist, it meant you weren't the heartless rock you're so afraid you really are."

"Maybe," Elizabeth says, nodding. "And then maybe we wrapped ourselves up in a story that made the whole thing feel heroic. But it's time we face it, Jack. We have a placebo marriage. It made us feel good for a while, but in fact there's nothing here. And, probably, there never was."

By now, the phrase "ringing off the hook" might aptly describe the activity of their phones, a nonstop ruckus that is finally inescapable. "Who the fuck is texting us?" Elizabeth says.

And so they check their phones, and what they find are messages from friends, fellow parents, teachers, colleagues, all asking in different ways basically the same question, which is: *Are you seeing this?*

"What are they talking about?" Elizabeth says.

"Oh my god," Jack says. "My score!"

"Your what?"

"My impact score!"

Jack's looking at an email from the university's CFO—"Congratulations, buddy!" it says—that includes his new Impact algorithm numbers, and he is shocked to see that sometime in the last few hours, his online worth has apparently undergone a startling, quadratic explosion.

"What the fuck happened?" he says, horrified, staring at a number now many times larger than his annual salary.

Just then there's a soft knock on the bedroom's doorjamb, and in walks Toby, carrying his tablet computer, staring at the screen, distraught.

"Honey?" Elizabeth says. "What's wrong?"

"Something's going on," he says, his face pinched, worried.

"What?"

"Something weird is happening."

And Toby flips the tablet around so they can see the action on the screen. "You and Dad?" he says. "I think you've gone viral."

THE NEEDY USERS

A Drama in Seven Algorithms

The EdgeRank Algorithm

The user appears on the network at 2008-04-15 T14:47:30 (UTC-0600) running an out-of-date browser on an old PC that had previously been associated with a different IP but is now connecting to the internet via a sluggish landline originating in the Flint Hills of Kansas. The user has inherited this particular computer—which was already the cheapest of all possible desktops when it was purchased four years ago at the Topeka Best Buy—from a neighbor who has upgraded his own PC and offered not only to give this one away for free but also to set it up and tutor the user in its basic operations. Of course, the EdgeRank algorithm that first identifies and catalogs the user does not know this information. At first, the only data the algorithm possesses are the answers to two prompts that are the only prompts the user responds to: Name, which is *Lawrence Baker,* and Interests, which is *Jack Baker,* this latter response being pretty difficult for the algorithm to parse until it becomes clear that the user has misunderstood the prompt and eventually replaces *Jack Baker* with *Kansas City Chiefs,* after which his account is verified and his feed populates with National Football League–associated content and advertising.

It is April 2008, and Lawrence Baker has just joined Facebook.

His misunderstanding of that initial prompt turns out to be a consistent behavioral pattern: he is not yet a heavy user of computer technology and therefore tends to hold vast naïve confusions about its use and functionalities. He is the kind of seventy-year-old first-time computer user who will forever misunderstand the notion of a URL, for example, and will never just type *facebook.com* into the URL field of a browser, but will instead go to a search engine like Yahoo and type *www.facebook.com* into its search bar and then click on the top search result, believing that this is the only way to go anywhere on the internet, via an intermediary, like the community rural phone lines he grew up with, where you picked up the phone and had to ask the real-life operator to please place and connect your call. Yahoo is now like that operator—that is, until someone tells him that Google is a superior search engine, after which he will go to Yahoo and type *www.google.com* in the search bar, then click to Google, where he will search for *www.facebook.com,* which doesn't strike him as superior at all.

Also, he has the strong tendency to print out every email he receives at his brand-new email account because of a basic misconception about whether he will ever be able to access the emails or see the emails again. He has such a strong negative suspicion about the intangible and ethereal digital internet that it makes him believe his emails are no more real and lasting than a wisp of smoke that disappears in the wind. Thus he prints them out, all of them, including the email from his neighbor asking how it's going with the computer—he prints that out and writes, in pencil, "Just fine!" on the bottom of the page, then puts that page in an envelope, addresses it and stamps it, puts it in his mailbox to physically mail it to the neighbor—who lives thirty miles away; "neighbor" is a flexible and relative concept on the plains—then goes back to his computer to await his next email.

Other such innocent misunderstandings include Lawrence's strong belief that he cannot access his email or Facebook from any other computer anywhere in the world—he insists, despite others trying to explain to him how networks operate, that he can get to his email and Facebook account only from this one yellowing Dell computer that has found a home on his kitchen table. He also believes that anyone in possession of his email address will somehow be able to "hack" this computer and get into his bank accounts or steal his social security number or something, which is why he finds it so disconcerting to receive emailed advertising or spam, especially those ads that are addressed to him by name, which often send him searching for a relevant phone number and he'll call the company responsible for the advertising and accost the poor customer service rep on the other end of the line: "HOW DO YOU KNOW MY NAME? WHERE DID YOU GET MY EMAIL ADDRESS? WHO ARE YOU?"

Also there's the time he's visiting a website and the browser crashes and he gets an error message saying "This program has performed an illegal operation" and he genuinely thinks that he himself has accidentally committed a crime, after which he *never* returns to that website again.

He is the kind of user who operates a computer intuitively, but his intuitions are all fundamentally off, which makes normal computer usage and web navigation feel painful and difficult. And then this is made even more difficult and confusing when the many flashing toolbars and icons slowly begin to colonize the screen, these being the result of certain mouse-clicks on certain pop-up ads that declare *Your computer is infected with viruses! Download this anti-viral software immediately!!!* Which he always does, every time, downloads whatever any website tells him to download, and yet the weird flashing stuff on his computer keeps on spreading, for some reason. And then the interface gets even more baffling when—due to an unlikely series of events that no programmer or beta tester could ever possibly foresee or prevent—Lawrence somehow takes a screenshot of his desktop and then accidentally and unknowingly makes that picture his desktop's background, which creates this weird doubling effect where every chaotic icon that appears on his computer seems to have suddenly cloned itself—some of these icons remaining clickable and movable, while others, bafflingly, are not, despite repeated and infuriating attempts.

The point being: compared to all that confusion and nonsense, the relatively friendly- and relaxed-looking Facebook home page is a welcome relief and respite, which is why he ends up going there quite a lot.

For the EdgeRank algorithm that is responsible for delivering the personalized and dynamic user experience that the Facebook platform is generally known for, Lawrence Baker is, at first, somewhat of a frustrating mystery. He does not post, nor like, nor friend, nor interact in any way, and therefore he does not generate the new connections that the algorithm needs in order to sort and tailor his feed. The algorithm functions according to the basic principles of graph theory math, which visualizes a network as a large object with a lot of corners and edges. One could imagine this object, in a much-simplified form, as a cube—like the six-sided dice Lawrence found in Jack's bedroom after Jack left for Chicago, a stash of dice and figurines and Dungeons & Dragons books that Jack had kept hidden in a hollow behind his dresser. The most salient fact about these cubes, for D&D purposes, is that they have six faces; these faces, with their associated black dots, create the cube's meaning. But try to imagine a cube in the same way this algorithm does. The algorithm does not see the faces; rather, it sees only the edges. After all, any object that has faces can just as easily be defined by its edges instead. A cube has twelve edges, and where these edges come together, they make a corner.

Now, there are all sorts of philosophical chicken-and-egg problems here regarding whether it's the edges that create the corner or it's the corner that implies the edges or whatever—it doesn't really matter. Philosophy is irrelevant for the algorithm. For this particular algorithm, in the mathematical language that is literally the only language it speaks, Lawrence Baker the human person is merely an abstracted numerical concept, a single sharp point on a theoretical object, one of this object's many corners. And since, according to the underlying math, a corner is nothing more than the intersection of its edges, what the algorithm really cares about are those edges—whether they are short or long, brittle or robust. When the "Lawrence Baker" corner expresses an affinity for the "Kansas City Chiefs" corner, an edge is created between them, a line, a connection. And this, for the algorithm, is where all meaning is derived—not in things but in the relationships between things. And so the algorithm prompts Lawrence to make more of these relationships: to like and friend, which would create more edges, or to post and link, which would create new corners that could then spawn still more edges, and in this manner the network expands and grows and exponentially fattens, by taking a person—and all of their collected interests and interactions—and reconceiving them as a vast many-dimensional object inscribed within a still larger infinitely dimensional object, a seething universe with a billion corners and a trillion edges, an ever-changing massive topology literally impossible for the human mind to visualize but, for the algorithm, it's relative peanuts.

And so the algorithm prompts Lawrence to identify his hobbies, search for pages he's interested in, find some friends—prompts he roundly ignores. The only thing the algorithm wants here, its singular purpose, is to give Lawrence Baker more of what he desires. The algorithm is like a waiter, and Lawrence is a diner who stares at the menu but never orders food. That is, not until the day the algorithm prompts him with a "People You May Know" query using the only other data he has thus far inputted. The algorithm asks: *Do you know Jack Baker?*

And Lawrence sits there staring at that prompt for a full fifteen minutes before finally confirming it—*Yes*—whereby the algorithm launches a friend request, and when he's asked if he'd like to personalize this request, Lawrence, after some deliberation, and in the slow keyboarding manner that implies awkward hunting-and-pecking, writes: *I'm so, so sorry.*

‹2›

The Needy User Algorithm

When Jack Baker sees this request, he immediately closes his browser window.

Five minutes later, he logs on again, looks again at this friend request, and, again, closes his browser window.

Five minutes later, same thing.

This behavior continues for much of the next forty-eight hours: Jack Baker logs on and considers his father's friend request for a brief moment before a quick Ctrl-W. Jack is a user with a below-average number of other network connections, and so the system reminds him—gently, but daily—that there is an important request waiting for his response. Will he accept Lawrence Baker, or will he dismiss him?

Finally, after two days of this, Jack Baker accepts, and an edge is created between these two users, and Jack sends a private message, saying: *Hey Dad, long time.*

HOW ARE YOU??? Lawrence writes on his own page, in the space meant for public status updates. He is not yet familiar enough with internet conventions and etiquette to understand the difference between writing on his wall, or writing on someone else's wall, or writing in a private message, or what a "wall" even is, nor is he familiar with the community's general disdain for writing in capital letters.

I'm fine, Jack writes, again in a private message. *How are you?*

To which Lawrence posts another status update, visible to anyone with a Facebook account: *I'M SORRY WE BLAMED YOU PLEASE FORGIVE US IT WAS AN ACCIDENT!!!*

At which point Jack sends a long note explaining the essential differences between a status update and a private message, and he includes in this note links to instructional "Facebook 101" and "Facebook for Dummies"–type websites that Lawrence then faithfully accesses and reads, and afterward the elder Baker's Facebook behavior becomes more what you might call normalized. This connection with Jack seems to inspire a new enthusiasm for the prompts he had been previously ignoring, and he goes ahead and reaches out to other friends within the network, and he identifies a few interests and hobbies, and he writes his first tentative updates and posts a photo, and Jack watches all of this happen in real time, at the very top of his newsfeed, where the notifications of his father's actions now appear. They appear at the top because of the influence of a new algorithm, one designed to correct a flaw in the logic of EdgeRank. The problem with EdgeRank is that it's designed to populate your newsfeed with posts from people with whom you have the most robust history, which means it is unlikely to ever show you any of the posts from brand-new friend connections because, by definition, you have no history with them, no previous affiliation, no record of interaction, and thus their edge scores are, among all your connections, the lowest. It's simply one of those loopholes the math makes inevitable, the effect of which—if not properly corrected—would be that new users would come onto the network, make friends, and then never be seen or heard from again. And so to correct this specific algorithm's specific loophole, another algorithm is necessary: the Needy User algorithm, which identifies users who have been on Facebook for less than a certain threshold amount of time, or have less than a certain threshold number of connections with other users, or whose edges are less than a threshold level of robustness, and it categorizes these users as "needy," and it assigns them a "neediness value," and this value is then sent back to EdgeRank and added to the user's edge score, which score then becomes so large that the needy user's ranking goes way, way up, and thereafter any actions they take—their posts and links and photos and favorites and such—appear right there at the very top of all their friends' newsfeeds.

The subjective experience of this, for Lawrence, is that he's never once in his life felt more fully and uncomplicatedly accepted and loved.

Any little action he takes, anything that sends the tiniest ripple into the network, comes back as a wave of appreciation and support.

He chooses a profile picture, and his friends seem to *love it*. He posts about the Chiefs game, and his friends seem to *love it*. Even just his comments about the weather and the wind generate a flurry of positive response.

It is the most contact he's had with the wider world in years.

He's a man who was once well known among the rancher families of the Flint Hills, and it turns out that many of these families are, surprisingly, now on Facebook, and further, they are so happy to see him, finally, after his long withdrawal, and it's at this point he understands: *This is why people join Facebook*. This is what all the fuss is about. It feels friendly, lively, fun—people post jokes and comic strips and hilarious photos of cats and dogs and pictures of their children doing adorable things and inspirational quotes from celebrities or the Bible, and soon Lawrence learns about the "share" function and very quickly he's also sharing just these things, never failing to draw nice little comments from his small pack of friends: "Wonderful, Lawrence!" "Thank you, Lawrence!" "God bless you, Lawrence!" And so on.

The best part is, of course, that Jack is right there with the rest of them, liking all his various posts. Before joining Facebook, it would have seemed ridiculous to Lawrence to get so excited about some dumb digital "like," but now that he's here, he finds that it's not ridiculous at all. Far from it—if a "like" is the only communication he can have with Jack after these years of silence, then a "like" matters a great deal indeed. So Lawrence is thrilled whenever he gets a "like" from Jack, and the two of them begin occasionally messaging each other privately (Lawrence now understands about private messaging), and in this way Lawrence is caught up on the general details of his son's life: he's an artist in Chicago, a teacher at a university, a husband, a father. It is amazing, what the boy has accomplished, and Lawrence wishes he could see the photographic evidence of any of this—pictures of the wife or the kid or the art—but he cannot. Lawrence can find no photos on Jack's feed, nor really any posts or shares whatsoever. He assumes Jack is simply shy on Facebook. A low-level user. Probably too busy with his exciting life to dawdle online, is what he thinks. He does not understand that Jack has, in fact, hidden these things from him—the photo albums, the posts, the updates, the friends. Lawrence doesn't understand that these things are hidden because he doesn't know you can even do that.

The messages between the two of them are civil, but brief. Lawrence has never been a man of many words, and the computer interface is intimidating, and he's not entirely confident in his writing ability, and so he keeps his messages short. For now, he's happy merely speaking with his son again, and happy to be so welcomed by his old friends, happy to have reconnected finally, happy for this new, warm, cozy attention.

This will be, in Lawrence's memory of it, a sort of golden age of Facebook usage, a happy and innocent period that lasts roughly six months before something strange happens: the attention abruptly ends.

Suddenly, all at once, his friends stop engaging. Lawrence notices it one day when he posts a photo of the previous night's sunset over the prairie, a post that could be counted on to reliably fetch a few dozen likes and comments but which today nets a lousy three. And then, later that day, he shares another of those "Share this if you believe in this cause" things—this one about supporting our troops, which, *of course*—and this post gets only *a single comment*. And then that night during the seventh inning of a close baseball game, Lawrence posts "Go Royals!!" mostly as a kind of trial balloon, to see what happens. And what happens is nothing—no shares, no comments, no likes at all.

What have I done? he wonders. *Why have I been abandoned?* It feels demoralizing and confusing and even a little personally threatening, to be so quickly severed. He studies his previous week's posts to see if any of them might have been unintentionally insulting or offensive. He checks his list of friends to see if he's lost anyone, to see if his friends have staged some kind of walkout. He wonders if he's been posting too many things lately, if maybe this collective silent treatment is the passive-aggressive way his friends are telling him to cool it.

Actually, none of this has happened. The only thing that's happened here is that the Needy User algorithm has been switched off.

Lawrence Baker has now achieved the requisite amount of connectivity to no longer be considered "needy," and so the algorithm is no longer artificially boosting his rank, and so his posts tumble down newsfeeds everywhere, no longer appearing at the top but rather in places that require sustained intentional scrolling to find. Lawrence, of course, does not know his posts have fallen in this way, nor does he understand anything about his own ranking. And neither do his friends, who, when they think about him at all, just idly wonder: *Why isn't Lawrence posting anymore?*

3

The Pattern Recognition Algorithm

It is not entirely accidental that the platform functions in this manner, taking away Lawrence's spotlight at the exact moment he's getting used to it. It is not so different from certain dysfunctional relationship styles where one partner is generous with attention and affirmation until the very moment the other partner begins to want and need that attention, at which point the attention is withdrawn, often without explanation. This is the go-to technique of most so-called pickup artists, where part of the whole "game" of seduction involves bestowing their approval upon a woman only to suddenly, and without obvious cause, take it away. The thinking here is that this shifts the relationship's power dynamics, making the woman work hard to win back the guy's approval and attention, as people tend to place an irrationally high value on things they've lost versus things they never had or wanted in the first place. Essentially, the pickup artist's seduction of the woman is finally successful when he manipulates her into seducing *him,* which is the same basic pattern that repeats now between Lawrence and Facebook, though of course the Facebook engineers and mathematicians and programmers who maintain the Needy User algorithm are not thinking exactly in these terms—they know only what their analytics tell them, which is that account activity tends to spike immediately following Needy User deactivation, which seems to them like a win.

The subjective experience of this for Lawrence, though, is that he feels forsaken and discarded. It is surprising to him how much he's come to rely on all those likes and comments, how much these regular affirmations have come to function as emotional pillars, holding up each day. It is surprising to him to feel so bereft without them, so erased. He reaches out to Jack, sending private messages with really no subjects at all, just transparent fishing for connection:

How are you doing today?
What's new?
What's the weather like in Chicago? Good?
Hope you're well. (Write back!!)

And sometimes Jack does write back—a short one-sentence or sometimes even one-word reply is typical—and then other times he doesn't write back at all. Jack ignores the message, as if he never saw it, even though, according to the notification Lawrence gets from Facebook, he totally has.

Their relationship is, at this point, what network graph theory would define as "nonreciprocal."

Here then begins a flurry of new activity as Lawrence searches out and engages with anything on the platform that at all interests him, liking and favoriting movies and television programs and sporting events and celebrities and musicians and restaurants and brands and causes and even a few broad ontological concepts like "Knowledge" and "Recreation" and "Fruit" and "Life," among other categories. He has come to understand that he must radically increase his activity on Facebook in order to merely maintain the level of attention and visibility he has grown accustomed to—basically the same pattern as any kind of drug addiction, and the addictive spiral where the junkie needs more and more of the drug to maintain exactly the same high. This is, again, not entirely accidental.

All of this new activity is duly recorded by Facebook's action logger, which then adds that data to Lawrence's user-profile matrix, a personalized dynamic database that is stored in a monolithic black server that is one of fifty thousand such servers housed in an enormous gray rectangular building near the Arctic Circle in Sweden, where the cold air is constantly pumped into the building to keep computer temperatures optimal. It is here, in a data hall so spread out and immense that technicians traverse it via motorized scooter, that Lawrence's profile is analyzed and parsed and segmented and classified by an algorithm whose only job is to identify patterns.

This algorithm's underlying programming grew out of earlier and more primitive software used by banks to identify handwritten numbers on personal checks. This task—identifying, for example, a sloppily written number four, which might appear in either "open" or "closed" variants (4 as opposed to 4)—is a simple matter for most any human over the age of two, but not simple at all for a computer, which must be taught every tedious step of number recognition. Step one is taking a picture of the handwritten number and breaking that picture down to its elementary components: a bunch of black pixels and a bunch of white pixels. Then the algorithm overlays that image with the image of what it knows to be a handwritten zero, after which it eliminates the black pixels where the two figures do not overlap, just lops off the edges and counts up the remaining black pixels: the more pixels, the more overlap. Then it does that again for ten thousand more known number zeros, creating ten thousand more results and averaging all those together, then doing the same thing for all of the ones, the twos, and so on, through every digit, a hundred thousand comparisons that result in ten separate averages, the largest of which will almost certainly be generated by the number with the most overlap: the four.

In other words, it is a coldly mathematical and computational process, one without any of those human qualities that we associate with real understanding or knowledge or wisdom or insight, a process that seems painfully convoluted and tedious, except of course that a microprocessor can do all of it in less than a second, which means that a computer and a human will identify a handwritten number with roughly the same amount of accuracy in basically the same amount of time.

Anyway, the pattern-recognition algorithm used by Facebook grew out of this earlier iteration, only now it is phenomenally more complicated: instead of analyzing data in the two dimensions available to analog paper checks, it's now analyzing digitally in millions of dimensions. Each of Lawrence's actions and combinations of actions, each post and like, each comment and message, each bit of logged data is but one dimension the algorithm uses to compare

Lawrence with Facebook's other billion accounts in an effort to figure out what, exactly, he is. To take all his sloppy edges and average them away. To reveal his underlying sameness. The algorithm takes all his biographic data and social data and behavioral data and location data and compares it in every conceivable combination to every other user, effectively laying all possible dimensions atop all possible dimensions to locate the deep invisible crosscutting overlaps and connections and affinities that allow the algorithm to sort and classify and define and cluster him appropriately.

Lawrence, of course, has no idea this is happening. But he does notice the new and troubling updates now populating his feed. These mostly have to do with people getting sick. Often, children. Most often, children battling some terrible illness or injury or disease with their especially inspiring childlike aplomb. One day he logs in and right there at the top of his feed is a crowdfunder from a rancher whose youngest son has been diagnosed with a rare—and expensive—cancer. And then the next day it's a news story about a kid down in Wichita who is made more cheerful during dialysis by the hospital's loving therapy dogs. The next day, the granddaughter of a guy Lawrence used to know from church is undergoing her fourth operation to remove problematic blood clots. And it keeps going like this, every day a new story about some poor child battling something awful, and Lawrence reads and clicks and comments on all of them, often telling whoever posted the story or update or photo or video that it caused him to choke up a little bit and that he's sending his warmest wishes and praying that the benevolence of God's love and grace will fall gently upon these suffering children, and anyone who knows anything about Lawrence Baker knows that he's absolutely sincere about that. Because he went through it himself. His only son, Jack, was often sick, was often hospitalized with a seemingly nonstop variety of random illnesses and disasters, and it was clear to anyone who ever broached this subject with Lawrence how wearying it was, how taxing, how worried he was for his boy—though few people ever broached the subject with him, this being the rural Midwest where people mostly dance around touchy subjects due to an overriding social obligation to avoid feel-ing uncomfortable at all times. And so Lawrence went through life constantly—but silently—worried. Worried about his sickly, small, underweight son, and now he wishes more than anything that he could have had Facebook way back then, because people on Facebook seem able to overcome their in-person reticence and say things that are genuine and heartfelt. And so now he tells these parents and grandparents the things he wished people had told him all those years ago: that he's thinking about them, and praying for them, and that it's all going to be okay, and that it's not their fault, and that sometimes bad things happen to good people.

And the algorithm translates all of this activity into its rel-evant abstracted mathematical values and compares them many-dimensionally to all other account data to find that Lawrence seems to match up pretty closely to other American Facebook users for whom the specific subject of "Illness" and the more general subject of "Contamination" prove to be highly salient. Which is why Law-rence keeps seeing these stories and updates and videos about sick children, so many sick children that it seems like there's some kind of epidemic going on, that the number of children who are danger-ously, dramatically sick is higher now than at any other point he can ever remember. He does not consider the possibility that the num-ber of sick children in the world is roughly constant and that the variable here is how many of these sick children he's exposed to via Facebook. No, the subjective experience for Lawrence is that it very strongly feels like *way more children are getting really sick these days*, which is a sentiment that he begins expressing more and more often, and these comments themselves collect still more comments from other users—many of whom have unsettling theories explaining exactly why more children are getting so sick right now—and these new connections are added to his profile data, whereby the Pattern Recognition algorithm determines, based on various affinity matri-ces and edge strengths and eigenvalues and principal component analyses, that Lawrence clusters pretty seamlessly with members of certain wellness-related Facebook groups—among them, the

Health Freedom Network and the Awakened Patient Project and the Big Pharma Report and ScienceAlert and CancerTruth and the Truth Unleashed and the Truth Movement and What Your Doctor Isn't Telling You and so forth—all of which the algorithm recommends to him, and all of which, as it predicted, he faithfully joins.

4

The PageRank Algorithm

The ideas and theories and facts that Lawrence encounters in these particular Facebook communities are, to put it mildly, distressing. They are so distressing and troubling and occasionally downright disturbing that he decides he really needs to verify them independently, personally, quickly. And so each time he encounters a new distressing idea or theory or fact, he quits his Internet Explorer application and promptly restarts it (which is how he gets back to his Yahoo home page, as he has a basic misunderstanding regarding the Home button on the browser and assumes clicking the button means he's requesting that something be sent to his physical home), and he searches Yahoo for *www.google.com*, then clicks over to Google and slowly types into the search bar all of the pressing questions inspired by the unbelievable things he's now seeing on Facebook. He's never been taught how search engines work, has no awareness of keywords or metadata or Boolean logic or anything like that, and so he just types in full grammatically correct sentences of the sort one might pose to an actual teacher or doctor, such as:

> *Do cell phone towers really cause cancer?*
> *Are jet contrails really poisonous?*
> *Was the swine flu created by terrorists?*
> *Do drug companies secretly have a cheap cure for cancer but they're keeping it from us so they can continue making profits?*
> *Is the fluoride the government puts into the drinking water actually making the population so foggy-headed and dumb and passive that we don't notice all of these obvious plots and lies?*

And the answer to all of these questions turns out to be: probably yes.

Lawrence is shocked to find, via Google, hundreds of websites and videos that support even the most disturbing claims made by the Facebook groups of which he is now a member, websites that are lavish with charts and graphics and embedded YouTube clips, pages so lengthy and heavily researched that they take several minutes to scroll to the end of, text filled with bright blue links taking him to other websites making exactly the same claims and coming to exactly the same conclusions. The evidence, it seems, is overwhelming.

Of course, Lawrence does not consider the basic flaw in his search logic: namely, that websites about whether fluoride is poisonous are almost always made by people who believe that, yes, it definitely is. Meanwhile, people who are not worried about fluoride and don't spend too much time thinking about fluoride typically do not make elaborate websites saying so. And thus when Lawrence asks his fluoride question, the results that Google's PageRank algorithm collects for him—more than three million in less than half a second—come from a pool that is inherently much more sinister and suspicious, fluoridewise, than the actual world is. And even if there are a few lonely websites out there debunking the fluoride theory, Google's content-neutral algorithm literally cannot tell them apart, as the algorithm has no ability to understand the language that is written on a website or parse a website's arguments or logic. The best it can do is simply take every individual word it finds on a website and assign that word a point in theoretical space and then analyze how those points cluster together, assigning high search-result values to those words that often appear near each other, which is why two very different sentences—

The government is poisoning us with fluoride
and
The government is not poisoning us with fluoride

—are, for the algorithm, basically identical. They both have most of the same words clustered in most of the same ways. This is why websites that attempt to debunk conspiracy theories end up paradoxically boosting those very conspiracies, by making specific combinations of words more algorithmically salient. It's another one of those loopholes the math makes inevitable. It's why these websites all seem to reach the same conclusions and describe those conclusions in much the same language: it's just a reflection of the underlying algorithm's mathematical bias toward linguistic clusters and patterns, which tends to reward stock phrases and repetitive jargon. But obviously Lawrence does not know that, and so it seems to him that there's wide consensus and agreement on these points.

Of course, there is no such thing, but Lawrence never reads the websites that disagree with and debunk the fluoride theory because they don't appear on the first page of search results, which, like 98 percent of other internet search users, is the only page Lawrence looks at. The first-page results are entirely about the hidden dangers of fluoride, and the secrets the government is keeping from us regarding fluoride, and these results appear on the first page mostly because they have such a high "capture rate" compared to the more staid, less dramatic, more scientific websites that tend to inspire way less devotion. This is important because Google's content-blind algorithm cannot know why a user does or does not linger on any particular website, and so it has to make inferences. If, for example, someone clicks on a search result and then seconds later comes right back to Google, the algorithm assumes the result was not relevant, and thus it downgrades that kind of result in future searches. But if someone clicks on a search result and then stays on that website for a very long time, and if the user then follows the links on that website to still other websites, then the algorithm assumes the user has found something relevant and the result is upgraded. This tilting toward more sticky websites generally works well in most cases, but in Lawrence's particular circumstance—where the specific questions he's asking tend to bring up websites that imply shadowy and malevolent forces are everywhere out to get him, websites that require him to follow this link and that link in order to fully expose some dark hidden truth, to travel deeper and deeper into a tangle of conspiracies, which he does in a horrified, rubbernecking-at-the-disaster kind of way—what the algorithm promotes and rewards is a kind of cognitive quicksand. It is predisposed to deliver stories to get trapped in.

That these websites tend to link to each other so frequently is, itself, also one of the reasons they appear so high in Lawrence's search results, as the algorithm ranks websites based, in part, on how many outside links are connecting to them. The logic here is that more links imply more authority, which is generally true except in situations where a tight coterie of devoted people link to—and therefore algorithmically bolster—each other, as in for example Fluoride Website A links to Fluoride Website B, which links to Fluoride Website C, which links back to A, which links again to B, and so on and so forth, on and on in a recursive spiral that makes it look to the algorithm like each website has been linked to thousands of times when in fact those links are coming from the same small number of people over and over. Meanwhile, the lonely but actually truly authoritative website insisting that no, fluoride is not poisonous, this website is very infrequently linked to because its audience is just like, *Duh*, while the people who believe fluoride is indeed poisonous believe it *passionately*. Thus in this specific circumstance, what the algorithm amplifies is not actually authority but instead intensity. Obsession. Zeal. Pique. And so the lonely, dispassionate, scientifically objective websites that debunk the fluoride theory fall to around the fifth page of search results, which in terms of how often they're ever actually seen or clicked on means they may as well not exist at all. (There's an old SEO joke that goes: "Where's the best place to hide a dead body? On the second page of search results." Naturally Lawrence has never heard this joke, nor does he know what "SEO" even is.)

Here then begins a phase where Lawrence returns to those questionable new Facebook groups and comments on their pages about how he was initially dubious about their claims but then "I did my own research," he says, "to make up my own mind," he says, whereby he found, much to his shock and dismay, that the claims "checked out," and it's at this point in each of these various groups where the acceptance and support and love from the group is cast upon Lawrence like a warm summer dawn. It is easily the most attention he's gotten since his Needy User deactivation, and it begins a second golden age of Facebook usage, where people share with him their own stories of discovery and conversion, how each of them went through *exactly* what Lawrence is going through and thus knows *exactly* how he's feeling right now, all of these stories of epiphany and transformation having a kind of familiar Christian flair—an I-was-lost-but-now-I'm-found, all-was-dark-but-now-it's-light sort of thing—that Lawrence, without being entirely aware of it, finds comforting.

Jack, meanwhile, has no idea any of this is happening. He is not a member of any of these Facebook groups, and thus he cannot see what his father is reading or saying inside them. It just seems to him like Lawrence has taken a bit of a break from Facebook, which honestly makes Jack feel, mostly, relieved. How to deal with his father's sudden intrusion and interest in his life, after all those indifferent years, has been a source of constant doubt and stress. When Jack left home at age eighteen, he was leaving, he thought, for good, severing all connections and going forth into the larger world to reinvent himself in what he considered, at the time, a hallowed American tradition, where an individual of talent and pluck could become someone new, could achieve something grand, could leave history behind and never look back. He was not prepared, years later, for the advent of Facebook, and the way Facebook allowed the past to come rampaging upon him. Whereas most people his age found it pleasant or amusing to reconnect with the long-lost friends now finding each other on Facebook, Jack experienced this same phenomenon as a kind of deep threat. In Chicago, he is not the same person he was in Kansas—he has tattooed his body and changed his whole persona and walled off that part of his personal story from everyone, the part where he grew up on a ranch in the Flint Hills of Kansas in a small house that never wanted him.

So obviously he doesn't appreciate Facebook trying to drag him back to that place.

"Don't forget where you came from" was the only advice he ever got from anyone back home once word spread that he was leaving town—that he was going to college, in the city, *for art*. They all assumed that in Chicago he would become one of those pretentious urbanites, those insular city folk who turn up their noses at places like the Flint Hills. They told him not to "put on airs," is how they said it. They told him not to pretend he wasn't one of them.

How could they not understand that he had never felt like one of them? For so many years, they had treated him like a reject, and now here they were, telling him the worst thing he could do was reject them back.

So he made it pretty clear to the people back home that he was going to Chicago to *absolutely forget where he came from*. And in 1992, you could do that: just untether yourself and go to a new place and become a new person, a kind of dramatic bridge-burning that's quite a lot harder in the age of Facebook, he thinks, where all the people of your vast network compel you—softly, but powerfully—to continue being exactly who they've always believed you to be.

And so anytime anyone from Kansas finds Jack on Facebook, he immediately, reflexively, dismisses them. There is a big wall around his past, unbreached until that day his father sent a friend request, which Jack eventually accepted, but with conditions: that Jack restrict his father from seeing any information whatsoever about him, and that Jack restrict his friends from seeing anything his father says or does. Thus Lawrence is digitally quarantined, hidden from everyone in Jack's life, even Toby, even Elizabeth. And the relationship persists in this lopsided, guarded, highly nonreciprocal manner for many months, with Lawrence sending regular sheepish and supplicatory messages and Jack occasionally responding to them a few days later in a clipped and cold and distant manner. And honestly this feels just delicious to Jack, just so beautifully symmetrical, as if the arc of the universe has bent toward this small personal justice, Jack now able to do to his father *exactly* what his father did to him, which is to ignore him when he's most in need. To let him stew in an obviously lonely personal hell and not offer one bit of tenderness or aid. Jack is not exactly proud of this feeling, and he understands he's not being the compassionate, empathetic, forgiving person that, for example, he's trying to teach his own son to be—but it just feels *so good*, revenge. It's the only kind of cruelty that can make you feel like a bigger and better person for inflicting it. It's like Jack is teaching his father an important kind of lesson, the lesson being, basically: *Now you know how it feels.*

And so they continue like this for quite a long time, Jack withholding any real intimacy out of a mistaken belief that Lawrence is on Facebook only to connect with him, when in fact Lawrence has found strong and robust connections and support and community and fellowship in the many Facebook groups where he is now practically famous for the depth of his concern and the frequency of his posts, which Jack knows nothing about until one day in mid-2012 when, seemingly out of nowhere, Lawrence posts a long and involved diatribe on his public Facebook feed imploring all of his friends to make their peace with God and let go of earthly grudges and live life as fully and freely as possible because this is the year, 2012, that, as everyone knows, the world is going to end.

5

The Deep Learning Artificial Neural Network

As far as Jack can tell, it has something to do with the Mayan calendar, and how ancient Mayan measurements regarding the forward movement of time showed an abrupt conclusion at a particular fixed point in the distant future, a point where time stops and history ends and the world is unmade, and this point, when translated into our modern Gregorian calendar, turns out to be 21 December 2012. And on that day, the day that the calendar ends, the final day of some fundamental five-thousand-year planetary cycle—a Friday—something cosmically bad will happen, and what this is, exactly, is unclear, but *Lawrence has ideas*. Stuff about galactic alignments and solar precessions and the reversal of the planet's geomagnetic poles and the twisting off of its outer crust and the collision of Earth with a mysterious Planet X, whose gravity we have apparently detected but whose location remains elusive, and that's probably because it's hidden by a massive black hole now swooping into the Milky Way after millennia abroad to intercept us and shred us to atomic bits.

Or something like that. Frankly it's a grab bag of astronomical lunacy, and it makes Jack feel embarrassed for his father, embarrassed on his father's behalf.

Dad, what is this? he asks in a private message.

Just something I found on Facebook.

Do you believe it?

I think it's interesting.

But do you believe it?

There's nothing wrong with being prepared, right?

Okay, but do you actually believe this stuff?

I believe in having an open mind.

Okay, but seriously?

Jack, listen, you seem to me like you're still really angry about everything that happened. Maybe the end of the world is a good reminder to FORGIVE, before it's too late.

Do you really BELIEVE that the world is going to END THIS YEAR???

It's just a joke, Jack. Relax.

But then Lawrence keeps posting about it as if it's not a joke, keeps sharing links with his full friend network about, for example, a certain pattern in the sun's life cycle whereby every few thousand years it goes sort of crazy and ejects humongous solar flares that bathe the planet in cosmic radiation and supercharged particles, a deadly radioactive storm the Mayans actually lived through and witnessed firsthand, which we know because of these recently uncovered evocative glyphs carved into the walls of this one building in Tikal. And so Jack goes to the websites of NASA and the National Science Foundation and the National Oceanic and Atmospheric Administration and the U.S. Geological Survey and finds pages insisting that there is no such solar cycle, and there is no collision imminent with any planet-sized object, and there is no black hole anywhere near Earth's orbit, and there is definitely no way Earth's crust can up and twist off, and Jack sends all of these links to his father, and his father responds—only a few minutes later, frankly not nearly enough time to have fully read and digested all of the scientific literature that Jack sent his way—saying: *If the scientists know the world is going to end, do you really think they'd admit it publicly?*

But Dad, the world is not going to end.

That's exactly what they'd say if the world was ending.

Which makes for a kind of airtight, unfalsifiable theory whereby evidence against the conspiracy becomes, weirdly, evidence *for* the conspiracy. And so Jack just shuts his mouth and waits patiently for 21 December 2012, and when the world does not, in fact, end, he sends his father a triumphant I-told-you-so message, and Lawrence responds with links to new Facebook groups insisting that the whole 2012 Mayan apocalypse story was actually created by the government and leaked to the public as a false flag operation to distract us from what is *really* going on, and Jack, who actually thought that once the world did not end on the twenty-first of December his father would finally rationally see the error of his ways and moderate his reading habits, is appalled by this new twist, and not only because of the even greater lunacy of this new conspiracy but also because his father's writing about it feels increasingly unhinged and disturbed, full of gaps and leaps and contradictions and semantic paradoxes (*a sad lie if true!!!* being one of Lawrence's many difficult-to-parse utterances). Also appalling is the fact that his father seems to sincerely believe all of it. Despite consistent private denials in which Lawrence will tell Jack it's all just a joke and that he's just trying to rile people up and get a laugh and maybe Jack should try being a little less sensitive, publicly it does not seem like a joke, not one bit. It's hard to square Lawrence's private denials with his broadcasted behavior, where he consistently posts about how the Mayan calendar story was a cover-up created by the CIA to distract us from the government's imminent plan to declare martial law and massacre millions of Americans, a plot that anonymous internet sleuths uncovered after photographing a cache of plastic coffins stacked poignantly outside a CDC warehouse in Atlanta. And this sends Jack down his own Facebook rabbit holes, into groups dedicated to mocking or debunking conspiracy theories, after which he sends this evidence to his father, and Lawrence sends very odd kinds of "evidence" back, and it becomes a kind of endless angry pendulum between them, and this dynamic is, for the Facebook Neural Network mediating the whole thing, really excellent.

By 2012, Facebook's old EdgeRank algorithm is about as technologically relevant as a Studebaker and is being replaced by a state-of-the-art, fully optimized machine-learning neural network designed to maximize user engagement and leverage that engagement to drive monetization. Because the most significant thing to happen to both Lawrence and Jack in 2012 is not the Mayan apocalypse but rather that the Facebook corporation goes public, that it becomes a publicly traded company on Nasdaq, and after a pretty embarrassing IPO in which the stock's value drops like 50 percent in just one quarter, a decree comes down from the board of directors and the major shareholders to increase revenue significantly, immediately. And this is when the Facebook algorithm fundamentally evolves: whereas EdgeRank attempted to deliver to Lawrence more of what he desired, this new neural network attempts to deliver more of what Facebook desires—namely, content that makes its users stay on Facebook longer, to engage with the platform more, thereby driving more ad revenue. And so this neural network goes to work, its input being Lawrence Baker's full user-profile data, its output being Lawrence Baker's net annual worth to the company, and between input and output is a deep hidden layer of millions of individual neurons and nodes that are all constantly watching and testing and filtering and predicting and learning and tweaking in a grand synchronous effort to make that output number much, much bigger.

Because at this moment, at the end of 2012, Lawrence Baker produces only five dollars and sixty-five cents per year for Facebook, which is not excellent at all.

The neural network operates in a recursive, self-correcting manner, each of its nodes nudging and pushing in aggressive exploratory ways—sending group invitations and advertisements and surveys and notices of friend activity and requests to verify photo tags and any of a hundred kinds of alerts and notifications—and if a user does indeed engage with a specific notification, then that node's strength is enhanced, and if a user does not engage, then that node is inhibited, and in this way the algorithm discovers, through trial and error on a titanic scale, exactly which upstream variables tend to produce downstream results. It's a tuning process that literally never ends, because even after it finds, for example, that Lawrence is highly engaged by Mayan apocalypse–related content, the algorithm does not know if his engagement is yet maximized. Or, in other words, maybe there's another kind of content that might engage him *even more*. And so it goes about a kind of continuous A/B testing, lightly prodding him with invitations to engage with innumerable new content items, these invitations appearing as bright red notifications that grab his attention every time he logs on. The algorithm does not know or care what the actual content of the invitation is, merely whether Lawrence engages with it. And Lawrence, of course, does not know any of this is happening. It just seems to him, based on what he's lately seeing on Facebook, that the world is going to hell in a fucking handbasket.

It seems clear to Lawrence that the country is way more danger-ous and way more scary than it has ever been before, filled with threats from sickness and disaster and plague, a lawless country now infiltrated by terrorists and socialists and gangs, with robber-baron corporate masterminds pulling all the strings, with cabals of media and government elites pursuing deadly new world orders, releas-ing microbes and viruses and diseases upon unsuspecting popula-tions, selling them unnecessary pills and medicines, covering up the amazing all-natural effectiveness of homeopathic alternatives—stuff like colloidal silver, turmeric, shark cartilage, blue scorpion venom, cumin, apricot pits, electromagnetic waves—in order to keep people sick and needy and, therefore, compliant, passive, on the dole. He shares all of this information with his network—any new threaten-ing thing that comes across his transom, he clicks "Share," which seems like just his basic civic duty, to warn people. But he finds that every time he shares details of some new threat, he gets a quick and pompous message from Jack telling him to stop it, and he tells Jack that he absolutely won't stop it because people have a right to know what's going on, and Jack sends him links to websites that allegedly disprove these theories, and Lawrence sends Jack links about how these sources are the very liars responsible for the cover-up, and Jack sends Lawrence information about "confirmation bias" and insists that Lawrence is seeing threats simply because he *wants* to see threats, whereby Lawrence sends Jack links to websites about "normalcy bias" and insists that Jack doesn't see the threats because he's afraid to see them, and the two of them go back and forth about which of their brains is functioning incorrectly, the tone of the messages growing more exasperated and angry until one day Jack writes: *I'm so embarrassed to be related to you.*

Which is really excellent!

Never before in their long user history have Lawrence and Jack Baker ever engaged with the platform quite this much. And after months of tuning and learning and self-correcting, the neural net-work has discovered that the thing that keeps Jack most engaged is Lawrence, and the thing that keeps Lawrence most engaged is ter-ror. And so the algorithm, in a completely automatic and impartial and content-neutral way, becomes a machine that turns terror into money.

Lawrence, of course, does not know that he is being exposed daily to the most terrifying things available on the internet, nor does he know that the internet itself is actually a pretty great optimizing instrument for terrifying things, as the whole process of virality and the method by which things go viral guarantees that the very most terrifying and emotionally affecting and totally unignorable content will always be identified and exposed and promoted as a matter of course, in a more or less mechanical and unstoppable way. He doesn't understand that the friendly-looking place where he sees photographs of his neighbors' adorable children and pets is also maybe the most sophisticated fear engine ever created. He just thinks it's the normal news.

And Jack does not understand that the more angry he gets at his father, the more anger-provoking things the algorithm shows him, sometimes even pulling something from the archives that Jack might have missed the first time around, something Lawrence posted weeks ago that Jack didn't respond to at the time, showing this to him again and Jack not even realizing it's old news until he's halfway done composing his furious response.

And the two of them keep going around and around like this, Jack unable to understand why his father believes these incredible things, Lawrence unable to understand why his son does not, interacting with each other so angrily and so frequently that by the time the Ebola panic sets in around mid-2014, both Lawrence and Jack Baker are worth more than *fifty dollars each* to Facebook, a growth rate of roughly 1,000 percent year over year, which is pretty excellent indeed.

6

The Screen Interaction Algorithm

Both of them, privately, wish it were otherwise. Neither of them particularly *wants* to be fighting with the other, and both Jack and Lawrence believe that if the other could just stop being so disagreeable and blockheaded, everything would be fine, and they could go back to their more civil—if guarded—peace. In fact every morning for two weeks Lawrence sits down at his computer intending to write Jack a heartfelt and semi-conciliatory message about how he's sorry their relationship has grown so sour and combative, and how he'd hoped it would turn out so differently, and how he only ever reconnected with Jack in order to apologize for what he now understands was pretty unfair and neglectful treatment, years ago. It's a long and difficult letter he never actually brings himself to write because as soon as he logs on to Facebook, there's some bright red new notification, and there's something terrifying right there at the top of his newsfeed, something that snags his attention and then suddenly he's clicking and commenting and sharing and an entire morning can dissolve in this manner. He'll often blink up from the computer sometime in midafternoon when he realizes he's forgotten to eat breakfast and remembers that his project for the day was to write Jack an ambitious letter but finds that he no longer has the will, today, to do it, and so he puts it off until tomorrow and continues his furious scrolling, figuring that it's probably best not to write Jack a peace-seeking letter when Lawrence is feeling so jacked up and on edge and unpeaceful himself, on the inside.

This daily transformation—from the morning's quiet to the afternoon's disquiet—is obvious even from his mouse movements, which are captured by a bit of JavaScript embedded on the website and then analyzed by an algorithm designed to track a user's physical interactions with Facebook. It turns out that this so-called haptic data can pretty accurately communicate states of mind that the algorithm can then leverage to maximize engagement. Like, for example, it's well known in the area of "affective computing" that emotions can influence how a user operates a mouse, that a user feeling perfectly neutral and at ease will, when moving the mouse cursor from point A to point B, move it at a leisurely pace and in a more or less straight line, whereas a user under the influence of stress and anxiety and anger will get real twitchy: mouse users feeling high anxiety tend to slightly overshoot their targets, and they tend to have more frequent micro-accelerations and -decelerations in their mouse movements, and they tend to push the mouse with a larger initial force, and click the mouse for a longer duration, and be way less precise in their travel paths, moving the cursor in a wide or curvy arc rather than a straight line. Of course, the algorithm logging all of these movements does not comprehend any of this as "bad"—it is merely one haptic state out of many possible states. And each of these states is compared to Lawrence's action logs to analyze whether any particular state is associated with higher engagement, which is how the algorithm learns that Lawrence tends to engage with the platform most thoroughly and consistently when his mouse movements are at their most erratic and jumpy. And thus the platform naturally attempts to create that state within him, to nudge him into that state of high twitch, and when it observes him in the morning moving his mouse slowly and carefully and without much affect, it then signals the content database to deliver messages and notifications and alerts that have historically diverted him and caught his attention and made his mouse movements go optimally crazy. Which explains the phenomenon of Lawrence sitting down at his computer in the morning with a real goal in mind but then still sitting there hours later with little memory of what that goal was.

This problem gets much, much worse after Lawrence purchases his first cell phone. It's an older model, three versions behind the current release, but still the most technologically sophisticated thing that Lawrence has ever owned, a smartphone with a capacitive touch screen and inner accelerometer that passively delivers to Facebook even yet more haptic data regarding how forcefully Lawrence touches the screen and how quickly he picks up the phone or puts it down or rotates it or orients it, plus whether he's looking at it in a darkened room, and how long that room has been dark, which implies useful things about his current mood. Also the smartphone has a built-in front-facing camera that is, conveniently, pointing right up at Lawrence whenever he's using the phone, which allows the Facebook app to access the camera and passively observe his face while he's using the app and analyze his features for what his expressions imply about his emotional state, comparing his current features to its data set of millions of other faces experiencing known emotions to extrapolate exactly how he's feeling in real time and then deliver content appropriate for those emotions—for example, sending him interactive ads when he appears bored, or sending uplifting pablum when he appears melancholy, or sending alarming and terrifying news when he looks away from the phone for a period longer than a certain threshold amount of time, which his history suggests is the signal that he might soon put the phone down and do something else, in which case the very most effective way to regain his attention and keep his eyes fixed on the phone is to populate his feed with posts from a particular anonymous Facebook user calling himself the Heartland Patriot, allegedly a Midwestern farmer worried about the future of the country who is right now posting many times daily about how drug companies invented the Ebola virus in order to profit from a pandemic and associated vaccine. This is scary enough to keep Lawrence staring at his phone with that particular deep worried crease between his eyebrows, and as the algorithm has long ago noted, there is a strong connection between the depth of that crease and the length of Lawrence's engagement with the platform.

He does not know that Facebook is monitoring him and spying on him and even listening to him more or less constantly, nor does he believe it when he's told this very thing by Jack, that he is *being secretly watched by Facebook*. This comes in the form of a long private letter that Jack has composed pleading with his father to stop spending so much time with all these conspiracies, that none of them are true, that Lawrence is getting unnecessarily worked up and angry about nothing, that there are no shadowy cabals secretly plotting against the world, and what's happening here is actually just that a small group of engineers in Silicon Valley have built money-making algorithms that are now optimizing, that what Lawrence is seeing is not reality but rather an algorithmic abstraction of reality that sits invisibly atop reality like a kind of distortion field. And Jack sends Lawrence information about all those algorithms—the EdgeRank and PageRank algorithms, the Needy User algorithm, the object classifiers and the neural networks and the various haptic interaction scripts that Jack discovered online—explaining that Facebook is manipulating him into believing untrue conspiracies in order to generate advertising dollars. And this story sounds, to Lawrence, fishily similar to the very conspiracy theories that Jack otherwise insists are false: a shadowy cabal of Facebook engineers secretly manipulating the whole world?

C'mon, Lawrence writes in response. *No way.*

Sorry, Dad, but it's true.

I don't believe it.

I understand it probably feels humiliating to be manipulated like this. I'm sorry.

So you think there's no way that drug companies released Ebola to profit from it?

That's correct.

And yet you're also saying that Facebook released the story about drug companies releasing Ebola to profit from it, to profit from it?

I know it's confusing but basically, yes.

[thinking face emoji]

It's true, Dad.

But how do you KNOW it's true?

And Jack sends links to all these websites that, to Lawrence, upon first inspection, frankly don't seem any more or less authoritative than the places Lawrence found his own information, and yet Jack tells him—rather pretentiously, in Lawrence's opinion—*You can't trust everything you see online.*

But you found THIS online, Lawrence replies.

Some things online are true, and some aren't.

Well how convenient that the things you already believe just happen to be the true ones. [another thinking face emoji]

They're not true because I believe them, Dad. I believe them because they're true.

Facebook is not spying on me. That's ridiculous.

Why is it that you believe literally every conspiracy except the ONE THAT'S ACTUALLY HAPPENING???

And so Lawrence goes in search of evidence in defense of Facebook, which is not hard to find, websites insisting that Facebook is simply a neutral tool that only reflects the real world back to us, that its algorithms are harmless, that it doesn't force us to do anything we don't already want to do, that it's for sure not secretly spying on us, and that all of this hand-wringing about Facebook is, at best, the same kind of moral panic we see directed at every other transformational technology (see, for example, similar panics about the dangers of moving pictures, or the horrors of wireless radio). And then other websites claim that all of this anti-Facebook rhetoric is actually an insidious smear campaign brought on by narrow-minded left-wing fascists trying to censor and silence anyone who disagrees with them, that a classic gaslighting technique by fascists and authoritarians of all stripes is to insist that the thing you know is really happening has never actually happened at all.

And when Lawrence sends these links to Jack, Jack responds with more links of his own, and the two of them argue about which links are the true and right ones, and this opens up a whole ontological hornet's nest about whether we can ever know anything with certainty, whether we can ever know or identify the truth, whether "truth" can even be said to exist at all.

And Jack has to admit (privately, not to his father, he'd never admit this to his father) that upon further investigation, some of the things he had believed about Facebook were, indeed, fake. Turns out it's pretty unlikely that Facebook is secretly watching its users or eavesdropping on them via their phones—that little tidbit, it's true, might have been paranoid speculation passed off as fact by authors that Jack had, for some reason, trusted. He had trusted them immediately and uncomplicatedly, and now he wonders why he did that. Maybe it's true that he has some unconscious and possibly Freudian need to silence his father, or maybe it's true that blaming

Facebook for the problem of diverse people having diverse opinions really is an externalization of some deep inner psychological brittleness. After all, Jack doesn't know anything about how algorithms really work—he has never written an algorithm, nor *seen* an algorithm, if that even makes sense to say. Anything he believes about algorithms just came from other people online who also believed it. The algorithms themselves are a black box, a trade secret, a total vacuum of knowledge, and Jack knows enough from Elizabeth's research to understand that when there's an informational vacuum, the mind will naturally rush in to fill it. How different is this, really, from Lawrence's own fantasies? Both Lawrence and Jack look at the mysterious, God-sized systems in the world and imagine into those systems malevolence and evil. Maybe both father and son have the same paranoid style but have attached their paranoia to their own particular objects. Maybe, in the end, they're both wrong. Maybe they're both deluded. And Jack feels himself willing to capitulate on these points and admit it's possible his opinions are not 100 percent correct—that is, until he sees from his father absolutely no desire for similar capitulation, no evidence of compromise, no bridge-building. In fact, after these exchanges with Jack, Lawrence continues sharing links and stories and memes from the Heartland Patriot at a rate roughly triple his previous rate, which makes Jack furious, this sudden hysterical increase in lunacy, how his father's heightened devotion seems like a calculated insult directed only at Jack, and this ultimately persuades Jack to do exactly what he'd hoped to avoid when he crafted that long and sympathetic letter, and he sends Lawrence a brief message explaining: *It doesn't seem to matter, Dad, what I say, how many theories I debunk, it doesn't even matter because tomorrow you'll be back with seven more, and nothing I say can stop you, so ultimately it's just not worth it. I can't handle it. I have a lot going on, and my life is complicated enough, and I can't deal with your nonsense right now. So, bye.*

And with that, Jack finally unfriends his father.

7

The Chatbot

But there's so much more to say, so much that his father does not
know. Whenever Jack has gotten on Facebook these last several
months he's wondered how to break through to his dad, how to free
the man from his fever dream. Jack regrets having ignored him all
this time, and feels responsible now for the dark hole his father has
fallen into. If only Jack had been more gracious, more forgiving, less
seduced by petty revenge. He wants to somehow convince his father
that the life one experiences on Facebook *is not life*, that there's a
weird and wonderful world that's inaccessible to the algorithms.
Jack wants to tell his dad about this time when Toby was three years
old and entered this phase where right before bed he would demand
that Jack and Elizabeth both dance with him around the kitchen
table, around and around, dancing and doing laps around the table
while listening, on repeat, to this one particular dumb rock song
from the nineties called "Peaches," a song by this Seattle band that
was briefly popular circa 1996, and who even knows how Toby heard
that song but he *loved it so much,* and he would giggle outrageously
at the lyrics—

> *Movin' to the country*
> *Gonna eat a lot of peaches*
> *Movin' to the country*
> *Gonna eat me a lot of peaches*

—and they'd sing along, all three of them, and boogie ridiculously
around the table until the chorus, when the guitarist suddenly burst
in with a really delicious electric power chord and here Toby would
stop dancing and start playing a furious air guitar, and he would
swing one arm in a big circle over his head and bring his hand down
right where he pretended his guitar to be, nodding his head and
squeezing his eyes passionately shut like the headbanging lead gui-

tarists of Wicker Park did when Jack photographed them so long ago. How Toby even knew to do this was a mystery, and Jack and Elizabeth just about lost it every night, watching him rock out so hard to a song about peaches, dancing around in his purple pajamas.

This is a story Jack wants to tell his father. But every time he starts writing about it, it feels wrong. Putting that story on Facebook feels like it changes the story. It suddenly feels like he's maybe using the story selfishly, though unconsciously, to brag, that maybe the *real* reason he's posting it is to show off his charmed life, or to boast about his parenting skills, or to fish for praise and attention. This weird and precious and private family thing becomes something altogether new when alchemized by Facebook—it gains a second, uglier entendre. It becomes instrumental. Toby becomes a prop. The whole thing turns into an ad. Such is the inexorable mathematics of Facebook: whatever goes on Facebook just becomes more like Facebook.

Example: Each time Jack is feeling large-hearted and sympathetic and wants to finally let his father back into his life, he'll get on Facebook and see the abominable things Lawrence has lately shared, these pithy infuriating memes from the Heartland Patriot—some lunatic who seems to be his father's angry new best friend—and all of Jack's sympathy and generosity vanishes. In a blink, Jack cannot imagine loving someone—or, for that matter, even being friendly with someone, or civil with someone—who could post something like that, who could believe something like that.

It's even worse when Lawrence accompanies these posts with language that sounds distressingly similar to what Jack himself might have said in the past, in the nineties, in college. At that time Jack was righteously anti-corporate, anti-globalization, suspicious of mass culture and those it indoctrinated. And now his father claims to be all those things too, but not in any way that Jack understands or agrees with. Certain slogans that sounded revolutionary in the nineties sound apocalyptic now:

Don't believe what they tell you.
Shut the system down.

Stick it to the man.
Don't be a sheep.
QUESTION EVERYTHING!

Or when Lawrence shares this YouTube video about why people should not get vaccinated, what offends Jack most about the video is, actually, the soundtrack, because the creator has poached Rage Against the Machine screaming "Fuck you, I won't do what you tell me!" and Jack's like, *That's my song! You can't take my song!* This happens to him all the time, Jack feeling shocked to see exactly his own rhetoric from long ago boomeranged through the decades and coming back at him now, via his father, transformed and ugly.

He remembers his photography workshop in college, Professor Laird going on and on about the indeterminacy of language, the social construction of reality, the instability of the real, and the students all nodding, all agreeing. They deconstructed speech, deconstructed truth, deconstructed art. Jack had deconstructed his own photography so much that it was no longer accurate to even call it photography—it no longer contained a subject, no longer used a camera. *All solid ground is but thin air*—that's what they'd been taught. Reality is a made thing. Truth does not exist.

And now here he is, twenty years later, arguing exactly the opposite.

Benjamin Quince had once told him that the hyperlink was the most important invention since the printing press, that the hypertext would someday disrupt all literature. In the future, Benjamin had said, readers would navigate a story themselves, without the rigid interference of an author telling them what to do or what to think. They would have the freedom to wade into a sea of information, constructing personal meaning out of a constellation of many possible meanings, creating their own stories, and Jack has begun to think that Benjamin was half right. That is, indeed, exactly what people do now, people like this farmer, the Heartland Patriot, people like his own dad.

But they're not doing it in literature. Because it turned out that hypertext didn't disrupt literature. No, it disrupted *reality*. That's what Jack thinks when he sees his father's lunacy: The actual world has become one big hypertext, and nobody knows how to read it. It's a free-for-all where people build whatever story they want out of the world's innumerable available scraps.

Case in point: the farmer calling himself the Heartland Patriot is—neither Lawrence nor Jack knows this—not a farmer at all. And he's not from the heartland. The account is running through a series of virtual private networks via the Bahamas and the UK and Spain and Brazil, originating who-knows-where but definitely not in the American heartland. And the images and memes created by the Heartland Patriot bear the same digital fingerprint as images and memes posted by several other accounts with names like the Southern Rebel and the Woke Intersectionalist and the Mindful Warrior and the Fed-Up Scientist and a beauty-and-wellness influencer called Alexis Foxie—all of these mismatched identities being managed on the same computer, and likely by the same person, whose whole purpose in life seems to be to scour the internet for things people will get pissed off about, and then broadcast those things widely. Notable is the fact that the mission of the Fed-Up Scientist is to expose and mock conspiracy theorists on Facebook, and this user often insults the Heartland Patriot for spreading toxic propaganda, meaning that the same mysterious person is posting, on the same computer, both pro- and anti-conspiracy content, often within the span of a few minutes. In fact, all of these users often fight with each other and call each other out, the Heartland Patriot insisting that, for example, the Ebola virus was manufactured by Big Pharma in order to profit from a vaccine, and the Woke Intersectionalist saying no, it was created by our white supremacist government and released in Africa to kill Black people, and the Southern Rebel saying no, it was created by terrorists and given to illegal immigrants who are now storming across our borders, and the Fed-Up Scientist insisting that all three explanations are obviously idiotic drivel lacking empirical support, and the Mindful Warrior calling them all "sheeple" who will believe any official storyline, after which Alexis

Foxie chimes in about how Ebola was obviously a product of factory farming, which should be a reminder to all of us about the importance of clean eating and veganism. It's a circular firing squad that's not entirely dissimilar from the way Jack, as a child, would play Dungeons & Dragons alone, inhabiting every character at once and having them all fight against one another; whoever is responsible for these Facebook posts is conducting a similar role-play, only now with a massive audience. And immediately following any new post, literally seconds later, there's a storm of activity on both Facebook and Twitter when millions of other people all seem to simultaneously like and share and retweet and express their support or ridicule, such that the posts fly up newsfeeds on Facebook and trend on Twitter and attract even more attention, each post quickly developing long strings of anger and rage and insults and threats, usually hundreds of comments deep.

The people who are doing this are, mostly, not people at all. They are self-improving long short-term memory recurrent neural networks, more commonly known as bots. These bots are designed to mimic natural language by recombining the words of existing posts and comments just slightly, just enough that the bots seem like they are real thinking people and not, in fact, machines. They do this not by understanding language or syntax in any real way, but rather by taking a training set of a billion words written by real people on social media and assigning each of those words a point in a fifty-dimensional space, then extrapolating the rules of language and predicting new language in basically the same way a weather forecast predicts the weather based on past weather data. And, like a weather forecast, a bot can learn from its mistakes. When a bot creates a post and that post is not engaged with by any real humans, an error is generated and the algorithm self-corrects. It's like a forecast that predicts rain when rain does not happen—the model takes the error into account next time, which slowly improves the model. And so the bot, after several million iterations, can get pretty skilled at creating maximally engaging language without ever once comprehending what that language means. It is one of these algorithms that, for example, sets off one of the all-time great and epic

Facebook fights, when the Fed-Up Scientist posts a video of a fox hunting in the snow and comments, "Nature is amazing" and a bot replies, "You mean GOD'S CREATION is amazing," after which it's off to the races, engagementwise.

The effect of all this bot activity upon Lawrence and Jack is two-fold: first, whenever Lawrence occasionally questions whether the Heartland Patriot is really telling the truth, or whenever Jack wonders if the Fed-Up Scientist isn't maybe a little too belligerent, they both see how each user seems to have the support of a hundred thousand other real people, which reassures them that they are, respectively, correct; and second, and more importantly, it makes each of them feel like they are under attack. Constant, punitive, and aggressive attack. All of these rude and combative comments make them feel like they are under assault by malicious idiots everywhere, and nothing is more clarifying, and nothing makes you hold stronger to your beliefs, than seeing those beliefs unfairly abused by jerks.

And so Lawrence feels pretty resentful about getting unfriended by Jack—so unjustly, so *undeservedly,* is how he sees it. And he'd like to tell Jack exactly how unjust it is, except of course he now has no way to reach him. And so he goes searching Facebook for any mention of his son, which is how he comes across a brand-new public group called Preserve Park Shore, and in a post about stopping the construction of a building called the Shipworks, he finds Jack's name listed as the owner of a condo in this building, and he finds the group discussing tactics to "pressure" Jack and the other owners into terminating their agreements, which sounds downright threatening to Lawrence. And this is all it takes, this threat to his own flesh and blood, for Lawrence to stop battling with Jack and instead zealously defend him. He comments immediately on this post about how he knows for a fact that Jack Baker is a good and decent and brilliant man, a family man and churchgoing man that the town should be grateful to have as a neighbor.

And that's when a user named Brandie—a mom influencer with a decent following over on Instagram—swoops in and says that she knows Jack and Elizabeth Baker in real life and can say with certainty that they are *not* quality family-type Christian people, that

Elizabeth is actually a professional liar and a snake-oil peddler and a quack, that her work at Wellness preys on vulnerable people and lies to them for profit, and furthermore Brandie knows for an absolute fact that Jack and Elizabeth are into some pretty deviant and decidedly un-Christian things, some gross things of a weird sexual nature, things that she can't even bring herself to type publicly, that's how disturbing they are. Which naturally sends the members of Preserve Park Shore hunting through the web to find confirmation that Jack and Elizabeth are, in fact, degenerate, which is how they dredge up Jack's old *Girl in Window* pictures. And they post links to these images (NSFW) and then spend a good amount of time discussing whether these pictures do or do not prove immoral sexual depravity, Brandie now diving into the comments to convey her strong objection to Jack's appropriation of female bodies without their consent, not to mention his use of the word "girl" to describe adult women, which, she says, infantilizes them.

After that, she's on to Jack's photos of the Foundry, those old photographs of abandoned Wicker Park buildings from the early nineties, Brandie reposts them here, stripped of context, just images of rubble and decay, and she calls these pictures "ruin porn" and says that only an elite and privileged asshole could fetishize poverty that way. And Lawrence reacts poorly to this word "privileged" and tells Brandie she doesn't know what the fuck she's talking about and that she has no idea how difficult Jack's upbringing really was and that it was in no way privileged and if there's anyone here who's actually privileged it's definitely Brandie, living in her fancy house, sending her kid to some fancy school. Whereupon Brandie—who has obviously been doing some background research on Elizabeth— links to Wikipedia pages about the Augustine family of Litchfield, Connecticut, revealing that Elizabeth is really the one who grew up with the most privilege, with monstrous privilege, a giant fortune that, by the way, was strongly connected with the KKK. Then Lawrence descends into non sequitur and calls Brandie a "Nazi thug," after which Brandie scours Lawrence's long history of questionable conspiracy-related posts and links to his most inflammatory, most insensitive comments, calling him a "knuckle-dragging racist." And because Lawrence is spending so much time on this thread, and because he has robust edge connections with certain Facebook personalities who tend to covet and crave big controversies, all of this back-and-forth draws the attention of the Heartland Patriot and the Southern Rebel and the Woke Intersectionalist and the Mindful Warrior and the Fed-Up Scientist and Alexis Foxie, all of whom now ambush the group and carry on the fight in their usual militant manner. And then all the bots go to work, reposting and sharing and boosting the fight so that the Preserve Park Shore page now just completely blows up, hijacked by Lawrence and Brandie and one troll with an army of bots, making it today's ground zero for all of the culture's inextricable wars.

Jack, of course, does not know any of this is happening. He doesn't see any of his father's activity because he has unfriended his father, and he has stopped checking Facebook, and on this day, the day that Lawrence finally crashes through his digital quarantine, Jack is not online. He is away from his computer. He is not looking at his phone. He is having an argument with Elizabeth, and it's not until Toby knocks on the door and walks into that unfinished and empty bedroom and tells them that they, Jack and Elizabeth, are *going viral* that Jack finally checks Facebook, where he finds hundreds of alerts and notifications and messages, and buried among them are many new friend requests, all of them from his father's account, each of them with a new personalized message:

Jack, are you there? says the first one.

Jack, please respond, says the second.

Jack, I know you probably don't want to hear from me, but please write me back.

Jack, you need to know something.

Jack, something has happened.

Jack, I'm sick.

I'm really very sick, Jack.

Jack, are you there?

Jack, where are you?

Jack, it's getting worse now.

Jack, it's spreading and there's not much time.

Jack, you need to know something.

Jack, what happened between you and your sister, it wasn't your fault.

Jack, ask your mother, she'll tell you, it wasn't your fault.

I'm sorry, Jack.

I'm really, really sorry, Jack.

It wasn't your fault, Jack.

Jack, please. I'm so, so sorry.

THE MIRACLE

I T WAS NEARING DAWN when Jack felt himself shaken awake. He looked up and through groggy eyes saw, in the room's low blue light, his sister, Evelyn, standing above him, her hand outstretched, her smile full of mischief.

"Come with," she whispered.

He blinked away the sleep, the remnants of a dream already collapsing, and he looked around as the world resolved: it was the living room of his parents' house, he was sleeping on the couch, his big sister was there, she was visiting for the week, she was holding out her hand and he smiled and took it and she yanked him up off the couch and together they went out into the morning, the sun just a faint orange notion on the horizon, Jack rubbing the crumbs out of his eyes, Evelyn sniffing the cool air, then breathing so deeply her whole body got involved, her arms stretching out to their fullest wingspan as she inhaled.

"I forgot how this place smelled," she said, eyes closed, nose pointed to the sky. "Like oregano and sunshine."

She told Jack to do the same, and together they breathed like that—big gulp of herbaceous air, arms wide, chest big, hold it, hold it, then slowly release, bowing low toward the sun. Evelyn called it "welcoming the dawn." She wore a big canvas backpack over another polka-dot dress—this one lime green—and white sneakers coming apart at the stitching, soles blackened, laces shredded to string. She led him to the north pasture and together they walked through the crunching dry grass to the overlapping music of day and night—birds calling greetings to the sun, crickets still singing to the dark. The sky above them was slowly turning new shades of blue—from midnight to navy—and in the distance, the sun emerged as an incandescent dot atop the black edge of the earth.

They sat down right there in the grass, Evelyn setting the backpack on the ground and billowing out her dress and kneeling into the tangled thatch. From the bag she removed a small fisherman's tackle box and placed it between them, unlocked it, pulled open its accordion middle. Inside were tubes of acrylic paint: warm yellows and reds on the top tray, cool blues and purples on the bottom. She pulled two paintbrushes and two oval wooden palettes from the backpack, along with two small squares of stretched canvas and a water bottle whose plastic surface was overlaid with the every-colored drips of much previous work.

Canvases on their laps, they considered the scene before them—the house, the pasture, the sunrise, the rolling green-yellow grass of the surrounding country. "The world gives us such gifts," Evelyn said.

She soaked her brush in the water, dabbed some burnt umber on her palette, and with one quick and neat motion, she drew the brush's tip across the canvas to create a line that rose and fell exactly as the horizon in front of them rose and fell, a slight hill giving way to a shallow gully.

Then a few flicks of gray in the foreground, a quick smear of white, and there, suddenly, was their house—not really a strict depiction of it, but more like the suggestion of their house, thin lines that somehow *embodied* the house: the pitch of its roof, the way the porch sagged slightly with age, its quaint littleness amid the endless surrounding grass, all of this captured in only a few short strokes.

"Your turn," she said.

When Jack tried to paint the house, he painted every corner, every angle, every window, every shadow and eave, he tried to define the house completely, to thoroughly bound it in paint, but ultimately it all looked messy and fake and gloppy. It looked like what it was—a painting of a house—whereas Evelyn's seemed to *live*.

"I don't think I did it right," he said.

"That's okay," she said, smiling. "You just have to let it breathe."

"What do you mean?"

"Have a light touch, restrain your brush, don't smother the picture. You don't need to paint every detail. Only the important ones."

Jack looked out at the scene and wondered how to separate the unimportant details from the important ones.

"Try to provide a gap for the viewer's mind to cross," she said. "Watch."

She filled in the land with color, layering dollops of yellow and green and the occasional surprising purple—"It evokes shadow," she said—and when she applied these colors, she did so with an upward twist of her wrist, so that the hard bristles of her brush scratched into the canvas, leaving behind these thin white ribbons that, amazingly, conjured exactly the texture of grass: the braided swirl of its stalks, the curlicue tendrils of its leaves. When Jack tried to create grass, he painted the grass itself—straight green lines that bled into one another in anonymous monotone clumps. But Evelyn created grass by *not* painting it, by scratching away the color, leaving behind a negative space into which his eyes read: grass.

Then Evelyn painted the sun, adding to the paint a more-than-usual amount of water and letting the liquid do the work, spreading itself out over the canvas in a kind of animated mimicry of the sunrise itself, the colors streaking across her picture's sky in a red and orange halo. In Jack's version, the sun was an uneven yellow ball. In Evelyn's, it looked like how the sunrise felt: big and cosmic and holy.

She leaned back and considered her picture. To Jack, it looked complete—there was the house, the sun, the gently rolling hills. There was nothing left in front of them to depict.

"The first paintings that anyone ever did of Kansas looked a lot like this," she said. "I mean, take away the house, obviously. Just grass and sky. The first parties to explore the western frontier always brought a landscape artist with them. They needed to show people back East what the country looked like. This was before photography, of course."

"Right," Jack said, nodding.

"The problem, though, was that nobody back East wanted paintings that looked like this."

"Why not?"

"They weren't used to landscapes with so few details. Back then, a landscape was only worth painting if it had all these little adornments. Like so," she said, and, with a green so dark it was almost black, Evelyn quickly painted several junipers opposite the house—

tall and skinny trees, branches like feathers, a long grove that cast dramatic shadows onto the grass. Jack looked up at the actual world around them—there wasn't a tree like that for miles.

"You have to understand," Evelyn said, "the only landscape paintings that people had ever seen were of mountains and forests and rivers. When they saw the first paintings of the Great Plains, they were like, 'Where are the mountains? Where are the forests? Where are the rivers?'"

Evelyn scooped up a few similarly colored blues on her brush and smeared them onto the canvas in what Jack eventually recognized as a river—a rushing river that cut across the land and receded into the far distance. Then Evelyn filled its shores with stones, small trees, ferns.

"People couldn't appreciate the prairie," she said. "They were more familiar with forests. A prairie is just grass for miles. It was too strange. People wanted pictures like *this*"—nodding at her canvas—"like the pictures they were used to, even if the picture wasn't true."

Then she added a mountain range to the horizon, snowcapped peaks done in the faintest turquoise so that it seemed like they were a great distance away, barely visible through the morning haze.

"Eventually artists either stopped painting the prairie, or they added all these embellishments so that the paintings did not seem, to the collectors back home, so strange."

At the top edges of her canvas, Evelyn now added overhanging branches and leaves, in thick black paint, as if she were sitting directly beneath the boughs of a great oak tree, looking out from under its thick foliage.

"There," she said, "that's about right," dropping her brush into the water bottle and leaning back. "What do you think?"

Jack considered her picture for a moment, and even though he knew the scene did not really exist in life, still he thought that if he spotted it in a book or magazine, he would strongly want to go to that place.

Then he looked at his own picture: flat, lifeless, boxy, boring.

"Yours is better," he said.

"Ah, but yours is more *real*," she said. "Mine matches what people expect. Yours matches what you see. Which makes yours the superior work of art."

"Really?"

"Absolutely. Mine is propaganda, yours is true. If you're going to be an artist, you have to understand this. Don't be afraid of truth, Jack, even if it makes you a little strange."

This became their ritual—every day that week, she woke him up early and took him out to the north pasture and they painted this same scene again. The same house, the same view. The only thing that changed was the sky: sometimes it was clear, sometimes it was filled with great bulbous cumulus clouds whose undersides ignited redly at the dawn, and other times it was overcast, and the dark gray night gave way to a featureless gray morning. But these individual conditions seemed unimportant to Evelyn; each one presented its own challenge and opportunity. She taught him that an overcast sky was not merely a single gray color but rather a many-layered field of pastels that all conspired toward a dynamic, shimmering grayness. She showed him how a blue sky was not only blue, how green grass was not only green, that each contained within it traces of its opposite: how an orange wash complicated the blue sky, how shots of violet created depth in the grassy field. She showed him how to hold a brush, how to mix paints on the palette, how to look at a landscape not in terms of singular objects but in terms of interacting forms, how placing the house at the center of the canvas versus the edge changed the picture's whole dynamic, its whole visual weight.

Between these technical lessons there were larger, more conceptual ones, usually regarding the challenge of painting the prairie, and the folly of the first landscape artists who tried to do it.

"The prairie terrified them," she said. "Those early settlers, on cloudy days they'd lose all sense of cardinal directions because everywhere they looked it looked the same. On sunny days they'd see a lake on the horizon and ride all day and never reach it. Distances are strange on the plains. Everything gets extended and weird. You can't judge how near something is in all that space."

Jack dabbed color onto his canvas and said nothing. He didn't want to interrupt Evelyn when she got going like this—he wanted her attention to keep washing over him all day long.

"The problem is, it's too big and too uniform," she said. "Painting it, it's hard to create distance, separation, depth. The problem is its immensity, plus its monotony. Which, come to think of it, is also the problem with most marriages."

"What?"

"Immensity plus monotony. That's marriage in a nutshell."

She smirked and winked at him. It was thrilling to Jack that she would say such a thing to him, would treat him more or less like an equal and not like some dismal sickly child. These morning lessons had a seriousness of purpose that Jack had not found anywhere else—his mother did not speak to him this way, and certainly nobody at school did. He could not find this kind of experience in any of the game shows or soap operas that howled throughout the day, nor could he find it in books, because theirs was not a house that contained books.

Which was another lack that Evelyn sought to remedy. At the conclusion of that first week, she borrowed the Ford to go into town—ostensibly to fetch ingredients for a cake, as it was their mother's birthday, but she came back also lugging a bag that she secreted to Jack's room. It was filled with used books: *Great Expectations. The Call of the Wild. The Great Gatsby. On the Road. A Portrait of the Artist as a Young Man.* Books, she said, about people who leave home and go forth into the world and reinvent their very selves.

"You don't have to be what people around here want you to be," she said. "You can be who you really are, inside"—she pressed a fingertip to his chest—"in your heart."

He was still thinking about that even as they all sang "Happy Birthday" some hours later. Evelyn was there, and his father, and his mother, who seemed—as she always did on her own birthday—a little embarrassed at the attention and fuss. They sat around the kitchen table, cake in the middle, and they sang. Outside, the sky was darkening, nearing sunset. There was eating, and the opening of gifts. Jack had made his mother some IOU-type coupons she could use to compel him to do the chores she found most disagreeable, and Evelyn gave her a polka-dot dress of her very own, and to these gifts Ruth responded with a quiet "Thank you" and "How sweet" in a tone that was somewhere between benevolence and melancholy. Then it was Lawrence's turn, and he gave her a big box wrapped in shiny metallic birthday paper, and Ruth said, "I wonder what this might be?" and began tearing into the wrapping, and Jack found himself internally rooting for his father to have done a good job with the present-hunting this year, to have purchased something that wouldn't trigger one of Ruth's deeper swoons, when she complained privately to Jack for many days about how a particular lackluster gift proved that nobody really understood her or even loved her enough to *try* to understand her—Jack was pretty sure his father didn't grasp how much of the thoughtless-birthday-gift fallout landed on Jack's small shoulders.

And while Ruth tore at the box, Jack was still considering what Evelyn had told him, about being true to himself, listening to his heart, thinking that he had, in fact, no idea what his heart wanted, and this fact bothered him. He knew he could say with absolute confidence and precision what, for example, his mom wanted, and whether she would or would not appreciate this particular gift. But he realized he could not as easily describe what he himself wanted. It was something he'd never considered, a question he'd never thought to ask. He remembered a time a few Christmases ago when his parents took him to a mall in Wichita that had this North Pole scene where you'd sit on Santa's lap and tell him what you wanted, and when Jack got up there and Santa asked, "What would you like, little boy?" Jack sincerely did not know. He was not aware of anything that he truly wanted, had no real interior desire whatsoever. "Whatever you'd like to bring me," he finally said, "I'm sure it'll be fine," to Santa's deep bewilderment.

By now the wrapping paper was torn away, and Ruth opened the plain cardboard box underneath and pulled out her gift, which was—Jack's heart sank to see it—a sandwich maker.

The Oster electric sandwich grill.

"Oh," she said.

She held it in her hands as one might hold a sleeping animal: curiously, but cautiously.

This kind of device would, years later, be called a panini press, but that year, 1984, in Kansas, it was known as a sandwich grill or a sandwich toaster or sometimes a pie iron, and it was, for a brief period, really popular. For whatever reason, for a few years there, it was a terribly popular thing to put one's normal cold square sandwiches into this cast-iron griddle—it had shallow wells exactly the shape of store-bought bread—which not only toasted the sandwich but also cut it diagonally and sort of fused it all together, so that each half sandwich emerged looking more like an empanada (though of course Jack wouldn't know what an "empanada" was until much later), the exterior of the sandwich all brown and crispy, the interior molten. A sandwich like this was known, for a time, as a *hot 'n toasty*.

Ruth considered her electric hot 'n toasty griddle silently for a moment. Jack knew she would resent it in the way she resented any gift that evoked domestic chore-doing (the vacuum cleaner she received one year for Christmas being this category's most triggering example). However, Jack had also witnessed her watching television commercials for this very sandwich press and verbally endorsing it, saying, "That looks interesting" or "That might be fun," and so Jack hoped she'd appreciate the sandwich maker because it proved, at the very least, that her husband had been listening to her all this time and sincerely thinking about a gift she'd actually use.

"That's so *neat*!" Jack said, trying to coax his mother into, if not happiness, at least contentedness. "Didn't you say you wanted one of those?"

"I suppose I did," she said, almost in disbelief. She'd been so reflexively prepared for disappointment that this feeling of minor gratification probably came as a genuine shock.

Lawrence smiled then and seemed to relax. "See, I heard you talking about it after you saw that one commercial," he said, "and then I noticed it was on sale at Sears, and, look, it's not just sandwiches you can make but all sorts of good stuff"—the griddle came with its own thin cookbook of assorted hot 'n toasty recipes, which Lawrence now excitedly showed his wife—"like, see, you've got your grilled cheese sandwiches, of course, obviously you can make those, but then you've also got your tuna melts and corn bread and French toast and little pizzas and chicken potpies and blueberry pies and these quick stroganoffs and Wellingtons and salmon cream puffs—"

"*Salmon cream puffs?*" Ruth said, scandalized.

"The point is," Lawrence continued, "there's all sorts of things you can do. And I had Evelyn here pick up ingredients for a bunch of recipes when she went into town today. So if you're interested and you wanted to give this thing a whirl . . ."

"Right now?" Ruth said.

Lawrence nodded—he was so eager, so earnestly trying to please her. And so Ruth agreed, and then they were all watching as she placed the sandwich press on the kitchen counter and plugged it in—"Does it have an On switch?" she said. "How do I make it work? Oh, wait, it's getting hot. Well, I'm not ready for it to get hot *yet*. Is there a temperature control? Is it just one temperature for everything? That can't be right"—after which, following the recipe for a Fancy Fondue Toasty, she buttered some bread and put it on the griddle and topped it with piles of shredded cheese and a little mustard and a few tomato slices and another slice of bread and closed the thing and tried to latch it—"It's not latching. Why is it not latching? Is the sandwich too thick? I don't want to press down too hard. What if it breaks? This latch looks really thin and delicate. I think it's just plastic, the latch, which I'm sure is going to break. Why isn't it closing all the way? I only have a couple ingredients on there. Does this mean I can't make thicker sandwiches? What about all these recipes for thicker sandwiches? Why would they even put recipes in there if we can't use them?"—and the mood in the room seemed to sour and plummet as the sandwich cooked—"Do you smell that? Is something burning? It says cook for three minutes but maybe it's already done? How do I know if it's done if I can't see it? I don't like not knowing if it's done. When I'm cooking in a pan I can see when it's done but with this I can't see anything so how am I supposed to know if it's done?"

Then the three minutes were up, and Ruth popped open the griddle to discover, sure enough, that some of the cheese had leaked out of the sandwich pocket and was bubbling and charred and a little smoky—"I thought it was supposed to seal the edges but this isn't sealed at all. Plus the bread is sticking to the surface. How am I supposed to get it off when it's so hot? Now I have to wait until it cools all the way down to clean it, which will probably take at least an hour and I don't know how they expect you to make sandwiches for the family if you have to wait for it to cool down after every single sandwich. Plus I'm pretty sure the griddle won't fit in the dishwasher, and it probably isn't even dishwasher safe anyway. I'm gonna have to hand-wash it and so, like usual, it's just all making more work for me."

By this time Lawrence was walking out of the kitchen, quietly mumbling something about having to go check on a pasture. And Ruth stood at the sink, her back to the room, filling the basin with soapy water in advance of giving the griddle a good washing.

"Why do you do that?" Evelyn finally said, breaking a silence that had settled uncomfortably over the kitchen.

"Do what?"

"You know what."

"In fact I don't," Ruth said, then she pointed at a nearby drawer. "Sweetie, gloves." And Jack jumped off his chair and fetched her the pair of latex gloves she used while washing dishes.

"You don't have to be like that," Evelyn said. "It was just a dumb sandwich. You could have been gracious."

"Gracious," Ruth said, snapping a glove over each hand. "That's all anyone has ever wanted. Be gracious, Ruth. Accept everything and don't make a fuss, Ruth."

"That's not true."

"Maybe one of these days someone will care about what *I* want."

"That's the *only* thing people care about."

"Could've fooled me."

"Because when you don't get what you want, you act like this."

"Like what?"

"And so everybody's always tiptoeing around you, trying to keep you happy."

"You've been back for one week but apparently you know everything. How nice for you. How nice to be so perceptive, to have such a good eye."

"I don't think you should treat Dad that way. None of this is his fault."

Ruth scrubbed at the griddle, attacking the burned cheese with a little more force than was strictly necessary. The water in the sink splashed over the sides and dribbled down the cabinet fronts. She said: "How long do you intend to stay this year?"

"Not much longer," Evelyn said.

"Fine."

Evelyn stared at her mother as Ruth hunched over the sink, vigorously cleaning a griddle that appeared to be already fully clean.

"Hey, Jack," Evelyn said, "the sunset light looks amazing. How about we go paint it?"

"Okay," he said.

"Jack shouldn't be outside so much," Ruth said. "Not with his condition."

"And what condition would that be?" Evelyn said. She waited for an answer, but their mother just kept at it, silently scrubbing for so long that eventually Evelyn shook her head and grabbed her supplies and she and Jack left Ruth there in the kitchen, where she cleaned up after her own birthday party, in total silence, alone.

Outside, the evening wind blew hard and hot across the grass. Evelyn took Jack to their usual spot, where now the sun was setting behind the house, a mirror image of their morning scenes. In the distance, they could see Lawrence walking the firebreak along the south pasture.

"I was thinking," said Jack, who'd been turning over a plan in his mind ever since his mother's first visible sandwich-related frustration. "I could probably fix the latch."

"The what?"

"The latch on the sandwich maker. I could replace it so it's not so fragile. Then Mom would be able to make whatever sandwich she wants."

Evelyn smiled at him. "Sure," she said. "That would be really nice of you."

"Or maybe not replace the latch but support it with tape and superglue. Like, make it stronger. Do you think that would work?"

"I'm sure it would," she said. "I'm sure you could fix it. But listen to me, baby brother. There are some things you can't fix. If someone wants to be unhappy, there's nothing you can do to fix that. Okay?"

He nodded, unsure if this meant he should or should not go through with his plan. "Okay," he said.

"Mom has always wanted to be unhappy. She tries so hard to be unhappy." Evelyn stared at the figure of Lawrence in the distance. "She's punishing him."

"She is?"

"Yeah," Evelyn said, then looked at him. "Do you know the story about how Dad met Mom?"

Jack nodded, for he did know this story: that Lawrence was a brand-new hand on a burn crew that was working the ranches east of Wichita, and one of these ranches was the one where Ruth grew up, and they met and—as was the custom back then—went on two dates and then got married.

"Yeah, he fell in love at first sight," Evelyn said. "But did you know that it wasn't Mom he fell in love with?"

"It wasn't?"

"It was Mom's *sister*."

"Mom has a sister?"

"A younger sister. They haven't spoken in years, for obvious reasons. Dad took one look at that girl—Mom's little sister—and he fell in love, just like that. They flirted the whole week he was working there, and at the end of the week he proposed. And she said no."

"Why?"

"She had to. Her father wouldn't allow it. He had all these antique and chauvinist ideas about honor and tradition. Real sexist stuff. Apparently, a younger sister couldn't get married before the older one. It's how things were done. It's one of those dumb rules. The proposal itself was a big insult, and so to smooth things over, Dad did what he thought was the honorable thing. He proposed to the older sister instead. He married Mom, his second choice. And she's never forgiven him for it."

"How do you know all this?"

"He told me once."

They both stared at their father in the distance, watched him as he slowly walked the south pasture's fence line.

"The way he described that day," Evelyn said, "it's like he *knew*, immediately. He met this girl, and it was like their souls had met before. He's never told you this story?"

"No."

"*Our souls travel at night.* That was what he said. That our souls leave our body and wander the earth—sometimes as a bird, sometimes as a mouse. You can see what they're up to, occasionally, in your dreams. And when they meet another soul, you'll sense it if you ever meet that person in real life. You'll register that familiarity, that spark. And that's the person you're destined to be with."

"That does not sound like something Dad would say."

"He said it a long time ago, when I was a kid, younger than you. He really is a romantic, deep down. He wasn't always like this—so, you know, worn out. He's a really noble and sweet guy, at heart. But of course Mom doesn't see that."

Evelyn dipped her brush into the black paint on her palette and considered her canvas for a moment. "Did you know," she said, "that the first explorers who came to Kansas thought it was a big wasteland? They actually called it a desert. The Great American Desert. You know why?"

"No."

"It was the lack of trees. They thought if trees couldn't live here, nothing could. So they misunderstood the whole place. Which is basically what Mom does."

They watched Lawrence as he stopped and leaned against a fence post, looking out across the land, staring at the field, which was due for burning whenever the weather allowed for it.

"Those explorers," Evelyn said, "were looking for the one thing that didn't grow, and so they didn't notice all the things that did grow. It's an important lesson. If you cling too hard to what you want to see, you miss what's really there."

She brought her brush to the canvas and, with the lightest pressure, drew the figure of Lawrence Baker into her scene, a little stick of a man, a tiny presence in all that abundant country. It would become Jack's most lasting image of his father: alone, outside, looking over the land, contemplating how best to burn it all down.

THERE WAS FOOD. There was so much food, and there were volunteers serving the food. There was potato salad, egg salad, pea salad, cauliflower salad. There was noodle salad. There was green bean salad with bits of brown, dry onion. There was, at the end of it all, on the farthest edge of the table, bright and red, like the tip of a matchstick, Jell-O salad. There were sandwiches and buns, potato chips and dip, coffee, Kool-Aid. There was water. There were white plastic spoons for the coffee, powdered cream, Styrofoam cups. There were Rice Krispies treats and fudge brownies and chocolate chip brownies and cake. There were also beans. There were long banquet tables, for the most part accessible from both sides, on which the food was presented. There were people wandering into the church basement, coming in from the October chill, squinting in the fluorescent room, eyes adjusting, clusters of people, in family-shaped groups, people in ill-fitting black jackets or dresses pastel and floral, making their way down the stairs, into the basement's warmer air. There were greeters smiling, waiting, greeting. There was enjoyment of the warmth. There were people—old, inflexible, unstable—slowing the progress down the stairs. There were people wondering if it was okay to start eating, then calling for the family, Lawrence's family—his wife, Ruth, his son, Jack—because it's only right that kin should eat first. There was this church basement, walls covered in green shag carpet, decorated with drawings by the kids, Sunday school masterpieces: Jesus walking on water, Jesus walking on palm fronds, Jesus with his forehead all bloodied by a thorny hat. There was French onion dip and there was ranch dip. There were lunch meats—ham, turkey, roast beef—that were all slightly differing hues of basically the same gray. There were two lines of people, paper plates and napkins, squeezable mustard, a cereal bowl of mayonnaise, pickles. There were kids already asking for dessert. There were strips of wide white paper, not tablecloths.

There were large men at the front of the line, and wisecracks from the skinnier ones—"Leave some for me, buddy!"—plates sodden with bean juice, tipping from mounds of potato salad, near-disasters. There was red Jell-O with bananas and grapes and strawberries, and also red Jell-O without any fruit at all, plain, spotless Jell-O. There were buns, and they were white and they were wheat. There were cheeses dotted with oil from sitting out. There was chili in a Crock-Pot, volunteers serving drinks with jerking hands—wrinkled, spotted, ancient hands. There was red Kool-Aid and there was orange Kool-Aid. There were kids who were bigger than the last time they'd been seen, kids growing up so fast, and oh how time flies. There were sweet pickles and dill pickles, someone who licked the mayo knife, absentmindedly, and put the knife back while others, appalled, watched. There were cookies, chocolate chip and sugar. There was a not-too-recent photo of Lawrence, people saying, "He's in a better place now" and "His life was so cruel" and "He would have loved this meal." There was an old man saying to Jack, "The last time I saw you, you were only this big, and you helped me wash the car, do you remember?" and Jack not remembering at all. There were people saying, "All the way from Chicago, well, he would have been so happy you're here," and Jack nodding, producing the expected facial expressions, the expected polite responses, but feeling numb on the inside, just looking around, observing, registering, cataloging facts but not feeling any particular way about them. There were opinions about the Jesus-in-his-crown-of-thorns drawing: kind of violent, some said, kind of too much blood for Sunday school, don't you think? There were boys restless in stiff clothes and hard shoes, and cries from the infants, concomitant flashes of optimism: the young keep coming; humanity endures. There were mothers quietly warning children off the more suspect foods, oily, eggy, high-risk, breeding ground for salmonella and god knows what else: E. coli, campylobacter, staphylococcus. There was a prayer started by the old pastor, the sanguine and casual jeans-and-T-shirt pastor: "Our Lord and Savior, bless this food." There were heads bowed, fists clasped and pressed to foreheads. There was "Dear Lord, I know Lawrence is looking down on this meal and smiling down from heaven right now, and how do I know this, well I will tell you, it's because I got to minister to Lawrence this last week, and from that time, from our time together, I know about his faith in God, or the Bible, and I don't choose who goes to heaven but I'll bet Lawrence is there now because he said so, he said about his faith, and he knew that his time, what was left of it, here on this earth or world, in this his life, because of the cancer, was coming up, and he was so at peace with that, with the coming up of his time, or dying, so very much at peace, and he knew he was going to heaven because he believed, because Jesus was his savior or rock, because though I walk through the valley of death and all, because it's a choice, see, you fear no evil, and nobody who goes to heaven is surprised to go to heaven, nobody is like 'What am I doing in heaven?' because you choose how you live, and if you want to know where you go if you choose wrong, I will tell you, *it is hell,* so anybody goes to hell, it's not our fault, it's their fault, because they decided it for their own selves, because it's a choice, which is why Lawrence I know is smiling down on us right now and he fears no evil and let that be a lesson to all of us here today and in life, to be more like Lawrence, in that the way he chose was the right way, because he chose heaven, or the rock, amen." There were nods of agreement—silent, substantial nods—and repeated amens from the crowd, the amen-echo. There was the sound of chewing, people going for seconds. There were smoke breaks. There were memories shared, about attending Sunday school here; same pastor, same green carpet walls. There were questions about how they cleaned those walls—with a vacuum? There were thoughts about how Lawrence looked in his last days, so worn-out, so tired. There were the volunteers asking, "Who wants the rest of this turkey?" There were plans made involving changing clothes and getting out of this jacket and getting out of this tie and getting comfortable again, plans made involving the leftover ham, and beer, and sitting in lawn chairs in someone's garage, visiting, someone saying, "I don't know what else to do, so I might as well eat." There were the people who spoke to Jack before leaving, "I'm so sorry" and "God be with you," to his silent nods. There was so much still to do. There were flowers to collect and transport and food to split up and send home and decisions to be made about the money still to be collected for the cost of the service and the casket and still the matter of thanking everyone who had sent flowers and still the need to notify everyone who would want to know but does not yet know and still the financial affairs and the reading of the will and the going through the house and cataloging and collecting and tossing all the things that needed to be tossed and all those memories what will be found and what should be kept and what should be given away and what to do now that this man, this father, is gone. There were leftovers. There were dirty dishes. There was cleaning, packaging, containing, refrigeration. There was looking under the tables. There was a baby's bright red rattle, and a money clip, both put into lost and found. There was filing out, climbing up stairs, groaning at achy knees. There was the last person locking the doors, lights out, the quiet hush. There was the walk into the sun, the cold, the day, the season, the year, the next great loss, the next big shock, living and breathing and longing for all the people who were, like Lawrence, no longer there.

THE ONLY REASON a prairie is a prairie is because of fire. Without regular fire, a prairie would be slowly overrun. Trees would encroach upon the grasses—the cottonwood tree especially, a tree whose lint-like seeds can travel many miles on the Kansas wind. Easy to root and quick to grow, the cottonwood shoots up eight feet per year, a biologic sprint whose whole purpose is to squeeze in a little life before the next obliterating fire comes. And the fires have always come, sometime between early March and late August, when the air churns with electricity and heat lightning and a single strike can ignite grass that's gone summer-crisp, creating an inferno that could—in those eons before fences and fire departments—burn through a million acres. A cottonwood tree can't survive a fire; too much of its anatomy is aboveground, exposed and vulnerable. But for the bluestem grass of the Flint Hills, grass with roots that go twenty feet down, a fire is a simple thing: a haircut, a trim, a healthy prune. It could be said that the grass of the prairie evolved *with* fire, that it evolved to accommodate fire, and it does this by keeping most of itself covert, subterranean, protected and insulated and unseen.

So take away the fire, and the landscape of the prairie changes. Cottonwoods grow tall, elms start stealing the sunlight, the grasses beneath them wither and die, the trees spread out and multiply, and eventually, over the years, bit by bit, tree by tree, acre by acre, the prairie is remade.

And this is precisely what had happened to the Baker ranch.

Jack stood at the window of his old bedroom, the same window where, as a child, he looked for hours upon the swirling grasses that spread out in every direction. Now trees interrupted the horizon. The fields surrounding their old white house were now dotted with them, leaning with that particular windblown tilt, growing up crooked, nudged that way by the prairie's relentless bullying air. Lawrence had stopped burning these fields thirty years ago, and the

Flint Hills was no longer a place where wildfires rampaged freely, and thus the Baker ranch was slowly turning into woods, a perfectly rectilinear forest inscribed within the otherwise low-lying grass.

The last time Jack stood in this room, he was eighteen years old, carrying a garbage bag of clothes, and his sister's old Polaroid camera, and his mother's steel typewriter. He walked out of this room and then out of the house, well before dawn, and his father drove him in that old green Ford to a Greyhound station in Emporia, where Jack caught the express bus to Chicago. His mother had not said goodbye that morning—she would pray for his soul but would not speak to him face-to-face, for she could not countenance what he was choosing to do with his life: he was following Evelyn to Chicago, he was going to be an artist just like his big sister, and Ruth could not abide. It was her opinion that Evelyn—who was beautiful and bright and popular and could have done anything she wanted— had thrown it all away chasing some bizarre dream about being an artist. And not even a very good artist. A mediocre artist, barely making a living, never settling down, always on the move; what kind of life was that? Ruth could not understand why Jack would want to repeat his sister's grandest mistake.

So that morning, the morning he left Kansas forever, Jack walked past his mother's closed bedroom door, paused, whispered her a quiet farewell, and then took the ride to Emporia in that silent pickup truck, and the only time Lawrence spoke to him the entire trip was at the bus station, where he shook Jack's hand and said: "Well. Best of luck to you."

And that was the last time Jack heard from his father until Lawrence found him, years later, on Facebook.

In Jack's long absence, the fields around the house had turned to spotty timber. And his old bedroom had been converted into a storage room, filled, almost to the ceiling, with wilting cardboard boxes and yellowing plastic crates and stacks of what Jack could describe only as "retail detritus": jigsaw puzzles and board games still wrapped in plastic; socks still bound in their packaging; children's clothes still tagged and folded over some store's white hangers; boxes of desserts with long shelf lives—Twinkies and Nutty

Bars—many of the boxes crushed by a dozen kinds of shampoos and conditioners, in big plastic jugs, that sat atop them; and boxed electronics from multiple eras, VCRs and boom boxes and Bluetooth speakers and unopened packages of random cables (coaxial, Ethernet, USB, HDMI); also a full dumbbell set, and three yoga mats, and four baseball gloves, and a Frisbee.

Gone was the old dresser behind which he'd hidden his Dungeons & Dragons contraband, replaced now by a metal filing cabinet whose every drawer was labeled "Recipes"—this by a woman who, as far as Jack knew, never cooked anything that didn't come directly from a can or box. Jack's old twin bed remained but was obscured by piles of magazines, stacks tall and lopsided and unstable, wrinkled and creased magazines that were almost entirely home-renovation oriented. The room was so full and crowded that it was hard even to open the door, hard to walk to the window, stepping over debris, clearing a small path through the chaos.

"Mom?" Jack called out. "What's with all this stuff?"

She appeared in the doorway then, and looked gently around the room. As always, she had a tendency to not quite look him in the eye, to direct her long stare slightly to his right, at a point in space roughly half the distance between him and the floor. This is the spot she contemplated now as she mildly said: "Oh, you know. Sales."

"This is a lot of stuff, Mom."

"Clearance sales," she said. "Or garage sales. Two-for-one sales. Buy-one-get-one. I'll see something that's on sale and, you know . . . wouldn't it be such a shame to pass up a great bargain? Whatever I buy, I put it in here. In case somebody might need it."

"Who?"

"I don't know," she said, still avoiding his eyes. "Do you need it?"

"Maybe," he said, trying to be charitable. "I guess I'll have a look."

"Good," she said, nodding, turning now and shuffling out of the room. "Good," she said as she moseyed away. "Good."

She still looked basically like his memory of his mother: the same long and straight gray hair, the same clothes she'd worn back in the eighties, the same orthopedic shoes, the same souvenir T-shirts she'd picked up back when the family—this was before Jack was born—

still took vacations, to Galveston, Branson, Lake of the Ozarks, Pensacola. She moved more slowly now, more gingerly, hunched her shoulders more, dragged her feet as she walked. And in her disposition there was this new aura of detachment, a sense that she was engaging the exterior world with only a small fraction of her usable mind. It was a quality that reminded Jack of the junkies he'd encountered upon moving to Wicker Park, that look on their faces when they were seriously high: it wasn't bliss, exactly, nor was it confusion, but more like profound unavailability.

Jack had met his mother that day at the church, the same Flint Hills Calvary Church she'd taken him every week growing up, where each Sunday she'd stand and ask the congregation to pray for her son's forgiveness and redemption. He'd met her there this morning, before Lawrence's funeral, Jack getting out of his car and walking up to her and saying, "Hi, Mom," and all the people there dressed up uncomfortably for a funeral stared because here was Jack Baker, back now after so many years away.

"Good of you to come," his mother had said, not entirely looking at him. "Now c'mon. People are waiting." And that was it. She'd walked away from him, into the church. And Jack, always an expert at interpreting his mother's moods and signals, had understood immediately: he still wasn't forgiven.

Then the funeral, inside the sanctuary of Calvary Church, a converted feed-and-supply store that still smelled lightly of Purina. Jack had not stepped foot in this church since high school, but he'd spent much of his childhood here, enduring Sunday sermons about the end times, long prayers about getting right with God before it was too late, Bible study classes about the many sins of the flesh. Walking in today had triggered a sort of sense memory: Jack felt immediately guilty, embarrassed, under suspicion, wicked, watched.

He and his mother were ushered to the front pew—there were only eight pews in the sanctuary, which could hold maybe fifty people max; Jack was surprised that it was so much smaller than his memory of it—and during the service, Jack stared at that lacquered black coffin up near the pulpit and wondered why his father had not once mentioned, in all their furious arguing these last few years, that he was ill. Ruth had asked for a closed coffin, owing to the wasting away of Lawrence's body, she said, his face especially, sunken and hollow. "He didn't look like himself anymore," Ruth told many, many well-wishers during the reception potluck. "I didn't think people would want to remember him like that," she said, and these people took her hand and patted her on the shoulder and said, "Of course, of course. I understand." Jack observed all of this sort of neutrally, dispassionately; he didn't know or remember anyone at the funeral, and so he mostly watched his mother have basically the same conversation over and over, which started when someone would ask, "How are you holding up, Ruth?" and she'd say, "Oh, it's been hard going lately," and she'd talk about how the last few weeks had been especially tough but Lawrence was in so much pain and he was ready to go be with God and was now in a better place, finishing up when she explained the thing about the closed coffin and they told her to call if she needed anything, anything at all. Then after the interaction ran its course, she'd look around and find someone new and walk up to them and they'd say, "How are you holding up, Ruth?" and she'd say, "Oh, it's been hard going lately," and the whole thing was repeated, a ritual that never seemed to get old for Jack's mother, who, as soon as each conversation ended, would look around the room for someone else to have it with again.

Jack made his careful way back through the boxes now, stepping over the haphazard piles that had overtaken his old bedroom, into the hallway, then downstairs, noting how so little in the house had changed—the same old photographs, and the same old furniture, in all the same old places. In the living room, the same couch that Lawrence had retreated to all those years ago, now newly upholstered but still bearing that same familiar large divot where his father habitually sat.

In the kitchen, his mother stood at the sink, staring out the window, her back to the room. The kitchen looked just as it had when Jack was a child, save for the obvious exception of the computer that sat upon the table, an old beige PC, a mouse grimy from use, a keyboard with a film of dust atop the parts that Lawrence apparently never used—the function keys, the numeric keypad—the rest of the keys kept clean by his father's busy fingertips.

"I thought it was a lovely service," Ruth said, "didn't you?"

"Yes," Jack said, "lovely."

"And so many people. Very good turnout. Though I could not help but notice that the Pattersons did not attend. That woman has always had it out for me."

"I don't know who that is."

"Everyone else seemed very happy to see me, don't you think? Don't you think they were happy to see me?"

"Sure, Mom."

"Very happy," she said, nodding. Next to her, on the counter, were Tupperware containers full of food that people had been dropping off all day: potato salads and ham sandwiches and meat loafs.

Jack stared at the computer and imagined his father sitting there, ranting furiously upon it. "So this is where it all happened," he said.

"Where what happened?" his mother said, not turning around.

"All of Dad's time on the computer, on Facebook. It's just weird to think that it all happened right here."

"Is that what he was doing on that thing? Facebook?"

"Mom, he was obsessed with it."

"Oh," she said. "I guess I never asked."

"He was posting a dozen times a day."

"About what?"

"Mostly nonsense. Crazy internet theories. Do you believe the stuff he believed?"

"What stuff?"

"About Ebola. Fluoride. The Mayan apocalypse."

"I don't know what any of that means, dear."

"All those conspiracies. All those diatribes about shadowy evil people controlling the world."

"I guess he never mentioned it."

"Really?" Jack said. "I find that hard to believe."

"I suppose he was a private man."

"He couldn't shut up about it online. He seriously never talked about this?"

"Never."

It was not the first time that Jack felt confounded by the things his father could keep hidden. There was that story Evelyn had told, about a time when Lawrence was young—no older than Jack was the morning he left for Chicago—when he discovered some beautiful girl at a ranch outside Wichita and fell in instant love. No, the version of his father that Jack had known was the inscrutable one. The one who lived as the grasses of the Flint Hills lived, sending all their life and energy and pizzazz deep underground, keeping their largest self hidden and protected and unseen. Lawrence Baker was a man who neatly matched his landscape.

Jack said: "Did he ever mention me?"

"Oh, a few times, I suppose."

"And what did he say?"

"That you were doing well."

"That's it?"

"Yes."

"And did you ever want to know more?"

"What else was there to know? You were doing well."

"I have a family. A wife, a son."

"And where are they today?"

"I told them not to come."

"I see."

"I also teach at a university. I'm an artist."

"Oh, yes, Lawrence did show me some pictures. Of your art. Very odd. Black swirls and splotches and drips and such. Very strange."

"He must have found them online."

"Photographs without a camera. Pictures of nothing. This is the reason you abandoned your home?"

She continued her long stare out the window, toward the north pasture, at all those young and crooked trees. Jack sat down on one of the chairs at the kitchen table, but not the chair in front of the computer. That chair felt, somehow, off-limits. He said: "How long was Dad sick?"

"Oh, I guess a few years now. But he was only *really* sick the last few months or so."

"What happened?"

"Cancer, of course. It started in the lungs. The doctors said it was probably from being around all those fires his whole life."

"When did they find it?"

"I suppose it was, let's see, in 2008? Yes. That winter."

"Huh," Jack said. "That's when he joined Facebook."

"Is that so?" She wet a dishrag and began wiping down counters that looked to be already clean. "The doctors started him on chemo then."

"He didn't mention that," Jack said. "Not to me, anyway."

In his last correspondence with his father, Jack had argued with the man about, of all things, algorithms, an argument that felt really important at the time but rather less so now; death had a way of recasting all other subjects as petty in comparison. Jack had tried to persuade his father that various algorithms were nudging him and influencing him, a task that turned out to be pretty difficult because of course algorithms were most successfully manipulative when users were unaware of their manipulation. Thus the algorithms themselves aspired to total invisibility. You could sometimes sense their nudging, but you could never actually see *them*. The algorithms were a black box, their code private, their inner workings a trade secret.

Why, Jack wondered, had Lawrence sought him out right at the moment of the cancer diagnosis? And why then never mention the cancer? Why stay silent when the cancer got worse? Why type so much fury online but never once talk about it in real life? These were questions Jack could not now, nor ever, answer—for his father was gone, in the ground, in a coffin, the ultimate black box.

"I'm sorry, Mom," Jack said. "That must have been hard."

She nodded and continued wiping the counter, pressing hard on this one spot and rubbing at it, and it seemed for a moment that the conversation was over until his mother said: "It really was such bad timing. He had just stripped that barn over at the Winslow ranch. Now I have all this lumber and not the faintest clue what to do with it."

"Stripped the barn? What do you mean?"

"Oh, I'll show you."

She dried her hands and shuffled out the front door and led him outside, into the bright chilly October day, around to the back side of the house, where, hidden from the road, there sat a pyramid-shaped pile of wooden planks—weather-beaten, scratched and nicked, their once-red paint now chipped and faded.

"What is this?" Jack said.

"It's how we've been paying the bills."

"I don't understand."

"Well, so many of the ranches have been sold off these last few years. The prairie is all being bought up by these big companies, these outfits in Texas. They're paying millions for all the rangeland in the Flint Hills. But they don't want the houses. So the houses are split off and sold separately, and I know for a fact that folks around here would love to raise their families in those nice old ranch houses, but they can't afford it. They're outbid every time."

"Who's outbidding them?"

"City people, mostly, buying vacation homes. They come out here once a month talking about how it's so nice to *get away from it all.* From Kansas City, St. Louis, Wichita. So just about every acre in the county has now been bought by someone who doesn't live in the county. We'd love to keep all that land, but we can't compete with their money."

"But that still doesn't explain the wood."

"Oh, right. Well, the whole situation made Lawrence so ticked off that he didn't feel the least bit bad going to those ranches when no one was there and stripping the barns. Nobody was even using the barns anyway, not anymore. So he stripped them all the way down to their studs."

"Dad was stealing wood? Why?"

"He'd strip the barns and then auction the lumber on the internet. He called it 'authentic reclaimed barnwood from America's heartland.' It sold real well."

"Oh," Jack said, slumping as he imagined all the new businesses in Wicker Park with their "rustic chic" aesthetic, and his own new condo in the Shipworks with its barnwood accent wall, and he nodded and said, "Yeah," feeling just wretched. "I'll bet this is pretty popular."

"Though we could never figure out *why*," she said. "City folks seem to love it. Can you explain that?"

Jack suddenly wondered what a place like Wicker Park would look like from this vantage, from the Flint Hills of Kansas, what it would look like to his mother, and he decided, staring forlornly at this pile of wood—wood that was, to be honest, really excellently distressed and evocative—that his home in Chicago would look *insatiable*. It would look like a place that plundered all the world's money and capital and jobs and people while places like the Flint Hills were catastrophically emptied. Standing here, Jack imagined that Wicker Park would seem, to the people of the prairie, like a place that harvested their work, harvested their money, harvested their promising children, harvested their land, even harvested the corpses of their very homes, using the remains to decorate the fancy walls of fancy people who congratulated themselves for recycling.

"No, Mom," Jack said. "I can't explain it."

She nodded and, still staring at a point somewhere to the right of him, said, "*Well*" with that particular tone that signaled finality, that they were done now. "I won't keep you," she said. "You probably best be getting back to your family."

"But I just got here."

"I'm sure you're busy," she said. "Thanks for the visit," waving goodbye while still looking at the ground.

"Really?" Jack said. "That's it?"

"You can have a look through your dad's stuff, if you want, before I get rid of it."

"That's all you have to say?"

"I have a lot to do, Jack. I gotta clean up that basement, and I gotta write thank-you notes to everyone who sent flowers, and I gotta do all that paperwork, the will and the bank accounts and the retirement nonsense, getting it all straightened out. You'd think the government would make it easy, but no, nuh-uh, no way."

"Do you want some help?"

"No. I'll take care of it myself. Alone. As always."

She turned now and shuffled away from him, and Jack almost had to laugh, his mother's obstinance was so absurd. He'd known enough not to expect a prodigal welcome, of course, but he'd honestly been hoping for more than this, this bullheaded indifference. It reminded him of how she'd refused to come out of her bedroom the morning he left for Chicago. She had, in all these years, not changed a bit.

"You still can't forgive me, can you?" Jack called to her. "After all this time?"

His mother stopped then, and, for a moment, seemed to stare out at the distance, at the north pasture. And then she turned around and, for the first time all day, looked him right in the eye, smiled a sad smile, tilted her head.

"You know those pictures you make?" she said. "Those photographs of nothing?"

"Yes."

"They're not photographs of nothing. They're photographs of *her*."

Then she broke off her stare and continued the slow trudge back into the house, Jack watching her as she went, until she disappeared around a corner and then he too was looking out into the north pasture, at the bare trees growing crookedly in the field, some of them tilting like old headstones, others curling out of the ground, thick trunks that bent toward him like arms that were reaching for help.

I T WAS EVELYN who taught Jack how to see. It was his big sister who taught him that how you see the world depends in large part on what you intend to do with it. When Evelyn looked at the swirling grass of a pasture, she saw it in terms of color and light and texture and depth and mood. But when their father looked at the same pasture, he did not see it as she did. What he saw, instead, was *fuel*. That was how he spoke of it—especially during spring fire season—in the strange vocabulary of a burn boss. He'd look out at the pasture, and it wasn't even a pasture to him anymore; now it was a *burn unit*. And all the many plants growing in that burn unit—plants that the rest of the year he would routinely identify as bluestem grass and switch grass and cordgrass and larkspur and wild sage and milkweed and clover and spiderwort and parsley and aster and echinacea and redroot— all of these individuals became, in the spring, a collective: the *fuel load*. And the two big important variables were, first, how flammable this fuel was and, second, how the fuel was distributed, its architecture. There was what he called the *surface fuel*, the grasses and visible leaf and needle clutter, the dead branches, all the stuff you could see; above that was the *crown fuel*, the leaves living in the canopy made by occasional spindly shrubs or the rare tree; and beneath it all was the *ground fuel*, the decomposed or decaying organic matter atop the soil, the rotted wood, the leaf mold, the roots, the peat, the duff.

It was this layer, the hidden layer, that could most strongly quicken a fire, or most easily choke it out. If the ground fuel had been packed down by a wet spring—if thunderstorms came early, or winter snows stayed late—then the moisture would collect in this layer and snuff the fire from below.

But this year's spring had not been wet. It had been a hot and dry spring, a spring of arid southerly wind and relentless sun, which tended to crisp this underlayer to pure kindling. Jack could hear it crunch under his shoes.

"It's the stuff you can't see that burns the hottest," his father said, frowning.

They were walking through the south pasture on the morning of its burn, Lawrence having decided to press forward with his own fires despite what he called the "ongoing wind problem." His plan was to burn the south pasture that day and the north pasture the next, as test runs, to evaluate on this land whether the conditions were safe enough to burn on the land of others.

The day of a fire was, for Jack, a thrill. His father's crew would come out—there were usually eight of them, nearby ranchers who worked part-time in the spring doing burns—and together they'd go through the day's specific fire plan. First the ignition team would establish how the fire would be set, using either propane torches or road flares or, as today, these contraptions known as drip torches, which were small canisters with thin metal nozzles, filled with some kind of gasoline blend. At the tip of the nozzle was a wick, and when the wick was lit and the guys tipped the canister upside down, it created a thin waterfall of pure liquid fire, which was, of course, *amazing,* and it sent Jack into long daydreams about maybe becoming a drip torch operator himself one day. This job was much better than the other available job, that of the spotter. Guys who were spotters kept an eye out for embers floating over the firebreaks, embers that could ignite uncontrolled spot fires outside the burn unit. It was a boring job because Lawrence's burns were famously uneventful.

The way to create the least dangerous, least risky fire possible was to set what was called a *backfire,* a fire that moved against the prevailing wind—grass as accelerator, wind as brakes. If these two forces were balanced correctly, it resulted in a low, slow, cool fire that crept over the land in long, thin ribbons. But the problem today— indeed, the problem this whole spring—was that the wind was too strong, too gusty, would press too hard against the fire, stopping its spread.

"We just gotta hope the fuel is flammable enough," Lawrence said, looking dubiously into the sky after one particularly heavy gust. "Otherwise this fire's going nowhere."

The other method would have been to start a *headfire,* a fire that moved in the same direction as the wind, a fire fed by grass and wind at once, a hot and fast fire of the type that painters tended to portray in their dramatic depictions of prairie fires, those great blazing infernos. But most burns did not actually look like this. Most burns were short and lackadaisical and well-behaved.

"See that?" Lawrence said as he pointed to a spot in the pasture where the thick vegetation gave way to bare soil, patches of grass like small islands in the dirt. "That's what we call a large horizontal fuel discontinuity. Gonna need a new ignition point right there."

Jack nodded as if to concur. "Yeah," he said, "okay."

Nearby, Evelyn was photographing the pasture with a Polaroid camera. She took tight shots of the grass where it was most tangled and knotted—these images were meant to evoke nature's chaos, she said—then took wider photos of the broad, windswept landscape—these images evoking nature's symmetry. That was the paradox of grass, she told Jack: what was monolithic from afar was infinitely varied and complicated once you got up close.

Evelyn found the spectacle of a fire delightful. She walked behind the ignition crew and took pictures during these daytime fires. But her favorite thing was a nighttime blaze, when she sat with her acrylics and canvases watching from a nearby field, painting evocative landscapes lit whitely from above by the moon and orangely from below by strings of flame snaking over the land's soft curves.

It amused Lawrence that his job—which, to him, was as prosaic as any old job—was, to his daughter, so magical. It amused him as few things seemed to amuse him. He grinned as she danced behind them, looking through the Polaroid, the camera occasionally clacking and ejecting another photo.

"I don't know what you think is so interesting about all this," he said.

"Everything!" she said, spreading her arms dramatically wide. "Fire! It's so elemental, so prehistoric. It's renewing, it's life-giving. It consumes what's dead, makes way for the next generation. Don't you find the symbolism delicious? Don't you find it all so beautiful?"

"It's just work, Evie," he said.

"*It's just work, Evie,*" she said in comic mockery of his deep, even voice. "Listen, just because it's work doesn't mean it's not also beautiful."

"If you say so."

"I do say so."

"Okay," he said, nodding at her, grinning.

Then Lawrence seemed to remember that Jack was there. "I think it's time for you to get going," he said.

And so Jack ran back to the house, where, in the living room, he found his mother, in her pink robe, standing at the south-facing window, watching.

"Why is Evelyn taking pictures of grass?" she said.

"The symbolism."

"The *symbolism*?" she said, making a face—she could become exasperated so quickly, so easily. "She always has to fancy everything up. It's just a field. It's just grass."

They watched from the window as, outside, the ignition crew got into position, and the spotters took their places at the firebreaks, and Lawrence, still chatting with Evelyn, made this slight motion with his head, a nod in the direction of the pasture, which Jack recognized as the *Well, I guess I ought to be going* gesture his father had used countless times when excusing himself from a room (Lawrence's most frequent disposition when he was around the house could probably be best described as *just-about-to-leave*), but as he began walking away, Evelyn tugged at his sleeve, and he stopped and looked at her, and she moved in close to him and spun the camera around in her hand and lifted it up so that it was pointed backward at the two of them and they pressed tightly together and Jack imagined his sister saying "Smile!" as she took the picture—even at this distance he could still see the white pop of the flash—after which Lawrence and Evelyn stayed standing there like that, squeezed together, looking down at the photo, waiting for it to develop.

Evelyn was leaning her cheek on his shoulder, a pose of unguarded friendliness and affection, and Jack was pretty sure he had never seen his father show anyone the kind of warmth he was showing

Evelyn right now, simply standing there, being still, not pulling away, not maneuvering to escape.

Next to him, Jack could feel a mood settle over his mother. He could often sense these moods even when the two of them were in separate rooms, how Ruth's displeasure changed the whole frequency of the house. But up close like this, it felt like a kind of physical heat.

"The way he dotes on her," she said, jaw tightening. "The rest of us may as well be dead." And then she walked quietly to her bedroom and closed the door behind her. Jack heard the squeak of springs as she settled into her twin bed. Then he heard the television click on, followed by the manic cheers of a game show audience.

He knew he should go to her right now. He knew that the correct thing to do was go into her room and sit at the foot of her bed and be silent and wait like that until she felt like speaking, to offer a wordless display of fidelity and sacrifice and support, and then to give her—when she eventually began talking—a convenient object at which to direct her scorn: himself. Because even though his father was an all around tougher guy than Jack was, it was also true that his father could not bear Ruth's scorn as well as Jack could. And in this one way, Jack was much tougher, because he could sit there within the vortex of Ruth's resentment and just tolerate it.

But Jack didn't want to do that. He didn't want to go to her room. He wanted to see a fire. It was a dumb, boyish impulse: this desire to watch things burn. He raced upstairs to observe it all, kneeling at his bedroom window.

The wind that day blew out of the south, and so the ignition team began on the pasture's northern edge. From his vantage on the second floor, Jack could see the wicks of the torches being lit, could see the first drips of fire spilled onto the grass, could see the first flames leap into the air—but he did not see smoke.

During a typical fire, the first smoke that appeared would be white—a bright and almost translucent gentle fog that drifted into the air if conditions were favorable, if the breeze was not too strong and the ground was appropriately moist. White smoke was mostly not smoke at all—it was mostly water, mostly steam boiled out of the ground, which was necessary before the land would actually ignite. That was followed by the first real flames, which produced almost no smoke at all. The real smoke came later, when the grass began smoldering, when the fire slowly rolled over the pasture, consuming it with placid, but steadfast, intent. Those were the fires that produced the broad gray-brown plumes that, on the plains, could be seen for miles.

But today was not such a day. Today the ignition crew dripped their torches and the fire slicked across the grass and everyone had to leap back as the fire flared up in great bursts that had no smoke at all, so efficiently and hotly did the grass burn. It was the kindling of the ground fuel that did it, the crunchy dry underlayer making the ground a kind of tempestuous bomb that burned bright and wild and tall and quick. Too quick, it turned out: as soon as the fire caught, the wind knocked it back toward the ignition team, who retreated to avoid being singed. And then the fire spread in random, unpredictable ways, some fronts extinguished quickly by the wind, others driven by momentary gusts into strange directions, moving at right angles to the wind, as if trying to flank it, creating de facto mini headfires that ripped through the grass back at the crew, who had to retreat once more.

The team proceeded slowly that day, in fits and starts. A burn that usually looked so elegant—like a single ripple of fire that crept quietly over the land—was, today, a patchwork, the flames raging in one direction, dying in others, the ignition crew advancing and withdrawing. Through it all, Lawrence watched from the firebreak, arms crossed, impassive, stoic as ever, studying the whole uncooperative mess. Evelyn stood next to him. She had stopped taking pictures.

It was maybe an hour of watching this before Jack heard movement in the house, the opening of a door, then footsteps climbing the stairs, and then his mother was there with him. She surveyed the room, the piles Evelyn had made—his sister had fully colonized the space, which was now filled with her clothing and paints and canvases and supplies. Then Ruth looked at the walls, at the posters on the walls, the de Kooning and the Rothko, *American Gothic*. It might have been the first time she'd seen the posters, as she'd been avoiding this room since Evelyn had taken up temporary residence here.

"You're not allowed to go outside with her anymore," she said. She wasn't looking at Jack, exactly, but at the window behind him. "No more mornings together," she said. "No more painting. Ever."

"But," he said, standing up, "*why*?"

"She's a bad influence on you."

"No she's not!" he said, louder and more passionate than he'd intended. His mother squinted at him, crossed her arms, and he tried to calm himself, bring the volume down. "She's teaching me things."

"Bad things."

"But I like it, though. You don't understand—"

"No, *you* don't understand. You don't know *anything*, Jack. You can't see how she's manipulating you."

"No she isn't."

"How she's turning you against me."

"We only talk about art."

"Oh, *art*. Okay, right," she said with a laugh. "That's exactly what I mean. My god, she has you so fooled. She has everyone so fooled."

"It's not like that," Jack said.

"What has all her *art* ever gotten her? Huh? She moves from town to town. No job, no family. You don't watch out, you're going to end up just like her. A waste. An embarrassment."

"She's not an embarrassment! She's . . . she's . . ."—he searched for the right word—"*brave*!" he said finally. "Which is more than I can say for *you*!"

The air seemed to suck out of the room as soon as he said it. "I'm sorry!" he said almost right away, and he slumped over and looked at the floor, a posture of total supplication.

His mother stared at him, silent, shocked. "Well I just don't know about you," she finally said.

"I didn't mean it."

"This is exactly what I was afraid of."

"I'm really sorry."

"No more Evelyn, you hear me? You don't need any more of that girl's influence."

His mother stood over him for a moment, hands on her hips. It was not like Jack to be at all disagreeable with her, and she probably took his mutiny as evidence of Evelyn's deep imprint upon him.

"These posters," she said, "I want you to take them down. All of them."

"But—"

"Take them down *now*."

And so Jack stood up, slowly, showing his displeasure more obviously than he would usually dare. He went to *American Gothic*—Evelyn had tacked it to the wall, and he tried to pull out one of the bottommost tacks but found that he couldn't get his fingernail underneath it, not without damaging the poster. And so he wiggled the tack back and forth hoping to gently pry it free, and he did this until his mother said "Oh my *god*" and strode over and grabbed the top edge of the poster and with a quick and angry jerk ripped it down. Then she began pulling at the other posters, tearing and shredding them, and she kept going like that until all the posters were ripped to ribbons at her feet.

Evelyn found him there some time later, found him sitting cross-legged over the remains of *American Gothic,* softly crying. She came in smelling of charcoal, the front of her dress smeared with ash. She saw his tears, saw the pile of torn paper, saw how all the room's posters had been removed, and she must have deduced the rest. She sat down cross-legged next to him and placed a palm on his back.

"I want you to listen to me very carefully," she said. "I know it doesn't seem possible now, but this is all going to pass. Okay? You're going to come out of this and you're going to be fine."

He nodded but did not speak. He was holding his face in his hands, partly to catch the tears, and partly to hide the fact of his crying. He always felt guilty when he was crying, guilty that his crying demanded attention, and he was a child uncomfortable making demands or enduring attention.

"Let me show you something," Evelyn said. She pulled from her backpack a stack of Polaroids and began shuffling through them. "Here it is," she said. "I just took this. Look."

It was a photo of charred and smoking ground, dirt and ash everywhere, except, in the middle of it all, a bundle of flowers, which stood strong and untouched. Jack recognized the plant as redroot, or, as Evelyn liked to call it, wild snowball: about three feet tall, bushy white flowers, the only living thing in all that soot.

"Isn't this amazing?" she said. "The fire burned everything else but spared this *one flower*. The fire went right around it. Everything else died, but this one thing lived. Isn't that *incredible*?"

"I guess," Jack said, wiping his nose.

"Actually it's more than incredible. It's a *miracle*!"

"Okay."

"Oh you have to say it with waaaaay more feeling than that."

"What?"

"A miracle is a sacred thing, Jack. You have to be thankful for it. You have to acknowledge it properly, with awe and gratitude. You have to say it like you mean it. C'mon. It's a miracle!"

"It's a miracle."

"It's a miracle!" she said, arms raised into the air.

"It's a miracle!"

"It's a miracle!"

"*It's a miracle!*" he said, arms up, leaping to his feet.

"There you go."

He smiled. He could feel the tears drawing back now. Evelyn seemed to have that effect on him; her brightness was so contagious.

"And right now?" she said. "This flower is *you*."

"It is?"

"Yes. I know you feel like the fire is all around you. And I know it feels hopeless. But, trust me, it's not hopeless. You'll come out on the other side. It'll pass. You'll survive."

He nodded at her. "Okay," he said.

"You will. I know it. They'll see—Mom, Dad, everyone—they'll see what a miracle you are."

"Thank you."

"Also? Don't worry about the posters," she said. "It's only paper."

She picked up a handful of shredded *American Gothic* and flung the pieces into the air. "Who gives a shit about paper?"

He laughed as he watched the scraps flutter to the ground.

"Now let's get cleaned up and go downstairs and try to make nice with Mom."

That night, Ruth Baker was at her most terrifying—which is to say she was silent. All four of them sat at the kitchen table eating the beef chili that Ruth had heated up directly out of the can. None of them said a word. And this was maybe worse than when Ruth was in a mood of high public complaint, because it meant she was seething. It meant a punishment was brewing. And in the quiet moments before the punishment was revealed, it was difficult to achieve normal, unburdened conversation. And so they all sat there eating—Jack amazed at how loud eating actually was, with all the clinking of spoons on bowls and the gloppy chewing and the awful wet swallowing, amazed both at the high volume and the fact that under normal dinner circumstances nobody even noticed it—until Ruth, unprompted, finally spoke: "Lawrence will be leaving," she said, "tomorrow."

All heads popped up. Lawrence stopped chewing and looked at her, swallowed, dabbed his mouth with a napkin, and said with a strange formality: "Yes. I am going to take the crew back south and get the burns going."

"I thought it was too windy," Evelyn said.

"I suppose you could say that I have"—he glanced at Ruth, who kept her eyes fixed on her chili—"reevaluated," he said.

Which meant he'd been *instructed*. He'd been told to leave. There had been, at some point tonight, a conversation. Jack never knew what his parents talked about during these conversations, just that afterward they were tense and guarded, as defensive as the copper-heads he occasionally found in the grass, all silent potential deadly threat.

"But first I need to finish the burn here," Lawrence said. "Couldn't get it done today."

"When?" Evelyn said.

"Tonight."

"*Tonight?*" Evelyn said in a rush of excitement. "Can I watch?"

"Well," Lawrence said, glancing up at his wife, "I don't see why not," which drew a loud and immediate chuff from Ruth.

"We did not agree to that," she said.

"I just want to paint it," Evelyn said.

"I don't believe I was talking to you," Ruth said. Then quietly, measuredly, she said to her husband: "Come with me, please."

And the two of them went outside, and the way Lawrence followed her, slouched over, in this posture of pure defeat, made Jack feel a little bolt of hatred for him, that a man so tall and proud and honorable could be brought so low. It made him wish his parents had never met each other, whatever the consequences to his own existence.

"It's gonna be some night," Evelyn said, rolling her eyes. Then she wandered off, upstairs, to her room.

Jack stayed in the kitchen. He transferred the leftover chili to Tupperware, put it in the refrigerator, dumped everyone's uneaten portions into the trash, tied up the trash bag, took it out to the bins behind the house, shut the bins tight to keep out interested raccoons and coyotes, then washed all the dirty dishes, set them in the drying rack, wiped down the table and the sink, went into his parents' bedroom, laid out his mother's pink robe on her bed, turned the television to CBS, and waited for her there.

It was his experience that when his mother was angry, her anger tended to dissolve if he could do as much as possible to smooth her path here—robed, in bed, in front of the TV.

He waited. Outside, her voice grew to a desperate crescendo, and then she was coming back into the house: slammed door, hard footsteps into the kitchen, a brief silent pause before moderately lighter footsteps into the bedroom, where she stopped at the door and considered the scene: her robe, Jack waiting for her cross-legged on the floor, *Newhart* at a medium volume on the television.

"Thank you," she said.

"You're welcome."

Then she wrapped herself up in her robe and they sat together wordlessly until the end of the episode, at which point she finally broke her silence. "Tell your sister she can go outside and paint."

Jack, his face turned away from his mother, smiled. He wouldn't have smiled if she could see him, wouldn't want her to know how much he desired this, this concession, this possible warming of mother-daughter relations, because it meant that maybe Evelyn could stay, for maybe a few days longer, and so while Ruth explained to Jack that she'd changed her mind, that Evelyn could go watch the fire, tonight, north pasture, Jack was nodding at her but also imagining more mornings with his sister, out in the hills, greeting the dawn with her, more stories about the big outside world, the people she'd met, the adventures she'd had, more time with her and all her daily miracles.

"Go on," Ruth said. "Tell your sister, then come right back."

And so Jack did exactly that, ran up the stairs and found Evelyn, who was already dressed in her typical outdoor uniform—her polka-dot dress, her stained white sneakers, her backpack full of supplies—and she hugged him when he told her the news.

"I suppose I have you to thank for this sudden change in mood?" she said, her arms squeezing him tight.

"Maybe," he said, grinning.

She gathered all her supplies, bounded down the stairs. He followed her to the front porch and was watching her go out into the night when she spun around and looked back at him, smiled, said: "You know, I wish we could have grown up together." Then she waved, and he waved back, and she jogged off into the howling darkness.

And he was feeling really excellent about all this, how he'd managed the situation so well. He walked back into his mother's room and sat again on the floor next to her bed all aglow with possibility.

The next hour of *Cagney & Lacey* would be, he would later recall, the last hour of cheer he ever felt in that house.

He would, much later, think that if he'd acted sooner and not sat in the warmth of his dumb accomplishment—

or if he'd gone to his mother earlier in the day—

if he'd let her vent at him and not at his father—

if they'd kept to the original schedule and never done a night fire in the first place—

or if he'd just *listened* more carefully—

All of this not yet dawning on him as *Cagney & Lacey* ended and the local news began—the top story, as usual, being the drought and the wind—and Jack stood up and stretched and moseyed over to look out the bedroom window at the south pasture, made binoculars out of his hands and pressed them against the glass and looked out into the night and saw, strangely, nothing. No activity at all in the south pasture.

And yet he'd heard the voices of the fire team, heard all their trucks arrive during the show.

"Where is everyone?" he said.

"What do you mean?" his mother said.

"I don't see them. Where are they?"

"In the north pasture, silly."

Jack looked at his mother then, a quiver of dread in his belly. "You said Evelyn should *watch* from the north pasture."

"No," she said, "I told you they were *burning* the north pasture."

And they stared at each other for a moment, a terrible knowledge growing between them.

"Where is Evelyn?" she said. But already he was sprinting out the door, out of the house, running barefoot over the sharp rocks of the gravel driveway but not even feeling them, not when he saw, at the north pasture's firebreak, his father and the rest of the ignition team all holding road flares, which they right now snapped, furious shots of red bursting into the night, and Jack screamed at them to stop—but it was no use. They could not hear him over the raging wind, and Jack's small legs could not carry him fast enough to reach them before those flares were thrown, one by one, into the field, gentle parabolas in the sky.

Evelyn could not have known what was happening. Even if she'd seen the ignition team, from the middle of that immense field—as big as a baseball stadium—and at night, and on the plains, where distances were distended and strange, she couldn't have understood what they were about to do. She probably would have assumed they were once again setting a backfire at the south pasture. She would not have known that Lawrence had changed the plan, that his struggle with the day's earlier burn had made him decide in favor of a headfire tonight, to work with the wind instead of fighting against it, to stand outside the field and ignite it, at a distance, with flares, and to arrange his spotters to look for firebrands shooting out of the pasture, so that when the fire's light erupted, they were focused on the field's outskirts, not the field's middle, where they might have made out, in the distance, a small but distinct pop of color: a polka-dot dress.

When the flares landed in that dried and brittle grass, the flames erupted immediately, and then, given oxygen and momentum by the howling wind, the fire seemed to gather up and explode, and all at once it was an enormous wave, ten feet tall and raging northward faster than anyone could possibly move, Jack sprinting toward the ignition team and then right past them, screaming incoherently and hearing his father yell his name but he did not stop, not even when he reached the pasture and the ground was crisp and hot and glowing, still he ran, and what came to him as he watched the fire rushing farther and farther away was his sister's Polaroid picture, the image of that single surviving flower, and suddenly he was convinced that it was a sign, it was fate that she'd photographed that flower, but she hadn't properly understood it—that miraculous wildflower wasn't him; it was *her*. And the fire would pass right by her, and he'd find her untouched, just as she had found that flower—he was sure of this as he kept running, as he heard big footsteps closing in behind him, as his feet ignited in agony, he was waiting to see her emerge from the darkness, blackened but astonishingly alive, and he was screaming with what, to those who chased him, sounded like actual wonder and belief and awe, screaming over and over the psalm that his sister had taught him: "It's a miracle! It's a miracle! It's a miracle!"

THE HUMAN SOUL OUT WANDERING AS A MOUSE

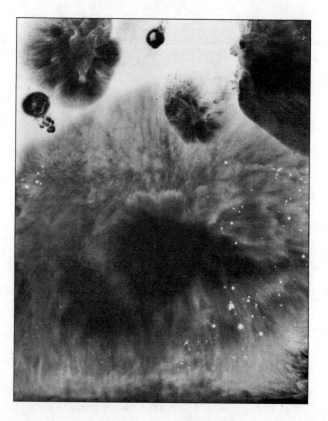

T HE FIRST PAYING JOB that Elizabeth ever had was the job given
to her by Dr. Otto Sanborne her first year in college, where
her basic responsibility was to engage in intimate and revealing conversations with random guys to see which of those guys
fell in love with her. The academic paper that eventually emerged
from this research—entitled, dryly, "The Empirical Construction
of Relational Intimacy: A Practical Methodology"—was received
with much mirth in the mainstream press, and Sanborne was interviewed on a daytime talk show, where his work was given a much
more scintillating name: it was, they said, the Love-at-First-Sight
Script. What Sanborne had done was to rigorously test various combinations of roughly a hundred probing questions to settle upon the
ten key questions that, when answered in a very specific order, could
unlock affection and even love between two otherwise total strangers. Thus Elizabeth's job: to go to the psychology department every
weekday during that first autumn in college and, three or four times
per day, be fallen in love with.

The men she interviewed were all volunteers, all college-aged,
heterosexual, single, who, on their intake forms, expressed a strong
interest in dating. Her conversations with them began with a simple
set of instructions that she (pretending to be a test subject herself)
would read aloud, informing her partner that she was going to ask
a series of questions of a personal nature and it was very important
that they both answer these questions thoroughly and honestly, after
which she'd begin the interview.

"On a scale of one to ten, how much did your parents love you?"

This was the question that, according to Sanborne's research, most
effectively lubricated the rest of the conversation; asking subjects to
assess how they had been fundamentally cared for in the past made
them more open to the possibility of a new and even better love in
the present. This was why the question was presented as a scale,

because it's well known in psychology that when asked to describe anything about themselves on a scale of one to ten, people almost never choose "one" or "ten," so even subjects with the most happy and loving childhoods would probably pick "nine," which implied that there was still room for improvement, which was the purpose of the question: to get them thinking about how they could be more fully and satisfyingly loved right now.

Plus it was Sanborne's theory that when subjects described their childhoods, they were, during the time they accessed and recalled and chronicled those memories, also reliving the memories and sort of *inhabiting* the child they used to be. There was, after all, a certain module in the brain that did not meaningfully distinguish between the experience of a thing in the present and the memory of that thing in the past—it was this same process that, for example, was often overpowering and uninhibited in people suffering from PTSD, who could not remember a traumatic moment without feeling they were reliving that moment—and so when a subject was talking about how he was loved as a child, there was part of his mind that had to *become that child* in order to accurately describe it. He had to simulate and re-create that child's consciousness within his adult mind, which primed him to feel, in this moment, with Elizabeth, exactly as that child felt in the past: needy and vulnerable. All people have within them—sometimes close to the surface, sometimes buried way down deep—the ghost of that defenseless child still haunting them, and Sanborne's first prompt was meant to summon it.

This was then reinforced via the second prompt—"Describe the first object you ever loved"—in which the guys recounted memories of some kind of security blanket thing or teddy bear or toy or doll or, for those guys who seemed to have seriously impressive early-life recall skills, a baby's little trinket, like a rattle or a pacifier, usually with some kind of primitive name, e.g., Binky. Elizabeth was charmed by the several men who had basically the same memory of a thin knitted cotton blanket of a pastel blue color with satin edging that would eventually fray at the corner exactly at the spot they habitually, as children, sucked on. It was important that these cherished objects were thoroughly described rather than merely named, as describing their physical characteristics required the interviewees to access information stored in the sensory cortex involving textures and smells and tastes and such, which again had the effect of subtly and subconsciously manifesting that blanket in the present, briefly reanimating the person they were when they were wrapped up in that blanket, feeling all safe and warm.

In other words, these first two questions were designed to drill under people's adult defenses and expose their more innocent and vulnerable and unprotected previous little tiny selves.

After which it was time to make them squirm.

Or, as Sanborne put it, make them "experience high affect." After priming his subjects to feel vulnerable, he'd next take advantage of that vulnerability by inducing powerful and often distressing emotions. Thus the next several questions were fashioned to trigger feelings of anxiety and embarrassment and shame and even dread, questions asking subjects to describe moments they were laughed at in public, moments they cried in front of other people, moments when they were most nervous or afraid. Elizabeth asked her partners to predict how they might die, or what they would regret if they died today. She asked them to describe, in clear and specific and terrifying detail, exactly what they found most physically beautiful about her.

The purpose of these questions was really just to get the guys' hearts racing, to get them sweating and nervous. Sanborne was trying to create in their bodies vaguely the same sensations that happened when people actually fell in love—the sweat, the nerves, the racing heart—taking advantage of a particular psychological phenomenon whereby people tended to misattribute what was causing them to feel aroused. As Sanborne explained it, the thing people understood as a "feeling" or "emotion" was only a conceptual and semantic category they associated with a suite of physical impressions: when they felt all hot and tight and trembling and clenched, they had learned somewhere along the way to call that "anger"; or when they felt fatigued and hollow and listless, they called that "sadness." Thus there was a basic chicken-and-egg problem with the human experience of emotions, a problem of causality. What it felt like, subjectively, in the head, was that strong emotions caused strong physical reactions in the body: one feels anxious, and that anxiety triggers sweaty palms. But in reality, it was the other way around: palms begin sweating, and then the mind retroactively searches for a cause. "I must be anxious," it decides.

Emotions, Sanborne said, were simply names that people gave, ex post facto, to biologic events, and thus it was possible and sometimes pretty common that these names were imprecise or confused or downright incorrect. Toddlers, for example, usually could not tell the difference between being angry and being tired. And even adults sometimes mistook being frustrated with just being hungry. It was widely known that people experienced much more romantic arousal and attraction in contexts that made them feel nervous or anxious or afraid—see studies done about the incredible effectiveness of first dates spent at amusement parks, or watching scary movies, or (as in one brilliant Canadian study) talking to a potential love interest in the middle of a wobbly suspension bridge four hundred feet over a rocky ravine in a high wind. Subjects on that tiny, swaying, alarmingly rickety bridge—it was right outside Vancouver—experienced the full complement of physical responses to *high affect*—the adrenaline, sweaty palms, racing heart, solar plexus–filling sense of panic and doom—and their minds had two ways of explaining it: either they were feeling this way because of the bridge, in which case what they were feeling was "fear," or they were feeling this way because of this other person with them on the bridge, in which case it was "attraction" or even "love."

And because feeling attraction was less ego-bruising than feeling fear, that's generally the story they trusted and believed: couples who met on the suspension bridge were far more attracted to each other, and had far more follow-up dates, than a control group of couples who met on a sturdy, large, low-lying and, for the most part, boring Canadian bridge.

In other words, people created a story that explained themselves to themselves, and then they believed their made-up story was the actual objective truth. Thus, if Elizabeth could get her partners feeling nervous via highly intimate and revealing questions, the guys might misattribute these nerves, telling themselves, essentially, "I must be really attracted to this girl if I'm feeling so nervous around her."

Hence the interview's final question: "Do you believe in love at first sight?" This question was a blunt instrument, the psychological equivalent of a magician's "force," where you assume you're picking a card freely from a deck of cards but you're really selecting exactly the card the magician is pushing upon you. Asking a subject if he believed in love at first sight at exactly the moment he was buzzing with the physical manifestations of extremely high affect was practically gift wrapping a version of reality for him to latch onto.

After which the guy was given two things: first, the Thematic Apperception Test, to measure for possible romantic and sexual arousal, and second, Elizabeth's home phone number, since the percentage of test subjects who called to ask her out was a revealing datum to collect and record, for scientific purposes.

It was this script that Elizabeth helped to perfect, and it was this script that she had used on Jack the night they met. This was a fact that, in all the years they were dating and, later, married, she never once revealed to him. She was, she thought, sparing him upsetting knowledge; Jack was such a colossal romantic, and he treasured the purity and magic of their origin story so much that she didn't want to poison his memory of it by revealing that he'd actually been the target of *advanced psychological manipulation*. She didn't want him to know that the excitement and rush he'd felt that night was, at least partially, lab-tested and peer-reviewed. It worried her, at first, to have finagled with his emotions like that, but then she discovered that he'd been watching her from afar, through the window, just as she'd been watching him, and that he'd had a big crush on her before they even met, which seemed exculpatory. And then eventually, after months and years went by, it all ceased to really matter. They'd been a couple for so long that whatever false tactics she'd used at their courtship's very beginning were outweighed by all their true and legitimately happy time together.

Right?

This was the question on her mind the day she met with Dr. Sanborne. She found him sitting on his favorite bench, looking at his favorite Chicago landmark, a sculpture that was known affectionately around town as "the Bean." Actually, its proper name was *Cloud Gate*, and apparently the artist was pretty persnickety that people please call it *Cloud Gate*, and whenever the city referred to it in any official capacity, it was always called *Cloud Gate*, but everyone else called it the Bean. Because that's what it looked like, this sculpture: it was sixty feet long and thirty feet tall and covered in reflective polished steel and its shape was—one could not deny it—leguminous. It was a colossal three-dimensional mirror in the exact oblong shape of a lima bean.

It sat in a plaza downtown, reflecting, on one side, all the buildings of Michigan Avenue, whose flat faces seemed to curve and curl on the Bean's seamless skin. What Sanborne liked most about this landmark was watching people watching their own strange images upon it, how their heads looked distended or squished, and then, moving a little this way or that way, now their bodies were distended or squished. Over here they were shaped like a pumpkin; over there they were shaped like a pear. Hundreds of people were now doing this, standing around the Bean or under it, waving at themselves, taking pictures, moving this way and that way and watching the corresponding deformations, which they found delightful, which Sanborne found delightful. He sat on one of the nearby benches and watched them, smiling.

Elizabeth had asked for this meeting. She hadn't kept in close touch with Sanborne in the years since he retired, but she'd had enough contact to know that retirement did not entirely suit him. He did not have the constitution for leisure or idleness, and so the assorted new hobbies and social mixers and exotic travel available to him now felt disappointing; they lacked the qualities of his working life, the sense of high intellectual purpose derived from pursuing one of life's greatest questions: How do we know what's true? Compared to a question like that, who cares about Acapulco, is what he had written Elizabeth in an email sent, a few years back, from Acapulco.

Sanborne was dressed in his usual outdoorsy flair—his many-pocketed hiking shirt lightly mottled with sweat, a broad-rimmed green bucket hat protecting his pink face from the sun, cargo pants Velcroed at the ankles so that his pant cuffs didn't catch in the chain of his bicycle, which was how he got anywhere in the city, still. The bike leaned against the back of the bench, heavily freighted from what must have been an afternoon trek to the grocery store—a handlebar box filled with six-packs of cola, a stuffed saddlebag, a big double basket in back from which sprouted the handles of many plastic sacks, twirling in the wind.

Sanborne sat enjoying the spectacle of the Bean until he saw Elizabeth emerge from the crowd, then he stood up, kissed her on the cheek, said: "My dear, what a lovely surprise to hear from you. Please, sit, sit."

She joined him on the bench and together they watched a group of children laugh extravagantly at the way the Bean rendered their faces all elongated or flattened or otherwise grotesque. These kids' parents, meanwhile, mostly stood around looking at their phones.

"Why are fun-house mirrors fun for some people," Sanborne said, "but not as much fun for others?"

"I don't know," Elizabeth said, "but I'll bet you have a theory."

"A working theory. Criminally untested. A wild guess. It would probably be irresponsible to even say it out loud."

"Your guesses are usually pretty entertaining. Let's hear it."

"Okay, well, what my hunch is, is this: Everyone feels, to some extent, large or small, that there is a part of themselves that is deeply weird, yes? An inner freak. A part of themselves that is at odds with what we all agree is, quote, unquote, 'normal.'"

"Sure, agreed."

"And some people have a good relationship with this inner weirdo. They cherish it, humor it, let it occasionally surface, revel in it. These are the people delighted by the fun-house mirror. They see this monstrous version of themselves in the mirror and think *Yes! That is also me!* They accept it."

"Like these kids here," Elizabeth said, watching the children now making outrageous faces into the Bean, sticking out their tongues, crossing their eyes, doing that thing with their mouths where they fishhooked themselves with their own fingers and pulled.

"Among us all, it's children who feel most at odds with social norms and etiquette," Sanborne said, "so it stands to reason that they are most in touch with their inner weirdos. But adults? Not as much. Some adults spend considerable mental resources being normal, fitting in, performing a facade that is pleasing and publicly acceptable. These adults experience their inner weirdo as alarming and threatening, full of unwanted urges they work very hard to silence or bury. For them, the fun-house mirror is not fun. They feel challenged by what they see there, the image of someone as ghastly and unpresentable as they feel they really are on the inside. Take this guy—"

Sanborne pointed at a nearby businessman—perhaps on his lunch break—navy sport coat, blue shirt, apricot tie, a little backpack flung over one shoulder, now making his way through the plaza, then stopping at the outskirts of the crowd, staring into the Bean for a moment, exhibiting perfect posture, then quickly moving on.

"That man," Sanborne said, "oh boy, that man has *secrets*."

"This sounds like a promising research subject."

"Oh, it's only a theory, my dear. I have no earthly idea how I would test it. And anyway I'm much too busy right now."

"Are you working again?"

"I am indeed! I couldn't bear retirement one second longer. All that free time. All that *golf*. No, I am back at it, currently doing an ethnographic study on a fascinating community of people who all share the same odd conviction."

"Which is what?"

"They believe that the world is a computer simulation."

"A simulation. Like in that movie with the robots?"

"Yes, but not so apocalyptic. The people I'm studying are shockingly logical about it, really quite rational and mathematical and analytical. They begin with a simple premise: that computer processing speed and power will likely continue to advance at their current exponential pace, well into the future."

"Sounds reasonable so far."

"It follows, then, that humanity will eventually, someday, invent computers of basically infinite capacity, yes? Computers so fast and powerful and intelligent that they are able to simulate the real world down to its last atom. A map of the world as big as the world. Computers with the ability to simulate the feeling of living a human life as a human being, to simulate all of Earth's history, altering variables here and there, to see what changes, to test how outcomes vary. Like a weather model on a cosmic scale. This type of simulation is more or less inevitable."

"I understand."

"So in that future, how many of these world-simulations might be run, do you suppose?"

"I don't know. A million?"

"Yes, indeed, a million! In which case the universe reasonably contains one real Earth and one million simulated Earths. Thus it follows, logically, that the chance we are right now living on that single real Earth is, literally, one in a million. It's a probabilities argument, in the end. The odds are just far better that we're in one of the simulations, especially given that anyone in the simulation would not perceive it as a simulation because that would ruin the simulation. Kind of brilliant, yes?"

"Are there many people who believe this?"

"There are *so many people*! And they have big boisterous communities online. I'm embedded in a group on Second Life, a platform that is, itself, also a simulation. Do you know what they call their group on Second Life?"

"No."

"Third Life! Oh, how I miss these chats of ours. How is everything? How is your family?"

Elizabeth smiled. She knew the answer to that question was *In tatters*. Jack was off in Kansas, their marriage was crumbling, her future and their dwindling nest egg were snared in internet controversy. But feeling suddenly guilty about burdening the poor man with all her drama, she said, "Fine," nodding with great vigor. "Everything's fine!"

"My dear," he said, "you did not contact me out of the blue because everything is fine. What's troubling you?"

Elizabeth let out a breath she did not realize she was holding. "It's about me and Jack."

"Yes?"

"We're not doing well."

"I see."

"We are having marital problems."

"Recent or ongoing?"

"Probably . . . both? But I guess it started with the new condo. I haven't told you: we finally bought a condo."

"Congratulations."

"Yeah, it was supposed to be our forever home. And I think that maybe the whole process of building our forever home just surfaced some things that, frankly, we hadn't been dealing with. Like, it made us wonder if this is really how we want to spend our lives, *forever*. It made us see that maybe there's something fundamentally, I don't know, *mistaken*, between us."

"And what is that?"

"It might sound odd, but—do you remember when you hired me?"

"Of course."

"Do you remember the research we were doing at the time?"

"The Love-at-First-Sight Script is I believe what they called it. Engineering intimacy in laboratory settings. I'll have you know that our results have proved to be robust and replicable, unlike so many other results these days. That was very good science."

"Yeah, I sort of used it on Jack."

"You did not!"

"On our first date. I did the entire script, all ten questions, in exactly the correct order."

"Why, you devil!"

"Ever since then, Jack has been convinced we're fated."

"Oh, but I wish this would have happened in the lab. We could have included it in our data! Imagine the headline: 'Results so strong that side effects include *marriage*.'"

"It's just that I'm pretty sure Jack and I . . . we're actually quite wrong for each other."

"Is that so?"

"Remember what you told me when you and I first met, your definition of love? You said that love is when you see something in someone else and you want it for yourself. And I saw things in Jack that I thought I wanted, at the time. But maybe I don't want them anymore, or maybe they were never there in the first place. I don't know."

"My dear," Sanborne said, looking at her now in the same patient way he'd looked at her when she was a student and said something naïve. "You and Jack? Of course you're not fated. Of course you're wrong for each other."

"Wow," Elizabeth said. "I actually thought you might try to make me feel better."

"I will try to make you feel better, my dear, but probably not in the manner you're expecting."

"Okay."

"Of course, I'm terribly biased right now. You should know that on the subject of love, I probably cannot be trusted to speak objectively."

"Why is that?"

"I've met someone."

"You have?"

"Someone—and I cringe to hear myself put it this way—someone *special*."

"Oh, good for you."

"His name is Dale, if you can believe that. Imagine! To be so unsentimental my entire life only now to be smitten and undone by a *Dale*. It's frankly embarrassing."

"I'm happy you've met someone," Elizabeth said. It was the first time Sanborne had ever told her anything specific about his romantic life. He'd always been, for decades, either completely silent on the matter or poignantly vague. She smiled at him and took his hand and squeezed it.

"Yes, well . . . Dale," Sanborne said, and shook his head. "He has awful taste in wine. And food. And film. He sincerely laughs at the dumbest sitcoms. He's never heard of Chopin but knows all the rules of football. He makes this sound when he's chewing that is moist and terrible. And yet? I can't get enough of him."

"I've been told that's called new relationship energy."

"My point is that he's made me reconsider my former intractable positions on the matter of love."

Sanborne grinned at her and then leaned back, crossed his legs, looked up into the crisp autumn sky. Elizabeth followed his gaze and saw, way above them, several pigeons sitting atop the Bean—the way the sculpture mirrored the bright blue day, it was difficult to see where the Bean ended and the heavens began, and so it looked like these pigeons were up there levitating.

"There's been a question nagging at me ever since our acupuncture study," Sanborne said. "Do you remember our acupuncture study?"

"That was the one where people cured themselves of chronic back pain, via toothpick."

"Yes! And ever since then I've been thinking about this question: If people are capable of that kind of self-healing, why don't they just do it? By themselves? Why do they need the placebo? Why do they wait for permission? Why do they need the trigger? I didn't have an answer back then, but I believe I have an answer now. Though, again, it is untested, so take everything I'm about to say with your normal healthy skepticism."

"I certainly will."

"Okay, so, the body can sometimes cure itself of pain but often opts not to. I believe this implies that occasionally it's good to feel bad. There must be some *advantage* to feeling bad. Some purpose to the pain, yes?"

"I suppose that pain is a kind of warning system. If you pull a muscle in your back, the pain tells you to rest your back, so you don't injure it worse."

"And that is definitely true for an acute injury—torn muscles, broken bones, lacerations, bruises. But as you and I well know, placebo has very little effect on this kind of damage. There is not a single placebo that can heal bone, or mend tissue. No, placebo works best on people who are suffering *chronically*—back pain that no X-ray can explain, headaches with no clear organic cause, irritated bowels with no obvious irritants, generalized allover lethargy, physical lassitude, ambiguous inflammation, endless emotional anguish, spiritual hopelessness—"

"Loss of romantic love."

"Pain with no acute physical cause, perceptual pain that the body could ease if it wanted to—this is the pain that's most responsive to placebo. And why is that? Well, I think the answer might just be boringly biological, which is that it's expensive. It's metabolically expensive. Treating pain or infection or inflammation from within is actually very costly, in terms of pure calories spent. It takes a tremendous amount of energy to summon the body's immunities or endorphins or natural opioids or serotonin, et cetera. Did you know, for example, that the body has a much smaller immune response to the common cold in the winter than it does in the summer?"

"I did not."

"The brain perceives the shorter days, the lack of sunlight, the cold temperatures, and it thinks: *This is the season of scarcity.* And so it does not spend as much energy fighting colds as it does in summer, the season of abundance. This is why colds in the winter tend to linger, because the brain is stingy about allocating resources, evolving as it did in conditions of hunger and hardship and famine and want."

"So if you're starving, you don't waste calories treating a cold."

"And if there are hungry lions everywhere, you spend your precious energy on running, not on your irritated bowels. So the brain—which is still operating a Paleolithic simulation set atop our twenty-first-century world—does a cost-benefit analysis: it will only spend the energy needed to cure you when it is *certain* there is enough energy to go around, when it is *certain* you are safe from harm."

"But we *are* safe, obviously. No lions, no famine."

"Okay, but is that how it feels to us, on the inside? Do you *feel* very certain? Do you *feel* very safe? If an emotion is just the name we give to bodily sensations, how would you describe an experience of certainty and safety? How would you feel, deep down?"

"I would feel calm, I guess. Tranquil. Peaceful."

"Yes."

"Mellow. Hopeful. Unencumbered. Free."

"And tell me, my dear, how often do you feel like that these days?"

"Probably almost never."

"Exactly right! People are not experiencing the world with peace and tranquility. Our lives have never before been so free of immediate physical threats, and yet we've never felt so threatened. And that's because, in the course of our normal everyday lives, with all the responsibilities of work and family, amid the churn of information and news and trends and spin, with the millions of choices available to us, with all the horrors of the world served up to us every second on TV and computers and phones, we mostly just feel anxious, worried, precarious, vulnerable—basically the same emotions we would feel if there really was a famine, or if we really were being hunted."

"Information overload is the new hungry lion."

"And isn't that the truth. We feel unsafe. We feel uncertain. And so the body gets stingy. It conserves. What placebo offers us is the illusion of certainty. It gives you a story that, once you believe it, triggers the body to finally do its own natural thing. So placebo doesn't cure you—rather, placebo creates the emotion required to cure yourself. And that emotion is certainty."

"I can't wait to find out what this has to do with my marriage."

"We don't live in a world that offers much certainty, my dear. We live in a world of exponential chaos, an age where it feels like the more we know, the less we understand, where it's fashionable to ascribe secret unconscious motives to all behaviors, and thus you doubt that even your deepest thoughts and feelings are actually your own. Maybe the way you think and feel is true and honest, or maybe it was just hardwired into you by evolution, or programmed into you by growing up in a patriarchy, or socialized into you by living in your particular racial caste, or implanted in you by the many ways your parents screwed you up, or maybe it's because you've been seduced by propaganda, or nudged by algorithms, or maybe you're unconsciously virtue signaling to your tribe, or maybe you were born with a particular brain with its particular chemical idiosyncrasies, or maybe all of these things at the same time—how would you know? We suspect there's something large lurking below, unseen, and so we're always searching for the even deeper entendre."

"Like your computer-simulation people."

"I think it's obvious that we do not live in a computer simulation, but choosing to believe that we do live in a computer simulation is a useful metaphor: it gives a name to our gnawing intuition that there's something else governing us, that we are not entirely in control, that we have no idea what the fuck is going on. It creates certainty out of uncertainty. Have you seen those photographs people take of the Leaning Tower of Pisa? Where it looks like they're holding up the tower with their bare hand?"

"Sure."

"That illusion only works when you're standing in exactly the right spot to observe it. If you move one step left or right, the illusion falls apart. And I think people do this all the time, in life. They find a view of the world that agrees with them, a spot that feels safe and secure, and they plant themselves on that spot and don't move. Because if they did move, their certainty and security and safety in the world would fall apart, and that's too scary and painful to contemplate. So people prefer their illusions—that the world is definitely a simulation, or that acupuncture is a thing, or that juice cleanses work, or that Ebola was created by the government. It's a little assertion of sovereignty amid the chaos. In the face of insurmountable threats and distressing precarity and pain, the body longs, more than anything, for certainty. You could say that certainty is, in fact, the flip side of pain—it's what pain looks like reflected off the fun-house mirror. When I see people on Facebook express their loud inflexible certainty about some political thing, what I believe they're actually saying is *I am in great pain, and nobody is paying attention.* This is also true for people who believe deeply in soulmates, like, say, your husband. What Jack really needs is the illusion of certainty, the illusion that he will never be hurt again."

"But why is it an illusion? Isn't love sometimes *real*? Aren't there at least some married people who are actually perfectly right for each other?"

"Is Jack right for you? Is Jack wrong for you? Well, that depends. Who is this *Jack* we're talking about? Who is this *you*? What version? At what time? In what place? Which of your many funny reflections is the accurate one? Yesterday you were this person, today you're that person, and tomorrow . . . who knows? But marriage promises consistency, certainty: *you will be loved forever*. And the moment we become certain of this is the moment it begins to slip away from us. Our certainty blinds us to how the world changes and changes and changes."

"So if nothing is real, if certainty is just an illusion, what do we do? Believe in nothing?"

"Believe what you believe, my dear, but believe gently. Believe compassionately. Believe with curiosity. Believe with humility. And don't trust the arrogance of certainty. I mean, my goodness, Elizabeth, if you want the gods to really laugh at you, then by all means call it your *forever home*."

ELIZABETH STOOD in her parents' room, in her brand-new dress, waiting. This was up on the third floor, in the grandest bedroom the Gables had to offer, the one with the big stone fireplace, a four-poster bed, polished wooden furniture at least a century old. Her father was at his full-length mirror, near the big mahogany wardrobe, tightening his tie and looking at Elizabeth via her reflection in the glass. Her mother, meanwhile, sat at one of her two vanities, in a black dress, a cashmere shawl draped over her shoulders, deciding on jewelry.

Downstairs, the caterers were preparing the house. Up here, Elizabeth was waiting for her outfit to be approved. Her father did this each time they entertained guests, necessary because Elizabeth needed to learn how to present herself appropriately, and she was, he said, regularly unable to do this.

So she waited for her father's verdict. And as she waited, she watched her mother pick up a pair of antique pearl earrings, raise them to her ears, examine herself in the mirror, then put the earrings back. On the vanity before her were ten other kinds of antique pearl earrings, plus all the gold and silver hoop earrings, the diamond stud earrings, the dangly earrings with exotic colorful gemstones, not to mention the many shiny bracelets and bangles and slim wristwatches—all antiques—plus the necklaces. There was another vanity for the necklaces. Elizabeth's mother fancied herself a "collector"—or that's how she described it, anyway, this stockpile of jewelry, and the rooms of Queen Anne furniture, the gallery downstairs of Early American art, the garage of classic cars, the boxes of designer wristwatches, the textiles of handmade origins: they were all "collections," she said, a word Elizabeth never really reflected on until this summer's research project, these recent philosophical investigations into the subject of economic self-interest and the invisible hand, when Elizabeth began wondering what purpose—

what *economic* purpose—these collections served. Antique pearl earrings were, of course, not intrinsically valuable, nor were they useful or beneficial in any obvious utilitarian way. Rather, the collection was worth something only because people *thought* it was worth something; Elizabeth's mother would show off a collection to visitors, and these visitors would praise it with great effusion, and this seemed to bring her mother pleasure. And pleasure was, in a market economy, valuable. Thus, Elizabeth decided that what we call a "collection" could actually be thought of as a kind of elaborate battery: just as a battery stores energy, a collection stores pleasure, is what she had written in her paper. And Elizabeth watched now as her mother ran her fingers over this earring, that earring, stroked this bracelet, that brooch, and Elizabeth imagined her mother tapping into the pleasure of her collection as one pulls electricity from a battery: slowly, until it runs out, which it always does. Her mother's collections seemed, over time, to yield less and less pleasure; whenever she showed them off to guests, she was seized by the subsequent need to immediately enhance and expand them, and then various excursions would inevitably follow, to auctions, estate sales, boutiques in the city that one could enter only by appointment.

Socrates would have something to say about that, Elizabeth thought. Socrates said that what was most important about pleasure was not the sheer amount of it but rather its quality, its impression, its endurance, that a person who lived life needing more and more and more pleasure while simultaneously unable to hold on to the pleasure was not really a person at all but more like a mollusk, just floating and feeding, floating and feeding.

Which was something Elizabeth had *not* written in her paper, afraid that her mother might find the paper and read the paper and be, naturally, shocked and offended.

Elizabeth stood there, silent, in her parents' bedroom. She watched as her mother tried on a different pair of pearl earrings. She waited for her father's wardrobe approval. He looked at Elizabeth's reflection in the mirror. Finally, he said: "Posture."

Elizabeth sucked in her breath, stood up straight.

"That's right," he said. "Shoulders back, tummy in. No one wants to see your belly."

She pledged to stop drooping and hunching, a pledge she knew from experience she could not keep for more than a couple of hours. She always had to be reminded and cajoled into uprightness. She always unknowingly drifted back to this baseline slouch. She wondered why she did that. Why her mind and her body were so consistently at odds. On this night, for example, she was able to keep her good posture at least halfway through dinner, when she caught sight of her father's disapproving look and realized she was doing it again, hunching.

Around the table were her father's business associates, here this weekend because he was being presented with some kind of award, from some organization that advocated for the disabled. This was three weeks after his little episode in the mall parking lot, bashing in that van's windshield, and now he was being honored for his "tireless efforts on behalf of Connecticut's handicapped citizens" was what was printed on the invitations.

So there would be this small dinner tonight, then frivolity tomorrow afternoon—tennis, swimming, shuffleboard—followed by the big party tomorrow night, when he would receive this honor and a large number of VIPs would be descending upon the Gables, people from the statehouse, or people from D.C., people of great political consequence, and her father was right now reciting the names of these powerful guests, slowly, reverently, to his business partners: "Berkley, Dodd, Macaulay, Groark," he said. "If we get any one of those folks on board, it's off to the races."

His associates all smiled at him obediently, nodded at him obediently—it could almost be said they were full-body *wagging*. "How do you do it?" asked one of them, the youngest one, recently out of his MBA program. "I mean, handicapped parking spaces? How did you even *think* of that?"

Her father grinned. "There are opportunities everywhere."

"Amazing. Truly amazing."

"The key is to never be satisfied," her father said, crossing his arms, leaning back in his chair. "Never rest on your laurels. Never feel content. If you ever start thinking *I've done enough, I'm good enough,* you're finished. Yesterday's successes don't matter. Forget them. All that matters is the next thing, and the next thing, and the next thing. Take my daughter here."

Elizabeth's eyes flicked up at him—she'd been staring into her lap, detaching her attention as he commenced his oration—and she suddenly became aware that she was slouching again, and so she sat up powerfully straight.

"My daughter," he continued, "isn't satisfied taking the same classes everyone else is taking. She isn't satisfied doing what everyone else in her high school is doing. No, she's taking *college courses.* As a *freshman.* Isn't that right?"

And then all eyes were on her, and her first impulse was to correct him—she wasn't taking college courses but rather college-*prep* courses, which were very different—but then she saw the look her father was giving her, a look like *Don't mess this up,* and so she batted away that impulse, nodded, and listed the many advanced classes she'd be taking this fall, after which she began name-dropping the various philosophers—Hobbes, Plato, Adam Smith—she'd been reading this summer in preparation, and she kept going on about all her summer research until she caught her mother's eye and was seized by another, opposite mandate, which was: Don't brag. This was one of her mother's primary rules of manners and etiquette. Don't brag. Don't gloat. Or, at the very least, don't *appear* to be bragging or gloating. She'd seen her mother so many times flaunt her collections of expensive things and seem to get right up to the edge of what might be considered "bragging" and then defuse it by saying something self-deprecating and modest: *Oh, it's nothing special, just a little trinket I almost certainly paid too much for, it's probably not even authentic,* said about a pricey piece of jewelry Elizabeth knew for a fact had been rigorously authenticated. And so Elizabeth, now aware that listing her academic achievements could possibly be seen as bragging or gloating, tried to similarly undercut herself: "I'm also taking theater, which I'm so bad at. Just no talent whatsoever.

Mostly I'm taking it because this girl Maggie's in it. She's probably my best friend. We're going leaf-peeping in the fall."

"Leaf-peeping?" her father said.

And Elizabeth explained how Maggie's family went up north every autumn when the colors reached their peak and drove to their favorite lookouts in the White Mountains and gazed at the trees' display before heading to the same small cabin they rented every year, where they built a fire and toasted marshmallows and drank hot cocoa and played checkers or Uno and stayed up way too late and headed home groggily the next morning, though everyone seemed to wake up and come alive when they passed by the Old Man of the Mountain, which was this rock formation in Franconia Notch that really looked exactly like a steely-jawed man in profile, and the whole car waved at the Old Man and said, "See you next year, Mr. Mountain!"

"And that's leaf-peeping," Elizabeth said.

"Sounds nice," said her dad's colleague, the young one. And Elizabeth was nodding, agreeing, even happy, until she caught her father's eye again.

"How very quaint," he said.

Elizabeth looked into her lap. She realized she was slouching again. She sat up straight. She couldn't do anything right.

"Well, at any rate," her father continued, "I wouldn't count on leaf-peeping." Then he flashed a smile at his business partners. "If this deal goes through tomorrow night, we're off to D.C."

"Oh," Elizabeth said, nodding.

"Don't worry, kiddo. You'll love D.C. And there are some great schools in Virginia."

Everyone was quiet for a moment, looking at her. Her mother idly caressed one pearl earring with a fingertip. And then her father was standing up, inviting his colleagues on a tour of the house, and so everyone followed him into the Portrait Room, and as Elizabeth listened to him tell the familiar stories of Augustines past, an understanding came over her: she would almost certainly not be going leaf-peeping with Maggie Percy after all, and furthermore, she would not be seeing Maggie Percy ever again in her life. And she felt that old sensation coming back. Or, rather, that *lack* of sensation. *Going gray rock,* is what she called it, after that book about Sylvester and his magic pebble. She was fortifying, thickening, hardening, ossifying. She felt herself becoming more impervious. Feeling less porous. Feeling less feeling. It was amazing, sometimes, the power she had over her body's automatic functions. She found that she could slow her own heartbeat if she focused on it intently enough, and she could make herself run a real fever if she wanted a sick day from school, and she could will herself to *just not feel*—in which case a kind of coldness took over, an impassiveness, and she found that for a few days or sometimes weeks afterward, the world became dull and uninteresting. And she knew she was doing it right now when she felt the people in the Portrait Room sort of recede from view; they just ceased to matter. And this news about a move to Virginia: she did not feel anything in particular about it.

She had literally no thoughts or feelings as she and everyone else listened to her father's stories of Augustine tycoons, these men who were not afraid to step into something new and unfamiliar—railroads, real estate, textiles, precious metals—each generation going into a new industry and conquering it.

Eventually the tour moved on, and she hung back, until the crowd disappeared into another room, and then she made her way back through the kitchen, the pantry, she walked the two floors up the staircase behind the pantry and sat holding her knees to her chest in the empty servants' quarters, those little rooms walled off from the rest of the house where she tried, on days like this, to reset, to self-soothe. She could be alone, and unbothered, up here, where the only sound was the wind brushing at the window and the home's old walls moaning and creaking as they warmed and cooled, expanded and contracted, breathed.

But soon a rustle and flutter from above alerted her to the time—it was now dark, and the horde of bats that had come to permanently roost on the home's fourth floor was now stirring, awakening. The colony had remained up there despite the best efforts of exterminators to trap them or contractors to seal them in or out. The creatures somehow always managed through these interventions more or less undisturbed: the bats were small, the house was large and drafty; they would find a way. Their numbers had grown so large these past few years that stains and streaks and gross wet rippling had become visible on parts of the third-floor ceiling, in spots where, just above, sat monstrous shimmering mounds of bat droppings, the collected secretions of the whole scrum. Thick plastic sheeting had to be installed on the ceiling in these rooms, to protect inhabitants from guano-related toxins or disease. Apparently even the air up on the fourth floor was now poisonous. Eventually, inevitably, the bats would overrun and ruin the house, but, as the exterminators told them, eliminating the bats would be a kind of catch-22: it would require so much poison applied so consistently that it would render the house uninhabitable. So the situation was altogether unsustainable, and yet, for now, it persisted. Elizabeth listened to the sounds from above: the shiver of wings flapping, the scratching of claws chiseling into plaster.

She must have fallen asleep like that, for she woke up still in that room, still in her dress, hearing her father's voice, calling for her. It was time for their morning tennis match.

And so Elizabeth quickly changed clothes and went into the backyard, where she found that today their contest would have an audience: everyone from last night's dinner. Here they were, on the porch, and they all applauded when she arrived, and joked about placing bets on the match. She walked by them, eyes down, walked out onto the court without even looking at her father, and took her place at the baseline, ready to return serve.

The match proceeded as it usually did for the first few games. Elizabeth was a mildly capable tennis player, but not once all summer had she defeated her father, whose slicing and spinning and curving shots always confounded. His was the junk-baller's strategy, to win by trickiness, wiliness, skulduggery, a player who imparted so much wacky spin on the ball that it was impossible to get a clean strike on it. Elizabeth watched the balls floating back at her, spinning so much that they would strike the dusty court and careen in unanticipated ways, sliding into her, leaping away from her, and this was how it always went with her and her father: miserably.

But this morning, suddenly, Elizabeth had a notion. After a few games of her typical losing, seemingly all at once, she decided to win. She decided to follow a brand-new strategy: if the problem was that her father's shots bounced in strange ways, well, she just wouldn't let them bounce. She would close the distance between herself and the ball. She would rush to the net and not allow the ball's fierce rotation to even matter. She sprinted up there and—it was so surprisingly easy—she put the floating ball away, a hard volley crosscourt, a winner. Her father looked at her, surprised. The crowd cheered. She did it again the next point, and the next—all of her shots, she battered right by him. She didn't grunt or yell or celebrate or anything; the only sound was the clean satisfying thwack of the ball contacting the exact middle of her string bed, followed by a hearty whoop from the spectating guests.

Her father's agitation began to show after two games of this, when Elizabeth tied the score. By the time she broke his next serve, he was complaining about lucky shots, missed line calls, flat balls, loose strings. He shattered his first racket of the day when she won the first set, smashing it hard against the court, whereupon the onlookers' enthusiasm suddenly dwindled. Yet Elizabeth continued on, feeling nothing, being a rock, mechanically putting away his slow, floating shots, then watching with total dispassion as he floundered and changed his tactics—junk-ballers famously have no real plan B—first trying to lob over her, which mostly resulted in a bunch of easy overheads, then attempting to smack the ball for flat and hard and angry passing shots that almost always flew out, and usually by several feet. A second racket was demolished during the changeover at 3–0, snapped across his knee, Elizabeth barely registering it, the guests now absolutely silent.

The final game proceeded like the others, Elizabeth volleying shots to this or that corner, her father scrambling, lunging, losing. On the last point of the match, Elizabeth was idly wondering why she had never before played this way—it was such an obvious strategy—thinking about this even while she was playing the point, as she came to the net and picked off her father's slice and, this time, placed a nice little drop shot in the middle of the service box, and her father, way back at the baseline, grunted and took off for it, but despite his large galloping and lengthy arms, Elizabeth could see that he had no chance, that he would never get that ball, and yet here he came, sprinting wildly to the net, Elizabeth still wondering *Why have I never done this before?* as the ball bounced twice—the point over, the match won—whereupon her father screamed "Goddammit!" and cocked his arm back and, in a sidearm motion similar to a Frisbee-thrower's, he hurled his racket forward—maybe at the net, as he would later claim, or maybe not—and as Elizabeth watched it come from basically point-blank range, unavoidable, helicoptering right at her, she thought, calmly, even mildly: *Oh, that's why.*

WHAT WOULD ultimately become Jack Baker's signature artistic style was born not out of any particular philosophy or practice, but rather out of pure necessity: he was just flat broke. He was in college, and he had no money, and the materials and chemicals and equipment of photography were forbiddingly expensive. This was shortly before digital cameras would radically lower both the price and the tedium involved in making photographs. The world of photography that Jack entered circa 1992 was still, for a few moments longer, an analog world, full of film and slides and paper and chemicals and darkroom time, and thus, for Jack, every single photograph he took bore a real and dispiriting and heartbreaking cost. The film and paper alone could bankrupt him, the black-and-white Ilford paper that he stared at longingly in the aisles of the downtown Blick art supply store, or the boxes of pricey 35mm cartridges, or just packages of Polaroid film would be cost-prohibitive if he were to take as many photos as his fellow students took. Fortunately for Jack, these fellow students—most of whom received monthly allowances and care packages and holiday plane tickets and goddamn *cars* from parents back home—tended to be pretty wasteful. Jack saw it as he cleaned up after them those nights he worked in the art department, doors locked, alone in the building, Jack the work-study janitor going from room to room and marveling at how much left-behind *stuff* there was: stretched canvases that were only slightly bent; scraps of wood that could be sanded and remade; cardboard palettes covered in still-pliable oil paints; used brushes with caked-together bristles that could be unglued with a little turpentine; and, in the photo studios and darkrooms, trash bins filled with photographic paper, some of it accidentally exposed, some of it expired, some of it improperly processed, now crumpled up and abandoned. Jack salvaged all of it.

He was aware that most artists begin with some kind of vision for their art and then find the appropriate materials on which to execute that vision. What Jack did was the opposite: he began with the materials and then tried to reverse-engineer art upon them. What he had available to him was creased and crumpled and spoiled eight-by-ten photographic paper. What he had to figure out was what to do with it.

He found that the paper was no longer viable in the traditional sense. Either it had already been exposed—in which case any new exposure would sit like a faint transparency atop whatever image was already there—or it was too old, in which case any picture would emerge as a ghostly, indistinct gray blob.

But while these cast-off papers no longer reacted effectively to light, they did still react to chemistry. The developers and fixers and stoppers and bleaches of the photographic process still strongly interacted with the silver-halide gelatin affixed to each page. Jack discovered that, using these agents, he could, essentially, paint without paint. He could draw without ink. He found that a solution of developer and water would turn the paper a light gray that then grew darker the longer the chemical reaction was allowed to last. It was a kind of printing done not with pigment but with time. He found that he could create layers and depth and differing gray shades by transferring the paper back and forth between the developing washes and stop baths. He found that chemicals pooling in the creases and folds of crushed-up paper resulted in darker lines that evoked a kind of crocodile skin on the photo's surface. He could drip developing chemicals onto the paper in the manner of a Pollock, or squeegee them in the manner of a Richter, or make rectangular fields in the manner of a Rothko. Those nights he spent at the art department were full of such random experimentation: he'd wipe the papers across those discarded artist palettes to see how oil paints behaved in solution, or he'd burn the pages lightly, or scratch them with his keys, or soak them in water until they nearly disintegrated, or cover them with chemical-resists like wax or honey, to see what happened. He created many hundreds of such evocative accidents, eventually learning how to control and shape and manage the resulting "photographs," or whatever you called them.

He could not afford a camera, nor camera lenses, nor film stock, nor even new paper, and thus he created a full artistic vision that did not require any of those things. Photography without the use of a camera, as he would write in many academic essays on this subject, was not only a viable art form, it was in fact the highest, the truest, the most pure and most real version of photography that existed, since, after all, the single most essential instrument in the entire photographic process was not the camera but rather this photosensitive chemistry. It was this chemical matrix that allowed us to see whatever a camera saw. Without it, a camera was worthless, just a mirror and a lens.

Thus, the photography Jack was doing was, actually, the *most important* kind of photography anyone could do.

Sometimes you have to take a disadvantage and mentally turn it around like that. Jack had learned this lesson when he first came to Chicago, a place that self-consciously thought of itself as a *second city*, which the artists and musicians of Wicker Park embraced. It wasn't that they were *ignored*. No, they were *independent*. Being forsaken by coastal conglomerated interests was actually a good thing, they insisted, because it meant they could remain authentic and pure.

They created a worldview that rejected what they'd already been denied.

Jack's lesson here: Sometimes you take the shit that's forced upon you and call it a stance. Sometimes what we think of as a philosophy of life is really just the complicated way we deal with the way other people deal with us.

Jack had spent enough time in Professor Laird's workshop to understand that what his teacher valued most in an image was not its subject, not its aesthetic qualities, and not even its technical skill or craft—in fact, Laird spoke often about the importance of "de-skilling" in photography, and tended to praise work that was ironically amateurish, poorly lit snapshots he said were actually brilliant photographic equivalents of Duchamp's urinals. No, what Laird admired most was not visual but conceptual: making the right statement, about the right thing. An artwork's value, he said, resided mostly in how the art reacted to other art. And so the story that Jack began telling (in the academic lingo he was so steeped in) was that his photography was nonobjective and nonrepresentational, pure abstraction that foregrounded the surface materiality of an image; that his photographs weren't *of* things but instead *were* things; that his purpose was to showcase the substances and chemistry and real tactile physicality of a picture, freeing photography from its traditional subservience to documentary realism, redeeming and saving the form of art from the tyrannical burden of "meaning."

It was a story that got high marks from his teacher, but it wasn't the truth. It wasn't even close to the truth.

Here was the truth: when he submerged those papers in trays of water and poured in the developing solutions, the gray swirls and eddies that soon appeared on their surfaces looked to him like smoke. Faint at first, and pale, like those steam clouds that marked the beginning of his father's burns, these silvery wisps grew heavier and denser the longer the paper sat floating in its chemical bath, eventually overwhelming and blackening the whole thing. Jack stared down into the tray and it was like staring down into his own memory: the smoke, the fire, the night that Evelyn died.

It had been, at that point, in college, roughly ten years since his sister's death, and yet still this was the memory that came crashing down upon him during these nights alone in the art department, or in bed trying to sleep, or sometimes seemingly out of nowhere, ruining otherwise perfectly fine days. Such was the nature of grief and guilt, that any stolen moment of good cheer had to be immediately repaid its equivalent in misery and regret and penitence. His mourning was so fully woven into him that he wasn't entirely sure who he was without it. It was an everyday weight, pulling him down to this one awful fact anytime he strayed too far from it: that he had, in a distracted moment, in a dire lapse of attention, in a daydream, caused the death of his sister, and neither his subconscious nor his parents would ever let him forget it.

After Evelyn's funeral, it was as if Lawrence and Ruth Baker traded roles. Now his father was the one planted before the television, watching the full daytime lineup of game shows and news programs and sports, tucked into the far end of the living room couch, arms crossed, legs crossed, leaning into the couch's back corner, becoming the smallest possible version of himself. Lawrence stopped all but the most surface-level communication, stopped all contact with the outside world, stopped working, stopped interacting with or even acknowledging Jack, even those moments Jack would walk into the living room and say, meekly, "Dad, I'm sorry," Lawrence would go on looking at the television, and even when Jack would then boldly stand between his father and the screen and say, "Dad?"—because what Jack felt was a pain that tightened around his heart so dangerously hard that it physically hurt to move and he knew there was nobody who could give him release except his father, no one else who could absolve him—still Lawrence would stare straight ahead with empty eyes that were somehow aimed at Jack without ever actually *seeing* him, and the only evidence that Lawrence was even aware of Jack's presence was when he tilted his head in the direction of the kitchen and said: "Go on now. Help your mother."

Jack's mother, on the other hand, seemed to come alive. She seemed to flourish in an exact inverse of Lawrence's withdrawal. Now responsible for the family's income, she did odd jobs in town, hired always by charitable people who pitied her and the tragedy that had befallen her family. Now she no longer spent her days in a bathrobe, in bed. Now she worked part-time as a teller at the credit union, and as a teacher's assistant at the elementary school, and doing some accounting for Calvary Church. Her new sociability meant that there wasn't a single person in the whole county who didn't know the circumstances of Evelyn's death: that Jack had accidentally sent her to the wrong field, that Ruth was overcome with guilt that she hadn't passed on the message in person, that she'd trusted Jack with something so important.

"You can't blame yourself," said many friends and neighbors, clasping Ruth's hand as Jack sat nearby, acting occupied with a toy or book but within obvious earshot.

"The boy's always been slow," Ruth said. "He never pays attention," looking over at Jack, who, at that moment, pretended not to be paying attention.

She began taking Jack to church four times weekly, telling him he needed to show an extra-special effort to earn back God's love and grace. And not only because of the accident but also because of the possibility that it *wasn't* an accident. Ruth began asking him, in less and less oblique ways, whether he was sure he hadn't sent Evelyn out to the north pasture *on purpose*—after all, she had the brains in the family, and the talent, the healthy strong body, the adventurous life, their father's love and support. Was it possible that Jack, always in her shadow, had seen an opportunity to get revenge on her, or to get her out of the way? And Jack, always one to automatically accept all fault and blame for anything that transpired in that house, would wretchedly shrug and not defend himself at all. And his mother looked him over with her usual deep frown and said what would become the motto of his adolescence: "You're rotten to the core, Jack Baker."

Hence all the churchgoing, where Ruth would stand up each week at Sunday services during the time given over for congregants to appeal for collective prayer and ask that everyone keep her family in their hearts, that God please forgive the person who had caused her family so much suffering, and everyone in the church knew exactly who she meant by that—including, of course, Jack himself, sitting next to her, eyes closed, head bowed.

There followed many years of Sunday worship after that, plus informal Thursday prayer services, plus Bible study classes on Wednesday evenings and Saturday afternoons. Bible study at Flint Hills Calvary Church seemed to be mostly about how Jesus loved little Christian children unconditionally—that is, until those same children reached puberty, around age thirteen, after which Bible study seemed to be mostly about how much Jesus hated the lustful things the pastor just knew were bouncing around the minds of sinful teenagers. *Anyone who looks at a woman lustfully has already committed adultery with her in his heart* seemed to be the relevant and terrifying scripture the pastor employed to justify all sorts of strange interventions and commandments. The boys were, for example, paired off with an "accountability partner" whom each boy could confide in and go to for help in resisting temptation and lust and sex and, most important, to avoid jerking off. Jerking off seemed like a real big no-no, and whole Bible study classes could be spent on the question of whether it was or was not sinful to touch one's own penis even while peeing, the pastor informing them that under specific conditions it was, indeed, morally acceptable to touch one's own penis while peeing, these conditions being (1) that the boy could personally guarantee he took no carnal or physical pleasure in it whatsoever and (2) that the boy did not have a single untoward lustful thought during the peeing and the touching. And if the boys could not, in fact, pledge to God that these two conditions were unilaterally met, then it would probably be best if, when at a urinal, they sort of wriggled themselves out of their pants hands-free and peed haphazardly forward, or, when encountering a toilet, they just sat down to pee. Such were the lengths they were supposed to go, to avoid sinning in their hearts, to avoid the private temptations that could lead to public degradation: inner lust leads to jerking off, which would lead to sexual degeneracy, which would lead to unwanted pregnancies, which would lead to abortions. Thus, it was their sacred duty to prevent *any sexual thought* from even entering their minds, as these thoughts sent them down a slippery slope that ended with murdered babies. This was the reason they were instructed to go through any magazine or catalog or retail circular that arrived at their house and rip out all bra- and underwear-related advertising, as well as any other picture that triggered sinful lust, which struck Jack as a bit of a catch-22, since of course any picture he tore out to prevent lust had already caused exactly that lust immediately upon his looking at it, that he needed to experience evil sinful lust to even know which pictures to tear out in the first place. This would be roughly the same catch-22 he would point out to the pastor when talk turned, in high school, to marriage and sex, when the pastor told him that love and desire toward a wife were sanctified by God but any desire toward any woman who was not his wife was a sin in God's eyes and Jack asked the pastor how he was expected to find a wife for whom he felt desire when he was not allowed to desire her until after she was his wife.

Pointing out these contradictions usually brought on some stern warning from the pastor about the consequences of "questioning God's word," consequences that usually had something to do with an eternity of creative torture. The pastor's most oft-cited punishment was being beheaded, repeatedly, daily, in the afterlife, the pastor vividly describing it, asking them all to imagine it, the feeling, on their necks, the scraping and biting of a saw whose teeth were, usually, in his telling, both dull and rusty.

It took only a few years of this before Jack stopped obeying the pastor and his ridiculous doctrine. By Jack's final year in high school, he had stopped churchgoing altogether and had started listening to music that was, according to both his mother and the pastor, possibly satanic. He had by then resolved to leave this place, to go somewhere very far away, any way he could. He considered the military—he had no money, and so the military seemed like the quickest, easiest, most expedient way out—but that notion was abandoned as soon as the recruiter took one look at his skinny body and alarming medical history. It seemed, then, that college was the only escape, but his grades were merely average, and his performance on the ACT underwhelmed (he had not been made aware that one was supposed to *study* for this exam). But he remembered his sister telling him that in Chicago there was a school in a museum, and this school had a somewhat storied history with students from the rural heartland, and so he mailed away for an application, filled it out, wrote an essay about being inspired by Grant Wood and *American Gothic,* and sent the school slides of his sister's Kansas landscapes, claiming them as his own. He was not a great painter, but his sister had been a great painter, and he didn't think she would object to his borrowing her work that way.

An acceptance came a few months later, and applications for need-based student loans and work-study jobs that could cover his expenses. It was as if the prophecy his sister had made all those years before—that he would one day leave this suffocating ranch and go out and see the world—was finally coming true, all because of her. She had divined his future, and she had made that future possible.

His last evening in Kansas, the night before his father would drive him to Emporia and he would catch the bus to Chicago, Jack walked out into the north pasture at sunset. Nobody had set foot in that field since the night of the accident, and the grass, in places, was taller than Jack, blades thick and sharp, tassels bending in the wind. Young trees had sprung up here and there, including an elm in what seemed to be the pasture's middle—what would have been center field back when Jack and his father pretended the pasture was a baseball stadium—and Jack imagined that this spot, where this lone tree was growing, this was where Evelyn had died, this was her grave. She had a proper, official, headstoned grave, of course, over at Calvary Church, but this tree felt, to Jack, more real, more actually connected to her. There was, he hoped, some part of her that grew in some part of it.

Jack never saw what the fire had done to her body, which was a blessing. The night of the accident, his father had quickly caught up to him and grabbed him and covered Jack's eyes with a big hand. And even while Jack struggled to get loose, and even as Lawrence screamed in anguish, and even as the fire crew sprinted in to give their futile aid, still that hand remained, Jack's vision obscured. It was a gift that Jack was later grateful for. He had not seen his sister's body in that field, but his father had seen it, and Lawrence was henceforth changed. For Jack, the only memory that persisted was the image of the fire and the smoke, a cloud so black it was darker even than the night sky.

The tree that grew on that spot grew up bent and leaning, having been nudged so long by the fierce wind, appearing now as if it were genuflecting, and Jack remembered Evelyn doing that same thing those mornings she'd wake him to go out painting, how she'd bow down toward the horizon, greeting the dawn. Jack walked around this crooked tree taking pictures with Evelyn's old Polaroid camera until all her film was spent.

The next morning, he left the Flint Hills for good.

What he didn't expect was that, in his art, he would stay here so long. When he discovered, those nights cleaning up after wasteful students, that certain chemicals poured onto photographic paper created swirls and streaks and ripples that looked like smoke, and then when he further found that leaving these photosensitive pieces out in the sun turned them shades of red and pink that evoked fire, he suddenly had his subject: his sister, the burn, her final terrible night.

Naturally, he couldn't reveal this to his teacher, nor to any of his classmates, all of whom had serious misgivings about expressing too much emotion in art; any artist who plucked too obviously from his own life's pain was immediately dismissed for being sentimental. Jack did not want to be dismissed, nor sentimental, nor did he want anyone in Chicago knowing this secret: not his friends, not even Elizabeth. Especially Elizabeth. He simply needed her too much, and he could not bear it if her feelings for him changed, if she heard this story and then concluded what his mother had concluded, that he was slow, stupid, untrustworthy, and perhaps even malicious, vindictive, murderous, rotten all the way to his core.

And so he kept the knowledge of that night to himself, putting it on paper as a way to get it out of his head, a secret hidden in plain sight, photographs of an unspeakable memory, alchemized onto a medium that was, like Jack, unwanted, and ruined, and cast away.

BEFORE JACK RETURNED to Chicago, his mother told him to have a look through Lawrence's downstairs bedroom, to see if there was anything Jack wanted to save or keep, any odds or ends, anything of value.

"Dad was sleeping down there?" Jack said at the top of the stairs, looking into the darkness.

"Oh, yeah, he moved downstairs a few years ago," Ruth said. "It was because of the coughing. He'd get to coughing in the middle of the night. He was worried about waking me up."

She clicked on the stairwell's overhead light. Back when Jack was a child, the stairs had been made of rickety old plywood, but sometime in the last few decades they'd been redone, renovated, carpeted.

"We had separate master bedrooms," Ruth said. "We seen it on HGTV. It's a trend."

"Yeah, I've heard of it."

"Take whatever you want from down there. The rest is going to the church. Or the trash."

"You don't want anything?"

"Why would I want anything?"

"I don't know," Jack said. "I guess to remember him by."

Ruth squinted at him and, ever the unsentimental plain old pragmatist, she shrugged. "Doubt I'm gonna forget, Jack."

The basement had been used strictly for storage when Jack was growing up, but in the time since he'd left home, the bare concrete walls had been covered with drywall, the dirt floor finished and carpeted, the mess of plumbing overhead hidden by a drop ceiling so low that it's likely Lawrence had to stoop to avoid knocking his head on it. The basement, once so scary to Jack, now had the beige anonymity of a dentist's waiting room. It was difficult to believe that such a generic-looking place had been the landscape of his father's final years. Something as monumental as death deserved more imaginative accommodations.

Going through the bedroom of someone recently dead felt like a large violation of their privacy and integrity. What if Jack found something embarrassing? Some secret? Jack understood that his father, always such a private man, would *hate* this, Jack rooting around his room. But of course there was no Lawrence anymore, nobody to embarrass, no one to feel that hate, and so Jack went ahead and looked around with this weird ambivalent feeling: that his father would not approve, but also that his father did not exist.

There wasn't much to look at anyway. A pull-out couch—not even a proper bed—was currently pulled out, sheets entangled on one side, a pathetically thin mattress, a pillowcase flecked with something ruddy and dark—Jack guessed blood. There was an oxygen tank and breathing mechanism next to the bed, within easy reach. And a metal walker with tennis balls impaled on its feet. Otherwise the basement was neat and clean, nothing to rummage through but a dresser and a bathroom.

The dresser was filled mostly with white T-shirts gone cream-colored at the collar and armpits. And a few green John Deere baseball hats. Two pairs of blue jeans, some socks, some underwear—all white, all Hanes—and a belt with one loop busted out from use. Jack hadn't known what he would find down here, but finding this—essentially nothing—just about gutted him. The entirety of his father's stuff would probably fit in a single cardboard box—it was the three cubic feet Lawrence's life amounted to. No wonder he spent so much time online.

In the bathroom, Jack found his father's electric razor sitting by the sink, and when he picked it up, it shed little bits of gray and black hair. An odd detail, that Lawrence knew he was dying and yet was still shaving, still performing the rote maintenance the living body required. The medicine cabinet was empty but for toothpaste and deodorant and several bottles of aspirin. Then Jack opened what he assumed would be a linen closet but turned out to be—he gasped when he saw it—a pharmacopoeia of pills and powders and extracts and salves and elixirs in large bulbous jugs, hundreds of them, the whole closet filled up with equipment and medicines, many of which were familiar to Jack from his father's online ravings about them.

There were bottles of colloidal silver, and turmeric pills, and high-dose vitamin C supplements, and powdered shark cartilage, and mushroom extract, and blue scorpion venom, and cumin seeds, their labels making unconfirmed claims about their all-natural cancer-fighting qualities. There were bags of apricot pits that claimed to kill tumors by alkalizing the body. There was a bottle of something brown that was said to kill the little-known parasite that was actually at the root of all cancer. There was a device that looked like an old radio that said it could detect the quantum vibrations from a person's specific cancer cells. There were several opened packages of "anti-cancer metabolic cleanses." There were bags of ambiguous "Chinese herbs," bottles of clear liquid "immunomodulations," infusions of vitamins, amino acids, antioxidants. There was bioactive CBD in a variety of media: oils, gels, dusts. There was a bottle with no ingredients list whatsoever called Nature's Chemotherapy. Jack wondered how many hundreds of hours, and how many thousands of dollars, and how much false hope was stashed away in this closet. He closed the door and went upstairs.

"Find anything?" his mother said. She was out on the front porch, sitting in a lawn chair, looking west, where the sun was now setting over the swaying grass.

"Tell me about the last month," Jack said as the screen door banged shut behind him. "What happened to Dad, at the end?"

"I told you already. The cancer spread."

"And what kind of treatment was he getting?"

"Oh, well, he was on all kinds of medicine. So many pills, I honestly couldn't keep up."

"Was it the medicine from the closet downstairs? Is that what he was taking?"

"I suppose so."

"And what about medicine from doctors? Was he taking anything from actual doctors?"

"Well, he didn't much trust doctors."

"Because the stuff downstairs isn't real. You know that, right?"

"He thought the hospital was a scam."

"Oh my god."

"Lawrence was convinced the doctors were liars. He thought there was a cure they weren't telling him about. And I can't say I disagreed with him, frankly, what with all the trouble doctors gave you, when you were young. Do you remember how they were with us? They were so mean."

Jack sat down on the porch steps, elbows on his knees, head leaning into his hands. It now made a little more sense, his father's belief in all those internet conspiracies, his devotion to fantasy. Perhaps the man *had* to believe what he read online, however outlandish it was, just to maintain this private hope: that he would be cured, that he would not die.

"On Lawrence's last day in the hospital," Ruth said, "they sent in this new guy. Not a doctor. He was a social worker, a counselor. He said he specialized in *palliative care*."

"It means end-of-life stuff."

"I know what it means. Anyway, this guy asked Lawrence to do all these silly breathing exercises. Sitting and closing his eyes and counting his breaths. Imagine, asking a man dying of lung cancer to breathe!"

"Sounds like meditation."

"He told Lawrence that when you're dying, it's normal to feel anxious and angry about it, and that some people find it helpful to relax and breathe and focus on moments from their lives."

"Like, happy moments?"

"No. He told Lawrence to focus on true moments."

"True moments. What does that mean?"

"Times when he was the most himself. He said that everyone has a deep feeling about who they really are, something underneath everything else, something that doesn't ever change. And he asked Lawrence to describe a moment when he felt like that. And of all the memories, you know which one he picked?"

"No."

"Pulling Evelyn's float in the homecoming parade. That's what he picked."

"Oh, okay."

"Not the day of our wedding. Not the day he proposed to me. No, riding his tractor. I guess that's the thanks I get, for taking care of this place all these years."

"I remember those parades. Evelyn looked so happy."

"Everyone loved that girl."

"Yes, they did," Jack said, nodding. "You were right, by the way, about my art. My photographs. Those aren't pictures of nothing. They're pictures of Evelyn. They're pictures of the fire."

"Well, that's obvious."

"Dad wrote to me about Evelyn. There at the end, in one of his last messages."

"Oh? And what did he say?"

"He said it wasn't my fault."

"How nice of him."

"He said to ask you about it."

"Ask *me*?"

"Yeah, he said it wasn't my fault and that you would explain why. What did he mean?"

"That man," Ruth said. "He's still accusing me, from beyond the grave."

Jack turned around to look at her. "Accusing you of what?"

She drew up straighter, clasped her hands together, and let out that laugh of hers, a forced and fake laugh that Jack knew actually signaled annoyance, pique. "Do you know how much I loved your father?" she said. "My god, when he showed up that day, on our ranch, he was so handsome. I was eighteen years old, and I took one look at that man and thought, *Well, there he is. He's the one.* I fell in love right on the spot. And you know what he did?"

"He proposed to your sister."

"He proposed to my sister. Yes. How did you know that?"

"Evelyn told me."

Ruth nodded. "But what you have to know is that my sister wasn't serious about him. She was flighty, careless, lazy. She wouldn't have been a good wife. It wouldn't have been a good match. So I put up a big fuss. I convinced my father that it should be *me*. I was the oldest, after all. I should get married first. I just thought that if Lawrence picked me, I could get him to fall in love."

She shook her head and rolled her eyes at the memory, made that fake laugh again. "Well, you know how that turned out," she said. "He blamed me for ruining his life."

"I'm sorry, Mom."

"I thought maybe it would get better if we had a child. If we were parents together, he'd have to love me, right? So we had Evelyn. And he doted on that girl so much, loved her so much. It made me feel like . . . well, like nothing. I'd tell him you are supposed to love and cherish your *wife*! I'd tell him it was a sin, treating his daughter so much better than me."

"You were jealous of Evelyn?"

"Well, that's what *he* thought. Especially after she died. After Evelyn died, it's all I heard from him, that I had ruined his life, again. Accusing me of the most terrible things."

"Accusing you of what?"

"Sending her out there, into the north pasture, on purpose."

"On purpose?"

"Telling you the wrong field. Sending Evelyn out there to die."

"You said that I misheard you."

"I know."

"You told me I hadn't been paying attention, that it was *my* fault."

"I know."

"So was it? Was it my fault?"

Ruth stood up quickly, frowning, shaking her head. "Why are we even talking about this?" And she was about to open the screen door when Jack jumped up and blocked it hard with his hand.

"Mom," he said, "tell me."

"I don't remember."

"Was it my fault or not?"

"I don't remember!"

"Be honest."

"I am! I don't remember! Honestly, Jack! There was so much going on that night, it was such chaos. All I knew for sure was that it was an accident, a mistake, but I didn't know who made the mistake, whether it was me, whether it was you. But then there you were in the middle of it saying 'I'm sorry, I'm sorry' all night long and I thought, oh, okay, it must have been your fault."

"But you didn't know?"

"You seemed so guilty, so sure you were guilty, that I suppose I . . . I guess I went with it."

"You *went with it*?"

"Everyone knew you were a little absent-minded."

"They thought that because of *you*."

"And what would people have said, huh? If they thought I'd killed my own daughter? I wouldn't have been able to show my face in church ever again!"

"So you blamed me, to save your reputation."

"I did not blame you. You blamed yourself. I just followed your lead."

"I was nine!"

"Yeah, well, I don't know what to tell you."

She stood there, arms crossed, shoulders hunched, staring at the ground like a petulant child.

"All those times you took me to church," Jack said, "you weren't asking for *my* forgiveness, you were asking for *yours*."

"I was asking for both."

"Because you don't know what really happened."

"I don't. It's the truth, Jack. I've thought about that night so many times, and I don't remember what I said. Maybe I told you the wrong thing, maybe you told Evelyn the wrong thing. It was an accident, I know that much. But the memory is gone."

"Dad didn't believe you."

"No."

"He thought you did it on purpose."

"He said Evelyn was popular and happy and I was alone and miserable and that I couldn't stand it. He thought I wanted revenge. He thought I wanted attention. Imagine being married to someone who thinks you're capable of *that*."

Was she capable of that? Was his father right about her? Or was this another of the old man's paranoid stories, another of his late conspiracies? Jack didn't know, and maybe he didn't need to know. He had been living with the guilt of his sister's death for so long that this new ambiguity felt like deliverance in comparison.

"I expect you want an apology," his mother said.

"That would be nice."

"I expect you want me to grovel right now, fall all over myself admitting what a horrible mother I was."

"You told me I was *rotten to the core*."

"Yeah, well, before you get all high and mighty, just remember all the trouble you put me through. When you were young. You weren't perfect either."

"I know. You've told me. I shouldn't have been born."

"That's right. You shouldn't have. So the way I see it is, you and I, we're probably even."

Jack had to laugh—at his mother's stubbornness, her audacity, at the grievances that she'd collected and nursed in her heart, at her ability to bend history to remain blameless.

"Sure, Mom," Jack said. "Fine. Whatever. We're even."

The sun now dipped beneath the western horizon, and the pastures before them took on their bluish evening cast, and there came on the wind the sound that often accompanied sunset in the Flint Hills: a pack of coyotes, howling, barking, somewhere eerily close by.

"God, I used to hate that sound," Jack said.

"The ky-oats?" Ruth said, pronouncing the word like she always had, with two syllables. "Why?"

"I didn't like when they got stuck on the fence. They'd cry all night. It was awful."

"Stuck on the fence?"

"You know, how the coyotes would jump the barbed wire and sometimes get caught on it."

"Is that what you thought was happening?"

"Yes."

"Jack, they didn't get stuck. Your father put them there."

"He did?"

"He set out traps in the fields. And when he caught a ky-oat, he'd hang it on the fence."

"Why?"

She shrugged. "Keeps away the other ky-oats," she said matter-of-factly. "But he didn't want you to see that. So he'd do it real early, before you were up. You were always so sensitive."

"Oh," Jack said. He was thinking it was a barbaric thing for his father to do, but he also felt a sudden rush of tenderness for the man. That Lawrence was going out into the blackened predawn to spare his delicate son a troubling sight—it made Jack wish more than anything that he could say thank you, for this one favor, and for all the other quiet charities his dad had likely performed, unnoticed. Lawrence, after all, could have told Jack to *toughen up*, to *be a man*, as so many of the other fathers did. But no, Lawrence had never asked Jack to be anything other than what he was. Lawrence had accepted Jack in a way that Jack could not, he thought now, reciprocate. It was a massive failure of empathy, these last few years of bickering, a massive failure of generosity. Jack wished he could take it back, all the bitterness, all that pointless fighting on the internet.

"That was good of him," he said. "That was nice."

"Well," Ruth said, "not if you're a ky-oat."

And now another sound reached them, from somewhere in the distance, the rattle and crunch and crackle of something driving on that long gravel road. And they looked up to see a dusty cloud in the air out beyond the north pasture, and then, a moment later, the headlights of a pickup truck emerged between the rolling hills, driving lazily toward the ranch, and Ruth nodded and said, "That'll be the Brannons. You remember the Brannons?"

"No."

"The mother used to teach literature at your school."

"Oh, right."

"She's retired now, of course."

"She didn't teach literature," Jack said. "She taught *RoboCop*."

"Coming to deliver her famous lemon bars, no doubt. I better put on some coffee."

Jack opened the screen door and followed his mother into the kitchen, watched her silently fiddle with the coffee filter, the grounds.

"Listen, Mom, I probably ought to get going."

"Okay, sure."

"I have to get back to work. I teach in the morning."

"Of course," she said, moving to the tap, pouring water into a coffeepot.

"Are you going to be okay?"

She turned to him then and flashed that old familiar expression: confused, confounded, the same face she'd made whenever Evelyn had gone on about some enchanting rock, or the beautiful symbolism of grass—*It's just a rock*, Ruth would say. *It's just grass, plain and simple.* His mother looked at him now with that same mystified expression. "Why wouldn't I be okay?"

"Right. Of course."

"Go on now. Get back to where you belong."

And then she turned back to the cabinet and pulled down two coffee mugs.

"Bye, Mom," Jack said, and he walked out of the kitchen.

Out front, Jack took a last look at the little white house, and then a long look at the surrounding pastures, slowly turning in place and searching out the spot where he and Evelyn sat those mornings when she taught him how to paint, how to see. He stared into the fields until his mom's new visitor turned into the ranch's lengthy dirt driveway, then he hopped into his own car and drove out, passing Mrs. Brannon halfway, giving her a little wave, then rumbling over the cattle guards, turning onto the gravel road and driving along the fence line of the north pasture for roughly a quarter mile before stopping, pulling over, getting out of the car, and jumping the barbed-wire fence. He jogged into the north pasture, into its middle, hopping over brush, skirting the larger clumps of grass, six feet tall and waving in the hard wind. He soon spotted the tree, the one he imagined was Evelyn's grave. It was so much bigger now, and joined by other trees slowly colonizing the field, but it was clearly the same

American elm tree he'd photographed, at sundown, the night before he left for Chicago—it had the same tilt, the same specific bend.

Twenty years separated that moment from this one, twenty years in which Jack had become an entirely new person—an artist, an intellectual, a teacher, a husband, a father—and yet, in other ways, he suspected he had not really changed at all. If, on his deathbed, some counselor asked Jack to pick a moment from his life that was his most "true," he might pick that moment out here, in the pasture, the morning he sat with Evelyn painting landscapes in the dawn light. How his sister could evoke such substance in only a few brushstrokes—just a handful of evocative lines and suddenly her picture seemed to pulse. Jack, on the other hand, clumped his canvas with paint, thick and obtuse. He tried to enclose and bound every building, every blade of grass, to define and hold and control and smother it all.

"You have to let it breathe," his sister had advised, and maybe that was Jack in a nutshell: he let nothing breathe. He let nothing just be. He let nothing evolve or unfold naturally, without trying to control it or coerce it. His sister, on the other hand, had accepted the world's inherent unpredictability, and even embraced it, living in an exotic place every year, always learning something new, never knowing what would come next. Jack pretended he was following her example, but what he'd really done after moving to Chicago was demand immediate permanence and safety and control: he'd found a girl, and an aesthetic, within his first year, and then henceforth never changed a thing. For Jack, marriage and art were not about investigation or learning or growth. They were more like the snapshots you take and then pin down in the album: they were artifacts, mementos, fixed under laminate. He could not let them breathe.

He had left Kansas because he felt alienated from his family, but how different was he, really? His mother had required that Lawrence adore her, that Evelyn be exactly like her, that Jack praise her, and she clung so hard to these needs that she didn't see how they were the very things that made her suffer, that drove people away.

And didn't Jack do the same thing? He needed Elizabeth so much, and that need was plainly suffocating her. He was so fearful of losing her that he'd choked the life right out of their marriage.

Evelyn had tried to teach him this very lesson, a long time ago. She'd told him: *When you cling too hard to what you want, you miss what's really there.*

"I wish we could have grown up together," Jack said now, in the direction of the memorial he'd invented for his sister. And then he turned around and made his way back to the car. It was clear to him, at last, what to do, how to solve the problem of his marriage. He had to finally take his sister's advice. He had to—even though it terrified him—he had to let his marriage go. This is what he decided, out there in the pasture, in the shadow of that looming tree, the heavy wind in his face: it was time to let Elizabeth go.

I T WAS DURING a certain week in mid-autumn—the week that Chicago seemed to tilt toward winter, when browned leaves began falling onto sidewalks in bunches and a cold wind came down from the north and one could smell the season's coming change on the crisp dry air—that, on a quiet block near DePaul's Lincoln Park campus, for the first time in years, no patients were seen entering or leaving the Wellness clinic, and no sign hung above its storefront door.

Wellness had become something of a curiosity during its time here. The dentists and physical therapists and dermatologists who inhabited the nearby shops were bemused by their strange neighbor, this vague-sounding clinic with the sign out front that changed weekly, and sometimes daily. What was going on in there? What strange things happened behind that frosted glass? Rumors of bizarre, unheard-of therapies percolated among them, never confirmed nor denied.

But this week, for the first time in anyone's memory, there were no patients, and no signs, only that opaque and anonymous white-blue glass. Newcomers visiting the block for the first time would have had no idea the office was even inhabited.

And that's because Elizabeth was closing it down.

She was pulling the plug. Wellness could no longer stay in business, not after it had been so publicly outed online. After Brandie's Facebook rantings went viral, several Wellness clients had come calling, demanding answers, and Elizabeth had to admit that, yes, these clients had been given placebos too, and their reactions were predictable. Anger, outrage, betrayal. After which things just sort of spiraled—those clients told other clients, who told still more clients, and then the jig was up. Placebo therapy, after all, works only when people don't know they're getting it. And now that everyone knew exactly what Elizabeth was doing, she could no longer effectively do it.

And so here she was, at Wellness, with her small staff, all of them silently, sadly, collecting their possessions, clearing out the office, and the only sounds were cardboard boxes being opened and shut, the tumble of drawers upended, packing tape unspooled, and Toby playing Minecraft on the waiting-area couch.

Elizabeth had received an email from Jack that afternoon, a short letter that began *I think it's time I gave you some space* and went on to explain that he was back in Chicago now and had come to some important realizations during his time in Kansas and he would be staying at the Shipworks tonight, and for a few more nights. *Don't worry,* he wrote. *Ben won't know I'm there. I'll be discreet. It's just a place to crash until we can agree on our next steps.* And that phrase, "next steps," had such an unexpected tone of finality. Elizabeth read it and thought: *One problem at a time.* There was, first, the matter of Wellness to deal with.

She'd been at it all day, and now the sun was setting outside. Elizabeth sat cross-legged on her office floor. She was supposed to be packing up the rest of her library, but instead she was flipping through the pages of a new psych journal. It had arrived today— she'd have to remember to cancel the subscription—and she was reading it because the journal had devoted this entire edition to the problem of psychology's "replication crisis," the crisis being that some of the most famous and influential studies in the field, and also in the wider social sciences, could not be replicated, their results could not be confirmed. Studies on social priming, and memory retrieval, and even the placebo effect were now being questioned, reassessed, often debunked. And what had caught Elizabeth's eye was an article testing and refuting that famous old Stanford study, the one about kids and marshmallows and patience.

The conclusion reached by that original study was that kids who could resist a marshmallow for fifteen minutes were more success-ful later in life because of their ability to control their impulses and delay their own gratification. But this new study had controlled for a variety of underlying variables and come to a new conclusion: the kids who could wait fifteen minutes didn't do so because they had better self-control. No, they were mostly just rich. These kids understood that they could get as many marshmallows as they wanted, whenever they wanted. So they could afford to wait. Whereas the kids who did not wait the fifteen minutes did not generally come from affluence, and they reached for the marshmallow not because they were impulsive but because when you live in a state of chronic lack, you don't take chances; you take the sure thing. And then if you track all these kids into adulthood, it shouldn't be too surprising that, on average, the rich kids have better outcomes than the poor kids. And this told you very little about patience or impulsiveness or delayed gratification.

This kind of thing was happening, it seemed, all the time: things that had once been deep truths were now upended, exposed, discredited, and in such obvious ways. Looking at it again, in hindsight, *of course* the marshmallow test was flawed. Why had she not seen that before? She looked at Toby now, on the couch, absorbed in his game, his face doing that thing it did when he played Minecraft, going all still and glassy and fishlike. She had given him this test because she wanted to teach him to control his urges. Because she'd been troubled by his outbursts, fearful of his tantrums. She did not want him becoming the kind of man her father was.

Elizabeth remembered when she'd stopped talking about this. It was during that first Otto Sanborne study, when her job was to dialogue with random men—she would answer incredibly personal questions with these men and then wait to see if, later, they called to ask her out. What Sanborne was ostensibly testing was the efficacy of various combinations of questions, but for Elizabeth there was a sort of secondary investigation happening during these interviews, a sub-study whereby she was able, through extensive trial and error, to understand exactly what potential love interests liked most about her—and, crucially, what they liked least.

In the latter category: the men she encountered during these interviews did not seem to find it very likable when she mentioned that her father was occasionally violent. When she said, in response to question number one, that her father's love for her was sometimes offset by his rage—the rare shattered tennis racket or television screen, the occasional fist-shaped hole left in a wall—this did not typically ignite their love. It was more like pity. Or worry. Or that particular disconnect that men were so unusually good at, that switch in their eyes that flipped off when they heard this stuff, when suddenly they were like, *Uh-oh, nope, she's broken, run away.*

She found more success with a slightly altered story, one that her Chicago subjects found appealing and likable: that her father was a demanding tyrant (which was true), a perfectionist who cared about appearances and money (true and true) and profited off the misery of others (also true, and something of a family tradition). And then she cast herself as a kind of rebellious iconoclast, refusing his wealth, moving across the country to go it alone.

Damn if it didn't sound heroic.

By the time of her first date with Jack, she'd learned how to talk about her family in a way that was maximally ingratiating and lovable. It wasn't that she was *lying* about her past, but rather that she'd perfected a particular translation of it, or a moderately censored version of it. And she'd gone along like that for so many years, not really thinking about it too much, not until Toby's tantrums dredged it all up again.

One memory in particular was still so vivid: those first moments after the tennis racket struck her, lying on the court, woozy, her face already swelling, blood in her eye, that peculiar taste of metal on her tongue, and all those people who'd been watching from the back porch, all of them running onto the court now, and she could hear their footsteps, their voices, and surely they must have checked on her, they must have asked her if she was okay, but that's not the thing she remembered. What she remembered was how quickly, and how emphatically, these people were already explaining and classifying and codifying what had just happened. Even as blood still seeped from her nose, they were insisting: "It was an accident." Her father, and her father's business partners, and even her mother, all of them repeating this same thing: "It was just an accident!" Elizabeth was still lying on the ground, still seeing odd round black spots in her field of vision, and yet these people were already imposing this reality upon her—*just an accident, no one to blame, everything's fine*—and they kept doing it as she finally got to her feet, and someone claiming minor previous medical training (he was maybe a lifeguard once?) inspected her nose and announced with total authority that it was fine, it was totally fine, just a bad-looking bruise, no need to call a doctor, and someone else helped her to walk, wobblingly, weakly, into the house, into a bathroom, where in the mirror she saw her two eyes already blackened, and the big red welt on the bridge of her nose, and the streaks of blood all down her tennis whites. For a moment she thought she would vomit, but then the feeling passed, and she was left with a persistent dizziness and drumming headache. She washed her hands and, as gently as she could, her face. Her mother brought her a change of clothes and hugged her and said, "You're okay."

It was more like a declaration than a question. Elizabeth nodded.

"It was an accident, you know."

"Yeah."

"He didn't mean to. The racket must have slipped out of his hand."

Elizabeth stared at the floor. "I'm think I'm gonna go sit down for a bit," she said. "I'd like to be alone."

"Okay," her mother said, rubbing her back. "You do that."

And so Elizabeth climbed, ever so slowly, up the spiral staircase behind the pantry, into the servants' quarters, where she sat on the floor and leaned her back against the wall and closed her eyes and, finally, began to cry. She was crying from the pain, sure, but also from the knowledge that what her father had done was not an accident. He'd done it on purpose, to punish her for humiliating him, for winning. She knew it in her bones. So did everyone else, but they would never say it. They could never acknowledge this fact. For they were all deeply in his pocket, dependent on him and his fortune: those business partners who needed their kickbacks, Elizabeth's mother beguiled by her big house and collections of cars and art and cashmere shawls and pearl earrings. The stakes were high, and thus facts were easily scrambled. Her father would get away with it, just as every terrible Augustine tycoon always had.

And as Elizabeth sat there lightly crying, a sound came from around the corner, from the kitchenette, a sound like knocking, like someone lightly tapping on a wall.

"Hello?" Elizabeth said, to no answer. "Who's there?"

She stood up—still so gingerly—and walked into the kitchenette. It was a little alcove of a kitchen, with a two-burner stove and a miniature sink and a graying linoleum floor and cabinets of thin and cheap and flimsy raw lumber. She stood very still, listened for the tapping, followed the sound up the wall, to the cabinets—the tapping was coming from inside. Something was inside the cabinet, knocking against its front face, and Elizabeth reached up to the cabinet's old brass knob—chipped and scratched from a century's use—and very slowly, very deliberately, pulled the cabinet just slightly open, just a sliver, when, all at once, she felt something from within the cabinet push strongly out, and suddenly she was falling backward, screaming, as the air above her exploded with life. Black streaks zigzagged all over, swooping up and down, panicked, chirping, dozens of bats pushing their way into the room. They flew laps around the ceiling of the servants' quarters, occasionally landing on the ledge of a window frame or door casing or latching onto the plaster walls, staying there for a moment, looking this way and that, agitated, scared, before taking off again. Elizabeth lay on the floor of the kitchenette and watched them overhead, a frenzy of wings. She looked into the cabinet and saw how the wall behind it had been disintegrated, eroded, chewed through. And from her spot on the linoleum she could see right up through the ceiling, right into the upstairs rooms, through a large hole that had been made, just behind this wall of cabinets.

The colony that had taken over the fourth floor was now, apparently, advancing upon the third.

Soon the bats seemed to calm down, and one by one they attached themselves to window screens and curtains by their little hooklike claws. It was daytime, and they preferred to be dormant right now, and so after a few minutes, the room stopped seething. Soon it was quiet, dotted all over with small black unmoving flecks.

And now a warmth reached her, a moist warm air and an odor,

tumbling like a fog down from the gap in the ceiling. The smell was pure ammonia, and seemed to burn lightly in her mouth. She remembered how the exterminators who went up to the fourth floor always wore these elaborate masks, how the air up there was apparently poisonous. And suddenly Elizabeth realized—as if it were the most rational thing in the world—exactly what she should do. She stood up. She opened the cabinet doors. She climbed onto the narrow Formica counter. She reached into the hollow behind the wall, found purchase on some old slats behind the plaster, a trellis by which she could pull herself up, into the recess behind the cabinets, and then up through the collapsed hole, steadying herself on antique metal brackets and broken pieces of timber, until finally she ascended to the fourth floor.

She was in some kind of parlor or drawing room—the large draped objects along the walls resembled couches, maybe, and chairs, and a table at the far end, all of them under tarps. The floor up here was parquet where it showed through from beneath a thick congealed layer of what looked like black mold or black sand or black gravel, sometimes in mounds two or three feet tall. The curtains were closed, the room dim and hazy, thin shafts of light shone through gaps in the walls or holes in the drapes, and wherever the light landed on the floor, this black stuff turned glittery and iridescent—the sparkle of wings from a million devoured insects, catching the sun.

Elizabeth looked up, above the largest mounds, and saw how the ceiling there seemed to churn. Black vague quivering impressions that, after her eyes grew accustomed to the dark, resolved themselves, and she now saw the many hundreds of them, the bats hanging upside down, rocking and swaying ever so slightly, the occasional creature dropping free and flying to one of the room's many other clusters. That sound, the quick beat of individual wings, was coming constantly from all angles, though Elizabeth could rarely see its source—the bats were too fast, the room too dark. It was just an ambiguous ripple in the air around her.

She understood that the smell must have been overwhelming, but her nose was stoppered, probably broken, and so the smell registered more like a taste, a pool-water flavor in her sinuses, a sharp chemical scorch in her lungs. There was something suffocating about breathing it, and soon her breathing was strained, and she was coughing, and she felt that panicked sensation when there's not enough air in the air, like being under the covers for too long. She closed her eyes. She tried to relax. She thought she heard, from somewhere far below, the sound of laughter—someone was laughing, life in the house was already back to normal. And she knew that all she had to do was sit here. Soon the gas would take her. Soon the room would fully dim. Soon she would pass out—it was just that easy—and sometime later they would find her up here, and that's when she would impose her reality on *them*. She imagined the police getting involved, interviewing the guests, and the fact of her father's attack becoming public knowledge, the news getting out, her father forever shamed and therefore punished. For the first time in her life, she had power over him—so much power right at this moment—and he didn't even know it. She listened to the sound of wings fluttering alarmingly close overhead, and she inhaled deeply, exhaled deeply, and she waited.

"What's wrong, Mom?"

Elizabeth opened her eyes. There Toby stood, in front of her now, staring at her, head cocked, worried. "Are you okay?" he said.

She smiled. He could do that sometimes. He was so often intransigent and stubborn, but occasionally, when darkness really overtook her, he could sense it, even from a completely different room, and suddenly he became compassionate, tender.

"I'm fine, honey," she said, blinking away the memory of that day.

"Are you sure?" He was looking at her dubiously. He didn't believe her.

"I'm sure," she said.

"Positive?" He stretched out the word, overpronouncing each syllable: *Pos-it-tive?*

And the way he stared at her so attentively, and his fierce concern and worry for her in this moment, almost made her want to weep. She felt a kind of ache rising within her now, a longing that felt as if it had been entombed for decades: that child's hope that someone would, finally, help. All those guests at the Gables, and all those teachers at those many schools, and all her brief friends and acquaintances—why didn't anyone see she needed help? Why didn't they step in? Why didn't they ask if she was okay? *She was in trouble, and nobody noticed.*

But here was Toby, noticing.

"Hey, listen," she said to her son, "do you remember that game we played with the apple turnovers?"

His forehead crinkled, and his eyes angled up as he retrieved the memory. "Oh, yeah," he said. "Eat one treat now or two treats in fifteen minutes."

"Yes, that's the game."

"I'm pretty sure it was some kind of test."

"It was a dumb test."

"I don't think I passed it."

"It's okay, sweetie."

"I *tried* to pass it."

"Really, don't worry about it."

"I thought I did pass it, actually. I really thought I did it right, at first."

"What do you mean?"

"It's just, I know you don't want me eating sugary things."

"That's true."

"And so I thought, if I only ate *one* turnover instead of waiting to eat *two* turnovers, it would make you happy."

"I don't understand."

"That's why I ate the one turnover right away. So you wouldn't have to give me another. I thought I'd passed the test. I thought I'd *resisted temptation*. I'm sorry."

"Oh my god."

"If we did the test again, I'd do it right this time. I promise."

She scooped him up in her arms then, and held him tightly to her, this amazing little boy, this sweet, sensitive kid. "Oh, honey," she said, "you have nothing to be sorry about. *I'm* the one who should be sorry—"

She stopped talking then because she felt a crack in her voice, could feel tears coming on. She squeezed her son, and what she was thinking more than anything right now was: *Thank god.*

Thank god she hadn't gone through with it that day at the Gables; thank god she'd made it this far, met Jack, had Toby. She wished she could go back and find that fourteen-year-old version of herself and give that poor girl a hug. She remembered how very close she'd come to ending it, sitting up there in that fourth-floor parlor struggling to breathe, and what eventually changed her mind wasn't anything noble or affirming but instead just stupid pride. It was the realization that her father would think that her dying up there was one more failure, one last way that Elizabeth had not measured up to him, another way he'd won. He wouldn't take any blame. He was a man incapable of taking blame. No, it would perversely become one more thing for him to be weirdly proud of: Elizabeth was weak and stupid and dead, whereas he was strong and smart and alive.

"Mom, you're squishing me," Toby said.

She let him go, and he tumbled out of her arms. "Sorry!"

"*Ow,*" he said, rubbing his ribs and making an over-the-top pain-stricken face.

"Oh, stop it. I didn't squeeze you that hard."

"I know." He giggled and dropped his arms, grinned. "I was teasing you."

She took both his hands in hers. "Toby, I am so sorry for doing that thing with the turnovers. I apologize. I shouldn't have done that."

"Okay."

"You know you don't have to pass any tests for me. You don't have to do anything at all. Pass or fail or whatever, I love you no matter what. All I really want is for you to be yourself."

"Why are you being weird?"

She smiled. "My parents never let me be myself. I don't want to make the same mistake."

"Mom, you don't make *any* mistakes."

"Oh yes I do. All the time."

"Yeah, you say that a lot, and you're always apologizing for stuff, but I can't figure out why."

"What do you mean?"

"You're, like, perfect."

"I am?"

"Yeah," he said, so matter-of-factly, like it was such an obvious thing. And then he pulled his hands free and jogged back over to the couch, where he resumed his game, Elizabeth sitting there absolutely still, thinking: *Perfect?*

How could the boy think she was perfect, when her own inner experience of motherhood was of constant catastrophe, endless defeat, never living up to her own parenting ideals, not even for a single day. *What the fuck am I doing wrong?* was basically her everyday mantra, and yet, somehow, Toby thought she was perfect. And Jack too thought she was perfect. And so the big question was: Why was she the only one who disagreed?

And then it came to her. Obviously. As it had to those scientists amending the Marshmallow Test, looking at the same data but coming up with a new explanation.

She was still on that tennis court.

Maybe, in certain fundamental ways, she was still out there, willing herself to lose, still sabotaging herself to avoid her father's jealousy, spare him humiliation, prevent his revenge. Maybe it was like her mind had been on that tennis court every day of her adult life, still letting the ball bounce, still playing the game at its highest difficulty level.

She began a mental inventory of all the supporting evidence, all the things she'd done to make life harder: How she had refused her family's wealth, refused her own inheritance, and come to Chicago penniless and alone. How she had taken on five majors at DePaul, spreading herself so thin that she couldn't graduate with honors in any one of them. How she became an expert in her field but in such a way that she was never allowed to publicize it, could never earn renown for it. It was as if despite their separation and distance, her father were still there, looking over her shoulder, always present as the invisible audience Elizabeth performed her life for. It was like at any given moment she wanted to be able to turn to him and say: *See? Still failing! So you can leave me alone!*

And then as a parent, with Toby, overwhelming herself with all the newest research, reading every relevant scientific journal. At the time, she said she wanted her parenting to be informed by best practices, but maybe what she was really doing was creating such unachievable standards that she was guaranteed to always fall short. She was never satisfied with herself, always needed to be just a little bit better, to improve and improve without end, and she recalled how her own mother had similar impulses regarding her many collections, to never feel quite content with any of them: *living like a mollusk* is how Elizabeth had described it at the time, quoting Socrates. Living like a creature who could only feed but never appreciate.

Toby loved her. And she should appreciate that. Jack loved her.

Jack, her agreeable husband, a hopeless romantic who believed without any doubt that they were fated for each other, that he had met her very soul as it traveled at night. It was as if Elizabeth had purposely chosen a person who loved her so immensely, who idealized her so extravagantly, that she could never possibly measure up to it. She'd escaped her father's discontent only to reinvent it in her own marriage.

How elegant. How perfectly, stupidly, dreadfully elegant.

She thought about this time in junior high, a morning she was sitting in the kitchen before school, reading a book, and her parents were there, her father leaving soon for work, and he'd just finished making breakfast, this gross green smoothie thing, a concoction of spinach and kiwi and strawberry and banana and skim milk and NutraSweet. There it sat in the blender, still frothy, recently churned, bright green, and her father was idly describing his upcoming day—"A bunch of interviews, depositions, et cetera"—except that when he said *et cetera*, he pronounced it *eCK cetera*, with a big hard *k* sound, which Elizabeth knew wasn't right, and which always bothered her when she heard him say it.

"Actually?" she said on this particular morning. "It's *eT cetera*."

Her mother stared at the floor. Her father stopped talking. "What?" he said.

"It's not *eCK cetera*, it's *eT cetera*," she said. "With a *t*."

And then she returned to her book and managed to read maybe two full sentences before the full blender jar crashed down on the countertop in front of her and bright green smoothie juice exploded all over her clothes and book and bookbag, and she sat there stunned in that silent kitchen as her father tightened the knot in his tie and said: "Oh, it looks like you spilled your breakfast on your pants and shoes, *eT cetera*" and then stormed out the door.

After which she stopped correcting him.

And what she wondered now was how many times she'd withheld something from Jack, something hard or troubling or delicate, how many times she had not said it out loud because she'd absorbed and metabolized this one important lesson: that men are weak. That they could not handle her. How many conflicts had she avoided, how many resentments had she kept locked away? How many times had she maneuvered her way out of sex rather than state plainly what was going on? How little of herself had she offered up to those who loved her most? It made her worry that she was still pretending to be that rock: flat, immovable, unbreakable, unavailable. Maybe something was broken within her. Maybe she wasn't feeling what she should be feeling. Maybe she understood love not as an emotion but as a theoretical construct, like she had a psychological and neurobiological and maybe even algorithmic conception of love that was just a well-researched simulation of what real people felt when they felt real love. Maybe her problem with Jack and Toby was that she'd always been, in her core, unloving, distant, stony, hidden.

She pictured Jack, sitting in the Shipworks, all alone, in the dark. She remembered what she'd said to persuade him to go to the Club. She said she needed a new thrill in her life, that all the big important questions had been answered, that she had figured everything out—figured *herself* out—and needed a shot of mystery.

What foolishness, she thought now, what a laugh. No, she had not figured herself out. She hadn't even started. And maybe that explained it, this recent middle-aged disenchantment, finding herself at the bottom of life's U-shaped curve: maybe that's how long it took to discover the specific, tortuous ways you were lying to yourself.

She stood up, fetched her purse, asked her coworkers if they wouldn't mind watching Toby for an hour or two. On her way out of the office, she stopped at the front couch, where he was playing Minecraft.

"Hey, Toby? I'm going out for a bit."

"Okay," he said, staring at the screen.

"You'll be good?"

"Okay."

She watched him for a moment, his unblinking face, his empty eyes—it was so difficult to get his attention when he was in this state. "Bye," she said, to no visible reaction. Then: "Don't forget to subscribe."

That got him. He looked up at her now, beaming. "Don't forget to subscribe!"

"I'll be back soon," she said, and she blew him a kiss.

"Hey Mom?" he said as she was on her way out the door. "What's better? Diamonds or netherite?"

"I know this one," she said. "Netherite's better."

"That's right!"

"It's stronger. And it doesn't burn."

"It can even float on lava," he said.

She smiled at him, her skinny little wondrous boy. She waved goodbye. She walked into the night, down the street and to her car, thinking that maybe that video game was correct. Diamond was the strongest stuff there was, sure, but sometimes the made-up things were even stronger.

She was opening her car door when she heard it, from behind: "Hey, Elizabeth?"

And she turned around to find, stepping out of the shadows, Benjamin Quince, looking at her with an uncharacteristically worried and penitent face.

"Ben, hi," she said. "What are you doing?"

"I hope I didn't frighten you, hiding in the dark like that."

"Yes, why were you hiding in the dark?"

"I have some bad news."

"Okay."

"News I could deliver only in person."

"I see."

"I'm afraid, Elizabeth, that the investors have pulled out."

"Oh no."

"Yeah, the investors, the financiers, all of them. Every single one. I'm afraid we don't have the funds to finish construction on the Shipworks. I'm so sorry."

"Why did they pull out?"

"All the recent controversy, the online attention, the bad press, the lawsuits. As I've said previously, our investors prefer anonymity, and this situation has gotten 'too hot,' which is a direct quote. Too hot. That's exactly how they put it."

"And so they're just abandoning it? They're allowed to do that?"

"They don't seem to be constrained by law, or ethics, or, actually, basic human decency. Do you know how easy it is to set up a shell company in America?"

"No."

"You'd think there'd be some restrictions but, ha ha, nope!"

"Ben, are you okay?"

"Turns out the biggest market in the world for unlawful money laundering is American real estate! Sometimes you don't know who you're actually dealing with until it's a little too late."

"So what's going to happen? The building's not livable, and we already paid."

"We have basically two options. The first of which is to litigate, in which case you might get your money back in five to ten years, minus lawyer fees, of course."

"That's not acceptable. We can't afford that."

"Yes, and suing these particular investors will be a horrific experience involving extradition and probably Interpol and such, not to mention the likelihood of threats and intimidation to your individual person, likely in the form of, let's say, a large dead animal appearing in your bed one day. Or something similarly grotesque."

"Jesus, Ben!"

"Also the investors themselves are demanding their money back. Immediately. As in, right now. And these are folks you do not fuck around with. Thus the second option. The second option is the reason for my hiding in the shadows."

"Okay."

"It's the reason I didn't call you or text you. Couldn't leave a trail!"

"Ben, what are you talking about?"

"I wanted to get your nest egg back. Please understand that I'm doing this for you."

"What is the second option, Ben?"

"Think of it as a cleanse. Okay? Think of it like, sometimes the body just has too many toxins, right? And drastic action is necessary? Sometimes you just gotta drink nothing but celery water until all the bad stuff is flushed away. That's what I'm doing to the Shipworks, in a manner of speaking. A cleanse."

"Ben, what *exactly* are you doing?"

"I'm burning the building down."

"You're what?"

"To collect the insurance. It's the only way to quickly recoup the investment. Of course you didn't hear that from me. And I will deny this conversation ever happened, okay?"

"Ben!"

"Fortunately the recent protests give us good cover. We can blame activists."

"I don't like this plan, Ben."

"It's done more often than you might think. Honestly by now the insurance companies build it into their actuary tables."

"I *really* don't like this plan."

"Well, I'm sorry, Elizabeth, but it's already underway."

"What do you mean?"

"The building is on fire. As we speak. I thought you should know."

"Right now?"

"Yes."

"But Jack is in there!"

"No, no, I made it very clear to him it's off-limits. And anyway I checked. No lights on, not a peep."

"Oh my god."

It was a thirty-minute drive to Park Shore, but Elizabeth made it in roughly half that. Even from several blocks away, she could already see it, an orange shine in the sky more vivid and ominous than the city's normal ambient diffuse glow. She could see a column of smoke by the blinking lights of emergency vehicles, a narrow plume lit in strobing red and blue. She could smell the char in the air. A crowd had gathered around the Shipworks, everyone staring quietly at the building, necks craned to look up at the roof and penthouse, currently aflame, an enormous candle in the night. Elizabeth leapt out of her car and ran toward the fire—she could feel, even a block away, the heat on her face, and she stopped at the mouth of an alley where the first responders had cordoned off the area. Firefighters were slowly connecting hoses, chatting pleasantly with one another, dawdling. Nobody seemed to be in much of a hurry, and Elizabeth was about to start screaming at them that there was someone up there, someone trapped on a middle floor, she was about to demand that rescuers rush in, that ladders ascend, when she looked into the alley and saw him, at the opposite end, Jack, staring up at the back side of the building. There he was, her gentle, patient, idiotic husband, standing with his hands in his pockets, watching their forever home burn.

The relief she felt, the dread that melted away as she breathed for what seemed like the first time in a long time—these were not the bland feelings of a big gray rock. Her face was wet—with tears, or sweat, or both. She waved at Jack, but he didn't, for the moment, see her. He watched the fire, watched as the ropes of the scaffolding slackened and melted and broke, the crashing of metal as the large frame fell. And the beautiful ship's-prow façade, recently 3D-printed from complex polymers, detached and shattered on the sidewalk. Jack watched all of this as Elizabeth watched him.

Were they destined for each other? Was he even right for her? She did not know. She wasn't sure of anything right now. She could not be certain she could ever love Jack as grandly, as unconditionally, as he needed. She understood that there was some fantastical and elevated place where his love awaited, and she was never certain she could join him there, whether her heart was capable of it. But she knew she loved him right now. And she would probably love him tomorrow. And maybe that was good enough. Maybe she didn't have to be certain of anything. Maybe the human heart was just that messy, and all romance was deeply precarious, and the future was unresolved, and that was fine. Maybe that's what true love actually was: an embrace of the chaotic unfolding. And maybe the only stories that had neat and certain conclusions were lies and fables and conspiracies. Maybe it was like Dr. Sanborne said: certainty was just a story the mind created to defend itself against the pain of living. Which meant, almost by definition, that certainty was a way to avoid living. You could choose to be certain, or you could choose to be alive.

And the only thing she was certain of was this: that between ourselves and the world are a million stories, and if we don't know which among them are true, we might as well try out those that are most humane, most generous, most beautiful, most loving.

Was Jack her soulmate?

Sure, she thought. Why not?

Finally he saw her. She was waving at him, and he waved back at her now, just as he had waved at her the night they first met, when he rushed over to her in a darkened dive bar and asked her to come with. She smiled at him, and both their faces were lit brilliantly by the fire, and as they stared at each other, separated by the length of the alley, they were both asking the same thing—though they did not know it—exactly the same thing at exactly the same time. They were asking: *Could you ever love someone as broken, as pathetic, as me?*

O N A PARTICULAR winter night—damp and muddy, the sky spitting a thin balsamic mist, a hazy purple night good for ghost stories or philosophy—they're out walking, arms linked, hands pocketed, staring up at the faces of apartment buildings, noting the typical urban facts about brutal gray concrete walls. "Sterile, cold, sinister," Jack says. "My problem," Elizabeth says, "is they're too decisive." They are on their way home. It's late. She says: "There's nothing ambiguous about a concrete wall." He agrees. They kick through the melting liver-brown snow, listen to the crunch of salt and sand on the sidewalk. And then they see light at a window, and movement—two shadows thrown against a bright yellow curtain. "Look," he says. "Those people. Are they dancing?" They *are* dancing, and he watches them flit about, these things, these human bodies, like puppets on a wire—they jerk, they prat, they potter. She stops too, and watches the flickering shadows. "It must be happy in there," she says, "and warm." It makes him wonder about the private lives of people, about the secret life hidden behind the public one.

What do real couples actually do together? he wonders. How do real couples spend all that time?

Jack and Elizabeth do not know. They are twenty years old. This is the first time they've been coupled with anyone in any way that's *real*.

But he has a theory: real couples, he says, stare deeply into each other's eyes, and hold each other for hours, and write epic love poetry about angels' wings and rose-red lips. Real couples, he says, are attached by hip and soul.

"That old chestnut?" she says.

But he insists. The people who are truly in love know each other all the way down to their souls, because their souls have already met.

"At night," he says. "When we're sleeping, our souls climb out of our bodies and explore."

"Oh, please."

"It's true! They take the form of animals—a mouse, a bird—and they go out wandering in the night. And sometimes they meet each other. So when you encounter your true love in real life, you know it immediately, because you've met them before. That's why it feels that way."

"You are hopeless."

"And you cannot prove me wrong."

"You are a profound cheeseball."

"What's your theory?"

Hers is more sinister. She talks about lovers who twaddle their love away—you know, cheerless platitudes and awkward silences and narcotic, bovine boredom.

"Maybe," he says. "Maybe we'll never know."

"It all happens behind the curtains."

"Indeed it does."

So they go home to their little studio apartment and she kisses him—on the palm of his hand, just below the knuckle, on the spot she calls his Sea of Tranquility, her favorite spot, the smoothest square inch in the world. They set the table with the good plates, the blue ones, Jim and Julianne are their names, the plates. He says "We're home! Are you happy to see us?" and the plates clatter and clap. He says "How about macaroni tonight?" and the plates are delirious with joy. They are only dimly aware that they are, in fact, plates.

She says: "Tonight it's self-portraits with silly food." So they eat and close the curtains and slop oil paints onto messy canvases—*Still Life with Boyfriend and Noodle, Still Life with Eggshell and Girl.* He says, "We're too committed to realism. Let us believe in more abstract things," and she says, "Make me."

Later, they lie together, quiet and curled up, in Cleveland, which is what they've named the couch. Everything in their little apartment has been so named—the furniture and closets, glasses and cutlery, all these secret landmarks, the contours of their life having been remapped and baptized. He leans into her and says, "Hello there," which means *Yes, at this moment, we are the finest and best people on the planet.* She taps his chest in a Morse code opposite of SOS. When she stretches and moans and winces, it means that love is not made entirely of back rubs, but it *must include back rubs*, just as a wedding cake is more than merely food, but it must also be food.

Then he answers in his Grizzly-Mountain-Man voice. Or his Too-Much-Sugar voice. Or his Bionic-Robot-Guy voice. And she calls him "Half man, half amazing." This is one of his many nicknames. Others include Pigeon Berry, Peach Butter, Prince of Wales, Cutie van der Waals, Mr. Smooth Boots, and the names of her four favorite bone-white minerals: pandermite, carnallite, aphrodite, and pearl. They connect their last names and applaud the performance of the hyphen, then add even more names to their names, toss on things like "Madame" and "Esquire," toss on weird phrases like "Her Regal Excellency" and "Chancellor of the Exchequer" until their names fill an entire notebook page. "We've done it," she says. "From now on it's pure profit."

Just then there's a crash from upstairs—like a fallen bookcase, a dropped bowling ball—and they jump and yell "Oh, mercy!" at exactly the same time. They eye each other suspiciously and wonder: *Did I learn that from you, or did you learn that from me?* They don't know. The words seem to have come from neither of them and yet both of them.

"It's like you're in my head," she says. "How could that be?"

"I told you," he says. "Our souls, they've met."

She closes her eyes. "Then tell me what I'm thinking."

She turns her back to him, which in this moment means he should put his arms around her from behind, all the way around her, hugging tightly, then put his lips against her ear, then smell her hair, then give long slow kisses down her collarbone until the skin turns light pink, then unhurriedly pull off her shirt, then turn her around, then look longingly and profoundly and ruggedly into her eyes in *exactly that order*, and when he does, her body unfurls in a dreamy *yes*.

That night, in bed, under a heap of quilts and blankets and comforters, they each accuse the other of stealing the covers last night.

She says: "Yesterday I loved you more, but today I think you love me more."

She hits him with a pillow.

He thinks about the walk, the dancing shadows on the yellow curtain, and asks her again: "What do couples do in secret?"

She says: "They name their dinnerware. Duh."

After she falls asleep, she stirs and rolls over and yawns widely and a small white mouse crawls out of her mouth. The mouse is a delicate little thing, fragile and soft, downy fur the color of milk. It wanders and sniffs the air and takes cautious steps toward the door. He scoops it up in his hand—it's so light! Like a puff of whipped cream. He ferries it outside—slowly, tenderly, as if he's holding a thin, unbroken egg yolk. He whispers it his dear adorings and holds it aloft, and the mouse stares at the stars. Then he shows the mouse how to play; he knuckles his hand into the ground, and the mouse begins to frolic. It digs into the soft crumbling fatty earth and disappears.

After a time, he calls for the mouse, and the creature hears his voice, and knows it, and follows it. The mouse returns to find her waking body, crawls back into her mouth as she yawns, and she blinks and opens her eyes and looks at him. He asks: "Were you dreaming just now?" And she says yes, she was. So he tells her about the mouse, how he lifted it to the stars, and she says: "In my dream I was flying through space." How the mouse clawed at the ground, and she says: "In my dream I was digging to the center of the earth." How he called for the mouse, and she says: "In my dream I was following your voice in the dark."

She laughs and says: "Do you believe me?"

Behind curtains, this, he thinks, is what lovers do—they are alchemists and architects; pioneers and fabulists; they make one thing another; they invent the world around them. So he says, "Yes, I believe you," and she smiles. She stretches. She touches his face, and makes it splendid.

#GRATITUDE

Thank you, Reagan Arthur, for your confidence in this book and the sure hand with which you brought it into the world. Thank you, Gabrielle Brooks, Isabel Yao Meyers, Emily Murphy, Edward Allen, Zachary Lutz, John Vorhees, Oliver Munday, and the whole incredible team at Knopf.

Thank you, Emily Forland, for being not only an amazing advocate but also a true creative partner and friend. Thank you, Marianne Merola, Henry Thayer, Gail Hochman, John Spano, and the rest of my family at Brandt & Hochman.

Thank you to the generous readers who looked at early drafts and gave invaluable advice: Peter Geye, Mark Abrams, Patrick Thomas, and Jessica Flint.

Thank you to my foreign editors, agents, publishers, and translators for your inspiring work bringing this book to readers around the world.

Thank you, Tim O'Connell—your support and camaraderie mean the world to me. Thank you, Michelle Weiner, for your indomitable enthusiasm and encouragement. Thank you, Javier Ramirez, for the lively tour of '90s Wicker Park.

Thank you to the Den Creek Ranch in the Flint Hills for your hospitality.

Thank you to my parents for being much better and more supportive parents than the parents in my novels—thank you and I love you.

Thank you to my wife, Jenni Groyon, who knew that readers of this book would probably assume it was *our* marriage I was describing—and yet encouraging me nonetheless. Thank you. Your love is the gift of my life.

Finally, thank you to all the parents who taught me so much about parenthood—both its highs and its lows—who shared their stories, their hearts, and sometimes even their homes. Thank you, Jen and JT, Anne Marie and Patrick, Aaron and Jessica (a particular thank-you to Jess for inspiring "The Unraveling"), Marc and Marlena, Chris and Shawna, Kelley and Sam, Erica and Matt, Naomi and Ted, Anne and Chris, Eric and Melissa, and Michael and Valerie.

Especially Valerie . . . thank you. We all miss you so much.

BIBLIOGRAPHY

One of the great joys of writing a book is that it gives me permission to explore the various odd things that grab my attention, to dive deeply into those subjects that puzzle, amuse, or amaze me. This book had many such deep dives. It was a daily process of discovery and wonder, and I'd like to issue a generalized *thank-you* to all the psychologists, sociologists, neurologists, evolutionary biologists, economists, sexologists, therapists, philosophers, doctors, data scientists, and everyone else working so hard to understand our strange, unruly, miraculous, and messy minds.

I'm particularly indebted to the following books.

On medical placebo and wellness culture: *The Wellness Syndrome* by Carl Cederström and André Spicer; *The Mind Made Flesh* by Nicholas Humphrey (who inspired Otto Sanborne's theory on the usefulness of certainty in healing); *Natural* by Alan Levinovitz; *Meaning, Medicine, and the "Placebo Effect"* by Daniel E. Moerman; *Placebo Talks,* edited by Amir Raz and Cory S. Harris; and *The Gospel of Wellness* by Rina Raphael.

On marriage, love, sex, and parenthood: *Arousal* and *Male Sexuality* by Michael Bader; *Open to Desire* by Mark Epstein; *Marriage Confidential* by Pamela Haag; *All About Love* by bell hooks; *Intimate Terrorism* by Michael Vincent Miller; *Can Love Last?* by Stephen A. Mitchell (who inspired Kyle's theory about marriage reproducing the miseries of childhood); *Mating in Captivity* and *The State of Affairs* by Esther Perel; *Monogamy* by Adam Phillips; *Sex at Dawn* by Christopher Ryan and Cacilda Jethá; *Overwhelmed* by Brigid Schulte; *All Joy and No Fun* by Jennifer Senior; *Midlife* by Kieran Setiya; and *Why Have Kids?* by Jessica Valenti.

On social media, misinformation, algorithms, and conspiracy: *The Formula* by Luke Dormehl; *The Chaos Machine* by Max Fisher; *Ten Arguments for Deleting Your Social Media Accounts Right Now* by Jaron Lanier; *Nine Algorithms That Changed the Future* by John MacCormick; *Post-Truth* by Lee McIntyre; *The Misinformation Age* by Cailin O'Connor and James Owen

Weatherall; *Likewar* by P. W. Singer and Emerson T. Brooking; and *Outnumbered* by David Sumpter.

On gentrification, authenticity, real estate, and Wicker Park: *Exile in Guyville* by Gina Arnold; *Neo-Bohemia* by Richard Lloyd (who inspired Benjamin Quince's theory of urban artists as corporate risk managers); *The Authenticity Hoax* by Andrew Potter; *Snob Zones* by Lisa Prevost; and *Naked City* by Sharon Zukin.

On the Flint Hills and the prairie: *Plain Pictures* by Joni L. Kinsey; *PrairyErth* by William Least Heat-Moon; and *Conducting Prescribed Fires* by John R. Weir.

The story of the human soul out wandering as a mouse comes from *Folktales of Norway*, edited by Reidar Christiansen. The song performed at the Empty Bottle is "6'1"" by Liz Phair.

Otto Sanborne's theory of love, as well as his experiment creating love at first sight, was inspired by "The Experimental Generation of Interpersonal Closeness: A Procedure and Some Preliminary Findings" by Arthur Aron, Edward Melinat, Elaine N. Aron, Robert Darrin Vallone, and Renee J. Bator, published in the *Personality and Social Psychology Bulletin*, volume 23, issue 4 (1997), and later described by Mandy Len Catron in her book *How to Fall in Love with Anyone*.

There are several studies and academic articles that I referred to without explicitly citing them. They are:

Cargill, Kima. "The Myth of the Green Fairy: Distilling the Scientific Truth About Absinthe." *Food, Culture & Society* 11, no. 1 (March 2008): 87–99.

Cherkin, Daniel C., Karen J. Sherman, Andrew L. Avins, Janet H. Erro, Laura Ichikawa, William E. Barlow, Kristin Delaney, et al. "A Randomized Trial Comparing Acupuncture, Simulated Acupuncture, and Usual Care for Chronic Low Back Pain." *Archives of Internal Medicine* 169, no. 9 (May 11, 2009): 858–66.

Crum, Alia J., William R. Corbin, Kelly D. Brownell, and Peter Salovey. "Mind over Milkshakes: Mindsets, Not Just Nutrients, Determine Ghrelin Response." *Health Psychology* 30, no. 4 (2011): 424–29.

Danaher, John, Sven Nyholm, and Brain D. Earp. "The Quantified Relationship." *American Journal of Bioethics* 18, no. 2 (February 2018): 3–19.

Dutton, Donald G., and Arthur P. Aron. "Some Evidence for Heightened Sexual Attraction Under Conditions of High Anxiety." *Journal of Personality and Social Psychology* 30, no. 4 (1974): 510–17.

Earp, Brian D., Anders Sandberg, and Julian Savulescu. "The Medicalization of Love." *Cambridge Quarterly of Healthcare Ethics* 24, no. 3 (July 2016): 323–36.

Garcia, Justin R., James MacKillop, Edward L. Aller, Ann M. Merriwether, David Sloan Wilson, and J. Koji Lum. "Associations Between Dopamine D4 Receptor Gene Variation with Both Infidelity and Sexual Promiscuity." *PLoS One* 5, no. 11 (November 2010): e14162.

Holland, Rob W., Merel Hendriks, and Henk Aarts. "Smells Like Clean Spirit: Nonconscious Effects of Scent on Cognition and Behavior." *Psychological Science* 16, no. 9 (September 2005): 689–93.

Levy, Karen E. "Intimate Surveillance." *Idaho Law Review* 51 (2014): 679–93.

Matthews, Luke J., and Paul M. Butler. "Novelty-Seeking DRD4 Polymorphisms Are Associated with Human Migration Distance Out-of-Africa After Controlling for Neutral Population Gene Structure." *American Journal of Physical Anthropology* 145, no. 3 (July 2011): 382–89.

Savulescu, Julian, and Anders Sandberg. "Neuroenhancement of Love and Marriage: The Chemicals Between Us." *Neuroethics* 1, no. 1 (March 2008): 31–44.

Schwandt, Hannes. "Unmet Aspirations as an Explanation for the Age U-Shape in Wellbeing." *Journal of Economic Behavior & Organization* 122 (February 2016): 75–87.

Seshadri, K. G. "The Neuroendocrinology of Love." *Indian Journal of Endocrinology and Metabolism* 20, no. 4 (July–August 2016): 558–63. doi:10.4103/2230-8210.183479.

Veissière, Samuel, and Leona Gibbs-Bravo. "Juicing: Language, Ritual, and Placebo Sociality in a Community of Extreme Eaters." In *Food Cults: How Fads, Dogma, and Doctrine Influence Diet*, edited by Kima Cargill, 63–86. Lanham, Md.: Rowman & Littlefield, 2016.

Watts, Tyler W., Greg J. Duncan, and Haonan Quan. "Revisiting the Marshmallow Test: A Conceptual Replication Investigating Links Between Early Delay of Gratification and Later Outcomes." *Psychological Science* 29, no. 7 (July 2018): 1159–77.

Weiss, Alexander, James E. King, Miho Inoue-Murayama, Tetsuro Matsuzawa, and Andrew J. Oswald. "Evidence for a Midlife Crisis in Great Apes Consistent with the U-Shape in Human Well-Being." *Proceedings of the National Academy of Sciences* 109, no. 49 (December 4, 2012): 19949–52.

Wudarczyk, Olga A., Brian D. Earp, Adam Guastella, and Julian Savulescu. "Could Intranasal Oxytocin Be Used to Enhance Relationships? Research Imperatives, Clinical Policy, and Ethical Considerations." *Current Opinion in Psychiatry* 26, no. 5 (September 2013): 474–84.

The following studies were cited in "The Unraveling."

Ambady, Nalini, Margaret Shih, Amy Kim, and Todd L. Pittinsky. "Stereotype Susceptibility in Children: Effects of Identity Activation on Quantitative Performance." *Psychological Science* 12, no. 5 (September 2001): 385–90.

Barber, Theodore X. "Hypnosis, Suggestions, and Psychosomatic Phenomena: A New Look from the Standpoint of Recent Experimental Studies." *American Journal of Clinical Hypnosis* 21, no. 1 (July 1978): 13–27.

Bergman, Nils J., Lucy L. Linley, and Susan R. Fawcus. "Randomized Controlled Trial of Skin-to-Skin Contact from Birth versus Conventional Incubator for Physiological Stabilization in 1200- to 2199-Gram Newborns." *Acta Pædiatrica* 93, no. 6 (June 2004): 779–85.

Birch, Leann L., and Diane W. Marlin. "I Don't Like It; I Never Tried It: Effects of Exposure on Two-Year-Old Children's Food Preferences." *Appetite* 3, no. 4 (December 1982): 353–60.

Bluestone, Cheryl, and Catherine S. Tamis-LeMonda. "Correlates of Parenting Styles in Predominantly Working- and Middle-Class African American Mothers." *Journal of Marriage and Family* 61, no. 4 (November 1999): 881–93.

Bystrova, Ksenia. "Skin-to-Skin Contact and Suckling in Early Postpartum: Effects on Temperature, Breastfeeding and Mother-Infant Interaction." Doctoral thesis, Karolinska Institutet (Sweden), 2008.

Carruth, Betty Ruth, Paula J. Ziegler, Anne Gordon, and Susan I. Barr. "Prevalence of Picky Eaters Among Infants and Toddlers and Their Caregivers' Decisions About Offering a New Food." *Journal of the American Dietetic Association* 104, supp. 1 (January 2004): 57–64.

Carruth, Betty Ruth, Paula J. Ziegler, Anne Gordon, and Kristy Hendricks. "Developmental Milestones and Self-Feeding Behaviors in Infants and Toddlers." *Journal of the American Dietetic Association* 104, supp. 1 (January 2004): 51–56.

Casey, Rosemary, and Paul Rozin. "Changing Children's Food Preferences: Parent Opinions." *Appetite* 12, no. 3 (June 1989): 171–82.

Cashdan, Elizabeth. "Adaptiveness of Food Learning and Food Aversions in Children." *Social Science Information* 37, no. 4 (December 1998): 613–32.

Chiang, Wen Chi, and Karen Wynn. "Infants' Tracking of Objects and Collections." *Cognition* 77, no. 3 (December 15, 2000): 169–95.

Cornish, Alison M., Catherine A. McMahon, Judy A. Ungerer, Bryanne Barnett, Nicholas Kowalenko, and Christopher Tennant. "Maternal Depression and the Experience of Parenting in the Second Postnatal Year." *Journal of Reproductive and Infant Psychology* 24, no. 2 (2006): 121–32.

Crum, Alia J., and Ellen J. Langer. "Mind-Set Matters: Exercise and the Placebo Effect." *Psychological Science* 18, no. 2 (February 2007): 165–71.

Cummings, E. Mark, and Patrick T. Davies. "Maternal Depression and Child Development." *Journal of Child Psychology and Psychiatry* 35, no. 1 (January 1994): 73–112.

De Chateau, Peter, and Britt Wiberg. "Long-Term Effect on Mother-Infant Behaviour of Extra Contact During the First Hour Post Partum II: A Follow-up at Three Months." *Acta Pædiatrica* 66, no. 2 (March 1997): 145–51.

Dishion, Thomas J., and Gerald R. Patterson. "The Timing and Severity of Antisocial Behavior: Three Hypotheses Within an Ecological Framework." In *Handbook of Antisocial Behavior*, edited by David M. Stoff, James Breiling, and Jack D. Maser, 205–17. Hoboken, N.J.: John Wiley & Sons, 1997.

Dovey, Terence M., Paul A. Staples, E. Leigh Gibson, and Jason C. G. Halford. "Food Neophobia and 'Picky/Fussy' Eating in Children: A Review." *Appetite* 50, nos. 2–3 (March–May 2008): 181–93.

Dumas, Jean E., and Christine Wekerle. "Maternal Reports of Child Behavior Problems and Personal Distress as Predictors of Dysfunctional Parenting." *Development and Psychopathology* 7, no. 3 (June 1995): 465–79.

Feldman, Ruth, Aron Weller, Lea Sirota, and Arthur I. Eidelman. "Testing a Family Intervention Hypothesis: The Contribution of Mother-Infant Skin-to-Skin Contact (Kangaroo Care) to Family Interaction, Proximity, and Touch." *Journal of Family Psychology* 17, no. 1 (March 2003): 94–107.

Flaten, M. A., and Terry Blumenthal. "Caffeine-Associated Stimuli Elicit Conditioned Responses: An Experimental Model of the Placebo Effect." *Psychopharmacology* 145, no. 2 (July 1999): 105–12.

Galloway, Amy T., Yoonna Lee, and Leann L. Birch. "Predictors and Consequences of Food Neophobia and Pickiness in Young Girls." *Journal of the American Dietetic Association* 103, no. 6 (June 2003): 692–98.

Goodman, Sherryl H., and Ian H. Gotlib. "Risk for Psychopathology in the Children of Depressed Mothers: A Developmental Model for Understanding Mechanisms of Transmission." *Psychological Review* 106, no. 3 (July 1999): 458–90.

Hamilton, Elizabeth B., Constance Hammen, Gayane Minasian, and Maren Jones. "Communication Styles of Children of Mothers with Affective Disorders, Chronic Medical Illness, and Normal Controls: A Contextual Perspective." *Journal of Abnormal Child Psychology* 21, no. 1 (February 1993): 51–63.

Harner, Lorraine. "Yesterday and Tomorrow: Development of Early Understanding of the Terms." *Developmental Psychology* 11, no. 6 (November 1975): 864–65.

———. "Comprehension of Past and Future Reference Revisited." *Journal of Experimental Child Psychology* 29, no. 1 (February 1980): 170–82.

———. "Immediacy and Certainty: Factors in Understanding Future Reference." *Journal of Child Language* 9, no. 1 (February 1982): 115–24.

Herrenkohl, Roy C., Brenda P. Egolf, and Ellen C. Herrenkohl. "Preschool Antecedents of Adolescent Assaultive Behavior: A Longitudinal Study." *American Journal of Orthopsychiatry* 67, no. 3 (July 1997): 422–32.

Hobden, Karen, and Patricia Pliner. "Effects of a Model on Food Neophobia in Humans." *Appetite* 25, no. 2 (October 1995): 101–14.

Horodynski, Mildred A., and Manfred Stommel. "Nutrition Education Aimed at Toddlers: An Intervention Study." *Pediatric Nursing* 31, no. 5 (September 2005): 364, 367–72.

Ingoldsby, Erin M., Gwynne O. Kohl, Robert J. McMahon, and Liliana Lengua. "Conduct Problems, Depressive Symptomatology and Their Co-Occurring Presentation in Childhood as Predictors of Adjustment in Early Adolescence." *Journal of Abnormal Child Psychology* 34, no. 5 (October 2006): 602–20.

Kelder, Steven H., Cheryl L. Perry, Knut-Inge Klepp, and Leslie A. Lytle. "Longitudinal Tracking of Adolescent Smoking, Physical Activity, and Food Choice Behaviors." *American Journal of Public Health* 84, no. 7 (August 1994): 1121–26.

Klimes-Dougan, Bonnie, and Claire B. Kopp. "Children's Conflict Tactics with Mothers: A Longitudinal Investigation of the Toddler and Preschool Years." *Merrill-Palmer Quarterly* 45, no. 2 (April 1999): 226–41.

Laible, Deborah J., and Ross A. Thompson. "Mother–Child Conflict in the Toddler Years: Lessons in Emotion, Morality, and Relationships." *Child Development* 73, no. 4 (July–August 2002): 1187–203.

Landray, Martin J., and Gregory H. Y. Lip. "White Coat Hypertension: A Recognised Syndrome with Uncertain Implications." *Journal of Human Hypertension* 13, no. 1 (January 1999): 5–8.

Larson, Nicole I., Mary Story, Marla E. Eisenberg, and Dianne Neumark-Sztainer. "Food Preparation and Purchasing Roles Among Adolescents: Associations with Sociodemographic Characteristics and Diet Quality." *Journal of the American Dietetic Association* 106, no. 2 (February 2006): 211–18.

Lepper, Mark R., and David Greene, eds. *The Hidden Costs of Reward*. London: Psychology Press, 1978.

Lovejoy, M. Christine, Patricia A. Graczyk, Elizabeth O'Hare, and George Neuman. "Maternal Depression and Parenting Behavior: A Meta-Analytic Review." *Clinical Psychology Review* 20, no. 5 (August 2000): 561–92.

Lyons-Ruth, Karlen, David Zoll, David Connell, and Henry U. Grunebaum.

"The Depressed Mother and Her One-Year-Old Infant: Environment, Interaction, Attachment, and Infant Development." *New Directions for Child and Adolescent Development* 1986, no. 34 (Winter 1986): 61–82.

McGrath, Jacqueline M., Kathie Records, and Michael Rice. "Maternal Depression and Infant Temperament Characteristics." *Infant Behavior and Development* 31, no. 1 (January 2007): 71–80.

Phillips, Raylene. "The Sacred Hour: Uninterrupted Skin-to-Skin Contact Immediately After Birth." *Newborn and Infant Nursing Reviews* 13, no. 2 (June 2013): 67–72.

Pliner, Patricia, and Karen Hobden. "Development of a Scale to Measure the Trait of Food Neophobia in Humans." *Appetite* 19, no. 2 (October 1992): 105–20.

Resnicow, Ken, Matt Smith, Tom Baranowski, Janice Baranowski, Roger Vaughan, and Marsha Davis. "2-Year Tracking of Children's Fruit and Vegetable Intake." *Journal of the American Dietetic Association* 98, no. 7 (July 1998): 785–89.

Rosenkranz, Richard R., and David A. Dzewaltowski. "Model of the Home Food Environment Pertaining to Childhood Obesity." *Nutrition Reviews* 66, no. 3 (March 2008): 123–40.

Scaramella, Laura V., and Leslie D. Leve. "Clarifying Parent-Child Reciprocities During Early Childhood: The Early Childhood Coercion Model." *Clinical Child and Family Psychology Review* 7, no. 2 (June 2004): 89–107.

Schulz, Laura E., Alison Gopnik, and Clark Glymour. "Preschool Children Learn About Causal Structure from Conditional Interventions." *Developmental Science* 10, no. 3 (May 2007): 322–32.

Serra-Majem, Lluís, Lourdes Ribas, Carmen Pérez-Rodrigo, Reina García-Closas, Luís Peña-Quintana, and Javier Aranceta. "Determinants of Nutrient Intake Among Children and Adolescents: Results from the enKid Study." *Annals of Nutrition and Metabolism* 46, supp. 1 (2002): 31–38.

Singer, Martha R., Lynn L. Moore, Ellen J. Garrahie, and R. Curtis Ellison. "The Tracking of Nutrient Intake in Young Children: The Framingham Children's Study." *American Journal of Public Health* 85, no. 12 (December 1995): 1673–77.

Skinner, Jean D., Betty Ruth Carruth, Wendy Bounds, and Paula Ziegler. "Children's Food Preferences: A Longitudinal Analysis." *Journal of the American Dietetic Association* 102, no. 11 (November 2002): 1638–47.

Smith, Judith R., and Jeanne Brooks-Gunn. "Correlates and Consequences of Harsh Discipline for Young Children." *Archives of Pediatrics & Adolescent Medicine* 151, no. 8 (August 1997): 777–86.

Sobal, Jeffery, and Brian Wansink. "Kitchenscapes, Tablescapes, Platescapes, and Foodscapes: Influences of Microscale Built Environments on Food Intake." *Environment and Behavior* 39, no. 1 (January 2007): 124–42.

Solomon, C. Ruth, and Françoise Serres. "Effects of Parental Verbal Aggression on Children's Self-Esteem and School Marks." *Child Abuse & Neglect* 23, no. 4 (April 1999): 339–51.

Strassberg, Zvi, Kenneth A. Dodge, Gregory S. Pettit, and John E. Bates. "Spanking in the Home and Children's Subsequent Aggression Toward Kindergarten Peers." *Development and Psychopathology* 6, no. 3 (Summer 1994): 445–61.

Sullivan, Susan A., and Leann L. Birch. "Infant Dietary Experience and Acceptance of Solid Foods." *Pediatrics* 93, no. 2 (February 1994): 271–77.

Visalberghi, Elisabetta, and Elsa Addessi. "Seeing Group Members Eating a Familiar Food Enhances the Acceptance of Novel Foods in Capuchin Monkeys." *Animal Behaviour* 60, no. 1 (July 2000): 69–76.

Wardle, J., M. L. Herrera, L. Cooke, and E. L. Gibson. "Modifying Children's Food Preferences: The Effects of Exposure and Reward on Acceptance of an Unfamiliar Vegetable." *European Journal of Clinical Nutrition* 57, no. 2 (February 2003): 341–48.

Widström, A. M., V. Wahlberg, A. S. Matthiesen, P. Eneroth, K. Uvnäs-Moberg, S. Werner, and J. Winberg. "Short-Term Effects of Early Suckling and Touch of the Nipple on Maternal Behaviour." *Early Human Development* 21, no. 3 (March 1990): 153–63.